About Hana

The Hana Du Rose Mysteries Book 1

K T BOWES

K T Bowes

Copyright © 2013 by K T Bowes

ISBN 978-0-9951190-0-0

All rights reserved.

No portion of this book may be reproduced in any form without written permission from the publisher or author.

Acknowledgement

I dedicate this book to my husband, who inspires all the best traits of Logan Du Rose.

Chapter 1

The New Zealand sunrise did not disappoint Logan Du Rose. He perched on the edge of the elevated ridge and dangled his long legs over the precipice, his angular face pointed out towards the sea. Muscular biceps moved beneath the light summer shirt, causing ripples in the cloth as he fidgeted as usual. Orange and yellow bled into the navy and cobalt of the sky behind him, justifying his decision to make the half hour trek up the mountain on his white mare. She snuffed at sweet blades of grass in the dim light, her coat glistening with sweat from the uphill climb.

The man took a handful of the loose soil beneath him; his soil, bequeathed to him by the Māori elder over three decades earlier. It crumbled in his fingers, cascading back to earth as dust. He was high enough above the rugged, green landscape to face east, but instead he craved the effect of the sunrise on the Tasman Sea as it cast its glow over the familiar, comforting waves. He never tired of the constancy of the mountain which grounded him in the tangata whenua; his ancestors, the people of the land.

Logan held the next handful of soil in his long, scarred fingers before tossing it away on the wind, sending with it his hopes and dreams into the scattered blaze of colour. "Twenty-six years," he murmured. "Searching for nothing. It stops here."

He recounted the moments in his memory, wasted years spent scouring the earth for his soul mate. From England to New Zealand and back again, seeking her out after a single meeting in which he'd known she belonged to him. After twenty-six years he relinquished his precious dream to the breeze and watched the shards of his heart drift away, fragmented and broken like the crumbled loam.

Turning, he greeted the new day. He whistled to the mare whose ears pricked forward in anticipation of the gallop down the mountain at their usual breakneck speed. The people of the township called him King of the Maunga, the Māori word for mountain. They whispered he would die one day, hurled from his crazy horse at speed on a landscape which had swallowed his forebears for generations.

As Logan crashed through the bush undergrowth on the capable mare, the old kauri tree on the topmost part of the mountain basked in the early rays of sunshine from the east. It warmed its aged knots and the scarred trunk bore the names of the family, carved into its smooth, branchless bark. A family tree in the truest sense, its history beginning with the mark of a tribal chief, a rangatira and his offspring. An aged tui bird cackled from the lower branches, sensing the disquiet in the earth as the man left the tapu sacred site, not just to grace the homestead with his presence but to leave; heading south for pastures new. It pained the earth as he fled yet again, his heritage and his ancestors crying out in dismay for a higher power to intervene.

In the city which lured Logan to a different future, a striking redhead rued the irritating sound of the alarm. It pulled her from a comfortable sleep and into the first day of a new school term. "Oh crap," she groaned, knocking it to the carpet in her efforts to mute it. After a six-week summer holiday, Hana Johal struggled to face the day, idling in bed and making herself late. In her haste, she burned her toast, spilled a mug of coffee and laddered her stockings, flying from the house feeling rumpled and unprepared for work. "It's a new year," she muttered to herself. "New resolutions and a nice, new start."

She tripped over a black and white cat on the front steps and saved herself by grasping the metal banister at the last minute. Grimacing at the welt rising on her shin where it contacted the metal, Hana stopped to catch her breath. "I am not a failure; I'm a strong, independent woman." She chanted the mantra under her breath and tried to believe it.

Shaking off the spectre of loneliness as she gripped the steering wheel of the people mover, Hana fixed a smile onto her rosebud lips and studied her green eyes in the rear-view mirror, galvanising herself against the growing sense of disquiet. "Get a grip, Hana."

With a sigh which betrayed her sense of futility, she started the engine and headed off to work at the desirable, private boys' school in a different suburb from her own.

A battered, white saloon drew into the heavy traffic behind her, lurching with imperfect gear changes as it switched lanes to keep up. The driver's head wobbled as he argued with his passenger. Their fortuitous interception was a thing of pure chance and they bickered as they shadowed an oblivious Hana into the staff car park. "I told you she'd go this way!" the driver exclaimed, blaming the passenger for time wasted watching a different road into the grid locked city.

"Well, just stick close," the passenger bit. "But don't attract attention. We need to get it back now; it's urgent!"

In the seven seater, Hana's auburn hair blew in the breeze from her open driver's window and she hummed to a tune on the radio and wedged the vehicle into her usual space. The white car poised in the entrance to the car park and staff vehicles bunched behind it.

Hana navigated her slender figure between her vehicle and the car next to it. While attempting to squeeze past without dirtying her clothes, she caught the strap of her handbag on the high wing mirror. She took a few steps into the car park before it yanked her backwards and she missed the white blur which passed far too close.

"Hana!" A colleague cried out in alarm as the car missed her with millimetres to spare. The school typist clapped her hand over her mouth in shock as the white car sped out onto the main road, tyres screeching as it blended into the rush hour traffic. Oblivious, Hana fumbled with her spewing handbag, its strap caught around the mirror and the pockets disgorging contents onto the floor. "That car almost hit you!" The woman squatted next to her and retrieved four stray pens and a packet of tissues from beneath the adjacent vehicle.

"Thanks. I'm such an idiot!" With a sigh of exasperation, Hana snatched her bag away from the mirror, mortified when the action sent its remaining contents tumbling to the ground. "I didn't see a car."

"Yeah, well thank your handbag strap otherwise you'd be its new hood ornament. Probably a parent dropping off their darling son. I swear some of these mothers don't think their precious boy's legs can carry him as far as the front doors. They get as close as they can."

Another pair of smart shoes arrived in Hana's peripheral vision as she chased down her mobile phone and clipped the battery back in. "That was close. I didn't see any students in the car. Did you get the registration number, Hana?"

"No. I'm fine. Just leave it." Grovelling on the floor in her smart suit and stiletto heels for lipstick and coins, Hana missed the astonished grey-eyed gaze of the tall newcomer as he stood transfixed to the spot. The other women eyed him with interest, their gaze taking in his impressive height and muscular build. He didn't even look their way, focussing on Hana as she retrieved her belongings, her fingers shoving a sanitary item into a ripped pocket in the hope nobody noticed. A lipstick rolled towards the scuffed toe of his cowboy boot and he watched it without moving.

Logan's shaking hand clutched his motorbike helmet, his eyes wide and sparkling with the revival of a lost hope. Twenty-six wasted years of searching and there she knelt, grappling on the dirty car park floor for the contents of her bag. She looked no older than he remembered, the New Zealand sun streaking red highlights in her hair and setting her aglow. Embarrassed, Hana gathered her belongings, unaware that a man who had loved her since her eighteenth year, watched her in agony.

Chapter 2

"Hana, please can you answer that phone? I'm stuck. Some kid shoved a half-eaten apple behind this shelf and my hands are filthy!" The blonde woman knelt in front of a brochure rack; her hands buried deep in the pile of dog-eared papers. "It's disgusting. It's gone soft over the holidays and stuck to the shelf."

"Yuk." Hana dropped her bundle of papers onto the floor and ran to answer the phone. Behind her, the newspapers slid into a graceful arc across the walkway. She returned within a few seconds, chewing her lip with anxiety and her cheeks pink with embarrassment. "Sheila, it's your husband. For you. He has an emergency."

"I bet I know what." Sheila hauled herself upright and Hana avoided her sticky, outstretched hands. She watched her boss saunter into the office and winced at the thought of the phone call, having already taken the full force of the caller's discomfort. Sheila's voice reverberated through the glass partition from the office. "You did what?"

The high beamed, vaulted roof left the partition walls hanging, stopping in mid-air as though the builders walked off the job half-finished a century earlier. Intricate wooden shapes decorated the ceiling like the inside of a church. Little angels and imps perched on the cross beams or hung from the apex, painstakingly carved into the wood of the Presbyterian school.

Hana tossed her red hair and bit her lip as Sheila's words filtered over the partition, "What do you mean, you thought you just farted?"

Hana tried not to eavesdrop and gathered the newspapers, stacking them in the brochure rack. Sheila returned sporting a rubber glove and the hint of a smirk. "Did he tell you?"

Hana nodded and then dissolved into giggles.

"Stupid idiot," the faithless wife remarked as she went back to the rotten apple. "I told him not to come in with a stomach upset, but he wouldn't listen. He's gone home to change his underwear."

"Where's Rory today?" Hana asked, referring to the Year 13 dean.

"I don't bloody know," Sheila replied with venom and Hana winced.

"How long until your house is finished?" She changed the subject.

"Another few months. We should've rented somewhere. Moving in with our daughter and Rory was a stupid idea. He tolerated us before and now he hates us for sure."

"I doubt that." Hana pictured the gentle dean fighting Sheila for the bathroom and wondered if they'd manage to keep their personal differences out of the office.

The peace shattered as a loud booming voice split the air like an axe and left the molecules vibrating. "Mrs Jennings, where's Martin? I've just found 9MJ without a teacher and they were trashing the place. Where's your husband? I swear I saw him at staff briefing this morning."

Sheila gave the angry male a disarming smile, using her Swedish charm to good effect. She used his outstretched arm to raise herself from her awkward kneeling position, then completed her manoeuvre by placing the disintegrating, fly infested apple remains into his open hand. The deputy principal stared at the rotting apple and considered its slimy vileness for a split second before dropping it into the bin. He looked at Sheila without repeating his question, his face unreadable. She smiled with enough sweetness to disarm a charging, wounded bull. "He's sick. I can cover his class, Alan."

Alan Dobbs grunted and breezed from the common room as quickly as he arrived. His incredible hairpiece wobbled on his head as he stalked away, in danger of blowing off as the doors slammed. It was blond and curly, stark against his dark features and black eyebrows. Hana knitted her brow and turned to Sheila. "Is his wig on back to front?"

Sheila shrugged with disinterest, used to the incongruous appendage. She muttered something under her breath and strutted off, disappearing through the double doors which slammed behind her. Hana's eyes widened in horror. "Sheila, the glove! Take the rubber glove off!" Receiving no reply, she poked a strand of red hair behind her ear in exasperation, "First Martin leaves the classroom with diarrhoea and then his wife turns up wearing a rubber glove."

Sheila returned at the end of lunch, flustered and still wearing the glove. "I made those unruly Year 9 boys stay in for a lunchtime detention," she complained. "It's the first bloody day of term and they're starting to play up! I coerced other staff members to cover Martin's classes." She sighed. "He can't get off the toilet."

Hurling herself into her office chair, she reached into her desk drawer and retrieved her sandwiches, staring at the gloved hand as though it belonged to someone else. With a shake of her head, she dropped it into the dustbin and bit into her sandwich. "Give them a month and that will be the worst class in the school, little buggers. What's the world coming to?" Airborne crumbs flew across the desk and hit the computer screen as Sheila berated the class of fourteen-year-olds. "I'd prefer diarrhoea to teaching them." Chutney oozed from the sandwich wrapper onto a significant memo which already sported a coffee cup ring over the words, 'For your urgent attention.'

Hana smiled to herself. "Thank goodness I don't have to teach," she commented. "I'd be rubbish at it."

"Ooh, talking of teaching, or teach-ers." Sheila grinned, unaware of the blob of chutney on her chin. "Have you noticed the new English teacher? Logan something. He's gorgeous!"

"Oh." Hana looked embarrassed. "Tall, dark and wearing cowboy boots?"

"Yep, yep, that's him. Did you see that body? He used the school gym this morning during his free period. I might join so I can watch. When did you see him?" Sheila peered up at Hana as the redhead hovered in the doorway.

"I dropped my handbag on the floor right in front of him. Anka and the school nurse said a car almost ran me over, but I didn't see it. I crawled around the chapel carpark putting the crap back in my bag and only saw his shoes."

"Yummy!" Sheila exclaimed. "He wears cowboy boots? So sexy. Did he help you?"

"No." Hana shook her head as her embarrassment grew. "He just watched, like he'd never seen anyone grovel on the ground for a lipstick before. It was mortifying. I laddered my tights."

Sheila poked at her squashed sandwich and then hurled it into the bin next to her. "I can't stop looking at him. He's got the nicest backside I've ever seen. Just like two little peaches in a...ahh back again Mr Dobbs?"

The afternoon whizzed by with administration jobs, keeping the budget straight and making posters advertising a visiting speaker for the next week. Hana left it until just before five o'clock to make her way back to the leafy suburb in the north of the city, to her empty house and equally hollow life.

Chapter 3

The first week of term passed in a blur. On Friday, the staff and students assembled outside in the courtyard for the first of the whole school assemblies. The principal welcomed new students and reminded those from last year what he expected.

The day loomed hot and humid. Tempers snapped amongst the staff, even before the exercise of aligning six hundred chairs outside in the baking sun. Alan Dobbs ran around booming orders and introducing his unique brand of confusion. One minute there weren't enough chairs. Then too many appeared and needed to be carried back inside by a troop of giggling boys. The invited guests arrived, but nobody remembered to greet them. A beaming set of new parents were sent in the wrong direction and later discovered sitting in the stands by the swimming pool.

So began the lengthy pōwhiri, the colourful welcoming of new students and staff by the impressive Kapa Haka boys. Garbed in their traditional feathered cloaks and loin coverings, the group of older students performed their school haka, filling the airwaves with guttural noises and fearsome display of aggression.

The principal's address to staff and students proved rousing as always. He conducted his whaikōrero, or formal speech, in flawless Māori and repeated in his gentle Scottish lilt. Angus Blair spoke with conviction about his vision. "It is our intention to make the young men in our care into valuable contributors of society..."

Hana's mind wandered as the principal outlined his expectations for the year, having heard it for the last fifteen years. Angus had made Waikato Presbyterian School for Boys into one of the best schools in the North Island. Parents boarded their children in the St Bartholomew's boarding house from as far afield as Australia and Germany, to enjoy the strong academic and sporting acumen of the school. Angus' strong Christian principles permeated every fibre of the school ethos and he was a man with infinite patience. Hana once overheard him say to a troublesome student,

"You may have bounced out of every school in the district, but you're here to stay. You'll leave when your time is up and this school has turned you into the useful young man I know you can be. I have all the time in the world and nowhere else I'd rather be!"

When Hana's husband died in a car accident nine years before, Angus called round to her house. She opened the door to him with reluctance, accepting his visit as the rudimentary five-minute-duty-call. He stayed for five hours, consumed most of a large bottle of red and shared his own experience of losing his wife to cancer months before. "We have to press on, dear," he told her in a slurred Scots accent, the wine working its magic on both of them. "Otherwise, what's the point of living?"

The ceremony went without a visible hitch from the perspective of the enamoured new parents. Those members of staff unfortunate enough to be near Sheila Jennings and son-in-law, Rory Kingston were privy to the resounding slap she meted out to him somewhere between the whaikōrero and waiata. The latter drowned out the argument with its rowdy singing. Both possessed faces like thunder and from her distant viewpoint, Hana anticipated the day going downhill fast.

Bored, she studied the new staff members seated on the steps whilst fanning herself with a programme. Angus favoured male teachers in his elite school for boys and this year they looked fresh out of university. Apart from one. The new head of English was Māori and handsome. He looked in his late thirties with jet black hair and olive skin. Even from the other side of the courtyard, Hana noticed his striking eyes. She shifted in her chair to admire the shapely bottom Sheila described with such enthusiasm, but unfortunately, he was sitting on it.

Hana peered too long, deciding if the man's eyes looked blue or green. The new head boy gushed his acceptance speech at the lectern and sweated ribbons of fluid which left wet patches under his armpits. The handsome male teacher moved and Hana should have averted her gaze out of decency. Slow on the uptake, she discovered his full attention turned on her, as though he sensed her gaze. She gulped. Perched on a small library chair behind the Year 12s, she bobbed her head, sensing the pink blush begin in her cheeks.

Curiosity got the better of her and she peered between boys' shoulders for another look. Hana stared straight into a pair of piercing grey eyes whose influence crossed the entire distance between them and drilled straight into her soul. She took a sharp intake of breath, causing the boys to look round as an unsettling déjà vu washed over her. The man smiled, an awkward, lop-sided expression, more from his eyes than his mouth. He pulled his gaze away and focussed on the head boy. Hana missed her opportunity to return the smile, convincing herself it was directed at someone else. Much as she wanted to appraise the striking man more, she resisted the urge in case she got caught again. She distracted herself with the excitement of a mental grocery shopping list.

Chapter 4

A study class occupied the common room, overseen by the tall Māori teacher. He stood with his hands in the pockets of expensively cut trousers, his famous backside resting against the wall. The sole of his black cowboy boot rested against the wall behind him and he looked casual and yet dangerous.

Hana dashed past carrying a box of university brochures and sensed a small electrical current go through her body. She stopped, perplexed. A grey-eyed gaze met her confused expression and she experienced that odd sense of déjà vu again. Hana faltered, her brow creasing as she corrected herself, realising her staring bordered on rudeness. Feeling unsure of herself, she turned away and a student requesting help diverted the teacher's attention. Drawn to the man in some inexplicable way, Hana dismissed the warmth of the schoolgirl-crush, which rose inside her, as ridiculous.

"I'm in my forties! This is stupid." Hana flung her wares onto her desk and rested a hand over her chest, feeling the heightened thud of her heart through her porcelain skin. She eyed the back of her colleague's head. Peter North snoozed with his wet cheek welded to a pile of reports. "Pete!" Hana shouted, wincing as he woke up with a start.

"What? What?" he screamed, standing up, his eyes wide and his wispy hair on end. "What happened?"

"I said I'm in my forties," Hana repeated and Pete looked confused.

"You were yesterday too. It's not an emergency!"

"No, but it's also half past ten in the morning and you went to sleep after staff briefing. If Alan Dobbs catches you napping at work again, he'll make sure Angus sacks you."

"Oh, yeah. Right." Pete sat with a thud, shedding a storm of dandruff around his chair. He pulled the reports towards him and peered at them.

"Pete?" Hana walked to his desk and stood next to him, pushing a few pieces of random paper with a slender finger. "Who's that new teacher in the English department, the tall one?"

Pete's eyes lit up with a mischievous smirk. "Why? Do you fancy him?"

Hana jumped back as though slapped. "I'm a happily...widowed woman." It sounded wrong and she cringed. "Forget it, I only wanted to know where he came from." She floundered. "He looks Māori and I wondered which tribe he belonged to."

"Whatever!" Pete snorted with derision. "What would an Englishwoman know about tribes?"

Hana slapped him on the top of his fluffy head, regretting it as she unleashed another snowstorm. She wiped her hand on her skirt. "I'm half Irish and half Scots and if you call me English again, I'll never cover for you with Dobbs for as long as you live!"

"Ngāpuhi!" Pete shouted, spinning his chair as Hana stalked back to her desk. "Ngāpuhi, but he's from the mountains in the north of the Waikato. His family has links to Tainui and Logan's fluent in four languages. He grew up on a farm and can teach sport, English, French, accounting and maths."

Hana hugged the knowledge to herself, a flush creeping up her neck. She faced her computer screen and tapped out a memo Sheila asked her to send. Sensing Pete still staring, she glanced in his direction. "What?"

"Nothing." He smirked. "I'll tell him you asked."

"Don't you dare!" Hana hissed. "That's mean! I'm not interested, in fact, I wish I'd never asked! I should've known I couldn't trust you."

"Hana!" Sheila's voice issued from her office in the corner and with a glare at Pete, Hana trotted over to the open door and poked her head through. "Have you balanced that budget from last year yet? We need to close it off and I can't get it to tally."

Hana's shoulders sank. "No, I'm still a hundred dollars short and I can't work out where it's gone." She bit her lip in nervous anticipation.

"Well neither of us enjoyed a surprise holiday in Fiji over the summer, so it must be here."

"I'll keep looking," Hana said, pulling her head from the gap and turning away.

"Oh, Hana! Gwynne Jeffs from media studies offered to fix the centre's computers for free. I've told him if we've got money left, he can have that photographic equipment he asked for last year." Sheila came to the door, biting at her thumb nail as realisation dawned. "I know where it went!" She fanned her face with her hand. "I got the student from the International department onto the barista course last term at late notice. James. We paid up-front so there wasn't an invoice. I bet that's the extra hundred dollars. Sorry, I forgot to tell you."

Hana smiled with relief, faith in her budgeting ability restored. As she sat back at her desk, Pete leaned towards her and whispered, "He fancies you."

Hana's eyes widened and the flush began again, her heart dancing a wild tattoo. "Who does?"

Pete bit into a cookie and waited until his mouth was full before answering, muffling the words. "Gwynne Jeffs. That's why he's offered to mend the computers; he wants to see more of your lovely legs under the table."

"Don't be disgusting!" Hana snapped, the withdrawal of adrenaline behaving like a hideous sapping of energy. "No, he doesn't."

Pete spat crumbs into the gap between their desks as he leaned sideways again. His face held a knowing look. "You thought I meant him, didn't you? You thought I meant Logan Du Rose fancied you."

Hana's face glowed beet red and she turned back to her screen, hating the silly sports teacher with every fibre of her being. "No, I didn't," she replied through gritted teeth. "I've had and lost one husband. I don't need another."

"Liar," he replied, shoving another cookie into his mouth whole. "I've known you fifteen years and I know when you're lying."

"Teach sport or something," Hana bit, dealing with the aftermath of her disappointment. "Or better still, finish writing those reports from last year! Dobbs came here looking for you earlier."

"Did he?" The other half of Pete's cookie plunged to the carpet and his eyes bulged in terror.

"No," Hana retorted. "I thought you could tell when I lied."

Pete turned around in disgust, halted by Sheila's shout from her office. "Pete, Dobbs wanted you earlier. He said he wants those reports you messed up last year and they need to be on his desk by this afternoon, otherwise you're fired."

Pete inhaled with shock and looked at Hana in accusation. His mouth opened and closed like a goldfish and Hana tried not to smirk. "I made it up," she sniggered. "How bizarre."

The spindly sports teacher picked up the wad of rumpled reports and tucked them under his arm, ignoring the few which tumbled back onto his desk. "Fine then!" he said, sticking his pudgy nose in the air. "I won't tell you what Logan said about you."

The smile disappeared from Hana's lips and she turned back to her work, knowing she didn't want to hear. It couldn't be flattering; not coming from a man much younger than her. Pete stomped from the room in temper when she refused to retype his reports and disappeared for a few hours.

Lunchtime saw the return of James, the Korean exchange student and prospective McDonald's employee. He greeted Hana with a beaming smile. "I guess that means you got the job?" she congratulated him.

"Yes, Miss, I will be doing buggers for my first week." He seemed ecstatic with his success, so she didn't have the heart to point out the obvious errors in his speech.

"Who told you that?" She enquired, her voice wavering. Her prayers for another Korean speaking employee failing before they reached heaven.

"Fat checkout girl," he answered. "She has big baps. I happy there."

"You mean she butters the bread rolls?" Hana's voice wavered.

"No." James shook his dark head and screwed up his face. He lifted his hands up in front of his chest and did an exaggerated squeezing movement. "She has big baps. I like."

"Ok." Hana swallowed and her mouth dried up.

"Oh! I have new English teacher," James said, his face breaking into a wide grin. "He wonderful. He help me get scholarship." The student pulled a sad face and patted Hana's upper arm in kindness. "Mr Johal die. You should marry Mr..." He faltered over the name. "Marry English Mr."

"It doesn't work that way, James, but thanks for the advice. I'd need to fall in love and I'm too old and jaded for that to happen." She'd said too much to a student and Hana's colour pinked, highlighting her porcelain complexion.

"In my culture, parents choose partner. Ask your dad."

Hana gulped and bit her lip. Robert McIntyre died long ago and Hana knew even if he lived, her choice of partner wouldn't be up for discussion. He made his opinion of her clear twenty-six years before when he attacked Vikram Johal. She straightened her spine and smiled at the thoughtful young man. "I'm glad about the job, James. Make sure you write to your mother and tell her. It'll take the pressure of the school fees off her shoulders a little. Well done."

James smiled. "Thank you muchly for your help." He pressed his palms together and touched his nose with his middle fingers, dropping from the waist in an elegant bow. "I love you, Missus Johal," he said.

Hana smiled and watched him leave the student centre. "I'm glad someone does," she whispered.

Chapter 5

Mid-February arrived and the weather broke, bringing with it disappointment and the reminder that summer waned. Autumn threatened in a nonchalant, foreboding way. Crickets began their endless night calling, which added to the heaviness as something enjoyed, dwindled.

The morning started humid due to the rain; the evening not much better. The day proved too long already for Hana as she sought escape from work. She had struggled to catch up on paperwork after a frantic deluge of boys called into the office wanting help with subject changes before the deadline. Pressure increased with her workload for the guidance counselling staff, who required her to make appointments and take their phone calls while they led sessions for the boys.

With an empty house awaiting her, Hana put off the moment for leaving, aware of a yawning middle-aged loneliness seizing her. Her soul mate died, her chicks flew the nest and made nests of their own without her. Little else occupied her life apart from church, work and a passion for knitting strange things which never turned out like the picture on the pattern. Hana recognised a need for change and kept delaying the dreadful hour.

Evening settled on the school grounds, throwing long shadows out from the buildings and Hana's striding figure, as she moved towards the chapel car park. That morning, with the radio station blaring out the Bee Gees and boys milling off buses, no hint of foreboding found a foothold. A storm brewed overhead, stripping out the daylight and creating a lonely, eerie atmosphere around Hana's lone car. As she neared the passenger side, Hana sensed danger too late, already distracted by the sound of shifting feet grinding loose gravel near the front tyre.

Hana's blood pounded in her ears and throat as a figure loomed up, seeming to rise out of the ground. The air choked with pervading evil. She smelled alcohol as a female voice swore at her, "Give it here, bitch!"

Hana's handbag jerked away from her, taking her upper body with it as she clung on. Instinct made her turn her body sideways and let out a small cry, refusing to let go. In response, she received a violent push from the woman, who let out another curse. Clutching her bag tighter, Hana released the less important item in her arms and there followed the startling crash of breaking pottery. The office plant hit the concrete floor and smashed into myriad tinkling pieces, needing resurrecting rather than repotting. Her attacker started at the noise and hesitated, but she wasn't alone. "Get it away from her!" the female hissed and renewed her tug-of-war action.

Hana heard heavy male breathing behind her and then the pressure on her handbag as he prised it from beneath her elbow. He jabbed her hard in the ribs with a sideways punch but still she clung on, revived by a fleeting picture of the contents of her bag. Her breath came in heaves of pain as he shoved her hard enough to dent the side wing of her passenger door, but her fingers clawed at the smooth leather. A lipstick popped from an open pocket and cracked underfoot and Hana gave a fortifying yank, fighting for her wallet, her keys, her driving licence and the picture of her daughter's new baby. She gripped her bag with determination, slipping grasping fingers inside the zipper of the front pocket and resolving not to lose; whatever the cost.

As adrenaline helped Hana face the danger, her attackers assumed human shape. The large caucasian female possessed a hard, unkind face. Her male companion maintained a crazed look of purpose in his vivid blue eyes. The woman drew so near to Hana's frightened face, she nauseated her with gin laden breath. Hard fingers closed around Hana's throat, constricting and pinching whilst the male rived harder at the handbag. He grunted as he tugged at the leather strap, hearing the stitching tear beneath her shoulder.

"Let go or you'll be sorry!" The woman's stench made Hana hold her breath, negating the effect of the throttling. She heard the pottery crunch underfoot and clung to her bag with everything she possessed. As her head crashed back against the vehicle bodywork, she bit her lip and tasted blood. Hana gagged on the metallic tang and choked for breath.

"Hey, what the hell?" A sudden shout sounded in the guilty silence of the car park and the man's grasp on the bag ended. A grunt followed and his body dropped to the ground. Oxygen flooded into Hana's airway and she bent over gasping, still clutching her bag with a hysterical sense of achievement. Through her peripheral vision, she caught sight of the woman's large shape waddling across the grass towards the road. She croaked out a warning but the ensuing chaos covered her feeble squeak.

When she looked at her feet, the male attacker lay prostrate on the floor, his right cheek pressed into the gravel. "It's not over!" he growled and fear tightened her chest to painful proportions.

"Shut it!" A dark figure sat astride him, bending his thieving arm up his back. The sound of running and voices streamed from the lighted chapel as others arrived on the scene, milling around and joining the confusion. "Help me get him up. Don't let go."

Hana took a step backwards as several pairs of hands reached in to haul her attacker upright. She contacted the wide wing mirror for the second time that day and stifled a groan of pain. The urge to get into her vehicle and drive away felt overwhelming and a dreadful tremor began in her knees as the adrenaline withdrew. The media studies teacher pushed himself off the floor and Hana recognised Gwynne Jeffs' friendly smile. But as the face of her attacker turned towards her, she saw a frightened teenager, eyes darting around with undisguised panic and the act of bravado gone.

Hana stared around, struggling to control the unfortunate tremble in her legs. She sank backwards against her car but taking the pressure off her legs just sent the shudder into her lower back. Her fingers strayed to her throat, which throbbed and felt sore to the touch. Her trembling fingers contacted stickiness. Hana fumbled in her handbag seeking a tissue and her fingers closed on the familiar glossy paper, out of which beamed her ecstatic daughter Isobel and her sleeping baby Elizabeth. With a force stronger than a body blow, it hit her. "They tried to steal my handbag." Her voice sounded disjointed and strange.

Hana sensed the tears surface and shame blushed her cheeks. Six people stared in silence at her discomfort. Gwynne handed the teenager over to a man Hana recognised as a parent. "Don't let him go!" he ordered. With a nod, the man shoved him forwards up the stairs to the meeting room above the chapel. The teenager tripped twice and the parent kept a tight hold, using the boy's arm bent behind his back like a rudder. Hana covered her face with shaking fingers but jumped at a gentle pressure over her wrist. Gwynne kept his voice light, the Welsh accent familiar and comforting. "Come on, let's get you into the light. You're bleeding."

Gwynne's knees oozed from his scuffle with the attacker and shards of broken pottery clung to his hairy legs.

"I'm so sorry, what a mess." Hana pointed at his wrecked skin. "It's my fault."

As they breached the stairs and light bathed them in a yellow glow, Hana saw blood staining Gwynne's cricket whites and a large run beginning in the hem of his creamy pullover. He guided her up the steps with a tentative hand in the small of her back, but Hana faltered at the top. "Please, can I just go home? I don't want a fuss."

"The cops are coming." Gwynne seized Hana's arm and moved her forward.

Hana held her breath as she stepped over the threshold, dreading an audience to her misery. The bright room above the chapel buzzed with activity, but its occupants averted their gaze from her stricken face. "Did you get the cops, Eddie?" Gwynne asked the head of the sports department. He nodded his frizzy curls in reply and continued to speak into his mobile phone. Two members of his department sat either side of the teenager like bodyguards. Hana eyed her attacker from her position by the door, studying his slumped body language. She readied herself to run if he moved, fixating on his black jeans and dark blue hoodie from beneath her lashes. Feeling for a reflex of hatred inside her chest, she discovered only numbness towards him. The teenager nursed his right arm and looked smaller in captivity than in the terror of the car park scene.

"Take a seat, Hana." Evie Douglas, one of the school's guidance counsellors indicated a chair near the kitchenette and set about producing tea-making noises with crockery and spoons.

Hana exhaled with relief and perched on the edge of the seat. "Where are the rest of the cricket team? I thought they might all be here."

Gwynne frowned and patted Hana's shoulder. He grimaced and wiped at the cuts on his knee with the fingers of his other hand. "No, thank goodness. Just a management briefing. We heard sounds from outside and went onto the balcony to investigate. I'm glad we did now." He threw her a sideways smile. Hana closed her eyes against the realisation that help might not have arrived on a different night.

Her hand shook as she dabbed at her lip with a tissue, grateful for the tea Evie thrust into her hand, the chipped mug wobbled without control and spilled hot, burning liquid onto her skirt. Gwynne sat next to her on one of the hard backed visitors' chairs, scowling across at the teenager but saying nothing. A few times he shook his head and tutted. Hana felt grateful for the lack of conversation and concentrated on not letting her drink shake out of her hand.

The police refrained from using sirens but appeared within fifteen minutes with radios, notebooks, and questions. A female officer talked Hana through the event. She looked unsurprised when Hana apologised and brushed tears away. They rolled down her cheeks and swollen neck, spreading blood stains from her cut lip onto her blouse.

"We'll take you to the police station on Bridge Street," the officer said. "Perhaps one of your colleagues can drive your car home? I need the police surgeon to photograph your injuries and check you out. We've got a special unit; there's no need to go to the hospital."

"I'll drive it for you," Eddie McLay volunteered. "Evie will drop me back here for my car. Do you have a spare set of keys at home?"

Hana nodded. "Yes, I'll take the front door key off the bunch and use Vic's set tomorrow." Her chin wobbled at the sound of her husband's name. "Please can you leave mine in the mail room?"

Hana filled the uneventful journey to the police station with recriminations. Somehow, she managed to make everything her fault.

"Is there someone I can call for you?" the officer asked as the police surgeon finished examining Hana's throat and lip.

Hana shook her head and winced as the doctor pressed her sore ribs. "Not broken," the medic concluded. "Just bruised. Good news is they heal but the bad news is they hurt while they do it. They protect your breathing muscles which are always moving."

"There must be someone," the police officer pressed. "You won't want to be alone tonight."

"There's nobody," Hana admitted, staring at the tiled floor and pushing her misery behind a mask of indifference. "My son's a policeman in the north and my daughter can't come home in a hurry. She has a tiny baby and lives in Invercargill."

With desolation pricking at her soul, Hana walked into the clinical waiting room at the front of the building. Darkness shrouded the street outside and she shivered.

"I'll drive you home," the police woman offered. "Unless you have a friend you can stay with?"

Hana's spine tightened at the question and she sighed in defeat. "I don't."

"You could go to Anka's house." Gwynne rose from a grey, ripped bench. He smiled and his Welsh lilt sounded more pronounced because of his tiredness. His face showed strain. "I'll drive you. They've taken my statement."

The police officer nodded and looked at her watch. "Take my card," she said, pressing the white rectangle into Hana's fingers. "My name's Shelley and I'll be in touch." Her gaze passed over Hana's handbag, which sported a rip from zipper to seam and a missing pocket from the front.

"Please just take me home," Hana begged and with a nod, Gwynne drove in silence. She offered halting directions and he made the turns until cutting the engine on her driveway.

"Are you sure about this?" he asked and reached for her hand.

"Yes." Hana stared at his hairy fingers and covered the awkwardness by using both hands to squash her handbag closed and shove it under her arm. Gwynne withdrew his hand and let it fall into his lap. Hana glanced up at the dark frontage of her home. "I should start leaving lights on," she rebuked herself. "I didn't expect to be so late."

Gwynne walked her to the door, standing back as Hana leaned in and put the entry lights on. "I can take a look around, if you want," he offered.

"I'm fine," Hana said, faking joviality and pretending to brush off the night's events.

Gwynne narrowed his eyes with doubt. "You should have a glass of something strong before you try to sleep," he advised with a smile.

The silence of her bedroom almost overpowered Hana as she readied herself for bed. Tears soaked her pillow as loneliness and exhaustion mingled in her tortured thoughts.

***

Gwynne sighed as he started the engine of his truck and it roared to life on the steep gradient of Hana's driveway. Disappointment ate away at his heart. Disappointment and regret at the state of the world. His phone rang and he grappled to retrieve it from his jacket pocket. "Hey Eddie," he said with a sigh. "Yeah, I just dropped Hana home." His brow furrowed at something the other teacher said and his reply sounded terse. "No, she didn't invite me in. Stop it, man. She's had a terrible shock." He backed the truck out one handed into the dark street and shook his head, watching for traffic. "Yeah, it makes ya sick, doesn't it?" He trapped the phone between his chin and shoulder and cranked the gear leaver into first. "Hana didn't recognise the kid; she probably never came across him. Yeah, of course I told the cops. I had high hopes for that boy and then his mother pulled him out of school." Gwynne swore and checked the road at the intersection. "I'm on my way home. Don't say anything to Hana for now. See what the cops do."

He turned right and drove home, his heart heavy for a multitude of reasons.

Chapter 6

Hana arrived at work late the next morning, flustered and apologetic. She failed to cover the angry welts on her throat or the tender cut on her lower lip, despite desperate efforts in the mirror. Angus accosted her as soon as her feet hit the parquet floor of the reception. "A quick word, Hana," he said, ushering her into his inner sanctum.

Hana sent up a silent prayer he wouldn't require the gory details and wasn't disappointed. Angus settled into his worn leather chair and eyed her over steepled fingers. "Take a few days of leave on full pay while your injuries heal," he suggested.

Hana took a moment to contemplate her empty home and far too much time spent gawking in the mirror. She anticipated the unhealthy cycle of staring, prodding, crying and staring some more at her sore parts. "No thanks. If you don't mind, I'd rather keep busy. I'll stay in the office, so nobody sees me; I know I look hideous."

"Hana, Hana, that's not even a consideration. Do whatever you think best but go home if you feel unwell."

Her morning went fast. Hana was thankful for the activities which kept her mind off the night's events and the disquiet she found creeping into her thoughts at inopportune moments. She took a phone call from the nice police lady around mid-morning. "We're still pursuing our enquiries, Mrs Johal. The youth apprehended last night won't talk. He's going through the magistrates' court this afternoon, but I think he'll just get a slap on the wrist or youth custody. I'll keep you updated though."

Hana thanked Shelley for her promise and fervently hoped she wouldn't. She nursed a desire to never hear another word about it. On that note, she avoided the staffroom teeming with people and gossip, choosing to take her short breaks in the relative safety of the student centre.

Logan Du Rose sat at the table nearest the ranch slider, marking exercise books with a frown as Hana slipped past on the way to the post room. She clutched a scarf to her bruised throat and skittered by, dreading the attention of his unnerving grey eyes. Skirting the kitchen, she focussed on the rear doors, allowing herself five minutes before the next bell rang for lesson change. Logan ran his right hand through his hair and from the corner of her eye, Hana noticed the dark, glossy curls tumble over his long fingers.

"Oh, bloody hell!" There was a crash as the double doors at the end of the staffroom opened into her face and a large, fleshy body cannoned into Hana, sending her flying backwards into the staff whiteboard.

Hana grunted in pain as her back contacted the metal and it bent underneath her. A whoosh of air left her lungs and her ribs sent out distress signals which bent her body into a ball of pain. The staff member she collided with drew herself up to her full height and glared at Hana with spiteful, gimlet eyes. "You support staffs is useless," Alberta Lenska screeched in her broken English. She waved a chemistry textbook in Hana's face. "Stupid leetle voman! You bend it."

Hana moaned an apology and forced her body upright, performing a mental check to see if her poor body had shattered under the second onslaught in less than twenty-four-hours. The whiteboard behind her made popping noises as gravity reshaped it. Alberta pushed her threatening face into Hana's, ignoring the shortened breaths issuing from Hana's lungs or the look of agony on her face. The terrifying Russian woman was capable of reducing both students and staff to tears with her jaded outlook on life and unsmiling persona. In fifteen years, Hana witnessed enough whiplash injuries from Alberta's violent tongue to know she should extricate herself from the situation with haste.

"It was an accident; I'm sorry," Hana managed as the woman loomed in front of her. She pressed herself backwards, smelling the whiteboard marker pen as it transferred itself to her white blouse.

"Just get out of way!" Alberta bit. "I need to see board!" She advanced, shoving Hana roughly aside like flotsam. Hana's face reddened with humiliation at seeing Logan's distinctive cowboy boots appear behind the Russian.

"What's your problem?" he asked, advancing into the chemistry teacher's personal space and dwarfing her. "Don't talk to her like that!"

Alberta fluffed up like an offended porcupine and her eyes bulged. She lifted her famous prodding finger and Logan shook his head. "Keep it to yourself," he said, his tone acerbic. He offered his hand to Hana and she gripped the long fingers, allowing him to ease her free from the tiny space between Alberta and the whiteboard. She edged around the chemistry teacher's florid body and found her flushed cheek against Logan's hard chest. He kept hold of Hana's hand and leaned in towards Alberta's face, his voice deep and resonant. Hana gulped. "If I ever hear you speak to anyone in this school like that again, I'll put in a formal disciplinary complaint."

Alberta bristled and stuck her nose in the air. "Nobody listen to support staffs," she smirked. "They is nothing. Is been tried before." Her multiple chins wobbled and the blonde bun bounced on the back of her head. She glanced in Hana's direction with a look of sly victory. Logan jerked his head towards Hana.

"Not her, me!" He took a step closer to Alberta and Hana shimmied sideways, unable to break the grip of his hand on hers. "I'm not scared of you, lady. Do you wanna test me?"

The colour faded from Alberta's face and the chemistry book shook in her hand. Hana steeled herself for the woman to throw one of her familiar tantrums, but for once it didn't come. Power surged from Logan's body and the other two staff members in the room watched in fascination as Alberta shook her head. "No. You is not scared of anyone." She lowered her eyes to Hana's face and wariness replaced spite. "Excuse me," she said to Hana with a modicum of politeness and waited for her to move.

Hana exhaled a ragged breath and shifted from in front of the list of events on the whiteboard. Her whole body trembled and she peered in confusion at Logan's hand. His olive fingers were long and beautifully formed, but ruined by myriad cuts and scars which criss-crossed the flesh as though he'd pushed his hand through glass. She felt the scarf at her neck slip and snatched her hand back, working the soft material into a knot to cover her throat injury. The cut on her bottom lip oozed and she pressed her top teeth over it, desperate to hide her weakness. "Thank you," she whispered in a small voice. Without looking up, she turned and ran from the room. The English teacher's grey eyes bored into her back as she let the double doors slam behind her, taking refuge in the bathroom instead of the post room.

Seeking refuge in the furthest cubicle, it was fortunate she couldn't see the back of her white blouse which now bore the words 'Swimming Sports' backwards in purple whiteboard marker. Hana peered at her hand in confusion, aware of the thrill of electricity which still coursed through her fingers. She lifted them to her nose and smelled the faint scent of aftershave. Despite herself, she smiled.

Chapter 7

The next day heralded a visitor from a North Island catering college and Miss Henrietta Dawlish arrived on the dot of twelve o'clock, in plenty of time to set up in the common room. Anka phoned Hana from reception, holding her hand over the receiver. "That massive woman's here," she stage-whispered. "She's even bigger than last year."

Anka pulled a face from behind the counter as Hana glided downstairs and shook Miss Dawlish's meaty hand. Then she turned her attention to a dying student bearing the hallmarks of 'Sickness-of-PE-Disease.' He gripped the counter and gesticulated towards the sick bay. "I'm not ringing your parents again!" Anka exclaimed. "You'll have to do PE at some point in the next five years."

"How many boys do we have this year?" Miss Dawlish asked. "Last year saw a tremendous turnout. Nobody enrolled though; very strange."

"A few boys expressed an interest," Hana lied and fixed a smile onto her lips. Miss Dawlish's talks were dull, although the previous year a rainstorm provided the incentive to sit indoors. The boys grew bored when they realised the college representative intended to talk about food and not actually provide any. "She ate 'em herself," one boy remarked. "Then she ate the baker."

"Such a long way up," Miss Dawlish puffed, hauling herself up the stairs and clinging feverishly to the banister. Her mound of fluffy hair breached the last step, attached to her nodding and perspiring head. She reached her destination gasping and pretended to look through the floor length windows. "More stairs than last year," she grumbled, forcing Hana to halt in surprise. She showed no real interest in the panoramic views of the rugby, soccer and cricket fields, but used the time to catch her breath and mop her damp brow.

"I'll fetch you a glass of water," Hana offered, wincing at the spreading sweat stain under the woman's armpits. "Just wait there for a moment; I'll be quick." She hovered in the doorway for a second, wondering if she should get the designated first aider as Miss Dawlish heaved in giant breaths and shuddered on her tiny feet.

Making for the water cooler, Hana noticed Peter North sitting on the veranda picking fluff from his belly button. Hana groaned. He'd forgotten the sixty curious male occupants watching from their study period in the Year 13 common room. Anka wandered in for her lunch break and Hana called to her. "Can you stop Pete from making a fool of himself? The Year 13s are watching him through the window again."

Anka strode towards the balcony doors, turning to give Hana a wink. "Call me on my mobile phone if you need the defibrillator for your guest. It's in my office." She stepped out onto the balcony and Hana heard her loud rebuke, "Pete you dirty pig, stop that! No! Don't eat it!"

Miss Dawlish stood in the same spot when Hana returned, but her breathing sounded regular. Hana sighed with relief. "Through here," she said, indicating the doors to the common room. "Start setting your data projector up and I'll grab an extension cord from the office."

Hana scrabbled around in the corner cupboard, bending to reveal a curvaceous pair of legs as she searched for the cord. "Come on, I know you're here somewhere," she muttered to herself.

"Nice legs," Pete commented as he ambled into the room behind her. "Shame about the face."

"Shame about your face!" Hana retorted, yanking hard on the tangled spaghetti of cables and plugs. She stood up and rounded on Pete, brushing her curls away from her face while clinging to the extension cable. Gulping, she faced a victorious Pete and the grey-eyed English teacher.

"What about my face?" Pete demanded. "It's lovely." He stroked his own cheek and Hana grimaced as he found a spot and began to pick at it.

"Nothing." She inhaled. "Nothing at all." Her gaze flicked towards Logan and she watched his eyes narrow as they caressed the cut to her lip. Anger flashed across his face, leaving a trail of heightened colour. Hana pulled the neck scarf closer to hide the horrid marks on her throat, self-consciousness blossoming. Logan's lips parted as though desperate to question her, but Hana evaded his piercing grey eyes with painful deliberateness. Between them the men blocked the door to the common room and Hana felt panic flutter in her breast at Logan's magnetic proximity. His familiar Māori authority snaked across the room towards her, enveloping her in his mana, the ethereal sense of power which came with tribal leadership. Instinct told her that within his culture, he held great importance to someone.

"Who's the hottie out there, aye?" Pete asked, jerking his chin upwards. Hana looked at him in confusion and Logan Du Rose peered at his friend, his lips parting in surprise.

"What? Who?" Hana said.

"Woman out there bending over." To Hana's horror, Pete held cupped hands up to his chest and wiggled his fingers in a graphical display. "Gorgeous!"

Hana's mouth gaped open and the English teacher turned away and rubbed his hand over his face, his shoulders shaking. His white shirt rustled against strong biceps, the material sumptuous and expensive. Hana narrowed her eyes as she heard him stifle a snort.

She looked at Pete, misunderstanding. "Sorry, who's gorgeous?" Miss Dawlish's shambling mound didn't seem to qualify as a 'hottie' and Hana assumed she'd missed someone else's arrival.

"Oh, there you are. Do you have that cable?" Miss Dawlish popped her broad face around the door and the look of pure lust on Peter North's weathered face, left Hana feeling nauseous.

As Miss Dawlish simpered into the cramped room through the front door, the English teacher headed for the back. His tall, muscular shape slid past Hana with incredible grace. "See ya," he said, his fingers brushing her wrist. His full lips suited the look of amusement, banishing his customary severity. "Who knew?" he whispered, raising an eyebrow in Pete's direction. "True love in the strangest of places."

Hana gulped and swallowed, sensing great weight in the statement. She'd sampled true love. Sampled and lost it. She pressed herself against the cupboard, feeling the sharp edges of the shelves against the backs of her legs. A shutter crashed down over her emotions, not liking her attraction to Logan Du Rose or the suspicion that she might be at the centre of an awful joke. He sensed her sudden reticence and a frown crossed his expression. His reassuring smile melted Hana's insides, an awkward, lop-sided motion which showed lovely teeth and defined cheekbones. Hana felt the aching pang in her stomach, a craving to be held and loved. She bit her lip in confusion, but by the time she looked up he'd gone.

Behind her, Henrietta Dawlish warmed to the appraising smile of Peter North and they stood in front of each other like blind date contestants.

"Excuse me. Please excuse me." Hana squeezed between them to retrieve her evaluation sheets from the desk. "I'll hand these out so the boys can rate your talk afterwards."

Pete snatched for one and missed as Hana pulled them away. "But I want to rate her now."

"Not that kind of rating," Hana hissed.

"I'm Henrietta." The woman smiled with encouragement at the sports teacher and he rose to the occasion.

North's chat up lines were basic and often invited a slap at staff parties, but Hana gave him ten out of ten for persistence. "Do you come here often?"

Hana kept her eyes facing the carpet to hide her snigger as he worked up to asking Henrietta to look at his etchings. Or worse. The one which achieved the most slaps was...

"They tell me I'm hung like a..."

"Pete!" Hana screamed. Miss Dawlish jumped. "Get the boys ready for the presentation, please?"

Henrietta assumed a ballerina pose and acted like a horse in season, sticking her proverbial tail in the air as invitation. Hana brandished the power cable like a bucket of water over amorous dogs, thrusting it between them without looking. Both reached out for it, missed and let it clatter to the floor. Hana used the diversion to say one more, "Excuse me." She escaped to the common room to greet the few boys who used their lunch hour to learn about the school for hotel management.

Twenty boys graced the common room to hear Miss Dawlish. She proved scintillating and entertaining. Sheila appeared towards the end and waggled her eyebrows at the laughing boys hanging off Henrietta's every word. "Is this the same woman as last year?" she whispered and Hana nodded.

"I know! You wouldn't think so."

"I wish I'd supervised her talk now. It's that crusty chap from the student loan office tomorrow," Sheila sulked. "I should make you sit and listen to him as punishment."

Hana grinned in victory and watched Henrietta answer questions about fees and food science. Three Year 12s signed up for more information and a Year 13 seemed keen to join at the end of the year. "That went well." Hana sounded impressed as she congratulated Henrietta. She dodged sideways and slapped Peter North's hand as he reached for an enrolment pack. "No. You can't go, you're too old. Sort out Miss Dawlish's belongings for her please. And don't steal anything!"

Chapter 8

Hana knew of the forthcoming swimming event, even before conceding the purple marker would not wash out of her blouse.

Sheila Jennings rushed around, calling boys and press-ganging them into entering various underwater exploits in the name of competition. She cajoled and entreated with the practiced expertise of a mother. "I want our tutor group to beat my husband's," she stated with maniacal insistence.

Peter North skived in the office and enjoyed a post lunch nap under the guise of student mentoring. He sulked at the constant foot traffic as boys responded to the flurry of notes generated by Sheila. "Why are you doing this to me?" he bawled, ushering another knot of scrawny Year 9s into his darkened boudoir. He greeted their polite knock with an angry demeanour, glaring from beneath bushy eyebrows.

"Come in, come in, ignore him." Sheila bustled the boys into her office and closed the door.

"That was a group of six and her office only seats two. Do you think she's wall mounting them?" Hana turned to face an irritated Pete and he growled in reply.

"I don't bloody know. Why does she have to do it here?" he grumbled.

"Because it's her office?" Hana retorted and Pete laid his head on his desk and covered it with a textbook. Each new arrival intensified his irritation and eventually he slammed out of the office. Hana heard him attack a group of Year 13s in the common room.

"Why are you drawing tits on that brochure?" he yelled. "Can't you see it's a dude? What's wrong with your generation? You just want it all!" He left a nervous hush in his wake and Hana delayed her need to pass through on the way to reception.

"Right, don't forget to meet by the stands at the swimming pool after school. We need to run through our game plan." Sheila pushed the boys out of her room and emerged flapping her hand in front of her face. "Gosh, it gets hot in there."

Hana indicated the pile of slips on her desk. "I'll take these down to reception in a minute. Pete just had a tantrum in the common room so I'm waiting for the dust to settle."

"Did he fart?" Sheila lifted her eyebrows in horror. "If he farted, I'd use the back stairs and not go in there until tomorrow."

Hana shook her head. "Na, he exploded in a different way this time. It's fine. I'll go now." She wandered to reception armed with yet another pile of notes calling for Sheila's boys.

"Not more," the receptionist groaned. "Everyone else dealt with this during tutor class."

"She wants to beat Martin," Hana said with a grimace. "She's got some secret plan."

"I could tell you a secret about him." The receptionist's eyes glinted with mischief behind her spectacles. She opened her mouth to speak and then closed it again. "But you don't listen to gossip. I won't waste my breath." She placed the slips on her desk. "Anka will be here to relieve me for my break soon. I'll leave them for her to do."

As Hana turned away, the unmistakable sound of tinkling glass heralded something shattered beyond repair. She glanced at the receptionist, who shrugged. "Someone with a rugby ball. Yesterday it was the door at the back of Q block."

"But everyone's in class," Hana replied with confusion.

Moments later, a student ran in through the doors, twisting his body as he cast around him for something. His eyes rested on Hana and he barrelled towards her with relief. "Miss, someone's busted your window!"

Believing she'd find a group of guilty boys wielding a rugby ball, or a cricketer shifting from foot to foot, Hana walked towards the chapel and her parking space. The Year 10 boy bounced up and down next to her in agitation. "It's fine Rewa, accidents happen, love," she said. "The windscreen company will fix it on my insurance. It's happened before."

The boy bustled along next to her as they made their way across the courtyard towards Hana's car. At a turn off the main thoroughfare, a window in the science block opened and a teacher stuck her head out. "He wore a hood and ran away before we realised what he'd done."

Hana's steady footsteps halted. "What? Someone did it on purpose?"

The teacher nodded and pulled her head back in, turning to rebuke the boys behind her who rubber necked through the glass.

Hana's smashed windscreen hung like a crystal curtain across the front of her truck. Glass glittered on every surface and she approached the stricken vehicle, hearing shards crunch beneath her shoes.

"Told ya, miss." Rewa bounced on the balls of his feet. "Someone busted it." He jabbed his finger at a clay brick sitting atop a dent in the hood. "Look." Before Hana could react, the boy reached across and hefted it in his palm. "He chucked it but the glass repelled it enough to bounce it back onto the bonnet. Did you know that windscreen glass is designed to shatter and stay in place in case of accidents? We learned about it in physics. It's clever, in'it?"

Hana nodded. "Very clever."

Sickness rose into Hana's throat, not helped by Rewa's excited tactlessness. "Did you upset a gang, miss? I can ask my bro' to sort it out for you. He'll put the word out."

"No, I don't believe I've upset anyone, Rewa," Hana said, her hands shaking as she plucked the brick from his hand. A note clung to it beneath a child's elastic hair tie. Hana slipped it free. 'Give it back!' the note stated.

With a nervous gulp, Hana shoved the note back into place and sat the brick in the centre of the dent. "Someone's being silly," she said, forcing calm and dignity into her poise.

"Is it the same person what made them marks on youse neck and lip?" the boy asked and Hana's blood pressure hiked.

"No," she replied, offering reassurance she didn't believe. She walked back to reception on trembling legs, her pulse pounding in her head.

Anka, already ensconced behind the reception desk, rose to greet Hana's pale face and wooden expression. "What's happened?"

"Please could you put a call through to the police?" Hana replied. Again.

She climbed the winding staircase up to her office on shaken legs, feeling victimised and afraid. She heard Rewa recounting her misfortune with the added details of gangs and shoot outs. At the top of the stairs, Hana heard Anka ask, "Why were you out of class?"

Hana brushed her hand across her face, catching her lip and wincing in pain. She closed her eyes and let the heavy door shut behind her.

"Hana?" Gwynne Jeffs sat in her chair, displaying an unfortunate pair of stubby grey shorts which didn't match his neat shirt and tie. She glanced at the reason; a series of painful looking grazes on his bare legs and knees. They oozed liquid stuff from beneath fragile scabs.

Hana's conscious mind formed a sentence filled with thanks and platitudes for the ride home a few days earlier, but her subconscious had other ideas. She blurted, "Someone smashed my windscreen on purpose."

Gwynne rose, his eyes narrowed to form a perplexed expression. The computer chair swivelled itself around and crashed into the desk. "Why?"

"I don't know. But it can't be a coincidence. They left a brick with a note on it." Hana sank into Rory's empty seat and nausea filled her chest.

The police arrived within a short time, not because it was the crime of the century, but because they maintained a community office up the road at Waikato Anglican Girls' Grammar. Two male officers walked around Hana's vehicle, taking photos and scratching their heads. One confiscated the brick, his fingers encased in latex gloves. Hana cringed and admitted that both she and the student touched it. Rewa seemed reluctant to share his observations with the boys in blue and hung behind Hana, feigning disinterest. The cop shoved the brick and its note into a clear plastic bag with a look of disgust. Behind the crime scene, a full class of boys rubber necked out of an abandoned lesson.

"What's with the injuries?" One of the officers waved his hand to encompass Hana's bruised neck and weeping lip. She opened her mouth to speak but unable to contain himself any longer, Rewa beat her to it.

"She upset the gangs. They smashed her and now they've smashed her car. They'll go after every member of her family until they feel vindicated." Pleased with himself, the boy took a step forward. "Did you know that windscreens are designed to do that thing where they hang like a curtain?"

"Okay, Rewa." Gwynne shut him down. "You should get back to class."

The boy shrugged. "Ah no, I'm wagging this afternoon, anyway." He coloured beetroot red, realising his error amidst all the excitement. He shifted from foot to foot. "I might go to maths, actually." He slunk away with Gwynne's eyes boring holes into his back.

The cops subjected Hana to numerous questions regarding this crime and the attempted mugging a few nights earlier. Hana gave short replies, desperate to forget both matters as soon as her swollen lip and neck allowed it.

Gwynne stood next to her and commented only when spoken to. The officers circled the car again, drawing few conclusions. "Can I suggest you speak to the boys from there?" Gwynne pointed towards the science classroom. "They probably saw the whole thing. You'll need to hurry before the bell goes or they'll disperse to other lessons and you'll have a bugger of a time finding them all then."

They wandered across to Y block without urgency, failing to arrive before the bell sounded and sixty potential witnesses stomped away to different classes.

"This is a nightmare!" Hana hissed. "Vik bought that car for me. Why would someone damage it?" She buttoned up her emotions, resenting her body for its desire to show weakness through tears.

"It's ok. I know how you feel." Gwynne rubbed Hana's shoulder as the police shrugged and talked amongst themselves amidst swirling teenage bodies, their attitude nonchalant.

"No, no you don't!" Hana panicked. "After the accident, the insurance company wrote Vik's car off. This and the house is all I have left!" She pressed her hands over her eyes and concentrated on her breathing as boys walked past, staring with childish interest.

Gwynne caught her arm and led her back towards the school building. "Come on, let's get out of here."

"Why me?" Hana complained, hearing the ugly whine in her voice as Gwynne nudged her towards his car. "Everyone will think I've done something wrong. Rewa's telling them I've upset a gang!"

"Hana, everyone who knows you will dismiss that theory. Don't worry about it." Gwynne's started his truck's engine and they left the grounds, heading north towards Chartwell. The mall hummed with daytime shoppers and Gwynne steered Hana towards the lift and the first floor food court. They headed for Starbucks and Hana found a seat in a corner while Gwynne ordered.

She stared at his back while he waited for drinks at the rounded servery, pondering the awkwardness of the other night. His loneliness called to hers but she resisted. Eight years of widowhood rested on her slender shoulders, apart from one small foray into relationship which ended without explanation after a few dates. Gwynne's wife, Tessa died just after Vik, equally unexpectedly leaving them both nipping at the edges of isolation. Older than Hana, he looked wiry and capable. His blond hair greyed at the temples and into his sideburns and Hana felt for slumbering emotions within her chest. She wondered if Pete was right about Gwynne liking her. When she reached for a response from her heart, she received nothing outside of the usual numbness.

A vision of the commanding English teacher rose unbidden into her mind. She saw the taut fabric of his trousers stretch across his neat backside as he wedged long, thin fingers into his pockets and the muscular torso which strained against his shirt. She remembered the smell of his aftershave and the sense of maleness he exuded, experiencing a peculiar tingle begin in her stomach. His attractive grey eyes could stop her in her tracks with the force of his questing. She felt like she'd seen him before but knew she'd remember someone as imposing as him. "You're a fantasist. He's too young to be interested in you", she told herself out loud, a familiar mantra over the last few weeks.

"Pardon?" Gwynne turned at the counter and Hana blushed red to the roots of her hair.

"Nothing," she replied, closing her eyes against the embarrassment.

While Gwynne waited for their drinks and shot looks of interest at Hana, she consoled herself with people-watching. A young couple occupied a sofa, their baby parked next to them in a buggy. The infant mouthed on a toy in relative contentment while his parents argued in hushed voices overhead. The male sipped a latte, but the mother left her drink untouched. Hana sent up a silent, agonised prayer they sorted out their problems. At least they had each other. Vik went to work one morning and never came home.

Gwynne returned with the drinks. He bought Hana a hot chocolate and as she sipped it, she sought self-control. The couple with the baby left and Hana turned her thoughts to the brick through her windscreen. Gwynne broke into her reverie with his own conclusions. "This must be related to the other night." He paused and observed Hana. "Not that I want to bring it all back for you."

"I'm coming to the same conclusion," she replied with a sigh. "Who have I upset? And why aren't the police more interested? Those two cops didn't seem bothered, did they?"

"Not really. But we're a school and stuff gets broken all the time." Gwynne raised his eyebrows and Hana saw, her heart sinking.

"Yeah, I know," she said. "The female officer rang once to say they'd had problems with the boy you caught. They haven't contacted me since."

"Me neither," he admitted. "But I turned my phone off yesterday because I went to Auckland with the media boys. I assumed they'd talked to you. What did the cop say?"

Hana shook her head. "Just that the boy was going to the magistrates' court yesterday afternoon. Nothing since then."

Gwynne rolled his eyes in frustration. "We know what that means. A few hours washing graffiti off community buildings, a slap on the wrist and away you go."

The green corduroy chairs felt comfortable and safe in their unashamed simplicity. As Hana stared at the fabric, she registered the stains and crumbs thousands of people contributed to and pulled herself back to her own stark reality. She started and her jarring movement slopped chocolate from the white mug and onto the arm of the squashy chair. Hana fumbled for a tissue and dabbed at the sinking stain. "I should get back," she said, guilt lacing her voice. "I left an hour ago on an errand for Sheila. She'll think you kidnapped me."

Gwynne gave a small smile and started to say something. Then he changed his mind and closed his lips. Hana laid her mug on a table decorated with sentences in different fonts. 'Enjoy life - keep it simple' the words said.

If only, Hana thought to herself.

Chapter 9

The deserted school grounds condemned Hana by the time she and Gwynne returned. The final bell sent boys dribbling onto waiting buses, leaving the building and grounds silent. "I'm in so much trouble," Hana muttered under her breath.

Gwynne patted her shoulder and smiled with paternal reassurance. "I'll square it away. Don't worry."

Hana found her car keys sitting amidst a pile of detritus on her desk. Sheila had raided each of Hana's drawers in her errand of mercy and created a mountain of stationery to be sorted through and replaced. But Hana's truck stood where she left it that morning, sporting a brand new windscreen. A note stuck to her monitor told Hana she owed Sheila fifty dollars for the windscreen excess.

Donald, the formidable director of administration and Hana's boss, accepted her apology for the desertion of her post. He answered the telephone call and told her to go home. Unbeknown to Hana, Alan Dobbs didn't extend the same disregard for Gwynne's casual abandonment of his notorious Year 10 class. "I taught them myself," he boomed, traumatised by the experience and his blond wig on sideways. "Do they always behave like that?"

Gwynne refrained from commenting, apologising in the face of a fury he'd encountered numerous times. Experience told him it would blow over once Dobbs realised he wouldn't argue back. Dobbs resorted to cruelty instead. "I don't know why you're wasting time on that admin assistant. Anyone can see she's not interested in you."

Gwynne set his jaw but refused to engage, waiting until Dobbs ran dry and then exiting as the man became bored with his passive opponent.

Back in the student centre, Hana contemplated her ransacked desk and upended belongings. She tinkered with the paperwork littered around the fringes of the mess, remembering her new year's resolutions filled with courage and fresh new starts. Her mind strayed back to the tearful young constable who broke the news of Vik's accident to her eight years before. The female probationer cried for Hana's loss, great tears of sadness rolling down cheeks filled with horror. She knew Shelley didn't remember. Perhaps it was better that way.

Hana walked into her kitchen just in time to stop her daughter disconnecting the phone call. "Mum, I love the sleep-suit. Elizabeth looks cute in it," Isobel gushed. As they chatted, Hana grappled one-handed in her handbag for the photograph she fought so hard to keep possession of, deciding it was worth the cuts and bruises. Her stunning daughter smiled up from the creased picture, cradling her newborn in a possessive embrace. Baby Elizabeth's name meant 'the fullness of God.' She'd already brought joy to her family and the tiny church Izzie's husband pastored in Invercargill. Her name countered the frail understanding of people who would always view Elizabeth as incomplete. Her Down syndrome made her half an able person to them, instead of the complete, but handicapped blessing she would always be.

"I miss you all. Give Beth a kiss for me and I suppose you'd better give that errant husband of yours a hug. I know he'll expect one." Hana sounded wistful, her fingers straying to her throat as the picture fluttered to the table. Isobel rang off leaving her mother feeling empty and contemplating a long soak in the bath, a well-deserved glass of wine and the remains of a novel.

Bubbles pumped into the deep bath and the room assumed the lovely mist accompanying the promise of luxury. Sipping her wine, Hana felt vibrations through the floor and heard the ominous sound of the garage door opening downstairs. The motor whirred, hinges clanked and a car crunched over the plastic pegs she dropped that morning as she flung washing over the indoor line. Hana snatched up her dressing gown, fumbling to cover herself. Voices echoed downstairs and the garage door closed with a whir and a grunt. She halted at the top of the stairs, holding her breath and trying to hear over the pounding of her heart in her ear drums.

Bodie's face appeared around the stairwell, his short, clipped black hair and his smart policeman's uniform making him appear even younger than his twenty-six years. He smiled and chatted over his shoulder to someone following him up the stairs from the garage. As they appeared one by one, three more startled men stared up at the terrified woman clad in a dressing gown. Embarrassed, Hana pulled it closer round her body and swallowed, unable to speak.

"Mum?" Bodie stared at her in curiosity, picking up her fear like an invisible thread. "What's wrong?"

"Nothing. Nothing." Hana yanked the gown under her throat to hide the fading bruises and stem her humiliation. "I didn't realise it was you."

"I rang the school earlier. The receptionist said she'd pass on my message." He continued to climb the stairs and reaching her level, held out his arms to her. His body felt rigid with suspicion. "Who else could it be?"

Mortified by her state of undress, Hana allowed him to fold her into his embrace.

"Nobody. The receptionist didn't mention it. I'm sorry." Her voice sounded muffled by Bodie's smart uniform.

"Mum, it's fine." He eyed her with a veiled expression which reminded Hana of his adolescent secrecy. The master of spin, he could always justify why the bedroom she sent him to tidy, looked no different after an hour of apparent cleaning. He indicated his companions with a nonchalant wave of his arm. "We're here to look for something in the river. We could get a hotel or go into the boarding house, but I hoped we could bunk here?"

"How many are we?" Hana replied, covering her awkwardness with a joking tone.

"Oh, just us four," Bodie replied. He shared Vik's Indian features and turbulent nature, growing more like his father as he matured. The reminder caused Hana's heart to clench in pain and she nodded in acceptance of the plan, eager to be out of the spotlight.

The sound of the bathwater still running called her back from the past. Hana moved towards the bathroom calling over her shoulder, "Of course you can stay. The beds are ready."

As she shut the bathroom door, Hana heard Bodie sorting out rooms and people. She smiled at the thought of having her son home for a few days and the temporary abatement of the paralysing loneliness. She sank into the steaming hot bubbles and soothed away the cares and bruises of the past few days, analysing Bodie's words and particularly the ones he didn't say. He wasn't in Hamilton to look for something in the Waikato River, but someone. She shook off the ghoulish memory of Vik's grey face on the mortuary slab and immersed herself under the welcoming foam.

Later, after his colleagues went to bed, Bodie broached the bruising on Hana's neck and the cut lip which still oozed when she smiled. Hana gave him her account of the attempted bag snatch and subsequent broken windscreen. "I can't think of anyone who might be upset with me," she mused. "But two incidents directed at me is strange." Her pretty face clouded with confusion and Bodie shook his head.

"It's more than coincidental, but why you? Why now?" He made her describe her attackers again, but time warped the memory and turned them both into monsters. Hana found to her surprise, she remembered little of use.

"They took the boy into custody but I don't know what happened to him in court." Hana sighed. "Gwynne thought he'd get a few hours' community service and disappear."

Bodie rolled his eyes. "Yeah, public perception is a bummer."

Later on when the house was dark and closed up for the night, Hana heard him moving around downstairs in the garage, looking over her people mover and inspecting the window replacement. In the peace of the silent garage, disturbed only by the occasional night noises of passing cars or chirping crickets, Bodie nosed around the familiar vehicle and turned the story over in his head. "What's the link?" he muttered to himself, searching for connections which seemed futile.

He leaned against the wall, gritting his teeth at the memory of the cut lip Hana tried to blank out with makeup and the livid red and black bruise on her neck, which moved into sight when she tilted her head. "Two attacks in a short space of time." His voice echoed into the cavernous space. "Something's not right. This isn't coincidence."

Sleep proved elusive for the policeman as he lay in his childhood bed. The light blue paint gleamed in the moonlight and through the open curtains the stars winked in merry oblivion. "Geez!" He ran a hand through his dark hair and tried to distract himself from the morning's ominous task, rendering the features of the missing elderly grandmother to just another emotionless job. Her fluffy white hair and sweet face wafted past his inner vision, blending with Hana's injuries, her smiling face interchanging with his mother's. "Stop!" he hissed into the darkness and put his hands over his ears, pressing his face into the pillow.

Hana didn't sleep well either. The house creaked and groaned with the additional guests and every sound woke her with a start of fear. But company over breakfast lifted her spirits and her son's cooking involved most of the contents of the fridge and pantry. Hana's hospitable child made his usual brand of chaos in the kitchen as he served his colleagues a decent breakfast, intended to sustain them until dinner. "How long have you all been diving?" Hana asked, making conversation as she buttered her toast.

The youngest police officer, Jarrad, answered first. "I'm new to the team but the others are showing me the ropes." He pushed bacon into his mouth. "I can't eat lunch when I'm diving." He swallowed and looked apologetic. "It makes me throw up."

"Right," Hana replied, shuddering at what he might discover in the depths of the mighty river which could turn a grown man's stomach.

"Yeah, you're not meant to," Graeme commented with his mouth full of bacon. The older policeman winked at Hana. "There's a lag time after you've eaten but we tag team so it works out okay. We're on a time limit with this dive though. They've given us two days and we'll be pushed to get the area covered."

Jarrad sighed. "Our last dive was in a lake up north. That was pitch black and in an old quarry, kilometres deep. The river's shallow compared to that."

"What were you looking for?" Hana asked, almost missing the frantic shake of her son's head at the younger man. She regretted the question. Bodie's work over the last five years included retrieving bodies and objects from water courses all over New Zealand. He'd wanted to do nothing else since his first day of diving in an outdoor education class at school and followed his dreams despite Hana's concerned opposition. Watching him fulfil his probationary period in Hamilton, Hana had lured herself into a false sense of security. It seemed he enjoyed general policing in the sprawling city, but a late night phone call preceded his hurried transfer north to the dive team. Despite the advanced warning, his sudden move both perplexed and worried Hana. Something happened, but she doubted she'd ever discover what.

An older, plain clothes officer accompanied the dive team. "Just call me Odering," he said, watching Hana with interest. Blond, smartly dressed and quiet, he exuded efficiency even in the consumption of his cereal. An air of tension and expectation hovered around the men and as seven o'clock approached, Odering became twitchy and silent, readying himself to leave.

"You okay?" Hana asked Bodie, knotting a different scarf at her throat.

He nodded and offered her a wooden smile. "Yeah. We just get on with it." His words held a quiet resignation of horrors seen and dealt with, but not forgotten. Even the bright, clear day could deliver a grisly discovery. The divers grew somber as they mentally prepared themselves to enter the threatening Waikato and persuade it to release its secrets. "Right boys, into the breach," Bodie said, rounding up the men. "See you tonight, Mum. Can we take you out for dinner?"

"Depends if we find her," Odering muttered and Hana paused in confusion.

"I'll be at work and then home around four," she said, feeling silly at the policeman's look of amusement. An involuntary shiver rocked her body as she realised what he meant. The lost item in the depths of the Mighty Waikato was a woman.

The police car slipped from the garage, reversing onto the quiet cul-de-sac and alarming the woman next door as she hustled her children into the waiting people carrier. The two older children ceased their bickering, temporarily silenced at the sight of the smart police officers. They looked at their frantic, frazzled mother for reassurance as she stuffed the grizzling baby into his car seat. The children stared after the retreating vehicle, silenced by the automatic guilt a police car engendered. "Do you think Mrs Next-door was arrested?" the boy asked and his sister shrugged. The poor mother, comforted by the sudden decrease in volume and remembering she left the baby's milk bottle in the microwave, slammed the side door and scurried off up the garage steps to retrieve it. The baby wailed while its siblings pulled knowing faces at each other. Then they resumed their important dispute.

"Give me back my toy frog!"

"No! You threw it at me."

Metres away in the upstairs kitchen, Hana finished wiping crumbs from the surfaces and tidying. The house trained visitors took care of most of their own mess. Just like his father though, Bodie inherited the need to use every plate, cup and item of cutlery in his grand culinary masterpieces. Hana dropped a tablet into the dishwasher and set it cleaning the plates.

She cracked open the high kitchen windows to let out the cooking aromas, stealing a moment to admire the early morning mists shrouding the mottled hills of the Hakarimata Ranges. It promised to be a fine, blue-sky day with temperatures pushing back into the late twenties. Hana wondered if she'd see the English teacher on his regular shift in the Year 13 common room and felt a flicker of excitement. Keeping loneliness and rejection at bay, Hana armed the burglar alarm and set off for work in the heavy traffic weaving its way like a fuming, metallic snake to the south end of town. "There's nothing wrong with admiring him from a distance," she told herself.

Chapter 10

The term proceeded with its usual hustle and bustle. Chapel services recommenced with their signature gusto, challenging the school towards higher goals whilst classes raced along, pointing at earthlier destinations.

Sheila and Rory sported a fragile peace during working hours although the grapevine told of intriguing battles behind the confines of Rory's not-so-private front door. There were odd moments of veiled tension. Rory rushed off to class in a hurry leaving the photocopier jammed and Sheila spent a whole period trying to remove the mashed paper. She exacted her revenge by filling the printer drawer with A5 paper and hiding the A4, forcing an embarrassed Rory to Sellotape a multi-page document in front of a parent.

The office flooded with information from colleges and universities. Bulletins popped onto the common room notice board, got defaced and then popped off again. Meanwhile, the weather pushed its way into the realms of unbearably hot, as summer engaged in its final fling before bowing out to the onslaught of a wet autumn. The girls from the Anglican school chosen to represent their fair sex in the annual joint production, came in and out of the Great Hall. They caused mayhem amongst the assembled testosterone and turned the staff toilets into a hairdresser-come-beauty clinic. Romances flourished and lifted the atmosphere in the male territory, keeping Dobbs on his toes as he hunted down flouters of the rules.

Hana bumped into Logan Du Rose most days. He seemed to be everywhere she wanted to be as though anticipating her route and getting there first. His brooding grey eyes studied her with frightening intensity and she both loved and hated it. His presence confused her. She hankered after seeing him and then when she sensed his gaze on her, all confidence ebbed away and she drowned in embarrassment. Something about him nagged at her memory as though she knew him from somewhere, but the recollection wouldn't come.

"He's staring at you again." Anka glanced across the staffroom as Hana struggled through her soup, trying not to spill the liquid down her blouse and embarrass herself. "You're very distant of late. Is he bothering you? I can tell him to stop."

Hana shrugged. "No, it's not him. It's other stuff, nothing major."

"Logan Du Rose spends too much time looking in your direction," her friend commented. "What's going on?" Her voice sounded sharp and Hana looked up in surprise.

"I don't know. I've seldom spoken to him."

"Well don't!" Anka hissed under her breath, avoiding the eager ears of their table companions. "He's bad news. Stay away from him."

"Why? What's wrong with him?" Hana leaned forwards hoping for more detail but Anka clammed up, turning to speak to the woman on her other side. Her continued determination to avoid the subject frustrated Hana and she grew irritated with Anka. Her friend showed no desire to share whatever she knew about Logan Du Rose.

In a small act of rebellion, Hana distanced herself from Anka's judgement, walking instead with one of the science assistants. Indian by birth, Sunita possessed a slender build and the stunning chocolate skin of her kin. Hana missed her half Indian children and Sunita's company eased the knot of pain in her stomach. The lunchtime walks provided a source of mild sanity, when the cobwebs of the school blew away for a short interlude. For an hour, Hana avoided the scrutiny of the serious grey eyes which set her heart pounding in an unnerving rhythm. She subconsciously anticipated the moment when the joke unfolded over her head and everyone laughed at her presumption that such a gorgeous man could possibly be interested in her.

"I won't be able to walk for a few weeks," Sunita announced. "Gudrun's going away so I need to nip home and check on my son during lunch. I go at morning tea usually, but I must do both visits while he's away."

Hana smiled. "Careful. You make it sound like Amrit's home alone."

"Oh, no!" Sunita widened her eyes in horror. "Gudrun's mother lives with us."

"I know!" Hana shoved her arm and Sunita relaxed. "Let's walk as far as the shop today. I fancy a fizzy drink."

"Okay." They set off at a brisk walk with the midday sun burning through their clothes.

"What's this I hear about Gwynne Jeffs asking you out on a date?" Sunita waggled her eyebrows and Hana cringed.

"So awkward." Hana swallowed and focussed on her footsteps. "I suppose it's all round the staffroom?"

"Of course! But what we don't know is your answer."

Hana sighed. "I said no. He's a sweet man and I value his friendship. I couldn't see myself involved with him in any other way, but I hated disappointing him."

"He'll live. I think he's turned his amorous gaze elsewhere." Sunita crinkled her pretty nose.

"Wow." Hana laid a delicate hand over her heart. "I'm so easily forgotten."

Sunita snorted. "You should come to staff briefing in the morning. That new English teacher's worth being bored rigid by Donald Watson for. He stood up and spoke this morning and he's really hot."

"Oh, what did he say?" Hana asked, "Admin staff can only attend on Mondays. You're special."

"No idea what came out of his mouth," her companion replied with a sigh. "I spent my time looking at his muscles. He must be over six feet tall and built like a Greek god. I hear he works out in the school gym."

"I bet he's married," Hana said, keeping her tone light and telling herself she didn't care. "Someone like him can't be single."

Turning left through the gates and heading south promised a pleasant stroll, punctuated twice by traffic lights and pedestrian crossings. At the end of the road beckoned the mysterious Waikato River with its undercurrents and swirling dark waters, fascinating to watch and hypnotic in its unrelenting movement. But an hour was never enough time to reach the river and return, so the goal was futile, but persuasive. The women put off their homeward journey until the last possible moment. "We should start back," Hana said, staring at her watch with a grimace. "Donald Watson roasted that poor girl from the canteen last week for running to the toilet outside break time."

"Yeah, I heard. He's no right to do things like that."

"You tell him." Hana shot a sideways look at Sunita. "I'll watch."

"Not likely!" Sunita picked up the pace, forcing Hana to jog to keep up.

The conversation continued as the women puffed along, turning towards the achievements of Sunita's toddler son. "Amrit used the potty this morning. Gudrun looked so proud. It can take months for them to do number twos sitting down. It's a sciatic nerve thing." Sunita continued with the detail and enthusiasm recounted only by a mother. As she slipped her untouched chocolate spread sandwich back into its wrapper, Hana endured the graphic description. "I've never seen one that shape before,"

Sunita claimed. "It was just like a Mr Whippy ice cream. All it needed was a flake."

Hana pulled an expression of distaste. "Gross! It's obvious you work in a laboratory setting. Ugh. That's disgusting."

Marching with purpose towards the traffic lights onto Maui Street, Hana spotted a smattering of familiar striped blazers occupying the low wall outside the dairy. The boys had raided the ice cream freezer inside and enjoyed the fruits of their labour. "They'll get a dean's detention for being off-site without permission," Hana mused, trying to identify the boys against the glare of the bright noonday sun. "Can you see who they are?"

"Stupid little idiots!" Sunita exclaimed. "Year 9s by the looks of it. They know they're not allowed to take themselves off to the shops when they feel like it."

Hana pressed the button to activate the pedestrian crossing lights, waiting as traffic streamed past. "They think we're cruel and boring," she said with a sigh. "Bodie thought I spent my time removing all traces of fun from his life." She eyed Sunita with sympathy. "You've got it to come."

"They've no idea," the slender Indian woman raged. "Yesterday, a man approached a group of Year 9s outside this dairy after school. He threatened them with a knife, stole their wallets and phones and punched one boy in the face."

"I didn't know that!" Hana stared at her aghast.

"Angus mentioned it at staff briefing this morning," Sunita confirmed. "Stupid little boys!"

"I thought you were busy ogling the new head of English," Hana joked and Sunita bobbled her head on her shoulders and smirked.

"I did my ogling after that. My Gudrun's fine, but eesh, that dude's hot. The lab assistants are going crazy over him. Pamela thinks he might be gay though." Sunita turned her lips downwards in distaste. "Such a waste."

"Why?" Disappointment laced Hana's voice and Sunita grinned. "She asked him out on a date and he said he was involved with someone. She stuck her boobs in his face and everything and he didn't bat an eyelid."

Hana gaped. "How did she manage that?"

"What? Asking him out? Easy, she just said, 'Will you come out with me for a drink?' He said no thank you and that was that." Leaning across Hana, Sunita jabbed at the button for the crossing again, trying to speed it up.

"No." Hana shook her head. "How did she stick her boobs in his face? She's tiny and he bumps his head on doorframes! Did she stand on a chair?"

"No, silly!" Sunita slapped her arm. "He sat down and she leaned across. Peter North practically put his face in her cleavage, but the other guy didn't even look. She's sure he's gay."

"These lights are taking ages." Hana fiddled with the button to no avail. "Has Angus told the boys about the assault?"

Sunita nodded. "Yes, all of them know. And he's sending a letter home for the parents tonight. The cops are keeping an eye out."

"Of course they are!" Hana mused, her voice heavy with sarcasm. "They haven't got a clue who broke my windscreen or tried to steal my handbag."

She looked across the road at six silly boys sitting on a wall, licking triple scoops of high calorie, artery clogging ice cream. A red stain on the pavement remained as evidence of the previous night's events.

"Oh, sod this!" Sunita snapped and launched herself off the curb and into the moving line of cars. As Hana froze at the crossing shielding her eyes from the sun, Sunita dodged traffic and made a swift beeline for the boys. Like sitting ducks, they didn't see her coming. As Sunita popped onto the pavement in front of them, the boys gazed up at her with indifference, an expression which changed the instant they realised she worked at the school.

The choices flashed across their faces. "Blag it out," one boy hissed, while three of his compatriots shouted, "Run!"

The latter choice had the required pulling power as chaos ensued. Two boys bent down for their rucksacks and bumped heads, resulting in one donating his triple scoop into the other's lap. The cold unpleasantness on his crotch caused that boy to leap up, smearing his cone up the side of the other boy's startled face. Sunita maintained her stern glare and rested her hands on her hips to accentuate the severity of the moment, while the other four boys decided having messed up the 'run' choice, they should 'blag it out.'

Arriving slower but no less determined, Hana surveyed the scene. Three boys stood frozen in time whilst large ice creams obeyed the law of physics relating to solids becoming liquids and dripped along their wrists. The melting mess headed for their elbows before making the dive towards the concrete floor. One child dripped over his open bag onto what looked like a maths book. A blond Year 9 stood with his legs bowed, suspicious looking chocolate-brown gunk covering the crotch of his shorts and dripping into his sandals. His olive skinned friend wore a helping of 'goody gum drops,' which began at his left eye and ended with a blue gumdrop in his nostril. A Somali boy stood in front of Sunita, licking his ice cream as though nothing happened.

"Stop licking!" Hana growled, with an exasperated edge to her voice.

The boy stopped, but continued to clean up his cone with his finger as she looked away.

"Let's walk them back to school," Sunita growled. "Dobbs can deal with them."

A terrified hush fell over the little group as the women trailed them along Maui Street. Ten minutes later, much interest greeted them in reception. A rainbow of ice cream stains graced the arms of the boys who, unable to find a bin along the route, hadn't deemed it appropriate under the circumstances to continue eating. Clutching empty but saturated cones, they crowded together on the polished parquet floor awaiting their fate. The child with the stained crotch endured complete humiliation, walking bow-legged past the rest of the school. The dark brown stain had run down his legs and resembled a bad diarrhoea attack. His accomplice snorted the jellybean from his nose but terrified of Sunita, ate the evidence.

Unperturbed, Sunita continued her potty dialogue until chocolate ice cream left the menu forever. The Somali boy devoured his melting cone during the journey and won the competition for the only one not wearing any of it.

As Sunita and Hana made arrangements to venture out again in a few weeks, the school grapevine summoned Alan Dobbs to the helm and they retired before the fireworks began. They stood on the front steps and basked in the sunshine for the last few minutes of lunch break. Sunita opened her mouth and Hana raised her hand. "No more poo talk. I can't take anymore."

"Who mentioned poo?" Sunita looked offended. "I was just going to point out that sexy English teacher. He's on duty in the courtyard." She dug Hana hard in the ribs. "Look, look. No don't look."

"Which do you want me to do?" Hana complained, rubbing her side.

"He's staring at you," she hissed and Hana felt her cheeks colour.

"Don't be ridiculous," Hana replied and stole a peek. The man's grey eyes fixed on hers and he offered the briefest smile. She returned it without looking an idiot for a change. He leaned against the wall with the sole of his left cowboy boot resting against the brick. His casual stance held tension, as though he might spring into action with little provocation. A scuffle broke out a short distance away and he put his foot down on the floor and straightened his jacket. Boys on the fringes of the scrap kept watch and nudged the perpetrators whilst looking at Logan Du Rose. Something about his stance made them nervous and they moved away, taking their dispute elsewhere.

"Talk to him," Sunita urged, giving Hana a small shove.

"No!" Hana clung to the hand rail. "I'm not twelve! We're grown adults." She drew herself up to her full height. "I'm a grandmother. Anyway, you said he was gay and involved with someone."

Sunita giggled. "He lied to get rid of Pam. Gorgeous as he is, he looks lost, if you know what I mean. So cut the crap and ask him out."

Hana's jaw dropped. "He can't be interested in me!"

Sunita stared at her in surprise. "You underestimate yourself, Hana. You're beautiful and unattached. He's looking at you again so he's interested. You need to jump on him."

Hana bit her lip and looked scandalised. "I will not!"

Sunita shrugged and turned towards the main building. "Well someone else will then, but at the moment it looks as though he'd like it to be you."

Hana stole a look at the grey-eyed man and he smiled again. She swallowed as her heart fluttered. The sunlight caught his dark hair and infused it with highlights. Hana's fingers twitched at the memory of his touch on her wrist and his fingers wrapped around hers. She offered another shy smile, surprised by the expression of relief which touched his face. Then her confidence failed her. She'd watched too many foolish women throw themselves at men. Foolish women, just like she'd once been.

Chapter 11

The aroma of unwashed boyhood wafted in mists around the main building before dispersing itself into the clear Waikato sky. Doors were propped open to encourage the scent's exit while birds twittered unconcerned from the huge oak trees lining Maui Street. During lessons the school appeared deserted, the silence punctuated by the occasional hum of voices or scrape of a chair.

Hana deemed it a safe time for a person of below average height to venture into the corridor and avoid the crowd of unpredictable males. Armed with a stack of prospectuses for the brochure racks, she opened the back door of the office and poked her face through the gap. "I'm going to the life skills classroom," she informed Pete. When he didn't answer, Hana bounced a poster off the back of his head. "Did you hear me?"

"Yesssss!" Pete complained, his face squashed against his desk. "I'm resting my eyes."

"You need to know where I am if Sheila or Evie want me," Hana retorted. "And I thought Dobbs wanted those reports redone."

"Type them for me," Pete begged. He lifted his head upright, revealing two paperclips and a row of staples stuck to the drivel on his cheek.

"You mean write them." Hana tossed her red hair. "No. I don't know the boys and it's your job." She pushed her way through the gap, snagging a stray booklet off the shelf as she went.

"I hope Nana talks you to death!" Pete shouted after her as the door clicked shut.

The matronly life skills teacher had worked at the school for almost thirty years, hence the nickname. One Year 9 claimed she'd taught three generations of his family. The portly Ethel Bowman denied the aspersion, only admitting to teaching two. The Year 9 claimed that all three generations in question called her 'Nana,' suggesting her wrinkled appearance and supersize dresses were not a thing of recent acquisition.

If gossip ever became an Olympic sport, Ethel Bowman would win gold every time. She loved to chat, engaging her listeners in a way which ensured they couldn't leave. She had perfected the fine art of conversation manipulation. As a spider injected its prey to paralyse it before cocooning, Ethel Bowman threw out a, "You'll never guess what," sentence, guaranteed to shock the victim into silence. Then she wound in her listener until their reputation became as maligned as hers in the filth she spewed. Hana never understood why people listened, but figured Mrs Bowman had pre-empted enough dirt to be considered mildly accurate.

Hana entered the classroom with caution, hoping to sneak over to the brochure rack and replenish it uninterrupted. The rack sat next to an ancient computer which served as the classroom's gateway to the Internet. Hana unloaded her heavy stock into the flimsy shelves; shifting the remaining ransacked brochures and pamphlets into their designated places. A Year 10 student sat at the computer desk surfing the web. As Hana glanced at the screen, she saw him flick from a chat room back to the careers website and frowned. "I'm sure that's not what you're supposed to be doing."

The child, suffering from a nasty cold, sniffed with vigour and looked guilty. He stood up to leave, wiping his runny nose on the sleeve of his grey school shirt. Bending to retrieve an errant sandal, he let out a huge sneeze and a large green gob of snot catapulted out of his swollen nose and landed in the middle of the screen. Before Hana could utter a word, he fled, sniffing and wiping his nose on his sleeves.

"Ah, Mrs Johal." Mrs Bowman's squawk cut through the airwaves and Hana sighed in defeat. She watched as the snot turned from a blob into a dribble and obeying the laws of gravity, headed downwards as a runny stripe. Mrs Bowman surveyed Hana with her hands on giant, wobbling hips. Noticing the alien on the screen, she wrinkled her face in distaste. "Would you like a tissue, dear?" she demanded.

"It wasn't me." Hana hated how the woman made her feel like a child. Nobody listened to her then and it jarred her nerves with the muscle memory of defeat. "I've restocked the brochure rack. Let Sheila know if you need more for the older boys."

Leaving the snot to bake on the screen, Mrs Bowman turned her attention back to Hana and appraised her like a bird of prey sizing up a mouse. Hana estimated she'd just kissed goodbye to the next half an hour of her life.

Flinging herself into her office chair much later, Hana oozed exhaustion. Pete eyed her sideways with a hint of satisfaction on his thin lips. "Yeah, thanks for cursing me!" Hana snapped. "I almost got away with it."

"You weren't as long as I thought you'd be." Sheila appeared from her office with a mug of coffee in her left hand and a ginger biscuit in the right. Pete's eyes widened and she shoved it in her mouth whole and swore at him through the crumbs. "It's like owning a dog," she spat. At least, that's what it sounded like.

"I shouted at her." Hana bit her lip and swung her chair around to face her computer screen. A collective gasp came from behind.

"You what?"

"I want to know everything." Sheila dragged a visitor's chair across the carpet and plonked herself in it. "You just made history." She picked at a scabby mark on the arm and then wrinkled her nose in disgust. Putting it back again, she stared around the room as though realising her empire looked tired and under funded.

"Life is complicated enough, without involving myself in other people's business!" Hana groaned. "I thought I'd never get away alive."

"What did she tell you?" Sheila struggled to curb her excitement and Hana frowned.

"You don't want to know!"

"Oh, well, if you're telling, I'm obviously happy to listen." Sheila walked across the room and sat in Rory's chair, deliberately fiddling with the settings. By the time she'd finished, Rory would plonk down after class and find himself kissing the edge of his desk in a laying position.

Hana shuddered as she remembered how Mrs Bowman's ample frame wobbled and shook with glee, armed with the delicious details of who in the dean's office fraternised out of hours with whom, where and when. Her cheeks coloured at a spiteful piece of gossip about the new head of English. Mrs Bowman brimmed with bile at her relayed tale of vice and spice, reliably told to her by someone in the administration corridor.

"Come on, tell us," Sheila urged. Hana shook her head and glanced sideways at Pete.

"No. I'm not spreading it."

"What did she say?" Pete's eyes narrowed and an alertness moved through his body. "Was it about Logan?"

Hana kept her head down and turned back to her computer. A horrible creak from Rory's chair marked the point of no return and Sheila looked guilty. "Oops, bugger!" she hissed. Rising with Swedish poise and grace, she edged nearer to Pete. "Rory's chair's broken," she announced. "Let's not tell him."

Hana put her head in her hands, feeling burdened by Ethel Bowman's words. 'That Logan Du Rose got publicly dumped at the altar. Have you seen the mess on his face? She's an Aucklander, so they say. What can you expect? They've got no morals up there. Who fights in a church? Aucklanders, that's who.'

"Come on, what did she say?" Sheila's eyes widened with curiosity.

Hana cringed. "She said the new head of English hurt his face." She felt Pete's gaze on the back of her head, burning pin holes through her scalp as she kept the most salient details to herself. "In a fight."

"In a fight?" Sheila clapped her hands. "Oh, how sexy! I bet he caned the other guy."

"Yeah, he did." Pete turned back to his paperwork as though the story bored him. "He always does."

"What else did Bowman say?" Sheila urged. "Why did you shout at her?"

"Because I don't like gossip; I never have." Hana blushed and busied herself with her work. Her shoulders slumping with disappointment, Sheila resorted to messing up Rory's desk. She switched items around to annoy him and then dripped coffee over the supporting documents for a student's scholarship.

Hana pinched the bridge of her nose, fighting the pressure build up behind her eyes. Ethel's words bit into her psyche, barbed and full of meaning. 'I can see you like him. Some of the science girls are working up to asking him out. You should get a move on.'

If Ethel Bowman saw her interest in Logan Du Rose, the rest of the staff would know too. Humiliation had flooded Hana's chest as she took the bait, falling into a carefully laid trap. 'I don't need a replacement for Vik, thank you. I'm tired of being told who I should and shouldn't date!' Hana had stomped from the classroom, snagging her tights on the rough doorframe during her escape. Many a marriage had been jeopardised through Ethel Bowman's bored fantasising, but the staff believed her, passing the gossip on and widening the net for the victims. Glancing back at the large woman's supercilious smile, Hana knew another story had taken a sordid twist in Ethel's imagination. Before home time, everyone would think she fancied Logan Du Rose. She'd become the butt of everyone's jokes; yet another poor, deluded woman. His looks would change to pity or awkwardness and she'd need to quit her job.

"Oh, no!" Hana let her head sink onto her forearms as Sheila moved out of earshot.

Pete swivelled his chair around. "He's been a boxer," he said and Hana peered sideways to look at him.

"Pardon?"

"Logan. He knows how to box. I've never known him lose a fight. You mustn't worry."

Hana sat upright. "I'm not worried. Why would I?"

"I dunno." Pete shrugged. "You just seem it. He's fine."

Needing peace, Hana glanced at the clock above Pete's desk. "Shouldn't you be teaching now?"

He shrugged. "Yeah. But I don't like the kids. They call me names."

Hana groaned and put her head back in her arms. "That's nothing compared to what Dobbs will do to you. Aren't you on a written warning next?"

Pete scraped his chair back and glared at Hana with injustice. "That's a low blow, Hana! Why did you have to mention that?" His indignation carried him through the back door and into the lobby. Quick footsteps took him down the stairs in the opposite direction to his health science class.

"I hate this place sometimes," Hana sighed to herself.

To cheer herself up, she created a wall display in the common room. Evie Douglas left a note asking for inspirational quotes and Hana spent a happy hour searching on the Internet and snipping out backgrounds from coloured cardboard. Needing the box of paper from beneath her desk, Hana contemplated the grotty carpet and prepared to retrieve it. Hunkering down, she noticed the ugly ladder snaking through her tights. She traced the line to her inner thigh and groaned. "It's just not my day."

Crouching under the desk revealed some benefits, she discovered. "Ah, interesting," she said to herself.

"I'm just going to class," Sheila called as she left the room.

"Okay." Hana's voice sounded muffled. Next to the skirting board lay a wrapped mint which should have been on her keyboard after the holiday, evidence the cleaner disinfected her keyboard and left this little goodwill gift. Everyone got one, but North always ate them before anyone else arrived on the first day of term. He came in especially early. "Ha-ha, ya missed this one, Pete," Hana snickered. "That's where it went!" she exclaimed, finding a missing list, neatly typed on yellow paper. "Shame, I already printed another one."

Reaching for the huge box of rolled paper, Hana spotted little raisin-like shapes near the back corner of her desk. Her fingers itched to pick one up but just in time, she spotted a sharp movement through her peripheral vision.

Beady eyes like blackcurrants stared at Hana almost in challenge as the rat weighed up its options. She froze in place, not daring to move her arm in case it attacked. A distant memory of her older brother chasing a black rat around the coal house with a shovel, sprang into her mind. The rat became airborne when cornered and appeared to dive for his throat. Mark used his cricket skills in self-defence, but the image left Hana with a terrible dilemma. A tell-tale stream of shredded paper led from the cardboard box to a hole in the skirting board and relief washed over her that she'd been spared putting her hand unwittingly into its nest. She held her breath and tried to edge out from underneath the desk, keeping the furry interloper in view. Her stiletto heel caught in a thread of the carpet and the rat jumped. Hana screamed.

She backed out from beneath the desk at a speed she didn't know was possible. Hitting her head on the underside of the table she shot out backwards, tangling up her legs and landing on her backside. Another ladder joined the first as Hana tried to roll out of danger, convinced the rat was in hot pursuit and would definitely bite her bum. Flipping onto her knees and scrabbling away, Hana's breaths came in frantic gasps. Reaching the door to the common room, she met the knees and hairy feet of senior boys, attracted to heroism by the screams of a woman. "There's a rat!" she insisted, pushing through their legs to escape on her hands and knees.

Like all males in the presence of female angst, they didn't believe her. "Na, miss. It's in your head. My mum sees all kinds of things that aren't there."

"Yeah! Mine does that," another boy agreed. "Noises in her car too that nobody else can hear, aye."

Hana shoved past the gathering throng and bolted through the double doors of the common room, making for the female toilets with an understandable desire to scrub her hands until they bled.

Recovering in the staffroom kitchen, Hana remembered she hadn't seen her sandwiches since she laid them on her desk that morning. "Oh, wonderful!"

"What's the matter?" Anka appeared with a tea tray and began filling it with mugs, milk and a sugar bowl. She jerked her head towards a box of tea bags. "Please can you shove some of those in the teapot? Angus' secretary's gone home with a migraine and he's got the trustees arriving in ten minutes."

Hana pushed tea bags into a pot and placed it on the tray. She found an empty bowl in the cupboard and filled it with coffee. "There's a rat in my office and it's eaten my sandwiches." Her brow furrowed. "And it's ripped up the paper in the box under my desk. Sheila refused to buy any more last year so I'll struggle to do wall displays."

"I meant what's the matter generally?" Anka filled another bowl with sugar. "You're avoiding me."

Hana shrugged. "I felt you were unfair about the new English teacher." She lowered her voice and cast around the sparse occupants of the staffroom. She spotted him near the windows, his head down as he placed red ticks and crosses in an exercise book at speed. His dark fringe covered his eyes and he didn't raise his head.

"I want what's best for you!" Anka hissed, following Hana's gaze. "And he's not it!"

Hana gritted her teeth and began the long count from ten backwards, ensuring she kept her opinion to herself. But Anka wouldn't let it lie. "You know nothing about him," she persisted. "He's really bad news."

"On whose say-so?" Hana demanded, dumping teaspoons onto the tray. "Why are you listening to gossip? We've never taken any notice of what other people say. What's changed?"

Anka's face altered. Her complexion paled to leave high spots of colour on her attractive cheek bones. Her jaw worked in an uncharacteristic loss of words and Hana watched in alarm as her friend snatched the tray and left the kitchen. Milk slopped over the side of the jug and dribbled off the tray, leaving a white trail across the worn carpet.

"What's with her?" Rory sounded grumpy as he fumbled for a mug and filled it with hot water from the urn. "I hate this place."

"Nothing." Hana gave him a look of sympathy and touched his arm. "Maybe stay out of the office for a while."

"Why?" Rory's brown eyes grew round like saucers. "What's she done now?"

Hana winced. "There's a rat under my desk. Also, you might need to tidy your in-tray and alter your chair before you sit down." She chewed her lip. "Maybe, don't sit down at all."

"She's booby trapped the photocopier again, hasn't she?" Rory raised his voice and Hana felt the burn of Logan's gaze on her cheek.

"No. Nothing like that." She swallowed and Rory bent his knees so he could look into her eyes and read the lie.

"Yes she did. And you put it right again, didn't you?"

Hana sighed and turned away. "I don't need this, Rory. If it carries on, I can't work with you both anymore." The revelation surprised her and her guts clenched in response.

Rory looked horrified, dumping his mug on the counter and pulling Hana into his arms. "I'm sorry, I'm sorry," he breathed. "Don't leave; I'll talk to Sheila and we'll sort it out."

He let her go and took a step back as Hana raised her eyebrows. "Then stop spraying deodorant on her sandwiches. She thinks she's got throat cancer because everything tastes metallic."

Rory's eyes widened and he nodded in response, beating a hasty retreat into the post room. Hana made herself coffee, heaping in a generous amount of sugar. "My mother always told me it worked for shock," she told a wide eyed science teacher. "Finding a rat under your desk is right up there."

She found only blue-topped milk left in the fridge and doubted the age of it when it left a floating scum on the surface of her drink. Sighing, she sipped the hot liquid and chewed the crusty bits whilst looking around the staffroom. An innocuous space, it was generously enough proportioned so that unsuspecting newcomers might believe they could sit anywhere. That was the lie. Each table, despite not being labelled, was designated to a particular faculty and each member commanded a chair which remained theirs for life. The epitome of hierarchy and regulation, it became the undoing of many a contract teacher who put their bum in the wrong unoccupied seat. Staff sat alone on their designated tables during free periods, calling across the room to one another or standing over each other to chat, never sitting down and committing the ultimate crime.

Hana sighed with impatience, lonely and resenting the ease with which everyone seemed able to push her around. Logan Du Rose glanced up from his marking and caught her studying the cut beneath his right eye and the bruising around his jaw line. He jerked his head upwards in the slightest of invitations and Hana took a deep breath before navigating the puzzle of chairs to his table. He leaned back in his seat, one eyebrow quirked higher than the other. "You're a brave woman, Ms McIntyre," he smiled. "Not afraid of committing cardinal sins then?"

Hana faltered, a look of confusion on her face. "How do you know my maiden name?" she asked. Her mug tilted and Logan reached up and took it from her.

"Sorry, is it a secret?" he replied, his tone casual.

Hana shook her head. "No. I'm not in witness protection, or anything. I just haven't heard it spoken for a long time."

Logan pulled out the chair next to him and Hana sat, noticing the second ladder in her tights and sighing. She sensed the tantalising increase in her heart rate as the teacher studied her with uncanny perception. He knew her other name and it caused a flutter in Hana's chest, part alarm and part gratitude that he seemed interested in who she was. His dark eyelashes fluttered as he looked at her and Hana babbled like an idiot as nerves took over.

She entertained him for the next five minutes with the tale of the rat, which to the best of her knowledge was still in the office. Logan relaxed as they chatted, losing some of the hard edges and awkwardness which made him appear severe. Close up, she guessed his age at five years younger than her and chastised herself for ever entertaining the idea of romance. A latent nervousness robbed him of the ease his looks should have given and his hand shook slightly holding the red pen. He seemed agitated in her presence, invoking a curious maternalism in her soul. A long Māori nose gave him the look of a chief from the history books and his olive skin further betrayed his heritage. Brown eyes would have suited his dark features but instead, grey irises glittered like precious stones, giving him an ethereal look. Long dark eyelashes touched his cheeks as he blinked, giving Logan a deceptive look of innocence.

The bruising on Logan's face gave a form of truth to Mrs Bowman's gossip, reduced by time and healing to the greenish hue heralding the end of the process. A nasty gash under his eye appeared held together by dark stitches and Hana tried not to stare.

In his nervousness, Logan touched a hand to it, a hand with bruised and swollen knuckles. He sighed and made a noise with his lips like a huff of exasperation.

"Sorry," Hana said, biting her lip with remorse. "I didn't mean to stare."

Logan's face clouded with contrition. His fingers rested close to hers on the table. "No, don't worry. It hurt when I laughed at your rat story. The doctor stitched the inside of my lip and you're funny. Anyone ever told you that?"

Hana bit her lip and shook her head. "Stupid, dumb, an idiot. Never funny."

Logan narrowed his eyes and hid his surprise. His irises shifted colour, from a gentle grey to the colour of grit. "You're none of those things," he replied. His soft tone resonated somewhere deep inside Hana's soul. She felt the overwhelming déjà vu `strengthen its hold as speechless, she watched with fascination as his irises lightened again with painful slowness.

Hana's stomach lurched as though she'd crested the highest point of a roller coaster ride and anticipated the fall. Myriad tiny scars littered his olive fingers and she sat on her hands to stop herself touching them. His immaculate clothing looked expensive to the point of perfection, but his aura screamed of emotional neglect. Hana pushed her own confused thoughts to the back of her mind, trying to listen to his words but mesmerised by the softness of his lips. "Sorry, pardon?"

Logan repeated himself. "I tackled him and won the ball. He didn't like it and took my legs out in the box. The referee pinged him for a penalty so he waited for me in the car park."

"Ohhhh!" Hana exclaimed.

"I've started playing for Rovers this year," Logan continued. "That was the plan, anyway. The indoor soccer's meant to increase our fitness with friendly games." Logan smiled ruefully, oblivious to the sordid make-believe-life invented for him by the gossip. "The locals don't seem that friendly though."

Hana struggled to shake off the dirtiness which Ethel Bowman's tittle tattling left on her psyche. She covered her wrong footedness with platitudes. "Hamilton folk are okay. You just need to be here a while."

"I'd like to be." He sounded wistful and the smile he gave her looked tight on his face.

"Is your role not permanent?" Hana felt a stab of fear in her heart and faltered, disobeying her own rules. She didn't get attached to men. Never again.

"It is," Logan confirmed. His grey eyes seemed to look straight into her soul. "I need another reason to stay."

Looking and feeling flustered, she finished her horrid coffee and pushed her chair back. Logan got to his feet as she stood and waited for her to leave before sitting back down. "Nice chatting," she said, cursing herself as the lame sentence emerged from her lips. She glanced back as she reached the sink, embarrassed to find him studying her.

Hana dumped her mug into the dishwasher, squeaking with alarm at the sound of an angry shout. Paul Mannings, the biology teacher stormed through from the common room, his face puce with rage. An empty cage dangled from his hand.

"What's happened?" Hana asked the elderly man who cleaned the kitchen.

He leaned in close and whispered, "Fluffy from the biology lab went missing a few days ago. Paul thinks the groundsman let him out on purpose."

"Oh no!" Realisation flooded across Hana's face. "Fluffy's not a rat, is he?"

The old man nodded and she clapped a hand over her mouth, heading back to the office at a run. The common room erupted into noisy chaos and boys crowded ten deep round the office door. Hana pushed her way through the tall bodies, desperate to see between the jumpers and rucksacks.

Larry Collins wore large gloves and dangled a dead rat from one of them. A Year 13 boy leaned down to give Hana the details. "The groundsman murdered Fluffy. He did it seconds before Mr Mannings arrived. It's a bit mean; he knew he was on his way."

"Why, Collins? Why?" a Year 13 shouted, impersonating Paul Mannings and laughing. The groundsman posed with the dead rat while boys snapped photos of him on their phones.

"Vermin!" he hissed with a sour expression, enjoying the attention.

Hana put her hands over her face and pushed her way back through the boys, spending the afternoon in the guidance foyer making a wonderful display discouraging suicide.

Isobel phoned later that evening as Hana enjoyed the last rays of sunshine on the deck. "You caught me finishing this bottle of red wine I've been working my way through," Hana sighed. "It's nice, but it got quite vinegary towards the end. There're bits of cork in my glass."

"You need someone to share it with," Izzie remarked, her tone sad. "Normal people don't take months to drink one bottle."

"Better that than an alcoholic," Hana reminded her tartly.

"Yeah, sorry. I feel down in the dumps. Being the wife of a pastor in such a small community is taking its toll. These people think they own us. The parish church committee's decided I can run the Mums' and Tweenies' group by myself." She sniffed and Hana sensed her holding back tears.

"Oh, Izzie," she sympathised. "It's too soon after delivering Elizabeth. Can't you explain how you're feeling?"

Elizabeth's handicap made her more demanding than other babies. Izzie made it look easy, but it wasn't. "The chairwoman left me sitting in a circle with thirty women and children and thought I'd sing nursery rhymes to them!" Izzie released the threatening deluge. "You know I can't sing," she wailed.

Hana tried to help by delivering the usual platitudes which mothers are hard wired to produce, but Izzie resisted consolation. "I need to leave here," she sobbed. "Can I come home?"

Hana took a deep breath. "No."

"No?" Izzie's voice rose to a squeal. "But Mum!"

"You can come home for a visit but you know I'll send you right back after a rest. Marcus is a great husband and this isn't his fault. You've only been there a few months. We show people how to treat us and if you don't like what you're getting, change what you'll accept." Hana crossed her fingers and rolled her eyes, wishing she could follow her own advice.

As Izzie rang off with the parish council chairwoman in her sights, Hana feared for the woman's safety. Her daughter burned slow like her father but became volatile under pressure. Mrs Chairwoman was heading for a battle and wouldn't see it coming. Hana thought of poor Marcus, bearing up in the middle of the debacle. He'd been so calm and strong when Elizabeth arrived, supportive of Izzie and loving and accepting of their baby girl. "He must feel stuck between a rock and a hard place," Hana muttered to herself.

Hanging the phone back on its cradle, Hana heard the doorbell chime. The imposing shape through the glass didn't look familiar, so Hana opened the door with more care than usual. Standing on her porch with an expression of guilt, she discovered the last person she expected to see.

"I'm not stalking you, I got your address from the staff list," Logan said, sounding apologetic. Then he bit his lip and hesitated. "Geez, that does sound stalky. Sorry."

Hana laughed and stepped back to allow him entry. As he stood in her hallway, she acknowledged his height at well over six feet, compared to her five foot nothing. She found herself looking at the buttons of his shirt. "I'd forgotten about the staff address list. A few of the social sciences teachers live in this area." She didn't add that none of them ever visited.

Logan removed his cowboy boots and waited for directions. A vein in his neck twitched with nervous energy and Hana fought the urge to touch it. Her old black and white cat hovered at the top of the stairs, examining the visitor through green saucer eyes. He looked funny, his neck extended so he could peep around the corner.

"Come out of the way, Tiger," Hana chided him in a gentle voice. She scooped him into her arms and led the way up the first flight of stairs, along the hallway and into her bright dining room. The cat struggled for release and fled through the open ranch slider, his tail pointing upwards like an arrow. Logan stepped onto the deck and looked at the Hakarimata Ranges in the distance. "Wow, what a view. Now I know why the house is so high from the street."

Hana nodded. "I love watching the mountains. The city is busy but lonely, yet it always feels like something's happening up there." Her eyes widened and she bit her lip, regretting the slip which revealed too much of herself. "What would you like to drink?"

"Water's fine." Logan smiled revealing a dimple in his right cheek. The lack of a partner on the left suggested it came from an old injury.

Hana surreptitiously lifted her wine glass from the dining table where she had abandoned it and laid it in the dishwasher. "Have you eaten?" she asked.

"No." Logan's brows knitted and he looked awkward again.

"Me neither," Hana confessed. "It's hard when you live alone, isn't it? I either eat everything in the fridge, or nothing at all."

"Oh, I don't live alone," Logan replied and Hana's heart plummeted into her stomach. She tried to hide her misery as it flopped like a dead fish inside her.

"Of course you don't," she whispered and Logan studied her face expression with something like surprise.

Hana made fried egg sandwiches which she passed off as an English delicacy. Logan relaxed and it made a pleasant change as they chatted, cooked and ate.

After they cleared up, he pointed out his Triumph Spitfire parked out on the driveway. "Most of the history department live in this road," Logan mused. "I remembered reading your address on the staff list weeks ago and then noticed your car out front. I've been exploring the city and giving the old car a blow-out."

They sat on the deck until well after dark when the cool night air bit along with the mosquitoes. Mrs Bowman's tale of the jilting proved right but like most things, she mangled it in the telling. "My fiancé worked at the same school. I couldn't face going back there. Our relationship ended in the summer holidays a fortnight before school started back. Planned for months and destroyed in a moment." He looked wistful and embarrassed, picking at a thread on his jeans with slender, scarred fingers.

"She must be crazy," Hana whispered, her cheeks burning with embarrassment straight away. "Sorry, I didn't mean to say that out loud."

Logan smiled at her, his grey eyes soft and expectant, as though she'd ticked some subconscious box or passed a test. "Thanks," he replied. "But five minutes after arriving in Hamilton, I'm relieved it happened." His intense look bruised her delicate features and Hana looked away, not sure what he meant.

"How did you end up at Waikato Boys'?" she asked, changing the subject.

"I travelled down a few weeks ago on my motorbike, saw the principal and gave him my CV. He called me back a few days later after his head of English left him in the lurch."

Hana nodded. "I bet he was glad to see you. Caitlin left without notice. Her husband secured a job in Dubai. There would've been a riot if Angus picked any of the others to be head of department." She shivered in the dropping temperature and Logan stood up to leave.

"You should go indoors. Thanks for dinner," he said and smiled, his grey eyes studying her face for something. Again, Hana felt that curious sensation of having been there before, shaking it off as she followed him to the front door. Logan turned and looked as though he wanted to say something, losing his nerve at the last second. He pushed his feet into his boots and walked onto the porch.

Hana caught his scent, a pleasant meadowy smell, like flowers and hay. It plagued her memory and she shivered as though touched by her past. He felt mixed up in the years she struggled to forget, causing conflict and at the same time, excitement and danger.

The car waited on the driveway, matt white with green leather interior. Hana stroked the paintwork. "It's cute," she said with a smile. "How do you fit your legs in?"

"With difficulty." Logan grinned and crammed his long frame into the front seat. The door groaned with age as he closed it and wound the window down with a handle. "See ya, Ms McIntyre," he said and winked.

With a splutter and a hiss, the car roared to life and reversed out onto the street. Logan waved and crunched through the gears. Hana stood on the drive for a while, staring at a patch of oil left by the car. It glinted in the light of the streetlamps. She shook herself and made her way indoors, still haunted by that inexplicable feeling of déjà vu which accompanied Logan Du Rose.

Chapter 12

Hana apologised to the biology teacher the next day for the loss of his pet rat. He acknowledged responsibility for the sandwiches and the expensive box of paper, which an angry Sheila marched to the skip in a temper.

The incident marked the start of a feud between the biology department and Larry Collins, sparking a series of spiteful retaliations. Paul Mannings maintained the rat could not escape his own cage without help.

"Collins wouldn't go through all that damn drama!" Sheila scoffed. "He'd just kill the thing. These science teachers are far too fond of their conspiracy theories!"

The Year 13 biology class attempted to keep the saga going, demanding a full funeral complete with chaplain, for the deceased Fluffy. Angus refused on the grounds of not encouraging stupidity. The boys arrived in class sporting tissues and vapour rub, which they spread near their eyes to induce real tears. Paul Mannings assumed Fluffy went into the dustbin, courtesy of Larry Collins. In fact, Fluffy returned to the laboratory next-door, retrieved by Sunita and laid to rest in the freezer. The other class dissected Fluffy numerous times without realising. His moment of fame ended as quickly as it began.

Hana bumped into Logan a few days later in the corridor outside the common room. She peered into one of the brochure racks, trying to work out how to retrieve the banana skin from inside a shelf without covering herself in its decaying components. Exasperated with boys who couldn't master the use of the dustbin, she stepped back in frustration and lost her footing, lurching backwards into the stairwell. Hana felt the sharp edge of the top step beneath the sole of her shoe, but her stiletto hampered her ability to gain purchase. Her arms flailed and she missed the solid wooden banister by millimetres.

Strong hands halted her disastrous tumble and pushed her upright. Glancing down with her heart fluttering in fear, Hana rested her hands over the fingers clasping her waist. "Thank you," she gasped, nausea roiling her stomach. A solid chest cradled her from behind and she took a tentative step forward, away from the top of the steps.

"That's okay." Logan's voice made her jump in embarrassment and Hana turned, finding herself closer than she should be to another member of staff. He quirked his lips upwards, his expression gentle. He didn't remove his hands from her waist, allowing his fingers to track around her body as she turned before resuming their possessive hold. "That rack is too near the top of the stairs," he said, his gaze remaining on her face.

"I know." Hana shot a nervous glance at her office door. "I've mentioned it before."

"You could've fallen." Logan's brow narrowed and his lip twitched. He reached up with one hand and pushed a stray red curl behind her ear. The action felt intimate and tender.

"They're the stairs of death," Hana said with a shiver. "A couple of people have died on them."

"Really?" Logan's brow knitted and he glanced backwards at the hard wooden edges and angular balustrade.

"Thank you for catching me." Hana's eyelashes fluttered and she listened to the sound of her blood pulsing past her eardrums.

"You're welcome, Ms McIntyre."

"Why do you call me that?" Hana cocked her head like a little bird and Logan pursed his lips.

"Isn't it your name?"

Pain pushed through the delicious feeling of Logan's hand on her waist and she sighed. "Not anymore. Not for a very long time." Her tone sounded sad and she tried to correct herself and gloss over the misery her maiden name engendered. "Johal is a Sikh name. I married Vik at eighteen."

Logan bowed his head and pulled her closer with his hands on her waist, leaning so his lips brushed the shell of her left ear. "I know," he whispered. His fingers rose to her cheek, the knuckles skimming the soft, porcelain skin. Hana shuddered at the gentle warmth of his breath on her neck and closed her eyes.

"Sir? Oh." The juvenile voice issued from behind Hana, causing a guilty flush to haze across her neck and cheeks. "Mr Dobbs is looking for you. He wants you to supervise the common room for study period."

Hana glanced up at Logan's strong jaw as he answered, peering from beneath her lashes. "When?"

"Now, sir. He's sent your Year 13 English class to the common room and told them to sit near the front. He said you could manage it."

Logan winced. "Okay. I'm coming now."

Hana heard the boy turn and amble away, his sandals slapping against the wooden boards. Logan smiled down at her with a gentleness in his eyes which touched her and melted some of the hardness in her soul. "No rest for the wicked," he said with a sigh. He brushed the pad of his thumb over her cheekbone and dropped it to his side with an expression of reluctance. His full lips opened as though to say something else, but the sound of raucous laughter broke out from the direction of the common room.

Logan shot Hana an apologetic glance and strode away, the fingers of his left hand caressing her waist as he let go. The double doors clanged shut behind him. "Sit down!" Hana heard him say with quiet authority. He didn't shout or threaten like the other male teachers, but as she watched through the glass, the boys scurried back to their desks in instant obedience. The hidden steel in his voice brooked no opposition and Hana watched power exude from the man like a physical thing. He seated himself at the front of the class and laid a pad of green detention slips on the desk with minute precision, shifting them until happy with their position. Silence descended on the room as one hundred boys turned back to their work.

Realising she stared like a moron, Hana forced herself back to work. She dug out the banana skin with a fork from the kitchen and squirted cleaning spray into the shelf. When the bell rang at the end of the period, she found herself in the post room with one of the art teachers whining at her in a high pitched voice. "They need to go on this course. There isn't another one for six months," the woman complained.

Hana smiled with practiced calm. "The forms went out to you at the end of last year and you didn't respond. The course is now full. There's nothing I can do."

"Well, that's just plain unreasonableness," the woman bristled and Hana walked away to avoid further argument. In the women's toilets she shook her head at herself in the mirror and washed her hands, imagining her delicate fingers throttling the stumpy neck of the arrogant art teacher.

"Bad thoughts!" she said to her reflection. "Stop it." She smirked at the idea of twenty-eight boys sitting in a tutorial full of girls from Waikato Anglican Girls'.

"What's funny?" asked Lorrie from the tuck shop as she washed her hands alongside Hana.

"I'm just imagining a Photoshop lesson at Wintec, with our boys sitting next to girls from up the road."

Lorrie snorted. "Would Dobbs allow that? He's so archaic. He'd insist on going with them and using his ruler to measure the distance between them!"

"That's what I thought." Hana smirked, drying her hands on a towel. "It's too late anyway. We missed the cut off date and they grabbed every available place. I couldn't tell Clare her counterpart at the girls' school beat her to it."

"Remember the play last year? Hamlet wasn't it? All those girls with sassy hair and attitude. And the lead actor came on stage with long, glossy straight hair."

"I know. Four years he rocked that curly Afro. Dobbs couldn't punish him because his parents claimed it was part of his cultural heritage; couldn't cut it or change the style."

"Yep." Lorrie nodded. "Then the Waikato Girls' straightened it for him. Looked like he'd put his finger in an electrical socket."

Hana put her hand over her mouth and sniggered at the memory of the most touching scene being ruined by snorts and giggles from the boy's classmates.

"Hilarious," Lorrie laughed. "See you later if you come to morning tea."

By the time Hana made it back to the common room, all that remained of Logan Du Rose was the heady scent of his expensive aftershave and the aura of clear mountain air which seemed to shroud him. Hana suppressed the flicker of disappointment and chastised herself, reminding her battered ego that it didn't need another kick.

Chapter 13

Bright sunshine promised a hot and sultry day, the New Zealand climate keeping its dishonourable intentions to itself. Hana cleaned her house before heading to the mall at Chartwell on foot to waste a lonely Saturday amongst busy shoppers.

As her walk progressed, bright azure skies blinked under cloud cover and the day degenerated into awkward showers and an unpleasant gusting wind. Hana arrived buffeted and blown, her umbrella inside out and her jacket soaked. Not excited about the forty-minute walk home, she ordered coffee and sat down to watch the world go by. It gave her a peculiar feeling of detachment for a woman who'd once felt too busy, watching other parents ushering along whinging children while she sat alone. Hana recognised the despondent slump of the mothers' shoulders as they hauled their youngsters past tempting sweet kiosks and she remembered the never-ending slog of provision and worry. She watched the mother-daughter-duos browsing in clothing shops and emerging with carrier bags wearing the shopaholics' satisfied look of contentment. Husbands hung around outside shops ready to collect the variety of bags, freeing up their women to proceed into the next glitzy store and repeat the process. The men looked bored with denting their wallets in a credit crunching weekend ritual.

Hana sipped her latte and regretted the anticipated aerobic workout, which became less attractive as she listened to the rain slam into the mall roof.

"Can I join you?" Before she could answer, Logan Du Rose slid into the seat opposite, clutching a metal rod with the laminated number forty-three clipped to the top. He saw her near empty cup and strode off to order her another. "Got you a latte," he smiled as he seated himself again. "I don't want to sit here on my own."

He pulled a cane sugar sachet from the cute pottery dish on the table and fiddled with it, trapping the contents up one end. Hana watched with casual interest, waiting for the inevitable moment when the wrapper split and the sugar spilled everywhere. When it happened, she smirked and looked away. She glanced back as Logan finished collecting the granules in his palm and tipped them into an empty cup on the next table. He made a snuffing sound. "You knew that would happen, didn't you?"

Hana smiled and nodded. "My son loved doing that. They always rip."

Logan wrinkled his nose and flipped his fringe out of his eyes with a shallow movement. A sullen teenage girl interrupted his possible retort by arriving with their drinks. She slapped the order on the wobbly table, unconcerned by the amount of coffee residing in the saucer. She snatched the numbered spindle from the table and returned to the counter.

"Millennials are such fun, aren't they?" Logan mused with sarcasm.

Hana thought back to her days at university when she spent the summer working in the Belle Vue Hotel on the sea front. It seemed like hard work for unattractive money. On a trip back to Aberystwyth on holiday with Vik and the children many years after they left the university, Hana stared in the familiar windows.

'Come on, let's eat there,' Vik urged, but as she gazed into the sunny bar, she felt the click of time moving on.

'Nobody will remember me!' she scoffed. 'I was just a pregnant student from years ago. They'll pretend and it will feel hollow.' Hana blanched as she thought of the stares and finger pointing, both in class and at work.

"Fancy getting pregnant in your first year," the gossips whispered. "She just made life harder for herself."

"Hana?" A light touch on her hand made her jump and her drink slopped. Logan mopped up the mess with a serviette one-handed, but kept hold of her fingers with the other. She shucked off the stressful memories and forced herself back to the present, liking the warm hand over hers far too much. Hana extracted her fingers and smiled at Logan, her heart thudding and her mind whispering permission to enjoy the simple pleasures. A woman in her late thirties walked by and stared at Logan, undressing him with her eyes. She smiled at him with unspoken invitation and he ignored her.

Hana's voice wobbled as she tried to wish away the pretty brunette as she lingered by the confectionary stand, ogling Logan without shame. "I worked in a bar in my first year at uni. One busy Saturday, I tripped up a step coming into the dining room and emptied a full bowl of tomato soup over a man wearing a cream safari suit. The hotel paid for his dry cleaning and the owner blamed me." Hana blanched, remembering why she'd tripped, her swollen stomach obscuring the step in those last few weeks. "It's a stupid story," she stammered. "Ignore me."

Logan asked polite questions, teasing information from Hana like easing the knots from a tangled necklace. "So," he said, his voice quiet. "You married young and worked in a bar. What did your husband do?"

Hana went quiet for a minute as the memories flooded back. "Engineering degree. He worked at the local supermarket between classes." She smiled. "He was so lazy with his uniform and only used to iron the front of his shirt, claiming his overalls hid the rest. This one time, they made him take the overall off to collect trolleys outside and he looked like someone dragged him through a hedge backwards."

Hearing Logan clear his throat, Hana glanced up feeling embarrassed and disloyal. Why did this man ask questions when he didn't want the answers? Logan's sparkling grey eyes fixed on her face with a look of curious longing. Vik died eight years earlier but still Hana couldn't throw off the ill-placed sense of guilt for enjoying Logan's nearness. Her slender, sun kissed hand strayed to the space over her heart and Hana bit her lip. Silence hung over them like a shroud and Logan's nervousness returned. "Wanna go for a walk?" he asked, peering out from under his long lashes, the trace of a stammer showing itself.

Deciding Vik's spirit couldn't deny her friendship, Hana walked around the mall with Logan until he headed off to the hardware store for a particular type of bolt. Hana moseyed around the card racks before moving onto the bookstore next door. The rack of politically incorrect cards caught her eye and Hana opened a few out of curiosity. Some were genuinely funny and she snorted and giggled to herself. One depicted a little girl with her nose screwed up and a disgusted look on her face. Inside it read, 'Monica couldn't stand her own farts–Happy birthday'

It was deliciously funny, but not appropriate for Mabel at church. Fate chose that moment for Logan to appear behind her and read the caption over her shoulder. Hana felt his closeness and the heat from his body as he leaned over and her heart fluttered in betrayal. Feeling chastened, Hana put it back in the rack and forced the smirk from her lips.

Logan shrugged at the caption and grabbed another one from the stack. "I like this one better," he grinned. "I sent it to my sister in Auckland." He put it back, adding, "She didn't find it funny."

The cover sported a black-and-white photo of a nineteen fifties couple and the inside was unrepeatable but hilarious. "Schoolboy humour," Hana remarked sanctimoniously with a twinkle in her eye. She sauntered towards the nice flowery cards with dull poems about friendship.

"Boring," Logan remarked as she flounced away.

Hana picked a card with red poppies in a field scene and paid for it. Logan followed her into the mall and she experienced a flicker of irrational pleasure at his desire to stick with her. "It sounds terrible outside," she said, turning to him with a frown. She used a cloth band from her wrist to tie her hair back into a loose ponytail, readying herself for the long walk home. "These late-summer storms blow up from nowhere, don't they?"

The atrocious rain hammered on the mall's tin roof above them as if to reinforce her point. Hana looked upwards, seeing only the underside of the second level as she tucked her hair inside her jacket collar and inspected the ratty umbrella.

"I dunno. The weather forecast predicted it. Let me give you a lift?" Logan added, "Please."

Hana wavered for a moment before accepting, wondering how his little Triumph managed in the wet without a hood. Her heart pounded in her chest with abandon, refusing to still at the proximity of the stunning male. A taxi might have saved her heart failure.

They left the mall, staying under cover as far as possible until the extended parking spaces further away. The day appeared grey and dirty, the rain deluging in sheets. "Wait here, I'll fetch the car," Logan insisted, running into the rain and shielding his dark hair with his jacket.

Minutes later, a maroon Toyota Hilux halted next to her and the driver beckoned Hana. At first, she stared in confusion, expecting the Triumph. When Logan lowered the rain-spattered window and called to her, Hana jumped in surprise and hauled herself onto the side rail, slipping into the passenger seat with wet trainers. "Sorry," she said, feeling foolish.

Logan gave her a quick smile and slid into the bunching traffic as a car horn expressed another motorist's irritation at his halting of the flow. The fuming snake of cars and exhaust fumes remained static and the windows misted up from their wet clothes. Noise from the air blower made conversation redundant. The busy mall shifted traffic through the exits with painful slowness. At the junction with Hukanui Road, Logan half turned to Hana. "Would you like to see my place?" He chewed on the inside of his cheek, betraying fear mingled with hope.

Hana panicked. She didn't want to return to her deserted house, but dreaded the awkwardness of relying on Logan for a lift home if she needed to escape. The idea pushed a sense of powerlessness into her mind and left her unable to decide. A honk from behind panicked Hana into a choice as Logan waited at the junction, his patience appearing endless. "Yes. Please." She heard the words emerge from her lips and blinked in surprise at the dreadful risks loneliness forced her to take.

Logan waited in the left lane while an impatient driver made rude gestures from his vehicle next to them. Hana watched Logan's blank expression from the side, his jaw set into a hard line as he turned his head to meet the driver's gaze. The man looked away with such rapidity, Hana wished she'd seen whatever he did. With no more eye contact, the man turned right and blasted away down the road.

"Everyone's got the same idea." Logan took a gap in the traffic and moved onto the main road, travelling with caution through the torrents and into the northern end of town. His diesel engine chugged along without issue, splashing through the deep puddles on its massive wheels without reluctance.

Misgivings flooded into Hana's heart. She didn't know Logan Du Rose well enough to visit his home, especially without telling someone first. Easing her mobile phone from her jacket pocket, she held it away from Logan and peered at the screen, seeing the low battery sign blinking feebly up at her. Driving for fifteen minutes through heavy traffic, Logan headed north towards Gordonton and open country. As Hana summoned up enough courage to at least request an address, Logan indicated left and pulled into a rutted track off the main road. The post box stood to attention, a re-purposed red paint pot with a slit cut in its metal lid. It looked as though it had seen better days. The rutted road went on for endless minutes and the vehicle bumped and smacked over pools and puddles that might have shaken a lesser car to bits.

"How old are you?" Hana blurted, with unexpected force as her subconscious worked to dispel any notion of romance with Logan Du Rose. Her cheeks pinked with instant embarrassment.

Logan's lips quirked upwards. "Old enough to drive a car."

"You can drive at fifteen!" Hana remarked, sounding like an irritated teenager.

"Older than that." Logan smirked, his eyes narrowing with mischief and his top teeth grazing his lower lip.

Hana turned to face the window, humiliation making her emerald eyes flash. Strong fingers settled over her right hand and she glanced across to meet Logan's earnest gaze. "I'm thirty-nine, Hana. I've got all my own teeth and am financially solvent. I'm jilted and single, too perfectionist for my own good and not keen on feet. What else do you need to know?"

Hana looked down at his brown fingers entwined around her porcelain skin. White scars criss-crossed them as though he'd put his hand through a broken window more than once. Her thumb smoothed over one of the soft ridges, her mind in turmoil. She exhaled slowly. Five years' difference seemed too much. "I'm a grandmother," she said and Logan snorted.

"Congratulations," he answered. He withdrew his hand, leaving Hana's fingers feeling the lack of warmth. The jolting stopped as the road culminated in a large open gateway and they crunched onto a gravel drive and up to a colonial villa, nestled amongst native Nikau palms. The exterior wooden panels of the building looked white enough for recent renovation, whilst the roof displayed its original green corrugated metal. A period veranda and decorative wooden mouldings wrapped around the structure like an embrace. Despite the sheet rain, the house oozed class and pride.

Logan strode round and opened the passenger door, offering his hand to help Hana climb onto the slippery runner. She accepted his help, gripping Logan's hand and praying she didn't hit the floor face first in front of him. Hana felt a familiar flicker run through her body like the essence of a low voltage current. If Logan perceived it he didn't react, sheltering her under his jacket as they ran up the front steps and onto a wide porch.

Hana shook water droplets from her ponytail as Logan pushed open the unlocked front door. "Welcome to the mad house," he said, driving her panic levels higher. Deciding that if he turned out to be a serial killer she'd be better off comfortable, Hana removed her shoes and added them to a surprisingly large pile by the door. Stepping onto the stripped rimu boards which graced the entrance hall, she looked up at a stunning chandelier which fitted the period of the house. The smell of frying bacon assaulted her nostrils and drew an embarrassing growl from her stomach.

Logan walked straight ahead and into the kitchen and Hana heard him begin a discussion with someone inside. She delayed, hearing a female voice and feeling awkward. Looking around for somewhere to hang her wet jacket, she settled on the banister rail. It brought back memories of her childhood and her family hanging their coats on the banister in England. Hana remembered bringing the whole collection down on her head and having to hang each one up again. Sometimes her brother would loosen them on purpose to get her into trouble. Her mother hated the practice. Despite her inability to hear or speak with any clarity, Judith McIntyre would sign with frantic fingers that it made their modest Lincolnshire vicarage look untidy.

"Hey, come through." Logan returned for her and took her right hand, tugging her away from the stairs. Hana pattered into the kitchen in her socks, nervousness robbing her of confidence.

"Hana!" A radiant Henrietta Dawlish greeted her whilst snipping up rashers of bacon into a frying pan. "Darling, how wonderful to see you again," she cooed, as Hana gulped air like a dying fish.

Moments later, Peter North burst in from outside, brandishing a dirty pumpkin as though it was a trophy and dripping rainwater onto the rimu floor. "Got one!" he cried.

Henrietta chortled with encouragement and bustled over, brandishing a tea towel which she used to mop North's brow. She relieved him of his prize and took it over to the sink while he removed his shoes and coat. "Hana, welcome to our humble bachelor pad." North smiled. Spying the subtle stiffening of Henrietta's back, he added, "Some of us won't be bachelors for long apart from Logan; he will."

"Thanks!" Logan retorted, the insult driven hard into his heart. He narrowed his eyes and mouthed something in Pete's direction which looked like a threat. The skinny man's eyes widened and he dashed to Henrietta's ample side. Once in the safety of her voluptuous vicinity, his nerve returned and he offered Logan a rude finger gesture.

Hana's curiosity burned, desperate to ask about their living arrangements but squashing the impulse. A clothes airer in the corner bore a limp rugby shirt alongside a nasty pair of purple Y-fronts. The red trainers on the floor next to it looked a replica of those worn by the German student teacher.

"Hey Hana!" cried Boris Lomax. Tall and carrot orange haired, the boys called him 'Red' and loved his no-nonsense style of teaching. A total lush, he sent female hearts thumping in the staffroom and already burned a few bridges since the previous September. He wrapped long arms around Hana and planted a kiss on her cheek. It appeared like a chaste maneuver until his fingers strayed below the small of her back. Hana pulled away and glanced at Logan, gratified to recognise a flash of jealousy in his grey eyes.

The open plan kitchen encompassed a dining table and sofas. A 1900s bay window surveyed the garden through rain-streaked, misted glass. "Would you like to look around?" Logan offered. "I'll pour you a drink first."

Hana nodded with enthusiasm, keen to escape Boris' wandering hands and Pete's sycophantical behaviour around Henrietta. Logan poured a generous glass of red wine and pressed it into her hand. Then he led her out of the kitchen and back into the lobby. "I think it's 1900s," he said, looking up at the high ceiling. "But I'm not completely sure."

"It is." Hana nodded. "Perhaps earlier but not much." She pointed out the decorative plaster moldings of the ceiling rose and characteristic coving. "I can't believe you live with Pete." Her lips twisted into a smile around her wine glass. "Good luck with that. He drives me mad after eight hours a day and he's asleep for most of that."

Logan licked his lips and grinned. "Yeah," he replied. "But beggars can't be choosers."

"You don't strike me as someone who has to beg for anything." The unfiltered words slipped from her lips having bypassed her brain and

Hana cringed at her own rudeness. She swallowed a large gulp of wine and concentrated on the striking autumn colours of the paintwork.

Logan's instant smile raised the tantalising dimple and the healing scar beneath his right eye crinkled, giving him a roguish look. He left Hana to her discomfort and concentrated on showing her the house. Aged tongue and groove decorated each room to shoulder height, original rimu restored with love and expertise. The antique furniture intrigued Hana, not least because the tenants fitted better into the beer-and-Formica category. Three roomy bedrooms showed signs of male occupation. North's room looked like his desk at work, full of crap with pieces missing, aesthetically chaotic. It proved impossible to see where his unmade bed ended and the clothes on the floor began. Boris owned little and lived out of an open suitcase, clothing crawling from its cavernous mouth like escapees from tee shirt hell. Logan's room surprised her. Always dressed in immaculate designer clothing, Logan's placing of an ironing board in the corner looked in vogue with his room. Nothing appeared out of kilter, furniture aligned and nothing out on show. In contrast to his, North's room looked positively burgled.

The fourth bedroom smelled of female deodorant and one of Henrietta's voluminous dresses peeked out from an overnight case on the bedside table. Logan wrinkled his nose. "I haven't seen Pete this in love with a chick since my sister made him pee his pants."

Hana's eyes widened in horror and Logan laughed. "She's five years older than us and very scary." He reached out and ran a hand down her upper arm, leaning closer to explain. "Pete loves women who boss him around." His fingers felt strong and forceful and Hana swallowed down a heady mixture of wine and desire. Oblivious, Logan jerked his head towards the bed. "He thinks she'll sleep with him but I know she won't."

"How do you know?" Hana's voice sounded husky.

Logan winked at her. "She told me. This girl's after a wedding ring."

Hana choked on her next mouthful, shaking as she struggled to seat the wine glass on a hall table and almost knocked it over. Logan pulled her close and patted her back with gentle strokes, waiting until she'd caught her breath. Then she embarrassed herself by snorting with laughter. "That won't happen," she choked. "Are we talking about the same man?"

Logan nodded and his smile looked rueful. "Yeah. I told her she's dreaming. I'll be married before he is."

The words sent an arrow of pain into Hana's heart and her eyes darted around in search of a ready escape. Her brain sent a bucket of cruel rebukes to cool her foolish romantic notions. She shivered and closed her eyes against her own stupidity, rosebud lips pursing to prevent further calamity.

"You're cold." From a dresser drawer revealing neatly rolled garments, Logan pulled out a sweater and offered it to her.

Hana hesitated and then accepted it, using it as a diversion. Logan's fingers brushed hers, making the awfulness worse. "Thank you." She pulled it on over her tee shirt and wondered how to extract herself from the house and the sense of having lost out yet again in life. Logan's sweater smelled of lavender fabric softener and outdoors. Hana lifted a sleeve to her nose and inhaled the comforting scent. He reached behind her and teased a long red tress from inside the collar, the curl bouncing against his touch. His hands contacted the back of her neck and Hana's eyes flared wide in embarrassment at the pleasure his touch invoked. Logan straightened out the lock of hair with care and smoothed it down her back with gentle fingers, stroking out the static. Hana gulped and moved away, breaking the connection with an act of will.

The tour of the house included the bathroom, living room and laundry and Hana revelled in the beauty of the restoration. "It's amazing!" she exclaimed, pressing her hands together and smiling at Logan. "I love period houses. I've always wanted to buy an old place like this and give it back its dignity." She spun in a circle beneath the ceiling rose in the lounge, peering up at the detail in the molding. Even folded over twice, Logan's sweater sleeves still sneaked over her palms and forced her to hold them at bay with curled fingers. "Who owns this?" she asked in hushed reverence. "Not Pete. He can't afford to pay his tuck shop bill from last year."

She hadn't expected Logan's answer. "Angus."

It rushed back to her like a river reclaiming its flood plain, the awful afternoon following Vik's funeral. Angus supped wine and gave in to a lonely, soul sucking grief. 'I can't face it,' he wept. 'Iris renovated it for us to retire in. It was our dream home. This is my punishment.'

Angus never qualified how he believed Iris' cancer to be his punishment but he vacated the house a year after her death. He bought a two-bedroom unit in a residential park, happy to woo lonely widows with his wit and charm whilst closing his front door on them at night.

"This is the house," Hana whispered, sadness washing over her. "Iris' house."

The mess of North's bedroom seemed more offensive for the lack of sensitivity it displayed in the abandonment of order there. Hana's chest tightened to the point of painfulness and her wine glass tilted sideways in her hand. Iris and Vik sat together at the staff Christmas dinner, never knowing it would be the last for both of them. Hana contemplated the void at her feet and the ugliness of what threatened to suck her back in.

She sighed and closed her eyes against the questions she still carried and which Vik would never answer; not this side of heaven.

Logan watched as the emotions flicked across Hana's face, poorly masked in her confusion. Her green eyes filled with pain and her guard dropped for long enough for him to see the turmoil hidden inside.

Realising too late, Hana forced a smile onto her lips and buried the feelings back in Pandora's Box. "Thanks for showing me around," she said, her tone clipped and professional. "I should probably go home."

Logan reached for her, one hand confiscating the lilting wine glass and the other closing around her wrist. "Tell me?" he asked, a hint of pleading beneath the surface. Time whipped past him as he lost seconds of opportunity, days, weeks, years and decades. He let go of her wrist and touched her cheek, soft fingers caressing and coasting over her flushed skin. Hana's eyelids fluttered closed as she remembered how good it felt to be touched.

Noises from the kitchen forced her back into reality and Hana jumped away from Logan. He watched the roiling conflict in her expression as he released his hold on her wrist. "Don't run away. Stay for dinner," he invited, struggling to lighten the mood. He jerked the wine glass towards the kitchen sounds. "Henrietta does the meanest pumpkin and bacon soup and she cooks for a small army." He stood in front of Hana, his body rigid as he blocked her exit. Fear enlarged his pupils until his eyes looked black and Hana inwardly questioned her importance to him.

"Why do you care?" she whispered and his fear worked its way back behind a convincing mask.

Logan shrugged and gritted his teeth, calling her bluff. "I'll take you home if that's what you want."

Hana's eyes darted towards the doorway and then back to Logan's face. She swallowed and shook her head, relenting. His eyelashes fluttered and he rested a hand on her shoulder as though afraid if he let go she might flee. Hana's body felt rigid, expecting grief like a silent shadow to sneak up on her, biting her when she least anticipated it and reminding her she was half of a pair, less than whole.

Dinner as promised, tasted superb. The pumpkin soup was exquisitely cooked as only New Zealanders know how, despite the noble attempts of others to better it. Henrietta's catering skills had much to do with it. North seemed besotted with her, oblivious to the veiled snorts of laughter his flatmates suppressed when she referred to him as 'Peteepoos' and 'Glove Puppet.'

Boris raised his eyebrows in such a look of intrigue when Henrietta asked 'Glove Puppet' for the salt, Hana dropped her spoon into the soup.

A glob ricocheted onto Logan's chin and her eyes widened in horror. He wrinkled his nose with indignation and wiped it off, but she saw the amusement in his face and masked her giggle as a cough.

Henrietta set dessert on the table with such a flourish, it wibbled and wobbled and almost plunged off the platter. The pink blancmange resembled its creator and the realisation set Hana giggling again.

"That looks exceptionally pink and vobbly," Boris concluded and Hana struggled not to explode. She buried her face into her favourite handkerchief with a long and pretentious sniffle which bought her time to recover and wipe the tears of laughter away. She pitied the little kiwi birds, hand stitched around the edges of the hanky for their part in her subterfuge.

Achieving a degree of sanity, Hana pulled the handkerchief away from her face and glanced sideways at Logan. She found his gaze fixed on the object in her fingers and his olive skin paled to a sickly hue. His irises darkened as he peered at the marching kiwis around the edge of the cloth and his fingers twitched as though he wanted to reach out and take it. Hana balled it into her hand like a possessive child, stuffing it into her jeans pocket and hauling the sweater down over it. When she stole a glance at Logan, she saw he'd stopped eating, laying his spoon alongside the pink mess and staring at his plate.

Silence shrouded them both as dinner conversation centred around which beer Peter North liked best although the topic died at a withering look from Henrietta. "No, Peteepoos," she complained, her eyes rounding with hurt. "You promised you'd only drink wine from now on; like a real connoisseur!"

Boris wiggled his eyebrows at Hana and she winced in return, Henrietta's choke hold on Pete making her heart heavy with remembered misery.

After the final clatter of spoons and satisfied sighs from appetites sated, the mood around the rimu dining table became laced with sadness and a finality which left Hana confused. Logan cleared away the bowls and cutlery while Boris loaded the dishwasher and ran water into the sunken Belfast sink. Unsure what to do, Hana sat at the table, embarrassed when Henrietta took North's hand in her large paw and began a private, hushed conversation. Writhing in discomfort, Hana excused herself and went to help the men. She stuck close to Logan and they worked to restore the kitchen back to order. Soon the dishwasher hummed in the corner, making hungry sloshing sounds as it gulped water from the tank beneath the front lawn.

Logan made coffee and led Hana into the living room overlooking the darkening driveway. A daffodil farm in the paddocks beyond showed ploughed furrows awaiting new bulbs. Boris went to his room with the intention of Skyping his brother. As New Zealand sunk into Saturday night, Dieter in Germany had his Saturday morning lie-in destroyed.

"Pete's dreaded her leaving," Logan explained. "Henrietta toured the Waikato advertising her college but her next port of call is Hastings." He tapped a nervous beat against his jeans and fidgeted long fingers covered in healed scars. Hana tried to count the myriad white lines but couldn't.

She felt the roughness of Logan's jeans through hers and resisted the urge to touch his thigh, chiding herself for her inappropriate forwardness. The derisive voice in her mind ridiculed her and drove her further inside herself.

Logan didn't broach the subject of her marriage and Hana felt grateful. But he talked about his own life and former fiancé. "I guess she was the girl-next-door. We ended up in the same course at uni and got jobs at Auckland North Shore Grammar, me in the English faculty and her in physical education." Logan became quiet and subdued. "It's for the best," he admitted.

Hana looked at him in confusion. "How?" She sounded doubtful. "How can being jilted at the altar ever be for the best? It's cruel and wicked." Her jaw set in a harsh line and her lips turned downwards. "It's betrayal and the worst way to treat anyone you've claimed to love."

Logan shook his head, his dark fringe bouncing in the movement from his eyelashes. "No, trust me. I'm glad." His voice sounded tight, but his expression contradicted it with a look of peace.

Hana felt lost for words, but Pete spared her the dilemma of answering by pushing his face around the lounge door. "Henrietta's leaving," he announced like a butler.

The housemates lined the steps in a scene from Victorian England. Pete fetched Henrietta's carriage from the shed, a little white Suzuki Swift emblazoned with the logo of her college. She squeezed and kissed each member of the assembled group with genuine fondness and then poured herself into the driver's seat with difficulty, trapping her dress in the door twice before starting the engine. North's shoulders slumped as she bumped and shook along the dreadful track to the main road. She beeped her horn in the distance as she turned right and her lights moved out of sight.

North resembled a broken man within seconds. He fortified himself against the light drizzle and declared, "I'm going for a run."

Hana's brow knitted in concern. "But there're no streetlights and visibility is non-existent. You'll get squashed!"

"Sokay," Boris reassured her, touching her shoulder. "He go tavern viz friend, Foggy. He only jog a few metres. See da lights on left through trees. Henriettas not know he go for beers." Boris punctuated his words with a fist in the air. Then he climbed onto the porch steps, calling over his broad shoulder, "I Skype my sister in Berlin and Mutter in Gutersloh now."

North made a show of tying his trainers extra tight and set off along the drive. Logan snorted. "You should've asked Henrietta for a lift. Want me to text her?"

"No!" Pete's eyes grew round with the threatened betrayal. "Don't!"

Logan shook his head. "He won't be back before work on Monday morning now."

"Yes, I will!" Pete hollered back in temper.

Hana caught sight of her trainers snuggled on the rimu boards next to Logan's cowboy boots. They looked comfy and she decided it was an appropriate time to leave. She grabbed her coat from the newel post and slipped on her trainers. Logan seemed saddened as they ventured off the veranda and back into the Hilux. He drove her to town but kept turning towards her as though wishing to say something. Hana saw the light of courage fail him and assuming it would be a polite brush off, didn't ask.

Passing the tavern in Gordonton, Hana watched as a sweaty, pink-faced Peter North ordered something from the barman.

Chapter 14

For some inexplicable reason, Hana agreed to lead Sunday school just once, the promise extracted under duress.

"But I don't like children," she protested. "Not unless they're blood relatives and none of these are."

"Please, Hana," Pastor Allen begged. "Christine's overseas. We've all taken a turn. The youngest is five and the oldest around nine. Two of them are mine. You love my kids, don't you?"

"Yours yes! But I've seen the others and it's all snot and bad manners. They cry over silly things and exact petty revenges we can never catch them doing."

"Hana, you work in a school; I promise it will be easy," the pastor informed her in his best, 'I'm–so–desperate–please–say–yes voice.' "All the stuff is there in the book. You just need to teach it on the day. You'll be perfect. Thanks so much."

Hana opened her mouth to refuse and spoke to an empty phone line. Off Alan fled on his next mission to coerce someone else into doing another job.

"I hate you," Hana groaned, knowing he'd set her up for failure.

She spent the week getting to grips with the lesson plan and produced a cut out Goliath and a smaller David for the children to colour. Anka's children posed under protest for the cut-outs, which meant laying on the concrete garage floor while Hana drew round them with felt tip. Charlotte dissolved into chronic giggles every time Hana went near her bare legs and arms with the pen. Gareth lay on his back and fell asleep with ear buds jammed into his ear holes.

Hana struggled into Oadby church early to set up before the children arrived. The bright, clear Sunday held little evidence of the previous day's endless rain. Super-heated air chased the puddles into the lower patches of ground, leaving mush in places where it hung around in the soil. Mount Pirongia stood over the Sunday school room, rising above Hamilton with a tiny speckling of snow at its tips. The little community church was still surrounded by fields and hills, untouched by a growing suburbia which extended its fingers outwards at a determined rate. The city grew more each year, swallowing small townships like a hungry monster.

Hana struggled to separate David and Goliath. They became entangled on the back seat of the car and she experienced despair as their arms and legs tore under pressure. It took half an hour to lay them out on rickety paste tables, side by side and tape up their wounds. Hana got the story straight in her head and laid her notes on the chair, thinking bad thoughts about Pastor Allen. "It's only an hour with the little darlings," she promised herself. "What can go wrong in that time?"

Hana entered the church through a side door and stopped in horror. The usual members of the congregation bunched to one side and strangers filled the rest of the pews, numbering over a hundred. Instead of the regular eight infants, at least twenty more sat on parents' knees dressed in their Sunday best. Pastor Allen saw Hana attempting to bolt and caught her by the elbow. "Sorry, there's a baptism. Didn't I mention it?"

"No!" Hana growled, her hiss rising to a wail. "You didn't!"

Allen shrugged and shoved her towards the front pew. Unused to sitting still and listening, the visiting children squirmed and writhed for the first twenty minutes, switched from mother to father and back again. Hana escaped during the second hymn to raid the cupboards for extra crayons and biscuits. She found it hard to concentrate, worrying about controlling the children by herself. Successive memories of Sunday mornings covered in biscuit crumbs and bogies ran unbidden through her brain. Bodie never bothered if Hana accompanied him or not, but Isobel required her mother's presence at all times. For a while, Hana served as the Sunday school teacher, but an accident with matches and a rubbish bin full of confessed sin encouraged the deacons to question the insurance liability surrounding her presence in such an important ministry.

With a brief prayer from Allen, he released the Sunday school crowd into Hana's dubious care. Anka watched Hana as she waited in the doorway for the little brigade to clatter across. Leaning towards Charlotte and Gareth, Anka whispered something and judging by their incredulous faces, they didn't like it. Hana observed failed but whispered resistance and then the teenagers hauled themselves to their feet and slouched towards her. She gave Anka a grateful smile across a sea of children's heads and left the church like the Pied Piper.

Everyone squashed into the tiny schoolroom and Hana didn't give them time to start getting bored. With haste, she picked out two reluctant actors. "Okay, gentleman with the smart blue shirt, you can be Goliath and you with the lovely orange dress can be David. I'm Hana. What are your names?"

They mimed what she read out loud and the result moved from pleasing to hilarious. A skinny visitor named Duncan played Goliath and enjoyed pushing the little David around far too much. Marcia played David, in the interests of sex equality and threw herself into the part with gusto. She proved an accurate shot with paper stones and an elastic-band slingshot.

"Ouch! My head!" Duncan Goliath wailed, smacked square in the forehead by a balled up paper lump. The squeals of delight from the children rose to a crescendo and threatened to disturb the service next door.

Hana's pleas of, "Let's be quieter," fell on selectively deaf ears as Marcia got into her rock slinging like a professional.

Gareth sat mute in the centre of the carpet listening to music on his phone. He appeared oblivious until the biscuits came out. Charlotte sat next to him texting. That's the reason the colouring activity went so horribly wrong.

Apart from an overenthusiastic Goliath, the visiting children seemed well behaved. The same wasn't true of the usual merry band of regulars, who worked hard to show off and impress their new audience. One family of four boys came from what Hana believed were a fine, upstanding home of godly principles. Yet their behaviour reminded her of all the reasons she said no to the gig in the first place. Not content with roughhousing each other on the carpet, they proved vocal and entertaining for the benefit of the visiting girls. The youngest expressed every filthy word in his vocabulary relating to toilet activities, encouraged by the snorted giggles of his brothers. Besotted by the glamorous presence of Marcia, he set out to impress in ways that only a seven-year-old might find acceptable. "Poo, bum, willy."

"I don't think so!" Hana pulled his reluctant body around to the other side of the table, standing him next to a quiet little boy with dark rimmed glasses whose good behaviour might rub off on the tearaway.

She fed and watered the group before letting them loose on the defenceless cut-outs with crayons. Gareth sat cross legged on the floor swaying to his music and Charlotte lounged on the only armchair, texting into the ether. The children coloured with great concentration, amidst a gentle hum of chatter. "No, I'm putting pink spots on his shirt."

They whispered to each other and Hana sighed with relief and checked her watch. The older church kids dropped into an authoritarian role, sorting out stolen crayons and directing the visiting children to legs and arms. Hana used the sink in the corner to wash up the plastic juice cups while they were busy. She examined the crack in one and contemplated the economy of reusing fragile disposable cups. A muffled cry from Charlotte caused her to whip round in alarm.

"Oh. My. God!"

"Charlotte!" Hana's eyes widened with shock. "Don't call him unless you need him." She dried her hands on a towel and walked towards the colouring table.

"Well, look!" Charlotte and Gareth stood at the table, examining one of the cut-outs over the children's heads. Charlotte's hand covered her mouth and Gareth looked away stifling a snort. A hush fell over those gathered around Goliath and Hana sensed all eyes ready to witness her reaction.

"David looks great," she began, observing a wild rainbow man of random blocks of colour. Children's names decorated his body like genealogical tattoos and a unicorn replaced his nose. Hana moved around to Goliath, standing shoulder to shoulder with Charlotte and peering over the children's heads.

The boy in front of Gareth scratched his hair with constant, seeking fingernails and the teenager took a cautious step back as his sister whispered, "Nits."

Hana admired Goliath's colourful armour and impressive soldier's helmet. Large and proud, between the bottom of his pink and purple breastplate sat the biggest genitalia Hana ever saw.

"Do you think that's normal?" Gareth asked. "It doesn't look in proportion."

Charlotte turned on the little group which stood in silent complicity with crayons at half mast. "Who put the dick on Goliath?"

Mutterings began until the group unanimously pointed fingers at the family of four boys, in particular the middle child. Instead of looking guilty, the boy announced, "It's my dad."

Hana swallowed and cast around for something to make a loin cloth out of. Her gaze settled on Gareth's scarf. "Give me that." She held her hand out but panicked when he turned away.

"No! I don't want my scarf next to some guy's nads!"

With his usual exuberance, Allen burst into the silent room, an expectant smile playing across his lips. "The whole church is excited to see what the Sunday school have done. David and Goliath, isn't it this week?" He glanced across at the tables, seeing the edge of a decorated foot. "Marvellous! Bring it out in about five minutes." He ignored the tragedy on the table and the ashen face of the adult who mouthed, 'I hate you.' He blasted back out to the sound of organ music cranking through the last verse of a hymn.

The group filed back into the church on cue, the children looking forward to their lunch and Hana traumatised by the whole experience. Having press ganged one of the older boys to explain what they'd learned, Hana held her breath and retreated into the shadows at the side of the stage. She edged nearer to the exit as Allen unrolled the giant Goliath and a congregation member stood to help with the rainbow David. "Oh," Allen said. "That's interesting."

Goliath's nether regions sported an enormous felt tipped bow of fluorescent green, with vivid black spots. The unmistakable shadow of hastily covered rude parts showed through the bow. Allen swallowed and avoided Hana's eye. "These would look nice on display in the coffee room," he suggested.

Humiliated, Hana slid through the side door and made a run for the Sunday School classroom. She snatched up her bag and car keys and bolted. Through the open doors she caught the shrill voice of the youngest member of the family from Hell shouting in an aggravated tone, "They maked Daddy's willy into a present!"

Chapter 15

Monday morning dawned with a pleasant warmth as fading summer blessed Hamilton city. Dashing into work early, Hana avoided the administration corridor and hoped Anka might have stopped laughing about Goliath's wedding tackle.

Running up the back stairs with her head down, she cannoned into the Year 10 dean. "I'm so sorry," Hana apologised and retrieved his crutches which flew in opposite directions. He balanced on the split-level landing, keeping his broken ankle off the floor.

"It's fine." He waved away her ministrations. His eyes sparkled with mischief and Hana grew wary, trying to pass him before he tainted her with the juicy piece of staffroom gossip she sensed on his lips. "Jeffs is getting married," he announced, watching Hana's reaction with interest. "To an internet bride!"

She shook her head, irritated that the men gossiped as much as the women and sucked her in just the same. "What? Gwynne?"

Telea faked contrition, eager to be the shoulder Hana cried on. "Oh sorry, you didn't know? You must feel gutted because we had you pegged as Mrs Jeffs number two. I didn't mean to shock you. Sorry."

Hana flushed with irritation, seeing his game plan laid out before her like a trap. "Gwynne and I are friends and that's all." Seeing the disbelief in his face and the smirk beginning on his lips, Hana shoved past him in the small space. She jabbed a finger into his face. "I've told you before; I'm not sleeping with you, not even as a consolation prize."

"But we'd be so good together!" Telea wailed. Hana kept moving, hearing the clang of his crutch as it hit the fire bucket at the bottom of the stairwell. She escaped into the deserted post room with a flush creeping up her neck.

"Yeah," she muttered to herself. "Because I love sharing my boyfriends with five other women desperate to sleep with an ex-has-been-rugby player."

"What?" Pete's eyes widened in horror and he stopped with a chocolate bar halfway to his lips. "You like orgies? How did I not know this?"

Choosing to ignore him, Hana grabbed a wooden chair from the corner and lamented the illogical administration which gave the smallest people in the school the highest pigeon holes. She pulled it over to the rack and climbed onto it in her high heels. Sticking her hand into the back, she discovered a few envelopes for the guidance counsellors and a careers newspaper for Sheila.

"You've got great legs for your age, Hana." Pete edged nearer the chair and reached out with a pudgy, chocolate covered hand. He ran a finger over her strappy sandal and Hana recoiled in disgust.

"Touch me again and you're dead." Hana's voice remained casual, but the hand kept moving towards her calves. She backed to the edge of the chair with a look of distaste on her face. "I mean it!"

Logan Du Rose walked into the room and halted, enjoying the sight of Hana's backside and trim, elegant legs. Then he spotted Pete's questing fingers and his expression darkened. He leaned against the door frame with his arms folded and directed his bile towards Pete. "You do that and I'll snap it off," he declared, voice low and sinister. "And you know I mean it."

Pete withdrew his hand and looked around him, his escape route blocked. "You said you wouldn't break bits of me again," he sulked. "I'm just looking."

"Well, don't." Logan's biceps flexed and he moved his head to the side, revealing a dangerous, pulsing vein. "It's sexual harassment and assault." He sniffed. "And I'll kill you."

"Not just for that!" Pete's expression morphed into one of dismay. "You'd kill me just for that?"

Logan jerked his head towards the doorway and Pete sidled across, his crablike movements jerky and awkward. He paused with distance still between them. "You need to move. I don't trust you."

Logan shrugged and pointed at the brown mess in Pete's fingers. "Dude, it's melting. Try getting hot over Henrietta and leave Hana alone."

At the reminder of his large girlfriend, Pete opened his mouth to speak and Logan silenced him with a shake of his head. "I don't want to know. Get out."

Pete sighed and edged past Logan, keeping a look out for repercussions. He walked backwards into the corridor and then when he felt safe, turned and jogged away. Hana observed from her position on the chair, her heels digging into the fabric. "Would you really hurt him?" she asked, her tone suspicious.

Logan shook his head. "Na. I broke his finger once messing about. He's like a wasp; keeps buzzing around your face and ducking the swats." His face relaxed and he crossed his legs at the ankle. "You look good up there, Ms McIntyre."

Hana chewed her lip and looked at the carpet. Her tight skirt made dismounting with elegance impossible with an audience. Logan's eyes flickered with amusement. "Need a hand?"

"Not the round of applause kind, but thanks." Hana clutched the envelopes and gripped the back of the chair, contemplating a jump.

"Not like that." Logan's voice sounded soft as he fixed strong hands around her waist and took her weight. Hana forced herself to trust him and allowed him to lift her from the chair, wincing as Logan slid her along the length of his body. Her breasts pushed against his rock hard stomach and the height difference between them left her staring at the buttons of another immaculate shirt.

"Thanks," she managed, inhaling his gorgeous, clean scent. When Logan released her, she felt as though an unseen hand cut her strings and she swayed on her high heels, feeling pathetic.

Logan walked to the window and looked out. "How was Sunday School?" he asked over his shoulder.

Hana scowled. "Fantastic! Apart from the children."

Logan put his head back and laughed, a low, husky sound that tickled the pit of Hana's stomach. "I heard the chick from downstairs telling the receptionist." He smiled. "What's her name?"

"The receptionist? That's Alma."

Logan shook his head. "Not her. The one with red bits in her hair."

"The typist? Anka?" Confusion spread across Hana's delicate features. "Don't you know her?"

"No, never spoken to her." The scar beneath his right eye crinkled with amusement. "Sounds like you had fun though. Is put-the-willy-on-the-man a Christian version of pin-the-tail-on-the-donkey?"

He brushed his fingers across her shoulder, the contact tantalising. Logan withdrew it as six other members of staff dashed into the post room, behaving like ants as they spread out towards their pigeon holes. Hana noticed the sidelong glance of Ethel Bowman as she bent her large body in half to reach her crammed-full box near the floor. She shot Hana a look of victory as she stashed her lavish lunch on top of paperwork. Hana read glee in the florid face and her heart sank.

Gwynne entered the room, sifting through his box and extracting a few sheets of interest. Hana smiled at him and he winked back at her. "Congratulations are in order, I hear," she said and he beamed and nodded.

"Yeah, thanks Hana."

She read relief in his eyes at her public acceptance and knitted her brow. He owed her nothing. "I'm pleased for you." Hana gave him a light kiss on the cheek, aware of the other staff watching. She knew the grapevine would deliver the right message so they could both get on with their lives. Logan leaned back against the rack, not hiding his interest. Hana felt his tension and destroyed the last possible obstacle between them. "See you later." She lowered her voice and smiled at Logan, issuing the veiled promise. She squeezed his forearm before leaving the room, feeling muscle and sinew flex beneath her fingers. He shot her a sultry look from under his lashes and relief flooded Hana's chest. She saw no ulterior motive in his expression.

In the hallway, Hana's shoulders slumped as she lost confidence and dropped into chastising herself. Ethel Bowman's gaze burned into her back as she touched the younger man and Hana quailed as the don't-care spirit abandoned her. She jumped at the sound of the post room window grinding open, followed by an ear splitting whistle. "Hey!" Logan yelled. "Prefects! Break up that tussle. I'll be out in a second."

Hana ran into the women's toilets to avoid him as he jogged downstairs to deal with the miscreants. A spirit of rebellion crept into her humiliation, reminding her she'd always wanted a man who could whistle through his fingers.

The staff gossip involved Gwynne and his shock announcement at briefing that morning.

"I'm glad for the guy," Rory muttered, chatting to Hana whilst typing an email to a parent. "There was a bit of an awkward hush and then people congratulated him. Old Gwynne loved it." Rory lost interest as he recalled the email so he could correct his spelling errors.

Sheila looked downcast and couldn't refer to Gwynne's new love without reference to his late wife, Tessa. It grew boring and took the shine off the news. "Whatever would Tess think?" she lamented for the hundredth time.

"Shut the hell up, woman!" Rory snapped, spinning around in a chair borrowed from the history department. An uneasy truce existed between them, but its fragile skin showed veritable cracks. Pete gathered up his car keys and a wad of reports and beat a hasty retreat, keen not to experience one of their endless arguments which often spilled over into frustration with him. Hana missed her opportunity and cursed Pete's disappearing spine through the window.

She regretted it within seconds. Smarting from Rory's rebuke, Sheila lashed out at Hana instead. "We thought Gwynne liked you. But why would you settle for an old duffer like him with younger fish to fry? I'd be careful; your toy boy's on one hell of a rebound, so I hear."

Hana whipped round from her photocopying but Rory beat her to it, throwing his pen at the wall and leaping to his feet. "Is nobody safe from your spite, woman?" He tripped over his chair as he strode towards Sheila. "How the hell do you know what 'poor Tess' would think? You didn't even like her. Just because your life sucks and your husband's a joke, doesn't mean you can take it out on Hana."

Deciding Rory looked able to mete out justice for the both of them, Hana fled, leaving Sheila open mouthed and ready to retort. She closed the student centre door behind her and sought fresh air, descending the back steps to the covered entryway and out onto the field. The last time Rory and Sheila fought so badly, Hana and Pete went for coffee at a local café to get out of the way. The argument raged all day and Hana ended up logging in from home to do her work. Something told her this time, she couldn't be bothered.

With no car keys or money, she left herself few alternatives and settled on a bench overlooking the soccer field. The sound of silence comforted Hana as she warmed herself. She kept one eye open for Dobbs or the admin director, aware they'd view her defection without sympathy. Preparing a ready story in her head, she relaxed.

The bell sounded for lesson change and boys moved around, their behaviour loud and bawdy as they pushed and jostled each other. Some ran and others rambled without urgency. She wondered if anyone in her world valued her as numerous human beings rushed past and disregarded her as though she was invisible. In a matter of minutes, the grounds silenced again as the five-minute allocation for lesson change ended. Sheila's words cut into Hana's psyche and an embarrassed flush kissed the delicate freckles across her nose.

"Hey." Logan slumped onto the bench next to her, their thighs touching as he leaned back to push keys deeper into his pocket. For once he dressed in tracksuit pants and a loose fitting tee shirt instead of Italian designer shirt and suit trousers. She caught his heady fragrance and her pulse quickened. "What's the matter?" He leaned forward and rested his elbows on his knees to look into her face.

Hana felt a weight on her chest. "You're the only person who's asked that," she said, her voice sad.

Logan glanced around them and nudged her elbow. "I'm the only one here, sweetheart."

Hana felt the weight move into her throat and avoided the urge to cry like a pathetic female, but the sense of emptiness clawed at her soul. "Yeah, now."

"So, what's up?" Logan persisted.

Hana shook her head. "Rory and Sheila are fighting in the office. It's best to get out of their way."

"Ah." Logan pulled an expression of sympathy and his pupils reduced against the glare of the sun.

"Why aren't you teaching?" Hana brushed a stray piece of grass from her bare shin and watched it flutter away on the breeze.

"I am." Logan winced and Hana grew curious.

"Where are the boys then?"

Logan turned towards her, worry etched in a furrow between his eyebrows. "What's the process when a member of staff loses an entire Year 10 class?"

Hana pulled a face and shrugged, "Throw a party? I'm not great at guessing joke endings."

Logan looked shifty. "Who says I'm joking?"

Hana sat forward and looked into his grey eyes, sensing his urgency. "Where did you look? Start at the beginning."

Logan sighed. "I took Rory's sports class first period because he's meant to be sorting out an issue with a parent. I guess he's not anymore. He didn't give me any suggestions, so I figured we'd go for a cross country run to wear them out. They set off full of purpose and I haven't seen them since. I got distracted by a kid who turned up without his kit."

Hana leaned back against the bench. "You said first period. We're into second period."

"Yep." Logan wrinkled his nose. "They're still missing. Some of them have metal tech now and I just checked; they didn't show up."

Hana sat for a moment pondering on likely hiding places. Logan opened his mouth to interrupt and she placed her index finger over his parted lips. "They never leave their bags unattended because they're scared of losing phones and wallets and they can't carry them in their sports kit."

"It's all still in the changing room." Logan spoke from behind her finger, his warm breath sending shivers along Hana's spine. "And I had to unlock it for the next class."

Hana nodded. "So wherever they are, they've lost track of time and forgotten about everything else."

Logan's eyes widened. "What would distract thirty kids to that extent?"

Her face creased into a smile and she let her finger slide down Logan's chin, leaving a blazing trail along his skin which his eyes betrayed. "I know where they are."

"I need to get them." Logan rose to his feet and held out his hand, clasping Hana's fingers and hauling her upright. "Please help me?"

Leading the way, she set off toward the back of the site and instead of turning alongside the swimming baths, headed towards the area marked as out of bounds to students by a decrepit sign clinging to a rotten post. Logan strode behind her, panic and curiosity mingling on his face. As they dropped below the level of the school and into the vegetation of the gully it grew more shaded, native trees masking the warmth of the sun.

"Wait!" Logan snatched at her hand and pulled her to a halt. "What makes you think they're here?"

Hana rolled her eyes. "Experience. This is where they'll be, I promise."

Logan raised their joined palms and pushed his fingers through hers. "You're sure?"

"Yeah." Hana's reply sounded hoarse and she bit her lower lip. "I'm sure."

A dedicated group saw the gully project as an ongoing labour of love, restoring the native ferns and trees which fed the minds of horticulture students over the last fifteen years. Reclaimed from a sad, derelict area of swamp where two local gullies met, the soil became a bog for most of the year but the boys loved it.

Amidst the speckled light which filtered through the delicate umbrella of ferns, the air felt still. The soil puffed up as dust in patches and as they hurried, Hana lost her footing and slipped. Her strappy sandal went out from under her and she saw the ground coming up fast to meet her. Logan, caught her by the elbow and hauled her upright, grabbing her around the waist as her blouse untucked itself from her skirt. Calloused fingers caressed her soft flesh, taking her breath away even more than the fall. She recovered her footing, heart racing and her lungs panting with fear from the near miss. Logan's grip felt secure around her. His eyes narrowed. "That's the third time you've fallen at my feet, Ms McIntyre," he breathed. "Should I read into it?"

Hana swallowed. "I don't know." Her voice sounded small and frightened, her answer relating to more than just her clumsiness. The familiar electricity arced through both of them and Hana felt that peculiar sense of déjà vu again, reaching for some opportunity she'd missed and erased from memory. Neither of them moved under the powerful spell which enveloped them in a timeless peace.

Logan reached down with every intention of kissing her. Hana held her breath, desperate for him to make the impossible attraction into a tangible action. She swallowed and waited for the contact but it didn't come. "Hana," he whispered, "I need to tell you something."

He jumped as the air split with the sound of squeals and screams from deeper in the gully. Logan swore and let go and Hana slipped in exactly the same spot as before. "Sorry, sorry," he said, sounding rattled and impatient. "What the hell are they doing?"

Hana knew but didn't waste time in the telling. She gripped Logan's tee shirt to right herself and set off ahead, leading the way towards the awful sound of dying children.

The ground changed underfoot, becoming sodden and heavy. Brown liquid resembling clay-slip oozed through Hana's delicate strappy sandals and coated Logan's trainers. The track wound through the trees and they followed, a cacophony of bird sounds hysterical overhead and the relentless screams of thirty boys.

Rounding a sharp downhill bend, Hana stopped with such abruptness, Logan ran into her spine and grabbed her by the shoulders to prevent him flattening her. Where the two gullies joined into a muddy, swampy pool, boys of varying height and weight appeared molded into a dirty ball. Their smart black and white sports shirts looked unrecognisable from the mud. Each boy looked light brown in colour, shining and slippery with the liquid which covered every inch of them from head to toe. Impossible to determine where their clothes began and ended, they slipped around in the filth without a care. They rolled in a heap like an enormous milk chocolate pudding, with punctuations where arms and feet poked from the scrum.

Hana laughed but Logan stood speechless, watching the teenage enjoyment with disbelief. He swore and shook his head. Mud flew in every direction and Hana took a step back, sheltering behind Logan as it came their way. One boy sensed their presence and looked up and Hana knew the moment at which the telepathic message passed through the group, ruining their fun. The first child leapt upright from the scrum and the pudding disbanded with a sucking noise. The writhing lump became separate units of dirty teenagers and they formed into a perfect line, knee deep in disgusting brown soup.

Hana shook her head. "Did anyone swallow water?" she asked.

Every hand rose and she sighed. "Then you probably have giardia. Tell your parents tonight and see a doctor."

"What's giardia, miss?" A tiny boy from the centre of the scrum raised his hand.

"A parasite in your gut," Logan said and the child paled. Another boy gagged and a titter went through the group, masking their uncertainty in the face of certain punishment.

"Come on," Hana said, taking control. "We need to get back to school." She set off up the track the same way they'd come, slipping and sliding as she made towards more solid ground. Like a giant brown snake, the line of boys followed, as though she was a mother duck about to cross a busy road. At the top of the hill she looked to Logan for direction, struck by the impossibility of sending the boys onto the polished parquet boards and pristine carpets. "You can't go into class like this," she said, her mind running through options. She chewed her lip and made a decision. "Logan, give me your keys."

"Okay." He nodded and drew them from an inner pocket in his pants, holding them aloft for her. Hana grabbed them and searched for a master key.

"Come on," she told the boys and set off walking, the line trailing after her. Logan didn't question her authority and it felt good to be treated as an equal for a change. At the swimming pool she stopped and unlocked the gate. The water temperature reading gave sixteen degrees and the boys filed past her as she motioned towards the water. "Get in! And no noise!"

The filthy boys slipped into the water and swam around. Hana wouldn't let them out until they'd dunked themselves fully and released the mud from their hair and faces. Their clothes looked stained beyond recovery and they collected in a line by the gate with teeth chattering and grey liquid pooling around their bare feet. "Don't expect sympathy from me!" she scolded them. "And we're not giving you absence passes so your next class teacher will give you a detention."

They nodded as one, looking at least passable as children. "Aren't you going to punish us, sir?" The boy shivered and hopped from foot to foot as he asked Logan the question, eliciting a groan from the rest of the class.

Logan shrugged. "Only if you involve me."

The boys nodded and filed past him, leaving a wet trail to the changing rooms. Hana took a broom from the pool shed and attempted to sweep the muddy footprints away, only smearing the brown paste around the tiles. Leaves and blobs of mud hung around the edge of the water like pond scum. "It's not coming off," she complained. "Larry Collins will kill us. He'll dispose of my body in the gully!"

"Just leave it. I'll take the blame." Logan confiscated the broom and seized her hand in warm fingers. He stood it up against the wall and led her through the gate, locking it up behind them. The sound of a quad bike revved in the distance and Hana panicked.

"He's coming!" she squeaked, looking around for somewhere to hide.

Logan snorted. "He doesn't scare me," he said, watching Hana's frenzied movements with interest.

"Well, he should!" she snapped. She grabbed his hand and bolted, hauling him along behind her. Boys emerged from the changing rooms and Hana sent them in a single direction. "Groundsman!" she hissed and the message went through the group like a ripple. Within seconds only a drying trail into the changing room remained as evidence, the last child scrambling for safety into the main building.

Reaching the deserted staircase up to the guidance counsellors' suite, Hana and Logan flattened themselves against the wall as the quad bike passed outside the door. Logan sniggered. "That was close."

Hana looked appalled. "It's not funny. He'll go mental!" She squared her shoulders. "I'll have to admit it. I won't involve you."

"Don't be daft." Logan pressed her back to the wall and stopped her leaving. "I said I'd take the blame."

Hana shook her head. "You're new. I'm a nobody. He'll complain to Donald and I'll get growled at but I'll survive. You might not."

Logan's hand moved up to her face and his thumb brushed Hana's cheek. His fingers dug into the back of her hair, releasing a torrent of red curls as her clip gave way. "You and Gwynne," he whispered, his tone hoarse and his irises flickering like storm water.

"There is no me and Gwynne," Hana breathed. "There never was."

Logan lowered his lips to hers and the stairwell melted away from view.

Five minutes later, Hana squelched into the student centre in soaked sandals streaked with gully mud. She hovered outside the closed door of the office. She'd forgotten how it felt to stroke a man's rough skin beneath her fingers or have her mouth teased by another's lips. Like riding too high on a swing and losing her stomach on the downward, Hana sank into oblivion beneath Logan's touch and she felt the spectre of Vikram Johal let go of her just a little. She thought about Logan's sensuous lips against hers and put her hand up to her mouth, stifling a grin.

"They're still at it."

"What?" Hana whipped around with guilt on her face.

"They're still at it. Rory and Sheila." Grant jerked his head towards the door and flapped his wad of detention slips in warning at two boys near the front of the common room. They silenced. "The first ten minutes sounded entertaining, but now we've gone past the usual insults and he's apparently a brown son of a bitch and she's something unrepeatable." He shrugged. "I don't know how you put up with them."

The shine of Logan's kiss didn't dim against the impossibility of her working environment and Hana sighed. "Nor do I."

She smiled at Grant and watched by fifty boys, opened the office door with caution. A tornado of paperwork greeted her, swishing around in the current from the overhead fan. The contents of her desk had joined Rory's on the carpet. Hana sighed and closed the door behind her, leaning against it to help the wobble in her legs. Her body thrummed with the excitement of her encounter with Logan and the disaster at her feet couldn't touch her. Sheila and Rory stopped their bickering to watch as Hana hummed to herself, her mind elsewhere. Then Rory ducked as Sheila threw the paperweight.

Chapter 16

Hana left work early on account of her saturated sandals growing painful as they dried. Blisters started where the straps met her foot, which was everywhere. Grant complained about Sheila and Rory after the paperweight cracked the glass in the office door and Dobbs hauled them off to his office.

In the car, Hana drove barefoot. At the lights on Maui Street heading north, a brown leaf fluttered onto her windscreen and she felt depressed with the passing of summer. Autumn threatened and after that came winter. She missed the northern hemisphere seasons and the ability to break long winters with the promise of Christmas. Her mind strayed to Boxing Day and Elizabeth's unexpected arrival on the floor of her bathroom. By the time the tiny girl came into the world, crying and squealing five weeks early, they already loved her despite knowing what lay ahead. The ambulance men shared looks of concern, not wanting to be the ones to burst their bubble. They shot glances at one another as they swaddled the tiny baby and helped Izzie onto their stretcher. Hana watched them wondering if the family realised the little girl had Down syndrome or whether they should mention it. The lights changed and Hana pressed on the gas. "We knew," she murmured to herself. "And we didn't care."

Indicating left after a fifteen minute drive, Hana pulled onto the hard shoulder, ready to enter her street. A black sedan followed close behind and she worried it might clip her bumper as she made the tight turn into her driveway. She slowed, indicating a warning, but her heart sank at the dreadful crunch which rocked her vehicle as the one behind ploughed into it. Hana jumped from her driver's seat to view the damage, her head foggy from the whiplash action of her skull hitting the head rest.

A tall blond man emerged from the vehicle, exuding apologies. "Sorry, I didn't see you indicate," he said, holding his arms out wide.

"I gave you plenty of warning," Hana bit, rubbing the back of her neck with her hand. "You followed much too close."

She watched as the passenger knelt down at the point where the vehicles still touched. His black hair glinted in the sunlight and oriental features pulled his face into a grimace.

"Sorry," the blond man said again, but Hana detected insincerity in his tone and her heart rate increased further.

"To hit me that hard, you must have sped up!" The words escaped without filter and she heard them and realised they made sense.

The other man poked and prodded at the bumper before moving around Hana's vehicle on his knees, looking underneath and tapping at the metal.

"What are you doing?" Hana felt vulnerable and looked around her, willing one of her neighbours to appear. The empty street heightened her sense of aloneness. She felt trapped, her handbag on the passenger seat and the remote for the garage door in the glove box. The rear bumper of her car looked cracked across the centre, but the sedan appeared undamaged apart from a small scrape. Through her panic she tried to memorise the registration number of the black car, the letters and numbers rearranging in her mind. She reached into her vehicle for the keys and her phone and slipped them into her pocket.

"We need to exchange insurance details," she said to the blond man, her words coming breathy and fast. "I'll need your name and address."

"No, you don't." He edged closer and his face assumed a hardness, a sneer touching his lips. The dark haired man with the Asian features continued to move around the vehicle, poking underneath as he went.

"Details please?" Hana demanded in her best school-voice. The blond remained silent and bunched her against the vehicle as his companion banged around the outside panels. Tall and imposing, he cast Hana into shade. His face looked ruggedly handsome, punctuated by striking blue eyes framed with dark lashes. Something about him looked familiar and Hana stared longer than he liked. His eyes blazed and Hana gulped in fear. She changed tack. "Never mind. It doesn't matter, it'll be cheaper to fix it myself."

"Yeah?" The man moved closer until his chest obscured Hana's vision of the street. He lifted angular fingers and stroked them down her cheek. "You're pretty hot," he whispered. "Pity."

Hana swallowed. "What's a pity?"

He smiled, a sliver of regret in the expression. The other man continued his intent examination, circling the Serena like a shark and shaking his head. Hana concentrated on breathing as the oddness of the situation communicated itself to her lungs and then the rest of her body. Nobody came to her aid. The intimidating blond man kept her trapped in the space between the open driver's door and his body but he didn't touch her again. He smelled of an aftershave she recognised, but couldn't recall and ash coloured stubble sprouted from the pores in his face. His latent hardness rendered his otherwise good looks unappealing.

His companion got to his feet with a shake of his head, dusting his trousers to remove the road debris. "Nothing," he spat with the hint of a Chinese accent. The blond man used his body to push Hana so hard into the door, she heard it creak on its hinges as it took the strain of their combined body weight.

"Where-is-it?" he hissed, stressing each word as though Hana might be intellectually limited. With each syllable, she felt his spittle land on her face and winced.

Something snapped in her brain and she pushed him back with both hands full in the chest. "Get away from me!" she screamed.

He stepped backwards while reaching to capture Hana's flailing arms. His full weight went onto his back foot and crushed the neat patent shoe of his companion standing behind him. Knowing she didn't have time to get home without them following, Hana slammed the driver's door hard and bolted around the vehicle, running for her neighbour's house and praying Andrea would be home.

As she ran, Hana pointed the car keys over her shoulder and pressed the remote control to activate the vehicle alarm. It didn't sound, confused by the growing distance between her and it, but she heard the central locking click to deny the men access. The blond man grappled with the driver's door handle, swearing in temper.

Hana didn't linger at Andrea's front door. She bolted around the side and into the back garden, terrifying Andrea's husband Paul as he emerged from the kitchen door with a washing basket. He dropped it in fright. The empty basket bounced on the concrete and hundreds of wooden pegs scattered far and wide. "I thought I heard you come home," he began as he bent to gather the pegs. "What was that bang?"

The open kitchen door behind Paul consumed Hana's attention and she pushed past him and into the safety of the house. Once inside, panic seized her body and adrenaline rendered her incoherent.

"Andrea's not home yet." Paul left the few remaining pegs on the ground and stepped over the threshold, eyeing Hana with a nervous expression. "She told me to get the washing in." Hana watched as he winced and knew he summoned his wife by a sheer act of will. "She said it might rain. It's not though, is it?"

Hana watched, one hand gripping the other as she struggled to stem the awful tremors. Paul edged towards his mobile phone on the counter. "She said they forecasted rain, so she left Ryan in the cot and drove to school to fetch Carlie and Daniel."

Hana's brain worked on overdrive and she noticed the open ranch slider. Darting across she slammed it closed and clicked the lock home. Paul's eyes widened in terror as though she might be a psychopath. "She won't be long." His voice raised at the edges. "She's knows we're here."

"Shut up, shut up, please." Hana spun around, trying to see over their ivy covered fence to the street.

"I need to get the washing." Eyes widening at the flat battery on his phone and nowhere near the land line, Paul made a bid for escape, prepared to leave his sleeping baby in the back bedroom with a serial killer. "I left it out yesterday and Andrea got very cross."

"I don't care." Hana cast around her. "I need to call the cops."

"Oh, great!" he looked relieved. "You want the cops?"

"Of course, I want the bloody cops!" Hana shrieked. "Two men just dinged my car and one of them touched me."

"Oh, shit!" Paul said. "My phone's dead."

The barefoot Hana paced around the kitchen while Paul located the handset for the land line. "It was in the bathroom," he admitted with a grimace. "But it's been there since yesterday so it needs time to charge."

Hana sank to the sofa with her head in her hands. Feeling under fire, Paul decided to investigate and wandered around to the front of the property, whereupon Hana locked him out. As he examined Hana's car, dumped half on her driveway and half on the pavement, Andrea spun round the corner and bounced onto their own driveway, her wipers working to dismiss the raindrops on the windscreen. "Did you even get the bloody washing in?" she snapped and he shook his head. "No. And her from next door's locked me out."

With capable female ingenuity, Andrea lifted the garage door using the remote from her glove box and left Paul to heft the children from the car. She hurried through the internal access door into the kitchen where she found Hana perched on the edge of the old sofa in the corner, wiping her eyes and nose on her sleeve. Some time later, Paul entered carrying Daniel and what appeared to be a paper snow-storm, Carlie trailing behind grizzling with a sticky lolly glued to her hand.

"I've called the cops," Andrea told him. "The other bloody handset was only in the bedroom." She cocked her head at the sound of a baby crying and jerked her head towards the door. "Get Ryan for me please?"

"But I'm supposed to be working from home." Paul's eyes bugged and Hana felt the tension in the room hike.

"I'm fine," she said, getting to her feet. "I'll go home and call Bodie."

"No, you won't!" Andrea snapped. "This is the most excitement I've had in six months." She pressed Hana back into the seat and glared at her husband. Paul looked insulted and wandered away to fetch the squalling baby which he dumped on Andrea who then plied him on Hana.

Hana remembered her own mobile in her skirt pocket and used it to call Bodie's number, choosing not to leave a message. "He'll only worry if he's on duty," she said, her tone sad. When her phone chirped seconds later, she balanced baby Ryan over her shoulder and answered it, expecting to hear her son's voice. She got Boris.

"Hey my vriend, vould you like to come for dinner zis evening? I am cooking and wezzer is miserable. Vas going to be BBQ but not nice. I do bratwurst indoors now."

Hana made feeble, pathetic excuses while the baby grabbed for the phone. Andrea reached over and Hana thought she might reclaim her child, but instead she took the phone and spoke into it, giving Boris a brief rundown of events. "We're just waiting for the cops," she added.

Hana groaned. "I didn't want him to know any of that."

"Don't be daft." Andrea swapped the phone for her baby. "There's nothing to be ashamed of."

The police responded within half an hour, even though the two men were long gone. Paul moved Hana's vehicle into the garage at her request and received a telling off from the officer. "You should've left it where it was, sir," he told him in a stern tone. "It's better for us to see it in situ and now your prints are on it."

Paul threw his hands up in the air with irritation. "I moved it off the footpath," he complained. He postured in the corner until Andrea released him back into his office to continue his work.

"Mad professor," she whispered to Hana, as though the explanation helped.

Andrea's children seemed fascinated with the police officers, both male and imposing. The baby crawled onto the sofa and tried to make free with the curly radio wire on the younger of the two. The older policeman eyed Hana with a knowing look and she squirmed in discomfort. "You've had a few calls recently, miss," he said, knitting his bushy black brows. "First someone tried to mug you and then we took a call when someone vandalised your windscreen. Now this."

"Mugged?" Andrea's eyes widened in shock. "You didn't tell me someone mugged you!"

"They tried to take my bag and didn't get it." Hana swallowed and fixed her attention on the officer.

"What did they want?" he asked for the third time in ten minutes. "They must have said something. Nobody crawls around under a vehicle they just hit without reason. Can you remember upsetting anyone?" he pressed. "This is too much of a coincidence. Are you sure you can't think of anyone? No niggling disputes or unpleasantness? No ex-husbands or estranged boyfriends?"

Hana's face hardened at the mention of ex-husbands and her hands balled at her sides. The officer continued his tirade. "That registration number you gave us is not coming up either. Are you sure you remembered it right?"

"I'm going home," Hana declared, getting to her feet.

"We haven't finished." The officer matched her stance, notebook at the ready. A knock on the front door interrupted his train of thought and Hana sidled towards the gap Andrea left as she answered it. She returned to the kitchen trailed by Logan, Boris and Peter North.

"What's happening?" Pete demanded. "Oh, sorry." He wafted his hand behind his bum and the baby gagged behind him. "Geez, that was a bad curry!"

The police retreated to Hana's garage to examine her car and returned to deliver the usual patter. "Ring us if you think of anything. You're required to sign a written statement. We'll be in touch with further developments." The older man nodded, fixed his hat back on his bald head and departed with his offsider.

"They don't believe me!" Hana's voice contained an unattractive whine and she closed her eyes in frustration. "I can tell." She set off towards the front door. "Hey, sorry everyone for the fuss. I'll be fine. See you tomorrow."

Everyone stopped and stared at her in surprise.

"Stay here," Andrea offered.

"No, stay viz us," Boris insisted. "Wir habe ein guest room."

"Thank you. I want to go home, feed the cat, take some pills for my banging headache and forget about this afternoon."

"I'll walk you home." Logan's gentle voice soothed her beneath the din of everyone else's objections. His steady, stroking touch on her wrist offered her reassurance and Hana felt a wave of gratitude.

"I'll come," Pete insisted.

"Me too." Boris took a guard position opposite Logan.

"Not with that ass!" Logan wrinkled his nose. "You can stay outside, North."

When Hana emerged from her bedroom having washed her face and changed her clothes, she found the men raiding the fridge and North clanging around with the electric frying pan. They sat around the dining table as dusk thickened and turned into night, eating bacon and fried eggs. "Can I have yours?" Pete asked, nudging Hana with his elbow. She nodded and pushed her plate towards him, her appetite gone. Between them, the men polished off the best part of two loaves of bread, a dozen eggs and a packet of bacon. Logan gave Hana encouraging smiles when the others weren't looking and kept his knee resting against hers beneath the table.

As the silence grew, Hana forced herself to make an effort. "I'm sorry," she conceded. "There's so much going round in my head, I can't think straight."

Boris suggested writing down everything she remembered, like a true school teacher. Pete opted to write in his scrawled hand, jotting down dates and incidents.

"That cop said someone mugged you." Logan's brow furrowed. "Is that why you had a cut lip and marks on your neck?" He glared at Pete, who shrugged.

"I didn't know. Nobody tells me anything!"

"Yeah." Hana touched the space on her throat which hurt for days. "I kept it hidden but it's gone now."

"So," Boris summarised, snatching the list from Pete. "Ze first attackers said nussing significant to Hana as zey tried to take her handbag, but Hana recalls zat zey vere hanging around ze truck. She assumed zat it vas to jump out at her, but vat if zey had been interested in somesing inside ze truck?"

"Logan, can't you find something out? You know, with your contacts," Pete began, wiggling his eyebrows. The look Logan shot him killed the sentence on his thin lips. Hana looked at the tall, good-looking man sideways and realised how little she knew about him.

Boris continued, but Pete interrupted him so often he gave up. "The second incident involving the brick through the windscreen came soon after the attempted mugging, but happened in daylight. They didn't try to get into the vehicle but left you a warning." Pete's animation rattled Hana's nerves.

"I'm glad my life is so entertaining," she bit as the men continued to debate her circumstances.

"There're more discreet ways of getting into a vehicle like that," Logan contributed, causing Hana to raise her eyebrows.

"Could you do it?" Pete demanded and Logan nodded.

"Yeah. It's easy. Why not look at the truck when it's parked somewhere else? They could break in and take whatever they wanted. They want

Hana involved; they want her to know what they're doing. What did the guy say to you, Hana?" Logan asked, fixing his grey eyes on her face.

Her voice sounded tired as she answered. "The blond man said something similar to the note on the brick. Something like, 'Where is it?' But then I ran, so I've made it look like I know what they want." Hana sighed, realising her escape had compounded the illusion of guilt.

"What was that guy doing underneath?" Pete commented, sounding frustrated.

"I took a look," Logan said. "The cops want to fingerprint it, so it's hard without touching. I couldn't see anything apart from the marks where you keep that little magnet thing. It's fallen off by the way."

Hana's face showed confusion. "What magnet thing?"

"You know, the metal box with the spare key in it. I've got one stuck on the farm truck with a magnet. The stockmen know where it is and put it back after they use it. I noticed last time we hoisted it to change the clutch that it left awful scratchy marks on the paintwork where they drag it off and put it back. Your car's got those marks right underneath the driver's door."

"I don't keep a spare key on the car!" Hana responded with sarcasm in her voice. "Not with a cop for a son. He'd think I'd gone nuts!"

"Your son's a cop?" Logan asked, his brow furrowing. An expression of discomfort crossed his face.

"Yes. Why?" Hana felt defensive and challenged him, but he masked his thoughts with a blank look.

"No reason. It's just a question."

"Maybe the previous owner kept losing their keys so used the magnet thing," North suggested, but Logan shrugged.

"Whatever. The marks from it are fresh and clean. No dirt, no rust. So unless you steam cleaned the underside of your car in the last six months, you've been carrying around a magnetised box of some description."

"So where is it then?" asked Hana, standing up to clear the table. Her patience grew thin with the interrogation and tiredness crept over her head like a blanket. She needed her guests to leave so she could contemplate alone and try Bodie again on his mobile.

The men washed up and loaded the dishwasher, displaying a reluctance to leave despite her protestations that Andrea and Paul were only next door. "I'll ring Bodie again," she promised. "As soon as you leave."

Boris fetched his car from next door's driveway and Peter North gave her an awkward but sincere hug. He ruined it by tripping over his untied shoelaces, falling down the front steps and waking the dead with his cursing. He pulled a large piece of hedging from the back of his pants and threw it onto the lawn. "See you tomorrow, Hana," he said. He wafted a hand behind his backside again and shook his head.

"Will you be okay?" Logan sat on the bottom step like a child to zip his cowboy boots up and Hana felt an unexpected moment of longing.

"I think so," she replied, peering out into the dark street. "It doesn't feel good that someone wants to hurt me."

"Yeah. I bet." He stood and rested a hand on her shoulder. Hana saw the concern in his eyes and bit her lip. She wanted him to kiss her again, to smooth away the day's events in a whirlpool of passion but he didn't. "Don't answer the door to anyone," he insisted. Hana felt warmth play on her cheeks as she contemplated asking him to stay. But the moment passed. "Tell the cops about the scratches under the car," he said. "It's worth a shot."

Hana shrugged in dismissal. "You saw them. They didn't listen to me. In their eyes it's a petty grudge or a series of coincidences. I can't ring and tell them that."

"But these guys sound dangerous." Logan's eyes narrowed and he cocked his head.

"I'll be fine." Irritation crept into Hana's voice. "I'll keep calling Bodie. He'll be on a night dive but he'll answer when he can. The local police won't be interested in scratches under the car which I can't swear weren't there before. Vik bought it ten years ago."

Logan shook his head. "The scratches are newer than that. Your mechanic might remember. Want me to ring him?" Logan dragged his thumb down Hana's cheek and the action made her want to scream with frustration. Her answer sounded biting.

"No. I don't want to involve him. I carried on using Doug after Vik died but I make appointments through the parts shop, get his junior to pick up the car and pay online."

"Why?" Logan's eyes narrowed.

Hana snapped. "Because he always wants to talk about Vik and I don't! I'm not ringing him and nor are you."

"Why don't you use a different garage?" Logan's question seemed so logical, Hana couldn't argue.

"I can't. He does a good job." She licked her top lip and glared at the wall, ending the conversation. She regretted the words which betrayed her imprisonment to a life long gone and felt hopelessness and self-pity descend on her shoulders.

"Oh, Hana." Logan leaned in and kissed her on the cheek. He lingered, the smell of his fading aftershave musky and addictive.

Hana's heart fluttered in her chest and she craved more of him. She didn't want to be alone anymore. She opened her mouth to speak, but he gave a casual shrug, missing the cue and leaving. "Lock it after me," he ordered, closing the door behind him.

Hana listened to his footsteps walk down the stairs and onto the driveway. She stood behind the door listening to Boris' car door open and close and the engine rev as the vehicle drove away. She stood in the dark, lacking the energy to move or lock the front door. A numbness gripped her like something just finished and left her grieving. Rousing herself, she turned the key in the lock and hung it on the back of the door in its usual place. She made her way upstairs to the kitchen as her phone finished its orchestral dance on the bench top.

Checking the missed call she saw Bodie's number, but didn't ring him back. She wasn't his responsibility, just his mother. Hana missed her husband's companionship and his ability to take control of problems and make them right. She felt his memory shrouding her and condemning her attraction to Logan. "Did you mean for me to end up alone?" she asked the empty room filled with his ghost. Her own answer brought no comfort. "Yes. You did."

Bodie texted later. 'What's wrong? I'm on a date. She's nipped to the bathroom.'

Hana texted back, lying to him and telling him she just fancied a chat. Against all sensible advice, she downed a large glass of white wine and swallowed some out-of-date sleeping pills. Huffing at the best before date of eight years ago, Hana swallowed them with the alcohol and hoped for the best. She'd either sleep or die.

She checked the doors and windows before the pills took effect. She also shut curtains she never worried about and double checked the doors again. Hana turned away from the front window only seconds before the truck slid into the street, turning at the top of the cul-de-sac and parking opposite her house. Its lights winked out, but no driver emerged.

The street settled for the night. Lights dwindled in the houses one by one and went out as occupants retired to bed. The darkness became dense and blue-black as clouds obscured the quarter moon. The occasional squawk from a pukeko punctuated the silence as it moved around in the reeds of a nearby lake, worried by the whirr of a morepork's wings as it hunted for dinner. The driver opposite scanned the street from his vehicle, alert and ready. A gloved hand turned the radio on and when its display lit up like a Christmas tree, switched it off again.

The out-of-date sleeping tablets did their job. Hana fell into bed just in time and woke hours later in the same position. She dreamed she heard noises in the garden outside her bedroom window and fought a monster who climbed over the gate.

The earth turned and night progressed as God decreed. The morepork caught his mate a juicy mouse and the pukeko gave up trying to rescue the fallen twig and settled down in the reeds.

Chapter 17

Hana awoke to the chirp of the dawn chorus. Sunrise grew later as autumn approached and six o'clock came and went before she opened her eyes, groggy from the sleeping tablets. Her head felt as though someone filled it with cotton wool and then kicked it around. On reaching the bathroom, she didn't recognise the woman in the mirror who resembled a harpy with sticking up hair and dark circles around her eyes. "Attractive," she muttered, scaring the cat who mewed at her and ran away.

Last night's wine glass sat on the bedside table next to the open bottle of pills. It mocked and condemned her in the early morning sunshine. Screwing on the childproof lid and debating whether to bin them or not, Hana noticed the instructions for use on the label, 'Take one with food. Seek medical advice in the event of overdose.' Hana's eyes widened. She'd disobeyed every instruction. "Hey, you lived to tell the tale," she told herself.

Hana blundered around the bedroom and kitchen getting dressed for work and sorting out the cat. Still feeling groggy and sick, she stared in the pantry at the array of cereal boxes and closed the door choosing nothing. She set the burglar alarm in the hallway and stumbled down the stairs to the garage. The sensor picked her up as she came around the corner and the light flicked on, illuminating the bottom of the stairs. Opening the internal garage door and stepping into the darkness, she saw her damaged truck for the first time. A crack across the back bumper didn't look too dire until Hana peered closer and noticed the dent. Jiggling the catch on her rear door proved futile as the lock fused with the impact on the chassis. She turned on the main light and contemplated searching for the scratches Logan mentioned but without a torch, it seemed a pointless exercise.

Patting the rear wing, she apologised in advance. "I'm sorry for having to use you today but I need to get to work. Please don't drop anything important on the road." Hana pressed the garage release on the wall and the door clanked upwards, letting in cool morning air. She fiddled with the keys in her hand and watched the widening gap as she worried the men might return. She'd be powerless if they got into the house.

A sudden flurry of movement caught her eye as a car bumped onto the driveway, its elderly suspension creaking and grinding up the slope. Panic rose in Hana's chest and taking short, gasping breaths, she edged backwards to jam herself between the rear wall and the freezer. Her heart pounded in her breast and she froze, knowing they'd come back for her. Her terrified gaze fixed on the switch and she leapt for it, slamming her hand down hard enough to depress it first time.

The motor kicked in and the door began its slow journey towards the floor, chains rattling overhead as it stirred itself to life as though disturbed from a deep sleep. A figure appeared in the narrowing gap, ducking beneath the metal door and touching the sensor on the bottom so it stopped at half-mast.

"No!" Hana screamed, failure sending anger to mingle with the fear. "Leave me alone!" She grappled with the door handle, feeling it slip from her grasp as she remembered she'd locked it from the inside before closing it behind her. In desperation, she cast around and seized a spade hanging with other garden implements on a set of wall hooks. She yanked it free, sending a fork and a rake tumbling down at her feet. Hana gritted her teeth and wielded it like a weapon, ready to take off her attacker's head this time.

"Bloody hell!" Logan exclaimed, raising his forearms in self-defence as he rounded the back of the vehicle and met Hana head on. Already in motion, she couldn't stop her arms swinging the shovel and watched it cut through the air and almost decapitate Logan. He ducked in time and snatched the wooden shaft from her one-handed.

"Sorry, sorry!" Hana gasped. "I thought you were them."

"I can see that." Logan flipped the spade upright and leaned it against the wall, eyeing Hana with a look of disbelief. Then he gave a decisive nod. "Good choice of weapon though. It took me by surprise, but I dodged it. Grab the rake next time and jab it forward. You might trip them up and the prongs can be useful." He bent and stood the other implements upright, glancing around the garage with interest.

"Use the rake," Hana repeated. She swallowed and put her hand over her mouth, her stomach roiling from the stress. "Use the bloody rake."

Logan quirked his mouth up on one side. "Sorry. Too factual." He pulled her hand away from her mouth with strong fingers and reeled her in, the movement slow and deliberate. Hana's feet moved in short, jerky steps until her nose touched the front of Logan's jacket. Then she turned her cheek to meet his chest and felt the shakes begin in her knees and work their way up her thighs into her lower back. She breathed through pursed lips and groaned with relief as Logan's strong arms enfolded her, burying her head in fabric and safety.

"You know they'll come back, don't you?" Her voice sounded small and muffled.

"Sorry, babe. I'm so sorry." He didn't deny her fears or reduce them to a figment of female overreaction. Instead, he held her shuddering body until she calmed. Hana breathed in his masculine scent and took massive gulps of air. Logan's voice sounded soft and soothing, resonating through her skull from his cheek against the top of her head. "We thought you might like a ride," he whispered. "Boris' car's got a flat, so we came in Pete's old banger. There's room if you want?" He touched his hand to her cheek. "I should have texted first. Sorry."

His brow knitted and Hana forced her head to nod, staring up at him with gratitude. Logan kept hold of her hand but bent to retrieve her fallen handbag, passing it to her and brushing the fingers of her other hand with a light touch. "You go," he said, jerking his head towards Pete's battered heap on the driveway. "I'll shut the door and duck out. Did you set your alarm?"

Hana nodded. "I did it from upstairs. It doesn't cover the garage."

Logan nodded. "Pity." He smiled and stroked her cheek with a tender action. His fingers brushed her skin and settled on the back of her neck beneath her hair. He leaned in and placed a kiss on her forehead which sent shivers down her spine and Hana held her breath. But the moment ended and Logan withdrew his hand, raising the garage door higher and then sending her under. As Hana settled in the back of Pete's car, she watched him lower the door again and duck under at the last moment.

Hana hoped nobody wanted to discuss the previous evening's events. She sat in the back with Logan as the car lurched in the traffic, Peter North fighting for clutch control at junctions and inclines.

"You've got a hole in your exhaust," Logan commented as the rasping noise caused pedestrians to stop and stare. "Sounds like it's at the baffle end."

"Na." Pete dismissed his diagnosis. "I like it. Makes me look like a boy racer. This is my ride, bro'. I love it."

"Bloody hell, man, grow up," Logan complained from the back as another loud grumble came from beneath his seat. "How can you be a boy racer when you're an overweight, balding guy accompanied by a car full of teachers from the local high school?" Logan shook his head in exasperation and put two fingers to his temple in a shoot-myself-in-the-head symbol.

Pete bristled, accepting he was overweight and balding but pulling Logan up on one small error. "Hana's not a teacher!" He wound the window down, ramped up the heavy beat on his screechy stereo and waved to a motorist in the queue next to him. "Yo, bro', how ya doin'?" he shouted.

Logan glanced at Hana and rolled his eyes. He slumped down in his seat a little lower and masked his identity to other road users by placing his elbow on the windowsill and covering his face. Hana smiled at his antics, knowing he meant it as a distraction. She stretched out her hand and touched his face; the first time she'd initiated something physical with him. He stirred as Hana's fingers traced the healing scar under his eye, feeling the knottiness of the line. She sighed, recognising the impossibility of a relationship, while knowing she fell deeper into something she couldn't extract herself from without pain. She moved her hand away and glanced down at her feet to avoid his perceptive gaze. "Oh no!" she groaned. "I've still got my slippers on."

Hana's white, fluffy clad feet were the least of the school's problems and even Donald Watson allowed them to pad by without mention. At interval, Hana stared down at her feet beneath the desk and wiggled her toes. "I might wear these tomorrow," she told Sheila. "My feet usually ache by now."

Sheila ignored her and continued to pull staples from the notice board and toss them onto Rory's seat.

"What's the matter?" Hana asked and Sheila shrugged.

"Nothing."

The final dress rehearsal for the joint production between the boys' and girls' schools took place during the third period. Mayhem reigned throughout the site with no one immune to the growing atmosphere of nervousness. Raw fear permeated the air, actors fled from toilet to Great Hall and back again clad in gaudy, surreal costumes. Boys wearing eyeliner and lipstick hung around in the corridors alongside girls who looked similar.

"Which Shakespeare play is this?" Hana asked a girl lounging outside the Great Hall.

The teenager fluttered false eyelashes and adjusted the dog collar tightened around her throat. "Romeo and Juliet."

An English major, Hana looked confused. "So, which character are you?" She took in the leather jacket and skin-tight black jeans, Gothic eye makeup and fake facial tattoos.

"Juliet!" the girl replied as though insulted.

Hana nodded and beat a hasty retreat, glad she missed out on buying tickets.

Dobbs policed the site, parting couples who looked too cosy between scenes, becoming more and more agitated as the day wore on. Adding to the flagrant disregard of school rules, drama teachers contributed to the melee, leaning against walls and blocking fire exits as they waited for scene changes and actors suffering stage fright.

With the floorshow downstairs, the student centre seemed eerily silent, offering peace and solace for Hana. She completed jobs which often got neglected and dusted the shelves of the office. When her phone rang, she answered it.

"Hi, Mrs Johal, it's Tom here. I attended the call to your neighbour's house last night."

"Oh, hi." Hana regretted her lack of enthusiasm, but couldn't muster up anything more excitable.

"Yeah," he continued, "I'm sending someone to fingerprint your vehicle. He might be able to identify the men."

"They didn't both touch it." Hana closed her eyes and thought back to the men's behaviour. "The dark haired man might've prodded the underside but the other one didn't."

"Ah well." The police officer sounded defeatist. "It's a long shot but my new boss feels it's important enough to try."

Hana lost her hard won sense of peace and agreed she'd be home by five, remembering too late that she needed Pete to give her a ride.

Wandering through the staffroom in her fluffy slippers she looked for Pete, realising he'd been absent all day. She spotted him laid across two chairs on the deck outside the staffroom, fast asleep and snoring. A line of curious faces watched through the common room window as the remaining Year 13s came in for their study class. Hana noticed a line of spit balls lying around him on the deck, still glistening in the sunshine. Some other class had used him for target practice.

Hana negotiated the obstacle course of tables and chairs, tripping over a pair of feet sticking out from under a table. "Sorry!" she cried, struggling to right herself before she hit the floor.

Boris rose like a monster from the deep, his hair on end and his eyes bleary. "What, what?" he shouted.

Hana rubbed her elbow and studied him with concern. "Are you ill?"

Boris snorted and wiped dribble from his chin, pushing himself off the carpet. Upright, he wavered on the spot like a blade of grass before noticing the clock. He uttered a loud expletive and collected a bag from next to him on the floor. "I'm late for ze class!" He staggered away, weaving himself across the staffroom like a drunk.

Wondering if she should wake North, Hana decided against it. His head lolled over the side of the seat and a long glob of spit formed a track from his open mouth to the floor. Drops of saliva travelled down it, making it look like an invisible escalator.

Rain began outside and knowing her slippers wouldn't cut it on a journey over to the English department, Hana phoned Logan in his classroom to see what time they planned to leave work. The phone in the English department office rang for a while until answered by the grumpy Bob Green. "He disappeared off before lunch and hasn't come back yet. Angus said not to worry, but Angus doesn't have to take Du Rose's classes as well as his own, does he? No, it's me who's forced to do two people's work, isn't it?"

"Okay, thanks. I just wanted to know when he planned to leave tonight. He's giving me a ride home."

"I'll tell you what I told that other woman," Bob ranted. "I don't know where the hell he's gone and if I wanted to be a messenger service, I'd get a job in a call centre."

"What other woman?" Hana asked, regretting the question the second it emerged from her lips.

"The one who keeps ringing!" Bob snapped. "His girlfriend." He ended the call and Hana dropped the phone as though it was contaminated.

The call left her rattled and Hana distracted herself with work, not allowing herself the luxury of searching for an explanation. A curious numbness sank into her soul and she beat herself up for almost making a fool of herself. When Logan appeared looking wasted with his hair sticking up around his head like a halo, Hana avoided any physical contact and treated him like any other colleague. He looked confused but picked up her obvious signals and didn't press her for answers. North staggered into the office with a spit ball on his forehead, slumping into his chair and resting his head on the table. He and Logan shared the barest of grunts.

"The cops rang me." Hana kept her tone clipped. "What time are you leaving, Pete?"

North got to his feet. "Now. Let's go now."

"You can't! You're already in trouble." Logan pressed him back into the chair where he closed his eyes and dozed off. He turned to Hana. "One of us will drive you home. What did your son say about it?"

Hana chewed her lip and tried not to look guilty. "I didn't speak to him," she admitted, fending off Logan's surprise with irritation. "He's a busy man. I can't involve him with every little problem I run into."

"Okay, okay." Logan held his hands out in front of him and backed away. "I'm teaching now. We'll talk later." His lips twitched as though he wanted to kiss her but he suppressed any desire to follow through and left the room. North woke up for long enough to stumble out of the office and disappear, maybe to a teaching engagement but then again perhaps not.

Towards the end of lunch, the school readied itself for the performance of a lifetime. 'Romeo and Juliet,' chez a group of spotty, hormonal teenagers, many of whom had transitioned from acting to real romance. That was the trouble with single sex schools. It resembled the diet fanatic avoiding chocolate. Should the unfortunate dieter get locked in a chocolate factory, there existed the potential for a never-to-be-forgotten binge session. The next day would bring forgotten promises and broken hearts.

Despite being four hours north, Bodie still had many colleagues and friends in Hamilton and unlimited access to a huge and all-encompassing computer database. He rang Hana mid-afternoon, his tone irritated. "How come I have to hear it from someone else, Mum?" he whined.

Hana sighed. "You sounded busy and I didn't want to bother you." She apologised and asked after his date. Demanding answers of a man trained in interrogation techniques proved fruitless; she learned nothing apart from the woman's rank and that she worked with him. Something about his tone told her it was casual and she'd be best not pressing further.

The conversation turned back to her recent one-woman crime wave. "Logan thinks it's something to do with scratches under the truck."

"What scratches?" Bodie demanded. "Who's Logan?"

Hana fudged the question, not wanting to admit to her monster crush on a colleague.

Coming to no useful conclusion about the attacks, Bodie rang off and promised to visit on his next shift rotation. Hana clutched the phone and wondered how to escape work, early, barefoot, without being spotted by Donald Watson and without a vehicle.

Chapter 18

Anka discovered Hana in the student centre and raised an eyebrow at her bare feet. "I brought some typing back for Sheila. I can't read some of her writing though." She placed the papers in Sheila's office and jerked her head towards Hana's feet. "New trend?"

Hana shook her head. "No, I came in my slippers by accident."

"Really?" Anka snorted. "I've got spares in my office. I'll get them." She let herself out and clattered away. Hana smiled to herself, realising she'd missed their easy friendship.

"I can't wear those thanks," exclaimed Hana trying not to seem too ungrateful when Anka returned later. "I'll break my neck. How do you walk in them?"

Anka held out the bright red, pointy-toed stilettos, pressing them into Hana's hands. "Just try them. They'll look awesome."

"No, I'll fall over." Hana kept hold of one but the other tumbled to the carpet. Anka retrieved it.

"Come on, Hana. You won't win Gwynne back in bare feet. His thing is killer heels."

Hana's jaw dropped. "I don't want Gwynne! I never did. Anyway, he's got an Internet bride."

Anka laughed, the sound hollow. "Intranet, Hana! It's the Chinese woman from food technology. They were chatting on the school system. You need to lift your game."

Hana shook her head. "I don't have game. How do you know he likes heels?"

Anka shrugged. "He just does. Put them on."

Hana pressed her foot into the right one and sighed. "They're a bit too big."

"They'll be fine. Put the other one on and practice walking."

Hana obeyed, shaking her finger at Anka. "I don't want Gwynne Jeffs thank you. But I do need some shoes to get home." She wobbled around for a minute. "I can't walk in them," she giggled. She teetered round the office tripping over empty boxes and fallen brochures whilst admiring her feet. "They're very you," she admitted, grinning at Anka. "Glitzy, debonair and bright. They don't really fit with the rest of what I'm wearing."

Dressed in fitted blue slacks and a white blouse, Hana wrinkled her nose. The red shoes glinted from beneath the hem of her slacks, daring her to naughtiness. "You could kill someone with these pointy toes!" She giggled and performed a dainty pirouette, bending her knee to prolong the spin.

Anka shrieked with laughter and Hana repeated the rusty ballet move, adding a high kick to the finale. Too late, she saw the office door open inwards. Peter North blundered towards her, looking behind him as he shouted abuse at a student in the common room. He took the full brunt of the pointed kick right in the crotch. With a roar of agony, he doubled over and fell to the ground, panting to catch his breath. Hana withdrew her foot but discovered the shoe no longer on it. Pete lay on the dirty carpet squirming and making an odd grunting sound.

Anka bolted through the back door like a guilty child, leaving Hana wearing one bright red shoe and palpitating. She balanced on one leg and put her hands on her hips. "It can't be that bad. I'm not rubbing it."

As Pete rolled over onto his other side, hands gripping his crotch, the moans grew in volume with a twang of hope resonating in there somewhere. "In your dreams, boy," Hana muttered. She spotted the shoe beneath him and bent to drag it out. "Oh man! You squashed it!" she complained. Hana grabbed her handbag and hopped around on one foot, pushing her bare toes into the other. "Sorry about this," she panted. "I have to leave."

In the common room, the study teacher rose to his feet, shooting alarmed looks at the student centre door. "Pete's not well," Hana muttered with as much conviction as she could muster. "Mysterious belly-ache." She looked back from the stairwell as the teacher strode towards the door and clip-clopped faster down the stairs. Everything wiggled and wobbled as she teetered into the car park, remembering only then she had no car. Clopping out onto Maui Street, she turned left and kept walking.

The journey took longer than usual and Hana arrived at the rest home on the corner of Powell Street with sore toes and a blister starting on her right heel. She nodded to the matron as the older woman sat at the front desk doing her endless paperwork. "Hi, Hana. Father Sinbad's in his room this afternoon."

"Thank you." Hana wobbled her way down a long corridor until she arrived outside Room 28. The space outside the door seemed dark and gloomy with only the light from the overhead bulb. An aroma of cleaning materials and death choked up the air. Hana knocked and opened the door. "Are you decent, Father?" she called.

The light was stronger in the room and the smell of coal tar soap and aftershave masked everything else. Nothing had changed in the past eleven years. The male occupant sat in a corner of the room in a metal-framed wheelchair, facing a window and a sunny garden. His face enjoyed the warmth, but his blind eyes saw nothing. His white clerical collar looked stark and clean against the neat black shirt. "Aye, I'm decent," his thick Irish voice rumbled.

Hana threw herself on the edge of the hospital bed with a sigh. The clean-shaven, wrinkled face turned towards her with a smile which betrayed the heart of a gentleman. "What ails me girl then?" he asked.

Hana shrugged. He couldn't see her, but she knew from experience the old man sensed how she felt. His blindness had finely tuned every other sense in his aging body. She could hide nothing from him and didn't have the energy to try.

Half an hour later, the priest asked, "So what's the crack wit' dis young man den? D'ya thinks he likes you as much as you like him?"

Hana turned to look at the old man, her mouth gaping. She had recounted her story from a visitors' chair next to his wheelchair. Blindness did little to diminish the old priest and a game of draughts was his favourite vice. Hana sat beside him, balancing the board game in her lap, responsible for moving both their counters and giving a running commentary. Fading grid numbers aided the task, written by a fourteen-year-old Bodie in vivid black marker pen. "Black 4 to C6," she replied, ignoring the question.

"White 3 to A4. Taking two of dem lovely black draughts I do believe," he chuckled, displaying the crinkly laugh lines round his useless eyes.

"Father Sinbad!" Hana exclaimed.

"That's me. Priest of de sinful and de bad. How me mammy would have giggled if she could a seen me in dat pulpit wit me collar and me smock. What a name for a man of God. Sinbad. I ask ye."

Hana smiled, but she'd heard it many times over the years.

"Aye, I know ye never tire of hearing me yarns but not today. Today I want to hear yourn. What's occurring in ye pretty heart, Hana Johal? Humour me and tell the old confessor what ye feel."

Hana thought before she spoke. She couldn't fool a man who'd listened to millions of confessions for the best part of sixty years. His blindness changed nothing in his ability to discern or read human emotion. "I miss Vik. I like Logan. A lot. But when I'm around Logan, I feel unfaithful to

Vik and when I think of Vik, I just get angry." She sighed in confusion. "Anyway, it's all academic. I think he has a girlfriend but isn't being on the level. I don't have the energy for games."

Sadness enveloped her and loneliness crowded back in. Giving up brought a sense of overwhelming loss, no longer because her husband died, but because she denied herself the comfort of waking in the night and hearing another person breathing next to her. Nobody listened to her recount the mishaps of her day or shared a laugh about it. A familiar grief caused the stray tear to roll down her cheek. She wiped it away with a spark of anger.

"Why won't ye release yerself?" asked the priest, his voice soothing. "Even Jesus released de widows from their marriages and let dem love again. Why not you, me darlin'? There's no wrong in what your heart feels. He's a God of second chances, so he is."

Hana's sigh betrayed her to the old man as did her silence as she wrestled with inner misgivings. "Vik's clothes are in my wardrobe," she admitted in a small voice. "Not them all," she qualified a little too fast. "But the things he treasured most, his favourite shirt, his best shoes, the tie he wore at Christmas which played Jingle Bells." Her smile looked sad. "He wore it to annoy the kids."

Every Christmas she sat in the wardrobe, allowing herself the luxury of squeezing the thing that made the tie play the song and every year she promised herself she'd get rid of it. One year she'd press it and it wouldn't play, the battery dead. She wasn't sure if she'd replace the battery or keep the tie even though it no longer played. Every year she dreaded it. It stayed in the wardrobe; her dirty secret.

The old priest went on in his quiet, reassuring way, his gentle but realist views having softened many an angry catholic heart or chastised a guilty one in love and compassion. He embodied the Father-heart of God in a man. "To love, Hana Johal, until death do us part," he whispered, but she put her hands over her ears, not wanting to hear the rest. Nobody said those words on her wedding day, not in the registry office or at the Sikh ceremony. As she nurtured the fragile life inside her which became Bodie, Hana ran into a marriage nobody else wanted to happen. And it worked, right up until the day after Vik's funeral; the day her heart died under a crushing weight of grief and anger.

Strong hands pulled her hands from her ears and held them in a vice like grip; firm for such a frail old man and yet so tender. "Till death do us part," he whispered, the faint scent of coffee and decay on his breath. "Death, Hana and Vik is dead, him and all his promises."

Hana sobbed under the cruelty of the words. "No," she sniffed. "I can't do it again. I gave a hundred percent. There's nothing left to give."

Father Sinbad held her hands until she ceased crying, cooing and whispering Latin words over her which she sensed were prayers. His overwhelming care filled her with gratitude and she cried for longer because of it. When she stopped crying, Father Sinbad let go of her hands and touched her forehead, muttering a benediction.

Hana felt embarrassed and made a joke, "Were those my last rites?"

He threw back his head and laughed, "Ye'll never know, Hana Johal. No, truly, t'was a blessing of peace. Now go home and ring dat young man. Give him a chance my dear, give him a chance. Because dat's what's holding ye back and we both know it. Love is a risk my dear and nobody likes pain." As she kissed his temple and turned to leave, he added a last gem of wisdom. "And while you're at it, get rid of dat car and dat ole house. Get something your own size and take me somewhere nice in de new car. Something yellow or purple. Your Lord God is purple, ye know."

Red shoes swinging from her hand, Hana padded through the rest home, Father Sinbad's jolly laughter ringing in her ears. His words gripped her as an idea. Changing the car seemed a great plan in the light of her recent troubles. Moving house might solve another issue. Hana nodded to the Matron as she passed.

"See ya, Hana," the woman said and gave a small wave. The calm and stability of the rest home were testament to her iron rule. The matron interviewed a sullen Bodie more than a decade earlier, assigning him to read for Father Sinbad Maloney. In exchange, she stamped his attendance book, wrote nice things about the schoolboy and made sure he got his service award certificate every year for the next four years. It began as a way of Angus forcing an out-of-control teenager to gain a sense of social responsibility and ended in one of those rare friendships some people never experience. Bodie always called to see the priest each time he visited Hamilton and the old man had become an anchor for him. Hana only met Father Sinbad after Vik died, accompanying her distraught child to the sunny room to support him. After an absence during the anger part of Bodie's grief, Hana visited and began by making excuses for her son's neglect. The need for apologies proved futile. She discovered for herself a man whose miseries equalled her own, but who learned like the Apostle Paul that whether in abundance or hardship, pain or joy, the grace of Christ was enough. Hana desired what the old priest possessed and in glimpses and snatches over the years, had shared his peace.

When Bodie returned to reading duty, Hana accompanied him and they shared the solace Sinbad offered. Grafted onto their family vine, it seemed as though he always belonged.

Donning the shoes once again and wincing against the blisters, Hana emerged from the manicured gardens and back onto Powell Street. School had emptied and the buses enjoyed a lull before work rush hour began. Hana crossed the main road and waited by the bus stop. A light drizzle attacked her hair and clothes, but Hana pondered the nuances of her life and ignored it. Tapping the heel of her right shoe against the pavement, she ran through her conversation with Father Sinbad, coming to some long overdue resolutions about her life. Beginning with the Jingle Bells tie.

The bus arrived empty but late. Hana got to her house, puffed and flustered, having removed the shoes half a kilometre earlier. She stopped at the sight of a car on her driveway and approached with caution. A man descended the front stairs with a clipboard in his hand. "Mrs Johal?" he asked and she gave a tiny nod. He heaved in an exasperated breath. "I'm meant to be examining a vehicle at this address but I can't get any answer."

"Sorry. The bus didn't come." Hana apologised and offered tea and biscuits as a consolation prize. The man remained abrupt and business-like, but accepted the tea.

The policeman dusted around the vehicle where Hana recalled the Asian-looking man touching the bodywork. He also examined the door where the other man leaned across her. Hana shuddered at the memory of the blond man's taut body forcing her into the metal and the look of malice in his eyes. "You shouldn't have moved the vehicle," the cop chastised her. "You've got a list of people who touched it after them."

"Oh." Hana cringed. "My neighbour Paul drove it off the pavement. Logan didn't touch it."

The man's eyebrows narrowed. "Logan who?" He peered at his list.

"Logan Du Rose." Hana swallowed at the flicker of interest which crossed his face. "Do you know him?" She asked the question and watched his expression shutter.

"No." He shook his head. "Just the name." Opening the door and flooding the garage with light, he photographed the cracked bumper and kept working with a fine brush and an array of powders.

Hana glanced around, embarrassed by the volume of detritus. In one corner sat a matching set of adults' and children's golf clubs, both dusty and unused. An old school bag hung on a nail beneath some shelving, bulging with something which hadn't seen the light of day for years. A pink eeling net, a broken tennis racquet, an exercise machine for toning abdominal muscles and drying washing occupied another corner. Hana sighed, remembering Sinbad's wisdom.

"How long have you lived here?" the cop asked, his pen hovering over a box on a form. Hana watched his gloved fingers twitching.

"Fifteen years," she answered. "But I'm selling up."

"Okay. Leave a forwarding address." He turned away and began packing up his gear.

The thought of telling her kids sent a cold shiver down her spine. Perhaps it wasn't a viable plan to abandon her marital home and start again. Hana felt her life venture into the great and frightening unknown, where the thoughts and needs of others fenced off her journey and contained her within their comfort zones, instead of letting her walk free.

The policeman finished his tea after taking Hana's prints on a mobile fingerprinting unit to rule out hers from her attackers. Then he left. Hana abandoned the messy garage, determined to tackle it at the weekend if the mood for change survived. She waved to the policeman and turned to press the switch for the garage door, starting in fright as a motorbike slid onto the driveway.

The rider waved before removing the black, tinted helmet. Logan's hair looked flat and dark circles underlined his grey eyes. Hana released the breath she held and gave him a feeble wave. Stubble shadowed the lower half of his face, adding to his ruggedness. He dismounted with ease and took the key from the ignition before walking into the garage. "I was just passing," he began and then stopped. "Na, that's not true. I came to see how you're feeling. You seemed off earlier and I wanted to make sure we're okay." His brow furrowed and he chewed on his lower lip.

Hana worked her jaw, maintaining the distance between them. "I rang the English department to ask for a lift and Bob said another woman's called numerous times. He said she's your girlfriend." She kept her face blank, feeling her heart speed up in her breast. The silence between them felt endless.

Logan ran slender fingers through his dark hair. His sigh betrayed frustration. "My ex thinks we have unfinished business." He spoke through gritted teeth. "We don't."

Hana shrugged. "I haven't the energy for messy relationships, Logan. I really don't."

Logan's lips parted in a smile. "Is this what it is, Hana? Are we having a relationship?"

Chapter 19

Hana swallowed, boxed into a corner with her own suspicions. "I don't know," she stammered.

Logan crossed the distance between them and placed his lips over hers, removing any objections with their gentle graze. Hana backed up against her stricken vehicle and leaned into him, praying her legs held her up long enough. His persuasive kisses addled her mind and reduced her objections to little more than a peripheral voice in the back of her brain.

"I don't want to lose you now," he whispered, their lips close and his fingers threading through her curls. "Please, give me a chance."

Hana closed the garage against her nosy neighbours opposite and Logan tied up the bumper on her car while she made dinner. He ate, the light leaving his eyes as he grew more exhausted.

"What's with you guys?" Hana demanded as Logan ran a hand over his face. "You're all shattered today. Did you stay up talking last night?"

Logan shook his head. "I wasn't going to say anything but I want you to trust me. We took it in turns to watch the house last night, in case the men came back."

Hana gaped. "You watched my house?"

"Yeah." Logan's smile drooped. "And we climbed the fence and checked the back garden heaps of times."

Hana pushed plates into the dishwasher and stood up. "I can't believe you did that. I'm guessing the men didn't come back."

"No." Logan shook his head and stood up, his imposing height making Hana feel safe. "We did it because we care about you."

"Did the cops drive around?" Hana asked, hope in her voice.

Logan wrinkled his nose. "Nope. Not even once." He held his arms out to her. "I need to go. Keep the doors locked and only the upstairs windows open."

Hana pressed her face into his shirt. "But what if someone climbs over the back gate like you did? What then?"

Logan snorted and pulled his shirt sleeve up to reveal a bandage. "Then they get cut like I did, or their pants ripped like Boris. There's more rusty metal in that gate than wood."

"Sorry." Hana reached for his arm but stopped just before she made contact. "What happened to Pete?"

"Who knows?" Logan shrugged. "If he fell and hit his head, we didn't notice."

"I'm glad I didn't wake up in the middle of the night and see someone in the garden. I'd have freaked out." Hana's eyes widened in fear, her green irises obscured by dark pupils. "Those sleeping tablets zonked me out. I might take more tonight."

"Don't do that." Logan stroked her cheek. "Just be sensible."

He held her beneath the photo of a youthful Vik and Hana on their wedding day. It felt odd for her and the sense of déjà vu vied with confusing feelings of betrayal. Logan pointed at a photo of a small, dark-skinned teenager in a familiar school uniform. "Your son went to our school? I hadn't realised," he said. His brow creased. "I guess there's a lot I need to learn about you, Ms McIntyre."

Hana nodded and floundered, not knowing where to begin. Logan stroked her cheek and pressed his soft lips over hers. "It's okay," he whispered. "I've got all the time in the world."

They sat on the bottom step while Logan fastened his heavy motorbike boots. The shiny red shoes winked under the hallway lights, nestled beneath the hall table. Logan jerked his head towards them and zipped up his leather jacket. "Ah, the weapons of mass destruction."

Hana laughed. "Poor Pete. How are his nuts?"

"Don't worry about him. He keeps his brains in his ass so I've no idea where his nuts are." He smiled, the scar beneath his eye wrinkling. "He complained you wouldn't rub them better."

Hana shuddered. "No thanks!"

Logan's eyes narrowed. "Good. I told him if you did, I'd snap them off."

"Did he believe you?" Hana smiled and Logan's nod looked slow and calculated.

"Oh yes."

Hana sighed. "What a day. What a year actually. It's been crap from the start."

"No it hasn't." Logan fitted his arm around her shoulders, crushing her into his side. His jacket smelled of leather and petrol and he kissed the side of her head. "I found you. It's been a good year so far and it can only get better."

Hana nodded and pushed herself closer. "Hold me," she whispered and he did.

Chapter 20

The grating voice of her sixty-six-year-old mother-in-law greeted Hana as she answered the midnight phone call. Roused from a deep sleep, her head felt foggy. "I almost rang off!" Indra complained, the irritating shrill quality still present after three years of no contact. "We're visiting New Zealand and staying with you." She laid it down like a gauntlet of challenge. Vik might be gone, but the game continued, forcing the unwanted wife to dance when she least felt like it. Anger rose within Hana and she fought for control.

"We want to see Vikram's children. We arrive on the Saturday after next. Get us from the airport at nine in the morning, your time."

Indra Johal rang off, leaving Hana furious with herself. "Your son's dead," she said to the silent handset. "I shouldn't have to see you anymore."

She stumbled back to bed with a glass of red wine and a detective novel, noticing a text from Izzie which had arrived fifteen minutes earlier. She replied. 'Are you still up?'

Her phone rang straight away. "Hey Mum. Just feeding Beth. Why are you up this late?"

"Bibi ji phoned me."

"What? Really?" Izzie chuckled. "What did she want?"

Hana relayed Indra's wishes and Isobel fell silent for a long moment. When she spoke, her voice held a tremor. "They won't come to Invercargill. It's too far."

"She said they're planning to." Hana yawned. "They want to see Beth."

"But they don't know!" Izzie sounded panicked. "I didn't tell them about the Down syndrome. What will they do?"

"What can they do?" Hana soothed. "She's their granddaughter, like she is mine. They'll love her."

"Please don't let them come down here," Izzie begged. "I can't face the interrogation about my deepest personal secrets. Elizabeth's enough of a reject in society without her own grandparents passing verdict!" Hana heard her swallow and calm herself. "Mum, tell them it's too cold down here. Winter's coming. They'll hate it."

Hana didn't like to burst her bubble by pointing out they lived in Britain. Trying to distract her, she decided to broach the subject of selling the house. "I need a change and feel like it's time. Logan said the market isn't great but I've asked a few agents to call round and give me a value."

Silence greeted her sentence and then Izzie sighed. "It's okay, Mum. You must do what you think is best. Who's Logan?"

Not quite ready for a full confession, Hana floundered. "I work with him. He's younger than me but seems to like me." She waited, hearing only silence.

The effort told in the small voice which came across the miles as Izzie fought to control her feelings. "Good luck, Mum. I hope it goes well. Just make sure he's not an axe murderer or a con artist."

"Okay, I will."

"Eight years is a long time Mum. And Dad loved you so much; I know he'd want you to find love again."

Hana settled down to sleep, hearing Izzie's words replaying in her head. "Would he?" she whispered into the darkness. "Would he really?" She thought about the feelings of inadequacy her husband's memory induced. She never believed she deserved him and couldn't bear to imagine him with anyone else. If she never intended for him to replace her, then perhaps she lived the life she deserved.

Hana likened herself to a lonely elephant, doomed after the death of her partner to wander the earth alone forever. The cruelty stung as once again Hana resorted to the sleeping tablets, only one this time to shut out the condemnation of her confused thoughts.

Chapter 21

After ten days of fitful, sleepless nights, Hana found herself exactly where she vowed she'd never go again; the arrivals' terminal of Auckland International Airport. A hellish journey through rolling fog over the Bombay Hills cut visibility to a few metres and smacked of horror movies where drivers roamed without hope of finding their destination. Hana sat in the queue for the airport ticket machine, eyeing her temperamental nemesis with terror. "It's gonna get me again," she wittered, chewing her bottom lip. "I know it is."

The ticket machine looked innocuous enough but still refused to clip and release her ticket. Just like last time. The previous car pulled away in a cloud of exhaust fumes and Hana pressed the big green button again. "Just give me the ticket!" she groaned through the open window. "Why do we always have to do this?"

Leaning down she spotted the cardboard ticket poking a few millimetres from the slot, but it stayed there, baiting her. "I did what you said!" Her voice rose a few octaves as the robotic command rebuked her in its automated tone.

"Pull up close to the machine and obey the instructions."

"I did!" Hana pushed her driver's door open, hearing it clang against the metal of the machine. "I pulled up close and now I can't get out!" She scooted across the centre of the car, entangling herself on the gear lever and cursing. Slamming the passenger door, she stalked around the back of her vehicle, trying to take the machine by surprise. She launched herself at it from the side and scrabbled at the ticket with her fingernails. Somebody behind honked their horn.

"Yes!" she punched the air in victory, feeling the shiny cardboard slide into her hand. "No!" Half a ticket sat in her palm, the other jagged half wedged in the hole.

Time marched on towards the arrival of the NZ001 flight from London Heathrow via Los Angeles and the traffic volume increased. Vehicles filled with curious occupants filed past the other ticket machine at a slow crawl, all eyes turned towards her like a bewildered theatre audience. Hana dug through her handbag for tweezers to extract the rest of her ticket. She'd pushed the green button eleven times but nothing happened. Unless she could make the barrier arm go up and fool the machine into thinking she'd gone and someone sensible had arrived, it wouldn't play. Jumping up and down in front of her vehicle didn't work either. The barrier stayed closed and the ticket remained stuck.

A shadow loomed from the fog, an imposing Māori with a moko tattoo dominating his cheeks and chin. His black hair was tied back in a ponytail. Gang insignia decorated his leather jacket and swear words abused her from the knuckles of both hands. He strode towards her, his lips a hard line and his nose, large and flat against his brown skin. Hana gulped and attempted a smile, gripping the handles of her bag in a death grip. "Hey, missus." His voice sounded deep and powerful. "Youse got trouble?" he asked.

She nodded and jerked a shaking finger at the slot. "It won't spit it out," she said, hearing the wobble in her voice. Her eyes grew wide as she imagined him ripping the machine from its pilings and hurling it across the car park. Security would come and she'd miss Indra and Deepak's flight.

The man squeezed into the tiny space between Hana's car and the machine, forcing her to slip out the other side. He jabbed his finger at the instructions.

1. Press green button for ticket.
2. Press red button to release ticket.
3. Proceed under barrier.
4. Pay at a machine located in the car park before leaving.

Hana gulped as a stubby finger pressed the red button and half a ticket popped from the slot, crumpled and ragged on one edge and neatly perforated on the other. Hana felt colour flush to the roots of her hair. "I'm so sorry. Thank you." She accepted the fragile leaf of cardboard residing in the giant palm and clambered back into her seat via the passenger side. Cranking the gear lever into first, she forgot to release the handbrake and the car made a terrible noise as the wheels spun. Removal of the ticket raised the barrier and it pointed jauntily skywards, starting its downward journey as Hana screeched underneath, leaving tyre marks on the asphalt. She fled the scene without her seatbelt and heard a clunk as her back bumper hit the car park floor.

Her heart pounded as she executed an appalling reverse turn into the last empty space in the arrivals car park, having almost ploughed into the vacant trolley bay adjacent. An airbus droned overhead as it came into land, sending her running for the double doors into the arrivals' lounge.

Flight NZ001 processed for ages and she prayed Indra hadn't smuggled in some Indian delicacy and met the border patrol close up. Hana sat near the doors and fidgeted, muttering admonishments to herself like a lunatic. She tried to watch the feet underneath the screens to identify an approaching sari, but they shifted around too quickly. The frosted arrival doors opened and closed, disgorging tired travellers in small denominations and Hana felt her chest grow tighter with each departure.

Auckland Airport depressed her as families arrived with smiles and departed with tears. Wonderful reunions happened in an area only twenty metres wide and she watched a small girl run under the barriers and hurl herself at a white haired old man. In the food court nearby, those departing held stiff conversations, avoiding the final goodbye and radiating fear and misery. Children grew bored and broke the rules, swinging on the barriers and hanging upside down from the railings. Some people laughed as they reunited with loved ones and others cried. The atmosphere shimmered with raw human emotion, tears and promises, sadness and broken hearts. Hana felt drained with the effort of sitting there.

They appeared in front of her, striding through the sliding doors with purpose and blinking in confusion. Slightly built and beautiful still, Indra exuded authority. Despite the long flight, her skin mirrored the colour of an excellent espresso and her dark eyes shone. Jet-black hair pulled back into a bun showed not a strand of grey and her red and gold sari made her stand out like royalty. The Indian matriarch bore the same imposing presence which confronted Hana twenty-six years earlier as she trembled through the family meeting. At the mention of her pregnancy, Indra's face had turned to stone and she terrified Hana with her screech of fury. She'd screamed in a language Hana grew to despise, until an aunty of Vik's led her to another part of the house. Hana still heard her even with the distance between them. She asked Vik later what Indra screamed and he lied to her. "Very bad, very bad," he translated and Hana chose to believe him. But her heart told her Indra wished her unborn child dead.

Hana jumped to her feet and met them at the end of the barrier. She wore a stunning amber dress, a neat jacket and heaps too much makeup. Her eyes widened in alarm as Indra let out a high-pitched wail and ran to her, throwing herself into her arms. Everyone in the terminal stopped to watch and Hana patted Indra's back with cautious taps. "Oh, Hana!" Indra bawled. "It's been too long."

Lost for words, Hana swallowed and took Indra's weight as the old woman draped herself over her.

"Hello my darling." Deepak strolled over with a laden trolley, casually handing a clean white handkerchief to his blithering wife. He leaned across to kiss Hana on the cheek. She felt stunned by their genuine greeting and somehow, they staggered and wheeled towards the exit doors.

Emerging into bright sunshine, Hana realised she'd forgotten the row number of her parking space. Glinting metal greeted her frantically searching gaze. "I'll find it in a minute," she said, hiding her growing dismay. Deepak and Indra drooped in the daylight and the twenty-six hour flight showed in the dark circles beneath their eyes. Hana scoured the car park, looking for landmarks to give her a clue.

A police car slid into the emergency vehicle bay and Indra gave another shriek as the single male occupant emerged. Bodie strode towards them, his physique solidified by a body-armoured vest. Indra entertained more onlookers as she collapsed in a heap, accompanied by wailing and crying. Hana cringed as members of the public assumed her arrivals were under arrest. A tourist stopped to snap photographs on his camera.

Bodie caught Hana's eye and winked as she toyed with the two bits of ticket. "The car's in row 12B, over that way." He indicated with a jerk of his head as Indra continued dripping and sobbing over his uniform. "Bring it here and we can save them a walk."

Hana eyed the parking warden as he picked a fight with an over stayer and looked doubtful. Bodie jerked his head at her, forcing her to trust him. Hana jogged to her car, finding it where her son promised. She sat for a moment inside before starting the engine, never imagining a meeting with her in-laws that didn't end in arguments and emotional bloodshed. Hana battled her way back to arrivals through the departing traffic. Her tattooed saviour watched as she made an illegal turn, having driven around the car park in the wrong direction.

Pulling up behind the police car, Hana observed her son supporting his grandmother's arm, laughing and talking to Deepak. The likeness between them took her breath away, the shared genetics running through their blood. Bodie's skin looked lighter, the darkness of his Indian heritage tempered and mellowed by Hana's fair Celtic genes. But the brown eyes which flashed like coals when he was angry were his grandmother's. Seeing them in comparison made her sad, wishing things had been different. Bodie shared Deepak's sturdy frame, solid shoulders and an effortless grace, the likeness striking. It made Vik feel nearer somehow and Hana pushed away the emotions which surfaced. She glanced down at her left hand and rubbed the space where her wedding ring used to lie, her gift to Izzie on her wedding day. Her finger seemed naked and she smoothed the dent which had never filled out.

"Where's the bumper?" Bodie jabbed at the empty space at the back of Hana's car.

"On the road near the entrance." Hana cringed. "And I can't open the rear door. We'll need to put the cases on the back seat." At his look of incredulity, Hana shook her head. "I didn't do it. Those men rear-ended it."

Bodie settled Indra in the back and packed the luggage around her. "You'll be okay, Bibi ji," he said with a smile. "It's not far."

Indra nodded and waved over the top of a lemon coloured suitcase and Bodie waggled his eyebrows at Hana. He leaned in close to her ear on the pretext of giving her a kiss. "She's sick, Mum. Papa ji said this is their last hurrah."

Hana swallowed and took in his news. Indra's sunny smile condemned her from the back seat. She nodded as Bodie enfolded her in a safe embrace. "Thanks. I'll make sure they have a good time."

He helped her settle into the driver's seat where she faced the prospect of the treacherous exit journey with her not-quite-symmetrical halves of ticket. Watching distress cloud her face, Bodie held out his hand. "Here, give it to me," he said, a smirk lighting his dark eyes. He emerged from the airport with a new ticket, the grin still on his lips. Hana gave him a grateful look and he shrugged. "Didn't even have to pull my gun," he whispered, for her ears only.

Hana's eyes widened in horror and he laughed. "Oh, Mum! You're so gullible."

Bodie kissed his grandparents through their open windows and promised to catch up with them after they'd made the journey to Invercargill to see Izzie. Hana left the car park without difficulty, heaving a sigh of relief as she filtered onto the highway towards Hamilton.

Hana drove for an hour with Deepak snorting out a random, snoring concerto and Indra chatting non stop about the family back home. Hana didn't ask about her illness, her heart filling with a sense of profound sadness at the wasteland between them. It could've been different. "The Johals have spread since you left, Hana," Indra called. She listed the relatives and respective children and Hana struggled to recall the disapproving faces from her history.

Arriving home, Hana drove straight into the garage, noticing a strange vehicle parked opposite her house. She dropped the garage door with the remote, recognising her nasty blond visitor as she passed. The black saloon car contained only him and he waved to her from the driver's window. Hana's fingers fluttered over her chest and she clambered from her vehicle on shaking legs. With Indra and Deepak both sleeping, she rushed upstairs to peer from the front windows, the empty street confounding her. No point calling the cops with nothing to see.

Hearing movement downstairs, Hana discovered a bewildered Indra trying to free her sari from the closed rear door. Hana helped her and then woke Deepak. Her mother-in-law continued her chatter about the family as though she'd only stopped to take a breath. "Jaspal married a dreadful Hindu girl," she complained, referring to Vik's older brother. "It ended in tears; she couldn't cook!" Indra's expression nailed the real deal-breaker and Hana sighed at the memory of Indra's constant picking at her culinary efforts.

Upstairs, Hana settled the elderly couple in the double room opposite hers where Izzie once slept. Exhaustion assailed her bones but Indra seemed refreshed and desperate for a sightseeing trip around the city. A revived Deepak agreed. Hana recovered with a mug of strong coffee while Indra made a dreadful mess in the bedroom, disgorging her suitcase and spreading its contents over every surface. She wanted Hana to approve of her offerings like a child seeking praise. "This is the special sari from Birmingham for visiting Izzie in the South Island." She dropped the sumptuous fabric onto the bed and dragged out another. "This is the special sari for seeing Bodie." Indra stopped, her face full of confusion. "Oh, he saw me." She brushed a hand across her majestic red and gold number. "Never mind. We can pretend." She shrugged off her ruined plans with aplomb. "This is the baby sari for Elizabeth." The fabric dripped from her dark fingers, a blue base with golden hoops and swirls overlaid throughout the expensive material. "I bought a matching one for Isobel. Do you think she will like it?"

Hana inhaled and nodded. "She'll love it."

Indra pulled out another sari, engaging in a tussle with a stray pair of knickers. Hana respectfully looked away as the hold-up-suck-in and don't-breathe-out panties twanged from the case and landed on the bedside lamp. To her surprise, Indra left them there.

"Ohhhh!" Indra exclaimed, producing a large photo album from her suitcase. "This is what I wanted."

For the next two hours, she sat on the double bed with Hana. She showed her daughter-in-law memories from every significant event she'd missed. Hana sat through Jaspal's wedding, Jaspal's two children, Jaspal's workplace, Jaspal's luxurious home. She showed no surprise when Indra produced a scanned copy of Jaspal's Decree Absolute, neatly labelled and compartmentalised as part of the snapshot of Jaspal's life. Hana felt weary of a saga she no longer took part in. She imagined Izzie faking interest in the lives of her distant uncles and cousins and hoped she made a more convincing audience.

The evening couldn't come soon enough. After a meal out, one lengthy trip into Hamilton, afternoon tea in a coffee shop, then a mouth incinerating curry cooked by Deepak, Hana admitted defeat. She crawled into bed, anticipating a trip to Waitomo Caves the next day. She woke once around two o'clock, sitting bolt upright at the unusual cacophony of sounds. Recognising the scraping of bowls at the other end of the house, Hana lay down smiling to herself as two jetlagged travellers ate cornflakes in the middle of the night.

Chapter 22

The visit to the glow worm caves at Waitomo proved entertaining and Hana didn't remember the last time she laughed until it hurt. Being around Indra and Deepak outside their natural habitat felt like accompanying two small children on a school trip. They asked the most bizarre questions without guile or shame and their lack of political correctness left her weak at the knees.

Introduced to the Māori guide who steered the underground boat, Indra grew more like her old self. "What is this Māori?" she complained, waving her arms. "You can't be one. You look just like a member of the Jat clan from Bristol. There must be some mistake." She wagged an elegant finger. "You're a closet Sikh, I know it. There's no need to be ashamed. It's a free world."

The female guide looked horrified at the affront to her cultural heritage and edged away from Indra, the action difficult in the restriction of the boat.

"This water is deep," Deepak yelled into the darkness, alarming the other tourists on the boat.

"No shouting!" the guide implored. "The glow worms don't like noise. They turn their lights out."

"Sorry!" Deepak called, the sound echoing around the underground cavern. Hana squirmed in the seat next to Indra and tried to pretend they weren't with her. She looked up as the guide yelled out a warning but Deepak appeared so engrossed in peering into the murky water, he cracked his head against an unforgiving cave wall in the narrow tunnel. He gasped in horror as with a plop, his turban fell into the water like a floating helmet. "Oh, no!" Deepak yelled. "Bibi ji, look!"

Indra appeared scandalised as Deepak's seventy years of hair growth unwound itself into the boat. She tried to hide it under her sari and the flimsy wooden vessel tipped from side to side. Passengers screamed and

Hana sank lower on her portion of the bench seat, hiding beneath the folds of her warm jacket.

A five-year-old girl came to the rescue, snatching the hair bobble from her ponytail and offering it to Indra. The boat tipped and rocked while they wound Deepak's mop into a tress thin enough to fit into the elastic band. The guide hung onto the underground rope system with both arms outstretched and a face expression of pure malice.

"I'm fine now." Deepak sank onto his bench and gave everyone a magnanimous wave. Indra's eyeballs looked strange in the darkness, the whites glinting like shiny orbs as she tottered back to her seat.

"It's his Kesh," she said to Hana, wrinkling her nose. "It represents the love of God."

"Well, for the love of God, sit down!" an English tourist hissed and Hana covered her mouth with her hand. The boat lurched as the guide resumed hauling it along the tunnel using the rope pulleys.

Another boat passed them in a wider part of the tunnel, returning the way it came. The guides had a whispered conversation. Indra looked over the side and screamed, taking to heart the ancient Māori legends of taniwha and water dragons. "Taniwha!" she screeched, mangling the word with her accent. "It's chasing you!"

The other boat tipped as its members leaned over to look, adding their terror to the mix. A man at the back pointed to a white shape moving behind the boat. "It's chasing us!"

Hana closed her eyes as Deepak made a swipe for his turban, trying to unhook it from the back of the other boat. It slid around in the water like an oversized eel and Hana felt the boat lurch beneath her. "I can get it!" he complained as the guide forbade him in a tight, high voice. She slapped his fingers as he reached back into the water and he sulked all the way to the mouth of the biggest cave.

"This is meant to be the grand finale!" The guide glared at Indra and Deepak. "The cave is lit by the hair-like strands of tiny glow worms which dangle down from the cave roof."

"Ooh, this is what we've come to see." Indra hugged herself as her words echoed around the dark, empty space. She tilted her head and peered upwards. "I don't see them."

"Nobody can see them!" the guide hissed. "They've stopped glowing because of the noise."

The guide spat them out at the gift shop amidst the foreboding silence of angry tourists. They'd bussed, flown and driven to see the famous glow worms which refused to glow. Confusion began in the ticket office as staff debated closing for the day. Three boat loads of tourists already sat in boats in the gloomy darkness, pointing and whispering at Deepak's unravelled turban, while another fifty people complained outside. Hana beat a hasty retreat into the gift shop with her guests, avoiding the ugly glares of her boat companions.

Indra shopped for souvenirs, snatching up thirty small plastic kiwi birds from a tray. They didn't fit in her slender hands so she tipped them into her sari. A child next to her burst into tears. "That lady took them all," he sobbed. "I wanted one."

Indra glanced down at his wide mouth and considered the indignant look on his mother's face. Deciding they didn't deserve her clemency, she shrugged and tottered across to the cashier.

"Why does she need so many?" Hana asked, watching as Deepak held his hair in one hand and tried on baseball caps with the other.

"For her sewing group." He winked. "I call it Bitch and Stitch."

Indra continued shopping and purchased most of the cosmetic shelf. When a near riot ensued, Hana opted to wait outside in the sunshine, listening to disgruntled tourists as they emerged, complaining about the woman who bought everything. Deepak followed her out, wearing his new hat. It sat about ten centimetres off his actual head, his long locks filling the gap between. Sweat frizzled the stray ends and he laughed at his reflection in the windows of the shop.

The visit flew past at speed. Hana lent Deepak her car so they could entertain themselves while she worked and they ventured to the popular tourist destinations on day trips. Hana asked Deepak about Indra's illness one evening and he waved off her concerns. "It's a little problem with her pancreas," he said, minimising the painful condition with mediocre words. "This is our last chance to catch up with family."

Hana nodded, unsure how to answer. Deepak smiled and patted her hand. "Seeing you has been good for her. In the absence of your own parents, we regret not making more of an effort."

Hana gulped. "I've thought a lot about how shocking it must have been for you both. With hindsight, I should be more grateful. You undid a long-standing betrothal and allowed Vik and I to marry. It can't have been easy. I know you suffered repercussions within your community because of it."

Deepak shrugged and looked suddenly old. "What does it matter now? Indra regrets it and it's not how she wants to be remembered. Losing Vikram changed us all." He reached across and gripped her fingers. "He rang us the night before he died. Jaspal spoke to him but won't reveal what he said." He leaned closer. "Do you know why he rang? The time difference meant we were at morning prayers and it's pained us ever since. The not knowing is destructive."

Hana shook her head, her expression sympathetic. "I wish I could help, but I wasn't well that night. I suffered a problem with my kidneys and Vik fetched the children from school and took them to dinner." Hana breathed through pursed lips, forcing herself to remain calm and not make an audible sound. The remembered events of the next day rose up to meet her like a slap from the past, robbing her of feeling in her extremities. Deepak smoothed her hair back from her forehead and guilt formed a knot in her chest. She swallowed. "Indra blamed me for Vik's death at his funeral."

Deepak nodded. "I'm sorry. We travelled for two days and almost didn't make it in time. We raised our son a Sikh, yet you farewelled a Christian. She felt we lost more than just his physical body."

Hana took a shuddering breath. "I'm sorry."

Deepak nodded and squeezed her fingers. "We know that now, Hana. It's okay."

The conversation left her numb inside and an unease settled over her. When Logan picked her up the next morning so Deepak could use her car for a trip to Rotorua, Hana remained silent throughout the journey to work.

"Did I do something wrong?" Logan asked, his voice low. He stopped at the traffic lights and Hana sighed, feeling his gaze on her.

She shook her head. "No. Don't worry." But when Logan reached for her hand, she withdrew it, the tumult in her heart overwhelming and painful.

New dents appeared in the bodywork of her car, one of them bearing the imprint of a parking meter. Hana let it go, adding it to the list of the vehicle's misfortunes. She kept everyone else at bay, investing time into her relationship with her in-laws, growing more silent and distant as the week passed. Memories of Vik assailed her, happy times filled with love and the sound of children's laughter. It made her ache as though his death happened yesterday and she forced herself to relive it over and over in the lonely double bed. Indra watched from the sunroom window as Logan pulled onto the driveway the day before they left. Hana waved at the window, but Indra didn't wave back. It compounded her guilt and left her floating in a sea of emptiness.

Deepak and Indra flew to Invercargill after a week in Hamilton. Hana woke with a sick feeling in the pit of her stomach. Leaving everything on the other side of the world, she'd discovered the goodbyes got worse instead of better. It wasn't something which became easier with practice, only harder as advancing years made the likelihood of meeting less. Some of her goodbyes proved to be more final than she realised.

Hana lay in bed feeling tearful and wondering how she would keep it together long enough to get them to Hamilton airport. Their trip to Wellington and on to Invercargill stung, as it took them to Isobel. Hana ached to hold her daughter with a tangible pain. So many things grieved her that she felt overwhelmed and only a sheer act of will pulled her from the bed and into the shower. The wasted years groaned with the weight of lost time, time she spent dreading her in-laws' interference instead of valuing their support.

"This is so unfair," she whispered into the bathroom mirror. "After a quarter of a century of avoiding them, I fall in love with them and risk never seeing them again."

An unwelcome voice in her head began its whispered mantra. 'They always leave you in the end.' Hana banished the tape which played on a constant loop in her brain, pushing it aside for the moment. But she knew it would return in the darkness and taunt her with her aloneness.

Hearing the sound of plates and cutlery in the kitchen, Hana dressed and joined Vik's parents for their last breakfast together.

Chapter 23

Hana drove herself to work, attempting to reclaim the fragile threads of her life again. She felt sad and remote from everyone, regretting her desire to push them all away. She decided to make amends with Anka and forgive her slighting of Logan, remembering the adage about not breaking important friendships over a man.

Hana arrived at Anka's office in time for morning tea, hoping they might walk up to the staffroom together. Anka's computer screen showed her latest document and a mound of paperwork covered her desk.

"Shop!" called a voice from under a table. Hana jumped and spied the soles of flip-flops poking out. "She's helping in the shop," continued the feet as they emerged from under the desk. A large bottom followed them, accompanied by a naked midriff, inappropriate tee shirt and arms filled with rubbish. "I put the ceiling fan on and everything flew everywhere. Made a right mess!" The girl hauled herself to her feet and puffed across to the dustbin.

The bell sounded for interval and disappointment crossed Hana's face. "Will she take her usual morning tea now or do you think she's covering someone?"

The girl looked straight at Hana as though she might be thick. "How do I know?" She thudded into her seat, but not before the papers tumbled from her grasp and the ceiling fan whipped them into another frenzy.

Hana flicked the switch to off and beat a hasty retreat. She reached the shop at the same time as a gaggle of Year 9s. A science teacher shouted for silence over their heads. "Line up by the wall. ID cards ready and no messing around. This is your break time you're wasting. I don't have a life so I don't mind."

Hana peered through the doorway but didn't see Anka. As she turned to leave, she caught Lief's eye and shouted over the boys' heads. "Where's Anka?"

The shop assistant rolled her eyes. "No idea. She went to the stockroom on the first floor to find something ages ago." Lief slapped a graphics calculator on the counter and nodded at the line of students. "I hope she comes back soon. Sandra's off sick and Donald sent her to help me."

Hana gave up all hope of morning tea and rebuilding friendships. "I'll try to find her," she promised and Lief nodded with gratitude. Deciding to start at the stockroom, Hana set off for the main building, navigating adolescent bodies in various stages of eating or playing.

Hana's heels clattered up the first set of stairs to the split-level landing. Too late, she remembered she needed the key code for the lock and groaned. The hockey coach skipped up behind her and paused as she blocked the stair well. "Sorry." Hana moved sideways and he squeezed past her.

"What's the matter?"

"I can't remember the number for the stockroom." Her brow furrowed and she turned to take the sharp left turn towards the student centre. "I wrote it down; I'll find it."

"It's unlocked." Stan jerked his head towards the door and Hana followed his gaze. "Someone's in there. Just watch you don't get smacked in the face as they come out." He rubbed his forehead. "Happened to me last week. They need to put a sliding door on there."

Hana nodded and stared at the door with relief. It stood ajar, the toe of a smart shoe keeping it open. "Thanks," she said, tapping herself on the temple. "Of course it's open. Anka's in there." She crossed the stairs towards it, giving Stan an apologetic eye roll over her shoulder.

She placed her hand on the door with caution, half expecting it to swing outwards and knock her down the stairs to the bottom. Part of the original building, the small dog-legged room hugged its roots as an anteroom to an office, turning its back on the smart brick structure which sprung up at its rear in the 1980s. The carpenter who turned it into a stockroom made a fantastic job of fitting bespoke floor to ceiling shelving, assuming it would open from its original side. But the architects ordered that doorway closed and opened one onto the stairs, giving it the tiniest of landings. They didn't think to tell the carpenter and his handiwork didn't factor in a door which opened inwards. Rough edges betrayed his temper as he carved a hole in the shelving unit to allow only slender bodies to squeeze through. He hung the door to open outwards, not caring about generations of boys who learned to dodge the hazard as they flew up or down stairs. Numerous accidents with bags catching on the handle led the groundsman to remove it, forcing anyone inside to rely on a rusty catch to hold fast, without locking them in.

Making sure she didn't knock anyone out as she pulled the door outwards, Hana slipped between the door and frame, peering into the darkness for Anka. Distracted by making sure the vibrant blue stiletto remained in place, she ran her finger over the catch to lock the door in the open position. It refused to budge and Hana sighed, realising the reason for the shoe's placement. Anka's voice rose in an irritated whisper and Hana paused, curiosity getting the better of her. She leaned towards the left, her view blocked by a wall of shelves filled with stationery and lost property.

"No!" Anka pleaded. "No. It just won't work anymore; I'll lose my job."

"Look," a male voice entreated, the tone soft and cajoling. "Nobody will know. I'll be out of this dump soon. We'll be fine."

"You know how I feel." Anka sounded sad, her South African accent more pronounced. "We can't do this anymore. It's wrong on too many levels."

"You're worried about him, aren't you?" the male voice asked, fear in his tone. "He won't find out, I promise."

"It's too risky now. It's getting dangerous."

Hana heard the strain in Anka's voice and intervened without making it obvious she overheard the whispered exchange. She swiped a stack of exercise books onto the floor with her hand and bent to retrieve them, making a great fuss of shuffling them all together to buy Anka time. "Oops!" she exclaimed. Through a gap between the bottom two shelves, Hana watched as the couple froze and then parted. Her heart sank and disappointment flooded through her veins. By the time she stood and replaced the exercise books, her hands shook and her brain shut down any hope of conversation.

A student in a white prefect's shirt emerged from around the end shelf. Rugged and dark haired, he walked with casual confidence as though his X factor lurked just under the surface. Already tall enough for his head to be in line with the top shelf, he observed Hana through eyes masked by anger and fear. He waved a lined refill pad over his shoulder. "Should I pay for this at the shop?" he demanded.

Anka appeared in Hana's eye line, her cheeks pink and flushed. She licked her lips once and floundered, darting her eyes from him to Hana and back again. She shook her head once in response. "No, don't worry. I'll sort it out."

The student squeezed past Hana, stumbling over the shoe in the doorway and swearing. He glanced back at Anka with a smirk which pushed him beyond good looking and into the realms of devastating. Hana stared at him, a peculiar sense of recognition knocking at the back of her brain. She'd seen him around lots but it wasn't that. His olive skin and the smiling curve of his eyes reminded her of someone. His shirt hung from the back of his pants, not long enough to cover his torso and he shoved it inside his waistband with long fingers. Half way down the stairs, he turned and gave Anka a pointed look.

Hana heard her friend let out the smallest exhale, hearing desperation and misery. She turned to look at her. "How much did you hear?" Anka asked, defeat sounding in every syllable.

Hana sighed, deciding on honesty. "Enough," she replied. She took a step forward. "What are you doing?"

Anka poked out her foot, seating the blue shoe over her toes without bending down. She spoke in a halting, dead tone as though the story might prove boring. "He's a friend of Gareth's."

Hana's brow knitted. "I thought we were friends, Anka."

Her friend looked up, the lie on the tip of her tongue. Her shoulders slumped in defeat. "We are. I couldn't tell you."

Hana swallowed and put a hand over her mouth. "I don't know what to say."

Anka waved a slender hand which displayed an expensive wedding ring; a forgotten casualty of her life-changing decision. "I can't talk here. It's too complicated."

Hana nodded. "Look Anka, they want you in the shop, but we do need to talk about this. Can we meet tonight, in Starbuck's at Chartwell?" Hana reached out to touch her friend's shoulder but at the contact, felt her stiffen.

"Fine. At seven o'clock after I get dinner finished." Anka sounded wooden and the chasm between them opened wider. She pushed past Hana and stepped out onto the stairs, stopping just long enough to issue her threat. "Don't you dare tell anyone, especially not your smart new toy-boy!"

"Why would I do that?" Hana whispered, sadness radiating from her eyes. "Then he'll be in the same awful position I am."

Anka tossed her hair and walked away, gliding elegantly down the stairs in her designer navy suit and high heels. Hana let the door close in her face, jamming a ruler in the gap to stop it locking her in. She leaned against the shelf opposite and rubbed her cheeks with shaking fingers. Shock paralysed her and her mind pushed the awful thought around her head without understanding. Her best friend had engaged in a relationship with a student. Hana closed her eyes and shook her head. "Not just against school rules but illegal," she breathed. The bell sounded and Hana pulled the stockroom door shut behind her, arriving back in the common room in a state of shock. She worked until home time without stopping and making numerous silly errors on her budgets.

Logan popped in to see Pete and ran a gentle hand across her shoulders. "Hey, how are you doing?" He studied her face for clues, hating the wall Hana threw up between them.

She shrugged. "I'm good, thanks. I don't know where Pete is."

Logan perched on the edge of her desk and crossed his legs at the ankles. "I didn't really come to see him."

"Oh." Hana chewed her lip and prodded at a stack of brochures in front of her. It felt like his eyes bored holes in her soul and she stood up, needing to break free. He snatched at her hand as she turned and kept her in place, his touch light but firm.

"Did I do something wrong?" He searched her face.

Hana inhaled. "No."

He raised his free hand and wagged a finger at her. "Don't give me the, 'it's not you, it's me' routine." His lips quirked upwards in a smile which didn't reach his eyes. He swallowed. "Do you want me to leave you alone?" Dark lashes swished down, shuttering his hurt from her.

Hana looked at his fingers wrapped around her hand and shook her head, the motion almost negligible. He ducked his head to peer up at her. "Was that a no, Ms McIntyre?"

She pursed her lips as a smile broke free, lighting her green eyes from within. He stood up, towering over her and lifted her chin with his index finger. His brow furrowed and a gentle thumb played across her cheek. "I don't want to give you up," he whispered. "But I don't want to make you sad either."

Hana blinked and confusion coursed through her. She sighed. "Stuff keeps coming back from my past and I don't like it." She reached up and fingered Logan's shirt button, feeling the smoothness ground her. His scent enveloped her in a comforting aura which felt right. Sunshine and meadows and the taste of summer. "I don't want you to leave me alone." Her eyes searched his face for confirmation, relieved when he relaxed. His arms wound around her shoulders and his heartbeat thudded through his chest wall and into her cheek, like the ticking of a clock.

"Good." He kissed the top of her head. "Because I lied. I can't leave you alone."

Hana smiled into his shirt and pushed her hands under his jacket. His presence made her feel safe and immunised her against the world and its insistent problems. "I have a dilemma," she whispered. "I could use your advice."

"Yeah." His hands caressed the back of her neck, fingers exploring the delicate nape and pushing upwards into her curls. "What?"

Hana struggled to concentrate. Her fingers strayed from the small of his back to the strong muscles either side of his spine. Bunched and thick, they distracted her. Logan's fingers fluttered down the smooth fabric of her blouse and he cleared his throat. "Hana?"

"Sorry." She licked her lips and pushed herself into her chair, attempting to control the wobble in her legs. Buried sensations rose up from a well she once believed bricked over. "Okay." She gathered her wits enough to speak. "If someone you knew did something bad and you found out about it, would you tell someone in authority?"

Logan's eyes widened and he stared at her hard, taking a step back. "Is this a trick question?"

"No." Hana shook her head in confusion. "It's my dilemma."

"It depends on the thing." Logan reached for a long curl which coiled past Hana's shoulder, twirling it in his fingers and focussing his attention on the way the light caught the different shades of red. When his eyes met hers, they contained a look of seriousness. "What's the thing?"

"I can't tell you." Hana chewed her lip. "I just found out."

"Is it illegal?" Logan studied her face and she nodded.

"Very. And immoral."

Logan shrugged. "Sleep on it. As long as nobody gets hurt in the meantime, see how you feel tomorrow."

Hana winced. "Whatever I do, people are gonna be hurt. Some more than others."

The bell interrupted her and Logan glanced at the closed office door in irritation. Then he leaned down and kissed her, lingering and communicating his reluctance to leave. Hana reached up and ran her fingers through the back of his hair, resting her other hand against his chest and feeling his heart rate increase as she parted her lips for him. The sound of boys outside forced them to break apart. Logan looked pained, his forehead creased and annoyance in his grey eyes. "Can I see you tonight?" he asked.

Hana closed her eyes and shook her head. Logan winced. "You're washing your hair?"

"No. Nothing like that." Hana sighed and rolled her eyes. "I'm meeting a friend about my dilemma."

"Okay." Logan opened his mouth to speak but Pete crashed through the office door, slamming it behind him and leaning against it, his arms splayed wide.

"If Dobbs asks where I was period 4, tell him I was writing reports right there." He jabbed a finger towards his chaotic desk.

Hana gave Logan a knowing look and spun her chair to face her computer. "No. That would be lying."

"It's not!" Pete lurched for her. "Omission of the truth is not lying."

"Yeah, it is." Hana dodged the greasy hand which tried to grab her arm. "It's the exact definition. Touch me and you're dead."

"You don't understand!" Pete protested. "I need help."

Hana heard Logan snort from behind her. "Understatement of the year," he muttered. "See ya, Hana." He grabbed Pete by the ear and spun him around, shoving him towards his desk. "You heard the lady, touch her and you're dead. I second it so be told!"

Hana turned to acknowledge Logan's support with a stunning smile and his shoulders relaxed. He gave her a one-fingered salute which best fitted a cowboy and left the room, closing the door behind him.

"Hana?" Pete began again and she shook her head.

"No, Pete." She wedged ear buds into her ears and pressed the switch on Evie's dictaphone, typing up minutes from a departmental briefing.

The meeting with Anka remained at bay until Hana closed down her computer and readied the office for leaving. Then the weight of it rolled up to greet her with a sense of foreboding and loss. She'd attempt to talk sense into her friend but if she failed, she knew what she needed to do. Despite the boy being at least eighteen and over the age of consent, his relationship with Anka put her in front of the trustees and possibly in court. Knowing and saying nothing made Hana an accomplice.

On her way through reception, Hana stopped to see Angus' personal assistant. The older woman huffed and puffed and complained, but pencilled a meeting with Hana in the principal's calendar for interval the next day.

Chapter 24

Hana dropped her car outside the garage and the mechanic drove her home. "Youse been rallying, missus?" he joked and Hana shook her head.

"She's been in the wars a wee bit lately. Please, can you sort out the dents in the wing as well as the rear bumper? I'll pay for them myself."

"Yeah, sure." He turned onto Achilles Rise and pulled up outside Hana's house.

"Oh." She poked her head back into the passenger door. "The boot isn't opening. They hit it quite hard."

The mechanic waved his hand in dismissal and executed a three-point turn. Hana sighed and walked up the driveway. She changed into walking gear ready for the trip to Chartwell and texted Anka. 'Are we still meeting at 7?' There seemed little point walking all the way there only to be stood up.

Anka texted back. 'Yes. Want me to pick you up?'

Hana peered at the message and felt a wave of relief. The offer gave her hope and lifted her spirits. She replied. 'I'm okay, thanks. I'll walk there but I'd appreciate a ride home. Car's in the mechanic's and it will be dark.'

'Okay. Sure.'

Feeling optimistic, Hana nurtured the belief she could convince Anka to end the relationship with the student. She hoped she wouldn't require the appointment with Angus. The pleasant walk in the evening sunshine gave her time to think and pray for wisdom. Hana arrived a few minutes early and found seats in Starbucks, feeling as nervous as if she'd come for a job interview.

Anka didn't show until much later, blasting in at a quarter to eight looking flushed and irritated. Hana rose from her chair to hug her friend, feeling wooden shoulders beneath her hands. Embarrassed, she sat down. "I thought you'd changed your mind." She offered a smile but regretted the comment as Anka's face morphed from irritation to anger.

"I did," she bit. "Then I decided to come and tell you to mind your own business."

Hana's jaw gaped, the attitude reversal unexpected. "I thought we agreed to meet up and talk." She cocked her head in confusion. "You don't want that now?"

Anka shrugged. "I had to play nice by text; Ivan knows we're meeting but not why. I don't ultimately care what you think, Hana. I assumed you'd bleat to your toy-boy, so I've taken evasive action."

Hana gritted her teeth. "Don't call him that!"

Anka looked magnificent in tailored jeans and an expensive jacket. Hana felt underdressed and inadequate in her stretchy track pants and hooded sweater. Her friend's constant attacks on Logan made her wary, not understanding the context. "Why don't you like him? He doesn't even know you; I asked him."

Anka snorted and shook her head. "Wow, Hana. Just wow. You've got a shock coming your way and you can't even see it."

Hana shook her head. "Don't turn this around on me. Logan's single and he's not underage!"

Anka stood. "This is stupid, I shouldn't have come."

"Then why did you?" Hana held her arms out to her sides in exasperation. "I thought perhaps I could help. We've been friends for years."

Anka closed her eyes and the hand she brushed across her brow shook. "You can't help me."

"Sit down." Hana took her forearm and pushed her back into the chair. "I'll order drinks and we can start again."

She watched over her shoulder as she ordered two hot chocolates, half-expecting Anka to bolt as soon as she turned her back. But to her credit, Anka waited for her, awkwardness and regret shrouding her like a cloak.

Hana sat and twisted a napkin in her fingers until the barista called their order. Anka busied herself with her phone and ignored Hana's presence; making her wonder if she should change the order to take-away cups. The exercise felt more futile the longer it dragged on. She sat their drinks on the table with a sigh and stirred sugar into hers. Anka's question surprised her. "How's it going with Logan?"

Hana felt defensive and frowned. "Good. He's a nice guy."

Anka's smile made her nervous. "If you say so."

"How do you know him when he doesn't know you?"

Anka sat back in her seat and sipped her drink. Red manicured nails obscured the logo on her mug. "I've known about him for years," she replied. Then she shrugged. "What do you want from me, Hana? An explanation? The gory details?"

"I don't know." Despite her planning and praying, Hana felt lost. "I want to be a good friend and help you sort this out." It died on her tongue. Anka's face expression and posture showed her unresponsiveness. An uncharacteristic hardness cloaked her which hadn't been there before. She seemed resolute and spiky, not her usual smiling self, always willing to see the best in people. That Anka was gone.

"I can see you judging me. You're no different to anyone else. I'm sleeping with an eighteen-year-old student and you're horrified."

"I'm surprised, I guess." Hana fumbled for words.

"Why? Because I'm the last person you expected to fall for someone else? I'm not without needs, Hana."

"You're married!" Hana burnt her lip on the drink and placed it on the table. "I don't know what to think."

She fudged yet another start to a sentence but Anka waded on, regardless. "I know he's only eighteen, but he's mature, maybe because of what he's been through at home and stuff. Sex with him is amazing. I've tried, but I can't give him up. He adores and trusts me and I'm not about to destroy him. Do you even know what it's like to be somebody's first?"

Hana reeled at the low blow, aimed at the heart with destruction in view. She ground her teeth and ignored the sleight, not wanting to drag her late husband's name through the mud in his absence. "How long, Anka?" she asked, her brow creased with worry. "When did it start?"

Anka tossed her dark hair, the pink streaks standing out like a rebellion. "It started before the summer but I've known him for years. He turned up with Gareth just after they turned fourteen; they share the same birthday. He's lived in the boarding house for the last five years and struggles to find somewhere to go during the holidays. He came home with Gareth a few years ago because his home life sucks, his mother abandoned him as a baby and his father beats him up. Nobody cares about him. I comforted him when he discovered the man who raised him isn't his father and I've been there for him more than anyone else."

Hana reached across and touched Anka's writhing fingers. "But that's different to what you're doing now. Can't you see that?"

Anka flared her nostrils and straightened her back. She shook off Hana's touch. "Ivan's never home, Gareth and Charlotte go out most of the time. I'm left alone and it's miserable. He turned up looking for Gareth, I was alone as usual and one thing led to another." Anka inhaled and closed her eyes. "I can't get enough of him. He makes me feel alive and wanted. I forgot how that felt."

"But what about Ivan?" interjected Hana, sensing Anka pivoting on the edge of disaster. "What about destroying your marriage and your children? What will Charlotte and Gareth think? This boy is your son's friend! You have the power to ruin a lot of lives, not least your own." Hana shook her head, sensing she'd already lost the battle.

"Look Hana, I know this all seems stupid to someone as spotless as you, but I didn't ask for any of this to happen. I love Tama. Don't think I haven't considered the consequences. I don't know what else to say."

"But it's wrong," countered Hana. "It's wrong on every level! Anka think about what you're saying, you're having sex with an eighteen-year-old student from the school you work in. Please think about how this could end?"

Hana's voice grew louder as she appealed to her friend and Anka's eyes darted around, anxious to protect herself. Inwardly, Hana kicked herself. She'd lost. She used a last ditch attempt to get Anka to see reason. "Let's see Pastor Allen together. I'll go with you. We can talk it out properly; he'll know what to do."

"No!" Anka's shriek drowned her out. Her voice dropped to a whispered but forceful hiss. "No way! Don't you dare tell him about this. I'll deal with it in my own way."

She left, striding through the food court towards the lift. As she pressed the down-button, she turned and stared Hana straight in the eye. The violence in the look reached across the thirty-metre distance, across the heads of families eating their fatty food. It pierced through years of friendship and Christian fellowship in good times and bad and through the glass surrounding the Starbucks enclosure. It severed something precious in Hana's chest. It was a look of warning and threat. Hana's face became ashen as she withered under Anka's gaze. The friendship died right there, drawing its last, gasping breath before expiring. Hana closed her eyes against the misery of a friendship destroyed by the oldest trick in the deceiver's book; sex. And with the current of madness would go Anka's faith, her marriage, her relationship with her children, her job and if the authorities got wind of it, her liberty.

Hana leaned forward in her chair with both hands over her eyes, doing battle with the hot, angry tears which threatened to disgrace her. The promised ride home forgotten, Hana observed the darkening skylights as she made for the lift doors and a long, lonely hike home.

Emerging from the brightly lit mall, Hana walked through the car park, careful to stick to areas lit by old-fashioned street lamps. She spotted the front of Anka's stylish black sports car glinting under the artificial haze and hesitated, desperate to mend something from the evening. She walked slowly towards the vehicle, forming an apology on her lips and preparing a sensible sentence in her head. A minibus filled with elderly people passed and Hana waited on the curb, losing sight of the vehicle for a moment. When the bus and its choking exhaust fumes disappeared, Hana looked closer and saw two occupants in the front seats. She moved away from the light and watched.

Anka sat in the passenger seat dabbing at her eyes with a handkerchief. Hana sighed, recognising the student in the driver's seat. His fingers tapped a beat on the steering wheel and he studied Anka's face as though hanging off her every word. Hana's heart clenched in fear, watching the disaster unfold in front of her. "Tama." She turned the name over on her tongue, recalling it from various class lists over the years. She remembered him as blacklisted at some point, a troubled child. Tama reached his arm behind Anka's neck and bowed his head, joining their lips in the darkness. He held her as though she was the finest and most delicate Dresden china. Their intimacy placed an invisible hedge around the car and Hana dare not trespass.

She changed direction and forgot her own safety, pushing through the perimeter bushes and out onto the road. Anxious and upset by the situation, she acknowledged an inexplicable feeling of jealousy at their intimacy, which made her feel lonely and sickened. Memories of Vik for once did nothing to lessen the emptiness. "It's never okay to break up a marriage like that," she fumed at the darkness.

The walk home seemed long and hazardous. In the eighty kilometre zones, streetlamps were far apart, leaving darkened gaps between. Hana passed three different recreation areas, tree lined and deserted, admonishing herself for her isolation and stupidity in walking alone. Bodie would tell her off if he ever found out she walked this way alone in the dark. Spooked by every night noise and fighting the urge to hide each time she saw headlights approach, Hana jogged home, reaching Achilles Rise long after night assumed its darkest cloak.

The lights she left on beckoned to her from the bright, enticing windows of the sunroom on the first floor and Hana felt a catch in her throat. A figure rose to meet her from the front steps and she gasped and backed away.

"It's okay, sorry, Hana, it's me!" Logan stepped out of the shadows and pointed to the truck she'd walked past. "I didn't mean to scare you."

"Are you checking up on me?" She sounded haggard and desperate and Hana masked the sadness with anger.

Logan walked into the light and his face showed only concern. "No. Yes." He slapped his thighs with his hands in irritation. "Both. I remembered you booked your car into the garage, but then you said you had a meeting tonight." He reached out a hand and hooked the front of her hoodie. "To sort out your dilemma. I wanted to make sure you were okay." He pulled her closer, reeling her in, millimetres at a time. "I can go now you're home." He pressed his lips against the front of her forehead and then let go.

"No!" Hana gripped the front of his shirt and pushed her face into his warmth. "Thank you."

"Did it not go well?" Logan kissed the top of her head.

"Awful," Hana groaned.

"Do you still have a dilemma?" He lowered his head and kissed her ear and Hana sighed and nodded.

"It got bigger."

"Can I help?" He lifted her hair and massaged the space beneath her ponytail, pushing his face into her neck and inhaling.

"No," she whispered. "Just hold me."

They progressed to the steps, linking hands and listening to the sound of the crickets playing their sounds for the night creatures.

"I'm selling this house," Hana said, the fear sounding in her voice. "I need to move on. I'm putting it up for auction and selling that damn car."

"Wow. Dilemmas must be good for you." Logan lifted her hand and kissed the tips of her fingers.

Hana shook her head and snuggled closer. "I'm living in the past, Logan. Vik created this life for me and left me to live it alone. I can't do it anymore."

"I'm sure he didn't mean to." A strange barb filled his voice as though he didn't mean it and Hana sat up to look at him.

"Maybe." She brought her lips to his cheek and kissed, sending a jolt of electricity through them both. "But I'm not doing it anymore. If I sell the house and car, those men will leave me alone. I'll start again some place else."

"Will you take your dilemma with you?" Logan's eyes followed her mouth, catching it as she leaned across to kiss his other cheek. He parted her lips with his and his hands snaked around her waist.

"No." Hana shook her head and sighed. "It's not my dilemma anymore. It belongs to someone else."

Logan pulled her into his lap and kissed her again and Hana felt her heart drop to her knees. She revelled in the sensation. A grown woman who had birthed two children, her body reminded her what attraction felt like as their kiss deepened and it made her hot and bothered. Logan ended it, backing off as though afraid to push her and Hana felt a stab of frustration mingled with relief. She wasn't yet ready to relinquish control to another man. He buried his face in her hair and held her close.

Hana wrapped her arms around his neck and rested her cheek on his shoulder. It brought the rusting banister rail into view. The task of selling up seemed overwhelming. "What am I doing?" she groaned. "It's too hard."

Logan stroked her back. "Na. What can I do to help?"

Hana shrugged. "I don't know. My thought process only got as far as the decision, not to rationalising it and following through."

"How long will the garage take to mend your car?" Logan's jacket rustled against her ear and he shifted his legs so she tipped further into him.

"I don't know. Deepak added to its misery so I'm not sure. I can't sell it until it comes back."

"Borrow my truck," Logan offered. "I'll use the bike or the Triumph. When it's fixed, I'll sell yours online."

Hana sat up, their faces close as she looked for the catch. "That's heaps of hassle for you." Her eyes narrowed in suspicion. "Why would you do that for me?"

Logan planted a kiss on the end of her nose and gave her a searching look. "Ooh, I dunno. Duh!"

Hana grinned. "Are you suggesting this relationship might be progressing towards financial trust, Mr Du Rose?"

He laughed, his eyes crinkling at the corners. "It might, Ms McIntyre. Let's see, shall we?" His expression grew serious. "Maybe it's best you don't have people coming round here to see the car, not when you're on your own. When it's fixed, I'll sell it for you and give you the money. They can look at it over at the rental house." As Hana watched him, she saw the confidence in his eyes dissipate. They'd been of one mind, happily planning Hana's future and it looked in danger of fizzling out like a damp firework. She resurrected it.

"Thanks so much. I'd appreciate it. Are you sure you don't mind me having your car? I'll pay the difference if you put me on the insurance."

Logan hugged her tighter, pleasure surging through his soul at her nearness. The bitter scabs of twenty-six years of worry and disappointment slipped from his heart and melted into his bloodstream. Peace enfolded them both and Logan sighed with happiness. "You're wearing my sweater." He tugged at the long cuff and Hana pursed her lips.

"So?"

"So, nothing." He kissed her again, inhaling long breaths of salvation from her warm skin. "I like you having my things."

"Things?" Hana sat up on his knee and narrowed her eyes. She prodded at the hoodie and looked down, her fringe falling into her eyes. "Only this."

Logan swallowed and Hana saw the open emotion in his eyes shutter closed. She put her hand on his cheek. "What did I say?"

"Nothing." He shook his head and dispelled the fog of fear. "I included my truck, that's all."

"Oh, yeah." Hana grinned with satisfaction and laid her head back on his shoulder, fancying she felt him shudder beneath her. "Thanks for trusting me; I'll try not to ding it."

Logan sighed. "It doesn't matter. People are more essential than shiny things. I learned that the hardest way possible."

"How?" Hana popped her head up to look at him again and Logan laughed.

"Another time, wahine," he whispered. "Another story."

"Wahine," Hana repeated. "Isn't it rude to call someone woman?"

Logan's head shifted against her neck. "Not in my culture. Wahine, means my woman."

"Your woman?" Hana sat up and wrinkled her nose in a cute expression. "Really?" She leaned in and kissed him. "Will you stick your tongue out at me?"

Logan shook his head in a slow dismissal, his lips raised at the edges. "Nope. Because if I do that, it means I want to take your head off."

"Oh." Hana squinted. "Maybe don't do that then."

"I won't." Logan's lips felt warm against hers and Hana pressed herself into his body, feeling the hard edges of his ribs against her breasts.

The night grew colder and they huddled together like teenagers on the steps till the last, sampling something new and exciting. The neighbourhood lights winked out in the houses opposite and curtains twitched shut. The truck fired up and carried Logan away, but not before he watched Hana safely inside the house. "No point taking chances now," he muttered to himself, replying to her wave from the sunroom window.

He'd searched the world for the hauntingly beautiful redhead and given up, acknowledging the futility of an unrealistic infatuation. Yet there she was, right under his nose when he finally came home. He shook himself as he left the street, terrified of scaring her off. Her secrets harried at her nerves and she wrestled daily. It pained him to watch her agonise, not able to tell her he already knew. He glanced back at the cream two-storey which housed all his hopes and dreams, forcing himself not to dwell on his gnawing disappointment. She didn't remember.

Chapter 25

Logan turned up bright and early with his truck in the morning, planting a scorching kiss on her lips before handing her the keys. Hana drove to school while he directed her on the finer points of the temperamental vehicle. It felt huge compared to her Serena and owned many more blind spots, one of which almost swallowed the head of art's Toyota Vitz. At the last moment, Hana spotted it in the side mirror and swerved to avoid shunting it.

"Maybe drive in, rather than reversing," Logan pointed out, trying to be helpful. He received a glare and a repeat of the experience as his reward.

"I always back in!" Hana retorted, mounting the curb and flattening a prize rose bush before coming to rest in her allocated parking space. "Last time I drove in, someone attacked me. At least this way, I can see them hiding from miles away."

"That's not logical," Logan said, narrowing his eyes. "They can still hide around the front end."

"What?" Hana's head shot up in horror and he amended the sentence.

"I'll walk you to your car," he offered. "Nothing will happen."

Hana sighed. "Thanks." Bending to retrieve the road kill rose and attempting to stand it up again, she missed the rest of the staff sitting in their vehicles, too afraid to get out. Frightened faces eyed her through misted windshields.

"It's fine, leave it." Logan hid his smirk, pulling her fingers away from the hooky thorns. "I'll see you later." He dipped his head as though to kiss her and then thought better of it, in view of their audience. He satisfied himself with a light touch on her hand.

Hana hurried to the office and dumped her handbag, sliding into a back seat in the staff briefing. At a nod from Angus, Donald Watson stood and the room hushed. "We've called this extraordinary meeting to make some announcements." He puffed up his chest and the dramatic blond comb-over slipped alongside his right ear, giving him a side ponytail. "It's with great sadness we must inform you that Anka van Blerk has left our school with immediate effect. She's been our typist for seventeen years and is leaving to concentrate on family issues. A card will circulate over the next few days, along with a collection which I know you will donate generously to."

Nodding his thanks in advance of an avalanche of money, which in reality never went into collections, Donald sat with a satisfied bump. Hana watched Angus, noticing how his face remained blank, giving nothing away. She stared at her feet and contemplated life at the school without her friend while other important notices held everyone's attention. A general buzz of concern went round the gathered crowd afterwards and many approached Hana, assuming she knew Anka's circumstances. She couldn't trust herself not to say the wrong thing, so she smiled and nodded, reassuring those who enquired. She extracted herself from the staffroom as soon as she could, attempting to avoid the sudden interest in Anka. First back in the office, she dialled the number for Angus' assistant. "I won't need that appointment with Angus, thanks," she said, lowering her voice as Pete and Sheila blasted through the door, followed by a sulking Rory.

"Yeah, I bet you won't," the spiteful woman replied and Hana's heart sank.

"I don't know what you're referring to," she said with dignity and slammed the phone down.

Sheila made a beeline for Hana, buzzing with questions. "Come on," she said, irritated at Hana's reticence. "She's your friend. You must know something!"

Hana absented herself from the office after jamming the photocopier on purpose, providing her with a ready excuse to go elsewhere. Her heart felt like a wooden lump in her chest and she sent Anka a text. 'Donald announced your resignation. Assuming he doesn't know why. Please stay in touch. I don't wish you any ill.'

She hid in the staff workroom on the second floor, copying questionnaires for Evie. No matter how Hana felt about her friend's behaviour, she wouldn't betray Anka's secret to gossip mongers but worried about her tendency to put her foot in it under pressure. She sighed and repeated the tape that played in her head. "They always leave you in the end."

The door to the workroom opened and Logan strode in with a bundle of books and papers under his arm. Hana welcomed the distraction, admiring his physique in smart shirt, black slacks and polished boots. His dark fringe stuck up as though he'd run frantic hands through it.

She smiled, seeing anger replace the tired expression in his eyes. Her welcome line faltered on her lips. He strode towards her, weaving through tables piled high with marking and clutter. His jaw ground through his cheek and his grey eyes heralded an unpredictable storm. Anka's words of warning returned to bite Hana.

"Did you know?" His muscles stretched the shirt fabric as he leaned across to dump the books next to someone else's abandoned pile.

"Know what?" Hana's eyes widened and she backed away, finding her spine pressed against the copier. It whirred and spat paper into the tray, rocking her body in a gentle, soothing motion. Her mind spun, sifting through the things she may or may not know, until settling on Anka's bombshell. She glanced away for only a second but Logan read the tell. "What are we talking about? Know what?"

"About the typist. You did!" He drew his own conclusions as she floundered, snorting like an angry stallion. "Of course, you bloody did." He backed away from her, disgust on his face in the shape of a dismissive sneer. "Thanks a lot, Mrs Johal!" he countered, wounding her with the use of her married name. In that alone he severed their connection. "Thanks, a bloody lot!"

He spun on his heel and blasted from the room, leaving his books on the table. The breeze from the corridor sent a precarious heap of papers cascading onto the floor. Hana's hands shook as she retrieved them, her heart numb. She stacked them back into a pile while dismay morphed into anger. "How dare he!" she hissed. "How dare he think I'll share gossip with him; it's none of his business."

Her mind spun with possibilities, remembering Anka's disparaging remarks about Logan Du Rose. His behaviour validated them and Hana sank into a chair. "I don't want to be Mrs Johal anymore," she sighed with a tremor in her voice. "I liked being Ms McIntyre again." Hana thumped her fist on the desk and two piles of books and papers toppled, mingling on the floor. "Damn it!" she exclaimed to the empty room, thumping the table again. It hurt just as much the second time.

Her sanctuary destroyed, Hana separated the piles best she could and contemplated her options. The workroom filled with teachers trying to squeeze marking or research into their already packed day, gulping cups of cold coffee and taking frenzied bites of sandwich as they worked. Hana left, grabbing the copied questionnaires and dumping them on top of Logan's abandoned pile. It hadn't appeared so heavy under his strong arm and Hana struggled with the combined weight of her work and his.

Passing the window facing the chapel, she groaned at the sight of Logan's truck parked in her space. It looked wonky, the rear wheel crossing the white line on the passenger side. "Can't drive it anyway," she muttered to herself in consolation. "And the bus is okay."

By the time she reached it with her armful of books, she'd convinced herself the deal would be off and she needed to fix an awkward situation up front. Battling not to drop the pile as she fought with the car key, alarm button and door, Hana felt the wave of sadness start in her chest and radiate outwards. Her conscience dictated that she safeguard the boys' work and she wrapped the seatbelt around the books before locking the door.

Engrossed in her silly mission, she didn't notice someone sneak up behind her. As she slammed the door and turned, she discovered herself nose to nose with Peter North. She squealed and he looked at her with curiosity, scratching a spot on his forehead. "What are you doing?" he asked, pointing as the top layer of papers slid off the pile and onto the floor of the car. Hana took a deep breath, grabbed his hand and thumped the keys in his palm.

"Give these to Logan, please." Leaving him gawking at her, she stomped towards the guidance counsellors' entrance, remembering too late that her own work was in with Logan's. She halted and glanced back as Peter North set off running after a group of Year 11s, disappearing through the front gates.

Hana used the counsellors' back door and climbed the stairs to the common room. The tranquil lobby of the guidance suite looked inviting and calm. She sat in a chair for a moment to catch her breath before braving the hundreds of eyes beyond the common room door. Evie's door snapped open and a small boy emerged. He giggled and Evie patted him on the shoulder. "Good boy, Kevin, remember what we've talked about. Use your strategies this week. Come back and tell me how it goes on Friday, will you?"

The Year 10 nodded with enthusiasm and waved from the open door to the stairs. He shouted over the balustrade to someone else on the ground floor and a tennis ball bounced up to meet him.

Evie turned to Hana. "Come in," she said, indicating her open door.

Awkwardness shrouded Hana. "Oh, I'm not staying. I wondered if you had another copy of the questionnaire for me to duplicate. You wanted fifty, didn't you?"

"Yes, please." Evie walked across to her sunny desk, the light creating highlights in her hair. She picked up a copy of the questionnaire and handed it to Hana. "Now sit down."

"I should get back to Sheila," Hana said, backing towards the doorway.

Evie regarded her with sympathy. "What, to the endless questions and guilt tripping for answers? Why would you rush back to that? Stay and have coffee with me. We can catch up."

Hana felt numb and experienced a sense of impending doom as she watched the new facets of her life crumble and twist before her eyes. Staleness, dull and choking, rose up to infill. She grabbed at the figurative lifeline and sat down with a bump.

Evie made coffee and they discussed work matters. Hana broke first, spewing her guts to the counsellor when she couldn't hold it in any longer. "I feel I have no right to be happy," she admitted. "I always felt that way. I crossed a line and I can't come back."

Bulging filing cabinets lined the walls, filled with secrets and confidences. Hana knew Evie was trustworthy.

"I liked Logan." Hana's voice sounded sad. "Anka tried to warn me in her cryptic way, but I ignored her. He got angry because I didn't tell him about her and the student. We've fallen at the first hurdle because I won't share other people's problems, especially not sensitive ones like that."

Evie raised her eyebrows. "How long have you known about Anka?"

Hana swallowed. "I found out yesterday, by accident. I walked in on them. We arranged to meet for coffee last night and I booked an appointment with Angus for interval today." She sighed. "She fell on her sword so it's academic now."

Evie nodded and her smile looked genuine. "Why do you think Logan reacted that way? Could there be another reason for his anger?"

"I have no idea." Hana's face screwed up in defence. "But he won't be getting a second chance!"

"Why?" Evie leaned forward. "You've allowed Anka to make a mistake but not Logan. What's the difference? Is it because he was angry, or something else?"

Hana swallowed. "He's not the person I thought he was. I feel a fool."

Evie's nod looked slowed down, a movie reel at half speed. "So, could your trigger be humiliation, Hana?"

She gasped, her faults laid bare and raw. The revelation shocked her and she blinked in horror. Her mouth opened and closed but no sound emerged. Evie leaned across and patted her knee. "We don't need to press further into where it comes from, Hana. But you should recognise the tapes playing in your head and reverse them."

Hana fought for air, relying on humour to extract her. "They always leave me in the end. How do I say that backwards?"

"Oh, Hana." Evie's smile radiated sympathy. "Change it to, I will love while I have the chance."

Hana looked at her hands, picking at a ratty nail and lacking the energy to bother. "Fat lot of good that's done me so far," she sighed. She rose to leave, unable to cope with the gentle probing and scared she may reveal something of her inner awfulness to the sweet woman with the fluffy hair.

"Hana, I don't usually give advice," Evie said. "It's not my role. But I feel a single conversation with Logan might prove important. Everyone deserves a second chance."

Hana pressed her fingers around the door handle and turned away, Evie's words bouncing off her hardened resolve. The smile she returned contained sadness and hurt. "Not always," she said and left.

Sheila gave Hana a ride home. They left late and Hana saw Logan's truck still outside the chapel. "Bloody Pete!" she hissed and Sheila rolled her eyes, eagerly diving into a list of North's many faults and foibles. As she rambled, Hana realised the gossip mongers knew nothing about Anka aside from speculation, assuming her family issues related to Ivan. They kinda did. But that didn't explain how Logan found out.

Izzie rang, buzzing with excitement because Elizabeth rolled onto her stomach unaided. "She's so gorgeous, Mum. I wish you could see her. She grunts something awful and doesn't give up until she rolls over onto her fat little tummy."

"I'm glad things are working out." Hana nosed through the cupboards and found a new bottle of red wine. She battled with the lid one-handed before admitting defeat and shoving it back in the cupboard. The tap water effervesced in the glass, entertaining her while Izzie chatted about how the ladies of the parish helped rather than hindered.

"I needed to be clear with them, that's all. Marcus helped me and now it makes perfect sense. They clean, bring food and all they want in return is company. One lady takes Beth for a walk while I mow her garden. I get some peace and physical exercise and she gets to play nana for an hour. Life is one big trade off."

"That's lovely darling." Hana's bland answer alerted her daughter.

"How are your plans going?" Izzie asked, trying to draw her out. Hana rolled her eyes and fished a speck from her water with a tentative finger.

"Ah, you know," she sighed. "These things take time."

The argument with Logan left a bitter taste in her mouth and a sick feeling inside her chest. Hana clambered into bed, swathed in her favourite flannelette pyjamas. Little monkeys carouseled around the pants. "You're too old for drama, girl," she whispered to herself. "You're nobody's woman. I think it's best if you stay on your own."

Chapter 26

Hana left home earlier and braved the bus service from Flagstaff to work. The Orbiter to Maui Street heaved with students from different schools and workers from the outer suburbs, mixing and mingling in a haze of muffled iPod music. Other commuters stood in the aisles, but a Year 13 from school recognised Hana and offered his seat. "Thanks, love. That's kind of you." She sank onto the tatty bench, avoiding a large rip in the seat material. Her high heels proved ineffective against the slippery, metallic bus floor and she experienced a wave of relief at not having to jerk and sway in the aisle with the other bodies.

The elderly gentleman next to the window leaned against her every time the bus took a corner, his breath smelling of tobacco and old cheese. After the eighth time, Hana gave an ill-tempered sigh and the Year 13 smirked. When the bus stopped outside school, Hana emerged coughing from the haze of boy sweat and veiled cigarette smoke. "I can't do that every day," she grumbled to herself.

Walking past the chapel car park, Hana spotted Logan's truck. She winced, assuming he'd arrived early and slowed her walk, wondering how to spend the rest of her life avoiding him. Noticing a mist covering the lower halves of the window and the wheel still broaching the white line, she realised it hadn't moved since the day before. She sighed with irritation and picked up speed.

Pete's empty desk greeted her as she banged through the door and Hana gritted her teeth. He'd made an awkward problem into a catastrophe, ensuring she looked like the bad guy. Logan lent her his truck and she left it overnight in a theft-prone part of town in revenge. She shook her fist at Pete's dandruff-covered chair and imagined the pleasure of throttling him. "Wearing gloves!" she added, wrinkling her nose. She pushed her handbag into her drawer and sank onto her chair, pressing a hand over her already thudding head. If Logan's anger intimidated her yesterday, today's would send her into orbit.

"Only he didn't intimidate me," she sighed. Closing her eyes, she remembered his flashing grey irises and the strong cut of his jaw. Everything about him exuded power and authority, his mana, life essence pouring off him in intoxicating waves. It excited and invigorated her but she wanted him on her side, not in the opposite camp. She knew they were doomed, yet her lips and cheeks remembered his kisses and her treacherous heart sent darts of desire to her gut.

Hana clumped around the office putting away stray brochures and paperwork. She fired up her computer and checked the bulletin for the day's events. Anka always did them early, giving a run sheet for the day. Another set of initials appeared in the footer, compounding Hana's misery. She printed a copy and hunted down a drawing pin to clip it to the common room notice board. One particular item caught her eye and she peered at it. 'New Zealand Police are visiting the common room today at 12.45, lunchtime. Students interested in a police career should attend. All year groups welcome.'

"No, they're not!" Hana logged onto her own calendar as dread mounted. The police visit showed up on the screen for the following week, alongside other items which were colour coded. She pulled up the bulletin and groaned. External courses for that day were also listed. Chaos threatened. Hana readied herself for the fireworks when Sheila returned from the imminent staff briefing.

Right on cue, Sheila stamped into the office. "What's the matter with this place?" she yelled. "The police visit is next week! Now Watson's whining at me." She performed an entertaining but not very accurate impression of Donald Watson grumbling, the voice a few octaves too high and squeaky, "I've already got the common room booked for a meeting then and I can't change it blah blah blah."

"It's a mistake," Hana reassured her. "The new typist has pulled up the wrong week in the calendar is all. Why don't I email all tutor staff and stop them reading out any notices relating to us?" She considered the blanket email which would arrive in Logan's inbox and shivered.

"They don't read bloody emails!" Sheila huffed. She repeated the process Hana had already gone through, checking and rechecking. She ground her teeth as valuable time trickled through their fingers. "Fine, email them then!" Sheila snapped and Hana sighed. She opened her mouth to speak and the bell rang for the start of tutor group.

With a wail, Sheila exited the office, flying down the corridor to impart the message to twelve individual classes with a personal appearance. Hana shook her head and dashed off the email, leaving Logan out of the list.

Peter North slouched through the door, offering Hana a vent for her guilt. "Could you not do one simple task?" she growled. His eyes grew wide and round and he scratched at an itch in his right armpit. "Why didn't you give the keys to Logan?"

North looked sheepish and dug around in his pocket, pulling out the offending keys, covered in a veil of pocket fluff. He shrugged. "I don't like it when he's sad. You made him sad." Pete gave her an accusing glare and Hana took a deep breath, holding out her hand for the keys.

"I'll give them to him myself," she said through gritted teeth. A voice in her head reprimanded her for not doing that in the first place.

"Don't!" Pete implored. He stepped in front of her with his arms outstretched in line with her boobs. Hana glanced at his waggling fingers in horror.

"Don't even think about it!" she snapped, taking a step out of range.

Pete shook his head and adjusted his arms so they dropped by his sides. "No, I want you to stop. You don't understand what he's been through."

"I don't care." Hana's jaw hardened. "I don't have to tell him jack! We aren't married and he doesn't command every thought I have. He crossed the line, Pete. Give me the keys."

He tipped them into her hand, dropping the fluff in too. Not trusting herself to comment further, Hana snatched a poster from the shelf and set off towards the back stairs and the art rooms. She loved the sweet, elderly art teacher and his haven of pretty things. He reminded her of a friend of her father's who brought her colourful rocks and little curios as a child. Buying time, Hana walked towards her distraction whilst wondering how to give the keys to Logan without making a fuss. She practised sentences in her head. "It's for the best," she whispered under her breath on repeat, reminding herself of the clause in her contract which decreed that staff members were not permitted to date.

Halfway up the stairs, Hana stopped and peered at the poster in her hand. Donald Watson paused on his way down. "What's the matter?"

"I think I picked up the wrong poster." Hana attempted to peer down the shaft, seeing only dark shapes. She glanced back the way she'd come, hundreds of steps and corridors swelling into an insurmountable distance. At the end of it waited Pete, with his misguided loyalty and groping hands.

"Well, don't waste time girl!" Donald bit. "Unravel it and take a look." He trotted off down the stairs, his tie blown over one shoulder and matching the strands of hair dangling from his head.

The stairs seemed a foolish place to unroll a flimsy poster, especially one almost as tall as Hana. She eyed up the landing ahead of her and realised she'd be vulnerable as soon as the bell rang, a prime target for stampeding students hurrying to class. She backtracked, finding herself at the door of the stockroom on the split-level landing.

This time she knocked. Receiving no answer, Hana pressed the keypad, relaying the number she'd seen on an all staff email that morning. The code changed monthly and she smirked at 666, the number of the beast. Someone had a sense of humour in a church school. Once inside, she jiggled the internal button and hissed an expletive at the groundsman who mended nothing. Pushing an exercise book into the gap to stop the door slamming on her, she rolled the poster onto the floorboards and squatted down to look. A Māori man in a reed skirt peered up at her, brandishing a Te Rakau. The rod looked powerful in his olive fingers, able to bring creativity or inflict punishment. Tattoos covered his chin and neck denoting his genealogical whakapapa and his pink tongue flattened against his lower lip in challenge. Hana stroked his cheek, remembering her conversation with Logan. The art teacher wouldn't want the poster but the head of Māori language would love him, especially as he bore an uncanny likeness to a student from a couple of years ago. Hana rolled the poster into its tube shape, fighting the elastic band around its girth. The language classrooms were next door to English, so she steeled herself to hand deliver the keys on her way there.

A shadow fell across her as someone yanked the door open, making her jump. Logan Du Rose stood in the gap, biting his lower lip and battling a shroud of awkwardness. A broken ruler in one hand and a shop receipt in the other revealed his mission. After a long moment of stunned silence, Hana broke it by shifting backwards so he could pass. The air crackled between them. Logan bent and scooped up the exercise book. "You dropped this," he said, holding it out towards her.

Hana's eyes widened as the door eased closed behind him, relaxing as it rested against the frame with the tiniest shaft of light showing through. "Excuse me," she said, avoiding his eyes. She moved closer, her gaze fixed on the glimmer of light from the stairwell. A twang heralded the rebellion of the elastic band and the poster began unrolling itself around her legs. Hana gathered up the edges and tried to fit the huge piece of shiny paper and herself past Logan's imposing frame.

He reached out a muscular arm and blocked her way, "Can we talk?"

"I've nothing to add to your monologue yesterday, thanks." Hana clung to the resolution which dictated she'd be better off alone. She couldn't date a colleague and would be foolish to try.

She fixed her gaze on the arm in front of her face and contemplated shoving it away. The bright paua cufflinks sparkled against the crisp linen and other thoughts strayed into her mind. Logan withdrew his arm and a wave of disappointment crashed over Hana's flustered confusion. The car keys chose that moment to dig into her thigh, moving in the tight pocket of her trousers as a reminder of her decision. Hana dropped her gaze and fumbled for them, losing control of the poster again. She held them out to him like an offering, exchanging them for the portion of her heart she'd foolishly already given. Long lashes swished over Logan's cheek as he looked down at them and then back up at her.

Hana closed her eyes, willing the awful minute over. She felt a breeze and caught a hint of Logan's aftershave; a gorgeous muskiness mingled with sweet meadows and summer. Her body reminded her how it felt on the steps of her house with his arm around her, conspiring to show her what she'd lost. What she always lost. She battled a sense of overwhelming distress and lurched for the door, dragging the poster behind her.

It ripped, tearing the fearsome Māori face from hair to neck. Rage obliterated all other emotions, carrying her through like a current of salvation and immunising her against hurt. Hana's green eyes flashed danger and she shoved at Logan's chest, meeting a rock hard wall of muscle. He snatched up her fist and bent her arm upwards, pressing it against the rough shelf behind. Hana dropped the poster and raised her other hand, losing that too in his firm grip. The keys dug into her palm. Logan switched so one strong hand captured both slender wrists and then he leaned down and kissed her. Hana turned her face away and he kissed her neck. "Trust me," he whispered.

She opened her mouth to deliver a barbed reply and his lips covered hers, taking her breath away. The car keys clanged to the dusty floorboards and Hana heard them settle, the rush of her heartbeat far louder. Logan teased her lips and tongue, making her feel out of control and alive. When he sensed her relax, he released her arms to rest on his shoulders. She felt like a ball of putty as he ravished her face with warm kisses, spreading her lipstick across her cheek and his. "It's not over," he whispered against her lips and she groaned.

The door clicked and the room darkened. Hana panicked.

The sound of the bell for the first period sent them skittering apart, Hana putting her hand up to her mouth in horror. "We need to stop." She sounded breathless and her heartbeat thudded in her ears.

Logan snaked his hands around her waist and pulled her into him, planting a kiss on her forehead. "What if I don't want to?" His lips were persuasive, the skin on his jaw soft from an early morning shave and his cologne intoxicating. Hana gasped as her stomach plunged downwards in a sensation of incredible longing. Logan's lips pressed against her ear. "What if I never let you go again?" he asked in a whisper.

"Stop it." Hana giggled, wriggling away as Logan bit her neck. "We'll get caught."

"Is there a light switch?" She heard his cowboy boots scuff against the floor and clatter into the keys.

"It's here." She felt along the shelves and touched the back of the door, fumbling her way right until she contacted the old, stubby switch. A dull light flared into existence from a single, dangling bulb near the back of the room. Corner shelves cast eerie shadows and Hana pressed herself against the solid door. It didn't budge. "Oh, no!"

Footsteps clumped past as six hundred boys dragged reluctant bodies to class. Bags slid against the door as they jostled on the stairs and around the dog leg.

Logan strode forward and knocked, but the stampeding males drowned out his efforts. He looked at Hana and then smiled. "You've smudged your lipstick." He dragged his thumb beneath her bottom lip, his grey irises disappearing behind black pupils.

Hana frowned. "No, you smudged my lipstick." Her face curled into a sly smile. "You're wearing it now too."

Logan reached for her and dragged her into his body. "It tasted like berries. Does it suit me?"

A flush of embarrassment lit Hana's cheeks in a soft pink and she shook her head. "No." She shifted her cheek against his chest. "I'm wiping it on your shirt."

"Don't!" He held onto her upper arms, keeping her far enough away to stop her. "Not unless you want me fired."

"Are you teaching next?" Realisation dawned and Hana's eyes opened wide.

"Meant to be." He chewed his lip. "How do we get out?"

"My phone's on my desk," Hana groaned. "Do you have yours?" She prodded at Logan's trouser pocket and he wrinkled his nose.

"No. I waited all last night for you to text and then left it at home in disgust." He reached for her again and she backed away.

"That wasn't my fault. I don't need to say sorry."

"Okay, okay." He pulled her into his chest and rubbed a hand across her tense shoulders. "Then I'm sorry, Hana. Okay? It turned into a doozy of a day and I apologise for taking it out on you."

"Fine." She made her reply sound grudging, loving it when Logan held her tighter. The noise outside lessened. "What do we say when someone opens the door?" She sounded fearful, biting her bottom lip with anxiety.

Logan leaned back and sighed. "Tell them we were making out."

"No!" Hana stamped her foot. "It's against the rules."

"What rules?"

Hana slapped him on the arm. "The no fraternising rule. It's in your contract."

"Not in mine." He rubbed sensuous circles on the back of her neck.

"It's in everyone's. It's a church school and they don't want trouble." Hana sighed. "I don't want trouble."

Logan gave a low snort and found the soft dip in the small of her back. "Then you should run now." His fingers felt warm and gentle and persuasive. "It's not in my contract."

Hana put her hands against his chest in a stop sign. "It's definitely in mine." Her voice dripped regret. "I thought you knew. We can't do this. It's stupid to start."

Logan snagged her again, hauling her into him. "We are doing this, Hana. We did start and it's non-negotiable. I'm not stopping and they can't enforce it."

Hana sighed and ran a nervous hand across her mouth, trying to rub away the errant lipstick. Logan inhaled and kept hold of her. "Are you frightened of Watson?" he asked, his gaze perceptive. She nodded.

"Yes. Aren't you?" She stared up at him, seeing the futility of the comment against his latent authority. She'd anticipated the shake of his dark head before it came. "He always calls me girl. I don't think after fifteen years he even knows my name. And he treats me like I'm time wasting, whatever he finds me doing. I can't win. He'll walk in any second and fire me for shirking. It might be a relief."

"Really?" Logan cocked his head and Hana shrugged.

"I sometimes think so. I own my house and I'm solvent. But working means I haven't touched Vik's life insurance yet." She shook her head. "Sorry. I shouldn't talk about stuff like that. Bodie says I'll attract a con artist who'll marry me and push me down the stairs."

Logan quirked an eyebrow. "Right. Because that's the kind of person you find in a school stockroom."

Hana shrugged. "You never know."

"I'm a lot of things, but not that." Logan turned to lean against the wall, keeping his left arm around her shoulder. He bent his knee and balanced the sole of his cowboy boot against a shelf. "Look, I'll take the blame," he offered. "I'm new; they'll figure I didn't know the catch was broken."

"Okay then," Hana replied without shame and Logan hid his smile.

She rested her palm against the front of his thigh and he closed his eyes, struggling not to react in the way he wanted. "Logan," Hana whispered and he opened his eyes and looked at her. "About before. Anka told me something in confidence. I try so hard not to gossip in this place." She swallowed, looking for the right words. Logan raised his hand, so she didn't have to finish.

"I don't like surprises and it knocked me sideways for a bit, that's all. You're right, a confidence is a confidence. It's fine." He pressed his lips to Hana's in forgiveness, shifting position so he could hold and kiss her, communicating his apology through his body.

Hana felt a flush of passion and remembered being eighteen again. She felt it once a long time ago, a naïve little girl in her first year at Aberystwyth University. That one reckless moment with the handsome Sikh boy heralded a world of trouble. Memories flooded her mind and she overrode the urge to flee, promising she wouldn't repeat her mistakes. Logan's breathing changed and she recognised the danger.

"Enough," she sighed, pulling away from him and biting her lip. "It's not a good look if someone comes in."

Logan raised his eyebrows and leaned back with a smug look on his face. "You wanna get out of here and go some place else?" He linked his fingers through hers and leaned back against the wall.

"What's with you?" Hana laughed and nudged him. He seized her fingers and kissed them.

"When was the last time anyone told you how beautiful you are?"

Hana's brow furrowed as she tried to remember. "I don't know."

Logan looked at her in horror. "Didn't your husband say it to you?"

She shifted in discomfort and floundered. "It's complicated. He's been dead a long time." She squirmed and pain crossed her face as she wriggled away from Logan, hiding beneath an expressionless mask.

"Hey." His voice sounded soft as he leaned into her and kissed her cheek. "I'll tell you every day for the rest of your life. You're the most beautiful woman I've ever known."

"I bet you say that to all the girls." Hana's voice sounded listless and faraway. Logan sensed the emotional distance grow between them. He dragged her back into his side.

"Actually, I've never said it to anyone." His eyes crinkled at the edges. "I've only ever wanted to say it to you." He kissed the top of her head and held her tight.

Hana sighed against his shoulder. "You're funny," she whispered and Logan hid his look of sadness at her disbelief.

"Let's get out of here," he said, pushing off from the wall and dragging her with him.

"How?" Hana put her hands on her hips, her eyes hidden in the shadow of her fringe.

"Trust me," Logan replied and winked at her.

Before he reached the door, it opened outwards with a creak. The newcomer stopped in her tracks and gaped in surprise. "Angus was worried about you. He asked me if you'd gone to the hospital." Sunita directed her question at Logan and Hana saw his shoulders stiffen.

"Hardly. I got locked in here."

Hana knew her face grew pinker by the second and hid behind Logan as Sunita pushed her way further into the cupboard. When they were at eye level, Sunita smirked. "Please could you pass me a bundle of those wooden rulers, Hana? The shop's run out and the last person they sent to fetch some never arrived back."

Hana watched Logan's eyes narrow behind the Indian woman's back and dropped her gaze to the shelf behind her. Logan watched as she bent down and Hana felt him appraising her legs through the smart slacks. A smile touched her lips and she accentuated the movement, making more of it than she needed to. The period bell sounded muffled as it tolled in the corridor, reminding Hana an hour had passed. "Grab the door!" She flapped her hand at Logan and he took a step forward, lurching backwards with a grunt as another body entered the cramped space.

"Party? Cool as!" squealed Peter North. He saw Hana bring a bundle of wooden rulers from the shelf and heft them in her hand, his face creasing in panic. He tried to cover his bases by pressing his hand over his crotch. "Hey, Logan, don't let her hit me. Hana asked me to give you your keys. Yesterday." His eyes darted from Hana and then back to Logan.

"So?" Logan narrowed his eyes and held his hand out. Pete put his fingers in his pants pocket and looked confused. Enlightenment dawned across his pale blue eyes.

"She's got them." He jabbed a finger at Hana. "I went to the shop for staples but Lief says I have to fetch rulers first. I'm stapling my zipper, look." He pointed at his crotch where an opening gaped. Dingy underpants poked through the gap.

"I'm getting rulers!" Sunita snatched them from Hana and cradled them to her chest like a child. "They asked me first."

"No!" North shoved his way past Logan, bobbing down to grab another bundle. "I'm getting them. Then I can staple my pants. I can't walk around like this!"

"You usually do." Irritation made Sunita's accent more pronounced and she straightened her back and gave Pete the spoiled-princess-look. Logan watched, his expression unreadable and Hana shrieked as the door behind him swung closed. The slap of a school bag ensured it clicked shut before any of them could move. The sound of students walking about on the staircase made Pete's ensuing shouts and hammering pointless. He screamed, a high-pitched operatic sound which made the women cover their ears. Logan slapped him across the back of the head and he stopped.

The cupboard felt small for two, but four adult bodies made it overheated and claustrophobic. North squished himself into the corner between the last shelf and the wall. "I'm taking the rulers," he maintained. Sunita humphed and folded her arms.

Logan leaned against the door, one leg bent and the sole of his cowboy boot resting against the wood. He snagged up his keys and shoved them in his pocket. "I can open it," he offered and both women recoiled in horror.

"Donald Watson will kill us if you break it down," Sunita breathed and Hana agreed. They huddled in the middle of the cupboard, listening for the sounds of anyone passing by. "We'll hammer on the door and shout the code," Sunita suggested. "Then swear them to secrecy."

Logan sighed and folded his arms, leaning his head back and closing his eyes against the room full of stupidity. Sunita cornered Hana, whispering in an undertone. "How long have you been seeing him?" she hissed. "I told you he liked you."

Hana shook her head, watching Logan through one eye. "We're not allowed to date other staff members," she whispered. Sunita snorted.

"Tell that to some of the others. Martin Jennings for one."

Hana rolled her eyes. "They're married!" she replied, her tone incredulous. She opened her mouth to say something else when the single, pathetic bulb winked out. "Fantastic!" she complained. The room pitched into darkness and all Hana felt for the next ten minutes was Sunita's elbow jabbing her in the ribs as she whispered gossip in hushed tones. Hana blanked it out with a nursery rhyme in her head, running through four or five before Sunita grew silent and jabbed her again.

"It's terrible, isn't it?"

"What is?" Hana felt Sunita's breath on her cheek and realised how close she must be. She shifted, her heels scraping on the wooden floor and the air became fraught with tension. Instinct told Hana it wasn't just hers.

"About Anka and that student. I don't know how Angus kept a lid on it. Angus' personal assistant said they've hushed it up."

Hana sighed and kept her body still. Misery flooded through her bones. Sunita leaned closer. "I won't tell anyone else. I figured you knew anyway." She jabbed Hana in the ribs again, making her groan in pain. Then she continued in a hushed voice, "Must have been hard for him too." She sighed. "Really embarrassing. The receptionist said he had no idea."

"I have no idea what you're talking about now." Hana let impatience flood her tone, hoping Sunita would shut up about it. No such luck. Sunita jabbed her again with a pointy elbow, getting her in the stomach as she breathed into Hana's face. "I thought they looked alike, but they have different surnames. I saw Logan last year when Tama got caught smoking at the boarding house. They've got the same eyes. I suppose they would look similar with the boy being his nephew. Angus' assistant said Logan's paid his fees for the last five years and now the little git has done this."

Hana choked on her own saliva, grateful for the darkness which hid her stunned reaction. The bombshell sent her body into a paroxysm of trembling, the drama slotting into place like the parts of a well-oiled machine. She swallowed, her silence speaking volumes. Anka's obvious animosity found an explanation, rooted in a way to protect her illicit affair. Hana sighed and Sunita jabbed her again. "You didn't know, did you?"

Hana shook her head, sickness working its way through her system. "No," she whispered. "No, I didn't."

"Oops!" A foul smell percolated from Pete's corner and Hana gagged.

"Pete!" she squeaked. "That's disgusting!" She lifted her blouse in the darkness and used it to cover her nose, panting into the fabric.

"Now can I open the bloody door?" Logan's feet ground against the dusty floor and Hana couldn't answer for fear of breathing in the stench.

"Are you telling me you could open it the whole time?" Sunita demanded. Hana concentrated through the haze of whatever crawled up Pete's bum and died there, her eyes watering.

"Yep," Logan replied. "I offered twice."

"Do it!" Sunita squealed. "Just do it!"

A click followed a shuffle and the women lurched towards the light, desperate for escape as the fog of death drifted towards them.

The child on the stairs regretted skipping class as the three shrieking banshees leapt from the cupboard, accompanied by the nauseating stench of death. As he shrank back against the bannister, he saw the cadaver lying slumped on the floor inside, its eyes rolled back in its rotting head. He ran to fetch the school nurse and quaked as she pressed the number of the beast into the keypad.

"Oh, thanks." Peter North walked through the open door, clutching four bundles of wooden rulers. "The shop sent me to fetch these. You don't need to get any." He jerked his head towards the shelf. "I've got all eighty."

The nurse took the child back to sick bay and rang his mother to fetch him. She wrote in the log that he'd suffered a medical episode including worrying delusions and hustled him off to the doctors with his concerned parent.

Logan ran the gauntlet with Alan Dobbs. "I covered your second class, Du Rose!" he raged. "The Year 12s talked for the whole bloody hour, but the Year 9s didn't report you missing. Instead, they made the damn classroom into an assault course and in the process, broke the legs off a desk and ripped those curtains from the long windows facing the courtyard. They turned it into a pirate ship!"

Logan stood his ground as Dobbs ranted, waiting for him to draw breath. "We've read Treasure Island," he replied. "I'm glad it got them thinking." He made the mistake of smirking and Dobbs flipped his lid.

"This is a private school, Du Rose, not a bloody kindergarten. The parents who pay our bloody exorbitant fees have certain bloody expectations."

Logan entertained himself counting the expletives in his superior's sentences. Every time Dobbs swore, the blond wig on his head moved further left. Logan wondered how many more would turn it into a beard.

"You got locked into the stock cupboard near the art rooms?" Dobbs peered at Logan with a quizzical expression. "You're sure it was that one?"

"Yeah." Logan nodded and cocked his head. "The weird one with the door that opens outward."

Dobbs prodded at his computer screen and dragged his glasses further down his nose. "A student took the nurse back there earlier. Said there were murderers and a body. She sent him home." Dobbs sat back and flung his glasses on the desk. A hairy hand rubbed across his face. "Probably another kid trying to get out of class; whole place is going down the toilet." He sighed. "Mrs Dobbs wondered if you wanted dinner one night this week. The neighbouring reserve has a rabbit problem. You up for it?"

Logan nodded. "Yeah. Just give me the details later and we'll go out there."

"Awesome." Dobbs looked pleased. "It's great to have a crack shot on the team."

Logan held his gaze with grey eyes the colour of grit. Realising he'd let his formidable guard down at work, Dobbs dismissed the English teacher with a warning. "I'm watching you! Let's have no more disappearing acts during school hours." His brow furrowed. "Apart from the necessary one's obviously. Angus explained. How's that all going?"

"Fine thanks," Logan replied with a smile. "Want me to bring my poppa's gun again?"

Dobbs sat back in his chair and observed him, a covetous look in his eyes. "Yes," he said in a calm tone. His fingers twitched at the memory of the eighty-year-old shotgun, clean lines and smooth firing action. "That would be wonderful."

Sheila taught for two periods and didn't notice Hana's absence, although Hana stayed back after hours to make up for it and got more work done without the constant interruptions. Nobody ever missed Pete, who spent the next hour in the toilet. Sunita got to the shop first with the rulers.

Hana felt like the stink of Pete's fart stuck in her nose for the rest of the day. Lying awake that night she decided next time she went in the cupboard, she'd borrow Anka's trick and leave her shoe in the entrance.

Chapter 27

Logan's truck proved a blessing, even if it was difficult to start first thing in the morning. As the term neared a close, the weather deteriorated. Frost threatened to put in an appearance and the nights gained a frozen edge.

Anka's husband rang Hana one evening to let her know she left him. "You must have known," he argued.

"I thought she stopped it," Hana replied. "I challenged her and she left the school. I thought she removed herself from temptation. We've had no contact since."

"You should've told me." He sounded bitter and Hana felt his pain.

"I'm sorry," she admitted. "You're right. In my defence, I assumed she'd stopped."

Ivan snorted. "I didn't know she'd quit her job until last weekend! She did it so the kid could stay at school and not get expelled."

"Oh, no." Hana sat on the sofa and smoothed the cat's tail between her fingers. He glared at her and hopped off the cushion. "He's still there?" She sighed, knowing she could have asked Logan but hadn't dared, pushing the subject as far from them as possible. It already did enough damage. He didn't mention it and nor would she.

"There will be repercussions from this," Ivan predicted. "I don't know how to deal with it. Gareth is livid. He reckons if Tama comes near him, he'll smack the snot out of him. I told him he'd get suspended and that will be the end of his school career and university. But I know how he feels. Apart from the fact Tama's a kid himself and I've thought of him like a son, I'd smack the snot out of him myself!"

The conversation ended with neither of them any the wiser. Hana sat in stunned silence for a while, grateful when the cat returned for a smooch. "People just don't realise, Tiger," she whispered, fondling his ears. "When they set off after their own desires, they implode so many other lives in the process." She thought about another time in another life and felt the chill begin in her soul.

Her mind drifted to Logan and warmth returned, stopping the ice regaining a hold. "Keep the truck, please?" he'd said, running his fingers up Hana's forearms with a feather light touch. "I don't go back on favours, that's not who I am."

"I just kind of assumed you would," Hana began and he looked hard into her green eyes with a serious expression on his face.

He faltered for a second and after running his tongue across his bottom lip, said, "You can't make assumptions about me, Hana. Sometimes things won't be as they seem. Just ask me if you need to know something and I'll tell you." He had exacted a promise from her with a heated kiss in the car park and Hana blushed at the memory.

Hana made good on her plans to change her circumstances and started clearing out the garage. In the absence of her car, stuff crept outwards from the walls and took up residence on the garage floor. She didn't even try to drive Logan's truck in. Vik's tools hung around the walls, rusting and unused. Hana's repertoire of tools included a hammer, some nails and the ability to run up the street and summon one of her poor male neighbours. The junk needed to go.

Izzie wanted nothing but Bodie wasn't sure. Hana spoke to him on the phone. "You need to come and look soon," she told him. "I can't keep it forever." She heard his sharp inhale on the other end of the line and tensed. He didn't like change and proved frosty over the house sale.

"I'll come down soon," he promised. Hana sighed. He'd been saying that for years, but had so far only ever turned up unexpectedly on his way to somewhere else.

"I'm planning a garage sale," she said with pride in her voice. "I've got the signs ready."

"You're really going through with it?" Bodie sounded surprised and Hana cringed at the doubt in his voice.

"Yes. The real estate agents came through last weekend. I'm giving their proposals to Angus. He'll look over them for me."

Bodie's silence spoke volumes and he changed the subject. "Any news on those two clowns who damaged the car?"

"No." Hana's brow furrowed. "I haven't heard from the garage either. I should ring them. It shouldn't take this long to repair Papa ji's dings and replace the bumper, should it?"

"Not really. What did it cost?"

"I don't know that either. I got busy clearing out the house and forgot about it. I'll get onto it soon." Hana didn't mention the car parked periodically across the street from her house; a black sedan with a white male driver. She wanted to tell Bodie, but the man never approached her, just watched from a distance. Hana rang her case officer with the registration number, but she never seemed to be available and hadn't yet returned the voicemail messages.

Logan's truck kangarooed Hana to work, choking in disgust at the high grade gas she put in it. The day proved long and frustrating as Sheila geared up for the annual careers expo for students. Everyone lived on a knife-edge around her of late and the office degenerated into an unhappy, toxic place as the year progressed.

Held in the evening during August, the expo involved endless administration for Hana and other school admin staff who helped. It hailed the start of hundreds of messages left on voicemail for prospective visitors, emails dashing forwards and back, notes made about who needed what on the night; frustration and success all rolled into one.

"Thank goodness we started early this year," Sheila sighed. "But it doesn't lessen the stress does it? It just drags it out longer. What will we do without Anka? She did the typing and sorted out the floor plan."

"It'll be okay," Hana reassured her. "It always is. We'll manage."

At interval, she saw Angus with her pile of real estate agreements and he went through them. One by one he poured over them, checking out the small print and the terms with his glasses perched on the end of his nose. "Even though we're in the middle of a recession, some of them have good terms but want to list the house at a very low asking price. Others are higher, but I suspect once they get the listing, the price will be lowered after a few weeks to your detriment."

"I don't pretend to understand this." Hana sighed and Angus observed her over his glasses. Then he slid them off his long nose.

"Can't Logan help you with this?" he asked. "He's got a good head for business."

Hana misunderstood. "No. It's okay if you don't have time. I can work it out." She stood and shuffled the agreements together in a bundle, shoving them back inside a manila folder. "We're not allowed relationships with other staff." Her jaw worked and Angus cocked his head and watched her like an eagle waiting for a sparrow to settle.

"It's not in his contract," he said, his lips lifting upwards in amusement.

Hana narrowed her eyes. "But it is in mine." Her jaw worked and she hid the disappointment in her eyes. She wanted to be honest. Wanted to tell him she'd found love after all this time. The sentence died on her lips and she asked another question. "Why isn't it in Logan's? What's different about him?"

Angus grinned and leaned forward. "If I tell you, Donald will be cross," he said and tapped the side of his nose.

Not liking the riddle, Hana shook her head and pushed her chair under the table. When she looked up again, Angus grinned. "It's simple, Hana. Our Mr Du Rose is a law unto himself. He crossed that line out and initialled it. Donald didn't expect it and so he didn't notice. He countersigned it, amendment and all."

Hana's brow furrowed. "That easy?"

Angus laughed, the sound issuing from deep inside his chest as though the matter really tickled him. "That easy," he said and winked. "Donald regrets the incident. I doubt it will happen again. I figure Mr Du Rose met someone on his first day here, someone he wished to get to know." He reached for his telephone handset and lifted a finger. "Wait there, Hana."

Angus called an old friend in real estate to ask his advice. The friend was expected back in the office at any moment and while they waited for his reply, Angus ordered tea from his personal assistant and relaxed in his battered old chair. "I found the business of Mrs van Blerk rather distressing," he said without preamble, watching Hana with interest. "I'm saddened to think you knew about the situation and didn't inform someone, even anonymously."

Hana's cheeks flared red and anger rose to the surface in defence. Ivan's accusations weren't easy to shake off. "I found out by accident the day before Anka resigned," Hana began, a barbed edge to her voice. "I met with her that night to get her to see sense, but she left after we argued. I haven't seen her since and I don't know where she is. It's not fair how everyone blames me. I almost lost everything." Hana stopped herself, staring at the fist resting in her lap and concentrating hard on her nails, which needed some serious care.

"I see," said Angus. And that was it. The tea arrived and he didn't mention it again. As his assistant thumped a cup in front of Hana and gave her a spiteful glare, Hana wondered what Angus did actually see. She suspected it might be the one thing she didn't want him to. Her relationship with Logan remained off limits for public discussion. Relationship. Hana recognised the plummeting in her stomach when she thought about Logan's kisses and steered her mind elsewhere, unable to disguise the flush on her neck. Angus studied her with predatory calm and Hana diverted her attention to her tea as though engrossed in the horrid tan colour and peculiar floaty bits. An occasional twitch of his lips told her she failed. The Scotsman missed nothing.

His friend called back and after a lengthy chat, Angus gave him Hana's address and phone number. "Mates' rates?" he enquired and then laughed.

Replacing the phone with a clatter, he smiled at Hana. "He'll meet you at home after school to do an independent appraisal. Come back to me if you need further help."

Hana felt the world drop out of her stomach at the sudden prospect. Her courage failed her and she nodded and thanked him, standing to end the meeting. "I'm grateful," she said, fear in her eyes. "It seems like a massive undertaking."

Angus accompanied her to the door and rested his hand on her shoulder. "And it is, Hana." His smile held understanding. He knew. "It is. Lean into the pain, dear. It doesn't last forever. We both know that."

Hana pulled the door open, running into the assistant whose wrinkled face oozed mischief. "Ah, headmaster," she said. "We have a little problem." She shot barbs of hatred in Hana's direction.

Hana left them to it and walked into reception, finding Ivan pacing in front of the counter. "What's happened?" she asked, responding to the misery in his expression.

Angus came out behind her and there was little time for Ivan to do more than raise his eyebrows and give Hana a look that said it all. Tama sat on the couch with a roll of tissue stuffed beneath a bleeding nose, his white shirt soaked through to the skin. Gareth stood in an opposite corner of the wide room, his body stiff and eyes unseeing. Bruised knuckles still curled into a fist at his chest and his anger boiled over into a tangible force.

Ivan disappeared into the office with Angus just as Logan strode from the stairwell. He didn't see Hana, his gaze fixed on the sorry kid with the blood nose. With a cursory glance over her shoulder, Hana left them to it.

Chapter 28

"Rent it out?" Hana's voice rose to a squeak at the end of her sentence.

"Yes dear," replied the agent, flicking through his pages of notes and ending up back where he started after a minor reshuffle. "It's the best solution for you at the moment. As you own the house outright, advertise it as a rental. Pay your new mortgage from the rent you get on this one, less upkeep. It's the best way to get value for money in the short term. Nothing's shifting in this area as you may have noticed."

"No." Hana slumped onto the sofa. "I hadn't noticed. I've paid no attention to the housing market before last week." Her face oozed frustration in a knitting of her brows and a valiant attempt to keep her trademark redheaded temper in check. The closest she'd come in eight years to leaving the past behind her and her courage seemed wasted.

The agent looked delicately boned, precise and careful in his movements as he closed his leather pad and placed it into his briefcase. His white fringe gave way to a darker grey at the back, making him appear fragile. "I'll leave this contract and a brochure about our services." He dropped the glitzy leaflets onto the table. "Come back with any questions. Or speak to Angus. We rent out his villa in Gordonton and offer a full managed property service. You can forget it's there."

The agent stopped on the threshold to hand Hana his card. A pretty female smiled out from a professional photo, shoulder to shoulder with this man. The card bore the words, 'Eric and Ingrid Tanner–Real Estate and Letting Agents.' Hana raised her eyebrows at the age difference, wondering if the five years between her and Logan looked so drastic on paper. "Call me or my wife, once you've decided what to do."

Hana waved him off and then leaned against the inside of the closed door, sighing in disappointment. She turned the business card over in her fingers, considering cutting her losses and just selling. The thought of keeping the house comforted her, like leaving a security blanket at home but knowing it still occupied a space on the bed. Hana groaned and ran a hand over her face. "You're avoiding the inevitable," she whispered. "Stop being a wimp. That's the road to ruined plans and another eight years holding your breath, instead of living life."

Hana's mind remained in turmoil the following day. She bounced between letting and selling and then back again. Logan offered encouragement as they cleaned Hana's garage. "It's releasing when you walk away from your past," he said, examining Vik's old golf clubs. "It worked for me." He winked at her and Hana sighed.

"I suppose. I'll concentrate on the garage sale for now and at least I'll feel I'm achieving something." Hana stuffed a pair of child's shoes into a dustbin bag. "If I can get your truck in the garage, it will be a start."

Logan stood up and jerked his head towards the bag in her hand. "Can't you give those away?" he asked.

"No." Hana shook her head and peered into the bag. "They're Bodie's. He walked through the soles. I don't know how old they are."

Logan lifted his arms above his head and stretched his back, his palms almost touching the ceiling. "The rest of your house is immaculate," he said. "Why did you keep old stuff down here?"

Hana shrugged. "The garage and my wardrobe. I don't know the answer to that question. I needed somewhere to put things that reminded me of what I lost. I'm looking at it now and it's mainly crap. I don't know what I was thinking." She dropped a pile of rags into the bag on top of the shoes, cloths made from Vik's old work shirts. Her eyes strayed to the tools hanging on the wall. "I don't think I can face those. Nobody's touched them since Vik last used them."

"It's okay." Logan's arms felt strong around her and Hana closed her eyes against his shirt. The night sounds continued beyond the screen of the metal door and Hana blocked them out, concentrating on the love she drew from Logan's presence.

"Have I got enough worth selling?" she asked, her voice betraying tiredness and emotional strain.

"Maybe." Logan stroked her back as she pulled away, settling his arm over her shoulder. "You can't do a garage sale though."

"Yeah, I can." Hana furrowed her brow and poked his ribs. "It's easy. You put a sign on the main road and open the garage door. People sift through and offer you cash for your trash." She grinned at her poetic skill and looked at Logan for approval. She got none.

"It's stupid." His eyes narrowed. "You've been mugged, crashed into and threatened. It's not the greatest idea to open your doors and let them walk in. Or am I missing something here?"

"I won't let them in, will I?" Hana rolled her eyes and Logan spun her around, facing her with determination in his face.

"Do you think you can stop them?" He cocked his head to one side. "You've not had much luck with that so far."

Hana pouted and waved an arm around the garage, taking in the boxes and rubbish bags. "What do I do with all this then?" She felt deflated, her efforts worthless and her plan reduced to foolishness.

Logan poked his tongue into the corner of his mouth and observed her through fathomless grey eyes. "I said I'd help and I will." He jerked his head towards the items nearest the door. "I'll load the truck tonight with the golf clubs and saleable stuff and you drive it to school tomorrow. I'll deal with it. We'll fit as much of the rubbish in as possible and I'll drive the truck to the dump in my free period. Yeah?" His knuckles felt hard against the skin of her cheek and she twisted her face to kiss them.

"I promised myself I'd let go of my past, but how can I if you're doing it all for me?"

Logan wrinkled his nose and gave her a lopsided smile. "Hana, you've done the worst bit. You chose what to trash and what to sell. Look at it." He pointed around the room. "Apart from the tools and those shelves by the door, it's clear."

"Oh, yeah." Hana looked around the empty garage, imagining it devoid of junk. Her smile appeared coy and Logan laughed at her, tickling her until she shrieked.

He left when their game got too heated, pushing the bags and gear into the back of the truck with a serious face. Hana watched him straddle the motorbike with narrowed eyes. "You look hot on a bike," she said, biting her lower lip. "Anyone ever tell you that?" She pushed her hands under his leather jacket, feeling a thrill at his cocooned heat.

He lifted his visor and braced his arms against the handlebars, revving the throttle. "Nobody I wanted to hear it from," he replied, his eyes smiling.

Hana pressed her lips against his, turning her face sideways to reach under his visor. "You'll keep," she said with a smile and stepped back to let him go. Logan winked as he backed the bike up and turned on the driveway, easing onto the road behind a neighbour's passing car. He gave a single wave and exited the street, not noticing the dark saloon which eased around the corner.

Hana's heart thudded in her chest as she ran into the garage and depressed the switch, dropping the door with its usual slowness. She watched until the last gap disappeared and then relaxed, running upstairs to watch through the front window. Keeping the lights off, she observed the dark car settle across the street. The blond driver got out and checked around him before ambling across in a casual walk. He climbed Hana's driveway and nosed around the truck, using his hand to shield the light from the streetlamps. He kicked the rear tyre and then glanced up at the window as though he knew Hana watched him. She crouched on the floor, her forehead barely above the windowsill and a leaden sickness began in her chest.

The car left but the sickness didn't. It took up permanent residence and stayed the night, ruining her sleep and destroying her sense of safety. She should've rung the cops or texted Logan but she did neither. The blond man looked straight at her, covetousness and possession in his eyes. How could she communicate that to someone else?

Rushing into the special briefing the next day, Hana seated herself amongst the other support staff only seconds before the bell rang. Alan Dobbs droned on about litter and detention supervision and Hana grew bored, her attention turning to her colleagues. The staff turnover proved minimal from year to year. A great place to work, people came in their thirties and stayed till retirement, coveting the gold plated carriage clock which bore the school crest. Hana picked out the faces who began as colleagues and finished as friends. Sunita poked her tongue out and crossed her eyes, making Hana smirk and look away. She missed Anka and peered sideways at the receptionist whose thighs spilled over the seat of the hard chair. The woman gave her a pompous look and Hana averted her gaze.

Gwynne sat just in front of Logan, arty and unkempt against the English teacher's pristine turnout. An expensive shirt fitted Logan like a glove, allowing for his strong chest and defined biceps. He leaned back in his chair and Hana detected boredom in his twinkling grey eyes. He noticed her looking and smiled a slight movement of the lips showing a dimple in his right cheek. She remembered the sensation of his lips on her neck the night before and fanned herself with a wad of bulletins, the unmistakable blush creeping up her neck and into her cheeks. "Hot flush," she hissed to the receptionist when the woman tipped forward to give her a curious look.

"Well, you're at that age," the gravelly voice of Angus' assistant growled from behind her. Hana resisted the urge to turn around, catching Logan's smile and the one raised eyebrow. He knew what ailed her and she covered her grin with the papers.

The blush under control, Hana avoided looking at Logan. Directly in her eye line, she sensed his penetrating gaze reading her face. Instead, she focussed on Peter North for entertainment and distraction, rewarded by his loud yawn. Donald Watson leaned sideways to glare at Pete and then looked straight at her as though making her culpable. Hana gulped and looked down at her hands, trying to stay out of trouble.

The meeting drew to a close and Hana peeked across at Angus. He squirmed in his chair as though afflicted with piles, his silence uncharacteristic. Donald waited for Dobbs to sit down and then bounced to his feet, grasping the moment as he unleashed his latest diktat. "The board of trustees wishes to remind all staff that relationships between staff members are strictly forbidden. They are an unnecessary distraction from the quality teaching and administration expected by our parents and students." He puffed himself up to his thickset height of not very much and issued his threat. "We are a Christian establishment. Fraternisation will not be tolerated." He sat down with a thud, a fine layer of dust guffing from his chair cushion.

Angus sat like a statue as silence resonated its nothingness around the hushed audience. He stared at a point on the ceiling where the rain came in the previous winter. Hana hid behind the notices, pretending to read them while concentrating on her breathing. She couldn't look at Logan, knowing this heralded the end of a beautiful thing. She couldn't leave and neither would he. Over before it started.

Hana waited until everyone else got up to leave and then bolted to the office. Behind her retreating back, she overheard the mutterings of dissent.

"They can't do that!"

"That's ridiculous!"

"I'm talking to the union about this!"

"There is no union stupid, it's a private school!"

"They can't enforce it."

"It's in our contracts. Remember, that paper you signed without reading while you celebrated getting the job?"

Hana sped to her desk and sat down with a thump. Her heart pounded and a mixture of embarrassment and disappointment consumed her. "Dead in the water," she said with a tearful sigh. "Shortest relationship since Alan Reeves in Year 2."

As she struggled with the bitterness which threatened to overthrow her, Hana heard footsteps. Thinking it was Sheila returning, she hauled herself together and put her password into the computer. A gentle hand on her shoulder made her turn, biting the inside of her cheek to distract her from the misery. Peter North followed the squeeze with a pat, a little too hard, but filled with compassion. "That sucks!" he said with conviction.

Hana found she couldn't answer. She excused herself and ran to the disabled toilet on the ground floor, spending the next hour watching herself cry into the mirror. Pitiful and not at all satisfying.

She emerged to a fire storm. Sheila's vast sense of overreaction flared and she ranted and raved to anyone with the time to listen. "How can I not have a relationship with my own husband?" she demanded. "I have to fraternise with him, otherwise how will I make him do what I want?"

"I wish I didn't have to fraternise with either of them," Rory grumbled. An idea popped into his head and his chin lifted as he thought it through. He caught Hana's gaze and grinned.

"It won't work," she said with a sigh, bursting his bubble. "Wrong sort of relationship."

Sheila ranted to anyone who showed an interest, including a bank recruiter who came to see boys and suffered an hour of it. She made a long distance and very heated phone call to her mother on the office phone, conducting it in fluent Swedish. Hana wished she'd shut up. In every language.

Pete remained silent on the matter until a teacher aide suggested Henrietta might be out of bounds. "She's a school recruitment officer," the woman said, as though Pete didn't know that. "Will it be allowed, or is that considered a 'school relationship'?" The small woman with large breasts escaping from her tiny tee shirt used her fingers to make inverted commas in the air.

"It?" Pete stood up and Hana tensed, knowing the signs. "I'm not getting any of it, so I wouldn't know!"

The woman ducked just in time and the paperweight missed her by a hair's breadth. "Bloody hell!" she shrieked as it hit the wall where her face sniggered seconds before.

"Shut up about it!" Pete yelled, a purplish flush spreading up his neck and through his wispy hair. "Just shut up!"

"What did you do?" Sheila emerged from her office to examine the hole in the wall, the paperweight stuck at a jaunty angle in the plasterboard. Pete skittered from the room in a mixture of temper and fear.

The teacher aide bristled. "That guy needs the opposite to Viagra," she stated and turned to leave. "Who needs a horny sports teacher?"

"Hana," Sheila called after her. She jerked her head in Hana's direction. "The toy-boy teaches sport sometimes."

Hana felt like her life upended in a single sentence, robbing her of rational thought. They weighed on her, the house sale and her feelings for Logan, intensifying the sickness in her chest.

"I know what this is about," Sheila stated, ramming the paper tray into the photocopier. "It's Anka van Blerk's fault. She started this."

Hana blinked at her screen and ignored the comment, recognising an obvious attempt to play her. She tapped away on her keyboard and drowned out Sheila's bile, maintaining a blank expression until she left for class. As soon as the door clicked closed, Hana jumped up to drop the catch and sat back down, letting her forehead sink onto the desk. "Why me?" she grumbled into the wooden surface, hearing the sound vibrate back to her.

"Is this a private desperate moment or can anyone join?" Logan's fingers smoothed Hana's hair aside and he kneaded her shoulders with a massage which drew a groan. He snorted. "If you make noises like that, you'll get fired for sure."

"I don't care anymore," she grumbled, her cheek against the table. "I'm going off this job."

"Na, you're not." Logan tickled her ribs. "Keys, Ms McIntyre. I'm using my free period to visit the dump."

"Do they accept dead bodies?" Hana reached into the drawer for her handbag. "I can think of a few candidates."

"Na." Logan held his hand out. "There are much better places for those."

Hana dropped the keys into his palm and stood, her nose at the same level as his third shirt button. She looked at him from under long lashes. "I locked the door. Yet here you are." She wagged her finger at him. "And you got us out of the stockroom in seconds." Hana cocked her head, her eyes demanding explanation.

Logan smirked and tapped the end of her nose with a scarred forefinger. "If I tell you that, Ms McIntyre, I'll have to kill you."

"Yeah, whatever!" Hana smiled at the door as he let himself out. All trace of happiness left with him.

Hana visited the post room after lunch. A bottleneck at the glass doors from the staffroom took ages to clear and the tiny space where staff collected mail and other important items such as their lunch, resembled a beehive. The pigeon-holes for careers and counselling sat together, one above the other. Hana couldn't reach either. The room swarmed with bodies and she stood on tiptoes and stretched, blindly shoving her fingers in the slots. "There's something there," she groaned, looking for her chair to stand on. Bodies moved around her, pushing, shoving and complaining as they jostled each other.

"Yeah, this." Gentle fingers closed around Hana's and she looked up into Logan's smile. He handed her two invoices from the back of the careers box and her heart sped up its rhythm. She swallowed, knowing he saw the conflict in her eyes. "It's okay," he whispered. "Nothing's changed."

Hana opened her mouth to contradict him. Her contract stated otherwise. She closed her eyes and remembered signing it fifteen years earlier, dismissing the tiny one-liner as irrelevant. Vik stood ready with a bottle of red wine to celebrate her new job and she dashed off a signature without thought. How could it ever relate to her?

Logan's departure coincided with the entry of Alan Dobbs and Donald Watson, a festival of grumpiness descending on the busy room. "Stop that right now!" Donald screeched, pointing somewhere beyond Hana.

From the centre of the small space, cheering and clapping bubbled outwards. Hana whipped round in time to see Gwynne with his arms locked around the tiny Chinese lab assistant from the food technology department. Their kiss ended to a host of wolf whistles.

Paddy Chatfield from the physics department grinned at Hana like a serial killer. "That showed Watson." He waggled his bushy eyebrows and Hana nodded, keeping her opinion to herself. She attempted to leave the room, Logan's wake already healed over. She squeezed between the gawking teachers as Dobbs and Watson pushed through the throng towards the offending lovers. Glancing back, she saw a triumphant look on Gwynne's face. Watson appeared ready to bust a blood vessel and Dobbs like he already had.

Hana called in to see Angus on her way home, the rental contract clutched in her hand. She couldn't get near his office. A line of staff snaked from his door to the cafeteria. She noticed established couples in the queue and her heart ached for them. She backtracked, her own dilemma sitting heavy on her shoulders.

A series of silent phone calls plagued her evening. When she picked up, she heard someone disconnect at the other end. On the fourth occasion, she lost her patience. "Are you enjoying yourself?" she demanded. She heard people in the background, laughing and talking.

After a pause, a voice came through the tired grey handset. "I can do this all year, baby. Unless you give it back, this will only get worse." The click of disconnection made Hana jump and robbed her of reply. Her heart rate increased, knowing the blond man meant business. She rushed to the front window and scoured the empty street.

Streetlights flicked on as dusk gave way to the darkness of night. Wrenching at the cords holding the blinds up, Hana dropped them to screen her from the road. They released a cloud of dust into the upstairs room. "Bloody hell!" she groaned. She hadn't closed them for years and stamped her foot as one of the aged strings snapped under the pressure and sent strands of bamboo scattering across the carpet. The clean up took her until after midnight and she didn't sleep, even after checking all doors and windows like a compulsive. At every little sound, her body filled with adrenaline, leaving her shaking and afraid as it receded. The night felt unreal and when she dozed, it seemed shallow and without rest.

Hana drove to work feeling uneasy. The school had cushioned and supported her after Vik's death, giving her a focus to dull the emptiness. Now it threatened her first worthwhile relationship and she felt the burden of hard choices. She needed to speak to Logan.

The lab assistant's car sat in the chapel car park and Hana spotted Gwynne's truck poking out from behind the gym. She assumed they'd be disciplined but their continued presence gave her hope. Inside the building, the atmosphere seemed tense and a storm brewed beneath the surface. The staffroom hummed with whispers, patience proved in short supply and teachers issued a record number of detention slips.

Even the boys seemed subdued at interval, not understanding why the adults growled like bears woken from hibernation. Hana busied herself with general tasks, arguing with a company claiming to have sold the school a complicated drill bit. She put the phone down, not realising someone else had entered the room until she heard the lock snap closed behind them.

Logan pulled her to her feet and nudged her alongside a filing cabinet out of view. Then he pressed warm lips to hers. Hana inhaled in horror. "You'll get me sacked!"

Logan placed an index finger on her lips to silence her. "Will you come home with me at the weekend, to meet my parents?"

She hesitated, watching the hope die in his eyes. When he took a step backwards, she clutched the front of his shirt. "Only if they're not a Māori version of Deepak and Indra," she said. "Are you ready for that?"

"Indian parents?" Logan bowed his head and kissed her neck. "Sure, babe. Whatever you think."

"No!" Hana shoved his shoulder. "For me to meet your parents."

Logan narrowed his eyes and cupped her face in his palms. "Ms McIntyre, I never say things I don't mean. Would you like a weekend away?"

"Yes please." When he smiled, she raised her finger in warning. "But Watson is vengeful. You might think it's not in your contract that we can't date, but he'll white it out and forge your signature or claim foul play. I don't want you risking your job for me."

Logan rested his hand on the wall above Hana's head, screening her with his arm. He leaned down and touched his lips to hers. His grey eyes were serious. "You have no idea how much I'd give up for you." His voice sounded hushed and sultry.

Hana's eyes danced. "Not your job though."

Logan's lips felt soft on her cheek. "Definitely my job."

She opened her mouth to protest and he placed his lips over hers, speaking into the tiny space between them. "I'm not giving you up now."

"I should've called you last night," Hana gushed, her green eyes wide. "But I got scared you might think it's too complicated."

Logan shook his head. "Don't be scared, Hana. We're good. Anyway, I went out of town on the bike. No phone signal." He rained soft kisses on her face and worked his way along her jaw to her sensitive neck. He ran his fingers underneath the back of her long hair and it rebelled, breaking free from its clip and cascading down to caress Logan's hand. Hana felt her stomach clunk into her shoes and she abandoned her usual reserve. She kissed him back, drinking in the proximity of her skin on his and the scent of his aftershave. Logan's other hand pressed into the small of Hana's back and she heard herself give a tiny moan.

"Who's locked the bloody door?" The handle rattled with violence and someone jiggled a key in the lock. Logan winked at Hana and reached out his arm, releasing the dead bolt. Hana heard the sound of metal on metal and Pete burst into the room.

Logan plonked himself in Rory's chair with casual ease, greeting Pete with his one-fingered salute. "Hey, bro'. How's things?"

Pete stopped in the doorway and eyed them both, Logan sitting with his hands in his pockets and Hana wedged between the filing cabinet and the wall. "You'll get fired," he said, staring from one to the other.

"Do I look like I care?" Logan drew an envelope from his jacket pocket and lobbed it onto Hana's desk. He stood and sauntered towards the door, winking at Hana as he slipped behind Pete.

"Guy's got a death wish," Pete muttered to himself, dusting flaked skin off his chair before sitting down. "Place is a mausoleum at the moment with Dobbs and Watson hunting couples."

Hana extracted herself from the tiny space and sat down at her computer. "Oh yeah, what happened to Gwynne?"

Pete grinned and licked his lips. "Tell ya if you do some reports for me."

"No thanks. I don't want to know anymore." Hana turned her attention to a spreadsheet and heard Pete sigh behind her.

"Okay, I'll tell you," he grumbled. "They got married last weekend. But they got a warning for snogging in public."

"Cool." Hana smiled. "That's awesome."

"It's what you should do." Pete spun around in his chair, misjudged the swing and kept going until Hana saw the back of his head again.

"Get married? Or get married in secret?"

"Both." Pete's eyes widened with enthusiasm. "She didn't get her hands on the wedding rings so Logan's maybe still got them."

Hana's jaw dropped in horror. "That's sick. Stop talking." She reached for the envelope Logan left. It contained $500 in cash for the golf clubs and other garage stuff. Her brow furrowed. "He sorted that out fast." She sifted through the notes. "Tell you a secret. I didn't want to do a garage sale anyway."

"Oh yeah, Logan Du Rose sorts things out real fast!" Pete's comment sounded jaded, an edge of jealousy making Hana shoot a look at his bowed head. He sifted through his paperwork and then used the corner of a bulletin to wipe his nose.

Hana cringed and settled into her work with renewed energy. Worry kicked in not long afterwards. For every objection, a solution presented itself but the effort drove her crazy. Hana started a list of things to organise. The neighbour opposite would feed Tiger and often did. She'd tell Bodie and Izzie she wouldn't be available for a few days. Her pen hovered over the page as other questions popped into her mind. One left her flushed and panicking. Hana turned to Pete, clearing her throat and waiting for him to turn around. "I'm going away with Logan for the weekend," she whispered. "Do you think he'll want separate rooms or to share?"

Pete squinted at her, one eyebrow raised. "What do you want?" he asked, the question loaded.

Hana swallowed. "Separate ones."

Pete rolled his eyes. "Great! Another one!" he spat. "I've got one of those too."

Hana turned back to her desk and swallowed. Like she always did, she spent the afternoon second guessing her decision. She ran through possible scenarios and then re-ran the tape with different answers, arguing with herself in her head until she went into a tailspin. She missed Anka's common sense and wondered if it would ever stop hurting. "Oh, Hana, just go!" she imagined her friend saying. A new voice broke through the turmoil, telling her she shouldn't anticipate trouble before it happened.

Pete's snoring cut through her musing and highlighted the ridiculousness of her mental wanderings. He slept face down with an assessment paper stuck to the dribble leaking from one side of his face.

A telephone call destroyed her afternoon. "Sorry, Darrell can you repeat that?" Hana felt vacant as she asked the mechanic to say it for the third time.

"Yeah, look, I'm sorry. I don't know how it happened."

"Someone nicked my car from your compound? But it only needed a couple of dents fixing and a new bumper."

Darrell's voice held an uncharacteristic wobble as he talked through the problem. "Yeah, I know. The Serena's bumper arrived, but we had other jobs on. You didn't seem in any rush."

Hana sighed. "Note to self not to be so complacent in the future."

Darrell coughed, his breath wheezing down the phone. "I scheduled the repairs for this afternoon. My trainee technician wandered around the compound for ages. I got annoyed with him but I couldn't find it either!"

"When did it go missing?" Hana asked, rubbing her eyes.

"Not sure." Darrel sounded real guilty. "And I haven't told Doug yet. He's gonna go mental."

Hana closed her eyes and imagined the scene. Doug would start up about Vik again. She suspected he felt more gutted about the immaculate Ford Mustang Vik wrecked than her husband, but she'd never been able to tell.

"I called the cops." Darrell's tone became defensive. "They walked around the garage and property, but they can't file a stolen report until you call them yourself."

"Hence the awkward phone call." Hana heard the barb in her voice and shame washed over her. "It's okay," she said with a sigh. "I'll call them."

Hana replaced the handset, drew in a deep breath and then dialled the number for the friendly officer, whose extension number never picked up. Then she texted Bodie, who also didn't reply. In frustration, she flicked an email to Donald explaining what happened and firing up Logan's truck, set off for the police station in Bridge Street to file her complaint.

After wasting yet another afternoon making a statement, Hana went straight home instead of heading back to work. She spent the rest of the evening on the phone to her insurer, who promised to talk to Darrell. "It's a complicated case, Mrs Johal," the customer service operator said. "There's an issue regarding responsibility at the time of the theft."

"So who's going to pay for a replacement?" she asked, receiving a blanket don't-know. "I wanted to sell it. I can't sell something I no longer have!"

After wine for dinner, Hana rummaged in her copious filing cabinet for the vehicle documents. She found everything but the original purchase agreement. The telephone sat on the floor next to her, its long grey cable trailing over the top of the cabinet like a strand of dirty spaghetti. Hana peered into the depths of the second drawer when the phone trilled. Remembering the odd phone calls, she hesitated before picking up the receiver then said nothing, waiting for the caller to speak first.

"Hana?" Logan's soft tones soothed her. "Are you okay? Where'd you go?"

She sighed and filled him in on the day's extraordinary turn of events. A weekend away became more attractive by the second as they contemplated each recent nasty surprise. "Hey, thanks for the money. Who did you sell the golf clubs and the garage stuff to?" Hana asked.

Logan seemed vague and non-committal, so she moved on to the announcement at staff briefing. "Donald made his point pretty clear." She couched her unease with a hopeless impression of Donald Watson, but Logan laughed it off.

"Na, don't worry. It'll blow over. I'll marry you and then it won't matter. It worked for Jeffs."

Logan couldn't see Hana's shocked expression and switched the conversation to the arrangements for the weekend, organising when they would leave.

Hana replaced the receiver again, realising she didn't know where Logan's parents lived. He'd ticked one thing off her worry list, anyway. "No babe, I promise we won't go on the motorbike."

Chapter 29

Despite Hana's nerves, Friday loomed and they set off straight from school. Hana felt Logan's eyes on her as he stole sideways glances, worrying she didn't let him down. She ran through her usual internal itinerary of what ifs, wasting time and missing the scenery.

"And right on cue," Logan said as the truck shuddered to a halt on a wide road. Boats, trailers and jet skis' rambled ahead on tow, crawling through the tail back. "Scenic Ngaruawahia, bottleneck for the Waikato." He reached across and stroked Hana's fingers as they writhed in her lap.

"I've never explored out here," she said, peering through the windscreen at the imposing mountain range ahead. "I can see the Hakarimatas from my house."

"Yep." Logan nodded. "And Taupiri Mountain. One side is the back door and the other is the front."

"Pardon?" Hana's brow knitted and she lifted her sunglasses for a better view, staring at the distant, knotty ridge.

"It refers to the burial sites," Logan said, craning his neck sideways to look around the truck in front. "We sound our car horn when we pass by, to acknowledge our dead."

Hana's eyes narrowed and her fingers fluttered over an imaginary button. "What, like, honk honk?"

Logan laughed, crow's feet showing in the corners of his grey eyes. "No. You press for each ancestor resting on the mountain."

"How many times do you press?" Hana asked, turning in her seat as curiosity bit. She bent her right knee and pushed it under her, relaxing at last.

"Once." Logan's jaw ground and he swallowed. "My tribe is from the north but allied with the Waikato tribes during the wars. The Du Roses have one member buried beneath the royal family."

"Oh." Hana peered at the mountain in the distance, a new interest in its history and landscape.

"A car's broken down," Logan mused. "It's blocking the first bend into Ngaruawahia." He put his arm around the back of her seat and he swivelled his head to peer through the rear window. "Backing up, buddy," he mouthed to the car behind and cranked the truck into reverse. The driver pressed his horn in warning and Hana closed her eyes as Logan edged back anyway, gaining clearance to swing out without hitting the car in front. He checked his side mirrors and angled the truck left, driving onto the hard shoulder and skirting the traffic for a few metres. Hana bit her lower lip and watched his capable hands throw the truck around, the scarred fingers depressing the indicator and then turning left. Other vehicles followed, peeling away from the growing queue.

"Where are we going?" Hana asked, seeing wide, tree-lined back streets and chocolate box houses passing by.

"Back route," Logan said, negotiating a roundabout and then a bridge. "It's the old rat run to Auckland. I come this way on the bike." He didn't reveal the ultimate destination and left her no choice but to trust him.

Logan crossed the Waipa River and turned right into a country road which followed the conjoined rivers north. From Hana's left rose the Hakarimata Ranges, bush covered and thriving, the road snaking precariously across their mountainous feet.

"This is beautiful," Hana breathed. "I've never been along here." Vik travelled for his work and often described places of unexpected beauty. He promised to show her, but didn't. Hana turned to Logan but bit her lip to silence herself, banishing thoughts of her dead husband and feeling the familiar wave of guilt.

Misunderstanding her unease, Logan reached across and snagged Hana's fidgeting fingers. "Stop worrying. Everything's gonna be fine," he soothed.

Occasional glimpses of the main road across the water showed slow moving traffic at a crawl. Hana pointed. "The tail back is still there. It can't be because of that car."

"Yeah." Logan glanced sideways and nodded his head. "Maybe that car overheated in the traffic. There's definitely something else. I'm glad we got off there." He concentrated on the approaching bend, wincing as the car behind overtook, despite the driver's blindness to oncoming hazards. Hana held her breath as a rock face filled her passenger window, close enough to touch. The other side of the skinny road met the wide Waikato River, its surging current containing the thing Bodie never found that day. Logan swore as the car raced him around the bend, lucky not to meet another vehicle. "Moron," he hissed. The car's brake lights flashed on for the next bend and Logan shook his head. "Never a cop when you need one," he muttered. "But always one when you don't."

Hana nestled on her seat facing him, watching his strong profile against the backdrop of the river. "Where do your parents live?" she asked.

Logan opened his mouth to speak, releasing a slew of expletives in lieu of a destination. Hana's belt locked, pinning her to the seat sideways and she turned her head to see the dirty bumper of a white van swerve in front of them. It missed the oncoming gravel lorry by mere centimetres. Logan's heavy braking locked the truck in a sideways motion and only by wrestling the wheel, he pulled it to a sliding stop at the bottom of a steep driveway.

He sat with his hands clamped over the steering wheel and let out a slow breath before turning to Hana. "You okay?"

She nodded, although her face expression and wide green eyes betrayed otherwise. Her fingers fluttered over the seat belt switch and Logan released it for her. "The belt caught my neck." Hana pulled down the passenger visor and examined the red welt in the mirror. "Serves me right for sitting sideways." She uncurled her leg from under her and leaned back in the seat. "Thank goodness you were driving. I swear my reactions are slower." Leaning forward, Hana stared into the wing mirror, seeing the jagged wall of rock which Logan managed to avoid. She sighed and rubbed her neck.

Logan undid his seat belt and removed his jacket, throwing it into the back seat. He ran his hands through his hair and leaned his head backwards. "I hope nobody comes down their drive and wants to get out," he remarked. "The engine's stalled."

Hana stared up the steep slope. "They won't, look. It's for sale. Vacant possession." She read the agent's board and peered at the photos. "It's a villa, like the one you live in."

"Na, it's a dump." Logan shrugged at the agent's attempt to showcase the property. Even the skill of the photographer couldn't disguise the dilapidated aura. "Maybe nice once, but not anymore."

"Mmmm," Hana replied, her eyes acquiring a faraway glaze.

Logan restarted the engine after a few tries, put the truck into gear and pulled out onto the road. Their journey on to Huntly proved uneventful. Logan stayed on the back roads until they reached Rangiriri, joining the motorway for a few minutes and then leaving it behind. They entered the tiny township after six o'clock, their stomachs rumbling. Logan bought food from a chip shop while Hana stretched her legs and looked around at the shuttered shops and empty street. Small town New Zealand attracted her like a magnet, where it sent others screaming in the other direction.

Logan returned with battered hoki fish and chips. They ate from the paper wrapper, washing it down with a shared bottle of cola. "I could do this," Hana commented, licking her fingers. She jerked her head towards the deserted shops. "I like small towns. I love the community feel; Hamilton's always felt too big for me."

Logan wiped his fingers on a handkerchief and put his arm around her shoulder. He rested his cheek on the top of her head. "Good," he said, Hana's hair masking the upward curve of his lips. She crumpled up the wrapper and shoved it into a nearby rubbish bin but remained standing, her posture betraying awkwardness.

"I want to talk about Anka," she said, her fingers writhing in front of her. Logan's body stiffened and the mask shuttered down over his emotions. "She said his father beat Tama up, but wasn't his real father after all. His mother abandoned him as a baby." She swallowed, seeing a strange warning flash across Logan's face. "But that's your family. They're related to you."

Logan leaned forward and placed his elbows on his knees with care, as though measuring the optimum pressure required to rest his jaw on his hand. He sighed. "Maybe we should've had this conversation before we left," he said.

Hana sat next to him on the bench, leaving a distance between them. "Sorry. Courage isn't my strong point."

Logan looked wrong footed, leaning back on the bench and stretching his arm out behind her. The action suggested possession and Hana swallowed. He studied her, holding her gaze with stormy grey eyes. "You won't see Tama," he said. "Or any of his family. My father and uncle haven't spoken for forty years."

"Oh." Hana contemplated his answer, drawing comfort. She wanted to probe more but daren't, diverting the conversation back to Anka. "She said Tama needed her, like a hurt puppy dog. He made her feel good about herself."

Logan inhaled, the sound like a hiss of irritation. He took a swig from the cola bottle. "He tells a different story." His eyes narrowed. "Things aren't always as they seem." A flame flickered in his eyes as he wiped his mouth with the back of his hand.

"She said she was his first." Hana chewed her lip, curiosity leading her down a hazardous route.

Logan snorted. "I don't think so, Hana." He looked away and she caught the tail end of a smirk. "That kid's had more sex than a prize bull. But he's a great actor."

Hana swallowed and leaned back against the bench. "Oh, dear. So it's all lies then?"

"No." Logan sounded nonchalant, a hint the candid moment drew to a close. "The rest is true. If it's any consolation, he's in love with her. I guess how he got there doesn't matter. They're both as addled as each other."

"If your family doesn't speak to his family, why are you involved?" The question hung between them, a knotty issue for another time.

"Because I am." Logan lifted his hand towards her face and Hana winced. He saw and his brows knitted. Finishing the action, Logan brushed her fringe away from her eyes. "I'll never hurt you, Hana," he said, his eyes blazing. "Never."

She nodded and her lashes flickered. "Okay."

Logan's jaw worked in his face and he forced a smile. "Are you ready?"

"Yep." She rose and slung the cola bottle into the dustbin, her footsteps heavy as she walked to the truck. It felt overwhelming, like stepping off a cliff into nothing. Logan's arms enfolded her as she reached for the door handle. He held her, pressing her into him and obliterating the small town from view.

"Trust me," he whispered into her ear. "Just trust me."

They left the town and turned towards Glen Murray, then left that road too. The lanes became narrow and twisted, navigating through harsher countryside as they drove west. After a while, Logan turned right onto an unsealed road and the truck bumped and lurched over potholes.

"In England, you get more warning of things," Hana mused. "Day gets lowered into night like God's putting away toys into a box. In New Zealand, you get no warning. Daylight winks out and the tide rushes around your feet. I don't get it. It's the same earth and the same moon, isn't it?"

"Yeah." Logan oozed tension and Hana's nerves hiked. He wanted her to trust him, whilst looking anxious himself. It didn't bode well. "You need to visit England to see what I mean," she concluded. "You just get more time for things."

Logan's eyes darted to her with a curious expression on his face. He said nothing, navigating the road with expertise and familiarity.

As night pursued them with a vengeance, Hana spotted bites out of the road which left her looking through gaping wash outs. They wound around the mountain until her ears ached with the altitude. The road spun downhill and she swallowed until her ears popped and normal hearing resumed. Logan's eyes glinted in the reflection of the headlights and she calmed herself with breathing exercises. If he heard, he didn't mention it.

Twinkling lights appeared in the basin of a distant valley. Bright and welcoming, they promised comfort and warmth. Still some distance away, the house appeared and disappeared as the truck picked its way around the mountain. On the final approach, they passed through magnificent wrought iron gates. Gravel scrunched beneath the truck tyres as the enormous floodlit house swung into view. Logan swept the truck around a circular driveway and slewed to a halt in front of sweeping steps crowned by carved, wooden doors.

"Breathe, Hana, breathe," she implored herself as Logan slammed the driver's door. "You can do this, you're not too old for him, you're not." She squeezed a finger and thumb either side of the bridge of her nose. "You are, you are."

Hana scrabbled at the internal handle as Logan opened the door. Her eyes looked huge in her pale face and she drew her legs away from him. He leaned into the vehicle and put his hands on the edge of her seat. "What's wrong, Hana?"

"I'm scared," she whispered. "I'm older than you; they'll notice."

Logan climbed onto the side rail and crouched down, holding onto the chassis. "Hana, it's all fine," he said with a sigh. "I've told them everything about you. My parents can't wait to meet you."

"Only to warn me off!" She ran her hands through her hair and panicked. Closing her eyes and wishing herself back to the safety of Achilles Rise didn't help. The prospect seemed grey and lonely.

Logan let out a soft snuff and clasped her chin in his fingers. "You're gorgeous and they'll approve. I'm happy; they'll be happy. Get out of the car."

Hana inhaled and opened her eyes. She swallowed. "But there are things you don't know. They might not understand."

"Hana, out." Logan tugged on her arm, a look of amusement on his face. He quirked an eyebrow upwards. "Do I need to put you over my shoulder like a caveman?"

"No." Hana backed away further, staring up at Logan's family home. Built of old stone with the symmetry and poise of an ancient European manor house, it rose in front of her. A fantastic fake, it mirrored an opulence non-existent in New Zealand's history. The windows and pillar work copied a spectacular Gothic emphasis, rising to three stories. "I'm old," she blurted, feeling like a teenager instead of a woman in her forties.

"No, you're gorgeous." Logan smiled at her, shyness in his face. He fondled her fingers and tugged her forwards. "It's gonna be fine."

The ornate wooden doors opened on the cold night and a woman in her seventies flew down the steps towards them. Small but agile, she oozed capability. Her hair had passed from black into grey, pulled back into a fluffy bun which created a halo around her head. Logan's enchanting grey eyes twinkled from her face. The outside lights illuminated her skin and Hana saw the black tattoo on her chin, denoting her family lineage. "Inside, tamariki," she said, rubbing Hana's upper arm. "It's cold out here."

Up the stairs and into a lobby, Hana followed Logan's lead. His mother clasped his hand, tiny and wizened against his. In the light from a glittering chandelier, she turned to scrutinize him. Not convinced about something, she seized bifocal glasses swinging from a neck-chain and perched them on her nose. "Better, much better. Haere mai," she declared.

She turned to Hana and grasped both her forearms, pressing her face forwards. Their foreheads met and the grey eyes flickered closed before opening and staring into Hana's soul. "Welcome," she said in English and then let go with a nod of satisfaction. She waved her arm towards a row of seats in front of a glowing fire. "Sit, sit," she said. "I'll fetch a tray."

Logan pushed Hana into a sofa nearest the fire, giving her a moment to acclimatise. Books lined the walls either side of the fireplace and the hearth matched her kitchen for size. "I'll build up the fire," he said, pulling away the guard and reaching into a basket of cut logs.

Hana felt an unsettling sense of misgiving grow. His mother seemed familiar, the lines on her chin invoking the faint dusting of a memory she couldn't retrieve. It came again, more powerful than before. Déjà vu. She'd only ever seen one woman with a chin tattoo, so long ago it felt like a movie starring someone else. "What's your mother's name?" she asked, desperate for answers.

Logan glanced up at her and then continued his work, deft fingers laying the logs in a pattern designed to let the flames breathe. "Miriam," he replied, caressing the name on his lips.

Nothing. Hana searched the annals of her brain and came up empty. Logan prodded the glowing embers with a metal poker. Hana sensed he watched her from beneath his eyelashes. She ran a shaking hand across her face and tried to settle. "I made this poker in metalwork at school," Logan said, hefting it over the guard. "Best thing I ever made." He twirled it, displaying the ornate twisting of the iron in the shaft and the perfect loop of the handle.

"Always good with your hands," his mother remarked, laying a tea tray on the coffee table before Hana. Logan quirked his eyebrow at Hana and she fought the urge to giggle.

"Where's Pa?" he asked, brushing ash from the hearth and tipping it into the fire. He rose and closed the guard, inspecting his sooty fingers.

"Toby rode up with him to the stock in the forty-eighth this afternoon. He'll be here soon." She pushed a spoon into the teapot and smiled at her son. "I'm glad you came; you look well. Hei koanga ngākau." She patted his hand with sturdy, work worn hands but Logan's eyes flashed towards Hana with unease. He drew his fingers away and nodded.

"I'll wash my hands."

Hana's brow knitted with confusion at the Māori phrase. She knew that one. Wonderful news. What wonderful news? She watched Logan disappear through a door in the distance and heard running water.

His mother's manner seemed excitable, like a child with a new toy. She squeezed her open, brown face up in pleasure and Hana allowed herself to relax. Logan returned and took the cushion next to Hana, his movement subtle as he forced Miriam to sit opposite. She didn't notice, pouring tea for Hana. "He doesn't drink tea." She jerked her head towards Logan and Hana nodded.

"I know."

The heat of the fire felt welcome, filling the cavernous lobby with rising heat. A set of ornate stairs curved behind a desk, rising out of sight in a beautiful arc. Hana followed the line with her eyes, sipping her tea in silence while Logan's mother observed her. The other woman searched for something in Hana's face and it unnerved her, feeling the gentle tug of recognition, yet unable to respond. The flames roared in the fireplace, rising and falling in their short-lived dance routine.

"Your house is gorgeous, Mrs Du Rose," Hana commented, unable to bear the heavy silence. She meant it. The furniture looked antique, but the effect seemed comfortable and relaxed, not showy and pretentious. Expensive but useful.

"Call me Miriam, Hana," Logan's mother stated, staring at her through piercing grey eyes.

Just as Hana reached breaking point, a man appeared from a corridor to the right, his face friendly and wrinkled. Dirt filled a crease on his forehead from a hat and the scent of horses arrived with him. "Son!" The quiet voice contained the strength of command, hidden beneath a smooth, lilting accent.

"Hey, Pa." Logan rose and they pressed noses in a hongi of greeting. When Logan released his father with a slap to his shoulder, Hana saw a wiry man with a strong Māori profile. In his seventies, he lacked his wife's vibrancy, the cares of the world bending his spine into a shallow question mark. A delicateness shrouded him as though the rigors of life and hardship wished to drag him to earth faster.

"Ah, the famous Hana." He held his right hand out to her and Hana stood, clasping it and strengthening her fingers to greet his. "Call me Alfred," he offered and she nodded. His eyes searched her face, the greyness of his irises identical to Logan's. His hand tilted over hers, seeking dominance whilst exerting no extra pressure. She glanced down, seeing the hammer shaped thumb with the stunted first knuckle. Genetics.

Alfred sat next to his wife and accepted tea. Logan sipped water from a tall glass. The conversation centred around beef stock and over-wintering and Hana drowned it out, staring at a portrait above the fireplace. A regal woman posed for the oil painting, vibrant grey eyes glaring from the canvas. Black hair cascaded past her shoulders in curves and lines accentuated by the painter's brush. The weight of the world sat on her shoulders and it showed in her face. Tattooed lines decorated her chin and continued into her lips to give them a darkened hue. Hana felt life in the grey eyes and shivered.

"That's the kuia," Miriam said, ignored by the men who continued to discuss cattle.

"Your female elder?" Hana translated, cocking her head.

Miriam nodded. "Logan's grandmother. She adored him. Alfie was the kuia's first son."

Hana removed her gaze from the painting, something about it leaving a haunting hollowness in her soul. She felt grateful when Miriam rose and carried the tray away, giving her space to relax. She returned with glasses and a bottle of exquisite red wine, doling out a double portion to Hana. The alcohol loosened her tongue and dispelled the nerves and Hana relaxed. Miriam asked her questions across the coffee table and Hana answered, telling her about Bodie and Izzie and their various achievements.

"Your husband died?" Miriam asked and Hana nodded, the action slow and otherworldly.

"Yes. Eight years ago. Car accident."

Miriam nodded and crossed her chest in a Catholic sign of the cross. She didn't express condolences, just that single action. Hana realised the third glass made her ramble and she bit her tongue to prevent anything important escaping. Logan noticed and made their excuses.

The journey upstairs seemed endless, walking past more doors than Hana could count. She felt drunk and foggy, not used to high-end plonk which went straight into her blood stream. Logan held her hand, brushing his thumb across the tops of her fingers as they walked. Hana heard noises from behind the closed doors and worried about other family members bouncing out to meet her in her sozzled state. "Your mum got me tipsy,"

Hana said with a hiccough as Logan stopped outside a door and kissed the ends of her fingers.

"You helped her." His lips quirked into a smile and he pushed the door open. "Come on, wahine."

"Am I your woman again?" Hana's voice wavered and her feet stumbled of their own accord.

"Yep." Logan caught her and swung her onto the bed. "You always were."

"No." Hana shook her head and a clip pinged across the room. She put her hand over her mouth and giggled. Pain entered her green eyes, widening them with innocence. "You called me Mrs Johal. I don't wanna be Mrs Johal."

Logan winced. He sighed and sat on the bed next to her. "I regret that," he said, his voice soft. "It won't happen again."

"It sucked!" Hana's shoulders slumped and she twisted her face into a pout.

Logan snorted and stroked her hair back from her face, tucking a long, curled strand behind her ear. "It did. Sorry."

He stood and hefted Hana's suitcase onto the bed. She stared at it, wondering how it got upstairs. "You'll be okay in here," he said, unzipping it and flopping the lid back on the bed. Hana's eyes widened at the sight of her tatty grey underwear nestled on top. She lurched for it as Logan turned away, relieved when he strode towards the enormous windows and dragged the curtains across the aperture. "Tomorrow you'll see the mountains. They look amazing the first time you see them." His voice sounded wistful and held a deep longing. "There's a bathroom and gear to make drinks." He prodded around in a basket and pulled up a regular tea bag amongst the herbals. "Milk's in the fridge under the desk."

He turned and his eyes widened as Hana shoved her pants under the pillow, so engrossed in her work, she didn't catch him watching. "Where are you sleeping?" she asked, the wine giving her a false dose of bravery.

"Front wing of the house." Logan nudged her aside and turned back the sheets on one side. "I always sleep in my old room."

The walk to the bedroom had sent the merlot swirling around Hana's body, intensifying the effect. Her co-ordination failed first and she giggled as a pair of knickers flicked across the room with the action of turning back the covers. She lurched for them, missed and landed at Logan's feet. "Oh no!" she grunted, pushing herself backwards into the nightstand.

"You're a mess, woman," he said with a smile, helping her off the rug. "I didn't know you couldn't hold your liquor."

Hana shrugged. "I buy cheap stuff." She wagged her index finger in his face. "And it lasts for months and months."

"Right." He smirked, holding her upright with his arms around her. She hiccoughed again and he smiled with his eyes. "My mother gets the best stuff out and you end up paralytic."

"Shorry," Hana said, attempting to appear contrite. She pushed at the waistband of her jeans and then remembered the zipper, hauling it down without shame. She stripped her blouse over her head, getting it stuck around her ears when she forgot to undo the buttons and Logan extracted her with gentleness and patience. Her jeans clung to her lower legs and he removed them, grinding his teeth into his lower lip and working his jaw as she flopped backwards and hummed to herself.

Hana sat on the edge of her bed in her bra and knickers and Logan fished around in her suitcase. He handed the claret coloured silky number over, retrieving it from the floor as she missed. "You should put this on," he said, a catch in his voice. She dropped the nightdress again and stood, pressing herself close into him. His jeans felt scratchy against her bare thighs. Standing on tiptoe, she kissed his lips. "I always feel like I know you," she said, drunkenness drawling her sentence. "Like déjà vu. You make me happy."

"Good." Logan's eyes softened to the colour of pewter and Hana watched the transition. "You make me happy too." His fingers stroked her shoulders and his gaze searched her face. His pupils dilated and he struggled to keep it decent between them. Hana experienced a strange surge of power as alarm bells clanged into her brain.

"I think I love you," she slurred and then hiccoughed. She tried to put her arms around his neck and missed.

Logan snorted and caught her flailing arms. "Yeah, you do," he replied and kissed her merlot-flavoured lips. "You just don't know it yet." He sighed. "But you're also worse for wear and need to sleep it off."

"Okay." Hana flopped onto the mattress in her bra and knickers and closed her eyes in obedience. Sleep sounded like a great idea as the room spun with her eyes open.

Logan stroked her hair and she missed the powerful look of longing in his eyes. "Bathroom light's on, wahine," he whispered and covered her with the sheets. "Night, babe." His voice sounded husky and Hana giggled because he called her babe.

She meant to use the bathroom to clean her teeth. In a minute. The light speckled the room with silver and Logan left, pulling the door closed behind him. The heady merlot swept Hana's worries away on the breeze and she slept sounder than she had for years.

The king size bed felt empty and cold when she woke next morning and the pounding headache reminded her of her student days. A pair of knickers were wrapped around her wrist like a tatty bracelet and Hana groaned. "He's seen my pants. I want to die."

Sunshine filtered around the heavy drapes and she lay for a while, staring at the ornate ceiling rose. Forced to face the day, she found activity dispersed the hangover, helped by a strong cup of coffee and a shower. Then Hana sat on the edge of the bed and stared at the mountain scene outside the window. "He's right," she whispered. "It does take your breath away.

Chapter 30

Opening the bedroom door and peeking out, Hana regretted not paying attention the night before when Logan walked her to her room. A long corridor stretched to the left and right on either side of her, flanked by doors. Hana hovered in the doorway, wondering whether to attempt to navigate her way downstairs or pull out her phone and text Logan. "I can't do that," she hissed at herself. "Embarrassing." She rolled her eyes at the memory of the previous night's drunkenness and cringed. The tablet she took to calm her nerves before leaving school hadn't played well with alcohol. The eight-year-old stash in her bathroom at home needed flushing.

Hana took her bearings, noting the number eleven on her door. She let it close behind her but then couldn't open it. Finding it locked, she had no choice but to venture onwards. Fixing her eyes on a vase of pink flowers at the other end of the corridor, Hana headed for it. It perched on an antique French table, which looked original and expensive. A long window with leaded glass cast prisms across the carpet and Hana saw a view of the mountain through the hand-blown panes.

Her socks padded along the corridor, passing door after door. Voices came from behind some of them and she shied away from knocking, imagining her first meeting with family members starting with, "Hi, I'm Hana and I'm lost."

The rooms numbered past twenty and Hana swallowed at the dawning realisation. A hotel. The corridor ended in an elegant sweeping staircase and the pale, stripped banister rail curved beneath her hand, carrying her downstairs.

On the ground floor, Hana found the lobby from the previous evening. The main doors stood wide open, the cool air kept at bay by inner glass doors. The desk she remembered contained an occupant. "Hello, can I help you?" The smart, uniformed girl's face creased into a smile. A telephone rang at her elbow and Hana's eyes strayed towards it.

"I'm looking for Mr Du Rose," she said, feeling like a child.

"Oh." The girl ignored the trilling phone. "Is something wrong? Can I help you?"

Hana shook her head and swallowed, embarrassment freezing her tongue. Her words came out jumbled. "I arrived with him last night. Where will I find him?"

To her credit, the girl's smile didn't falter. "Which Mr Du Rose?" she asked.

"The young one." Hana's cheeks flamed. Something in the girl's eyes made her feel like a hooker.

She shrugged. "Which young one? There's a few. Take your pick. If it's the one I'm thinking, you won't see him again."

Hana stood on one leg, pressing the toes of one foot over the other. She stifled a muffled scream which originated from her chest and threatened to come out. "But we came in his car," she said, her voice wobbling. "How will I get home?"

The receptionist rolled her eyes. "Dunno. I can call you a taxi. He usually leaves cash." She fluttered her fingers around the desk. "Nothing here."

Hana gulped and opened her mouth to speak, not trusting what might come out. Many thoughts powered through her brain. No shoes, no phone, locked out of her room.

"Hana?" Logan's voice sent her heart racing into orbit. She didn't know whether to hug him or slap him as he rested his hands on her shoulders and spun her around. His eyes widened at the sight of her distress. "What's wrong?"

"I'm sorry, Mr Du Rose." Hana heard the receptionist gulp. "I didn't realise you brought her. I thought she wanted a taxi."

Logan's eyes widened and his face darkened into a fearsome mask. "No." His voice sounded laced with ice.

Hana closed her eyes and counted to ten, allowing Logan to hustle her away from the embarrassed girl. He led her along a corridor with a quarry-tiled floor and Hana stiffened her legs to halt her progress. Her socks slid under her and she wobbled. The question formed on Logan's lips but Hana beat him to it. "She thinks I'm a tart!" she spat, her voice wavering. "What kind of people are you?"

"Did you ask for me?" Logan demanded. "By name?"

"I was getting to it," Hana bit. "I didn't know there were millions of you, all bringing women back to the middle of nowhere and then shipping them out by taxi the next morning." She collected herself, pulling the band from her ponytail as a distraction and then trying to put it back with shaking hands. Logan took it from her and kept it, lifting her chin with his finger.

"Not millions." His grey eyes looked sad. "Only two do that and they're not here. I'm sorry. I came to fetch you but used the back stairs and missed you."

Hana chewed her lip and regretted it as her tongue got a blast of berry lip-gloss. She breathed through pursed lips and waited for her heart to stop climbing through her chest wall. Logan stroked her cheek. "You okay?"

Hana shook her head and stared at the tiles. "I'm waiting to see the funny side." Her voice sounded petulant.

Logan sighed and pulled her into his chest. "You won't because there isn't one. My brother's a dick and so is Tama."

Hana shrugged. "She thought I spent the night with Tama? That's gross. My son's older than him."

Logan gave a sharp inhale. "She probably pitched for Michael. He's a year older than me."

"Great. So not you then?"

Logan snuffed into her hair. "No, Hana. I've never brought a woman here for the night. That's why she didn't put you with me." He raised his hand to silence her next objection. "Not because I'm too young for you."

"I shouldn't be here." Hana struggled out of his embrace and put distance between them. Logan's face clouded.

"Well you are. And I'm not driving you back yet, so come and get breakfast."

"I'm not hungry." She dug her heels in, feeling the cold tiles through her socks.

Logan rounded her up like a sheep dog, going behind and edging her forward. "I am," he said. "And if you don't eat, you'll regret it later." He nudged her along the corridor and she stared through doors as they passed. "This is the service corridor," he said, driving her forwards with his hands on her shoulders. "Lounge, dining room, ballroom. We use this corridor but guests access them from the other side, in that hallway with the glass roof. See." He pointed his index finger and interested, Hana followed his direction and nodded.

She moved with exaggerated slowness, feasting her eyes as she passed. A stylish lounge contained sofas and a coffee table. Magazines lay in a fan shape on the polished wooden surface. An expensive TV hogged the corner, opposite glass doors which took up a whole wall. They passed a dining room with multiple round tables set for a meal and other rooms with closed doors and numbers on the polished wood. Logan halted outside an open door to Hana's left and an original ballroom opened out before her. Magnificent parquet flooring made her want to dance and windows flanked both sides of the room. It jutted far beyond the bounds of the main building with a stage set up at the very end. "The first Du Rose built this room for his wife," Logan said. "She loved to dance. He modelled it on the one at Versailles, but on a smaller scale." He shrugged and Hana glanced up at him, seeing a smile in his eyes. "I rode my skateboard through here one winter and my mother chased me with a switch. She said she'd whoop my ass so bad I wouldn't sit down for a week. It marked all the floors and I spent my holiday sanding and varnishing it." He sighed as the memory washed over him.

"How old were you?" Hana's hair brushed his chin.

"Ten." The clang of steel sounded in his voice and it changed, becoming rougher. "When I still thought the world was a good place."

Hana's brow narrowed and she felt sadness descend over them like a cloak. She pointed to a courtyard outside, surrounded by imposing walls and windows. Flanked by paving stones, a stunning fountain of a naked woman with her arms above her head graced its geometric centre. The woman held a bird in her palms, its beauty diverting her stony-eyed attention. "That's stunning."

Logan nodded. "It's my grandmother. Her husband carved it for her before he went to war."

"What's the bird?"

"It's a tūī." Logan clutched her tighter and Hana looked up at him.

"You said that different to how I've heard it spoken before."

Logan smiled at her perception. "They say it wrong. The word they say and spell is tui, which is a binding or a string. They miss the accents off." He jerked his head towards the fountain. "That bird embraces both meanings. It's a bird of wisdom and foresight in my family, but it also represents a binding of us to our past. Our heritage and the lessons of our forefathers are in us and we in them." It sounded so reverent and honest, Hana craved that strong family bond. She gritted her jaw at all thoughts of family and forced herself not to remember.

"Oh crap!"

Hana jumped at the sudden clatter and Logan strode into the room. His father shot from a cupboard, nursing his hand and swearing. He froze at the sight of his audience and sucked a blood soaked finger. "Don't tell the wife?" he appealed, his expression hopeless.

"Tell her what?" Hana replied, her question genuine. That he swore or went into the cupboard? Which was the greater crime?

"What are you doing?" Logan poked his head into the cupboard and his voice echoed. "Why are you messing with these tables again?"

"They keep falling over." Alfred sucked his finger and peered into the dark interior. Hana stood in the entrance to the ballroom, feeling forgotten.

Logan disappeared inside and Hana heard him complaining. "That's because you don't clip them into the stand. I've shown you how to do it. Look." Hana saw Alfred lean forward, his head and shoulders disappearing into the cupboard. "I designed this thing and made it myself. It works. It's moron friendly."

Alfred pulled his head out and rolled his eyes at Hana. She smiled in response. "Come on," he said to her. "Let's get you some breakfast before my son tries to kill you."

Hana's jaw dropped and she floundered as the old man took her arm and led her into the corridor. He pushed her through a heavy fire door disguised in wood effect and she found herself in an industrial kitchen. Miriam dodged a girl carrying a heavy saucepan and waved. Then she spotted the way her husband sucked on his fingers. "Alfred, what have you done?"

He stared at fingers which oozed blood along his wrist as though surprised they belonged to him. "Oh," he said with feigned innocence. "I'm not sure."

Hana stayed quiet, but looked at Logan for help as he entered the room behind them. "Sit down here, babe," he said, his grey eyes smiling. He sat next to her at the enormous bleached wooden table and reached for a clean mug from the centre. "Here you go." He poured tea and gave it to her, brushing her fingers in the handover.

Miriam reached into a first aid cupboard on the wall and produced a battered box, setting about her husband's cut with wipes and plasters. "Bloody men bleeding in this house!" she complained.

Logan jerked his head in her direction and looked at her with an unreadable expression. Alfred shook his head at her. "Hush, wahine."

Miriam dressed the cut and then seized Alfred's head in both hands, kissing him on the forehead. "Stupid old man," she whispered.

Hana drank her tea and stared at the stainless steel appliances, feeling intrusive. She twitched in her nervousness and without looking up, Logan used his free hand to cover hers on the bleached wood, his warmth smoothing and massaging her fretful fingers. He infused her with calm and contentment and she accepted it, drinking tea and eating the toast he fetched for her. Staff milled around the kitchen, creating an atmosphere of busyness and chaos. They shot sidelong glances in her direction and Hana figured they all assumed she'd come for the night and would depart in a taxi of shame. She worked hard to ignore them, even when they whispered and jerked their heads in her direction.

Tension marched back into her soul and took up residence with Logan's unexpected question. "You're okay to trek a few kilometres aren't you?"

"Pardon." Her face told him she didn't understand. "Is that Martian for a walk?" Her look of disgust raised a smile on his face.

"Kinda. Don't you like exercise?"

Hana winced. "I like tennis." She shrugged. "And I like watching programmes about tennis."

Logan shook his head. "No tennis. And no TV." He got to his feet and took her hand. "Come outside and we'll get you kitted out."

Alfred patted Hana on the shoulder with his good hand, the other swathed in plasters and clamped around a large mug of tea. Then he unnerved Hana further by wagging his finger at his son and lifting his eyebrows. Hana dragged her feet at the onslaught of impending doom and wondered if she could fake sick for the day.

Logan led her along the corridor past the ballroom and kept walking until they reached a small room at the end. He opened a door with a keypad and stepped inside. Hana's socks slid to a halt on the dirty floor, smelling the scent of worn leather and horse. Shelves lined the walls, covered with riding boots, wax coats and hats. A work-table housed a dirty cloth, an open tub of saddle soap and a strap of some kind beneath a metal punch. The room seemed dark with only one long vertical window, but the door opened to outside. Logan grabbed a cowboy hat from a high shelf and stuffed it onto his head, sifting around the other shelves for a smaller one. "Borrow this," he said. "Ma won't mind." He pushed the leather jillaroo onto her head and Hana closed her eyes in disbelief.

She stared down at her socks and drew in a sigh of relief. Logan stopped at the door and stared back at her. "Sorry, no boots," Hana said, trying to sound sorry, but not really.

"Pick a pair from there." Logan pointed to a shelf behind her and Hana's heart sank.

"Don't they belong to people?" she asked, curling up her lip.

Logan shrugged. "They're not here, are they?" He dragged a pair of black jodhpur boots from a bottom shelf. "These are Liza's. They should fit."

Hana prayed they wouldn't, but God put his fingers in his ears and sang 'la la la.'

"Cool," Logan exclaimed with satisfaction as Hana's feet slid into them. "They're my sister's."

"Won't she mind?" Hana asked, casting around for a rescuer. "I would."

"Yeah, but she won't know." His eyes sparkled with mischief.

"Can I ring her and make sure?" Hana asked and Logan grinned.

"No. But full marks for trying."

Logan wore his trademark cowboy boots. Black for work and brown for other times. He looked like he fitted and defeated, Hana followed him into the courtyard, waiting while he shut the door behind them. "It's a long time since I rode," she ventured, feeling she might spectacularly fail this terrible test of acceptance. "I was eighteen." She tugged on his hand. Logan snagged her with an arm around her shoulder and Hana panicked inside. Eighteen and pregnant and she didn't know it.

"Will you dump me if I fall off?" she hissed under her breath.

The colour green surrounded the property. Green hills soared above it, covered with lush green grass. Green trees acted as the backdrop and the green bush-line added texture. The montage of hues and variations conspired to produce a picture book scene. Hana dawdled, fighting for control over the butterflies in her stomach. Logan strode off ahead, leaving her to follow. Hana rested a hand on her chest as she stood in the centre of a four-sided stable yard, wishing she'd accepted the hooker-taxi an hour ago. She'd be home by now.

Logan disappeared from view, but Hana heard him banging around in a room to the right. He appeared bearing a saddle over his left forearm, a bridle dangling from his fingers. Hana galvanised herself and followed him to a half door where a grey and black spotted Appaloosa peered over the top. Logan clicked at the horse to move back as he dumped the saddle over the ridge of the door and laid the bridle on top. The huge horse moved back a few steps, huffing and puffing at the saddle as though making sure it was the right one. Hana walked towards the huge beast, breathing in its musky scent as muscle memory returned. She loved riding. She'd missed it.

Hana smelled that sweet, perfumed aroma of horseflesh and it brought back happy memories of her life before she messed it up. Logan groomed the horse, running the plastic currycomb over its body and dislodging mud and clumps of hair. The animal flicked its ears back and forth with the rhythm of the brush, but edged closer to inspect Hana. She admired the proud head and the ears pointed forward as she leaned in towards the whiskery grey nose. The head lifted and reached out to sniff at her face, scenting her with tiny breaths before making up its mind. One long breath and the nose sank onto her shoulder, leaning hard and lazily against her while enjoying the ecstasy of Logan's vigorous brushing.

Hana reached up, stroking the hairy cheek with long downward movements. "You're pretty gorgeous," she crooned, liking the animal's kind face but hoping she got something nearer to ground level. The horse breathed out in long puffs and Hana felt the damp air on the side of her face.

"Can you tack up?" Logan stood and Hana saw his eyes watching her from beneath the shadow of his hat brim.

"No." She faked complete innocence and saw his smile spread across his face.

"You're such a liar," he replied.

"I don't know what you mean." Hana feigned ignorance and moved out of his way while he retrieved the saddle and bridle.

"What's he called?" She made herself sound disinterested.

"You know that much then?" Logan answered with a smile. Hana watched his lips move and fought the urge to kiss them.

"Yes," she replied with confidence. "He looks like a male, all adoration and puppy-dog eyes." She smirked and watched Logan as he settled the saddle on the pointed withers, laughing at her.

"Like that, is it?" he asked. He pulled up the girth and the horse stretched his long neck round to look at him, the furry lips twitching in threat. "Yeah, don't bother," Logan told him. He tucked the straps into the cross ties and glanced at Hana again. She leaned against the door and the horse rubbed the front of his broad forehead against her shoulder, satisfying an itch on that hard-to-reach place and covering Hana's hoodie in grey hair.

"His name's Digger." Logan's voice sounded casual. Hana nodded, scratching the knotty poll and rubbing the inside edges of his ears. The horse snuffed and sprayed her again with damp, snorted air.

The animal made Hana feel mellow and contented. Logan moved him back and fitted the bridle. Digger took the bit, clamping and champing on the metal as he got used to it in his mouth. Hana resurrected the names of bridle parts from memory in her head: throat lash, cheek piece, brow band, snaffle. "Why did you stop riding?" Logan asked.

"Who says I ever did?" Hana lied, determined not to play her aces at once.

Logan smirked and said nothing. Once he'd tacked Digger, he retrieved a hoof pick from his back jeans pocket and made sure the mount's feet were clean. The horse's unshod hooves looked smooth and neatly rasped. Hana watched Logan's backside as he worked. His shirt rode up and she fought the urge to touch his tanned skin. The veins of his forearms stood out as he supported the weight of the dinner plate hooves, flicking out muck and loose grit with his pick. Digger picked his feet up one at a time in response to Logan's tap on his leg, his brown eyes sleepy in their sockets.

Logan laid the reins over the pommel of the saddle and closed the door on Digger. He walked across the stable yard to a door opposite, peering into the darkness inside. The face of a beautiful white horse popped over the door in response. "Good girl. You missed me?" Logan spoke with gentleness, running his fingers over the tan bridle. "Did Jack get you ready?" he asked and the horse nodded her magnificent head. "Awesome," Logan said. "That'll save time."

Logan turned to Hana and held out his arm, encouraging her closer. "This is Sacha. I've had her for four years now. She's home bred here in the mountains and I broke her in myself." Casting about him, he said, "I wanted you to meet Jack." The white horse pushed her muzzle into his face and he kissed the end of it. "Where's Jack, baby?" he crooned and the mare whinnied, a low, deep sound.

"Bring Digger," Logan told Hana and she baulked at the instruction. He unlatched Sacha's door and she thrust herself through the gap, eager to get going.

Hana faltered, hearing the sound of clattering buckets and the hiss of feed being poured. She turned back to Digger's stable in time to see him pawing at the ground with impatience, using his front hoof to scrape down the stable door. "Okay, now I get it," Hana said. "You dig holes." With shaking hands, she unlatched the stable door and pulled his reins over his ears.

An old man appeared from the stable opposite, barring the door by using his foot to swing the catch across, bolting it at the top in the same fluid movement. He walked towards Hana, his wizened face screwed into an unreadable expression. Bowed and bent like a weathered tree, he snatched the reins from Hana, shoving the door open wide. He almost caught her with its edge and she jumped quickly out of the way. The horse followed him, hooves scraping and clattering against the concrete surface. Digger looked even bigger than Hana realised. He towered above the old man and way above Hana's head, jogging on the spot in his eagerness. Hana gulped.

Logan towed his horse behind him, jerking his head towards a dilapidated kauri table at the back of the stable yard. "Mount up on the table," he called over his shoulder to Hana. "It's easier."

"I'm not riding this horse am I?" Hana's voice held a note of panic as she did the maths.

"You can ride this one if you want," Logan offered, pointing a finger at the white head. One brown eye and one blue wall-eye glinted and threatened from either side of a forehead dappled with grey. "But I'm not sure if she'd deliberately scare you. She's got a reputation as a bitch."

Hana's palms sweated as the old man led the enormous beast towards the wooden picnic table. She wiped them on her jeans and fought the uncomfortable terror burgeoning in the pit of her stomach. Logan's horse waited while he stepped up and seated himself in the saddle, his long legs clearing the cantle without difficulty. Hana glanced at the tan stock saddle on Digger's back. Beautifully embroidered patterns were stitched into its leather and it held buckles and hooks for towing cattle or other horses. The pommel looked a winged affair protruding from either side. "I've never ridden Western," she squeaked, her anxiety communicating hidden fear to the horses. Digger twitched and danced and Sacha's eyes flashed mischief.

"You'll be fine." Logan sounded confident. "I won't let anything happen to you."

Hana stared at Sacha's rolling eyes as Logan sat astride her with ease. The sound of teeth on metal jarred her nerves and she wanted to back out. The taxi sounded amazing. He'd dump her, probably seconds after his horse did.

The old man beckoned to Hana with exaggerated movements and her moment of doom grew closer. As she passed Logan, he leaned down and spoke to her, his voice low. "His name's Jack and he lip reads."

For a second, Hana felt confusion add to her panic, realising with a flash of inspiration Logan meant the man, not the horse. Jack positioned Digger next to the table and looked around for the quaking rider, indicating again with his arm for Hana.

She dragged her feet and approached the deaf man. He jabbed a finger at the makeshift block. With a tiny groan of protest, Hana obeyed, clambering onto the tabletop on her hands and knees. The horse seemed smaller when she stood up, until she looked at the ground. Dust spun away from the fidgeting hooves below. Her face paled and Hana felt her blood launch into her feet and away from her brain. Jack slapped her calf and looked impatient and Hana panicked. Reaching into the annals of her memory for the sign language she shared with her mother, she signed, "I'm frightened."

Jack's face changed. His jaw dropped open and he regarded her with interest. Not a single tooth graced his mouth but the wizened face might once have been handsome. He nodded and reached for her leg. Expecting another slap, Hana stepped back, but he shook his head and lifted the reins in gnarled fingers. He touched his chest with his right hand and then the side of his head, nodding. "I know."

Hana relaxed and he jabbed a finger towards the saddle and the prancing horse. He didn't sign again but his muffled grunt encouraged her to trust him. Logan watched with interest, his grey eyes shadowed beneath his hat but his expression attentive. She swallowed and looked at Jack for help. Years since Hana last mounted a horse, she suffered a momentary mind blank. Jack pointed at the stirrup and grabbed at her left ankle, almost pitching her off the table. It began to look safer mounting the damn horse. Hana shoved her boot in the stirrup and launched herself with an undignified grunt as Jack rushed around the other side and grabbed hold of the opposite stirrup leather, stabilising the saddle. It seemed easier than she remembered.

Her mind flooded with memories of being a small child trying to mount a big pony, hopping around on one foot while the pony fidgeted and tried to run off. Jack yanked on her other leg, encouraging her to put her foot into the stirrup. "They're too long," Hana tried to say, but he shook his head and patted the stirrup leather with no intention of changing it. His face held determination and an element of do-as-you're-bloody-told-woman. He made strange sounds in his throat which reminded her of her mother.

Jack stepped back and waved them away with a dismissive shake of his head. But as Hana watched, he jabbed his index finger across his lips in an action she recognised. It confused her and she stared at him. His face dropped into a blank expression and turned away.

Rapid footsteps slapped on concrete, moving from the hotel courtyard and into the stables. The horses started, the jangle of tack adding to the confusion as Miriam puffed across the concrete. "Wear a hat, you foolish tāne!" she exclaimed. "I keep telling you!"

Logan pointed to his Jackaroo. "What's this, Ma?"

Miriam clucked and slapped his calf, pointing towards Hana. "What about your guest?" She rested her hands on her hips in victory. "That won't protect her head!"

Logan looked across at Hana and irritation flickered in his eyes. "She's not gonna fall off, so it doesn't matter. Stop winding her up."

"Ignore him." Miriam indicated Logan with a jerk of her head. "He's an idiot. They all say he'll break his neck one day on that bloody hōiho. He'll lay on the mountain waiting for help, but everyone will just enjoy the break from his perfectionism." She glared across at her son, but her expression softened at the last moment. She leaned close to Hana and stared up into her face. Digger turned his head and sniffed the back of Miriam's blouse, leaving a line of whiskery slobber. "This is important to him. He'll take good care of you."

Hana nodded and gulped, fear reaching out to touch the other woman's psyche. Miriam patted her knee. "Don't be scared. There's nothing to fear." The words left a leaden quality in the air as Miriam walked back to the house, stopping on the way to communicate with Jack. He beamed with pleasure and pointed to his mouth, nodding with a grin. He dropped his bucket and followed her like a puppy.

"What did she say to you?" Logan sounded concerned.

Hana shrugged, unable to read the expression in his grey eyes. "Nothing, just not to be scared."

Logan nodded and lost the crease in his brow. Growing restless, Digger wheeled around in a circle and Hana tightened her reins. He shuddered to a halt on the hard surface and backed up, almost unseating her. Logan trotted over, grasping the reins and lifting them in the air above the horse's neck. Digger ceased his prancing. "Relax," ordered Logan. "Hold the reins in your weakest hand and if you want to stop, lift them up." Hana did as he asked. "This is a stock horse." He pointed to the bridle. "We muster on him, so if you pull on the reins and put your legs on, he'll cut backwards."

Hana looked horrified. Wide green eyes shone from a porcelain complexion and Logan leaned across and touched her shoulder with a reassuring hand. "You're doing fine. I'll tell you stuff as we go along. Don't worry."

Embarrassment washed over her, making her temper flare in response. "Your grandfather just threw me up here," she protested. "He could've told me that."

Logan floundered and his lower jaw dropped. His reply sounded acerbic in the silent yard. "My grandfather died before I came along. And Jack's deaf and mute."

"He could've signed!" Hana bit. "And he called you son."

Logan shook his head and wheeled away from her, aiming for the open end of the yard. He turned alongside a gate into a lush paddock and waited. Digger clattered after him and Hana struggled to relax and seat herself in the unfamiliar saddle. Her stirrups felt way too long. If the horse got up any speed, she knew she'd fall.

Logan watched her expression as she approached, his confidence failing. "What's wrong?" he asked, appearing crestfallen. "You really don't want to do this?"

"My stirrups are too long," Hana complained, keeping the whine from her voice. "I can't relax because it doesn't feel right."

"Okay." Logan caught up her reins and steadied Digger, indicating with a pointed finger at her leg, "Shorten them. We ride long because your leg stretches as you ride further. Up here, the stockmen ride all day. Change them for now and maybe lengthen them later when you feel more confident."

Hana struggled, pulling the leather out to clip the buckle higher and then wrestling it back into its holder. Logan waited until she finished and then leaned down to test her girth. He jostled the horses together. "Put your leg forward and I'll tighten this." He sounded disappointed. Hana levered her leg over the flap and Logan tightened the girth straps. The thought of disappointing him frightened her more than falling off. She regretted making him pander to her fears, watching his face for further signs of exasperation. Sacha's girth hung slack beneath her belly, more like a teenager's belt than a safety device.

"Are you fed up of me?" she asked, her voice wavering.

Logan licked his lips and gave a slight shake of his head. "No. Just scared you might give up before we get going."

Digger expelled his excess wind in a noisy fart and Logan stifled a grin. "That's what he thinks," he said, injecting humour into Hana's fear. He pushed her leg back into position, his fingers comforting against her thigh. His touch lingered and Hana fought the urge to grab his hand and plead release from the disastrous equine excursion. Logan slapped Digger's neck. "You'll enjoy it, I promise," he said with a smile. He leaned forward and kissed Hana's lips, smelling of toothpaste and coffee. She reached for the front of his shirt to steady herself as the horse moved beneath her.

"If I break my neck, just leave me there," she pleaded. "Forget I ever existed."

Logan laughed, his warm breath mussing her fringe. "Yeah. Like I can do that, Hana." He smiled and straightened her hat. "Suits you." He turned and clicked to Sacha with his tongue. "Come on."

He didn't dismount to open the gate, unclipping it from in the saddle and using Sacha's chest to open it. His horse seemed unconcerned by the clanging metal. Hana passed through the gap and waited for Logan to fasten it closed. The horses skipped on the spot, desperate to leave. Open paddock stretched ahead of them for acres uphill. Logan jogged ahead and Hana used the distance between them to practice stopping Digger by raising her reins in the air. He responded with ease, skidding to a halt every time. Hana's confidence grew as she sensed the balance of control over the immense piece of horseflesh, reverting to her.

The saddle offered surprising comfort and Hana felt she might survive the journey. The wings on the pommel made rising to the trot impossible and she bounced like a rag doll as Digger jogged to catch up with Sacha. She discovered if she flexed her stomach muscles and relaxed her legs, she gained more control and settled at last.

Logan slowed as they approached another gate and Hana waited as they went through the same drill. The next paddock contained mares with foals at heel, all dapple white or black and grey like Digger. The curious foals bounced over to greet them, but their dams stamped and snorted at them to come away like school mums directing their offspring away from traffic. Logan moved across the paddock at a greater speed, accelerating into a lazy canter. Sacha seemed unperturbed, but Digger disliked his encounter with the females. The foals made him nervous and he skipped and pulled after Logan, forcing Hana to give him his head.

She sighed with relief as they reached another gate and Logan opened it. "Quick," he instructed, jerking his head at the approaching foals. They got braver with curiosity, crowding around until Hana feared they might escape.

"It's fine," Logan reassured her. "They won't leave their dams." Hana watched as the force of maternalism over-rode the will of the foals. One mare designated bad cop by the others trotted over and nipped their hocks until they returned to the group. They sprang away from the gate, herded back to the middle of the paddock where they surged with excitement, bucking and kicking with joy over nothing.

Logan wheeled Sacha around and headed downhill, rounding the bottom of a steep slope. The imposing bush rose up before them, signifying the start of the mountain slopes. Once inside the trees, the temperature dropped as the native palms and canopy cut out the breeze and air currents. Sunshine shone through the deep shades of green in dappled bursts of patterned light. It was darker in the bush and Hana's eyes struggled to adjust from the brightness outside. Digger plodded onwards, picking his way along the track and avoiding holes and stones without direction from his rider. Hana let him find his own path, figuring he knew the route better than her. She left her reins slack on his neck, not trusting herself to yank them by accident if he stumbled.

Logan looked back occasionally to check on her, pushing on at a brisk rate. When he skidded to a stop on a sharp downhill and called out, "Whoa!" Hana panicked. Digger scrabbled for purchase on the track and Hana grabbed the hardy wings on the pommel. Digger's chin rested on the backside of Logan's mare and Sacha twitched her feet in protest. Hana closed her eyes. With nowhere to back up, a kick from in front would pitch her off.

Logan pointed towards Sacha's front feet and Hana's eyes widened in horror at the gaping hole in front of them. It looked like a giant took a bite out of the earth. Hana looked behind her for a way to turn, seeing nothing but the slender, winding path downwards.

"Remember those rains a few weeks back?" Logan tilted his hat back on his head. "Something's blocked the stream, so the water came through here instead." He turned in his saddle to face Hana, greeted by her frightened green eyes.

"We need to turn around." She searched his face, not wanting to hear his denial. She got it anyway.

"No," he countered. "There's not enough room. We'll cross here. Leave your reins long and lean back. Hold onto the saddle if you can and trust the horse."

He saw the abject refusal in Hana's face and squashed it. "Look, you'll be fine. Just let the horse do the work. They bum slide all the time, just balance and let him go. I'll go first."

With that, he disappeared, plunging over the edge to the bottom. The drop looked sheer and an avalanche of earth followed him, catching in Sacha's tail and covering her thighs with orange clay. Hana held her breath. Sacha used her front feet to balance, dropping her rear in a sitting position and using her back legs as a rudder. As soon as her front feet hit solid ground, she bounced upright. It took seconds. Hana's stomach lurched into her mouth as she watched Logan and the mare pick their way up the other side, leaping and bouncing as they scrabbled through loose earth. The upward climb appeared more terrifying than the down, Logan leaning forward to help Sacha gain grip. He looked solid in the saddle, his reins loose in his right hand and his hat square on his head. Hana knew she'd be unseated on the uphill, even if she survived the slalom down. "I'm not bloody doing that," she said to the horse and he flicked his ears in response.

Picking her way between the edge of the precipice and a punga tree, Sacha's legs took Logan to the top of the bank. He turned and faced Hana across the void with expectation in his face. His horse oozed exhilaration, tossing her head and dancing around as though wanting to do it again. Hana felt nauseous. She turned in her saddle to look back, contemplating the narrow track and the safety of the hotel. "I'm not bum sliding on a horse, not at my age," she hissed. She closed her eyes and consigned herself to zimmer frames and liquidised food.

Logan saw her glance behind and an expression of panic crossed his face. "Hana, no!" he shouted across the void and she heard impatience in his voice.

"Your mum promised you'd take care of me!" she yelled back, betrayal in her face expression.

"And I will!" he snapped. "If you let me."

"This isn't taking care of me!" she screamed, her voice breaking in terror. "I'm not doing it, not without a proper helmet!"

Despite the danger, Logan laughed. Mistake. He saw rage burst into Hana's green eyes and watched her body turn in the saddle, her right heel pressing into Digger's flank.

"Hana! Trust me!" he yelled. Putting two fingers in his mouth, he emitted a sharp whistle.

Hana lurched forward, grabbing the pommel as Digger obeyed the call. He dived headlong down the bank with sure-footed enthusiasm. Hana lost the reins and one of her stirrups, gripping onto the saddle with white fingers through a primeval need to survive. Down they plunged, slipping and sliding and lurching upwards without waiting at the bottom for her to recover. Hana lost all control, bobbing around in the saddle like a rag doll. She prayed the end might be painless and closed her eyes against the dirt and spray. Her hat tipped forward over her eyes and she held her breath, feeling the bunched equine muscles operating beneath her on autopilot. Cresting the bank to safety, she kept her eyes closed and still held on, not realising she'd survived.

"You can look now." Logan peeled her white knuckled fingers from the pommel and Hana glanced up, mistaking his smirk of relief for mirth. She raised her hand to slap his face and he caught her wrist in strong fingers. His eyes twinkled, infuriating her further. "That's better," he whispered, appraising her flashing green eyes and the high flush lining her cheekbones. "That's what living feels like, Hana. Scaring yourself witless once in a while."

She dragged her hand from his grip and pushed the hat back on her head. Her fingers trembled as she dealt with escaped red curls full of clay and dead leaves. "I hate you!" she grumbled and he moved Sacha sideways until his boot rested against hers.

"No, you don't," he said with confidence. "We both know that."

His words left her floored and she hated the lack of control it fostered. When he kissed her, she turned her face away and instead, he bit her neck. The horses scraped their hooves on the crumbling track and tack clanked beneath them. Hana's green eyes flashed like emeralds but she looked away first.

Logan removed his hat with his left hand and wiped his brow using the hem of his shirt. The action exposed his brown stomach, defined muscle pressing through soft skin and a delicious line of black hair disappearing into his jeans. Flustered, Hana glanced away.

Logan's grey eyes sought her gaze and Hana felt powerless to stop the windows of her soul opening for him. Fear rendered her vulnerable and defenceless. Her stomach plunged as though she crested a roller coaster and exhilaration filled her blood. Logan raised his hand and stroked her cheek with his thumb, his other fingers fluttering against the side of her face. Hana forced herself to breathe and then looked down, breaking the connection in case she revealed more than she wanted.

"I haven't told you yet today." His voice sounded husky and soft.

Hana maintained the haughty expression, still angry and embarrassed. "Told me what?" she demanded.

"That you're beautiful." He smiled and his kiss felt gentle, their lips touching beneath the speckled canopy of distilled sunlight.

Chapter 31

Hana stalled, trying to slow her heart rate and deliberately disconnecting from Logan. She reached down to replace her right stirrup iron and wouldn't look at him again. She willed herself to hate him for putting her at risk, not understanding his end game. Alfred said she should eat before his son killed her and she'd taken it as a joke. Logan Du Rose seemed fathoms deep and at the back of the heart stopping attraction, something else lurked.

Her battle plan to distract her poor heart from Logan's magnetic power over it failed, as the clank of tack signified Sacha moving closer to Digger. They snuffed and breathed into each other's nostrils as though conversing. Logan's stirrup iron clinked against hers and Hana glanced up to find him still close. The air between them crackled with electricity and her resolve crumbled. "Stop running from me," Logan whispered. He put his hand up to Hana's face again and she felt the warmth of his fingers on her cheek. This time, she didn't pull away.

He ran his thumb under her eye and across her lips before letting his hand drop back to his side. He clicked his tongue to Sacha, moved away from the edge of the bank and turned his back on Hana. Emptiness shrouded her and her chest tightened as though the oxygen levels depleted in his absence. Hana fell in behind him, her emotions still plunging down the bank over and over. She'd been there before and it wrecked everything. "Get a grip, Hana," she hissed under her breath. "One big mistake was enough."

"Sorry?" Logan turned as Sacha picked her way over a decayed punga. He raised his eyebrow in question and Hana shook her head.

"Nothing. I said nothing." She swallowed and screwed her face into a look of passable blankness.

They rode for another hour, talking as often as the track permitted. "Why do you have a French surname?" Hana called, stopping to admire a view of the bluest skies and tops of young kauri trees.

Logan laughed, his eyes creasing against the sunshine. "Does it offend your English sensibilities?" he demanded and she shook her head.

"I'm half Scots and half Irish. I don't get hot under the collar about Frogs."

"Frogs!" Logan acted like he didn't know the English slur. "A French ship travelled into New Zealand waters in the early 1800s. Her captain, Jean Francois Langlois secured land and invited the Du Roses to return with him in 1840 as settlers. They arrived at Akaroa to discover the British had annexed the South Island for themselves."

Hana smirked behind his back. "Sounds about right."

Logan nodded and flicked a fallen cockroach off his sleeve, causing Hana to examine the overhead trees with alarm. She patted the surface of her hat and examined her clothing. Nothing. "Local Māori agreed to Langlois' original deed of purchase and he retained the land as a matter of honour. But the Du Rose family migrated north and headed for Auckland. Conditions were tough and all but one man died on the way. Local iwi took pity on the survivor and the chief befriended him, allowing him to marry his youngest daughter. He purchased the mountain for farming with the blessing of Māori. I'm fourth generation New Zealander, but we maintain our French heritage, although to lesser degrees as the younger generation loses interest. We still have family in France. The first Du Rose supported Māori in the Waikato Wars, offering a haven for women and children during the storming of Rangiriri Pā. After that, we became part of the landscape."

"That's some heritage," Hana agreed. "Did he build the hotel?"

Logan nodded. "Yeah. Cost a fortune to earthquake proof a couple of years ago. He built it into bedrock in the valley, so it's safe from most shakes anyway, but the local council took some convincing. We've poured money into holes in the ground and there's more concrete and steel in the thing now than he ever imagined possible. Auckland University used it as a test case for structural engineering students. We shut the place for twelve months and almost bankrupted it. I wanted to pull it down, but it's also listed now."

"How did your parents meet?" Hana asked, interest pricking her.

"Usual way." Logan glanced back, a cursory look to check on her. "Mum's from a local hapū and my paternal grandmother was the daughter of the rangatira."

"That's a Māori tribal leader by birth, isn't it?"

"Yeah, good girl."

"So, could they be related? Your parents. It's not a big town." A twang of jealousy budded in her soul. He owned a history, a place in time to call his own. Hana swallowed it, with difficulty.

"First cousins. It's how they maintained the French and Māori whakapapa. All that generation intermarried."

"Oh." Alarm bells went off in Hana's head. "Won't it be expected of you?"

Logan's jaw showed through his cheek as he ground his teeth. His features scrunched in pain. "I do what I want," he replied. "I'm done pleasing them."

Hana sighed, her mind straying to Vik and their situation. "I'm jealous of your heritage," she admitted. "Immigration robbed my children of that. We belong nowhere. For that first generation, everyone seated around our table at Christmas is all we had. We made our own history and traditions. It felt uphill at times."

Logan nodded, his tone harsh. "Yeah. Isolation is a bitch."

At the top of a long rise, they encountered a gate. Logan dismounted to open it, pressing numbers into a combination padlock. Hana's brow knitted. "A locked gate at the top of a mountain. It sounds like a riddle."

Logan didn't reply, leading Sacha through and waiting until Hana followed. He remounted by standing on top of the fence post like a dangerous circus trick. Hana needed the toilet and grew more and more uncomfortable the further they went. "Not far now," he said, jerking his head. "Just over there."

Hana looked at the back of Logan's head for inspiration. Nothing about the flat, open paddock suggested the presence of a toilet block with fresh running water. She cringed and the worry grew, intensifying the feeling of desperation. She studied Digger's bobbing ears and realised she needed to dismount first. That in itself loomed as an impossible feat, especially as one might lead to the other.

"Wow!" Hana exclaimed at the vast expanse of water laid out before her like an endless tablecloth. "The Tasman Sea, right?"

"Yep." Logan leaned on the horn of his saddle and lifted his feet from his stirrups, stretching his legs. He pointed to a wide estuary spewing out grey water. "That's Port Waikato."

"So your parents' land stretches from the hotel to the coast?" Hana sounded impressed and Logan shifted in his saddle, a flash of uncertainty there for a second and then gone. "Yep."

"Can I see it on a map?" she pressed, interested. "It might make more sense. It feels like we've gone around in circles and ended up here."

Logan gave a tight smile. "There's an ordinance survey map back at the hotel. Or you can look on Google Earth. Not up here though. There's no signal."

Hana nodded. "Yeah. I love that satellite view. I'll do it later." Her mind strayed to the decaying villa on the back road to Huntly. She'd check out that too.

Hana watched as Logan dismounted with ease, keeping one foot in the stirrup, throwing the other leg over the cantle and stepping down. She pretended to admire the view whilst her brain reminded her legs they needed to do more than dangle at the end of her hips.

Logan's activity distracted her and she stared in amazement as culinary delights appeared from pockets in the saddle blanket. Sacha's flanks held a picnic, one which had endured a terrifying bum slide. "The wine's a bit shook up." Logan held up a small bottle which frothed near the lid. "Might need to leave that a while." He pushed his hat back and raised an eyebrow at Hana. "After last night it could be a hair of the dog."

Hana shook her head. "I'll be fine today." She leaned forward and dragged the stirrup leather away from her bruised thigh. "I'm not drugged up. And I won't be doing that again." Digger's ear flicked back and forward and he snorted.

While Logan continued to produce food from his patient mount, Hana dealt with the ordeal of getting off. She released her right foot from the stirrup and attempted to swing it over the back of the cantle, finding her stiff leg unable to comply. She resembled an arthritic doing ballet. After three more tries, she looked for another route down.

As Logan removed Sacha's bridle and let her snuffle in the long grass, Digger became impatient. He wrenched his reins free and dropped his head, eager to copy. He munched with eagerness, not caring that his neck formed a slide and his arched back made dismounting even harder for Hana. "Thanks for that," she grumbled, grabbing a tuft of mane and making her move as Logan fiddled with a picnic blanket.

Hana threw her right leg over the back of the saddle with gusto. She slid down Digger's left side, banging every buckle as she descended. Too late, she realised keeping her left foot in the stirrup was a terrible idea. Her nose touched her shin and the top button of her jeans flung itself open. She dangled there, her right foot a good ruler length from the floor and the tuft of mane shedding stubby hairs into her rigid fingers. "Damn and blast it!" With a squeak, Hana let go, falling backwards into the squashy carpet of lush grass. With a clang, the stirrup released her left foot and she lay like a snow angel under the azure New Zealand sky.

Digger snuffed around her feet, nudging her boots away and snagging the grass beneath. Logan's anxious face appeared from behind the gelding's dappled rump. "You okay?" he enquired.

"Fine thanks." Hana tilted her chin upwards and avoided Logan's eyes. She pulled herself onto her elbows and pushed the hat off her left eye. "I love the New Zealand sky, it's enormous."

Logan shrugged. "I guess." His lips trembled as he resisted a smirk. "You fell, didn't you?"

"Nope, no. Absolutely not."

He went back to the picnic and Hana hid her face in her hands. "Big sky?" she groaned. Clambering onto her knees sent the toilet problem higher on the urgent list. Hana chewed her lower lip and wondered how to broach it. Logan removed Digger's saddle, standing it on its pommel and replacing his bridle with a head collar. Digger ignored him, moving off over the grass like a primary school child at choosing time.

"That looks amazing." Hana kept her legs crossed as she admired the fruits of Logan's labour. Paper plates sat on a patterned picnic rug with sandwiches in plastic wrappers. A pair of tiny wine bottles leaned at cheerful angles on the camber of the rug.

"You can sit down if you want." Logan pointed at the rug and then jerked his head towards the cliff edge. "I just need to pee." He disappeared and Hana stared around, desperate for a hiding place. She settled on a stand of trees to her left and ran there, her sigh of relief sending a flock of birds cascading into the sky.

The sun shone warm on their backs during lunch, hot despite the nagging breeze. Hana scarfed sandwiches and fruit, sipping expensive wine from the bottle. "Riding makes me starving," she commented, peering at the squashed chocolate muffin between her fingers.

Logan nodded. "The long musters are killers. All you think about is food."

"How long does the longest take?" Hana asked.

Logan's answer made her eyes bug. "Two days. The terrain is rough going in places so we ride out at dawn. Sometimes fences are down so the cattle spread further. We take what we need and stay out with the horses for as long as it takes." He shrugged. "It's what we've always done."

"Don't you use dogs?" Hana snagged a wet wipe from a rustling packet to clean her fingers. Digger ambled over, anticipating a treat. Logan swore as the horse nosed his apple from his fingers.

"No." He shook his head.

"Is that unusual?" Hana probed and he shrugged.

"Don't know. We just never have. The horses and stockmen work fine together. It's how my grandmother ran it."

"The kuia?" Hana cocked her head and remembered the portrait in the lobby.

Logan's eyes softened. "Yeah."

Hana lay on her back and closed her eyes. "Wasn't this an amazing place to grow up?" she asked, romantic visions of Enid Blyton novels in her mind's eye. Logan seemed slow to reply and she stared across at him, squinting against the sunshine.

"Sometimes," he said, his tone thoughtful. "But not always." He pushed a blade of grass into the corner of his mouth, his voice faraway and distracted. "I loved primary school in the township. Ma home-schooled us for intermediate. I rushed through my school work so I could ride with Jack and Pa." He sighed and Hana waited. "The others weren't interested. Eliza's five years older than me. My brother Barry didn't care about the farm. Michael suffered a bad fall as a kid. But I loved it. There's freedom out here in the mountains with a horse under you."

Hana nodded in understanding. "It sounds idyllic."

Logan shook his head. "Dirt poor, Hana. That's what we were. Never enough to go around." He flicked the grass away and Digger investigated it. "Just before my thirteenth birthday, Barry got sick. Ma sent Mike and I to study at North Shore Auckland Grammar and we boarded there while she looked after Barry. Liza went to Wellington to study Law. We all won scholarships and satisfied the underprivileged Māori quota." He shook his head and gave a disparaging snort. "We owned a mountain nobody wanted. Pa wasted money sub-dividing some of the front blocks, but nobody fancied living in a nothing town in the back end of nowhere. All that land and we were the kids in a private school with holes in our shorts."

Hana looked away, sensing he didn't want sympathy. Or words.

"We couldn't come home during the first holidays because Barry was too ill. Ma sent us to relatives in Whangamata. Michael couldn't behave and slept with the eldest daughter, so they turfed us out. We hitched back to school and camped out in the cricket pavilion for a week. Barry died, but she didn't fetch us home after the tangi. She sent us back to school with empty promises. 'Just use up this year's scholarship,' she said. Then next year's and the year after. She let us back for holidays after that, but never to stay."

"But you achieved?" Hana asked. "For yourself?"

Logan nodded and his face changed. "Yeah. I found a reason. I needed money and to get that, I needed transferable qualifications. Teaching and accounting were my ticket out."

"Yet you love it here." Hana rolled onto her side. "You fit."

Logan reached out a hand and stroked her cheek. "It's the tangata whenua. They make me return."

Hana cocked her head. "The people of the land?"

"Yeah." Logan concentrated on twirling a strand of her hair in his fingers. "My ancestors. I can go as far away as I like, but they bring me home every time. It's like a tug in my chest and I can ignore it for a while, but not forever."

Hana sighed. "That's amazing. There's nothing for me in England, or anywhere else. All I have is here."

Logan's voice lowered to a whisper. "Me too." He became quiet and Hana relaxed in the peace. She rolled onto her stomach and cushioned her head on her forearms. Her body touched Logan's and he stretched his arm across her back.

"Sorry about your brother," she whispered. "People dying sucks."

Logan didn't answer and Hana concentrated on the activities of a busy tūī bird making a nest in the top of a kauri tree. "Did you find homeschooling lonely?" she asked. "With only you and your brother."

Logan shook his head. "We were escape artists." He smirked. "My pa didn't talk to his brother and we weren't meant to associate with any of his family. But we had this friend, Linc. He helped us make a track through the mountain and we built a den. We all met up there."

"With your uncle?" Hana frowned.

"No. His kids. They live on the other side of this ridge. We got away with it for ages."

"How did they find out?" Hana kissed Logan's exposed wrist and he closed his eyes, shuttering his feelings from her.

"Something happened." He withdrew his arm and his fingers moved to his right side. He traced the seam of his shirt from armpit to hip as though a bug crawled over his flesh.

"What are their names?" Hana asked.

"Nev is the oldest. We always got along. My sister dated his younger brother, Kane. My pa found out and gave her such a whacking, she couldn't walk for a week." He sighed. "Kane raised Tama. He's a nasty drunk and drove the kid's mother off early on. He smokes weed and is real bad news. My uncle fostered a girl a few years older than me." Logan licked his lips. "He never adopted her though."

"I wonder why." Hana watched a ladybird crawl along her sleeve. "Maybe her parents never let her go."

Logan shrugged, the action dismissive. "Yep. She always wanted to be a Du Rose."

"That's sad. She could change her name by deed poll."

Logan's brow creased and he shook his head. "It's not the same though, is it? It's not acceptance."

"I guess. She's probably married and doesn't care now." Hana sighed. "This sun is gorgeous. I need a nana nap."

Logan enfolded her in his strong arms and rolled her on top of him. Hana felt attraction burgeon like a flower in her heart as she ran her hands across his chest. He put a steady pressure behind her head and lowered her face, his kiss firm but gentle on her trembling lips. He sensed her fear and stroked her hair back from her forehead. The tip of his tongue stroked her top lip, taking her breath away and driving her to the point of explosion. She knew he held all the aces, rendering her powerless to protest.

"You're beautiful," Logan sighed, brushing the side of her mouth with his lips. Hana wore her vulnerability in her expression and he smiled. "We've got all the time in the world," he promised as he pressed her cheek against his shoulder. "I don't want you to be scared."

His perception floored her and gratitude flooded her body. He'd wait. A cynical part of her brain wondered for how long, but she pushed it away, content for now. He held her under the warm sun and Hana sensed an ethereal presence surround them. God didn't sing 'la la la' with his fingers in his ears. Instead, he smiled with satisfaction.

Disappointment raged through her as Logan patted her back. "We need to leave," he said, his voice lazy.

"No!" Hana pushed her fingers behind his neck and held on. "I don't want to. Let's stay here forever."

Logan snorted. "I wish." He slapped her bum. "Come on, Ms McIntyre. It's a long ride back."

Hana rolled off him sideways and scrambled to her feet. "I'm not doing that slide again," she said, her eyes flashing in warning. "Send a helicopter or something. I can't do it."

"Idiot!" He chased her and pulled her struggling body into him, wrapping his arms around her. "There are other ways back."

"Now you tell me!" Hana's voice sounded muffled against his shirt. "Then why did we go that way?"

Logan shrugged. "It was the most scenic." His lips quirked upwards. "Now it's not."

Hana let him slide his fingers through hers. "You promise?"

"Yeah. I promise it was the most scenic route and now it's crap."

"No!" Hana dragged her fingers away and he turned and caught her wrist, a look of amusement on his face. She couldn't break free. "Promise you won't take me back that way."

"I won't." He kissed her, grey eyes laughing at her discomfort.

Logan whistled and the horses reappeared. Digger's muzzle dripped water and his hooves looked wet. "You've been in the stream, boy?" Logan said, slipping the halter over the flicking ears. The horse gave an answering snort which covered Logan's shirt in water spray.

Hana fetched the tack and waited while he sorted out the horses, their fingers brushing with each exchange. "Was the house always a hotel?" she asked.

"Dairy farm," Logan replied. "And beef. The whole family lived there when I was first born, but an argument between my father and uncle divided them. They left."

"That's sad." Hana's nose wrinkled.

"Broke my grandmother's heart," Logan replied, tightening Sacha's girth. "She never got over it."

"But the hotel works?" Hana said. "It looks amazing."

"Yeah, it works." Logan slapped Sacha's neck and handed the reins to Hana. "It's a money pit, but it's paying its own bills nowadays. Thank goodness."

Hana held the reins and waited for Logan to tighten Digger's girth. He left it loose and dangling and her heart clenched. "Pa started the hotel after the kids left," he said. "Best business idea he ever had." He winced. "No follow through though. No control over spending or budgets. He's like a kid in a lolly shop."

"What's the name of this mountain?" Hana waved her arm and Sacha glared at it with her blue eye, her head bouncing in annoyance.

"Mātakitaki." Logan said the name with pride. "It means to watch."

Hana gazed around her at the spectacular view and sighed. "It certainly does that." Logan's eyes sparkled and something in them made her blood fizz. She snatched at a memory infused with the worst day of her life but no, it danced away like sea mist.

Logan led Digger behind him and indicated they should walk. They stepped through the long grass with the horses tugging at occasional mouthfuls. Logan shot sideways glances at Hana and she felt panic rising. When he stopped, she wanted to scream at him to just do it. "Do you want to dump me?" she demanded, her jaw stiff.

"What?"

Hana swallowed. "You say all the right things, but sometimes your body language screams something else. I'm confused."

"Oh." Logan floundered, darting a look at Sacha and back at her. The horse blew out a sigh of contentment and snagged a mouthful of lush grass. He stepped in front of her, towing Digger. "I wanted to ask you if we have a future together. If you like me enough."

Hana closed her eyes against her idiocy. She shook her head and when she opened them again, saw the fear in Logan's face. "I'm cross with myself," she admitted. "Not you. I never feel good enough. Life is a balancing act of second-guessing and protecting myself against inevitable hurt. I anticipate pain and just want it over."

Logan squirmed with discomfort and his courage failed in his eyes so fast, Hana felt guilty. "Yes I like you." She reached out and caressed his cheek. "More than like you." Sadness flushed into her veins like cold water. "But I don't know what to do about work, or my kids, or anything." She swallowed and her voice became a whisper. "I want to keep seeing you, Logan. But I don't want to get hurt."

He nodded with understanding. "I know. But I'm not sure one comes without the other." The dimple showed in his right cheek as he winced.

Hana sighed. "That's what I'm afraid of."

His kiss banished all doubt and darts of pleasure filled Hana's stomach. His beard felt bristly against her chin and she rubbed the day old growth with her fingers. "When I'm around you, I get this feeling of déjà vu. It's so odd."

He kissed her one last time and shrugged. "Weird."

"Do you get it with me?" she asked, skipping to catch up. Sacha followed with her ears back.

"I get a lot of things around you," Logan replied with a smile. "I don't call them that."

Hana laughed and followed him to the fence, towing the white horse behind her. Her insides felt light as though they could lift off into the air and she smiled to herself like a giggly teenager with her first crush. Memories of Vik wiped the smile from her face and she banished him from her thoughts with difficulty. He left. He didn't get the right to ruin her future.

"You did good." Logan took Sacha's reins. "My horse likes you." He kissed the end of her nose.

"I didn't realise it was a test," Hana said, swapping them for Digger's.

"Life's a test," Logan replied with a wink. He spun her body and pushed her against Digger's side, running his hands down her waist. The sensation made Hana want to scream. Cupping her left knee in his hands, Logan counted to three and hoisted her into the saddle. "Do you want your stirrups longer now?" he asked, his tone serious.

"No." Hana denied him victory, even though her legs protested at being forced into the same position as before.

Logan slapped Digger's bum to send him through the gate, closing the padlock and then bouncing into Sacha's saddle.

"You promised," Hana reminded him and he laughed.

"Yep. I always keep my promises." He shot her a sultry look and turned left, skirting a track he knew by sight. The route continued downwards, much sharper than their ascent, with the horses picking their way through undergrowth and fallen trees. Hana leaned backwards to balance Digger and let him find his feet.

"I lied," Hana called to Logan, patting Digger's neck. The horse's ears flicked backwards and forwards at the sound of her voice.

"I know." Logan glanced back at her and smiled.

"How?"

He laughed. "The boots looked right on you. A couple of times you've mentioned a friend back in England with stables. I figured you could ride."

Hana sighed. "I started aged ten and stopped at eighteen. I helped every Saturday through school and taught the younger kids."

"Why did you stop?" His innocuous question wiped the coy smile from Hana's face and she searched for an answer.

"Life," she said. Logan didn't push it and she heaved a sigh of relief. Many women rode while pregnant and nothing happened. The bleeding which followed her afternoon of galloping and jumping, lulled her into a false sense of security and masked her pregnancy with Bodie. She blamed herself for many things, including those which didn't happen.

Trekking through the outer edges of bush, Hana noticed they followed a fence line. It seemed endless, a ribbon of posts and wire. In the distance she spotted a sprawling, timber clad house, spread out across a flat piece of land. "Who lives there?" she asked, pointing.

"It's Uncle Reuben's place," Logan told her, calling over his shoulder as though not wanting to attract attention. They followed its line until the route ended, severed by a fresh swathe of fencing which cut inwards.

"What the hell?" Logan dismounted and inspected the posts, shaking his head. A gravel road snaked alongside, circumnavigating a ridge which towered overhead.

"It looks like they couldn't go any other way," Hana said, eyeing the yellow chassis of a sleeping bulldozer. "They need access for that cul-de-sac."

Logan followed the direction of her pointed finger. He clambered onto a sturdy fence post to get higher and saw the curb edging and concrete piping ready to be buried for drainage.

"Will their water run-off affect your property?" Hana asked. "I suppose it already has. Perhaps their excavations caused the washout we came across."

Logan nodded, the movement short and jerky. He jumped from the fence post and mounted Sacha, whirling her across the uneven ground to regain the track. "Bloody bastard!" he hissed. Logan didn't mention the fence or road again, but his mood remained heavy and brooding for the rest of their descent.

Back at the stables, Hana dismounted with more elegance as Jack whipped Digger away. He took him into a loose box, leaving her redundant. She used the bottom of her shirt to dust Miriam's hat and watched Logan un-tack Sacha. He ran a hosepipe over her spine and Hana saw the flesh creep with pleasure, her head drooped and eyes closed in silent appreciation. Wanting to help with her mount, she popped her head over the door of the loose box and waited until she caught Jack's eye. "Can I help?" she asked using her hands and he shook his head.

As she turned to leave in disappointment, he put both thumbs up to her and beamed. The wizened face lost its angry edge and bright eyes twinkled out from beneath hooded lids. "Thank you," he signed in return. Hana nodded, gratified by his toothless smile.

Logan carried his heavy saddle to the tack room and Hana washed Sacha's bit under the yard tap. The tension between them felt palpable and again, she allowed it to gnaw at her confidence. Logan didn't notice her growing unease, hailing a dark-skinned man on a quad bike. "Toby, where's Alfred?"

"Fifteenth, boss," the man answered, eying Hana sideways. "Want me to get him on the radio?"

"Yes," Logan snapped, all gentle edges gone.

Hana's eyes widened in curiosity as the man roared away, speaking into a hand held device with a long aerial and doing Logan's bidding without question.

Logan took the bridle from her outstretched hand. "I've had a great day," he said. "You're everything I knew you would be."

Hana accepted the peculiar compliment and allowed him to hold her. His dismissal burned. "I'll walk you back to the house and then I need to see the old man."

"Okay." Hana tried to sound positive, helping with the picnic items and carrying the blanket back to the kitchen. Anxiety shrouded her at the sense of abandonment.

Logan's mother looked frazzled, wisps of hair ringing her face in a frizzy halo. "There's a party of eighty coming." She yanked Hana's arm to pull her away from the chiller as a woman emerged carrying a loaded tray of desserts. Logan's back disappeared through the kitchen door, leaving her.

"Do you want me to help?" Hana offered and Miriam shook her head.

"No. Just stay out of the way. I'll serve dinner for us when they're settled." She dragged Hana's sleeve and pulled her into the hallway. At the reception desk, Miriam waved her arm at the girl behind the desk. Hana cringed. "We're getting something from the office," Miriam snapped, hurrying past and dragging Hana behind her.

They passed a set of toilets and Miriam unlocked an office, closing the door behind them. "Help yourself to a nice bath," she said, jangling keys in a wide cupboard door. "There's one in your room." She turned to pat Hana's arm. "You'll be sore tomorrow."

The cupboard contained all manner of goodies and Hana's eyes bulged. From pharmacy to home wares, Miriam had it covered. "Here we are." She reached into the back and withdrew a packet of white powder. Hana's eyes widened.

"What's this?"

"Epsom salts." Miriam pushed it into her hand and tapped a bony finger on the label. "It'll help your muscles after riding all day." She locked the cupboard and patted Hana's back to make her move on, shooing her into reception.

Hana's body turned to jelly and the action repeated itself in her head on a loop. Miriam handing her something. The tattoos on her chin. Her brown fingers clasped around another object in her inner vision.

Pain and misery infused her psyche as the memory came nearer to revealing itself. Not a happy recollection, but one filled with anguish. Miriam bustled away and left Hana standing outside the office door, her fingers clutching an object which felt wrong. The same action but the wrong gift.

"Do you have a spare key to my room?" Hana asked the receptionist. She aimed for rude and dismissive and succeeded at haughty.

"Yes, miss," the girl responded. She turned to fumble in a cabinet behind her desk and retrieved a white card with a black stripe down the back of it. Her fingers shook as she handed it over, neat pink nails with white edges painted on.

Hana shoved the card in her pocket with the Epsom salts and sighed. "Thanks."

"I'm so sorry about before." The girl chewed her lower lip, blonde strands escaping her raggedy bun. "Mr Logan never brings people back."

Her affirmation lifted Hana's spirits and she nodded, forcing her face into a smile. "It's fine. No hard feelings."

She set off up the stairs in her socks, the grass stains and mud on her jeans making her less a part of the furnishings. Room eleven felt silent after the cacophony of the bush and Hana washed her dirty hands in the sink. The heaviness in her chest remained as her memory foxed her, giving her snapshots of Miriam's hands and then misting up the time and place. "I give up," she sighed, sinking into the deep bath.

Hana laid her phone in the soap tray and listened to music. Sounds from her childhood offered comfort and the eighties tunes reminded her of home. She hummed along, examining her bruises and soaking her tired muscles. She missed the gentle tap on her bedroom door.

Logan let himself into the room and sat on the bed, his boots dusty against the shaggy rug. He heard Hana singing and rubbed a hand across his face, leaving a streak of filth. His father's words rang in his ears. 'Youse weren't bloody here!' the old man shouted. 'Youse left, man! You ran away, just like you always do, so don't complain about the decisions I made in your absence!'

Logan stood, his jaw flexing. Hana sang through a terrible rendition of an eighties hit and he shook his head and smiled. "At least I know you can't sing," he whispered. He closed the door behind him and left no sign of his visit. In the hall outside, he felt someone watching him and saw the receptionist halt on her way to another room, a pair of pressed trousers on a hanger in her hand.

He raised an eyebrow and looked at her, seeing the colour drain from her face. "If I wanted monkeys, I'd pay peanuts," he bit and she nodded. He didn't wait to hear her apology.

Chapter 32

Hana felt refreshed after her bath. Her washed hair hung in long red ringlets down her back, almost to her waist.

The hotel guests arrived and Hana heard the party start downstairs. Many of them booked rooms and the surrounding noise increased. Loud music accompanied the banging of doors and squealing of women's voices. Hana sat on the bed fiddling with the TV remote, settling instead on the novel she brought.

She read to page four of the book before falling asleep, a feat considering the noise in the hallway. She woke with a start when the book fell from her hand and crashed to the floor. Her stomach urged her to check the clock, seeing the hands moving past seven. She made herself tea and ate the complimentary crackers, hoping they lasted her until morning.

Answering a knock on her door revealed Logan, balancing a tray against the wall and his stomach. "Hey," he said. "I've knocked a couple of times. Take this." He handed over a bottle of red wine.

"Yum. I love macaroni cheese," Hana said with enthusiasm, eying the hunk of fresh bread balanced on the tray. Logan set it down on the bed, producing cutlery from his back pocket.

"Hungry?" he asked and she nodded.

"Starving. I could lick the bowl."

Logan opened the doors onto the balcony and stepped outside, retreating as the guests either side of Hana shouted to each other across her balcony. "Bloody animals," he complained, his face clouding over. "We'll eat in here then."

"Who are they?" Hana asked, tearing off a hunk of bread and dipping it into the cheese sauce. She savoured the taste and sighed with happiness.

"Some IT company," Logan said. "They arrived drunk, so it doesn't bode well."

Hana wrinkled her nose in sympathy. "That sucks when it's your home."

Logan nodded. "Yeah. The best conferences are the Christian ones. We never have a problem with them. Ma's getting sick of the corporate stuff."

"I'm not surprised." Hana watched a shoe zing past her window.

Logan looked tired and careworn, dark stubble shrouding the lower part of his face. "I forgot the butter," he said.

"Doesn't need it," Hana reassured him, stuffing a crust between her lips and speaking with her mouth full. She used the last of the bread to mop the bowl, feeling full to bursting as she finished and laid it on the nightstand. "That was so nice," she sighed. She flopped back against the pillows and puffed her belly out. "I'm stuffed."

Logan watched her with a smile, relaxing against the backdrop of her innocent jocularity. He finished his dinner and scooted onto the bed next to her, lying on his side and twirling her hair in his fingers. "Tell me about your husband," he asked.

"I'm not sure where to start." Hana felt herself tense, both her worlds merging and causing her discomfort. "Do I have to?"

"No." Logan twirled her hair and his grey eyes bored into her soul. "Was he kind to you?" he asked. "That's what I'm asking."

Hana sighed. "Yes. He was."

"That's good then. Tell me about your kids." Logan probed with an air of casualness, as though it didn't matter what she revealed. Hana loosened up, speaking about Bodie and Izzie with the glow of love in her green eyes.

"They sound great," Logan said. "Bodie's your eldest? How old is he?"

Hana breathed through pursed lips. "He's twenty-six," she answered, her expression guarded.

Logan didn't react and the tense moment passed. "What about your parents?" he asked. "You said you're half Scots and half Irish. Tell me about them."

Hana swallowed and sat up, hugging her knees. "I find them harder to talk about than Vik, to be honest."

"That's okay, you don't have to." Logan rolled onto his back and rested a hand on his tight stomach. "I'm just interested in where you've come from."

Hana sighed. "I grew up in Lincolnshire in the UK. Mum was an amazing Irishwoman and I get my hair colour from her."

Logan smiled with his eyes. "What makes her amazing?"

Hana shook her head and rested her chin on her knees. "Past tense, Logan. She died after Bo was born." Hana's voice tailed off, remembering the last time she saw her mother. She shut her eyes against the old pain. "Mum was deaf and couldn't speak."

"Like Jack?" Logan cocked his head and understanding crossed his expression. "So, you signed with him?"

Hana nodded. "Kind of. I know British Sign Language but one of his signs appeared American. Maybe he's learned a mix of languages."

"Can you teach me some?" Logan asked. "I've learned to understand his noises, but it would be good to speak to him properly."

"Yeah sure." Hana's smile had a tight quality.

"What about your father?" Logan asked. "Is he still in England?"

Hana shook her head. "He was an Anglican minister. And he's dead too."

Logan's brow knitted at her tone. "Sorry, Hana. That must be hard. I can't imagine it."

She swallowed. "It doesn't matter. We didn't part on good terms."

"Still hurts though." Logan studied her face, watching as she skirted the edge of trusting him. Hana bit her lip harder than she intended, selecting her words with care.

"The last time I saw him, he said I was dead to him. I made a mistake. He couldn't forgive me and only cared about the impact on his reputation. He threw me out of his home and I didn't see my mother alive again."

"Wow. Sorry, Hana. We don't have to talk about it." Logan held his arms out to her and she edged nearer, allowing him to touch her. She heard her father's hysteria echo in her memory and the pain crushed her chest like a bag of frozen peas, still as fresh as the day he spoke the words.

"You should probably know what I did," she said, lowering her voice to a whisper. "It might affect how you feel."

Logan pulled her towards him in a fluid movement, his fingers gripping her left shoulder. "Nothing will change how I feel about you," he whispered, guiding her down so he could kiss her. She tasted the wine on his lips, felt her stomach drop to her knees and relaxed into the pleasure of his nearness. Hana opened her mouth to speak but Logan pressed his index finger over her lips. "I don't need to know," he whispered, kissing her lips, hair, neck and face. "Leave the past where it lies."

Hana acknowledged his acceptance by relaxing into his embrace. With every kiss, she fell a little more under his spell until the dangerous cliff edge passed beneath her without fanfare. She couldn't stop, even if she wanted to. The tap of Vik's memory in the back of her brain went unnoticed for the first time in eight years. Logan kissed her until she sounded breathless and then he held her.

Hana stilled, counting the scars on Logan's fingers. She asked about each of them in turn and he answered for those he remembered. There seemed so many. "Barbed wire. That one was a rusty nail in the tack shed. That one was a fight and needed four stitches."

"A fight? Were you a naughty boy?"

Logan smirked. "Sometimes. I took care of myself and those who mattered to me. Pete earned me a couple of hidings at school."

"Pete?" Hana waggled her eyebrows in surprise. Their easy friendship fell into place like a missing puzzle piece. "Ah."

A tap on the door disturbed them and Hana pulled away from Logan in fright. He laughed at her reaction and got up to answer it. Miriam stood in the hallway, bearing a tray with three tall mugs of hot cocoa. Hana ran a hand through her mussed hair, trying to put it straight as Logan took the tray.

Miriam grabbed the third mug and plonked herself down in an armchair by the window. "Geez, this lot are hard work," she sighed, slurping her drink. "They've eaten all the food, drunk all the drink the boss man paid for and are set on driving Alfie mad, wanting this, that and the other."

"Why's he dealing with them?" Logan didn't take the second mug but shoved his hands deep into his pockets and narrowed his eyes.

Miriam shrugged. "He said to leave you alone," she answered. Her brow furrowed. "He thinks they sneaked in their own drink. We'll lose our licence if anyone reports them." She jumped at the sound of squealing from the balcony. A trouser leg appeared over the railing separating Hana's from the rest, followed by a body and head. Hana watched in amazement as a man scaled the railing on the other side and banged on her neighbour's door. "It's too much," Miriam groaned. "They're out of control."

"Want me to deal with it?" Logan demanded.

At Miriam's almost imperceptible nod, Logan wrenched open Hana's ranch slider and vaulted the balcony. He grabbed the drunk by the shirt, snatching a decorative vase from his hand. "You gonna smash that window?" he asked, forcing the man out of sight. "No? Good choice." Hana heard the clunk of the pot on the balcony floor and Logan's fist hammering on the glass. "Management," he shouted. "Open up!"

Hana and Miriam heard the swish of curtains and the sliding door opened and closed. Hana held her breath as one-sided arguing ensued. Logan said nothing in reply. The commotion moved into the hallway. "Pack your gear," he ordered the room's occupants, his tone brooking no argument. "Leave before I get back up here or I'll throw you out."

"You can't do that," a female voice slurred.

They heard Logan laugh. "Can't I? I'm about to chuck your mate in the car park. I'm happy to come back up and do the same to you."

Chuntering followed his threat and Hana heard the zipper of a case opening next door. "Do you think he'll be okay?" she asked wide-eyed.

"He won't hit him," Miriam lowered her voice. "Not unless he needs to."

"I meant Logan!" Hana's eyes widened.

"Oh yes!" Miriam giggled. "Logan handles himself just fine."

Hana slumped onto the bed, her face ashen and she rubbed a hand over her eyes. "What do you mean by that? Does Logan fight a lot?"

Miriam shrugged and dismissed the question. She glanced behind her at the sliding door and moved to click it shut, securing the lock and pulling the curtains across. "We've met before." She laid out her sentence with deliberation, emphasising each word. "Do you remember?"

Hana's body stilled and her heart rate picked up, sensing a conclusion to her mystery. She leaned forward. "Yes. But where?"

Miriam nodded, a steady, regal dip of her head. She'd been beautiful once. "My brother got sick and sent for us. We travelled to London to visit. I took Logan and Michael. You sat opposite us with an Indian man." Miriam ran a hand over her own stomach to accentuate her meaning and the colour drained from Hana's cheeks. "You looked five months pregnant and pūkatokato."

"What's that?" Hana whispered, concentrating on the unfamiliar word to distract her from the unfolding disaster. "What does that word mean?"

"Heart broken." Miriam dropped her voice to translate the Māori words for utter devastation.

"No, no, no!" Hana stood, squeezing her cheeks between her hands. Her head felt ready to explode and sickness roiled the food in her stomach. The scene flooded back like an ice cold wave crashing over her head. "Not that day, not that day," she begged, her voice breaking.

"Why?" Miriam sounded innocent, her question innocuous.

Hana sank onto the bed as the memories rolled like a film reel, undoing her carefully crafted life at the seams. They rode the Circle Line train to Vik's parents, carrying news which already earned him a cut eyebrow and a split lip from Hana's father and brother. She remembered crying for most of the journey, wiping her eyes on her sleeve and hoping the rest of the train didn't see. It marked the day she lost her family, her reputation and control over her life. Her fragile sanity protected her, shrouding the hideous day in a fog of amnesia. Miriam's presence lingered beneath the surface, pricking at Hana's subconscious, but no more prevalent than the pattern on the ragged seats of the underground train.

Miriam watched her struggle. "Do you remember what happened?"

Hana's mind grappled, in too much pain to pull out the memory. "No." Her reply communicated exhaustion. "I don't." A glance at the grey eyes opposite filled her with chills. Her brain unlocked a picture of those eyes and it hurt like a physical pain.

"You cried and I gave you my handkerchief." Miriam swallowed. "Logan's really. He gave me a set as a gift. I lost the rest, but you took the last one."

Hana swallowed. "Kiwi birds," she said, her voice trembling. "Little navy blue ones marching around the edge."

Miriam nodded. "Yes, that's it."

"I still have it."

"That's nice." Miriam smiled. "I'm not asking for it back." She cocked her head and watched Hana wrestle.

It hit Hana like a freight train. "No! Oh no! Tell me that boy with you wasn't Logan?" Hana's green eyes flashed. She shook her head. "He wasn't there, was he?"

Miriam's slow nod tipped her over the edge and the veil fell. The dark haired teenager on the train watched her through unusual grey eyes the colour of grit. He stared at her, still fourteen and trapped inside her memory. Hana covered her mouth with her hand. "Please leave." She issued the directive to Miriam without looking up.

The old woman stood on bones which creaked as she moved. Her progress towards the door seemed endless. Hana kept her eyes closed, knowing she would run. Tonight. She knew that much, but not where.

"He died." Miriam's voice broke into Hana's turmoil like nails on a blackboard.

"What?" Tortured green eyes turned towards her and the old woman nodded.

"My brother," she said. "Logan wouldn't get off the train because of you. We missed our stop and my kauaemua died. We got there too late."

"You blame me?" Hana's voice sounded hoarse and her eyes closed against Miriam's shrug. "You do."

"I don't know anymore." Miriam opened the bedroom door and glanced back. "But it was the beginning of the end."

She left the room and Hana paced, unable to think through the confusion. She hugged herself tight, foolishness breeding rage. "The receptionist will call me a taxi," she said, speaking to herself in hushed tones, soothing her inner child. "It'll be okay."

Her toothbrush clattered into the sink as Hana shoved it into her wash bag with shaking hands. She retrieved it and added her other belongings, stuffing them in and cursing when the zipper stuck.

"What are you doing?" Logan's question made her jump and Hana screamed, fear and anger interchanging in her chest and confusing her thoughts.

"Leaving. Don't try to stop me."

Logan heaved out a sigh of defeat, pushing his hands into his pockets and leaning a muscular shoulder against the doorframe. "At least tell me why," he asked, his tone calmer than his expression.

"You know why!" Hana shouted, her face ashen. "Your mother told me."

Logan's lips pursed into a silent 'o' and he cursed. "She wasn't meant to."

Hana shook her head. "What is this?" She waved her arm around her, taking in the opulent hotel room and the handsome man in the doorway. "Is it a sick joke? Do you want to blackmail me?"

Logan laughed, the sound hollow. "For being pregnant at eighteen? Nobody gives a damn nowadays, Hana."

"Angus might. The board might." She gritted her teeth and ran cold water over her hands, pressing the soap into her palms hard enough to make the skin red. "Nobody knows. You could ruin my whole life."

"I don't want to." Logan gritted his jaw.

"What do you want?" Hana demanded. "What do you want, Logan?"

He swallowed and stared at her, his expression unchanging. His irises flashed like moving smoke. "I want to make you happy," he said. "I know it sounds lame, but I promised myself I'd find you and put it right."

"Put what right?" Hana left the water coursing over her fingers. "How?" It sounded like a plea.

Logan gritted his teeth. "Put right how you felt that day. You seemed so lost and that man you married? I hated him. He didn't care about you or your baby and it made me sick."

"Don't say that," Hana hissed. "He did love us, he did."

Logan nodded. "Then I'm glad, Hana. Because he didn't deserve you that day, babe. And how do I want to put it right? I want to love you better, to tell you you're beautiful every bloody day because you are."

"You've always known? The day of the assembly and the time I sat with you in the staffroom. You knew then?" Hana turned off the tap and stared at her fingers.

Logan nodded. "Yeah, I knew. Twenty-six years I searched for you, Hana. But here you were. I knew on the first day of term when you dropped your handbag at my feet."

"And you altered your contract." She closed her eyes, feeling hot tears near the surface. "Nobody knows," she said. "About Bodie. They never asked."

"It's not their business." Logan screwed up his face. "I'm not interested in them."

"Bodie doesn't know." Hana's whisper made his jaw clench. "Vik lied. He said our anniversary marked our Sikh wedding, but the registry office one took place months earlier." She swallowed. "After Vik died, I almost told him the truth but couldn't."

Logan edged towards her, working her like a frightened mare being rugged for the first time. Hana balled herself against the sink. "I need to go home," she said. "I can't think straight."

Logan nodded. "Okay." He paused in front of her and held out his arms, watching the conflict in her eyes. She stared at the offered warmth, old memories giving her eyes a wild quality. He kept his body still, willing her to trust him and attempting to communicate assurance across the distance between them. Hana closed her eyes and blocked him out, putting her index finger in her mouth like a child. Her hand shook.

"You never said you'd been to London." Her tone accused him.

"I never said I didn't."

"Where did you search for me?" Her eyes snapped open, seeking answers and wanting only truth.

"There." Logan edged closer. "As soon as I could. I taught in London and rode the trains every weekend, every line." He wrinkled his nose in distaste. "That sounds pathetic."

Hana shook her head. "It doesn't. Not pathetic."

"I was fourteen. My uncle wanted the eldest boy in the whānau but Barry died the summer before. I shouldn't have been there. Michael travelled with us, but faked sick. Ma ran out of money and I made us late for the train, drawing cash from my savings account. We got on the train and a girl got on at the next stop. A girl in a yellow dress. She sat opposite me, the most beautiful woman I'd ever seen. I couldn't take my eyes off her, but she cried from Epping Forest to the centre of London. I spent the journey trying not to stare, but I failed. Watching her eased the ache in my soul and I imagined what it might feel like, to love her and be loved in return. I fell in love, Hana. I fell in love with you."

Hana sniffed and reached for toilet roll, pushing a wad under her nose. "It's too strange," she whispered, her words stilted. "Nothing good came out of that day."

"It did for me." Logan cocked his head and edged nearer. "Trust me."

There it was, the sentence he repeated to her like a mantra, offering safety and hope, a lifeline to something else. She turned and faced him, collecting the pieces of herself into an acceptable state. "Why didn't you tell me in the first place?" she asked. "Why not just say we'd met?"

Logan quirked an eyebrow. "Really? Can you imagine that conversation, Hana?"

She shrugged and nodded, understanding pushing through the fog. "No. I'm glad you didn't."

Logan swept her hair off her shoulders, allowing his hands to replace the red swirls. "Do you want me to take you home? I can."

Hana swallowed and shook her head. "No. It's too late and you've been drinking. Maybe tomorrow."

Logan smiled and released his breath, feeling like he'd run a marathon. "Okay. We'll talk more in the morning. If you want." He searched her face for an answer, his grey irises shot with desperation and fear.

Hana glanced up at him, her eyes mirroring his confusion. "I can see that little boy and he's so young." Her green eyes sparkled with salty tears. "It makes me feel worse." She touched her chest with shaking fingers.

Logan shook his head. "Five years is nothing, Hana. I wouldn't care if it were twenty, but it isn't. Stop hiding. Let me love you."

She didn't object to his hands on her shoulders and he eased her closer until her cheek pressed against his chest. He pushed his fingers into her hair and kissed the top of her head. Hana sighed, her mind and body limp with exhaustion. "You're tired," Logan whispered. "Come on, lay on the bed."

Hana let him lead her to the centre of the room, sinking down into the mattress. Bone weariness afflicted her and images of her mother's face plagued her. The same one, over and over, not disappointment but love, aching, painful, silent love. Logan lay next to her and pulled her into his body, warming her as she shivered and gave up fighting sleep.

She disturbed as a different man ran across her balcony and tapped on next door's window. Logan slipped from the bed, covering Hana with a blanket. With a glance back at her beatific face, he slipped the catch on the door and closed it behind him. It took seconds to fell the fool with a punch to the face. The drunk dribbled as Logan stuffed him over the rail and jimmied the lock on the empty room next door. It stunk of cheap perfume belonging to the women he threw out earlier and Logan dragged the bleeding man through the same way as the first, giving him another slap for annoyance sake. He hauled him downstairs with a hand covering his mouth and dropped him on the floor before the deserted reception desk. Then he dialled the number for security. "Get him out," Logan told the retired army sergeant. "Tell them I've had enough. Their boss will pay us compensation and I want them all out first thing. Any more trouble and they go tonight. No more noise, no more disturbances. Last warning." He grunted at the man's reply and hung up the phone.

Then he returned to Hana, gratified when she snuggled in next to him. He covered them both with the sheets and held her, experiencing the motion of the dirty underground train in his dreams and remembering how powerlessness felt.

Chapter 33

"So much for giving you the best room in the house!" remarked Logan as they drove home the next morning. Hana smiled, tiredness in her eyes.

"I slept okay," she said with a sigh. "When did you leave?"

"I'm not sure," Logan lied. "Late. I helped the security guys with that party which caused so much trouble."

"Good job you were there," she mused.

"They can cope." Logan peered down at the bruised knuckles on his right hand and winced. A good punch up always cured frustration.

"I loved the trek."

Logan smiled across at her and squeezed her hand, reluctant to let go. He drove one-handed, their fingers entwined on his thigh. Hana didn't pull away and it gave him hope.

She sat up straighter at the sight of the Tainui Bridge. "Hakarimata Road is up there, isn't it?"

Logan nodded. Hana pulled her hand away. "Can we go there?" she begged, her face eager like a child's. "Please can we make a detour?"

They turned off the main road on a dangerous bend and Logan's truck revved up the steep gravel driveway. "Hana, it's a mess," Logan said, even before they crested the top of the hill. "It'll cost everything you have."

"You don't know that!" Hana argued. "You haven't seen it yet."

"I don't need to." He dodged another pothole and the truck sank into a rut, sending gravel flying as it pulled itself out. "Nice landslide," he commented, jerking his head towards the right of the track where fallen trees pivoted on a substantial mudslide.

"Fine!" Hana folded her arms and pouted. "Blow out my fragile candle of hope, why don't you?"

Logan laughed and pressed the accelerator, coaxing the truck around the final bend.

The Hakarimata Ranges loomed ahead, dark and forbidding. The house perched on a lower slope, a valley between it and the first of the foothills. Five hundred metres sat between the house and a thriving bush, surrounded by green, rolling hills and paddocks.

"Wow! It's just like Angus' villa!" Hana exclaimed. "It's gorgeous."

"It's derelict," Logan muttered, knowing she ignored him. "It didn't start out here. Someone transported it although I don't know how they got it up the slope." White, weather-boarded and with a fading pride, the house sported an original tin roof. A widow's walk wrapped around two sides, joining onto a balcony above a double garage. The doors hung sideways like a boxer's post-fight eyelids and the flashing sat on the driveway in front. "It's not even watertight."

Two of the side windows were cracked and the drive down to the garage looked treacherous, littered with builder's crap and pieces from a retaining wall. Nightmare. Logan sighed at the expression on Hana's face. "Sweetheart, don't even get out of the truck."

Logan cranked the gear lever into reverse and glanced behind him, ready to execute a turn small enough to face the downhill trip. "I bet the last person who tried to reverse down there is the reason those trees ended up flat on their backs." Logan's eyes crinkled with humour. "If you listen carefully, you can still hear the engine running."

Hana tossed her head and pushed the door open, slamming it behind her. Logan watched in amazement as she crunched across the gravel towards the front steps. An agent sat on a camping chair, her expression surprised at the presence of visitors. "Yeah, I bet you are, love," Logan hissed as he gave her a polite wave. He switched off the engine, locked the doors and made his way towards Hana. A lack of surety plagued him after the previous night. Damn his mother.

Deciding to keep his opinions about the house to himself, Logan let Hana follow the agent up the stairs. He felt lost, not knowing what she expected of him. She needed protecting, yet he knew she wouldn't accept it with any degree of trust. Not now. He cursed his mother again and shook his head. "Bloody women."

Logan felt awkward as he shook hands with the agent, not lessened by her assumption they were a married couple. She wore unsuitable stilettos which welded her to the gravel and her English accent reminded him of London. "Amazing timing," she said with a smile. "We've held open homes every Sunday lunchtime for the last six weeks. This is the last one."

"We saw the sale board on Friday," Hana admitted.

"The property has potential," the agent twittered as she and Hana moved around the rooms.

"Yep. As firewood," Logan mused, wandering in a different direction. He took in the practicalities, elderly wiring, rotten weatherboards and general, money-sucking dilapidation. The bay window at the front looked out over a spectacular view of the merging Waikato River and the Waipa, the grey water standing out against the orange hues of the latter. "Ngaruawahia." Logan sighed and tasted the name of the township on his tongue. Home of the kīngitanga movement and the current Māori king. Logan blew out his cheeks and shook his head.

The sky took on a pink glow as the sun dipped into the hills behind the house. Hana clattered around with the agent downstairs in the garage and Logan heard them laughing. When they climbed the stairs from the garage, Hana appeared alive and vibrant. The agent's eyes widened in hope. Logan kept his uncharitable thoughts about the source of that hope to himself, but it involved the listing from hell coming off her books.

His heart melted at the sight of Hana's excitement and he knew she'd fallen in love with it. "It's amazing," she said, her eyes shining. He daren't hold out his hand in case she rejected him in front of the agent, but the overwhelming need to touch her caused him physical pain.

"It's a great project," the agent said, beaming. "Are you looking for a family home?"

Hana giggled. "Not really." Her eyelashes fluttered at Logan. "But my partner's renovated before. His parents' place is beautiful."

Logan released the breath he didn't know he held. Perhaps he'd held it since the night before. His lungs emptied in an exhale which shook his body. Partner.

Back in the truck and skittering down the treacherous road, Hana chatted about the agent who migrated from the south of England. Logan remained silent, regrouping and gathering his shattered nerves. "She pointed out the areas where the previous owner sunk piles. He also put in some retaining walls." Hana jabbed a finger at the washout. "That's where the council rerouted a stream. It used to run across the road so they sent it underneath and it drains into the river. The agent said it's made a difference to the stability of the area."

Some long buried wisdom caused Logan to bite back the enormous, mounting reservations. Her bubble of hope seemed so fragile. "What did you see?" he asked. "What do you want?"

Hana faltered, glancing sideways at him as though not understanding the question. Then she turned away, staring through the window. He heard her whisper, "Myself. Freedom." Then she fell silent.

Logan turned off Hakarimata Road and crossed the railway line. He indicated left and instead of heading towards River Road and Hamilton, he drove further north. Before the Taupiri sign, he pulled into a makeshift lay-by, dodging gravel piles belonging to road construction gangs. The truck lurched through potholes and ground to a halt. Logan switched everything off, including his own brain, silencing the myriad warnings and objections.

He turned sideways in his seat and watched Hana as she gazed through the windscreen, her glassy eyes not seeing the grit piles. He waited, forcing himself into an unfamiliar state of patience.

Hana sighed. "The house is stuck. Someone loved it once and now it's rotting on the side of the mountain. That's how I feel. Previously loved, but stuck. I'm living a life mapped out for four people and I'm trying to live it alone. I needed you to rescue me, but didn't know that until this weekend." Hana sighed. "You make me feel whole. I've never given anyone the chance to accept me with all the bad parts, but you knew them." Her eyes narrowed in question. "You don't seem to care about my past." She glanced at Logan and he smiled, his lips twitching with the tension. Hana's face radiated hope. "I want to buy that house."

Logan reached out towards her, putting his hand over her fidgeting fingers and holding them still. He said nothing but stared out across the horizon, a slight smile playing on his parted lips.

"Say something." Hana looked up at him, gauging his reaction to her bizarre logic. She followed his gaze through the windscreen, across water sparkling in the dying embers of the sunshine. Her eyes rested on the white house set high in the hills and backed by dense bush. From a distance, none of its imperfections showed.

"Life's about perspective," Logan said. "Get a good surveyor."

Chapter 34

Before the first week of the holiday finished, Hana had engaged a solicitor, a surveyor and begun the purchase process for the old house. "Culver's Cottage?" she said in surprise, her pen hovering over the sale document. "Why?"

"Not sure." The agent shrugged.

"Previous owner's name." Logan sifted through papers attached to the file they'd obtained, his grey eyes flicking as he speed-read tiny print. "He moved the house from a location in Te Awamutu. The original soil samples are here and details of the piling specifications."

"The surveyor said it's sound." Hana bit her lower lip, already defending the house against scepticism.

Logan nodded. "It is." His eyes held amusement. "You were right; it's fine."

Hana relaxed and leaned towards the agent. "Why didn't Mr Culver finish the renovation?"

"Start," Logan asked. "Why didn't he start it?"

"Business failure." The agent eyed Hana's pen like a hungry bear. "He blames the recession but I can't comment on that. His wife left him around the same time and he lost heart with the house. He wants the sale completed within the month though."

"Okay." Hana's fingers twitched around the pen and the agent sighed.

"He fenced around the house itself, but if you want more garden, you can move it. Your land will go as far as the bush and down to the road. The council is responsible for the part adjoining the highway. They clear it back periodically to prevent slips." At Hana's hesitation, the woman fired up her hard-sell techniques. "Other clients are interested."

"Are they?" Hana cocked her head and the pen moved closer to the paper.

Logan smirked and turned his face so the women didn't see his silent amusement at their game. The agent nodded. "Yes. There are."

Hana glanced across at Logan, needing his assurance. Her nerve failed her at the last moment as the silver-plated pen twirled in her fingers. "Should I do this?" she asked him and the agent sighed.

"Do you want extra time?" He sat up, more concerned with Hana's interests than the agent's. The other woman panicked, fluttering her eyelashes at Logan for support. Wasted.

"I'm not sure." Hana wavered, confusion in her eyes. "It's a heap of money from Vik's estate. What if it all goes wrong?"

"Then we work it out, babe." Logan's brow furrowed and he rested a hand on her thigh under the table. "What does your gut say?"

"Do it." Hana swallowed. "But my head's screaming something different."

Logan inhaled. "It's up to you, Hana. If it feels right, it probably is, but don't blow half a million grand on something you can't manage."

Hana gulped. "It's a fortune."

The agent heaved out a ragged breath and nudged the brochure with an acrylic fingernail. She'd almost ditched the awful house and relieved herself of an eighteen-month millstone. Other prospective viewers fled at the steepness of the driveway and state of the exterior. Those who ventured inside added to the house's misfortunes, poking and prodding plaster and wood and making it look worse. The only other offer on the property got laughed out of the office. Until Hana's.

"I'm doing it." Hana raised the pen and signed her name, hovering over the surname. "I should've bought it in my old name," she said with a sigh. "McIntyre."

The agent sat up straight, worry flitting across her face. "You provided identification," she said, her tone terse. "You have other names?"

"Just my maiden name." Hana signed Johal with her usual flourish. "My first husband died."

The agent's liberal trowelling of makeup didn't hide the embarrassed flush which crawled up her throat. "Sorry," she said, her voice hushed. "You never said."

Logan sniffed and his grey eyes held a veiled warning. His body stiffened at any mention of Vikram Johal and although he kept his opinion private, he wished Hana never met the man. He gritted his teeth. "Ah well, when I make an honest woman of you, it won't matter." Logan kept his face straight, seeing a romantic haze descend across the agent's face which chased out the awkwardness.

"Oh, that's so sweet." She pressed her hands across her chest and clutched her heart. "You're so lucky, Hana." Her eyes roved over Logan's white tee shirt, undressing him with her eyes.

Hana noticed and frowned. "Thanks for the coffee and donuts," she said, pushing her chair back and standing. She held out her slender hand and the agent shook it.

"I'll get an envelope for your copy of the contract," she gushed, standing and disappearing into a side office.

"Stop it!" Hana said to Logan, giving him a sideways glare. "You know she fancies you."

"Are you jealous?" Logan's eyes flashed and Hana tried to read his twinkling grey eyes. She failed and he watched her give in.

"Yes. Very." Her face creased into a pout and Logan snorted, leaning across and planting a loud kiss on her cheek. His eyes still sparkled and the agent heaved a dreamy sigh on her return, handing a chunky envelope to Hana.

"Here's the key you requested." She held out a fob with the agency's logo emblazoned on it. "Any changes you make will become the owner's property if you default on the contract. You aren't allowed to take up residence or deny him access until the completion date. After that, it's all yours."

Hana nodded and accepted the key, turning it over in her fingers. "Thanks. I understand."

Logan maintained a possessive hand in the small of her back as they exited the office, surprised when they didn't walk to the truck straight away. Instead, Hana aimed for a bench nearby. She clutched the envelope to her chest and her face paled. "What did I just do?" she wailed as her courage failed. She sank onto the wooden slats with wobbly legs.

"You're priceless," Logan said with a smile. "You crack me up." He sat next to her and wrapped his arm around her shoulders. "I'm so proud of you."

Hana's jaw slackened and she turned to him, their faces close. "Are you?" she said and he heard the craving in her voice. "Are you really?"

Logan swallowed and nodded. "Really and truly, backwards and forwards." He pushed his fingers through the back of her hair and breathed in her flowery scent. His lips trembled against hers and Hana felt her stomach pitch. Stubble grazed her chin and she sighed.

"What would I do without you?" she whispered and Logan smiled and rested his forehead against hers.

"I don't intend for you to find out."

"Apparently not." Hana's fingers linked through his as she joked, "Nice move though. The wedding thing stopped her pining after you."

Their relationship progressed into something tangible and steady as they worked together on the house. Hana revelled in the physical thrill at his nearness, surprised to discover she still possessed love to give after the abrupt end of her marriage. The contract completion went through without a hitch and Culver's Cottage became the property of Mrs Hana Johal. In an act of rebellion, she gave her name as McIntyre to the service providers, ensuring electricity and phone bills arrived in her post box in her maiden name. It gave Hana a peculiar thrill, shedding facets of her past and preparing herself for a brighter future. But with it came guilt at abandoning her children's surname and a husband she'd loved.

Work proved business as usual, sorting out the pile of mail and appointment run sheets for the guidance counsellors. Rory took a term's sabbatical and brought in his new baby daughter for Hana to cuddle. Pete gave the child a cursory glance but complained when Rory wouldn't hand her over, losing interest in favour of picking his nose. "Nobody trusts me," he grumbled, eating the bogey off his index finger.

"Is Angus replacing you?" Hana asked, jerking her head towards Rory's empty seat. He shrugged and pointed at the mountain of boxes on his desk.

"Yeah, she's under there somewhere."

"She?" Pete's blue eyes widened with enthusiasm. "What kind of she? Old? Young? I hope she's hot and fit." He closed his eyes and let his imagination wander. Rory shuddered.

"Pete, promise us you'll never breed," he begged.

Hana laughed and jerked her head towards the desk as Sheila dumped another box of leaflets on top of the pile and glared at Rory. As she wandered back into her office, Hana winced. "I hoped things might get better after Amy arrived," she whispered. "I'm sorry."

Rory rolled his eyes. "Yeah. Me too. I'm not white and middle classed, Hana. I'll never be good enough."

"That's not it!" Hana seemed appalled; her eyes wide and green as emeralds. "She's not a racist."

"Maybe." Rory sighed and stroked his daughter's olive cheek. "But that feels like the problem."

Hana glanced at the back of Pete's head. "I have a Māori friend," she said, watching his ears twitch back like a dog's. "He said he couldn't speak Te Reo in school until the mid-90s. I didn't realise."

Rory nodded. "Yup. My father got caned for saying his own surname because it sounded too Māori. So they butchered it, dropping the first half to fit in." He shook his head. "People have no idea. On the one hand it was about getting brown people into qualifications and giving them scholarships, while on the other, training them to be a white, middle classed Pākehā, just like them."

"What's your full name then?" Hana asked, stroking the baby's black curls.

"Te Kanawa," Rory said with a sigh. "My father used Kana on my birth certificate, so I'd need to change it back by deed poll. Then there's my marriage licence and the children's names." He sighed and glanced at Sheila's office, his expression sad. "Life's hard enough without that."

Hana leaned forward and touched his hand. "I don't believe she's a racist," she whispered. "But she is deeply unhappy. Something else is going on."

"Maybe." Rory stood and collected his daughter from Hana's arms. "Best get Amy home for a feed." He walked across to Sheila's open doorway and spoke to his child. "Wanna say bye to granny?" he asked.

Sheila emerged, her face ethereal in the glow of grandparent-ship. Hana watched love for the little girl spill over, eradicating the aura of sadness for a moment. "Bye sweetpea," Sheila whispered and placed a gentle kiss on the perfect head. Hana watched tears bud in her eyes and her brow knitted in confusion.

"See you at home," Rory said, his tone gruff as he turned away.

After lunch, Hana heard the sound of Angus' Scottish lilt in the common room. It didn't concern her until his words hit home. "This is where the boys study during free periods. Rory supervised many of those classes but other staff are rostered on. You'll take over those duties as well as the role of Year 13 dean for this term. We'll talk again before Rory returns as it might be feasible to move you into the sports department, given your qualifications. There's a permanent role here for someone of your calibre."

Hana shot to her feet and ran to Sheila's door. "Quick! Rory's replacement is outside. Angus is bringing them in now!"

Sheila and Hana jostled each other in their attempt to rid Rory's desk of its considerable detritus. They gathered boxes into their arms and then stood in the middle of the room, searching for somewhere to hide the mess. Peter North sat at his desk playing with his phone, a sitting target. "Under here!" Sheila hissed and they dived for him, elbowing him sideways as they stashed it at his feet.

"We won't get it all in," Hana squeaked and Sheila bobbled her head on her shoulders, hurling another box across.

"We have to!" she stage whispered. "Oh, crap!" A box upended itself on Pete's desk as the women jostled, spewing leaflets like a paper-fall. Sheila snagged the box, lost its entire contents and then dropped the cardboard container on Pete's head.

"Ah, here we are." Angus appeared calm as he blocked the doorway, but his guest opened her eyes wide in alarm. "The student centre." His brows knitted at the sight of the women flanking Pete's seated body. Pete moved his head and the box swivelled on it, tilting backwards at a jaunty angle and blocking his view. A University of Waikato brochure slid onto the table in front of him and he opened it as though wearing a box was usual practice.

Hana froze with her back to the door, watching as Sheila swallowed and took evasive action. She slapped Pete on the back of the head, knocking the box forwards. "I can't breathe!" He made choking noises.

She slapped it again and glared at him. "Get this cleared up!" she snapped. "I'm sick of your mess." She dumped the empty box in front of him and stamped to her office, closing the door behind her. Hana fought the urge to laugh at the expression on Pete's face. She straightened her shoulders and with cool professionalism, turned to greet the principal and his newest staff member. Angus continued without faltering. "This is Caroline Marsh and she's acting for Rory this term," he stated. "She will also take physical education and science classes. I know you'll make her most welcome."

Angus left a breeze in his wake, abandoning the teacher to her fate. The room remained static as nobody moved and Hana heard Angus chatting to a student in the corridor. Sheila appeared from her office and pointed towards Rory's desk. Dust and stray papers littered it. "You can sit there," she said, jabbing her finger. "But my son-in-law will be back."

Hana gaped in surprise at the possession in Sheila's tone. Caroline Marsh didn't change her face expression at all. Hana smelled trouble as Sheila found a new enemy, one who might just fight back.

Short blonde hair suited the new teacher, giving her a boyish look. Everything about her screamed quality, from the cut of her suit to the expensive shoes on her feet. Hana glanced down at her store brand heels and winced. Caroline Marsh appeared athletic, her body toned to lush angles devoid of bulges. Hana sucked in her stomach and worried about her wrinkles. The new teacher wore no makeup, preferring the natural tones of her skin to reflect beauty and inner assurance.

Hana watched as she broke the deadlock, ignoring Sheila and dumping a bag of possessions on Rory's desk. The silence felt palpable and Hana sighed, preferring the tense truce between Rory and Sheila any day. "Sorry, Pete," she whispered, removing the box from his head and confiscating the leaflet. He sat like a statue, watching Caroline Marsh with an unreadable expression on his face. "Don't stare," Hana hissed in his ear. "She's probably married."

Pete's jaw flexed and Hana heard the distinct sound of his teeth grinding. She leapt back as he shoved his chair out from under the desk, almost running over her. "You bitch!" he snapped, malice in his usually gormless face. His gaze fixed on Caroline and anger made his thin shoulders rigid.

"Pete!" Hana couldn't mask her shock. She grabbed his wrist and stared at him, taking in the balled fists and rigid stance. He turned towards her, lips moving and finger jabbing.

"You'll find out!" he spat. Grabbing his car keys in a shaking hand, he slammed from the room, the glass trembling in the rear door with the force of his exit. Hana and Sheila exchanged a look of shock, but Ms Marsh continued sorting her possessions as though Pete's interjection happened in a parallel universe.

Picking up a cardboard tube containing posters, the woman held it between two fingers as though it was contaminated. Hana watched as she dropped it into the bin at her feet with a clang. Sheila stuck her head around the corner and inhaled in surprise, but instead of meeting the challenge as usual, she disappeared and left Hana with the problem. "I'll take that," she said, mustering the courage to snag the cardboard end and pull. No reaction. She stashed the tube in an end cupboard, her heart racing with uncertainty.

Sheila stayed in her office with the door closed and Hana shot worried glances behind her as the atmosphere in the room hung leaden on her shoulders. A visit from Logan during his free period lightened her mood. He walked through the open door and sat on a corner of her desk, a sheet of paper in his fingers. "This is a quote for the new roof," he began, placing it in front of her. "I've printed off the email." His brow furrowed at the tension on Hana's face, his fingers reaching across to brush a red curl off her shoulder. "It's the best quote we've had. Winter's coming and he's happy to start this week. What do you think?"

"That's brilliant!" Hana sighed with relief at the price. "I think that's doable." Her fingers strayed to the crease in his trousers, following the line from his knee to the middle of his thigh. At his look of amusement, she stopped herself. The familiar hum of their connection invigorated her and the effort of hiding their attraction at work took its toll. She wanted his arms around her, but Hana felt the new woman's eyes boring into her back and crushed the need. Logan pointed an olive finger to the start date and Hana forced herself to concentrate.

One second she stared at the paper and the next, Hana watched it flutter to the carpet. Confused, she followed its plight as Logan jumped away from her.

"Hello, Logan." Caroline Marsh stood close behind Hana's seat, her fingers clasping the back and preventing her from turning. Logan's body appeared rigid in her peripheral vision, his arm muscles bunching into a hard knot.

Hana pressed her legs against her chair, desperate to turn. Caroline's grip denied her. "I guess you didn't expect to see me here?"

The shock on Logan's face told Hana the question was rhetorical. He bent to retrieve the paper and she watched it vibrate in his hand as he laid it on the edge of her desk. A mantle of awkwardness descended over him, frightening Hana. She shoved at the chair, finding it rigid against her. Logan's sensuous lips worked, but no sound emerged. Hana's gaze was restricted to a mark on the wall behind Pete's desk, which resembled a stray bogey. She shoved hard with the backs of her legs and the wheels of her chair clattered against Caroline's shoes. The woman let go with a hiss of pain. Hana stood and whirled around, seeing the expression of victory on Caroline's face and the abject misery on Logan's. He shot them both a look of confusion and bolted, storming from the room without explanation. Hana's heart pounded in her chest, emotions running riot and whispering lies.

"What's going on?" Her green eyes flashed and Caroline saw the doubt and pain which she didn't mask in time.

"Nothing that concerns you." She turned away with a smile on her lips, returning to her desk and picking up her pen.

Hana glanced at Sheila's door, seeing her boss' face peeking through the narrow gap. Sheila's eyes blinked twice and then the door closed, leaving her alone and undefended. Hana pushed at the roofing quote with her index finger, confusion making her heart pound. Looking up, she caught the sideways glance from Caroline and felt sick at the animosity in the other woman's eyes.

Caroline left to teach Rory's classes and Sheila went too, leaving Hana with her fears and worries. She texted Logan but received no response. Her unease grew and she found it impossible to concentrate. As the final bell tolled, she gave up, collected her bag and wandered out to Logan's truck, the quote fluttering in her fingers.

Clattering across the uneven surface in her high heels, Hana noticed Logan in the distance. He walked towards Peter North's battered car, hands stuffed into his tight trouser pockets. The fabric pulled taut over his neat buttocks and his shoulders slumped in despondency.

"This is ridiculous!" Hana told herself, bolstering her courage. "You need to get this sorted." Knowing from experience her voice wouldn't carry, she began walking in his direction. Her right arm lifted in a ready wave, hoping he'd turn around.

"Logan!" Hana's lips parted in surprise at the shout, watching as Caroline Marsh approached from the other direction. She sashayed across the car park in her expensive heels, pink lips parting in a smile. She wiggled her hips like a catwalk model and Hana watched Logan pause. His body language was unreadable. Hana didn't hear Caroline's words, but saw her press her hands against Logan's chest in comfortable familiarity, gazing up into his eyes as her lips moved. Hana's heart rose into her throat, creating a lump which stopped her swallowing.

Caroline pressed closer, aligning her body against Logan's. They matched, their respective height complimenting each other's. Hana's chest hitched as after a short pause, Logan unlocked Pete's car. She saw Caroline's hand drag casually from his chest to his waist, lingering on his bum as Logan opened the boot and stowed his bag. She slipped into the passenger seat and the car doors slammed, sealing them both inside together. Logan started the engine and the reverse lights flicked on. At the same instant, pride and dignity flooded back into Hana's dismayed senses. "You idiotic, middle-aged fool!" she hissed at herself.

Her heels dug into the tarmac as Hana dropped her hand from its waving position and whirled around. She clip clopped to the truck, not wanting them to witness her devastation as they drove past. Her heart numb, she hid on the driver's side, bobbing down as though she'd dropped something. She knew the identity of Caroline Marsh with absolute positivity and an old chasm of misery opened up in her soul.

Hana drove the truck to Achilles Rise in a haze of distraction, remembering nothing of the journey when she finally pulled onto the driveway.

Chapter 35

Hana woke early after a restless night filled with worry. She made a number of decisions before she got out of bed, giving herself ready distractions and making life bearable.

She rang the mobile number on the roofer's quote just after seven, greeted by a cheery male voice. "Yeah, sure. We can start this afternoon. There's a halt on our other job."

"That doesn't sound good." Hana pursed her lips and watched her neighbour drag his rubbish bin to the curb, reminding her it was bin day.

"It isn't," the man retorted. "The bank foreclosed."

Hana winced. "Good timing then."

"Sure is. I'll see you at the house later. We own our own scaffolding so we'll get started, then talk about a deposit."

Hana glanced down at the quote in her hand. "I can talk about it now."

The roofer chuckled. "I know you're good for it. That guy of yours knows what he's about."

Hana swallowed and fought the knot of sickness in her stomach. She opened her mouth to deny Logan's affiliation to anything belonging to her and then closed it again.

Hana used the coffee maker to produce a passable latte and made the next decision of the day. "Chocolate for breakfast," she sighed, dipping the peanut slab into her coffee. "Decadence is my reward for being single. No husband will tolerate breakfast opposite a woman with a chocolate moustache."

Feeling nauseous from the chocolate, Hana stumbled to the garage and the sight of Logan's truck greeted her. She allowed herself a minor flutter of dismay before steeling her spine. "Next adventure, Hana. Car buying." She jabbed a finger at Logan's truck. "This can't go on."

At work early, Hana made a private call to a local hardware store and rented a floor sander. Every evening over the next week would involve stripping the rimu floors of Culver's Cottage. If that didn't cure a broken heart, a lung infection might at least distract it. Hana arranged to pick the machine up on the way to the house that evening and asked the man to leave some varnish at the Customer Service desk. "Sure, what sort?" he asked.

"I don't know." Hana faltered at the first hurdle and fiddled with her credit card. "What do you recommend?"

"If you're going to the trouble of stripping rimu, get a nice clear varnish and let the wood do the work," he said. "You know it's going to take you hours though, don't you?"

"Yep." Hana sighed. "Looking forward to it."

"Right you are then," the man responded. "I'll have it ready at the cash desk this afternoon. Good luck." He hung up.

Hana stared at the phone. "Good luck? I'm not going to bloody war!"

"What?" Sheila puffed into the room after briefing, a stack of notices in her hand.

Hana watched her cowed body language with concern. "Nothing," she replied. "Just talking to myself. You okay?"

Sheila walked into her office and slammed the door in reply. Hana got up to pursue her but Caroline Marsh appeared, a twinkle in her eyes. She flounced into the room, humming a happy tune to herself. She glanced at Hana as though she was little more than a bug on the wall and Hana swallowed and concentrated on her work. Deciding to care and not caring were poles apart.

Caroline stayed at her desk and dealt with the usual Year 13 problems. Improper uniform, hair outside the regulations and candidates with behavioural issues were sent her way from the deans' office. She dealt with the boys amidst an aura of decisiveness, refusing to listen to their practiced arguments or give sway to their usual bluster. She dispatched them like a hitman, which jarred with Rory's gentler approach.

At the start of third period, Caroline left to teach a physical education class and Hana sighed with relief. An urge to plant drawing tacks on Caroline's chair in a playschool-type display of aggression reared its ugly head. Hana chose the mature option of coffee. "Want tea or coffee, Sheila?" she called, receiving a grunt in reply. "Sorry, is that yes or no?" She put her head around Sheila's door and smiled as she waited. Sheila shook her head and pursed her lips, the venom in her face causing Hana to beat a hasty retreat.

Using the common room as the quickest route to the staffroom, Hana contemplated the school's greasy tea or floaty coffee, not fancying either option. The empty mug in her hand bore testament to the disgusting quality of one of them and she couldn't remember which. She waved to the teacher on duty and he waved back, putting an imaginary gun to his head and rolling his eyes. Hana laughed and turned late, protecting her face with her outstretched hands as the door swung towards her. The man stepping through caught it at the last minute, his face dark and foreboding. He steadied her with a hand on her forearm.

"Logan." Hana breathed out his name, hating herself for the emotion betrayed in the single word. She didn't have enough time to plan her facial expression and render it neutral. Logan's skin appeared sallow beneath his eyes and tiredness radiated out from him. His dark hair stuck up at the front where he'd run his hands through it. Even his pristine white shirt was buttoned up wrong, leaking from beneath his grey pullover.

"Hana," he said, his voice soft as he increased the pressure on her arm.

"No!" she hissed, yanking her arm away. The cup pinged from her fingers and bounced on the carpet, drawing the attention of the room's occupants. As their spat gained public traction, Hana lost her nerve and bolted, leaving the dregs of something brown leaking onto the floor. The hurt in Logan's eyes followed her as she plunged across the split-level landing and into the staffroom.

Hana lurked in the kitchen, deciding on hot water because she couldn't trust herself to wield a spoon. Her redheaded temper flared and it only saddened her more. Vik hated it, saying it reduced her effectiveness. She'd buried it so deep, it felt alien in her chest and she shook with the effort of suppressing it.

"Steady on, dear, you'll burn yourself." The old man who washed the dishes for busy and lazy staff alike, took Hana's cup from her trembling hand. He wiped the hot splashes from the counter top with a deft action. Adding a splash of cold, he peered into her face. "Don't you feel well, Hana?" he asked. "You look a little peaky."

She nodded, unable to summon the words. Despite the cold, Hana stepped onto the balcony with her drink, taking deep breaths to calm herself. Recriminations pinged around her brain like a pinball. After all these years she let someone into her life, beyond the gates of polite reserve into sharing her hopes and fears. The veil of happiness seemed so fragile in the face of Caroline Marsh's presence. Hana knew she couldn't win against Logan's fiancé, ex or otherwise. The breeze tossed Hana's hair into a frenzy of auburn curls, messing with her vulnerable state in a violent caress. She enjoyed a momentary lack of control as it shielded her face and closed her eyes against the force of it. The thought of Culver's Cottage invigorated her, taking away the bitter pill and replacing it with sweetness. All hers and a beacon for her newfound independence.

She leaned over the rail and allowed her water to tip just a little. A dribble cleared the banister and landed on the path below the balcony. Hana fought the urge to spit, wondering how great it would feel in the unemployment line afterwards. She pushed her hair back from her face and sighed, steeling her nerves for a return to the office. Guarding herself against running into Logan on a daily basis seemed an impossibility in a place she'd always considered home. The turn of the clock on New Year's Eve had edged out all her security and switched boring for terrifying, with challenges at every turn.

Hana sipped her drink and glanced across towards the chapel, seeing movement in her peripheral vision. Logan watched her through the long windows of the common room, his face a mask of confusion and unhappiness. He touched the door handle and Hana saw the frame move, his eyes never leaving her face. Boys glanced up around him and humiliation visited her soul. Fear of another public display caused her to avoid him, leaving the balcony before he closed the door behind him.

Hana skirted the counselling offices and used their entrance to her office, desperate to avoid any further quickening of her heart rate or dashing of her fragile spirits. "Please can I go, Sheila?" she begged. "I've got so much to do, I can't concentrate. You know I'll make the time up."

Sheila nodded. "I don't care, Hana. Oh, Mr Nice Bum came looking for you. He left you a note."

Hana swallowed. "Thanks." She returned to her desk and saw the envelope, Logan's neat left-handed slant spelling out her name. With a jerky movement, she snatched it up, tearing it into tiny pieces without opening it. Her fingers shook as she slid the shards of paper into the dustbin and dropped an old brochure on top. Then she wrote a quick email to Donald explaining she needed to source transport. Not waiting for a reply she left, unable to bear the thought of running into Logan again and having to listen to his excuses for choosing Caroline over her.

Driving the truck along Greenwood Street, Hana visited every car yard on its length before finding what she wanted. She admired the silver Honda CRV through the window and didn't hear the salesman's stealthy approach. "Nice car," he commented.

"Geez!" Hana jumped out of her skin and banged her face into the driver's window.

The salesman masked a smirk with his hand. "It's open," he said, leaning forward to jiggle the handle. Hana flushed with embarrassment and groaned.

"Thanks." She swallowed. "Tell me about the car. I'm interested."

The man rested a hand on the bonnet, getting into his stride. "Two point five horsepower, it looks like a four by four but isn't really. It's got the bodywork, tyres and all the hype but is actually a front wheel drive."

Hana shook her head and tried to follow his lingo. "Is that good or bad? I'm sensing bad."

He notched up his enthusiasm levels. "It's good. Are you wanting something to take off-road?"

"No." Hana thought of her new property, a glow of pleasure beginning in her chest. "My house is up a steep driveway which isn't sealed. It will need to cope with that a few times a day. Other than that, I need a normal car."

The salesman nodded. "That's fine. She'll do that no problem. You've got an automatic gearbox, but you can knock it into manual and override that on steep inclines." He eyed Logan's truck. "What you've got looks more than enough. That Hilux will drive across rivers."

Hana swallowed. "It's not mine. A friend lent it to me and wants it back."

The man's face brightened and he flashed Hana a coy wink. "How about a test drive? As soon as you get behind the wheel, you'll love it."

Hana agreed and sat in the plush reception, sipping a latte from a machine and flicking through a gossip magazine. He took the car to get ready. Hana sighed and glanced at her watch as the afternoon ticked by. Just as she considered giving it up as a bad job, the man appeared in the doorway. "Ready miss? Your ride awaits you." He made a dashing sight, his blond hair brushed back from his forehead and a cloud of aftershave hanging around his head. "This way." He threw his arm out in an act of gallantry and Hana tried not to cough at his halo of strong scent.

The Honda waited for her beneath the covered entranceway. The panels shone and the interior smelled like a tart's boudoir. He'd even shined off the smudge left by Hana's face-plant into the driver's window. A light rain fell, leaving smatterings of fine drizzle on the windscreen and he ushered Hana into the passenger seat. "You can call me Brian," he said. "I'll drive until we find somewhere safe to swap." He gave her a sideways smile. "You get a feel of being inside the vehicle and see if it suits you."

Hana liked the interior. With heaps of room at her feet, she stretched her legs, touching buttons and making Brian panic. As they headed into the suburb of Dinsdale, he distracted her fiddling with information about the vehicle. "It's a Japanese import, three years old, has a full service history and low mileage," he waxed. "Tow bar, alarm and three year warranty."

Hana nodded and her interest piqued. "I want a good price," she said, felling him with a wide smile.

"Yes, yes, we only do the very best prices," he gushed, straightening his tie.

They swapped seats in a lay-by on the Whatawhata Road and Hana put her foot down. "Let's go to Raglan," she suggested, mischief in her green eyes. Brian held onto the door handle and sweated.

"Not today," he said, a nervous twitch distorting his right eyelid. "But I'd love to take you for coffee at the weekend."

Hana winced. "Sorry, Brian. I wasn't propositioning you. I'm in a relationship." She gritted her teeth and lied, not able to think of good reasons to deny putting her foot back into the dirty ditch of over forties coupling.

"Oh, is it serious?" Brian appeared fed up. "My divorce came through last week."

"Very serious." Hana took a bend too fast and plastered Brian against the passenger door. "He's a cop," she added, detail giving weight to authenticity. "A big Indian cop with muscles." Her mind wandered to Bodie and she relaxed, describing someone familiar and figuring Brian would never meet him. "He's in the vice squad." She giggled, embellishing. "Now I've told you that, he'll have to kill you."

Brian gulped. "I'm not really divorced." He clung to the door handle with one hand and straightened his tie with the other. "Please can I drive now?"

Hana loved the car and the sense of freedom it offered. She peeled back the sunroof and put her head out. She felt euphoric at her ability to make decisions for herself, the new mindset enjoyable. Back at the sale yard, Hana drove a hard bargain. She used Brian's computer to transfer the money and agreed to pick the car up the next day. He eyed her like a puppy dog and threw in a full year's road tax under the influence of Hana's intoxicating happiness with her achievements.

Starting the engine of Logan's truck, Hana faced a reality check and her spirits lowered. She needed to get his vehicle out to Gordonton, avoid all awkwardness and somehow get home afterwards. "Tomorrow," she promised herself. "I can get a taxi back to town. I'll be fine."

Chapter 36

Hana climbed the steep driveway to Culver's Cottage, the truck whining with the effort as the floor sander clunked in the boot. At the top of the incline, she stopped to survey the house, noting parts of the rusty roof already covered with a large, multi-coloured parachute. The builder met her on the porch. "We'll need access to the house, but not for a few days. We got heaps done today from the outside."

"That's great, thank you." Hana's brow knitted in worry. "It feels daunting." She dug a spare key from her jeans pocket.

"Na." The builder took it, his gaze on a man climbing the scaffold with a length of wood on one shoulder. "Once the joists are strengthened, we'll get yer new roof on. It'll look amazing. It's nice to see these old places getting some love." He gave Hana an encouraging smile and she nodded in appreciation.

Hana met the labourers, signed the contract for work and admired how far they'd got. The men left in two vans after a quick game of move-the-cars. Hana drove down the steep slope towards the garage with care, not bothering to angle the truck towards the doors. Standing there it felt overwhelming, her decisions more foolhardy than brave as she faced them alone. "Damn it!" she yelled into the silence as she opened the boot and the sander dropped onto her foot. "He's gone, okay! It's over!" Logan's absence jarred with his promises of help and loyalty. He should be there, carrying the equipment and sanding the floor with her. Just like he said. Hana squeezed the bridge of her nose between thumb and forefinger, waiting for her brain to stop reminding her how it felt to see him at work. "I haven't been dumped since Year 3," she grumbled to herself, her mind running over the awkwardness on Logan's face and the wonky buttons. Hana inhaled and shook her head. "You're a stupid woman," she sighed. "Stay single, that's my advice."

Cumbersome and heavy, the sander fought her every step as she manhandled it up the back stairs to the upper level. She returned to retrieve the massive pot of varnish, turpentine and assortment of brushes, her resolve receding further with every footstep. "This can go one of two ways," she told the empty house. "I'll either make the floor look beautiful or delay my moving in date while the builders lay carpet!"

An hour later, she'd worked out how to change the sanding pads with a screw driver and sanded the master bedroom and lounge once. Two hours and four changes of pads revealed a smooth honey coloured rimu. She scuffed the hall floor and lobby and dented the wall of the bedroom in the back corner, by slipping and almost sending the sander through the plasterboard. Every muscle in her body complained and her eyes felt scratchy with dust.

Hana stood in the bay window at the front of the house and admired her handiwork. "Not bad for an amateur," she commented to her reflection in the window. "Even if self-praise is no praise." A woman looked back at her and she blinked, seeing a dust-covered banshee wearing a scarf over her nose and mouth. Her hair looked grey and Hana coughed, sending up a cloud of fine debris. She laughed and returned to her work, her legs dragging themselves back to the top of the rear stairs and the waiting machine.

It grew dark, forcing Hana to search for the light switch. A naked bulb in the third bedroom blinked to life, dangling from a length of brown cable. Sanding dust covered every surface and she reached for a broom and attempted to herd the mess into one corner. As she ceased sweeping to catch her breath, a door downstairs creaked and Hana froze with her hand on the broom handle. Quick footsteps mounted the stairs and fear banished all thoughts of autonomy and independence. Hana panicked and lifted the broom like a weapon, ready to whack whoever walked past the door.

"Mum?" Bodie's face appeared in the gap and Hana screamed. Having already begun a downwards swipe, she couldn't stop in time and he dodged aside as the broom head flew off and crashed into the opposite wall. Hana dropped the handle and put her hands over her mouth.

"Sorry, sorry," she gushed.

"Who did you think I was?" Bodie's eyes narrowed in suspicion and he pulled her hands away from her face. "Mum?"

"It doesn't matter." She pressed her face into his chest and heaved out a grateful sigh, banishing thoughts of the blond man who sat outside her house at random times, his presence threatening her and his air casual. "I'm glad you're here."

Bodie choked and waved his hands at the floating dust particles. "What are you doing?" He coughed. He walked into the hall and retrieved the grizzled broom head.

"Sanding." Hana ran her filthy hands through her hair. "It looks amazing but I wish I'd never started."

Bodie looked at her dirt-streaked face and grinned. "I bet." His eyes narrowed. "You didn't lock the downstairs door. There's nobody else out here. No one will hear you scream."

"Thanks for reminding me." Hana sighed. "Just as I felt safe."

Bodie confiscated the broom handle. "Interesting weapon of choice."

Hana eyed the sander. "I'm fed up of lifting that. I'll bring the rake up and use that to hit intruders instead."

Bodie nodded with approval. "Cumbersome, but used right, a rake might inflict enough injury to escape."

Hana closed her eyes and exhaled, releasing a puff of dust. Logan's advice returned with a bite. "Can we talk about something else?"

"Sure." Bodie stepped around the bedroom examining the floor. "I took a week off to help you."

Hana swallowed and gratitude melted some of the ice in her heart. She licked her lips and fought the lid on her emotions. Hearing nothing, Bodie turned to face her, confusion in his eyes. "Is that okay? Sorry, I should've spoken to you first."

"It's fine. Amazing actually." Hana breathed through pursed lips, her courage failing. "I think I've made a terrible mistake. It's a money pit and I thought I could renovate it myself." Her lower lip wobbled and her throat tightened. "I'm lost and overwhelmed."

"Mum, it's gonna be okay." Bodie's face softened and he crossed the short distance between them. His arms around her offered safety and consolation. He kissed the side of her face. "We can sort this out and it'll be fantastic. It's good to see you stepping out of your comfort zone."

Hana sniffed into the front of his tee shirt. "I bought a new car today."

"You what?" Bodie pulled away, holding her by the shoulders to look into her face. "Geez, Mum! Did you win the lottery and forget to mention it?"

"No." Hana shook her head. "I'm using the money Dad left. I wanted to sell the other house, but the market isn't great in Flagstaff at the moment. The agent says I need to keep it for a while and rent it out."

To her relief, Bodie smiled and squeezed her shoulders beneath strong fingers. "Best get this place sorted out then and you can move in."

Hana swallowed. "I'm glad you're here."

"Good." Bodie gave her a small shake. "Because I brought dinner." He left down the stairs and returned with a bottle of cheap champagne, a new box of wine glasses and a steaming packet of chips.

Hana watched as he unpacked the gift onto the dusty window seat, seeing his father in every facet of his body language and looks. Gorgeous and complicated. She sat next to him, releasing a cloud of dust from the windowsill. "Where's your car?"

"In the garage." Bodie pushed a chip into his mouth and closed his eyes. "These are nice. Got them from a place in Ngaruawahia."

"My garage?" Hana savoured the word on her lips and he nodded.

"Yep. Some gumby blocked the bottom of the slope with a Hilux. I didn't realise until I got half way down so I drove into the garage and parked."

"Made yourself at home already. Nice." Hana dipped a chip into a container of tomato sauce.

"Yep. I hope you didn't buy that Hilux today." He narrowed his eyes. "You didn't, did you?"

"Why? It's a cool man-wagon."

Bodie snorted. "It's a diesel fuel guzzler. It's a farm vehicle. Please tell me you didn't."

Hana rolled her eyes. "No. It belongs to a farmer. He lent it after mine went missing."

"Went missing?" Bodie stopped, a chip in mid-air. "Went missing where?"

Hana sighed and recounted the story. "I told you this."

"No you didn't!"

Her mind worked back over the last few weeks and she couldn't remember who knew what anymore. "I thought I did."

Hana ate until the chips masked the taste of wood dust. Then she leaned against the windowsill and rested her head on the cool glass. The dull ceiling bulb highlighted the small cuts healing on Bodie's cheek and more of the same on his fingers. "What happened?" she asked, taking his hand in hers.

"I don't wanna talk about it." The shutters slammed over her son's expression and Hana ran a hand over his hair.

"Fine," she said, her voice soft. "But are you okay otherwise?"

Bodie swallowed and shook his head. "No. I'll tell you later."

Hana kissed his cheek, using her hand to remove the dusty mark she left on his face. He snorted and reached for the champagne. "Let's drink to your new start, Mum," he said, lifting the foil from around the cap.

"I can't drink and drive." Hana raised a hand in protest and Bodie showed her the label.

"It's not real," he said, laughing at her. "I'm a cop, Mum. I can't drink and drive either. It's fizzy fruit drink."

Hana reached for the bottle and inspected it, seeing the letters rearranged in the label. "Oh," she said, her face breaking into a smile. "That's clever. Your brain reads it as champagne, not what it actually says."

Bodie nodded and filled a slim glass, handing it over and then pouring one for himself. "Yep," he said. "Perspective." Hana's smile faded as he lifted his glass to clink against hers, halting mid-way. "What's the matter?"

She sighed. "Someone else told me life was about perspective." Her eyes dulled with sadness. Logan's infidelity pained her, but at least she knew where she stood. "And it is." Hana raised her glass and the chink against Bodie's filled the room with a musical note. It soothed her heart and gave her hope. "It's all about perspective." She waved her glass around the room. "And this is my perspective from now on."

Hana grinned at her son and sipped her drink, studying him from beneath her eyelashes. He looked deflated and a familiar tick of worry began in the back of her head. She tried to respect his privacy, maternalism wanting to probe and comfort. "I needed you here," she whispered, sighing out her own concerns as dust particles bounced in the light. "I didn't know it though." Her fingers stroked his wrist through his jacket sleeve and she saw him wince. "Are you hurt?" she asked, the question tentative.

Bodie nodded and laid his glass on the floor. Then he rolled up his sleeve. Thin gouges covered the flesh of his forearm, deeper in some places than others. It wrapped around his arm and she recognised the marks. "Barbed wire?" Hana asked, reaching out her fingers and pulling away at the last moment.

"Yeah." Bodie inhaled. "A deep dive in a crater lake. A kid went missing from a family boat. We've searched that lake heaps of times for different reasons and stuff collects at one end. We spent a day looking, but the current sent me a different way just before the boss called time on it. Someone dumped a load of rusty wire on the bank and rising water levels pulled it under. He must've swum for the shore and would've made it, but the wire snagged the hem of his pants. Struggling would have dislodged more of it from the bank and he drowned there, less than a metre from the surface."

"That's so sad," Hana breathed. "How old was he?"

"Ten." Bodie's jaw worked in his cheek. "It never gets to me but this one did."

"Why?" Hana stroked his hair back from his face. "What's different?"

Bodie swallowed. "He looked like Marcus, Mum. I saw the photos before we dived and it became personal. It stopped being a body and became my best friend, my brother-in-law. It wasn't a job anymore, but something else."

"Oh, sweetheart." Hana's chest felt tight with the effort of not crying, of not making it all about her fears. She put her arms around Bodie's neck and he let her hold him, his face pushed into her soft hair.

"I got a tetanus jab," he muttered. "So you don't need to print off pictures of lock-jaw and sepsis."

Hana jabbed him in the ribs. "That was once! And it wasn't tetanus."

"I remember." Bodie sat up and rubbed his hands over his face. "You printed off a heap of pictures of athletes' foot when I refused to shower."

"They weren't feet," Hana began and Bodie covered her mouth with a large hand.

"No! They weren't. And I don't want to talk about those types of rotting body parts with my mother, thank you!"

Hana giggled. Her sentence sounded muffled. "You didn't want to talk about them back then either."

"No, I didn't!" Bodie removed his hand and reached for their glasses, topping them both up.

"It's hard when there's no father figure," Hana admitted. "I would've set Vik on you. He'd tell you how much you stunk."

"Man smell!" Bodie protested. "I liked it. He'd have liked it too."

Hana snorted and accepted her refilled glass. She raised it against the backdrop of the deepening night sky through the window and clinked it with Bodie's. "To a new future for both of us," she said, forcing positivity into her voice. "Gaining perspective and putting the past back where it belongs."

"Amen to that." Bodie clinked her glass again, planted a kiss on her dusty cheek and then sipped, closing his eyes and savouring the flavour. "This is nice."

"Jock-rot," Hana said, laying her glass on the windowsill. A peal of laughter escaped her lips at the horrified look on her son's face. "That's what the fungus is called. Boys get it when they don't wash!"

Bodie spat drink down his chin and his shirt and leaned forward, choking. "That's disgusting!" he cried, his body heaving with laughter. A giggling fit consumed them both and the sound carried outside to the lonely bush, floating away on the breeze. They each laughed away their troubles and the world felt a brighter place.

Chapter 37

The climb to the house appeared steep and unforgiving in the twilight. An unexpected visitor left his bike at the bottom of the driveway, fearful it might skid and slide on the loose gravel and tip him over one of the sharper faces of the hillside. Darkness grew around him without the soft haze of streetlights to break its impact and he stuck to the ridge of grass at the side of the driveway.

Finding Hana absent from Achilles Rise and only Tiger sitting in the first floor window, Logan drove to Ngaruawahia in pursuit. Her sudden animosity confused and frightened him. The house looked dark from the front, but the sloping driveway revealed his truck, parked askew. The back seats bent forwards and a dent from something heavy left a mark in the gravel behind the bumper. Walking forwards, Logan stopped at the sight of a smart silver BMW tucked into the garage.

The moon woke, making the silver paint on the flashy car glimmer and sparkle. It put his old truck to shame. Logan ran his hands through his hair, not recognising the vehicle and mindful of Hana's recent issues. He glanced up at the lighted window, hearing voices and making out two silhouettes back-lit by a single bulb. Hearing Hana's voice, Logan's jaw tensed and he tracked to the other side of the slope, clambering onto a retaining wall to get a better view through the window.

He recognised the back of Hana's head, her hair piled on top in a messy bun. She turned sideways and Logan saw her profile against the yellow glow of the light bulb. Her laughing profile. The other silhouette looked male and taller than Hana. He sat forwards so Logan could only see the ridge of his shoulders. The man lifted his forearm and Hana's head bobbed forward, giving him all her attention.

Logan watched, his heart pounding in his chest. He closed his eyes and imagined himself climbing the stairs and bursting in on them. Humiliation burgeoned like a heated flush and he knew he wouldn't follow through.

More laughter disturbed the darkness, followed by the clink of glasses. Then the profiles leaned together and kissed. Logan let out an audible sigh. "Shit, shit, shit!" he hissed under his breath. "What the hell happened?"

His body heavy, he returned the way he came, slipping and sliding in the grit without caring. "What did you do, Caroline?" he groaned. "What did you tell her about us?"

Of course, Hana would move on. Any man would be lucky to date her. But the speed of it made him nauseous.

Logan unlocked his bike and rested his hands on the seat. Sweat dripped from his forehead onto the leather. In anger he snatched his phone from his inside pocket and dialled a number, not waiting for a greeting from the other end. "What did you do?" he snapped, his anger palpable.

A sexy laugh filtered through the darkness. "Thanks for last night," she crooned. "I'd like a lift home next time."

"Go to hell!" Logan disconnected and slammed his helmet on his head. The expensive bike roared to life without a protest, infusing him with a sense of gratitude. One glimpse of loyalty in a cruel world.

His speed topped a tonne on the back road towards Huntly and he floored it, feeling the wind tug at his jacket. Curses ran through his head along with the realisation; so near but still too far.

Chapter 38

Bodie picked Hana up from work the next afternoon and drove her to the garage on Greenwood Street. Hana's heart sank at the alarmed expression on Brian's face as they pulled onto the forecourt. "Oh." She grabbed her son's arm and Bodie raised his eyebrows in suspicion. Hana swallowed. "I kinda made up a boyfriend," she said.

Bodie's eyes narrowed. "He hit on you?"

Hana squirmed. "Not exactly. More of a misunderstanding. Trouble is, I described you."

Bodie's eyes widened in horror and he shrank back against his seat. "Mum! That's gross."

"It wasn't you, someone just like you." Hana slapped his leg. "It popped out and then it seemed like a good idea. How was I meant to know you'd meet him?"

Brian walked towards the car and Hana whimpered high in her throat. "Shoot me. Shoot me now."

With a snort, Bodie jumped out and shook Brian's hand. His lips struggled against laughter and Hana endured her son's embellished tales about their incredible relationship. "Stop it!" she hissed, jabbing Bodie in the back as he joked about sugar mummies. Brian shot sideways glances at Hana until her discomfort levels went skywards.

Bodie peered in the Honda's side window and hid his smirk at the flowers and chocolates adorning the passenger seat. "I'll leave you to it," he announced, kissing Hana on the cheek. "See you at home. Darling."

Hana extracted herself from Brian's curiosity and drove to Achilles Rise, thrilled with her new vehicle and not disappointed by its performance. Bodie met her in the kitchen, sniggering at her with his face in the fridge. "Wow, Mum. I never knew how you felt about me. There's a law against that kind of thing though. I'll have to decline."

"Stop." Hana elbowed him in the ribs. "I started off describing your father, if you must know. Then I added cop as a job title and vice squad and it got worse. I knew he'd assume I'd described you because I said Indian."

Bodie clutched his heart like a dramatic Romeo and laughed at Hana's discomfort. His tone hardened at the same time as his eyes. "What kind of salesman hits on single women?"

Hana shook her head. "Don't worry about it. I need never see him again." She peered over his shoulder into the empty fridge. A hardened block of cheese lurked in the corner next to a packet of bread containing two crusts. "Cheese on toast?" she asked. "One each."

"No." Bodie withdrew his head and slammed the fridge door. "I'll take my hot date for dinner."

Hana groaned. "You're making it worse. I'm embarrassed enough." She covered her face with her hands and Bodie relented, wrapping his arms around her.

"Okay. I'll shut up. How about dinner though?"

Hana nodded and released a sigh. "I need to take the Hilux back first. I intended to get a taxi home afterwards."

"No need. I'm here now. I'll follow you in my car and take you to dinner."

Hana sniffed into Bodie's shirt and nodded. "Thanks. But can you drive the Honda? I can't wait to give it a blast."

"Okay." Bodie patted her back. "Let's do it. I'm starving."

They locked up after feeding Tiger and drove to the garage in convoy. They sipped coffee sitting in the truck as it went through the car wash. "Izzie said you met a guy at work." Bodie looked at Hana sideways over his cup and she winced.

"I did. It went nowhere. Nothing to worry about."

Bodie jerked his head upwards in acknowledgement. "I'll check him out, if you want."

"No need." Hana gritted her teeth and inhaled, driving further questions away with her tight body language.

She cleaned the interior with an autovac and Bodie watched her, leaning against the side of the truck. When she opened the rear door to vacuum the boot, he used the time to raid the glove box. His fingers closed around a crumpled letter from the tax office addressed to Mr Logan Du Rose. Keeping one eye on Hana, Bodie opened it out and speed-read it, scratching his head. He shoved it back and closed the flap as Hana fought the autovac into its cradle. "Here, let me help," he said, picking up the slack on the air hose. "Have you ever heard of Circle Line Holdings?"

Hana wrinkled her nose and shook her head. "No. That's a funny question. Why?"

"No reason." Bodie patted the side of the truck. "Do we need to fill this up?"

Hana bumped the vehicle along the driveway towards the villa in Gordonton. Every tilt and clatter through the potholes increased her heartbeat and tension formed a knot in the back of her neck. She pulled up outside the house and put the handbrake on, noticing a tremor in her hands. "Oh my gosh!" she groaned. "I can't do this!"

Bodie pulled in behind and waved, waiting for Hana to deliver the keys. Curiosity brightened his eyes and Hana felt him staring at her. She sat for so long, he got out and walked across. "What's the matter?"

"I can't do it!" Hana gushed. She jumped from the driver's seat and landed at his feet. "Please can you do it for me?"

Bodie backed away. "No. It's rude. Someone lent you a vehicle. You've cleaned it and filled it. Do it yourself."

"Bodie, please!" Hana's eyes filled with tears and she glanced across at the closed front door, fear in her eyes. "I can't. Do it, please? I made a mistake and got involved with someone who dumped me for his ex. I feel stupid." Her fingers shook as she pushed the keys into Bodie's chest. "They might be in there together. I'm humiliated enough."

Hana ignored his bewilderment and ran to the Honda, hurling herself into the passenger seat. Bodie blinked as Hana scooted into the foot well and disappeared from view. He gritted his teeth and climbed the porch steps, knocking on the wide front door with a decisive rap.

He waited a long while. When the door opened, a tall man eyed him with suspicion, his hair damp and sticking up. The scent of shower gel and aftershave hung around him and Bodie noticed his tee shirt clinging to his body in patches of damp. He'd tugged it over his head to answer the door and a wet line stained the neck a darker colour. "Sorry, in the shower," the man said.

Bodie's eyes narrowed. "I bet. Say hi to your new girlfriend and stay away from Hana Johal." He threw the keys, noticing the other man's fast reflexes as he caught them in mid-air. "Thanks for the loan of the car but leave her alone." Bodie's brown eyes flashed.

Logan Du Rose saw his truck on the driveway and regret budded in his grey eyes. "She sent the truck back." His jaw gritted, giving him a hard look. "But I said she could borrow it."

"Well, now she doesn't need it." The sarcastic edge in Bodie's voice sliced the air and the dark man studied his face.

"What's your problem?" Logan demanded, eyes narrowing as his hand formed a fist around the car keys. "Who the hell are you?"

Bodie snorted. "Someone you don't wanna mess with, dude." He turned to walk away, calling over his shoulder. "Stay away from my mother, loser."

Logan inhaled at the slur and his nostrils flared. He held onto his patience by the narrowest margin as the cocky punk climbed into the driver's seat of the Honda and revved the engine. Gravel spat from behind it, peppering the porch steps and Logan's mouth twitched in anger. But he said nothing.

"Don't dirty the car!" Hana hissed from the foot well. "That's naughty!"

Bodie waited until the end of the driveway to reply. "Where'd you find the bad boy?" he demanded as Hana sat up.

"Work." She curled her lower lip, looking ashamed of herself. "I shan't bother again."

Bodie shook his head. "Oh, Mum."

"You didn't like him?" She straightened her hair and scooped it back into a ponytail.

Bodie shrugged and his lips quirked upwards. "I can see the attraction for a chick." He raised an eyebrow in approval. "I baited him and he didn't go for it."

"What do you mean?" Hana unfastened her seatbelt. "Move over. I'm driving my new car."

Bodie walked around the outside while she jabbed herself on the gear lever and handbrake crossing the centre. "I expected him to smack me," he concluded, clicking the seatbelt closed. "But he didn't." His face twisted in a pensive look. "He could've. I saw it in his face. I called him a loser and he reacted. But he let it run."

Hana shrugged. "He's not a loser. He's a brilliant teacher and his parents own a massive hotel and farm above Rangiriri. From what I saw, he's an astute businessman. They rely on him."

"What farm and hotel?" Bodie's brows knitted and Hana shook her head, wagging her finger at him.

"Oh, no you don't, Officer Johal. Leave the poor man alone. They'll bust you down to kennel cleaner if you perform an illegal database search and you know it."

Bodie rolled his eyes. "Who said anything about illegal?" He winked at her. "His back light is out, that's all."

"Is it?" Hana's brow furrowed. "Is that my fault?"

Bodie laughed at her and tapped the dashboard. "No. Now feed me. You promised."

"Left or right?" Hana gave him the choice, a smirk on her lips and Bodie pointed right.

"Hamilton," he said. "Pizza." His smile mocked her. "I know what you're doing, Mum." He shook his head at her expression of wide-eyed innocence. "You're paying me back for my teenage years of sullen silences."

Hana winced. "No, I just don't wanna talk about it."

"Now you see how it feels." Bodie grinned at her and watched the villa shrink in the distance. His mind worked through a mystery he wanted to solve.

After a week of renovations, Hana looked forward to the weekend. She woke on Saturday morning and pulled the pillow over her head with a groan. Living in one house, working in the south of the city and driving half an hour north after work exhausted her. Bodie knocked on the door and brought her a cup of tea. "Get up, lazy-bones," he said, sitting on the end of the bed. "We've got stuff to do today."

Hana sat up and sipped her tea, rubbing her eyes with one hand. "I know. I'm exhausted. What time do you leave tomorrow?"

"Around tea time." Bodie scratched his stubbled chin and smiled at her. "That's the plan. Unless you need me to rescue you again." He laughed and Hana kicked him through the sheets.

"Not my fault. I varnished myself into a corner. It could happen to anyone!"

"No!" Bodie snorted. "These things only happen to you."

"I needed a wee so bad." Hana winced at the memory. "The varnish took ages to dry enough for me to escape. Damn stuff." Her face brightened at the memory of the smart new roof and guttering. Flashing green eyes gave her a youthfulness. "The builders worked hard. You kept them at it."

"Yep." Bodie lay backwards on the bed. "Decent guys. Today I'll replace the plasterboard on those ceilings with damp patches. We need to be up there by ten to meet the electrician. He wants to start on Monday."

Hana dragged herself out of bed and spent most of Saturday morning stripping aged wallpaper. She returned the rented sander to the store and swapped it for a steamer. The remaining thick flock caved in the face of such stiff opposition and peeled itself. She moved on to annoying Bodie, stealing his filler for the myriad holes and dents revealed underneath. Every time he left his ladder or tools unattended, she stole them. Around lunchtime, he kissed goodbye to the remnants of his patience. "I can't get anything done if you keep nicking my stuff! Go back to Hamilton and pack up the house. You're doing my head in! Once the electrician's finished you can move here for good. I'll finish the ceilings if you leave me alone."

"But they need plastering," Hana grumbled and Bodie jabbed a finger at her.

"Yes, he's coming in an hour."

"Who?" Hana put her hands on her hips. "Who's coming in an hour? It's Saturday."

"The guy to do the plastering!" Veins stuck out on Bodie's neck as frustration took over. "It's one or two patches. He doesn't need to do the whole house. You'll let it dry out for a few weeks and then paint over it when you do the rest of the room. Okay?"

Hana nodded. "How did you get someone to come on a Saturday?"

Bodie wiggled his eyebrows. "You're paying him extra."

Hana frowned. "You want me to leave?" she said, her lips twitching in a nervous tick. "But then you'll go home tomorrow and I won't get to spend time with you."

Bodie rolled his eyes and gathered her into his chest. "You're a nutter, Mum. I've been here all week. Do the packing and as soon as the plasterer leaves, I'll drive back for a shower and we'll go for food together. Yeah?"

"Okay." Hana nodded and ran a hand through her messy curls. "I'll take the steamer back on the way home. Apart from the master bedroom and lounge, the rest of the rooms were bare plaster. I've packed the rubbish into the Honda."

"Good. Now get!" Bodie shooed her onto the porch and locked the front door behind her.

Halfway home, Hana's mobile phone chirruped to itself in her pants pocket. She pulled over on River Road and answered it.

"I'm sorry," Angus began before Hana replied. "But I mentioned Achilles Rise to someone at school and they phoned me about it this morning."

"Okay. That's fine," Hana said.

"I am sorry," Angus repeated, but his apology sounded half-hearted. "My friend tells me his recommendation was for you to rent it."

"Yes." Hana opened her mouth to continue but Angus cut her off. "I've left numerous messages on your machine and you didn't answer your mobile."

She heard the tension in his voice and groaned. "You're outside the house with them, aren't you?" Her heart sank into her shoes.

"Yes, dear." Angus sounded unrepentant. "Logan mentioned your new house, so I figured you'd be leaving soon. They've looked around the outside and want to see indoors."

All coherent thought abandoned Hana. "I'm on River Road," she managed. "I'll be about ten minutes. Can't you go for coffee somewhere?"

"Oh, we've done that," Angus replied. "I'll tell them you're on your way."

Hana bounced onto the drive with plaster in her hair and a sticky mess on her tee shirt. The new biology teacher greeted her with enthusiasm. "We love your house, Hana," he gushed, unloading two small children from the back of the car. "Our landlord sold the house out from under us and we can't find anything suitable."

"When do you need to be out?" Hana asked, picking wallpaper from under her fingernails.

"End of the month." The teacher twisted his face into a grimace and Hana's eyes widened.

"That's ten days. I'm not ready." Her courage wavered as her emotional self demanded a foot in both camps while her rational self reminded her she went home to pack.

Hana unlocked the side gate. "Have a look around the garden while I tidy up." She waved in dismissal and bolted, spending the next five minutes running around the house and hiding things in strange places. The biology teacher chatted with Angus and tried to keep his small children off the flower beds. Tiger watched from Hana's pillow, making no attempt to help. Hana gathered up a pile of laundry, the folds of the clothing filled with sanding dust and lumps of plasterboard. "Damn!" she groaned, noticing a stain on her tee shirt where she used it to mop up a varnish spill. "You'll be sorry in a minute," she threatened Tiger, who gave a lazy blink. "When those two little kids get a look at you, it'll be a different matter!"

The messiest thing in the house was its owner, her hair hanging round her face having escaped its clip and her clothing covered in blobs of filler. Hana finished fussing and unlocked the ranch slider into the family room, noticing the biology teacher's heavily pregnant wife hauling herself up the slope from the driveway. She stood and caught her breath in the family room with Angus while her children bounced on their father in the garden.

Mrs Biology Teacher smiled at Hana. "I love it. Please can we rent it? We're desperate." Angus winced and the woman corrected herself, "I'm sorry, I shouldn't rush you." She pointed to her prominent bump. "I'm scared."

Hana exhaled, remembering her own traumatic pregnancy with Bodie. With so little support, she and Vik existed in a haze of misery, cowering beneath their shared disgrace. The couple raised Bodie in a grubby upstairs bedsit while they both finished their degrees, never sure where the next month's rent might appear from.

Hana smiled with sympathy at the hopeful woman. "I'll make tea," she said, attempting to buy thinking time and extract herself from Angus' unkind pressure tactics. Hana found milk in the fridge and rustled up tea and coffee for the adults and cold water for the children.

Tiger skulked through with his tail in the air and the two-year-old girl squealed, "Puss!" She sprayed her brother and the cat with a mouth full of water. Tiger beat a hasty retreat through the cat flap. Both children lunged for the open door and the cat fled over the back fence. A frantic barking heralded his arrival in the Rottweiler's yard and a yelp as the cat retaliated.

Hana felt sick with the pressure the family's visit put her under. "I haven't set a rental price yet," she said, defending herself against the barrage of questions. "I don't know what other people charge."

Angus shifted in his chair, affected by Hana's unease. He rose to leave. "I'm sorry, Hana, I've rushed you into it."

She glared at him, recognising a familiar glint in his eye. "No, you're not," she muttered. "You've no intention of losing a good teacher to homelessness and you're forcing me to make a decision. I bet you conspired with your agent friend."

The biology teacher and his wife stood, stepping in the garden as embarrassment shrouded them. Angus watched the children play and fixed his perceptive gaze on Hana's flushed face. "It's time to go, Hana," he said, his voice gentle.

"I'm doing just fine!" She stood and balled her fists. "I bought a house and a new car. I'm letting go. How can you do this to me? It's mean!"

The teacher and his wife walked inside as their children frolicked around the wide lawn. "We should leave," he said. "Sorry about this."

Hana watched his wife as she kept her eyes down and focussed on the carpet. She swallowed like she might cry. Angus waved his hand towards the hall. "Why don't you lovely people go and have a good look around? I'm sure Hana won't mind."

He observed Hana with a determined glint in his eyes and she glared in return. She waved her hand towards the hall door with an ineffectual wafting motion. For a woman who needed recovery time after the front steps, Mrs Biology Teacher moved like a racehorse when faced with possible success. She launched herself into the hallway and headed for the bedrooms, husband in tow.

"Angus!" Hana whipped round as soon as the couple moved out of earshot, "How could you? I'm not ready."

Angus rose from his sitting position on the sofa, watching the children chase each other round the garden and straight across another of Hana's flower beds. "My dear, you will never be ready." Smiling, he walked into the garden, climbing the steps to the upper terrace. He sat on the swing seat at the top, admiring the view in the bright sunshine. When the couple emerged from their inspection of the house, they found him with a child on either side, telling them tales about the dragons in Scotland when he was a boy.

By the time Bodie crawled home around five o'clock that night, he found Hana packing with frantic abandon. A box contained all the ornaments from the lounge and he tripped over the rolled up rug by the door.

"Did you finish?" Hana asked him and he nodded.

"Yeah. I finished the ceilings. It got easier when my equipment stopped disappearing." He sat on the sofa and watched Hana pack books from the Welsh dresser. "Far out, Mum. When I sent you home to pack, I kinda thought you'd mess around for hours. I'm amazed."

"Bloody Angus!" she groaned. "He gave me no choice!"

A necktie with a jovial Santa pattern flopped over one of the bin bags by the door and Bodie reached for it. He pressed the little squeaker at the back. "I wondered what happened to this," he mused. A gaudy Christmas tune bleated from it and Hana watched her son, trying to read his closed face. "It still works," he said to himself under his breath.

Hana nodded. "Dad's favourite tie," she whispered.

Bodie stood, tied the bag shut and carried it downstairs to the garage. Hana fought the urge to run after him, drag the tie from the bag and hug it to her chest. "You can't," she whispered into the empty room. "You're letting go, remember?" Hana gritted her teeth, praying she held out until the rubbish truck arrived on Tuesday.

After another day of snagging problems at Culver's Cottage, Bodie left, driving back up to Whangarei and his sparse room in a rental house. Hana found it hard to let him go, loneliness and devastation moving in as he hugged her goodbye. "I love you, darling," she told him in a whisper. "Keep safe."

Hana sat on the steps to the first floor and cried after Bodie drove away. Exhaustion nagged at her mind and body and weakness tugged at her heartstrings. She obeyed the urge to visit the rubbish bags in the garage, sinking to the concrete floor and sobbing when she couldn't find Vik's tie. After another hour of searching in the semi-darkness she knew she'd lost it. She also knew she couldn't ask for it back.

Work on Monday seemed dark and depressing. Smarting from Bodie's absence, Hana oozed misery.

"I need you to type this," Caroline demanded, placing a rough, handwritten report on Hana's desk with a flourish.

Hana kept her eyes on her computer and typed, her fingers flying across the keyboard with a report Sheila wanted. A form for Evie sat in her tray. "I'm too busy," she said, acid leaking from every word. "The typist is downstairs in the admin corridor. She types for the deans." Hana didn't raise her head and ignored Caroline's irritated sigh, causing Sheila's eyes to bug in her head with amazement.

"Do it!" Caroline pushed the paper in Hana's face and she ducked, fighting to maintain professionalism.

"Don't speak to her like that!" Sheila stepped across, offering unanimity as she faced Caroline. "She doesn't do typing for the deans. Go to the typist."

Caroline swallowed and Hana watched her consider her options. When she stalked away, Hana sighed in relief but knew she'd pushed too far. "I should've just done it," she said with a grimace and Sheila shook her head.

"No. I'm sick of doing what everyone else wants. Tell her to sod off if she tries it again." Sheila picked up her books and left, closing the door behind her as the bell rang for class.

Hana exhaled and put her head in her hands. "Why give her an excuse to get you fired?" she asked herself. "Just do her bloody typing. Be the bigger person." As if in response, a mobile phone bleeped into the silence and Hana traced it to Caroline's desk. Her conscience told her not to read the message but an uncharacteristic nastiness arose in her, accompanied by curiosity. Pressing a few buttons and finding no screen code, Hana's eyes widened at the message she read. 'Thx 4 last nite. When cn I see u again? Xxx'

For a techno-moron who couldn't work the DVD player, Hana managed to do geek like a professional. She deleted the message, replaced the phone and sat down in her chair. The cursor blinked on her computer screen and she ignored it, knowing in her heart the message came from Logan. She toyed with the idea of retrieving the phone again and checking the number against his. It showed on Caroline's as 'Hot Guy' but Hana shook her head and refused to give in. "You'll get caught," she told herself. "Just leave well alone now."

She cringed at the memory of her amazing weekend with Logan, prickling tears adding their weight to her stupidity. Another emotion wriggled to the surface and Hana knew she couldn't keep pushing it away. She worked in a church school and Logan knew about her past. A teenage pregnancy could get her fired. Hana's body tingled with terror at the possibility he might tell Caroline and let her do his dirty work.

Hana pulled herself together and dragged herself back to her new resolutions. She made her decision rather than watch her life crumble before her eyes, stomping down the front stairs and into reception.

"He's not to be disturbed!" The principal's assistant squeaked as Hana stormed past. Angus' door stood open and Hana marched through it, closing it with a slam behind her. Rushing forward to the heavy oak door to listen, the assistant heard Hana's loud exclamation.

"How could you do that to me? I thought we were friends."

The answering voice replied in lower tones and the assistant heard nothing more. The receptionist wandered over for a listen, but only recognised the sound of someone crying.

Angus gave Hana a painful reprimand. "I understand what it's like to lose a loved one and find yourself stuck in a life poorly lived. We wait for them to reappear and carry on as usual because moving on without them is excruciating." He handed her another tissue, perching on the corner of his desk and patting Hana's shoulder.

"But it's all gone wrong," she sobbed.

"Then start again!" he commanded. "And again and again and again. But at least do something, Hana!"

Hana dumped the ensuing legalities of the rental on Angus as punishment. "Fine," he capitulated. "I'll engage my agent, deal with the paperwork and present it to you for signing. Be ready to move out two weekends hence!"

Hana sat in his visitor's chair while he rang the removals company to book it. Angus replaced his handset and smiled in satisfaction. Hana felt like a bus drove over her chest. "Go home, darling Hana," he said with a grin. "I'll square it with Donald. Go home and pack. And stop wallowing girl!"

Hana emerged looking puffy eyed and flustered. The gossipy women spread rumours she'd got fired.

"No!" squeaked the alarmed biology teacher, overhearing their bile in the staffroom. "We want her house!"

Chapter 39

The following Sunday afternoon, Hana stood in her dining room and surveyed her home of many years. It appeared sad and empty, her possessions stacked in boxes around the room. All week she had flitted between work and two homes, running herself ragged in the process. Her phone rang and she retrieved it from the counter and answered.

"You packed yet?" Bodie sounded jovial and Hana smiled.

"Sort of," she replied, hedging.

"That's a no then." He laughed and Hana shook her head, realising he couldn't see her.

"It's an almost. I've finished the kitchen, dining room and lounge. I've stacked the boxes but can't get them down the stairs to the garage. The other bedrooms only contained furniture and that's all dismantled and downstairs. It's just my room now and I'm doing that next."

"Wow. Impressive." Music sounded in the background and Bodie spoke to someone else. "Sorry, Mum. Gotta go. Break's over and we just got a call."

"Okay. Take care." Hana sighed and surveyed the heavy boxes again as Bodie rang off. She hoped the removals men had big muscles. Bits of paper and weird stuff clung to the edges of the room, butted up to the skirting board and waiting for her to make decisions. "I hate this bit," Hana groaned. "Too many choices."

A sharp rap on the front door told Hana the battery had run out for the doorbell. She clattered down the stairs in her slippers, the lack of furniture making her footsteps echo. She opened the door, a vague smile plastered on her face to mask her irritation at the disturbance. Logan stood at the top of the steps sheltering under the small porch. Rain drove onto his back, plastering his hair to his head and his jacket looked damp across the shoulders. His eyes held Hana's in a firm gaze although his fingers shook as he ran a wet hand across his forehead. "We need to talk," he began. "I don't understand what happened between us." He stopped abruptly at the stunned expression on Hana's face.

"What happened between us?" she squawked and stuttered. "You cheated on me with your ex-fiancé! Go away. Leave me alone! And have a nice life!"

Hana launched herself inside and slammed the door. She stomped up the stairs, enjoying the sound her righteous indignation made in the echoing hallway. Having relished the slam of the front door, she repeated it with the hall and bedroom doors. "I don't believe it!" she fumed. Hana hurled herself on the bed in temper, remembering at the last moment it was dismantled. Her face-plant on the carpet robbed her of dignity and breath.

Logan lifted his hand to knock again. Then he thought better of it. He descended the front steps with an aura of heartbreak, shoulders bowed against the weight of disappointment. His truck dropped spots of oil onto the driveway and Logan glanced underneath and wrinkled his nose. He delayed the unlocking process, hoping Hana might reconsider. She didn't. He stood on the drive and listened to a mysterious series of loud bangs and crashes from inside.

The insistent hammering on the door ten minutes later sounded loud in the empty hallway. Hana pulled on the heavy box, hauling it with white knuckled fingers. Her entire collection of pullovers peeked from the hand holes, swathing her best china and offering woolly protection. "Bugger off, Logan!" she hissed, bending her knees and pulling with all her might. "How can you wonder what happened? Caroline bloody Marsh happened, you idiot!" She ignored the knocking, more occupied with manoeuvring the awkward cardboard weight through the door of the master bedroom. It wedged itself in the doorway, forcing her to tug it diagonally one way then the other. It emerged with a pop, sending the back of Hana's head into the wall behind her.

With gritted jaw and a heart full of determination, she pulled it the length of the hall, leaving dark pile tracks along the carpet. Her head throbbed, but she refused to quit. Going backwards, she increased momentum and shot onto the landing, almost pitching down the stairs to the front door. The frosted glass panels either side of it betrayed her presence and the knocking became more purposeful.

"Right! That's it!" Marching down the stairs for the second time, Hana wrenched the door open, her face a picture of anger as she readied herself to banish Logan forever.

The door banged hard against the little hall table behind it and knocked it into the wall. Hana followed it, the weight of the door hitting her in the face. She tasted blood and her vision distorted as her brain struggled to cope. "Hey sweetheart, going somewhere?" The big blond man moved with speed and precision, grabbing Hana around the throat as she reeled. "I tried to warn you," he said, his voice a level growl. He pushed her backwards onto the stairs to the first floor, laying her flat so the treads pushed into her spine. "Get that door shut!" He issued the order over his shoulder.

The dark haired man clicked the door closed and turned to survey the scene, his face impassive. Dismantled furniture lined the hallway and boxes wobbled in a stack at the top of the stairs. "Someone's doin' a runner." His Oriental accent mangled the words and dark eyes fixed on Hana's face as she choked and gagged beneath the blond man's fingers.

"Yep." He dug harder into her throat and Hana saw black spots dance in her vision. "Told you."

Hana felt the small bones along her spine crunch and creak, taking the impact of the stairs as the intruder flattened her. She knew it was hopeless when she heard herself gasp, her lungs fighting for oxygen.

"Let her go." The other man raised his voice to speak over Hana's gagging and the blond man's grip relaxed enough for her to hiss in a breath. But his weight on her body pinned her to the stairs. He bent his head close to her face, his eyes revealing a conflict between hatred and lust.

"Hello again," he whispered. The hardness in his gaze ruined the attractive masculine bone structure and twinkling blue eyes. He settled astride Hana on the stairs, his weight across her stomach. She wrestled her arms out from under her back, wrists sore from trying to soften her fall. Anger flashed in her eyes.

"You stole my car!" Her voice sounded choked and hoarse.

"Yeah, sorry about that. Hope you find it." The blond man winked and planted a kiss on Hana's lips, further cutting off her breathing. His grip on her throat relaxed. She brought her hands up as fists, slamming them into his arm on one side and head on the other. The small bones of her fingers ached from the impact of his cheekbone. He grunted in surprise and Hana bucked beneath him.

The blond man laughed and snatched up her wrists, pinning them above her head and immobilising her. "Feisty," he said, his voice catching with the effort of restraining her. "My favourite."

"Get off me!" Hana heard her heartbeat pounding in her eardrums as panic and helplessness merged together in her confused brain. Her anger against Logan could have proved useful, had it not deserted her the instant the man kissed her. She fell from the heights of justifiable anger to victim, a transition that made her soul feel damaged, as though dragged across broken glass. Powerlessness left a sickening taste in her mouth.

"Hey, don't kill her; she needs to tell us where it is." He sounded irritated.

"I wouldn't do it like this," the blond scoffed and he pinned Hana's arms beneath his knees and reached into his front pocket. A knife handle emerged in his long fingers and with a flick; the blade exposed its glossy metal face in the fading sunlight. He held the point to Hana's throat and smiled.

"Stop!" His companion lost patience. "Have fun when we find it."

With a sound of disappointment, the blond man stood, eyeing his companion with a veiled hatred which he brought under control with a flick of his long lashes. A severe expression graced the other man's face as he indicated the stairs with a pointed index finger. "Start up there."

The blond man hauled Hana up by her right arm, her legs dragging beneath her and an ache starting in her shoulder. He set her on unsteady feet and pushed her up the stairs in the same fluid motion. She stumbled at the top and he leaned in towards her terrified face, his voice a hoarse whisper. "Where is it? We can do this the easy way or the hard. It doesn't matter to me, sweetheart. I'll enjoy either."

Helplessness rose as acid inside Hana's throat as she realised she had nothing to bargain with. "I don't know," she heard herself squeak. "I don't know what you want."

Asian features stared at her with curiosity as she kneeled on the stairs ahead of him. He fixed his slitted gaze on her face as though weighing up her honesty or her ability to lie. He shook his head, irritation igniting his temper. "I don't know if she lies. Take her up there." He jerked his head towards the stairs.

"But she's running," the blond man insisted. "She's shipping out. I'm telling you, she's got it!"

Hana crawled up the remaining steps on her knees. The blond man yanked her upright again. He pushed her along the hallway where she fell over the abandoned box, hearing china smash within the confines of her many pullovers. In the family room, she remembered sitting with the biology teacher and his wife just a few days before. It felt surreal. Dismantled furniture leaned against the walls. Wall to wall boxes left only small walking areas and the man shoved Hana between them, digging his index finger into the back of her head as she missed her footing and fell countless times. The place looked like a bombsite.

The other man followed them into the room and looked around him in disgust. "Pull it apart!" he muttered, jabbing an angry finger at his partner.

Then he left the room. Hana heard crashes coming from the bedroom end of the house as he upended boxes and her belongings smashed against the carpet. The blond man did likewise in the kitchen. "Move and I'll cut you," he said, a spiteful glint in his eyes. He pushed Hana back against the oven, the handle digging into her spine. She knew he meant it. Then he lifted a box of crockery from the counter and upended it. Most of it smashed and the sound deafened Hana. She covered her ears with her hands as he tossed a box of kitchen items next. A little china spaniel which Bodie gave her their first Christmas in New Zealand, survived the first crashing fall. But the blond man's shoe crushed it with a deliberate stamp, shattering the brindle and white pieces without conscience.

Hana's senses stirred and she recaptured her latent anger. She edged sideways, moving away from the oven handle and making sure the man mistook it for fear of him. He glanced across at her once and sneered, turning back to his work with a commitment admirable in any other profession. He tossed a threat over his shoulder. "There's no way out. You can come past me or through me. I'll enjoy either."

Revulsion filled Hana and she bent her knees with deliberate slowness. She'd wrapped a knife block in drying towels and it lay on its side beneath the upturned box of kitchen items, the blades still sticking from the wood. Hana moved with care, pulling a large carving knife from beneath the towels. Her oak rolling pin sat next to the remains of the china dog and she hefted that in her left hand, standing up again and resting. The blond man glanced at her and she kept still, the implements tucked behind her back. The blade felt cold against her fingers and Hana focussed on the razor sharp edge to give her clarity. Smashing the dog snapped her last nerve and in her mind's eye, Hana imagined punishing the man who smirked as he tipped her belongings onto the carpet and trod them underfoot.

She regulated her ragged breathing. The stranglehold on her throat caused a dreadful soreness around her windpipe, but she couldn't touch it because of the weapons in her hands. She prayed for divine assistance and gripped the knife until her fingers bled.

A loud crash and a shout came from the other end of the house. The blond man looked towards the source of the noise, seeing nothing. "Get here!" He lurched towards Hana, intending to drag her with him, but she dug her heels in and resisted.

"No!" she screamed. She swung the rolling pin with everything she had. It contacted the side of his head with force and Hana followed through, lunging with the knife. The man's eyes widened in shock at the impact and then his eyes shuttered in his head. But it didn't fell him as Hana hoped. Made of strong stuff, he reeled for a second and then grappled for the rolling pin. The knife entangled itself in the sleeve of his dark coloured jacket, missing his heart by a country mile. They struggled together as Hana rained more blows against his temple one-handed, feeling every thudding contact. Enraged, the man grabbed her wrist and slammed it against the counter. Hana let out a scream of pain as her bones contacted the solid surface. The rolling pin spun from her grasp and skittered away, making a resounding clunk as it hit the wall.

Hana saw a dark shape move across the ranch-slider window, distracting her and making her miss her mark with the bare fist which replaced the rolling pin. She saw the dark haired man leap the low wall outside, running down the slope to the street below.

The blond man continued to fight her, overpowering her delicate frame and forcing her body backwards against the bench. He bled from a cut on his temple. The knife freed itself from his sleeve and sliced through the cloth, giving Hana the opportunity to raise it and slam it into his shoulder. The handle slipped in her fingers and the blade sliced her across the palm. Hana's scream contained pain and disappointment. She dropped the knife and it skittered away across the kitchen floor.

Hana saw the flash of fury in the man's eyes and knew she wouldn't survive whatever he did next. He raised his fist and Hana saw the flick knife blade spring to life in his hand. She closed her eyes, waiting for the blow to send her into oblivion. He gave a grunt and his other hand grappled against her sleeve, his fingers digging into her flesh as he pulled Hana into him. Confused, she opened her eyes and saw the blond man fall backwards.

The knife spun away and he clawed at his throat, the collar of his shirt digging into his flesh. She gasped at the sight of the newcomer, watching as he hauled the blond man to the carpet and then sprang on top of him. The sound of bone on bone filled the kitchen as the men fought. The blond man changed his priorities, wanting escape much more than hurting Hana. He squirmed away from his assailant, landing a spiteful right hook against the man's head and tipping him off sideways as he reeled. Hana's legs wobbled like a jelly, unable to sustain the weight of her body. The blond man staggered to his feet and lurched for his knife, landing a kick in his attacker's stomach as he tried to follow.

Hana slipped to the floor as her legs sagged, adrenaline making her gag. Her rescuer clambered to his feet and started to follow the blond man, halting as he heard her gasps of agony. Conflict crossed his face. He reached the ranch slider and then turned back, a different priority demanding his attention. Hana felt for the lino beneath her, the backs of her hands seeking solidity. Blood ran along her right wrist and into her sleeve as she raised her hands in front of her face.

Seeing the dilemma, the blond man stepped back over the threshold and launched himself at her rescuer's back, the knife outstretched. His reflection in a side window gave him away and he met a waiting elbow face first. Cutting his losses he picked himself up and ran, following his accomplice over the side gate and into their vehicle.

Logan approached Hana with care, squatting down in front of her. She saw the toes of his cowboy boots and her heart clenched in misery. She wrapped her arms around herself in the absence of anyone else's, spreading blood along her bare arms and onto the sleeve of her tee shirt.

Logan didn't touch her. "It's okay," he soothed. "It's gonna be okay." He reached into an upturned box and snatched up a drying towel, winding it around Hana's bleeding hand. Then he rose and locked the ranch slider to avoid any other unexpected visitors. "I climbed over the gate," he said, his voice soft. "Geez, Hana. I'm sorry this happened."

She looked up at him even though her throat smarted and her windpipe felt crushed. Gratitude mingled with regret and loss. Hana bowed her head and pressed her face into her knees, battling with overwhelming emotions she couldn't suppress. She heard Logan speaking to the emergency operator and closed her eyes.

Hana kept her face buried, making her battered body as tiny as possible. She missed the misery on Logan's face and the countless times he reached out towards her and then pulled back. "You're okay now, Hana," he soothed from nearby. "You're safe."

The police arrived, causing massive disruption. Two cars parked outside the house and the officers tramped inside without removing their shoes. Hana no longer cared. Twice she gave her statement to different men, the events muddling and changing their order in her brain. They hung around in her kitchen as their radios cackled coded messages and instructions. She watched Logan's boots moving around her, never far away. He answered questions in a low voice, his tone changing as they spoke of calling an ambulance. "She doesn't need any more drama," Logan maintained. "I'll take her to her own doctor when you're done here."

Everything stopped as a more senior officer arrived. His introduction reached Hana through mental static and she didn't register either his rank or name. She remembered Logan's reaction though. His boots scuffed against the floor and she looked up to see his fists balled by his sides. "Nice to see you again, Du Rose," the officer said. He squared his shoulders in his smart grey suit.

"Drop dead." Logan's words emerged as a whisper and Hana closed her eyes and leaned her head back against the cupboard. Every part of her body hurt, sending pain signals to her brain from the damaged parts. Her hand bled until it soaked the cloth Logan wrapped around it and her head and throat felt like they belonged to someone else. She stayed slumped on the floor in front of the sink, the gothic handles from last year's decorating project poking into her back. The lino felt safe and unchanging. Hana refused to move, despite being asked to numerous times.

The senior man in the grey suit took his officers into the lounge. Logan squatted next to Hana and she listened to the hushed conversation while staring at his boots. The policeman lowered his voice. "Her son came to see me ten days ago. Senior Sergeant Bodie Singh Johal. He wasn't pleased with you idiots and nor am I! Get the crime-scene guys in here. Go over it again. This isn't just a home invasion; it's a vendetta. Get this fiasco cleared up!"

"Are you ready?" Logan touched her knee with his index finger and Hana shrank away from him.

"Go away." She gritted her teeth and closed her eyes, cutting him out of her vision and her life.

"Your choice," he said. "But it's the doctors with me or an ambulance with them."

Logan drove Hana to the doctor's surgery. "I'm not going to hospital!" she growled through clenched teeth.

"Okay, okay," he soothed, his expression blank. "I promised."

"Don't you dare tell me to pull myself together either," Hana threatened, wiping her eyes with her bleeding hand. More leakage oozed from the open wound. "Don't tell me to calm down!"

"I haven't and I won't." Logan's voice sounded soft and reassuring despite the heartbreak in his eyes.

"Your promises suck!" she spat. "Nothing but lies."

Logan winced and ignored her. At the doctors, Hana experienced unexpected difficulties getting out of the truck. The distance from the rail to the floor confounded her and her body disobeyed her instructions to move. Her spine hurt and her throat burned like a fireball. She couldn't reach up and touch it because her left wrist ached and a drying towel swathed her right hand. Hana stared at the floor, remembering the flash of the policewoman's camera as she photographed Hana's latest injuries. "I loved this tea towel," she sobbed, sounding ridiculous even to her own addled mind. "Why did you use my Shakespeare one?"

"I'm sorry, Hana." Logan lifted her rigid body down from the truck, setting her on the floor as though she might break. He oozed competence, solidity and strength and after a pause, Hana allowed him to take her arm. Her frightened brain shut out everything but the necessities. Logan put his other hand in the small of her back, alarmed when Hana bashed it away. She overbalanced and hit the back of her head against the truck door. The blond man's abusive kiss filled her mind and Logan's possessive touch gave it life.

At the doctors, Hana went straight into triage without sitting in the waiting room. A nurse took Logan aside and Hana heard them through the curtains. "The police called," she said. "They warned us you'd be coming." Hana didn't hear Logan's reply, but he stayed outside the curtain as the woman continued speaking. "Are you okay? Do you need that stitched?"

"I have to stay with her." His answer sounded stilted.

"We can do it right here." The nurse lowered her voice. "But it needs fixing. We both know why."

The curtains swished open as a doctor walked in, snapping a pair of latex gloves over his hands. Hana panicked and drew her knees closer to her chin. "You're not touching me," she said, her voice wavering. "Stay over there!"

Logan put his head through the curtains and Hana noticed the blood on his shirt and the way he held his left hand. "Let him help you." His determination filtered through her brain and shame replaced the anger.

"I can't, Logan," she wailed. "I can't. I want to go home."

The nurse added her presence to the cramped space and touched the doctor on the arm. "It's okay, I'll do what I can for her. I'll call if I need help."

The doctor nodded and left the cubicle. He glanced at the front of Logan's shirt. "Come with me," he said.

Hana let the nurse examine her hand, feeling the cool fingers against her hot flesh. "This looks deep. It needs stitching," she mused. "Do you want an anaesthetic shot first?"

"I don't care!" Hana sniffed and turned away from the sight of the needle, her fear morphing into futile aggression. "He kissed me on the mouth. I need something to wipe my face."

Logan returned with thick plasters covering his knuckles, the blood already seeping through. He leaned against the sink with a clipboard and pen, struggling to fill in an accident claim form. Hana scrubbed at her lips with an antiseptic wipe, watching him withdraw his wallet from his tight jeans pocket and pay for her appointment in cash.

They called a technician to x-ray Hana's wrist. Bruising on her spine meant they checked that too. They found no broken bones but advised the sprain in her wrist would be painful for a while.

"Sprains can sometimes be worse than a break," the doctor ventured as the nurse wielded a sling. "I've prescribed a shot of pain relief and the nurse will administer that." He gave her a sad smile. "Get well soon. I hope the cops catch the bastard."

Hana swallowed and her gaze flicked to Logan. His jaw flexed and he avoided her eye. The pain killer created minor gaps in Hana's consciousness and she found herself back in the truck with only a foggy memory preceding it.

Logan remained silent but Hana caught him looking at her from under his lashes. "Am I going home now?" she pleaded, her voice pitiful.

"You can't. The cops don't want you there tonight. Trust me, I'm taking you somewhere safe." His expression remained neutral and detesting the weakness in her voice, Hana fell silent. Everything seemed so difficult. She dozed in the passenger seat, waking as her temple bumped against the window.

"The biology teacher won't move in now." She sniffed, wiping her nose on her sleeve. "He won't be safe. He's been my biggest fan all week, waving and smiling across the staffroom at me. I've let him down. His lovely family won't have anywhere to go. Who wants to live in a house after a home invasion?"

"It's fine, babe," Logan soothed. "Trust me."

"I don't trust you," Hana hiccoughed. "You tell lies."

"I don't, Hana." He frowned. "You let the house?"

Hana snorted. "That's right. You promised to help me with Culver's Cottage and my old house. But you didn't, did you?"

"You wouldn't let me!" Logan turned to her, his grey eyes wide with disbelief. "I've tried to speak to you so many times."

"I don't want to speak to you." Hana squeezed her eyes closed and focussed on the various pain sites in her body. Her speech sounded slurred and out of sync with her lips. She didn't register the route and Logan gave up speaking to her, her fear reaction working its way out in flashes of irrational temper.

The injection in Hana's butt made her pliable to the kind female hands which helped her undress and pull on a nightdress that wasn't hers. She descended into the soft, comfortable bed and a welcome pit of nothingness which held neither pain nor fear. Nothing but a drug fuelled haze would have induced her to end up there of all places.

Chapter 40

Hana woke with a clanger of a headache. It took an age for her to wake enough to regain reasonable control of her arms and legs. Sitting proved difficult, the lower half of her body mummified in a sheet. Her left wrist throbbed and her right hand stung beneath heavy bandages. Hana tried to bend her knees and couldn't. "Oh, help!" she squeaked. "I'm not dead. There's been a mistake."

Nobody came. Her bursting bladder needed urgent consideration and rolling onto her left side, Hana worked up enough traction to tip herself off the bed and onto her knees. Once there, she discovered an enormous white, old-fashioned nightdress shrouding her. Hana stuck her bottom in the air and straightened her back, feeling the tendons and ligaments complain against the stretch. She groaned and rested her forehead on her hands.

"Help! Help!" The screech behind her made Hana jump and the nightdress gave a hearty rip on the side seam. Henrietta sounded hysterical and refused to believe Hana didn't collapse.

"What's the time?" Hana groaned as Henrietta tried to stuff her back into bed. "Where am I?"

"You're at Pete's house," Henrietta assured her. "All safe. It's eleven in the morning."

"Eleven!" Hana tried to stand, the nightdress hampering her efforts. "On Monday? I need to go to work!"

Henrietta held her down until Hana gave in, begging to visit the bathroom. The younger woman dogged her footsteps and waited outside until she'd finished. "I need to go home," Hana said, holding onto the wall and attempting to find her way back to the bedroom.

"No, absolutely not." Henrietta remained steadfast and Hana wandered around the bedroom looking for her clothes. "Tiger's alone and defenceless," she complained. "My house isn't locked and I can't be here."

Henrietta tried to buy her off with a cup of tea, which proved pointless. Neither Hana's painful wrist nor her cut hand could support the mug of hot liquid and she gave up. "I'm not staying," Hana maintained. "I'm going home. I'll get a taxi. Where are my bloody clothes?"

Henrietta sighed and patted Hana's forearm. "Work is fine. Angus knows what happened and where you are. Your house is locked and my Peteepoos and Logan slept there last night. The police have access for fingerprinting and they also seized your clothes. Boris kept vigil over me and you." She smiled like the princess from Shrek.

"But Tiger." Hana stood and the mug tipped sideways, spilling brown tea onto the table. "I'm sorry." She put her hand up to her head and winced at the egg on the back of her skull. "How the hell did I do that?"

"Tiger's here." Henrietta waved towards the ranch slider. "Logan fetched him in his jacket. Darn cat ripped it to shreds." She sighed. "I only let him out for an hour and he brought back eleven dead mice."

"Logan?" The fog descended over Hana's brain. "Why?"

"No, the cat." Henrietta stared at her. "You don't look well, Hana. Why don't you have another sleep?"

The cat stalked towards Hana when Henrietta poked him and after his rude awakening, prowled the perimeter of the room. He finished by winding himself around Hana's legs, perplexed by the enormity of the nightdress. He amused himself by chasing threads dangling from the lacy hem until he tied himself in a knot. When Hana freed him, he strutted to a chair and settled down for another snooze.

Hana laid her forehead on her arms, remembering at the last minute to avoid her throbbing wrist and cut hand. Henrietta clucked with concern. "The doctor wants to speak to you. They've checked the x-ray again and think they've found a small break in your hand. I can take you back to repeat the x-ray this afternoon."

"No thanks." Hana sighed into her sleeves. "It doesn't feel broken. I'm not being poked and prodded again."

"Go back to bed for a while." Henrietta cajoled and persuaded but to no avail.

"Logan's bed? Where he slept with Caroline? No thanks." Hana stood, having decided. "I'm going home, although how I'll pack with no hands, I have no idea."

"What's left to do?" Henrietta asked and Hana groaned.

"The intruders wrecked everything at Achilles Rise and Culver's Cottage has no curtains and the place needs a damn good clean. I just need to get on with it."

Henrietta's brow narrowed. "I don't know anything about someone called Caroline, but I only arrived last night." She sighed. "Why can't men be faithful?"

"Not just men." Hana stood and pushed the chair in.

Tiger joined the conspiracy to keep her there as Hana stood and walked towards the hallway. He wound around her legs and knotted up the nightdress beneath her. "I'm still going," she muttered to herself. In the bathroom, she plied her tousled hair with water and mousse she found in the cupboard. Then she strip washed with a plastic bag over her stitches. "I need clothes," she complained, yanking off the bag.

"Oh, my life!" Henrietta exclaimed as Hana emerged from the bathroom with blood running up her arm.

"Oh man!" Hana wailed.

Henrietta patched up the damage with a new bandage and Hana began again. "Have you seen my clothes, please?"

"The cops didn't want your underwear," Henrietta whispered as though they'd bugged the house. "So I washed it for you."

"Thank you." Hana's sense of relief felt disproportionate to the small act of kindness, but it gave her one less thing to stress over. She retrieved her knickers and bra from an airer in the conservatory, nestled much too close to a pair of grubby Y-fronts, which she assumed were Pete's best.

"You can get dressed but you still need to stay here," Henrietta informed Hana as she stood in the bedroom in her undies.

"I can't," Hana insisted. "It's not appropriate."

"Logan said you weren't to leave!" Henrietta argued and Hana rolled her eyes.

"I'm not doing anything he says," she scoffed.

Henrietta looked scandalised. "The police officer who visited last night said he rescued you!" She bristled on his behalf.

"He did," Hana agreed. "But if I hadn't just slammed the door in his face, I might've been more careful before opening it a second time." She gritted her teeth and stuck her chin in the air, refusing to allow him any credit. "I'll get a taxi," she said, her tone stiff. Henrietta beat a hasty retreat and Hana sat on the bed, realising she had no purse or house keys. "Why me?" she groaned, lying on her side and pushing her sad face into Logan's pillow. His scent intoxicated her and emotional misery added to the physical ailments.

She lay for a while drowning in her own misery before galvanising the last of her energy. She opened cupboards and drawers looking for something to borrow. With a pang of guilt tainted by wistfulness, Logan's musky scent drifted up from the clothing and assaulted Hana's nostrils, filling her with regret. She held a tee shirt to her nose and missed him with a physical ache in her chest. The tee shirt bore the slogan, "Love is overrated" on the front and Hana slipped it over her bra, deciding it summed up how she felt. Finding a pair of Logan's track pants, Hana pushed her feet into them, folding the waistband over until she looked eight months pregnant. Her hand bled more and she stamped her foot at the unfairness.

Hana raided shelves in the compulsively tidy wardrobe and found the jumper Logan wore when he tried to dump her in the common room. For reasons known only to her subconscious, Hana slipped it on over the tee shirt. She borrowed socks and moved around, trying to put the room straight. The constant moving of her hand caused even more blood to leak through the bandage and she groaned at discovering drops on the nightdress. She folded it to take home and wash. The sheets she left, knowing she couldn't get them off without more bloodshed. As the bedroom clock ticked over onto the two, Hana tried to move faster, finding her trainers but struggling with the laces.

"I'm not taking you home and I won't lend you the phone to call a taxi," Henrietta declared. She made Hana sit at the kitchen table while she changed the dressing on her hand yet again, using an archaic but well-stocked first aid kit. She jerked her head towards the wound. "Grit your teeth. I'll pull this off and start at the beginning. There's only one bandage left. I'll see if a plaster will work."

"I can't stay here," Hana whined. "I don't want to see Logan!"

Henrietta shrugged. "Well, he wants to see you. I think you owe him that."

Hana sighed in frustration, but before she could answer, gravel crunched on the driveway and a car engine cut. Her heart leapt from calm to panic and she yanked her hand away from Henrietta before she finished with the plaster strip. The scissors Henrietta used to cut the gauze flipped across the table and landed on the parquet floor with a ting. Hana fled. She knew her behaviour looked ridiculous as she acted out the bizarre scene, searching for somewhere safe to hide.

"It's only me," Boris stated, creeping into the lounge with Henrietta clinging to his arm. He coaxed the sobbing Hana out from behind the curtains. "Zer is nussing to fear."

"You can't go home," Henrietta stated, shaking her head as though Hana's weird behaviour confirmed it. Boris nodded in agreement, sitting next to Hana on the sofa with his arm around her shoulders and a concerned look on his face.

"Nein," he said. "You vill be a...how you say...mit den nerven völlig am ende. Not happy all over ze place." He hugged her, patting her on the top of her head in the misguided belief he'd found the only place that didn't hurt on Hana's body. He glanced at Henrietta and raised his eyebrows.

"Look Hana, all that effort, getting dressed and sorting yourself out, it's exhausted you. Here, Logan picked up a prescription for more pain killers this morning." Henrietta produced a bottle of tablets and shook out two into her open hand. "Take these and have a lie down. Your neck looks painful." She faltered, stuck for further adjectives and Boris finished for her,

"It looks zer bad. Go back to ze bedroom and rest. I vill take you home if you vish later."

He waited until she swallowed the pills with the water Henrietta handed her. Then he hauled her to her feet and led her back to Logan's room. Hana lay on the bed and sensed the fog return. Fighting a growing fatigue, she knew she'd been tricked as she floundered and then drowned in the nothingness.

A worried Boris and Henrietta settled themselves in the kitchen and Boris pointed to the black and white cat sneaking along the hallway like a burglar. "Vy he bring dis?" he asked, raising his arms in question.

"He thought it might help," Henrietta replied, her eyes sad. "He said she loves it."

"Was ist das pill?" Boris held his hand out, finger and thumb pressed together as though holding a tablet. Henrietta blanched.

"One of the anti-depressants the doctor gave me after Mum died. I doubled the dose." She lifted her hand at the horror on Boris' face. "They're quite safe. I took two heaps of times and they made me tired. She needs to sleep right now, at least until Logan gets here. He'll know what to do."

Boris waggled his eyebrows in disapproval. The damage done, it seemed pointless to argue. Tiger found his mistress and sprung up onto the bed with her. He burrowed beneath the covers and made a nest behind her knees. Next time she needed him he wouldn't be chasing birds two streets away.

Hana dreamed Bodie whispered with Logan above her head. Anka appeared as a fairy and told her they could be friends again because Tama changed back into a frog. The fat cat weighed heavily against the backs of her knees and Hana dreamed she took part in a three-legged mothers' race on sports day but couldn't stay upright. The sight of Izzie's disappointed tears made her cry out in her sleep. A cool hand smoothed her brow and Hana reached for it, groaning as her wrist jarred. Hot sunshine beat down on an ice cream in her right hand and it melted up her arm and into the crook of her elbow. "Take it, Vik," she insisted. "It's for you." She heard him sigh and the cool hand disappeared from her forehead. "That's right," she slurred. "Just go. You always leave. Everyone leaves me."

She woke feeling wrung out, her brain addled and confused. The sticky plaster on her right hand showed blood instead of ice cream. An eerie half-light toned the room in shades of grey; the day disappeared from under her. Stretching out an aching hand to investigate the waist high paralysis revealed the snoring cat sprawled across her bottom half. Her legs felt bloodless and leaden. Hana prodded him and he sat up to lick himself clean after his nap, sniffing at the bloodied bandage with a disgusted look on his face. Hana persuaded her body to respond to her urgent signals for moving. "I need to leave, useless cat. Why can't you help me?" Tiger opened his mouth and gave a wide yawn which showed all his teeth.

The open door allowed a half-light to filter through from a lamp in the hallway. Hearing voices, Hana stirred herself and sat up. It felt easier than before to lever herself off the bed and pad to the hall. She fought the urge to escape through the front door and start walking home. Leaning against the wall at intervals, Hana moved along the hallway with surprising stealth. The kitchen door stood open and she forced her feet forwards, emerging into the bright room to the sound of awkward silence.

Nine people had squashed themselves around the large kitchen table. Nine expressions of concern turned towards her. Logan, Pete, Boris and Henrietta faced her as she leaned against the doorway and a police officer and his female counterpart sat opposite them. Angus sat with his back to her, but turned as she entered. The other two proved a complete surprise.

"Mum." Her son rose and walked towards her. He still wore his police issue shirt and slacks, but covered them with a jacket. Hana sank into his arms, all pretence at bravado wasted.

"Bodie," she whispered into the front of his jacket. She clung to the fabric to prevent the others seeing her grateful tears. "I'm sorry you got pulled into this nightmare."

"Hey, Hana." Her son-in-law waited his turn, the clerical collar around his neck glowing a peculiar white in the dim light. "Izzie and baby Elizabeth say hi." His voice sounded soft and reassuring but he looked tired, his blond hair tousled and his parting confused about where it should be. "Izzie's furious," he added. "I wouldn't let her come."

"There's nowhere for her to stay," Bodie added, frowning at Marcus. He thumped his arm. "Besides, she ruins our best mate time with her complaining."

"Why is everyone here?" Hana demanded, sounding ungrateful. "Did I miss my own funeral?" She noticed Logan look down at the table as she spat her bile and shame took a hold, making her squirm with discomfort.

"It's a council of war," Henrietta said. "I'll make more tea." She rose from the chair and flicked the switch on the kettle.

Hana sighed. "I'll be fine when I get home. Or I can move up to the other house and just rough it for a week." She glanced across at Angus. "I can't expect the biology teacher to move his family into Achilles Rise now. I'll sell it and cut my losses."

"Sit down." Bodie pulled up another chair and Hana lowered herself into it, every nerve ending in her spine screaming for relief. "Look at these photos, please." He pushed a folder filled with photographs in front of her and Hana reached out to fumble the first page. Bodie swore. "Geez, you're bleeding, Mum."

"It's dry." Hana peered at the disgusting plaster. "But it explains my dream."

"What dream?" He stood over her and waited for her to explain.

Hana shook her head, dismissing the foggy images. "I dreamed of your dad." She looked down at the blood and sighed, wanting to tell him the truth; his father didn't help her, not this time or the last.

"I've got more here too." Policewoman Shelley pushed an iPad towards her and Hana avoided her eye. It rankled that the cop didn't remember breaking her heart eight years ago, but perhaps she'd buried the awful experience somewhere deep along with all the other horrors of her job.

Bodie tapped the folder with an impatient finger. "Mum, we need to find these guys."

Hana heard the undertone which dictated urgency and blocked out thoughts of Vik and a whole other, safe life. While Henrietta brewed tea in an old yellow teapot, Hana trawled through the faces of men who'd trodden the line between societal good and bad and fallen off. The man with Asian features didn't appear, but her sharp intake of breath told everyone she'd seen the blond. Hana experienced a wave of nausea at his nonchalant image and her fingers fluttered against her lips to dispel the remembered kiss. In the photo, he wore his hair longer and looked clean-shaven. "This man," Hana said, her voice wavering. Her pupils dilated in a fear reaction. She saw Logan's fingers move towards her in her peripheral vision and then he stilled them, knowing she needed comfort but unable to deliver. "He pulled out a knife and the blade popped from the handle. He held it up to my throat and said he'd kill me." Hana gulped as her bandaged hand touched her jawline, feeling the tiny nick from the sharp point.

"It's okay, Hana. We took your statement last night. You don't have to go over it again for our benefit, but if you remember something else, please ring my direct number." Without looking up, Shelley made copious notes in her pocketbook and pushed a business card across the table to Hana.

"I've already got one," Hana said. She wanted to add, "But when I ring, you never call back." She refrained, the effort of speaking making her throat even sorer.

The male officer stepped outside, making an excuse as he went through the ranch slider. "Bad reception in here," he said, but Hana suspected he wanted privacy. She slurped her tea with difficulty, made even harder by her audience who watched. The policeman's return broke the tension, letting a great waft of cold air in and the cat out. Shelley gathered up her belongings to leave.

"You've both identified the same offender," she said. "We'll get him. Have a good night and Mrs Johal, sleep here. There are alternative places we can put you, but here is better for now."

They walked into the night with clinking belts and chirping radios. Moments later, the shrill sound of a siren in the distance took the pair to another call. Hana sneaked a look at Logan over her mug. He sat with a glass of water in front of him, avoiding eye contact with her. His eyes flickered at the sight of her in his clothes but other than that, he kept his head down. With practiced ease he banished the look of lingering pain as though it never existed. Plasters covered the knuckles of Logan's left hand, a blue bruise spreading along the middle finger. Hana remembered the doctor asking about his injuries the night before and shame flushed through her body, accompanied by guilt.

Around midnight, Bodie, Marcus and Boris set off for Achilles Rise. Hana protested. "I want to go home," she complained, emboldened by the idea of escaping Logan's brooding silence.

"Nope." Bodie turned his back on her, which only infuriated her more. She followed him onto the porch.

"You don't understand!" Hana hissed, petulance in her voice. "Please don't leave me here with him."

Her wide eyes alarmed him. "Why?" His body stiffened. "What did he do?"

"He dumped me for someone else. Please don't humiliate me by forcing me to stay here." Hana glanced back at the front door, seeing Logan leaning against the frame with his hands in his pockets. His expression looked blank.

"Your safety's more important right now." Bodie wore his cop's head and emotion didn't feature. "It's for one night. Better to be with him than the guys who attacked you. And anyway, if it weren't for him, you'd be in a worse mess." Bodie raised his eyebrows at the role reversal between mother and son. "Behave, Mum."

Powerlessness enveloped Hana as the vehicles pulled off the drive. "They tipped out all my packing," she insisted, hearing her plaintive repetition.

"I know, Hana." Angus put his arm around her and crushed her into his side. "The official work story is that you're ill. The police want no unnecessary interest in you at the moment. They intend to catch these men."

"They always go on TV and ask the public for help," Hana grumbled. "But they don't care about what happens to me. That police lady always gives me her card and never answers her phone." Hana felt herself stray into maudlin territory. "She doesn't even remember telling me my husband mashed himself on a sixteen wheeler like a hood ornament." Humour didn't lessen the pain and with understanding, Angus squeezed her harder.

"I'm so sorry, Hana," he breathed into her hair. "This is my fault. I shouldn't have interfered and forced you to change things."

Angus left, Henrietta padded off to her guest room and Pete retired to his dreadful pigsty at the other end of the house. Hana intercepted pointed looks between the couple and figured Henrietta was the driving force behind any purity vow. After the drugs and the monumental sleep, Hana didn't feel tired and hung around the kitchen alone. Logan appeared and washed up the cups, the tense atmosphere growing in density until it became a choking hazard.

A frantic scratching on the glass of the ranch slider caused them both to jump. Hana launched into panic mode and hid behind the sofa while Logan peered through the windows and saw nothing. He swore at the sight of two amber eyes staring through the glass near the bottom. Two padded feet beat an impatient tattoo. Logan opened the door but Hana shouted too late. "He's got a mouse!"

Tiger swaggered in, strutting his stuff like a feline prince. Logan spotted the wiggling tail dangling from his mouth and swore again as he chased him around the room. "Bloody hell! Where's he getting them from?"

"Just tell him he's a good boy and send him back out," Hana pleaded. She crouched behind the sofa, her body curled into a tight ball. Tiger hunted her out and spat the mouse on the floor in front of her, upset by her lack of enthusiasm. The mouse made a dash for it and the cat followed, both bounding along the hall and disappearing into the darkness.

"Did he go left or right?" Logan hissed as he reached the hall door. "I can't see him."

"Left," Hana answered. "Where does that go?"

Logan winced and amusement crossed his face. "Henrietta's room." He snorted and lifted a finger, calling for silence while he listened. "I can't hear anything. Maybe he lost it."

"He never loses them." Hana sighed and tried to run her hand over her eyes, groaning as the stitches in her palm passed across the bridge of her nose. Logan watched her in silence, his grey eyes mirroring her awkwardness.

"Oh well, Henrietta may have a little surprise in her bedroom tomorrow, but it won't be Pete!" Logan's laugh sounded hollow as he sat on the sofa.

Hana grabbed a piece of kitchen roll and mopped at the dried blood on her arm. It scratched and scraped but achieved nothing. She tore off another piece and tried to wet it first, soaking the bandage and wrist strap on her other hand. In temper, she snatched off the strap and flexed her wrist. The pain felt sickening, but the bones didn't grind.

"The doctor rang this morning," Logan said. He stood and fetched Henrietta's first aid kit from a cupboard over the microwave. "Someone else looked at the x-ray and found a small break. He's asked you to go back and he'll set it in a cast."

"No." Hana shook her head. "I don't want a cast. It doesn't feel broken." She flexed it again and the offending bone sent a twinge of pain as far as her shoulder.

"Liar." Logan thumped the kit on the table and pulled out a chair for her. "Let's get the other hand cleaned up."

Hana sat down and Logan took the wrist strap to an ancient radiator. He laid it over the hot metal with care. He undid the bandage and peered at the neat, black stitches, the ends sticking upwards like shocked polecats. The moment felt uncomfortable and intimate, their faces close as Logan leaned over to wipe away the blood with an antiseptic wipe.

Hana snatched another and tore the sachet open with her teeth. She closed her eyes against the pain in her wrist as she dabbed at her lips.

"Hana, don't." Logan clasped her fingers and confiscated the wipe. "Don't do that, babe."

She clenched her teeth, feeling the ache in her throat as misery sent tingles through her jaw and she fought to suppress tears. "He kissed me," she said, her tone wooden. "I can't make it go away."

Logan closed his eyes, his jaw showing as a hard outline against his cheek. When he opened them, the grey irises sparkled and danced like grit. "I'm sorry," he whispered. "I didn't come back soon enough."

Hana forced her back to straighten and fixed her face into a blank mask. "It's fine," she said, her tone clipped. "Thank you for coming back at all." She looked expectantly at her slashed palm as though telling him to finish the task or let go.

Logan shook his head. He pushed the fingers of his bruised left hand into her hair and massaged her temple. His thumb caressed her cheek before stroking her lips. He leaned forward and his kiss stole the damage of the blond man, replacing what he meant for harm with something sweet and pleasurable. Hana leaned in, hungry for more until her misfiring brain righted itself and reminded her of Caroline. She pulled away, shaking her head. "I'm not a cheat," she stated, her eyes narrowing to slits in accusation.

"Nor am I." Logan left his denial hanging, dragging her hand in front of him. He worked with his tongue trapped between his teeth as he concentrated on repairing the damage, producing a half-decent covering for the stitches. Hana held her breath against the lure of his musky scent, mentally blocking the feelings for him which still plagued her. Glancing up at the muted hoot of a morepork in the darkness outside, she noticed pillows stacked on the sofa and a sleeping bag laid next to them. She felt a wave of guilt.

"I can sleep on the sofa," she said, her tone prim.

"I'm fine." Logan sounded tired, dumping the reel of tape and scissors back into the first aid box. He felt the wrist strap and finding it dry, gave it to her.

"I insist." Hana examined his work, bending her fingers and finding it easier to move without the swathe of bloody plasters.

"No need to be a martyr." Logan walked to the kitchen and Hana watched his neat bum glide away. But he'd lit the blue touch paper and she flared.

"A martyr? You think I'm a martyr?"

"No." He shoved the kit back in the cupboard and stood. "I know you are."

"How dare you!" The chair scraped against the floorboards as Hana pushed it back with her knees and stood, holding her wounded hands in front of her like a boxer.

"Hana, I told you I loved you," Logan said, knocking the wind from her righteous sails. "And yet you still choose to believe ill of me."

"Because I can't do this!" Hana spat. "I won't let you make a fool of me."

"I'm not trying to!" He sounded frustrated, bitterness and anger lacing his voice.

Hana dropped her hands by her sides in defeat. "You and Caroline can get back together. It's nothing to do with me. I hope you have a good life, I really do." She stopped in alarm as Logan lurched forward over the counter as though he might vomit. Shaking hands covered his eyes. The atmosphere fizzed with electricity and Hana swallowed as Logan faced her, his eyes sparking with danger.

"Just go to bed, Hana!" he snapped.

Hana fled to the bedroom. She spent an endless night tossing and turning while sleep evaded her. She berated herself in a tireless loop and left no other options open as she planned her next few months. Sell her marital home, move into Culver's Cottage, resign, find a new job and start again. "You brought this on yourself," she murmured to herself in the darkness. "You didn't like boring and this is what you've ended up with. Be careful what you pray for."

Rejection brought a physical pain in her ribs, sickeningly familiar and all the more piercing for its repeat appearance. Hana cursed her own stupidity and vowed it was the last time. The cat turned up before morning as she nodded off, purring and kneading her stomach with the claws on all four feet. Hana pushed his nose out of her face. "Mouse breath. Lay down!"

She listened to Pete stumble from his bed just before seven thirty, seriously intending to leave at seven thirty-five. Hana met him at the car in her strange attire. "I'm going home and you're taking me," she informed him.

"Logan will kill me," he hissed. "He's shaving. I'll get him." He turned away and Hana grabbed his spindly arm, wincing at the pain in her wrist.

"It'll be the last thing you ever do," she threatened. "There's nothing between me and Logan, so get used to it."

Pete put his hands on his hips. "He doesn't think that. You're breaking his heart, Hana."

She shook her head and gave a nasty laugh, disturbing the wriggling cat stuffed under her pullover. A pitiful mewl came from inside and a claw poked through the stitching. "Just take me home, Pete," she wailed, threats turning to begging.

With a roll of his pale blue eyes, Pete opened the door for her and helped her into his car, muttering a list of all the things Logan would do to him when he found out. To his horror, Hana burst into tears. "I'm sorry," she sobbed, the effort of holding it in overwhelming her. "I'm sorry for everything."

Deciding he liked grumpy Hana much better than tearful Hana, Pete started the car and set off for Achilles Rise. It spared him witnessing the abject dismay on Logan's face when he saw his empty bedroom and the scream from Henrietta, who stepped out of bed and onto Tiger's little gift. Peckish whilst delivering the present, the generous cat ate the best bits, leaving the entrails in her slipper.

Chapter 41

Hana knocked on the front door and a startled Bodie opened it. Boris stood in the kitchen stuffing toast into his mouth and gave a feckless wave of a greasy hand. Tiger scratched his way out of the pullover and fled, leaving Hana extra injuries to her hands. He vented his irritation by tormenting sparrows on the roof, twenty metres above the street.

"I know! I know!" Pete followed Hana in and met Bodie's glare of annoyance. "She won't do as she's told!" He jostled Boris aside to push bread into the toaster.

"You got a letter from the insurance company," Bodie said, rubbing his eyes. "Want me to open it?"

Hana nodded, keeping her face blank. "I don't think it's a cheque." Her tone sounded leaden.

Bodie ripped the envelope and sighed. "Nope. Your car will need to remain missing for a total of three months before they settle the claim. Liability is being sought from the garage owner for negligence."

Hana nodded. "Why's the Honda on the driveway with your car?" she asked. "What if the men saw it?"

Bodie squeezed her forearm. "It's okay, Mum. They didn't come back."

"How do you know?" Her gaze darted towards the sunroom window and back to her son's face.

"Because someone kept watch all night." He jerked his head towards Boris and his voice hardened. "It's his turn now."

Hana's shoulders slumped. "He's not looking. He didn't even see us arrive," she wailed.

Boris said something with his mouthful, fighting Pete for the bread which popped free of the toaster and Bodie glared at his back. "Don't worry, Mum. It's okay. The local cops are keeping an eye out."

Hana rolled her eyes. "Great. I feel so safe now."

Pete shoved Boris into the oven handle and snatched the last piece of toast from his fingers. "Logan's gonna kill me," he declared. "And it's all

Hana's fault."

"Please stop it, Pete," Hana said, weariness making her irritable. "You're making my head ache. Wait for Boris in the car."

"But what about Logan?" Pete whined and Hana gritted her teeth.

"I don't want to hear his name."

Bodie turned Pete around and gave him a shove towards the door, snatching the toast from his outstretched fingers at the last moment. "Dude, know when to quit," he told him. "Some of us didn't get to sleep like babies." He passed the well-handled toast back to Boris, who pushed it into his mouth. Hana looked away and closed her eyes, fighting to control her gag reflex.

She found Marcus fast asleep in Izzie's old room, snoring like a motor in low gear. Hana glanced back at Bodie. "Keep an eye on him," she said. "You know he doesn't check his insulin levels without Izzie around to remind him."

Bodie nodded. "I will." He sighed and put his hand against Hana's bedroom door before she could push it open. "Your car's on the drive because the person on watch packed your gear to keep themselves awake. We loaded everything into the kitchen and kept going all night. It's done."

"All of it?" Hana paled. "Knickers and everything?"

Bodie nodded. "I did your knickers, Mum. What a revelation." He grinned and she slapped his arm. "I spread a towel over the drawers and stacked them in the back of my car. It seemed stupid to pack and then unpack them again. I wrote on the side which cupboard they came from, so just slide them back in when the frames arrive at the new house."

Hana cleared her throat. "Did you leave any knickers out for me?"

Bodie looked at her sideways. "Why?"

"I'm not moving until next weekend." She chewed her lip and considered her options. "It's okay. I probably need new ones, anyway."

Bodie snorted and faked surprise. "What? Is grey not the new black then?"

"Shut up. The washing machine did that." Hana smirked and her lip cracked. She closed her eyes and let Logan's kiss overwrite the blond man's, but the image hurt even more.

Bodie handed her a handkerchief, a pale blue square of cloth with navy kiwi birds marching around the edges. "I found this," he said. "Mop your lip with that and then wash it later. You're out of toilet roll."

Hana took the handkerchief, feeling the softness in her fingers. Her heart thudded in her breast and she slipped it into the pocket of the tracksuit pants and wiped her lip on the sleeve of Logan's pullover.

An eager Bodie showed her how they'd stacked the boxes five high in the garage. Hana's labelling system disappeared after the boys took over, but everything she owned sat inside a box. Hana looped her arm through Bodie's and smiled at him with gratitude. "So that's why Boris ate directly out of the toaster," she said. "I wondered why he spread margarine with the lid from the jam."

Bodie nodded. "We did a great job, aye?"

Hana rested her head against his shoulder and sighed. "I'm so relieved. I'm tired and I can't think straight."

"I know." Bodie kissed the top of her head. "How was last night? Did you sleep?"

Hana shook her head. "Awkward and no, I didn't." She sighed. "Is the big furniture still upstairs?"

"Yep. No point carrying it down here. The removals guys can take it through the ranch slider and along the slope to the driveway. It makes more sense."

Hana forced a wavering smile onto her lips and summoned up some enthusiasm. "You boys are amazing," she crooned, fondling the cardboard edge of an open box and ignoring the rubbish bin nestled against dessert bowls. "How much did those clowns break?" she asked, forcing the image of the blond man's face from her memory.

"Enough. But not everything." Bodie led her upstairs to the kitchen where he pulled a flower vase from the dishwasher. Hana squashed all comment when he brewed tea in it.

She turned her hand over and lifted the dressing so she could peek underneath. "Gross!" She wrinkled her nose. "I'm sure I could've found my own five-year-old to stitch this."

Bodie peered over her shoulder and laughed. "It looks clean though and it's stopped bleeding. Your neck is a mess." He jerked his head towards her throat and Hana resisted the urge to let her fingers follow his gaze. "Did you get the break in your wrist checked already, or do you want me to take you?"

"No!" Hana put her hand behind her back. "It's just sore, not broken. I'm not going back there." She reversed until her bum touched the two-seater sofa, which leaned against the wall on its side. Her Honda keys balanced on the uppermost edge. Hana reached for them and Bodie pounced.

"Oh no, you don't! You can't drive without at least one good hand. You'll wreck that new car before you've had it a fortnight!"

"Bo, I can't stay here," Hana begged. "I want to go to the new place." She looked around her with a sudden realisation. "I'm done here."

Bodie smiled and put his arm around her. He stared through the ranch-slider over the pile of furniture at the cat who rolled around in a patch of sand on the terrace. "I know what you mean," he said, his tone sad.

While the men showered, moaning and groaning as they realised every single towel got packed, Hana pottered around. She cleaned the empty rooms and wiped the skirting boards with her stitched right hand sealed inside a yellow rubber glove. She found two facecloths at the back of the airing cupboard and pulled them out from behind the hot water cylinder. "I've found some towels," she called over the noise of the shower. "I'll leave them outside the door."

Marcus yanked the bathroom door open naked. He squealed as he grabbed the nearest one and held it up in front of his face. "Is this it?"

"Ooh, vicar!" Bodie snorted, covering Hana's eyes with his hand.

"It's okay, I've already lost my appetite," Hana sighed.

"We'll take the vacuum over to the other place and bring it back when this house is empty," Bodie suggested. "I don't mind doing it. It should be a quick job with no furniture."

Hana nodded, exhaustion catching up with her. "What's left in the garage?" she asked, struggling to remember. "I should've checked when you showed me the boxes."

Bodie winced. "Dad's tools and the stuff on that shelf by the stairs door. I'll do it if you want."

Hana shook her head, giving his arm a feeble pat. "No. I'll do it. I don't mind."

Squeezing past the towers of boxes proved a mission, with only a narrow slit to push her body through. "Good job I didn't stop for breakfast this morning," Hana sighed. "I wouldn't fit."

"What?" Bodie stood on the bottom step to watch her progress. "You're sure you wanna do this?"

"Yep." Hana waved him away. "I think most of it's rubbish and the new owner might want the tools."

"Are you still selling?" Bodie sounded sad.

"I don't know. Angus promised to speak to the biology teacher this morning. He'll text me." Hana's brow knitted and she ducked between two boxes to get sight of Bodie again. "Did you find my phone?"

"Yes." His head nodded with certainty. "It's charging in the kitchen. Remind me to put it in the car when we leave."

"Okay." Hana gave him a forced smile. "I'm fine here. I won't be long. You can check on Marcus. Make sure he eats something, even if it's only toast."

Bodie nodded and disappeared, leaving Hana to her memories and the growing sense of loss which facing her husband's tool collection brought to the fore. Dusty from lack of use, they lined the walls as he left them, labelled and ready to work had Hana known how. A dusty shelf stood to attention beneath a shadow board, containing an ancient hand drill, now brown with age. Hana fingered Vik's shoe cleaning tin and picked up a bottle of liquid polish. She shook it and realised it defied the term 'liquid,' as a dry block rattled inside.

"My life sucks," she grumbled, bending down to swipe at a scrap of newspaper sticking out from under the shelf. The wrist and palm injury made both hands useless in fine motor skill activities and she knelt on the floor in frustration. "I only want to see the date," she complained to the silent boxes stacked around her. She knew why. It called to her from a happier time, from a day before her world ended and failed to restart. Hana pulled at the yellowing paper, feeling it crumble in her fingers. Desperation drove her on and she lurched forward, gripping it in her left hand before her wrist complained. The newspaper caught under the feet of the shelf and Hana gave a more forceful tug. A sharp pain shot through her wrist followed by a ripping sound and she overbalanced, falling against a stack of four boxes as the paper came away in her fingers. Hana slammed her right hand on the ground to steady herself. Bad mistake. "Ow!" she moaned. An old blue mouse block propelled through the air and hit her in the forehead, disintegrating into a shower of blue dust. "Well, thanks for the cancer to add to my problems," Hana grumbled, dusting herself off.

Another mouse block sat next to her on the floor, remaining whole even while its companion fell to pieces. Hana pushed at it with a lolly stick she found poking out from under the chest freezer. The block felt solid to the touch. Hana retrieved the handkerchief from her pocket and picked up the object. She gave a few cursory rubs, surprised to find it wasn't mouse poison but a metal box, beaten into a rectangular shape. Hana held it in clumsy fingers, something about it triggering a hazy memory relating to Bodie. "Metalwork," she breathed. "Fifth form."

In the time it took Bodie to shower, dry himself on the remaining facecloth and pull on clothes, Hana had stuffed most of the tools into bags and emptied the shelf in the garage. A call from Izzie delayed everything. "I'm fine, darling." Hana reassured her daughter. "It was very exciting."

"Bloody wasn't!" Bodie exclaimed and Hana pulled a face and put her finger up to her lips.

"Shut up!" she mouthed, before continuing her conversation with Izzie. "You know how your brother panics about everything." She side stepped

Bodie's grabbing fingers and ran into the corner of the kitchen counter, wincing in pain as he stuck his tongue out at her.

Hana stood at the top of the stairs with a handbag she'd wrestled from an open box in the garage. She pulled the metal box from her pocket and dropped it in. Marcus watched her with interest. "I made one of those at school," he said. "Fiddly things. Does Mr Harper still do that with the Fifth formers?"

"Year 11s," Bodie corrected. "Get with the times."

"Is it yours?" Hana retrieved it and turned it over in her fingers. Bodie shook his head.

"Na. I didn't do metal tech after Year 10. It didn't fit in with science."

Marcus snorted. "Whatever, dude. Harper banned you."

"What did I do?" Bodie cocked his head in confusion, brows knitted and brown eyes narrowed. "I welded something important to something else, didn't I?"

Marcus shrugged. "Dunno, can't remember."

Bodie shoulders slumped. "That was a total waste of time then, wasn't it? I bet I got detention. What's the point of a punishment if you can't remember the crime?"

Hana rolled her eyes and held the box out to Marcus. "It must be yours then."

He shook his head. "Na. Izzie's got mine. She keeps crap in it."

"Does she want another?"

"No thanks." Marcus bounded down the steps. "Our house is full of stuff like that. She'll kill me if I take home more."

Hana shrugged and dropped the box back into her handbag, quickly forgotten amongst the other pointless detritus.

Marcus blinked at the sight of Culver's Cottage as Hana pointed it out from across the river. "Impressive!" he exclaimed as they crossed the Waipa bridge. With only two opportunities to sneak a peek at it from Hakarimata Road, owing to the treacherous bends, Hana stopped him trying.

She grabbed at the steering wheel twice as he crossed the centre line. "Don't crash my new car!" she wailed. "You're doing it on purpose."

Marcus grinned and waggled his eyebrows, infuriating her. "Izzie said you'd found a boyfriend," he remarked as he slowed down for an oncoming gravel lorry. "Is he the dude who smashed his hand up on the guy's face?"

"Did he smash his hand up?" Hana's eyes grew wide with guilt. "I saw the plasters but thought maybe he just cut it a little."

Marcus shrugged. "Dunno. It was still bleeding last night and Pasty Pete said he smashed it."

"You shouldn't call him Pasty Pete," Hana chided and Marcus grinned.

"Because I'm all grown up?"

"No!" Hana turned in her seat to stare at him. "Because you're a vicar and it's not very nice."

"Oh, yeah." Marcus navigated the worst two bends and gave her a sideways look. "So, you didn't answer the question. Is he the same dude you're dating?"

"I'm not dating anyone." Hana gritted her teeth and faced the side window. "Can we talk about something else?"

Marcus gave her a sly look and Hana felt him staring at her back. She whipped round. "Eyes on the road, boy!" she snapped.

Bodie went ahead in his BMW, lurching over deep ruts and potholes. Twice the bumper scraped against the gravel and Hana cringed as they turned into the steep driveway behind him.

"Oops," Marcus laughed. "I'm not used to your car. I keep wiping the windows when I think I'm indicating. I just washed the windscreen instead of flashing Bodie."

"Don't flash anyone in my car." Hana sighed and watched her new investment slip in and out of view. Her car bit into the gravel and propelled up the slope just as Brian promised. She watched as Bodie almost lost his exhaust pipe.

"Wow, that's stunning!" Rounding the final bend, Marcus admired the old villa on its green hill, backed by the beautiful Hakarimata Ranges. Hills and valleys surrounded it until the outline of Ngaruawahia poked up in the distance. A shiny new roof perched atop the house like a hat; navy blue with matching pipe work. The villa occupied its section with latent pride, like a dog finally adopted from the pound.

"The painter started," Hana said, watching as Bodie knelt on the ground behind his car and prodded at his exhaust pipe. "The weather's been fine."

"Yep." Bodie stood and brushed dust from his jeans. His eyes roved over the weatherboard which gleamed with a shimmering new coat of white. "Looks good." He pointed at Hana's car. "I'll put my car in the garage. I don't want this idiot to ding it."

Marcus heaved in an indignant sigh and winked at Hana. "Don't speak about your mother like that."

"You'll need to unlock it. The builders hung new doors." Hana pushed her fingers into the Honda's glove box and withdrew a remote control, complete with sticking plaster. She groaned and stared at her palm. "I'll stop wrapping my hand up," she said, flapping the plaster.

Bodie cringed as she pulled it off and handed the remote to him. He wiped it on his trousers like a picky child.

Marcus had dispensed with the dog collar and dressed in jeans. Elizabeth shared his skin tones and the same unruly blond hair. Large framed and square, he looked a polar opposite to olive skinned, elfin Izzie with her father's dark hair and Indian heritage. Hana watched him from beneath her lashes and he raised a blond eyebrow. "I'm fine, Hana. I took my shot and ate a muesli bar for breakfast."

"Okay." Hana gave a tired smile. "Just looking out for you."

Marcus nodded and put his arm around her shoulders. "I know. Thank you." He pointed at the wrap around balcony. "This is a gorgeous house, Hana. Did you match the navy of the roof to the front door and handrail?"

Hana pressed her lips together with pleasure, a flush beginning in her pale cheeks. "Yes. Do you like it?" A stab of anguish reminded her of Logan's help sourcing the exact shade and she clenched her fists, regretting it as both hands sent sharp physical pain to distract her tortured heart.

Hana led the way up the steps to the front porch, pointing out Bodie's handiwork. "He sanded the deck once we finished the floors and the painter varnished it." She glowed under Marcus' nod of approval for her rash purchase. "Take a look around," she offered, unlocking the wide front door and pushing it open. It creaked with age and Hana felt a dart of welcome begin in her toes and tingle to the top of her head. Things would be okay.

Inside the house, Marcus stopped in surprise at the openness of the layout. "Wow," he said, spinning around. "You don't expect that." Individual rooms invited cosiness, leading from a magnificent lobby with high ceilings and the original architrave and ceiling rose. "Well done on snagging this!" He exhaled in approval, raising his eyebrows and winking at Hana. "Good on you."

"Go for a snoop," Hana invited, embarrassed by his enthusiasm. She imagined walking through the navy front door with Logan and bitterness replaced the sense of welcome. He would never see it painted. Hana listened to Marcus poking his head through doorways and chatting to Izzie on his phone.

"It's amazing," he enthused. "Each room opens onto the hallway as though it's the heartbeat of the house and instead of perpendicular openings; they're slanted, like being in an octagon. There are huge windows everywhere. Yeah, it's gorgeous."

"The rimu floors look fantastic." Bodie breached the stairs and nodded in approval. "Someone did a great job." He smirked at Hana and she summoned up a smile.

"Yeah, I love seeing the life of the wood in the knots. It shows all the stresses and lifelines of the original tree. A bit like me." She swallowed and the maudlin cloud swirled around her head and dripped its nasty condensation into her chest.

Bodie winced. "You'll be safe here; I'll make sure of it, Mum." He waved his arm towards the lounge, graced by the phenomenal views of the river and the sunshine. "You need to look at that each morning and let the fear and sadness go away."

"Is that what you do?" The words became airborne before Hana could stop them and she held her breath. A look of shock passed across Bodie's face at her uncanny perception and he shut it down with practiced expertise.

"No." He shook his head. "I'm a big boy. I let nothing make me feel that way." He jerked his head behind him. "I'll bring the cleaning stuff up from the car." His heavy footsteps down the stairs chided her.

Hana wiped her eyes on the sleeve of Logan's pullover, regretting her lack of control over her mouth. Bodie's unhappiness radiated outwards like an ethereal thread. It began in their shared past and the death of his father, but grew in intensity during those first years as a cop. The speed with which he headed north suggested something awful, but getting personal details from her son felt like major surgery. Hana didn't have the energy to wield an emotional scalpel. "Just leave it," she sighed and stared around her new home. "You've got your own problems."

Marcus reappeared from the kitchen, still giving Izzie a detailed description. "There's a dining room and laundry. Four bedrooms. Yes, I said four. What are you doing Izzie? Oh, give her a kiss from me. Tell Peggy hi too. No, don't kiss her. Do you want me to describe it, or not? Listen then." He wandered towards the front of the house, facing east. "The lounge is huge with a bay window that looks over the river. Your mum's stripped all the walls too. She just needs to decorate." He winked at Hana in appreciation of the massive task still ahead of her.

Hana sighed and walked into her basic kitchen, last updated in the 1960s. Old wooden cupboards and a metal draining board lined the walls. An open space in the middle left ample room for a kitchen table and an ancient cooker leaned against the wall looking decidedly unsafe. Evidence of patching on the plasterboard showed where the electrician had replaced much of the wiring and left new switches in his wake. She ran her fingers along a mantelshelf, knocking a host of dust and misplaced screws into the old hearth below. "What have I done?" she breathed to the empty room. "I can't do this alone."

Marcus moved through the house, admiring everything. Hana listened to his echoing voice and tried to catch a dose of his boundless enthusiasm. "There's an integral bathroom and toilet. Yes, it would work for us. I don't make a smell!" Marcus sounded huffy and his feet padded down the small hallway to the master bedroom on the right. "Ooh, this is big. No, no ensuite. The house is early 1900s. It's lucky to have an indoor bathroom. Yes, maybe they added it later; I'll ask." He walked towards the back of the house to where steps ran down to the garage. A rimu banister ran along the left side of the wall before the steps turned a dogleg and disappeared downwards. Hana followed and peered through the glass door onto the roof garden. Bitumen covered the surface and rickety wooden steps led down to an overgrown lawn. A huge overgrown lawn. Hana closed her eyes against the pressing need to mow it with her inadequate machine and poked her head into the bathroom.

"It's so authentic. I love it." Marcus made her jump as Hana wielded bleach and a cloth, wondering where to start. The enamelled iron bath looked like it craved more than bleach and the toilet seat needed changing. Wooden and old, it stank of pee. Hana wrinkled her nose.

"Where do I start?" She looked pitiful, leaning against the wood panelled wall with two damaged hands stuffed into yellow rubber gloves.

Marcus peered into the toilet at a cigarette end bobbing around in the water. "At the beginning," he answered and smiled. "We're here to help."

Hana swallowed. "I know. Just like always."

"Just like always." Marcus wrapped his arms around her and held her tight, infusing her with love and his usual brand of honesty. He never said anything he didn't mean. He kissed the top of her head and took the bottle of bleach from her fingers. "You've got a septic tank. You can't use this stuff."

He sent Hana to wipe down the kitchen cupboards with something less toxic to septic tank bacteria. Then he sought Bodie. The solid door at the bottom of the stairs led into the garage and he saw Bodie's car backed up to the entrance. Bird song piped in through the open doors. The sturdy concrete walls looked back at him with a blank expression, the vast space empty. At the sound of scuffling feet, Marcus located a half door leading under the house and followed the noise.

He pushed it with care, but like everything else in the old place, it creaked on its hinges.

Bodie reacted with a sidekick, deflected late. "Geez, bro, I nearly ended your fathering career!" Humour replaced discomfort as Marcus stood in the doorframe, protecting his groin with both hands.

"What the heck?" Marcus screwed his face up in annoyance and brushed the faint shoe mark from his jeans. His eyes narrowed. "Only guilt causes a reaction like that. Spill or I tell Hana."

Bodie blanched. "Please don't."

Marcus spread his legs and folded his arms, blocking the small doorway. He stooped to avoid the overhead joists. "I know you can go through me if you want to, but it'll make a noise and Hana will come downstairs." His lips quirked upwards and his blue eyes flashed.

Bodie exhaled, brushing the furthest wall with his hand and then inspecting the cobwebs and dust on his fingers. "Then you'd better not tell my sister!"

Marcus smiled like an angel. "As a man of the cloth, my word is my bond." He grunted as Bodie threatened his nether regions with another kick, forcing him to use his hands to protect his dignity again. Bodie snorted and got him in a headlock. They tussled and sparred like school boys before Marcus conceded. "I give up, okay I surrender. I won't tell. You can trust me!"

Bodie squeezed a lump of fat around Marcus' stomach and heard his friend grunt. "You'd better not," he threatened. "I'm letting go, but no retaliation. Okay?"

Marcus grunted again and stood up with a smirk. Bodie backed away and ran his hands through his hair. Cobwebs dotted the surface like a hairnet and he shivered, feeling a spider run up his wrist. He squeaked and Marcus hollered with laughter. "You're such a wimp!" he scoffed.

"Yeah?" Bodie collected the webs into his hand and Marcus lost his humour.

"No, don't!" he squealed as Bodie launched at him and stuffed the matted ball down his shirt. Marcus danced like a rhino in a tutu and Bodie laughed until his guts spasmed. He leaned against a dirty wall and the weight of the world settled back on his shoulders.

"What's up with you, man?" Marcus winced as he brushed the last of the web from his stomach and dropped his shirt. "What's the matter?"

Bodie sighed. "I want to store my gear in here."

Marcus couldn't resist the opportunity to mimic a high pitched voice. "Really officer, I'm surprised at you! I believed it when they told me the police incinerated all the drugs and guns."

Bodie didn't smile and Marcus shut up. "I dived a few weeks ago," Bodie said, his voice faltering. "I found this kid trapped in barbed wire and got caught up with him. The crew cut us both free and it's nothing new. It's happened before and it'll happen again. We put ourselves at risk to find them and sometimes end up in the same predicament; it goes with the territory. But that day in the water, I experienced this bone deep exhaustion and since then I've dreaded the calls. I've lost my nerve. It's no longer just a job, finding awful bloated, grey bodies that represent someone's daughter, someone's son. I can't look at the families anymore. It makes me physically ill, Marc. I can't explain it, but I see Mum's face instead of theirs. The day Dad died, Angus drove me home. We stopped to fetch Izzie and I sat in his car knowing it had to be bad. Mum sat us in the lounge and told us Dad wasn't coming home. Her face looked like plaster." Bodie rubbed a hand over his forehead and it came away damp. "Why's it coming back now?"

Marcus cocked his head. "Trauma is like frozen peas," he said, his eyes holding wisdom beyond his years. "We freeze dry the things we don't want to look at and that's okay for a time. But the day you get it back out is the day you discover it's just as fresh, just as painful as the day you put it in there." He pursed his lips. "Perhaps it's time to get it out and leave it out. Let it defrost."

Bodie nodded and swallowed. "There's something else." He breathed out through pursed lips and wouldn't look at Marcus. "Years ago before I left Hamilton, something happened." His eyes became gimlet hard. "I found new information a few weeks ago and it's eating me up."

Marcus watched his childhood friend, feeling the waves of sadness peel off him in a current of intoxicating misery. He didn't ask, sensing Bodie wouldn't tell him. "What will you do?" he said instead. "About the new thing."

Bodie inhaled. "I don't know. I've applied for a job with the Road Patrol guys." He bit his lip. "If I get it, I'll stay and deal with things. Properly."

"Good." Marcus nodded. "You know where I am if you need help." He cocked his head and Bodie saw into his soul, seeing the heartbroken blond teenager who loved Vik as much as he did. Marcus bawled at the funeral and Bodie supported him and Izzie, a seventeen-year-old bowed by secrets and pain, an arm around each of them.

"I know bro'. I know." He heard Hana moving overhead and sought to lighten the mood. He offered Marcus his hand, receiving a look of mistrust. The handshake forged on the fields of the Presbyterian Boys' High School decades earlier ended with them both picking their noses and Hana wrinkled hers in displeasure.

"That's gross!" she squeaked, pushing the door open. Her gaze took in the beamed ceiling and dirty block walls. "I didn't see this room on the plans," she said, wrinkling her nose. "Are you two making it into a den?"

Marcus laughed and widened his eyes at Bodie. "Can we?"

"No." Hana sighed. "But you can make yourselves useful. One of you can vacuum and the other will drive me to the shops. I need heavy duty cleaner for the bathroom and kitchen." She looked at them both in expectation, hands on hips.

Marcus bolted past her hauling the Honda keys from his pocket. "I'm driving!" he shouted. "Bo's the loser."

Hana's son rolled his eyes. "Who made that immature, un-Christian dude a vicar?"

An hour later, they leaned against the lounge wall while the sun poured into the room.

"Chips again," Bodie commented. "I need to do some serious exercise or I'll get as fat as Marcus."

Hana smiled and admired the vibrant red, shaggy rug adorning the centre of the room. Marcus pointed a chip at Bodie and then licked it until his friend cringed. "Okay, stop!" Bodie begged. "You're sick." He turned to Hana. "How did a trip to the supermarket for cleaning products end up with house furnishings? They don't sell this stuff."

Hana put her packet of chips on the floorboards. "Marcus forgot the difference between his left and right, so we went to Huntly. I found this amazing shop on the main street. We can get all the paint and building stuff there."

"I hope that's the royal 'we'," Bodie grumbled. "I'm over it now."

"Says the man who did a little vacuuming," Marcus retorted. "I did a crash course in putting the Honda's back seats down while the store owner balanced a three metre rug on his shoulder in the middle of the street. Not much pressure."

Hana leaned forward, her face alight. "This man stopped to help. He pointed out the folded picnic table under the floor mat in the boot. See, they think of everything, the Italians."

Marcus turned away sniggering and Hana smiled at him, not understanding. Bodie pointed a chip at his friend. "I loved watching you wrestle with it on the driveway," he said. "In the street would've been worth money."

Hana rolled her eyes as Marcus took the bait. "Telling a cleric where to stick it wasn't helpful."

"No, it wasn't." Hana narrowed her eyes at Bodie.

Marcus' face creased into a grin. "Your mummy told you off," he sang in a baby voice.

Hana groaned and left them to pick up the food wrappers, opening her purchases in the kitchen. Bottles of strong bleach lined up on the counter alongside a tub of horrid, thick, bacteria laden syrup for revitalising the septic tank after her killing spree. Bodie followed her in and whistled at the line-up, handling the new toilet seat with a look of disgust on his face.

"It's clean, idiot!" Hana said, laughing at his expression. "Please could you fit it for me?"

"No, make Marcus do it," he complained. "Don't clean the toilet first."

Hana sighed and carried her purchases to the bathroom.

"Have you thought about electronic gates," Bodie asked as they removed the packaging from the seat.

"Na," answered Hana. "They cost a fortune. I'd need to run the electrics all the way to the bottom of the drive. And how would I know if someone wanted to get in?"

"They install a monitor at the bottom." Bodie chewed his lip. "People should text first, anyway. Nobody just turns up on your doorstep when you live this far out."

"But what if they do and can't get in? They can't back out onto the main road. It's too dangerous."

Bodie sighed. "Okay then. Set them further back and gravel a decent turning circle."

Hana put her hands on her hips, bleach transferring from her gloves to Logan's track pants. "You've given this a lot of thought."

"Sure have." Bodie scratched his head and turned away. "They're being fitted on Monday."

"What?" Hana gulped. "I can't afford that."

"It's fine, Marcus is paying." He watched his brother-in-law turn uncomfortably pale, trying to swallow without choking. Bodie enjoyed Marcus' discomfort for a heartbeat longer. "Just kidding," he said. "I've got savings and I know you're dissolving the family trust. I chose the gate weeks ago so I hope you like it."

"The family trust isn't that big," Hana said, her face ashen. "It'll cost thousands."

Bodie wrapped his arms around her. Behind her back he gave Marcus the finger as his friend pretended to wipe tears from his cheeks with toilet roll. "Let me do this, Mum," he said. "You're so isolated up here. Dad would expect me to take care of you."

Hana felt a wave of sadness and regret. Vik's expectations always came back to bite them, his strong sense of family and moral obligation. She pushed her nose into Bodie's shoulder, using pain to block the mental wanderings. Pity her husband didn't stick around to look after her himself. "Thank you," she whispered, holding onto Bodie's muscular body to ground her. "It's too much, but I'm grateful."

"They're navy," he said. "Like the roof. Lightweight aluminium but they won't open without a remote or the code." He didn't tell her the slatted pattern discouraged climbing or that the spikes at the top were as purposeful as decorative. Only a brave assailant would climb the steep cliff either side of the gateway and plough through the dense bush and treacherous covering of nasty Supplejack vine. From any other direction, they'd approach across country, navigating the bush from the walking track and traversing paddocks before reaching the house. Bodie enthused Hana with a catalogue from the gate company and missed out the security details.

The afternoon continued in a haze of scrubbing. Marcus attempted to fit the toilet seat and failed, his skills lying in a different avenue. Hana decided a pastor reduced to swearing was distasteful and confiscated his tools. As teatime neared, Hana grew listless and Bodie knew the signs. "You don't intend to go back to Achilles Rise or Gordonton, do you?" he said, watching her colour flush.

"No." Hana shook her head. "I'm staying here. This is my home now." She sounded resolute, gritting her teeth and folding her arms.

An hour later, Bodie chased Tiger around the garden at Achilles Rise while Marcus giggled from the ranch-slider in the family room. "Bloody women!" Bodie shouted and Marcus snorted.

"The cat's a boy, stupid," he said, a dirty great smirk on his face.

For the tenth time, the cat shot tantalisingly out of reach and onto the roof above Bodie's head. "You're supposed to be getting the cat cage ready," he shouted at Marcus. "I'm gonna kill you now."

Bodie grabbed the door handle, listening to Marcus barfing up his afternoon tea behind the curtains as he laughed so hard. Bodie slapped the glass. "You sound like a sea lion!" he shouted. He jiggled the handle. "Let me in!"

Tears ran down Marcus' cheeks and he gripped his crotch as though adding wetting himself to the menu of distress. Bodie mouthed something at him through the glass, but Marcus didn't hear. Hana's neighbours did though, wondering how a vicar and a cop got to be so entertaining.

"I'm getting my sister to divorce you!" Bodie shouted, slapping the glass again.

Marcus froze and his blue eyes widened like saucers. "Doorbell!" he said.

Bodie watched in horror as he clambered through the furniture stacked in the room and out into the hallway. "No! Don't open it!" he shouted. "Marcus, no!" Bodie jumped the small wall by the window and ran down the slope to the locked gate. He clambered over the trellis, getting wrapped in the passion fruit vine that twisted and turned under his hands and feet.

He remembered his last tangle with the vine years ago, his body more agile as a teenager. Landing hard on the downward slope, he felt the wind knocked out of him and doubled over in pain. His ankles throbbed from the drop but he picked himself up, running past the garage door and up the front steps. Leaping the handrail gained him ground.

Logan Du Rose turned to stare at him. "Hi," he said, chewing his lower lip. He raised a box of beers in one hand and chocolates in the other. A bunch of flowers sat on the passenger seat of the truck, although he wasn't sure he wanted to wear them over his head quite yet. "Is Hana here?"

"She doesn't drink beer." Marcus swiped the box from Logan's hand and pitched forward with the weight.

"Nor do you, ass-wipe!" Bodie growled. "I'll tell your wife."

Marcus stuck his nose in the air. His eyes widened with mischief. "The secrets I could tell her about you."

Bodie groaned and leaned forward, resting his palms on his knees to get his breath back. Logan hefted the chocolates in his hand and stared between the two men. "Do you think I should get the flowers, or is there no point?"

Marcus smiled, the angelic expression practiced and effective. He gave Logan the full hundred-watt effect. "Just bring the chocolates," he said, holding out his hand. "If you've got Turkish Delight in there, I'll do or say whatever you want."

Chapter 42

In the absence of furniture, the three men leaned against the bench tops in the kitchen. They chatted about irrelevant issues and Marcus got stuck into the chocolate. Logan turned to Bodie. "Dude, I didn't realise who you were when you brought the truck back." A sense of guilt mixed with relief passed across his handsome face.

Bodie nodded. "You hurt my mum."

Logan scuffed his boot against the linoleum floor. "Yeah. I gather she thinks that. It's not true."

Bodie shrugged and narrowed his eyes into a macho challenge. "If I thought you did, you wouldn't be standing here."

Marcus pushed a chocolate into his mouth and closed his eyes. He dribbled as he spoke. "You two gonna fight? Can I keep these first?"

"They're for Hana!" Logan lurched for the box and missed.

"You're diabetic, you idiot!" Bodie caught it and Marcus' face crumpled with misery.

"I didn't find the Turkish Delight!"

Bodie peered into the box. "You found everything else. Geez, man!" He pointed towards the door. "Go check your insulin levels and I'm telling Izzie!"

Marcus sloped off and left Logan and Bodie eyeing each other. "Look," said Logan, spreading his hands. "It's getting dark and I presume Hana's up there on her own?"

Bodie squirmed with discomfort. "Yeah, we came home for the stupid cat." He glanced at the door Marcus left through. "I should check on my idiot friend."

Logan nodded. "I've got an idea."

Half an hour later, Logan headed north to Ngaruawahia with two sleeping bags and sleeping mats which Bodie retrieved from a box near the back of the garage. The other two men relinquished responsibility for Hana while Marcus recovered from his sugar overload. Bodie planned to spend the night looking for whatever Hana's attackers wanted; not yet knowing he'd come up empty handed again.

Logan rang the Gordonton house from his mobile on the way up to Culver's Cottage and met with resistance. "You promised!" he shouted down the phone.

Pete sounded far away. "It's Henri's last night before she goes to the South Island." Logan heard the sulk in his voice. "She's cooking my favourite dinner."

Logan sagged in his driver's seat. "You dick! Hana won't let me in by myself. Please mate."

"No." Pete hung up and when Logan dialled again, he got no reply. Logan glanced down at the bouquet on the front seat and his confidence wilted.

Hana placed her phone on the kitchen counter with a sigh. Bodie's text said to expect Pete and one other. She hoped it might be someone who could light a fire, as she couldn't trust Pete with responsible, grown-up activity.

When a sharp knock sounded twenty minutes later, she walked into the hall and peered through the window next to the front door. Nothing happened when she clicked the switch for the outside light. The visitor looked too tall for Peter North and Hana groaned as he turned to face the front door. "You've got to be kidding me!" she hissed.

"I know, I know!" Logan held his free hand up, palm outwards in supplication as Hana pulled the door open. "Pete bailed at the last minute." He stepped over the threshold and dumped two sleeping bags and mats on the hall floor. "I can leave if you want." With him came a blast of Antarctic air and Hana struggled to close the door after him.

"What happened to Bodie?" she demanded, her face pulled into an unattractive sulk.

Logan winced. "He's with Marcus. His blood stats went haywire."

"How haywire?" Hana narrowed her eyes. "He looked fine earlier." Understanding flooded her expression. "Chocolate? He's gorged on something naughty."

"Something like that." Logan looked around the hallway and gave a slow nod. "Floors look amazing. And you've fixed that ruined plasterboard on the ceiling. Well done."

Hana sighed and her eyes took on a hard glaze. "Yeah. All the things you planned to help me with."

Logan exhaled. "Hana. I tried to speak to you countless times and I even drove up here. What did you want me to do? Break in and sand the floors for you?"

"Very funny." Hana glared at him. "Make a joke of it, why don't you?"

"Just give me something to do now," Logan said, removing his jacket. "I'm here and willing to help. Where are you up to?"

Hana pointed towards the kitchen. "I've scrubbed and bleached out the old cupboards and lined them with cheap wallpaper off-cuts. Then I started sanding the fronts. I want to paint them and change the handles."

Logan pulled her right hand towards him and turned it over, exposing the stitches. "How did you keep that clean?"

"Rubber glove." Hana flapped the yellow gloves in her left hand. "Makes it sweat. Gloves don't help with the sore wrist though."

"Did you get that break checked again?" Logan reached for her other hand and she snatched it away.

"No. I'm not going back there." She pouted and Logan narrowed his eyes. To Hana's relief, he said nothing.

"Have you eaten?" His question came from left field and Hana floundered.

"Chips earlier," she said. "I brought the kettle and toaster from Achilles Rise. Do you want toast?"

Logan tutted. "I bought chocolates for you, but they had an accident."

"Shame." Hana looked disappointed. "I could murder some chocolate."

Logan followed her to the kitchen where she boiled the kettle for tea and coffee. Her new china cups from the hardware store looked cheerful against the darkness of the scene outside, white with bright red strawberries. They couldn't alter the black tension inside though.

"Thanks." Logan accepted the coffee and leaned back against the counter, looking at Hana as he sipped the hot liquid. The awkward moment lasted and lasted as neither of them wanted to speak first. Hana drank her tea too fast in her bloody-mindedness and burnt her mouth. Waiting for the pain to subside she stared into the mug, twisting it and watching how a stray tea leaf stayed in front of her, even though the liquid twisted with the cup.

Logan cleared his throat and Hana jumped, causing the brown tea to shoot upwards and splash onto the clean floor. Embarrassed about her overreaction, Hana dumped the mug on the counter and bolted.

"No, no, Hana. Don't run. I'm sorry." Logan crossed the room in four strides. He wrapped his arms around her and held her for a long time, stroking her hair and kissing the top of her head. "It doesn't last," he promised. "You're bound to be jumpy but it won't last forever."

Hana nestled into his chest and waited for her breathing to calm. He smelled as she remembered and his spell settled over her, muddying all thoughts outside of his influence. She wished she hated him more and tried to summon up the painful sense of betrayal and righteous indignation, without success.

"It's getting cold," Logan whispered and Hana stirred. "Should I light a fire?"

"Okay." She pulled out of his embrace, cool air filling the vacancy left by his warm body. "The builder checked the chimney and said it's fine."

Logan went outside to source wood and Hana used breathing exercises to reinstate her equilibrium. She failed. As long as she anticipated his footsteps, nothing worked to calm her nerves. When he stumbled up the back stairs with his arms filled with dusty logs and his biceps straining through his shirt, she lost herself again. "You should go," she suggested, her fingers writhing together and an anxious expression marring her looks. "I'm fine by myself."

"No." His single word answer threw her and left no clever comeback. Logan knelt before the fireplace and tipped the logs into the hearth. Hana sighed. She sat beside him and read newspaper clippings on a pretence of helping.

"There's a Zumba class in the community hall at Huntly," she commented, handing the sheet over with deliberate slowness so she could read an advert on the back for heat pumps. "I should get a heat pump for here."

Logan sighed and held his hand out for the paper, waiting while she finished and then scrunching it up with an irritated expression. It took ages for the paper to catch and light the sticks, instead of burning itself out after a tantalising show of temporary heat. "Done," Logan said, sitting back as the sticks crackled and burned.

"But is it?" Hana asked, peering at the logs on top. "You've said that twice. I thought you'd be good at this."

Logan's eyes widened. "I am good at this, cheeky tart! I made my first fire at the age of four."

"I was younger," Hana retorted, twisting her face into a pout. "But it was a gas fire and I pressed a switch."

"Townie!" Logan scoffed, his expression softening with humour. He glanced at his watch. "It's late. We should sleep."

"Okay. Turn around then." Hana dug her fingers in Logan's back and stood, hopping on the spot to remove the track pants. Then she slipped into a sleeping bag and pulled it up to her chin. She sighed in the warm softness and hopped towards the fire like a child in a sack race. She sat with difficulty and laid flat on her back.

"Don't be an egg." Logan shook his head at her and seizing the far edge of the sleeping bag, pulled her away from the fire. "If that gets going, it might spark and burn the bag. It's dangerous."

"Spoil sport." Hana pouted. "How can it be this cold for April?" she demanded, "It's crazy."

"Dunno," Logan replied. "Want another drink before I get into my sleeping bag?"

Hana shook her head. "No thanks," she said. She kept her eyes half closed and watched Logan flick the light off and then undress. He removed his work pants and folded them, balancing them on his cowboy boots. His work shirt lay over the top, but he kept the tight tee shirt on, its whiteness glowing against the light from the flames. Hana's gaze traced the outline of his long, muscular legs as he pushed his feet into the other sleeping bag, socks first.

"I stink of bleach," she complained to distract herself from his smooth skin and the way his shorts fitted snug to his bum. She pulled a hand free and sniffed her fingers. "It's horrid."

Logan wrinkled his nose, his eyes glinting in the darkness. He jerked his head towards the sleeping mats. "Do you want yours?"

Hana nodded and pushed herself up onto her elbows. "Yes please."

Logan hopped across to fetch both and butted them together, hauling Hana onto her half like a sack of potatoes. Her mouth dropped open in surprise. "I assumed you'd sleep over there." She jabbed a finger towards the other side of the room and watched Logan's left eyebrow quirk upwards in amusement.

"Did you?" he answered. He sat with more dignity than Hana managed and pulled himself down into the sleeping bag. His body felt solid and safe next to hers and she hissed out a sigh of mock annoyance before laying down and turning her back on him.

Despite herself, Hana felt comforted by his presence. He didn't just offer protection, but doubled as an unintentional draught excluder, helping her to maximise the heat from the healthy fire. He lay without touching her, but she heard him breathing and snuffling behind her. The spectre of Caroline rose and hung over them like an impending disaster, sucking any peace from the room.

Hana heard the change in Logan's breathing and knew he slept. Just like that, he shut his eyes and left. She groaned aloud at the unfairness which left her baking in front of a roaring fire with the suspicion she might need the toilet soon. Concentrating on the soporific assurance of Logan's steady breaths, Hana drifted into sleep. She woke with a start as a floorboard creaked nearby, panicking and snatching at the zipper of her sleeping bag.

"It's okay." Logan's whisper felt warm on her cheek and his fingers stroked her cool forehead. "I put more logs on the fire. It damped down too fast."

Hana lay back on something warm, realising his arm replaced the wooden floor beneath her head. Lacking the energy to argue, she settled, pushing her body back into his and enjoying the contact. "Thanks," she muttered.

"It's okay." He wrapped his other arm around her waist and tucked her in tight, creating a bubble of safety around her.

"I'd forgotten," she mused, her voice sleepy.

"Forgotten what?" Logan whispered.

"How nice it feels to listen to someone else breathe," she said, her sentence punctuated with a yawn. "Maybe that's why I can't sleep unless I'm exhausted."

Logan's arm pulled her closer, constricting her stomach until she levered her bottom against him. Then he leaned over and kissed her neck. He turned her in his arms, centimetres at a time until without resisting, she found herself facing him. His breath smelled of coffee and toothpaste, warm and inviting. When his lips found Hana's in the darkness, she responded, craving comfort and the need to feel loved. They kissed like teenagers on a time limit, putting everything into their stolen minutes together. "I don't want you thinking about sleeping with someone else," Logan whispered, breaking the kiss as his fingers strayed inside her sleeping bag. He found the bottom of the pullover and tugged.

"No!" Hana reacted, pushing herself backwards and knowing she'd almost fallen. Almost repeated the same mistake twice. 'Sin in haste, repent at leisure.' Her father's words wounded her like tiny needles in her flesh. Embarrassment made her spiteful. "How can you say that?" she snapped.

"Hana." Logan's fingers reached for her in the flickering orange glow and she slapped them away.

"No. You can't have your cake and eat it!" she bit. "You made your choice."

"What are you talking about?" Logan leaned up on one elbow, his expression unguarded for once.

Hana shuffled away in her sleeping bag, sliding off the mat and moving nearer the fire. "Did you mean everything you said at your parent's place?" she demanded. "Or was it lies to get me into bed and then ditch me?"

Logan exhaled and turned onto his back. He fixed his arms behind his head and his eyes glittered in the firelight. "I meant everything I said. Nothing's changed for me." He paused a moment. "What the hell happened, Hana?"

Hana shook her head. The memory of the touching scene in the car park made acid rise into her chest. She thought of how she hid behind the truck to avoid humiliation and anger replaced lust and the sense of hopelessness. Caroline's smug expression and the intercepted text message acted as the catalyst. "Caroline happened," she told him, her anger evident even in the darkness. "I saw you leave together. You looked like crap the next day with your shirt buttons done up in the wrong order. It doesn't take a genius, Logan! You humiliated me."

"Ah." Logan's tone sounded judgemental. "Right. So this isn't about me, is it? It's about you not wanting to look a fool."

Hana inhaled and balled her fists. Both hands sent darts of pain up her arms and exacerbated her fiery temper. "How dare you!" she shouted. "Don't make me the crazy in this relationship, Logan Du Rose! I know what I saw."

"No, you don't!" Logan sat up and faced her, his irises glinting in the orange glow. "Yes, you saw us leave together because she threatened to tell you a pack of lies. That's all you saw. We had a conversation and that was it."

Hana's laugh sounded cruel. The firelight bounced off her red hair, highlighting it in flames of its own. "Liar!" she shouted. "I saw the text you sent her."

"What?" Logan's brow narrowed. "What bloody text? I haven't texted her since the day after our wedding when I told her to go to hell."

"That's not very nice!" Hana bit, her childhood in her father's Sunday school classes coming home to roost. "You can't say that to people." She closed her eyes and gritted her teeth. "I want you to leave."

"Well, I'm not!" Logan snapped back. He lay down on the sleeping mat and stretched across to occupy Hana's half, condemning her to the hard floor. "It's late, I'm tired and I'm teaching in a few hours. Just go back to sleep."

"I don't have to if I don't want to." Hana stuck her nose in the air and folded her arms.

"Don't then," Logan replied. He gave a sigh that almost sounded like contentment and Hana resisted the urge to put her hands around his throat.

She lay on her side, her shoulder digging into the hard floorboard and losing the battle. Hana wondered why she didn't drag the large rug across and lay on that, but both her wrist and her hand punished her for the day's rough treatment.

"Hana." Logan's voice came through the darkness, leeching beneath her skin and sending tingles up her spine. "For what it's worth, I can see how it must have looked," he conceded, "I get it." He sighed and Hana tensed. An air of confession hung over them and she squeezed her eyes closed against it. She didn't want to hear. "I should've talked to you before now, but I didn't know how to say it. Will you let me explain something, please?"

Hana's heart plummeted down past her knees and dread replaced the void. She put her hands over her ears like a petulant toddler. "No. I don't care," she bit, raising her voice. Once he told her the thing which caught on his tongue and ruffled his confidence, they'd sleep like wooden planks cast together like flotsam in a swollen river. "Stop talking," she pleaded, her voice tearful. "Or go somewhere else. I've worked it out for myself, thanks. Just leave things the way they are. It's awkward enough at work without you making it worse."

Logan tried to pull her towards him but Hana resisted, snuggling deep into her bag and covering her head. Sadness drained away the anger and her tears dripped with muted plops into the fabric. She muffled the worst of her undignified sniffs but Logan heard, cuddling up behind her and reaching into her sleeping bag. With gentle hands, he stroked her hair back from her face, pulling her spine into his chest and forming a powerful rearguard against the draught pushing beneath the lounge door. Hana fell asleep with his arms around her. Despite the physical contact, she felt more alone than ever.

The next morning dawned grey and cold. Hana's pale complexion looked ghostlike and every bone in her body ached from sleeping on the floor. A draught slipped through the rimu boards from beneath the house and she rued the need for under floor insulation. The fire lay cold and dead in the grate, a pile of ashes beneath the iron basket the only evidence of its nocturnal activity. Logan slept on, his face pressed tight into the back of her neck. As Hana moved, he inhaled and roused himself and his grip tightened around her. She wriggled against him and he groaned. "Stay," he whispered and his tone sounded urgent.

"No," she bit. "Thanks for staying but it's time you left."

Logan snorted. "Oh, Hana! Why won't you let yourself trust me?"

"What, because you're trustworthy?" she retorted, yanking herself free of his grasp and backing out of the sleeping bag.

Logan sighed and rolled onto his stomach. Hana saw him glance at his watch, registering the time. Six-thirty felt like midnight and dark shadows circled his eyes in the dawn light. She pulled yesterday's track pants over her legs and hid in the kitchen.

Logan padded to the bathroom in his socks, his white tee shirt rumpled and his tight shorts clinging to every muscle and sinew. Hana turned her face towards the kitchen window and pretended not to stare. She brewed coffee, attempting to be pleasant to a man she'd reduced to the status of colleague, awaiting his appearance with a dull ache in her chest.

"I'm off now." Logan's voice sounded hard as he turned his shirt collar down and tucked it into his trousers. Stubble graced the lower half of his face, hardening his dark looks. His grey-eyed gaze flicked down to check his trousers and then up to rest on Hana's blushing face. The truck keys jangled in his hand.

"Thanks." Hana knew the word sounded lame. She swallowed and avoided looking at him. "For everything."

Logan snorted and shook his head. To her surprise, his expression softened. "You really think I'll walk away?" he asked. His tone sounded light and he leaned against the doorframe and stuck his hands in his pockets, his stature casual and relaxed. "You think it's that easy?"

Hana shrugged and avoided his gaze. "I don't know, Logan. I don't know anything anymore."

"Then know this." He pushed off from the doorframe and reached her in two strides, withdrawing his hands from his pockets in the same fluid movement. The pressure of his palms against Hana's upper arms and the small shake he gave her, unhooked the feeble clasp over her heart. "You're the one thing in this life I will not lose again." His voice sounded hoarse and he lifted her chin with an index finger, forcing her to see the gravity in his grey eyes. Logan tilted his head and Hana swallowed. "I'm in this for the long haul, Hana. I always was. Get used to it."

Hana breathed out through pursed lips and he kissed her, stalling the exhale mid-way. His fingers weaved through her hair, the plasters over his knuckles snagging until he snorted with exasperation. Hana opened up to him, her whole self in the kiss, a flower released from the restrictive casing of the bud she could've become if her life took a different route. Logan's pupils almost obscured his irises as he pulled away, resting his forehead against hers. Hana's palms against his chest felt the steady thrum of his heartbeat and she swallowed as fear sought to wreak havoc in the fleeting sense of peace. "I can't do this," she whispered, her voice catching. "I can't explain but I need to be alone."

She watched his eyes shutter closed but when he opened them, determination filled the space where dismay hovered before. Logan shook his head. "You're not listening Hana." He bowed his head and kissed her jaw. "I will not lose you." The corners of his lips lifted into a smile and déjà vu robbed her of voice. His teenage face returned to her inner vision, serious and intense with those haunting eyes and that same shy smile. Hana's lips parted and her resolve deserted her.

Logan's brow knitted and he glanced at his watch. "Gotta go," he said, stealing another kiss.

Hana pulled herself from his embrace, using his distraction against him. "I have to be alone," she repeated, the futility of her words hitting home.

"Why?" Logan cocked his head in confusion, the dimple appearing in his right cheek as he chewed his lip. "Why, Hana?"

She swallowed and repeated what she knew, what she'd always known. "It's what I deserve." Her words cut through the air like a knife. She swallowed and pointed a shaking finger at the front door. "Please go, Logan. I mean it."

He shook his head in disbelief. Rubbing the fingers of both hands beneath his eyes, he held the pose, drawing the grey windows of his soul into narrow, curved slits. "No," he said, as though to himself. "No." Logan let his hands fall, his fingers stroking the side of Hana's neck and tracing a line across her shoulder in retreat. An electric current passed through her, earthing itself to the floor through her stomach and snaking down her inner thigh. Logan reached the front door and unlocking it, he turned back to her. "You know where to find me, Hana. I love you and I've spent the last twenty-six years in love with you. This isn't about me or Caroline, but about you. I know what past hurts do, Hana. They cloud your judgement, lie to you and make you run." Logan waved his hand in her direction, taking in her rigid stance and flashing green eyes. "This is you running. So do it, babe. Do it. And when you're done running and find yourself standing still, look behind you. I'll still be here."

The door closed and Hana saw Logan pass the hall window, striding over the stairs two at a time. She heard the truck start with its familiar grunty roar like an accusation. Then it crunched away down the hillside. The silence Logan left behind him throbbed and hummed in the empty house and Hana stood right where he left her. The echo of her own jaded inner voice sought to make him a liar like all the others who trod in and out of her life just to trample the flowers. Her father, Vik, all of them. Liars.

Chapter 43

Hana's phone chirruped, dragging her from the awful pit of remembered pain. The device vibrated around the counter, stretching its cable taut against the new double-socket. Her fingers shook as she pulled it free and accepted the call.

"Hey Mum, how are you? Did Logan and Pete already leave?" Bodie asked. His tone sounded urgent.

Opting to explain nothing, Hana gave short, non-committal answers. "Yes, I'm fine. Yes, my visitors left for work. How's Marcus?" Her lips felt bruised from Logan's kiss and she pressed her fingers to them, filled with confusion and wanting what she couldn't have. She no longer thought of the blond man's kiss, the memory overwritten with the flare of a teenage crush. Her heart went to war with her head.

"Look Mum, I've booked a flight for Marcus. He's leaving tomorrow. I found him injecting in the night and he suffered a bit of a hypo. He's okay but struggling. Besides which, Izzie's threatening to fly up with Elizabeth and refuses to understand there's nowhere for them to sleep."

Hana put her hand up to her forehead and let out a huge sigh. "Poor Marcus, is he okay?"

"Don't give him sympathy!" Bodie snapped. "It's self-inflicted. Idiot ate a box of chocolates. He's begging me not to tell Izzie but I still might."

"Chocolates?" Hana rolled her eyes. "Why did you give him chocolates?"

"I didn't." Bodie paused. "Logan bought them for you. Did you like the flowers?"

"What flowers?"

"He had a massive bouquet on the front seat of his car." Bodie snorted. "Maybe he changed his mind."

Hana gritted her teeth and glanced around the bare kitchen. "Maybe they weren't for me," she snarled.

"He said they were, but that's not why I'm ringing." Hana heard his heavy intake of breath. "The removers rang me. Someone cancelled, so I changed the day. They arrive here in half an hour. They should be with you by about eleven." He waited for a response, unnerved by Hana's silence. "Mum? You still there?"

Hana clutched the phone with one hand and the bench top with the other. Her knuckles showed white through her porcelain skin. "I'm not ready!" she gasped. "The electrician hasn't finished."

Bodie continued, his tone cajoling. "I know you don't like last minute changes, but Culver's Cottage is as ready as it's gonna get at the moment. We all need a good night's sleep tonight, especially me. I have stuff to do tomorrow. For work."

"Sleep," Hana repeated and sighed. Her bones ached from last night's sleep, or lack of. She looked around at the bare walls showing patches of colour, the plaster sanded ready for painting. "I wanted to decorate the key areas first," she complained and Bodie snorted.

"You won't manage it before your actual moving day, Mum. Be realistic. Move in and then work around it." He paused. "Angus rang. He said the biology teacher still wants the house."

"Oh." Hana's mood lifted. "So I don't need to sell right now? That's amazing."

"It is but they're still moving in on Saturday. Finish up here and start again, Mum. You can do this."

Hana smirked at her son's attempts to encourage her. In a freaky role reversal, he even mimicked the same tone of voice she once used to get him to finish homework or run faster at sports' day. "Okay." She exhaled. "I'll get ready for the van arriving." She peered at her watch. "In three and a half hours. Should I drive back to Achilles Rise with the vacuum cleaner?"

"Nope," Bodie answered. "You can do that before the weekend. Just stay there. Decide where you want things so it's easier when the van arrives. There's one other thing."

Tension in Bodie's voice piqued Hana's interest. "What, Bo?"

Bodie lost his nerve. "It's fine. Nothing important. I'll tell ya later. You're amazing, Mum. You're taking this so well!"

The stack of black bin bags sat on next-door's trailer, attached to the tow bar of Bodie's BMW. The expensive car purred outside the city dump on Lincoln Road with Marcus at the wheel. It contained items Hana wouldn't want to lose. Bodie's packing wasn't as haphazard as his mother believed, but selective and careful. His dismantling of the family home uncovered morbid stacks of memorabilia which worried him; the newspaper clippings detailing the road accident which killed his father, cards of sympathy, fading and yellowing with age and a note from someone called Mark. He'd turned the paper over in his fingers, not having heard the name before. 'Mum died on Tuesday,' it read. 'Don't come to the funeral. You're not welcome. Mark.' He wanted to ask Hana about it, but knew he wouldn't. He sent it to the municipal dump, dreading the consequences once Marcus drove away.

Hana's reaction to the crushing of the little dog he gave her, alerted him to the fragility of her peace. He remembered buying it from a $2 store. His father gave them $5 each to buy Hana a birthday present, which for Izzie meant a $5 gift. For Bodie, it meant sweets and a panic after looking at the meagre change in his hand. So little thought went into the buying of the dog, yet she treasured it enough to die for against a man whose nickname reflected his skill with a blade.

Everything went into black bin bags and Marcus waited outside the dump, his body thrumming from the effects of his midnight hypo. Having grabbed a sneaky pie from the bakery, the cleric inspected Bodie's expensive ride for tell-tale crumbs on the driver's seat. He tuned the radio into a Christian music station and hiked the volume, guaranteed to upset his friend when he reclaimed the car and found himself blasted with a church choir. Then Marcus lay back in his seat outside the locked gates and belted out a hymn in a loud and entertaining baritone, much to the amusement of the council workers. "Oh, God," he bellowed and they looked at each other and sniggered.

"Yeah, you'll need him in a minute," stated the grumpy site manager and the others laughed.

By eleven o'clock, Hana felt ready. She wandered around the empty house looking at the rough walls and deciding how to place the furniture. Bodie rang her again. "They're almost there," he said, his voice distant and the sound of traffic in the background. "I've told them to leave a gap between the big furniture and walls so you can get behind it to decorate. Otherwise you'll kill yourself pulling the Welsh dresser out and in again."

Hana snorted. "You know me too well." At his lack of response, she cringed. "There're too many windows," she complained. "I don't know where I'll fit everything."

"You'll be fine," Bodie replied. "Almost there."

Hana heard the removal truck before she saw it. It whined and complained over every centimetre of the thousand metre driveway. Her mouth dropped open in horror as she waited on the porch, seeing the rear door come towards her. "Bloody hell!" she exclaimed. "He reversed up."

The huge removals van rounded the last bend and strained up the hill. The flat ridge at the top wasn't long enough to accommodate it, so the driver parked at a jaunty angle, with only just enough room to drop the loading ramp.

"Losers parked at the bottom," Marcus called to Hana, emerging from the middle seat of the removal van looking smug and self-satisfied. He poked his tongue out at Bodie, who stopped to catch his breath at the top of the rise. The other removals man appeared from the passenger seat looking sick. He crouched near the floor with a green complexion and Hana winced.

The driver punched the air in victory and high-fived Marcus. "Oosh, backwards bro'! I nearly lost it on that last bend! Good job you're a praying man."

Marcus laughed and Bodie stalked across, his face showing irritation. "That was irresponsible."

The driver shook his head. "Na. It's all good, mate. Rear wheel drive on this baby." He slapped the truck door with a loving hand.

"Mate, the handbrake's not on properly," Bodie interjected with urgency in his voice.

"Oops!" The driver dashed back into the cab, cranking the gears into reverse and ratcheting the handbrake up a few notches. The massive van leaned at a dangerous angle pointing down the hill.

Hana offered everyone a drink, but the removers declined. "I need to be in Hamilton by three o'clock to take my youngest son to soccer training." The driver smiled. "Otherwise, the wife will kill me."

The unloading began in earnest with Hana directing the furniture traffic to various locations. In the middle of the chaos, an unwelcome visitor arrived. Hana sighed at the sight of him and summoned up a blank look which didn't betray the salt rubbed into her wounds.

"Hey, Logan." Marcus wiped his hands down his thighs and offered his hand.

Logan shook it and nodded towards the house. "Need some help? I taught my first three classes and Angus let me go for today."

"Yeah, sure." Marcus glanced back at Hana's dark expression and cringed. "Come with me. I'm fixing up the double bed."

"Ooh, vicar!" Bodie retorted, hurrying past with a bedroom cabinet. "How very inappropriate."

Nobody stopped until two o'clock and the van sat empty. The driver's assistant proved entertaining in the slanted body, for as it emptied, he employed small wheels under his trainers to skate to the back and fetch the last items. At ten past two, the red brake lights of the van made a terrifying descent to the road, this time nose first. At the first bend, the driver took both hands off the wheel to give a cheery two-handed wave, shouting, "Invoice will be in the post!"

Hana felt her breath catch as he lurched around the corner and continued his unpredictable journey downhill. Inside, she heard the men shouting to each other as they reassembled the last of the cabinets and beds. They argued over the spanner and screwdriver which Marcus hogged. The dining table fitted in the centre of the kitchen and Hana hauled it into place and clapped her hands in pleasure.

"I'll put boxes in the dining room then," Bodie suggested, watching her from the hall. "They might get damp in the garage."

Marcus shot him an odd look, which he ignored. Hana frowned. "I don't think so. The surveyor found no sign of damp."

Bodie shook his head. "I don't want you carrying boxes up the stairs. It's dumb when you can sort them out up here."

Hana nodded. "Good plan." Her eyes narrowed. "There isn't as much as I thought there'd be. Did stuff get left at Achilles Rise?"

Bodie cringed and Marcus cleared his throat. Hana looked from one to the other. "Mum, can I borrow your car? I'll take Marcus to the dairy to get some lunch and fetch my car on the way back."

"Yeah sure." Hana dragged the keys from the counter and placed them into his upturned palm, watching his colour change enough to alert her. "What did you do?"

"Nothing!" Awkwardness made him laugh and they backed away, getting stuck side by side in the kitchen doorway.

Logan dodged out of their way as he arrived behind them. "The back bedroom is set up." He waved the spanner. "Easier once I got the tools."

Marcus waved to him from the front door. "Fancy a pie for lunch? Bo's buying."

Logan nodded. "Yeah, please."

The slam of the front door let silence flood back in and Hana kept her gaze on the floor. Logan edged nearer. "House looks great," he said. "Like you imagined."

Hana breathed out through pursed lips and nodded. "Kind of."

Logan cocked his head. "What does that mean?"

"Nothing." Her sharp retort shut down the discussion, the unspoken words hanging between them. The same loneliness but a different location. She hadn't planned to be there alone.

"Come on." Logan held his hand out to her and Hana's brow furrowed. "Show me where you packed the sheets and we can make some of the beds up."

They spent the next fifteen minutes in the dining room, opening boxes and looking for sheets and pillowcases. "This is ridiculous." Hana stopped and put her hands on her hips. "They must have left stuff."

"They didn't."

"How do you know?" she demanded and Logan shrugged. "I saw it all last night when I called by. There were twenty-eight boxes stacked up in the garage and that's what they brought. Plus your furniture." He yanked a double duvet and cover from a box, holding it up in front of her. "This is what we're looking for." He laid it over his arm and looked at her in expectation. "You coming?"

The tension between them eased and Hana felt herself thawing, despite her efforts not to. She grabbed pillows and cases and followed him into the bedroom. Logan flipped the duvet cover inside out and stuffed his hands into the corners. Hana laughed. "What are you doing?"

"Hey. My parents run a hotel. I know the quickest way to service a bedroom, Ms McIntyre. Don't doubt me."

She smiled and handed him the corners of the duvet inner. He seized them in his strong fingers and flicked the cover over the top, shaking the whole thing to encourage it to settle into place. "I don't do it like that," Hana said, watching the easy manoeuvre in surprise. "I'll try it that way when my hands feel better."

Logan smiled, the expression open and generous. They worked side by side to fasten the buttons at the bottom and Logan shook it out over the bed. Standing back to admire the effect, their hands touched. Hana jumped as though shot. "Sorry," she blurted and backed away.

"Don't be. I'm not." Logan took her slender forearms in his fingers and turned her hands over. "You're using your wrist easier," he remarked, his eyes moving across the stitches in her palm. "But you should cover this."

Hana watched his lips move as he spoke, remembering their kiss and horrifying herself by wishing he'd repeat it. He'd removed the plasters from his knuckles and the skin looked raw and ragged, less healed than any of her injuries. "Your hand looks sore," she said, her voice soft. "I never thanked you properly. You must've hit him hard."

Logan swallowed. "About average," he said. His eyes flashed something unreadable. His fingers gripped her forearms tighter.

"What did you want to say last night?" Hana asked, her voice tremulous. "We might as well get it over with."

Logan's eyebrows rose and then he shook his head. "Nothing important. Nothing to upset you, although you assumed it would."

Hana swallowed and looked at the floor, her teeth worrying at her lower lip. "So just say it."

"I don't need to." Logan's fingers roved up her arms, causing her to shiver with every fractional movement. They coasted up the side of her face, stopping to smooth the healing bruises before sliding into her hair and brushing the back of her neck. Hana felt a gentle tug as Logan loosed her ponytail and sat the long, red tresses over her shoulders. His work enveloped him, his mind entering another place and time and rendering his expression ethereal. Hana's resolve weakened a little further. Logan's dark hair flopped into his eyes and moved with the motion of his eyelashes as he stroked her hair into channels along her back. She reached up and pushed the fringe out of his eyes, wincing as her wrist complained.

Time stopped, holding the moment in its strong hands. Hana felt Logan's heart beating fast as he pressed her against the wall with his body. Her mind took her back to the green pasture of the mountain, invoking her feelings of excitement and promise. In real time, Logan bent and kissed the bruise beneath her jaw. Hana sighed. Pleasure mixed with pain as promises and a fractured relationship jarred. She lifted her palms to push him away, both hands objecting. "No," she sighed, her body stating otherwise.

"Okay." Logan spoke, his voice low and husky. "But it's not easy staying away from you." He hesitated as though afraid and then bent to press his lips against hers. Hana felt the pilot light flare behind her navel, at once breathless at the flick of his tongue against hers.

She jumped at the sound of the front door slamming and banged her head on the doorframe. "Ow!" she groaned, running her fingers over the bump on her skull. Her stitches caught in her hair and she cursed in frustration. Logan disentangled her, his grey eyes never leaving her face.

"Come on you guys," Bodie called. "Get it while it's hot!"

Logan smiled at Hana, his dark lashes sweeping upwards in a sultry movement. He didn't need to say anything, releasing her so she could yank the sweatshirt over her hips and take a steadying breath. It destroyed the moment and she slipped out into the hall, still tasting the pressure of Logan's lips against hers. She heard him exhale and clear his throat, waiting a moment before following her.

Hana found Marcus and Bodie arguing in the kitchen. Bodie tipped hot meat pies from a plastic bag onto paper plates and turned to complain to Hana. "Mum, he ate a pie on my leather interior."

"Marcus!" Hana gave him a hard stare. "A pie? Think of the cholesterol and hidden sugar. How will you ever control your condition if you don't take it seriously?"

Marcus looked ashamed but Bodie spoke through gritted teeth. "What about my seat? It's got a greasy stain right between where his fat legs were."

He spun around and eyeballed his friend. "And thanks for retuning my radio. I loved driving up here to doomsday music."

Marcus inhaled. "It's not doomsday! It's choir hour with Roger and Marjorie."

Logan snorted and both men glared at him. He shrugged. "Just give me some kai," he demanded.

Marcus pushed a plate towards him with a look of betrayal. "I'll have mine after I've checked my levels," he bit and stalked towards the bathroom.

"You're worse than children!" Hana groaned. She poured cola from a bottle into mugs and held one out to Logan.

"No, thanks," he said, shaking his head. "It's gut rot."

"So's that pie," she replied, jerking her head towards the cheese leaking from the pastry.

Logan shook his head. "Carbs." He spoke with his mouth full but covered the effect with his hand. "I'll burn them off."

"Shut up all of you!" Bodie snapped. "What about my car?"

Hana turned away with an eye roll, sharing a conspiratorial look with Logan. Bodie noticed and resentment stirred in his heart.

Logan left at six o'clock, but not before handing the bouquet to Hana on the porch steps. "I heard about these," she said, her eyes twinkling.

Logan cocked his head. "I'm surprised they survived in my car." His brow furrowed and he looked nervous. "I should've given them to you last night, but it never seemed like the right time."

"And it does now?" Hana winced, hearing the suspicion in her voice.

Logan shrugged. "I've decided it's never the right time. And if I die before tomorrow, I'll regret not giving them to you."

Hana's lips parted. "You won't will you? Die." Fear back-lit her expression and Logan closed his eyes at his tactlessness. Her husband went to work and didn't arrive home.

He shook his head. "No. Stupid example. Forget it." He leaned forward and kissed her over the flowers. "I'll see you tomorrow."

Logan watched Hana's pale face in his rear view mirror for as long as he could, feeling the cord between them stretch with the growing distance. He shook his head at his verbal fumbling and returned home via Achilles Rise as promised. He rang Bodie from the front garden. "Bloody cat went straight onto the roof," he said. "I don't know how you're gonna catch him. How's the unpacking going?"

"Good." Bodie surveyed the mess at Hana's feet. "Slow. Marcus took the cardboard boxes to the bottom of the driveway. It's recycling day tomorrow apparently, so that's good timing." He walked out into the hall and lowered his voice. "Does Mum seem a bit depressed to you?" he whispered.

Logan shrugged and shook his head. "I'm not sure," he answered, guilt kicking him in the guts. "I haven't known her long. What's she usually like?"

"Not like this." Bodie glanced into the dining room where Hana twirled a lock of hair and stared at the remaining boxes in confusion. "Did you say something to upset her?"

Logan's voice became hard. "No." He sighed. "I can't get the cat. Cheers." He disconnected the call and narrowed his eyes, sensing the younger man's jealousy in the airwaves. "I can see how this is going to go," he hissed to himself.

"The TV won't work." Marcus fiddled with the remote, his face a mask of dismay. "I always watch Police Ten Seven on Thursdays."

Hana shrugged. "There's no aerial." She ruffled Marcus' blond hair. "Why do you watch that rubbish, anyway?"

Bodie inhaled in horror. "It's not rubbish!" he bit. "I've been on there!"

"Yeah!" Marcus rushed to his friend's defence. "Bo's been on there."

Hana rolled her eyes. "It's all hyped up and psyched up for ratings. You went on it once about three years ago. If you went on more often I might bother, otherwise no." She walked away, her feet padding against the floorboards. "I don't need a TV, anyway."

Marcus' mouth dropped wide open in shock and he jabbed a finger at Hana's retreating back. "She doesn't need a TV!" he squeaked.

Bodie laughed at him, tackling him backwards on the sofa. A loud clunk signified it lifting onto two feet and then settling again.

"Stop it!" Hana shouted, her voice far away. "I can hear you!"

The cool night drew in and Bodie tried and failed to light a fire. "This sucks!" he exclaimed.

Hana remembered Logan's roaring blaze and pursed her lips. "It doesn't matter," she said, soothing his sore ego. "I've got fan heaters. We can run them for tonight."

Marcus turned in early, exhausted from the physical exercise and the mobile earache Izzie gave him for eating chocolate. "You told her," he grumbled and Bodie grinned.

"I didn't know she'd react like that," he agreed. "She's a bit off the wall at the moment. Why?"

"I dunno." Marcus tucked himself into the double bed, leaving only his eyes above the duvet. "Everything's a drama at the moment." He turned on his side away from the hall light and sighed.

"Yeah." Bodie closed the bedroom door. "Three guesses why, idiot."

Hana rang Angus. "Stay away until next week, Hana." He sounded firm. "People think you're still sick. Let's leave it like that and review it on Monday. Bodie said they still haven't caught those men."

Hana thanked him and rang off. The large mirror from Achilles Rise leaned against the wall in the lounge and she squatted down in front of it. Even its strange tilted angle showed the livid bruising and a graze across her throat. She sighed and ran a finger over the heated skin. "What did he want?" she asked herself, remembering the blue eyes boring into her soul. "What's stopping him coming back?"

She undressed in the bathroom, craving a hot shower. She'd removed the disgusting shower curtain earlier, placing towels next to the bath to absorb any overflow. Sighing in expectation, Hana clambered into the tin bath and pulled the lever upright, standing back to let the water heat. The noise sounded deafening. A plumber checked everything but didn't mention the caterwauling pipes. Hana endured a loud experience as warm, hot and then ice water spattered at her from above.

"You okay?" Bodie's concerned voice sounded muffled through the door.

"Yep. I'm hoping it lasts long enough to wash the shampoo out before blowing up," Hana called back.

"Awesome." Bodie's footsteps retreated and she closed her eyes and braced herself against another round of clanking and groaning as she rinsed her hair.

Hana pulled her dressing gown over her pyjamas as she walked into the kitchen, smiling at her son. "I'll get the plumber back," she said, filling the kettle with water. "I won't cope with that noise every morning."

"So what's the problem? Ring him," Bodie answered, hearing the reticence in her voice.

Hana bit her lip and glanced round, her expression pensive. "I don't have the number. Logan found him."

Bodie looked at his mother, suspicion budding in his brown eyes. "Ask him for the number." He shrugged and watched her reaction.

"Okay." Hana's smiled drooped and Bodie leaned back in his chair.

"What's going on between you, Mum? I can't work him out. Or you."

Hana sighed and shook her head. "Nothing. It's fine." She gazed through the glass at the dark mountains beyond, her head in turmoil.

"He's dodgy." Bodie licked his lips and considered divulging something he'd picked up. "He's not what you think."

"What's that?" Hana asked. "Because I don't know what I think."

Bodie shook his head. "Nothing. You don't need losers in your life." He waved his hand around the kitchen. "I've told you before, stay single. It's less complicated and you don't want to lose all this in a bad alliance. A lot of younger men prey on women your age until they've taken everything. Then they dump them."

His words struck Hana to her core and she forewent the promised cup of tea, kissing her son on the top of his head and taking herself to bed. She tossed and turned in her master bedroom, unable to get comfortable. Logan's arms around her on the cool, wooden boards of last night seemed preferable to her loveless, empty bed. She thought of his expensive clothes and the vastness of the mountain north of Rangiriri, dismissing Bodie's suspicions as groundless. Logan Du Rose might be guilty of many things, but her gut told her he wouldn't get into a relationship for cold, hard cash. They met on a train twenty-six-years earlier. She hugged the knowledge to herself, knowing she'd never share the reason for her distress that day with Bodie.

The proximity of Culver's Cottage to the bush lent itself to amplified night noises, coupled with every other sound bouncing off the surface of the river and reverberating. The railway line to the east sent freight trains every half an hour through the night, mimicking an earthquake as the sound arrived before the train.

Turning on the side lamp, Hana experienced a bubble of irritation. "I can't sleep in this mess," she muttered to herself. A tower of clothes sagged against the wall, the uppermost items losing their attempt to defy gravity. Pictures, more pictures and a wooden framed mirror leaned against the French windows. Hana stood in the centre of the chaos, shivering in her pyjamas. With a sigh of resolution, she tidied and continued until the first night in her new home disappeared from under her.

The day dawned clear and bright through the uncurtained windows, the orange orb reflecting its vibrant colour on the river below. It shone along the east of the house, warming those fortunate rooms at speed and causing condensation to pour as steam from wooden surfaces. Bodie and Marcus appeared together in the lounge, finding Hana's bed empty. "I'm hungry," Marcus announced, rubbing his eyes. "Is there any breakfast?"

Bodie elbowed him in the ribs and indicated his mother as she reached into the bottom of a cardboard box. Her dressing gown had slipped sideways and her hair stuck out at odd angles. The expression on her face merged tiredness with relief. She jumped as Marcus spoke, almost overbalancing into the bottom of the box and catching herself at the last minute. "Mum! What are you doing?" Bodie demanded.

Dark circles surrounded Hana's eyes and the increased paleness of her skin betrayed her nocturnal activities. "Look," she said, waving her right arm around the room. "I'm finished." Success infused her cheeks with radiance but Bodie noticed the way she cradled her left wrist, favouring the stitched right hand. He followed her gaze and saw the overall tidiness of the room, books neatly placed in the dresser, the furniture arranged and pictures leaned up against the patched walls in their designated places. "What do you think?" she asked, looking for their approval with childish need. The men looked around them, taking in the orderliness of the room while Hana resumed her foraging in the bottom of the box one-handed, uttering from its cardboard depths, "The trouble is, I can't find everything."

She looked up to find Bodie gone and a guilty looking Marcus standing in the doorway, too sleep befuddled to beat a hasty retreat with his partner in crime. "Pardon?" he said, as though not hearing the question. Bodie let out an undignified snort from the kitchen doorway.

The kitchen looked immaculate. With everything stored away, the surfaces became clear and free of debris. "Where's the toaster, Mum?" Bodie called, poking around in cupboards. The old-fashioned wooden doors creaked as he opened and closed them, some of the plastic handles hanging off. He banged door after door until Hana appeared.

"Over there!" She pointed at the cupboard nearest the sink.

"I would've got there eventually," he grumbled. He jerked his head towards the cupboards at ceiling height. "Did you use a chair to reach those shelves?" he asked.

Hana blanched. "I might have. Can if I want to."

"Mmmnnn." Bodie rolled his eyes. "So, when you fell off in the middle of the night and lay on the floor dying, we'd find your dead body the next day, would we?"

"It didn't happen." Hana pulled her painful wrist closer to her body. She oozed exhaustion and the bone ached. Changing the subject, she pointed out the location of everything he might need. "Crockery and pots are down there and I've stored those used least often on the top shelves."

"Jam?" Bodie raised his eyebrows in question.

Hana pointed towards the pantry next to the old fireplace. "Spreads are in there. Jam is in the fridge."

Marcus joined them at the table, the men eating and discussing their prospective plans. Bodie waved his toast at Marcus. "I can give you a ride to the airport," he offered. "I'm going to headquarters at midday."

"As long as you don't make me late like last time," Marcus grumbled.

"You did that yourself," Bodie retorted. "I can't be late, I've got an appointment and if you're ready, I'll take you. If not, get a cab."

"Why are we friends again? I've forgotten." Marcus opened his insulin case and messed around with the contents.

"We're not. You're my sister's husband and I'm stuck with you. And you left grease on my front seat."

Marcus stuck out his tongue in defiance, clicking a tiny scalpel blade into the knuckle of his index finger to draw blood. Bodie waved his toast at him in disgust. "Don't do that at the table! I'm eating. Mum! Mum, tell him!"

Hana rose to fetch a cup of tea, nodding approval of Bodie's use of the old brown teapot steaming on a coaster on the side. "Nice!" she exclaimed, ignoring the bickering men and pouring brown liquid into a strawberry decorated mug. "Anyone else for tea?"

"Me, please," Marcus said, examining his haemoglobin levels in a digital reader. "Ah, that's not good."

"What?" Hana turned with concern on her face.

"I'm still alive," Marcus commented and she narrowed her eyes.

"Hot damn," Bodie muttered over his toast and Hana frowned at him. He waved a greasy hand at her. "I know, I know. Don't joke about things you don't mean or you'll have to live with yourself after. That's a very pessimistic way of viewing life."

"Or realistic." Marcus cocked his head and made a choking sound deep in his throat like a dying swan.

Hana felt a heaviness descend over her. After Marcus, Bodie would leave too. The miserable bits of parenthood sometimes outweighed the exciting parts. Despite the loveliness of the house and Hana's bewildered excitement at her ownership of it, some part of her wanted to pack up and go away with the boys into their busy lives. Everyone left her in the end. It's what she deserved.

"I'll get a quick shower," Bodie said, dumping his plate in the washing up water. Minutes later, Hana recognised the awful banging and clanging of the pipes as he turned on the water. She looked alarmed, but Marcus shook his head and slurped the last of his tea dregs. He tipped the cup up, looking disappointed he'd finished. "Just an air lock," he stated with confidence. "It'll run off when the water gets going through the system." He licked a toast crumb off his finger. "Or tap the pipes. That sorts it."

"So I don't need a plumber?" Hana asked, relief flooding her face.

"I thought you got one." Marcus stood to pour himself more tea.

"I did, but he didn't fix the wailing pipes."

"He doesn't need to, Hana. It's an air lock."

Hana exhaled, a smile on her tired face. "Wouldn't it be amazing if life could be so simple?" she asked. "Tap once and all your problems disappear." She waved her hand as though it contained a wand and winced at the pain in her swollen wrist.

"But it is that easy." Marcus took his tea and walked towards the door. "It just depends what you're tapping with."

The shower behaved for Marcus and they gathered together in the hall, checking he had everything for his return flight.

"You'll text when you get there," Hana asked for the tenth time and Marcus rolled his eyes.

"Yes, mother."

Hana eyed her son with curiosity. "What's the monkey suit for?" she demanded, brushing lint from his full dress uniform. "Are you heading up a parade somewhere?"

"No." Bodie laughed her comment off. "Just seeing one of the seniors today."

"Ooh, medal time?" Marcus asked and Hana's eyes widened.

"Are you getting a medal? Can I come?"

"Now see what you did!" Bodie frowned at Marcus. "It's not a medal ceremony, Mum. I promise. I'd invite you to that. It's just a formal chat." He watched suspicion fill her eyes. "A good chat. Stop worrying." He kissed her cheek and went outside to load Marcus' suitcase into the boot of the BMW.

Hugging Marcus, Hana felt tearful and lost. "Tell Izzie I love her," she said, fighting the rising grief and managing an extra kiss for Elizabeth.

"Course I will, Hana." His arms felt strong and safe around her and he kissed the top of her head. "Come and see us again soon," he said, the invitation genuine.

Hana nodded and waved them off, mopping her eyes so they wouldn't see her tears as the car bumped around the bend and down into the bush. Pungas and ferns obstructed her view of their descent further.

Bright and pleasant after the cold and misery of the previous few days, Hana gave herself a mental shake. "Come on woman, get it together," she told herself aloud, her voice sounding incongruous amidst the squawking of birds and hissing of the breeze through the trees. Hana's wrist hurt after her night of hefting boxes and she wrapped it in a stretchy support, giving some relief. The stitches on her palm itched and she wondered about the merits of trying to remove them herself. The cut looked clean but as she prodded with the kitchen scissors, she noticed blood and lost confidence in her accuracy with her left hand. She washed the scissors and rued her own stupidity.

Hana cleared up the kitchen and bathroom after the boys, finding the floor soaked through lack of a shower curtain. She followed their example, showering and mopping the floor with a dry towel afterwards. Once dressed, she wrote a list of the things she still needed, adding a shower curtain to the bottom of the growing pile of problems. She sat at the kitchen table and surveyed the bare plaster and tired cupboard doors, her dissatisfaction beginning an impatient chant in her brain. Loneliness closed in on her, pouncing and using her boredom as leverage to gnaw at her insides.

Hana snapped. "This is my damn life!" she announced. "And I will live it!" She snatched up the Honda keys, activated the burglar alarm and locked the front door. Then she set off down her steep driveway and headed north towards her favourite shop in Huntly, driving without a single good hand to her name.

Chapter 44

Hana didn't hear the vehicle whine up the drive, too busy in the kitchen with her paintbrush. The loud knock on the front door made her start and jab the brush into her cheek. Her hands shook and she rested her shoulder against the wall, balancing on the draining board with one foot on the counter. The Honda sat on the driveway next to the porch, giving her away. Bodie took a key and said he'd be ages and Marcus texted from Invercargill to say he'd landed. Hana panicked.

"What can I do?" she hissed, reaching for the chair she used as a ladder. She glanced at the kitchen door standing ajar and knew the caller would see the muted light through the front windows. "Hide," she told herself. "Hide in the pantry." The cutlery drawer came into view as she reached the chair and Hana pictured the knife she'd grab. No mistakes this time.

Her phone vibrated in her pocket and she almost overbalanced trying to retrieve it, smearing paint from the wet brush onto the draining board. Her phone slipped in her wet fingers, reflecting the impressive shade of oilskin brown on the cupboard doors. Hana groaned as her fingers smeared the sticky mess across the screen and buttons and the phone stopped ringing. "No, no!" she hissed, watching her only lifeline disappear. She rubbed the screen against her pants and it stared up at her. Dead.

"Hana!" Logan's voice sounded urgent as he hammered on the door and Hana's heart lurched. "Are you okay? Hana!"

Logan smiled with relief as Hana pulled the door open. He'd positioned himself side on, ready to do battle with her front door. She wiped at the brown smudge and spread it across her cheek. "Sorry," he said, raising his hands, palms outwards. "I didn't want to break the door down but figured I'd have to."

"Why didn't you want to?" Hana stood back so he could pass. She stroked the glossy navy wood. "Because you'd mess up my door?"

Logan shook his head as he slipped off his cowboy boots. "No, wahine! My hand isn't mended yet." He held up his fingers, the knuckles still raw and painful.

Hana's eyes moved from the cracked, bruised skin to Logan's face. "But you would've?" she asked, her voice small. "If I needed you to?"

His slow nod offered reassurance. "Course," he replied, grey eyes raking her face. He smirked and prodded his own cheek. "Painting?" he asked. "Yourself or the walls?"

"Neither." She padded into the kitchen without replying, giving her nerves time to settle. Logan followed, issuing a low whistle of appreciation.

"Wow. This looks different. The brown is perfect for the cupboards." Logan spun around, nodding his head. "You've a good eye for colour."

"Thanks." Hana picked her brush out of the sink and laid it on the upturned lid of the paint tin. Her eyes strayed to the half-painted pantry door. "Would you like coffee?"

"Yeah, but I'll make it." Logan nudged her out of the way. "I'll stay for a while and help you paint. Leave that door near the window; it's too high. I'll finish it."

"Are you sure?" Hana eyed the pristine black jeans and casual sweater. "You'll ruin your clothes."

Logan shrugged and flicked the switch on the kettle. "It's just stuff, Hana. All replaceable. I'd like to help."

"Thanks." Hana placed her hand over her heart, feeling the frenetic beating slow to a dull throb. "The knock on the door scared me. I hate feeling this way."

"I can imagine." Logan's eyes narrowed. "How can I help?"

Hana jerked her head towards the pantry door. "Just paint that bit near the ceiling for me. I didn't like balancing on the draining board and my hands are sore."

His smile halted her instructions. "I didn't mean the painting. I'll do that anyway. But your security bothers me. How can I help with that?"

Hana swallowed. "I don't know, Logan. Bodie's paid for an expensive gate and they're installing it next week. He thinks it's impenetrable." Hana shrugged. "Other than that, I don't know. I'll be happier when I have control over who rocks up on my porch, but I can't stop that blond man finding me in town, at work or anywhere else for that matter."

"But they're public places," Logan assured her, cocking his head and folding his arms. "That's not gone well for him so far. The cops are watching out, so that limits him. If you get your home secure, the rest is easier."

Hana shook her head, doubt crossing her eyes. "Not really. He can run my car off the road or any number of things I've no control over. If he wants me dead, it won't prove hard."

The scar under Logan's right eye puckered as his brow furrowed. "But he doesn't want you dead, wahine. You have something he wants. Killing you makes no sense."

Hana rubbed her eye with her knuckle and winced. "But I don't know what it is; otherwise I'd give it back."

"I believe you." Logan's words struck a chord deep in her soul and emotion filled Hana's chest.

"Nobody's said that." She inhaled, flaring her nostrils to stem the tears. "It's on me. The cops look at me as though I'm the guilty one. Over and over again they ask me if I've offended anyone, taken something belonging to someone else, dated someone unsavoury." An ironic smile crossed her lips. "Fat chance. If you'd asked the same question last year, I'd say my husband died eight years ago, I go to work and home, have no social life and don't know anyone outside my church friends."

"What changed?" Logan cocked his head and his eyelashes remained unblinking.

Hana rolled her eyes and her laugh sounded jaded. "I still go to work and home and don't have a social life. But my best friend slept with a student, my boss thinks I knew and said nothing, I've changed house and car and seen more of my son in the last few months." Her eyelashes flickered. "And I thought I dated you."

"So, not all bad then." Logan's sarcasm forced a laugh from between Hana's lips and she relaxed.

"No. Not quite. But I still didn't take something from a crook."

"I know." Logan winked at her and turned away. "What am I making here? Tea or coffee?"

Three hours later and Logan finished painting the thirteenth cupboard door. "Half way there." He stood back to admire his work and glanced at Hana. She looked up at him and smiled, brown paint on her left cheek, forehead and the end of her nose.

"I bought some wrought iron handles which look gothic. Do you think they'll match?"

Logan looked around the room and nodded. "Yeah. I love that you didn't just rip it all out. Nobody appreciates the original stuff anymore."

Hana stood, grimacing as her knees creaked. Logan consigned her to the lower cupboards after witnessing another near tumble from the draining board. "Do you think the colour saps the light?" she asked him, worrying at her lower lip. "It's darker than it looked in the shop." She wiped her hand across her forehead and left another streak of paint.

Logan stepped back and looked at the difference between the finished doors and the old pale blue ones behind him. "I like it," he replied. "The wall paint will correct any lighting problems."

"What lighting problems?" Hana's eyes opened wide with dismay.

"No lighting problems, there aren't any. It's fine, don't worry." Logan laughed at her. "Geez, you're a sensitive artist, wahine. I'm not an expert."

Hana's green eyes narrowed to slits. "Are you messing with me, Du Rose?"

Logan's gaze darted to the brush in her hand. "No! Don't even think about it!"

"You have paint on your nose." Hana's eyes glinted.

"No, I don't." Logan squinted to peer at the end of his nose, seeing Hana move forward. His head snapped up and he raised an eyebrow in warning. "I'm wearing good clothes."

"You said you didn't care." Hana smirked, her lips quirking upwards. The brown brush dangled from her right hand and she still protected her left wrist, carrying it like a broken wing close to her body. Her giggle sounded childlike and Logan grinned.

"You'll lose."

"Yep." Hana's eyes sparkled with resignation. "Don't I always?" She lurched and Logan put his hand in front of his face, defending against her attack. Hana aimed for his sweatshirt and when he grunted and turned, she slotted the brush beneath his arm and drew a wonky line on his forehead. "A mono-brow!" she squealed with delight.

Logan's eyes narrowed, keeping watch as she skittered to the other side of the room in a hail of giggles. He bent in an exaggerated pretence of loading his brush with brown paint. Hana shrieked and ran around the table, laughing as he followed. Logan's long legged stride gained him ground as he shoved chairs out of the way. He pinned her against the kitchen door and she squirmed and giggled as he threatened her with the wet brush. "Where do you want it?" he asked, pretending to examine her face for the best location. "Your face is pretty full. Not much room left." His eyes narrowed with humour as he zeroed in on the gentle sweep of her neck and rounded curve of her breasts. He patted the empty brush around her collarbone and Hana screamed and writhed away.

Logan kept her pinned to the door with his body and raised the brush above her head. He formed an arch over her, his pupils dilating. "What now, Ms McIntyre?" His loaded question cut through the air.

"I don't know," Hana whispered, her eyes wide.

Holding her tight with his right arm snaked around her waist, Logan lowered his lips to hers. Even messing around with her drove him crazy. He kissed her with deliberate slowness and Hana relaxed under him, her body betraying her. She responded to his lips trembling against hers and the sensation of his fingers straying from her waist to the back of her neck. The kiss grew heated and urgent, the painting forgotten amidst their rising passion. The spectre of Caroline crashed to the floor with Logan's paintbrush.

The click of the front door closing made them jump apart. Hana's inhale sounded ragged. By the time Bodie removed his gleaming black shoes and padded across the hall, Logan stood at the sink washing his brush under running water. Hana leaned against the bench top with a guilty expression on her face.

"Hi." Bodie acknowledged Logan with a terse greeting and bent to kiss Hana's forehead. He stopped at the sight of her paint-streaked face but said nothing. He switched his attention to the altered room. "This is great, Mum." His eyes narrowed. "You didn't drive that car I hope."

Hana swallowed and waved her hand towards the paint tubs lined up on the draining board. "What do you think? Oilskin brown for the cupboards and cream for the walls. I think it matches, don't you?"

Bodie nodded. "Yeah, but did you drive? And what did you stand on to do the high cupboards?"

"I did all the hard stuff." Logan tapped his brush in the bottom of the sink and turned to stare at Bodie. The men locked egos and Hana cringed in a herald of the future. "Your mum's got good taste." Logan smiled at Hana and she peered at him from beneath her lashes.

"Fine." Bodie jerked his head towards the hall. "I'll get into casuals and help."

Hana exhaled as he left the room, taking the dark atmosphere with him. Logan brushed his hand across his forehead and smirked at her. "Did you ever imagine getting to our age and being caught snogging?" he whispered and she barked out a laugh, covering her mouth with her hand. The corners of her eyes crinkled and she shook her head. "Do you want me to leave?" Logan's brow narrowed at the question and Hana sobered.

"Not really," she admitted, glancing towards the door and lowering her voice. "Do you want to?"

"No." Logan smirked.

"Then don't." Mischief infused Hana's smile and Logan turned back to the sink to dry his abandoned brush.

Having lost both her smaller brushes, Hana cracked open the wall paint and applied it with liberal sweeps over the scarred walls. The slight sheen in the paint hid a multitude of defects in the ancient plasterboard. "I love this," she said, standing back and admiring her work. Logan and Bodie grunted from opposite ends of the room, their backs to each other. Hana rolled her eyes and wondered what might happen when they met in the middle.

The room took shape, the cupboards and walls blending with the rimu floor as though old friends. Even the metal bench tops seemed to fit. The yellow light from the single bulb bounced off each surface and the house settled with a sense of relief at finally experiencing love. The ceiling proved the worst job of all and the men took turns, interchanging in silence when they suffered neck ache. Every surface received a coat of paint and some of the luckier ones, two.

Around ten o'clock, Logan looked at his watch. "I need to make tracks to the Gordonton house," he said, his body language showing reluctance. He glanced at Bodie's rigid back and shrugged at receiving neither thanks nor argument. Hana followed him out onto the porch.

"I don't know what's wrong with Bo," she said, the apology whisked away by the cold breeze on the porch.

Logan's eyes narrowed. "Never apologise for others, Hana," he said, pulling her into him and kissing her cheek. "It's his burden, not yours." His lips felt warm over hers and Hana sighed into the kiss.

"But he seemed fine with you the other night. Grateful even." She inhaled and shook her head in confusion. "I don't know what changed."

"It doesn't bother me." Logan's thumb caressed her bottom lip and Hana shivered against him. His chest felt warm against her cheek. "I don't intend to get involved in how you deal with your family."

Hana nodded. "About Caroline," she began, gnawing on the inside of her cheek.

Logan shook his head. "She doesn't feature, Hana. I told you the truth."

Hana swallowed, her heart filling with dread and every ounce of good sense abandoning her. "I don't know what to do."

"Then do nothing." Logan's arms felt good around her shoulders and he rested his chin on the top of her head. "Especially don't dump me."

"I feel as though every time we reach some kind of comfortable place in our relationship, the whole barrow tips over," Hana complained, feeling Logan sigh against her.

"I know." He stroked her hair, his fingers snaking through the curls and following them almost to her waist. "I should stop trying so hard." He lifted her chin with his index finger. "But I'm scared."

Hana saw fear mix with sincerity in his eyes and nodded. "Me too." His stubble grazed her cheek and neck as he kissed her and darts of pleasure zapped through her stomach. The creak of chair legs dragging across the floorboards in the kitchen made her giggle. "I feel like a teenager. I expect my mother to appear and wag her finger at me." She grinned up at Logan and he kissed the end of her nose.

"When can I see you again, Ms McIntyre?" he whispered. "When are you next allowed out?"

"I'm not sure." Hana fluttered her eyelashes. "Please can we take it slower?"

"Okay." Logan caressed her cheek with the back of his right hand and gave her a reassuring smile. He glanced at his truck. "I think I can get her out without asking your son to move his car."

"Perhaps best." Hana took a step back and Logan released her with great reluctance. He climbed into the truck and started the engine. A few tight turns and he'd faced the Hilux downhill, saluting her with the side of his fingers to his head as she'd seen him do on the farm. He left, the heavy vehicle lumbering along the driveway, taking Hana's heart with it. Her chin stung from the roughness of Logan's stubble and her body tingled with his remembered touch. She ached to do it all again, but Caroline's snarky expression haunted her. Logan might claim not to be interested in the other woman, but Hana sensed it wasn't mutual. Caroline didn't follow him all the way to Hamilton just to stand aside without a fight. Hana sat on the porch steps and shivered against the cold, knowing she'd lose because she always did.

"Why are you sitting out here?" Bodie demanded, his tone one of surprise. "What did he say?"

Hana looked up at him and used the banister to haul herself upright. "Logan? Nothing. I'm enjoying the peace."

Bodie scoffed. "There's no peace with that guy, Mum. You need to kick him into touch."

"Why?" Hana's brow furrowed. "What do you know?"

Bodie pursed his lips and adopted a pious expression. "I can't tell you. But get rid of him."

Hana glanced across the river at the many car lights bouncing along the main road. She imagined one set might be Logan's as he headed south east. A dull ache began in the base of her skull and she sighed. "He's a good friend," she said, dismissing Bodie's harsh advice. "And I liked his family when I met them. They're good people."

"You met his family?" Bodie's eyes widened in horror. "When?"

"A while ago." Hana hugged her arms around her to stave off the cold. "That weekend I told you I'd be away." The thought of Logan's serious grey eyes, long dark lashes and his full lips pressing against hers, brought a warming rush of colour to Hana's cheeks. "I need to go inside," she said, pushing past Bodie as he blocked the front doorway.

Hana made tea in an old brown pot, responsible in part for her colour choices. She sat down at the table, trying not to cringe when Bodie sat opposite, wishing to continue his third degree interrogation. An old sheet covered the tabletop and Hana plonked her mug down, catching it as it tilted on something hidden beneath the shroud. "I'm tired Bo," she said, her tone pleading. "I haven't slept since the move."

"But what will you do about Du Rose?" Bodie demanded, his eyes narrowing. "He's bad news."

"Says who?" Hana snapped and her son recoiled. "Does he have a criminal record?"

"No." Bodie shook his head. "But he's got links to the Auckland underworld. There are whispers about him."

"Where? Who's whispering?" Hana felt her patience grow thin. "He's a school teacher, Bodie. According to Angus, he comes with a great pedigree and lots of experience. Unless you can give me hard facts, I won't do anything about him."

"You said he cheated on you." Bodie went back to the old ground and Hana closed her eyes.

"I thought he did. His ex fiancé turned up at work and is trying very hard to get under his skin. I misread something that happened."

"You mean he told you that you'd misread it?" Bodie sneered. "There's something very wrong about him, Mum. I don't want you to have regrets over this."

"Regrets?" Hana's face hardened. "Haven't we been here before, Bo?"

Bodie's cheeks flushed and he looked embarrassed. Hana didn't understand the words he muttered in response. She stood. "I don't want to argue. It's amazing having you here to help. Let's not ruin it?"

He nodded. "Okay. If you insist."

"I do."

He sighed and nodded, allowing Hana to escape. His conversation at the police station weighed on him, the detective's attitude towards Logan's involvement concerning. He also mulled over his discussion with Marcus at the airport over a different matter, running over the awkwardness and his friend's stunned reaction.

Frustrated and confused, Bodie picked up his brush and reloaded it with paint. He continued long into the night, adding a second coat to cupboard doors already dry and another to the walls and ceiling. The faded blue and yellow became a distant memory as though it never existed. Hana's phone disturbed him after midnight, vibrating itself around the table in a musical rendition. He snatched it up before it launched into its second phase.

Izzie's tearful voice wailed from the device and Bodie held it away from his ear. "I want Mum," she sobbed.

Bodie sighed. "She's asleep, Iz. Have me instead."

"How could you be so mean?" Izzie wailed. "Marcus turned up with an airport teddy for Beth and a pregnancy test for me."

"Oh." Bodie swallowed. "I assumed he'd be more subtle but hey, you know Marcus."

Izzie sniffed. "I thought I did."

"Yeah, you do." Bodie smiled at the thought of his best friend's poleaxed expression as he mentioned the possible reason for Izzie's unusual temper and inability to cope in recent months. "He loves you and he means well. Where is he? Hiding? Or did you bury his body under the house?"

Izzie blew her nose and sighed. "I picked him up from the airport and dropped him at the hospital."

"That sounds rather mean, Iz. Or did you cut out the middle man and just send him to the morgue?"

"Mrs Jones died and her husband asked for him."

"Oh." Bodie pulled out a chair and sat down, examining the brown paint under his fingernails. "So you're home alone and brooding about whether to do the test or wait for him."

"I did the test as soon as I got home," Izzie said. "Now I don't know what to do."

Bodie licked his lips. "It'll be okay, you know. It always is."

Izzie snorted. "Not like you to be the eternal optimist. You're usually the little rain cloud on the picnic."

"Not always." Bodie swallowed. "And I'm hoping it's true, that things do always work out okay."

"Any particular reason?" Izzie silenced, sensing tension across the huge physical distance. "What's happened?"

Bodie took a deep breath. "I've messed up, Iz. I've messed up bad."

"Work or personal?"

"Both. I'm trying to sort it out, but I'm years too late, Iz. I don't know if I can."

"Can you tell me about it?"

"Maybe. But not now. I feel raw. I can't sleep. Mum went to bed hours ago and I've almost finished painting her kitchen."

He heard his sister's smile in her voice. "Being busy helps, bro'. Take it from someone who knows. I'm here if you need me." She spoke to someone in the background, her voice sounding muffled and far away. "Marcus got a lift from Mrs Jones' son. He says he misses you already."

"No, he didn't." Bodie smirked. "You made that up."

"Yeah, I did." Izzie sniffed again, her emotions returning to their tumultuous state. "I'd best go and have a very difficult conversation. Wish me luck."

"Good luck," Bodie said, meaning it. "If you find you've more than you need, send some back for me, please."

"Always. I love you, Bo." Bodie closed his eyes and imagined Isobel's gentle olive face, black hair pulled into a ponytail with wisps surrounding her face. She reminded him of his father and he felt for the familiar ache in his gut, missing them both.

"Love you too," he said and ended the call.

Hana woke to a finished kitchen and a tired Bodie. She sent him for a nap while she cleaned up paintbrushes and spilled paint. A heaviness seeped into her bones at the thought of his impending departure and she pondered his animosity towards Logan. She regretted involving him in her disastrous relationship, casting Logan in a poor light because of her antics. Her casting of Logan as a serial cheat stuck and formed the basis of Bodie's harsh judgement. Or so she believed as she blamed herself.

When Bodie woke, he drove them to a cafe in Huntly and they ate and chatted through their last hour together. The cheerful blue walls and farming images contrasted with Bodie's dark mood and Hana resisted probing for answers. She ate her macaroni cheese and focussed on a lichen encrusted post and rail farm gate, affixed to the wall to add to the atmosphere. Hana imprinted the moment in her memory, grateful for their strengthened relationship and aware it might revert to strained at any moment.

Bodie leaned back, stuffed after his lasagne and garlic bread and stifled a belch behind his hand. Hana grimaced. "You'll never get a girlfriend," she jibed and he laughed, although she sensed it sounded false.

"That's what you think, Mum. My women do bigger burps and farts than me."

"Eugh!" Hana gave a mock shudder. "I'm sure there's a nice girl out there for you."

Bodie raised his eyebrow as though in warning, shutting down the conversation. Hana knew from experience to steer towards safer topics. He drove her back to Culver's Cottage and then left for Whangarei.

"Hello, Johal," said the detective in charge of Hana's case. "How can I help you?" His voice sounded tinny through the car speakers as he raced towards Hamilton and not Auckland as he'd told Hana.

"I can't rely on my mother to update me," Bodie snapped, moderating his tone with difficulty. "She doesn't want to worry me. She let slip how the blond guy sat outside her old house for weeks. She thinks you're not interested."

"Did she take the registration number of the vehicle?" The detective sergeant's tone sounded clipped.

Bodie sighed. "Check Shelley's voicemail. Mum said she called it in a few times but nobody rang back."

"Okay. Thanks." The man rang off and Bodie shook his head. His gut told him there was more to the story than two men terrorising his mother.

"What a mess." Bodie ran a hand through his dark hair and felt a stab of pain as he passed the sign for Hamilton. "Not long now," he promised himself, knowing his imminent return would shock many people, one in particular.

Bodie pressed his fingers to his lips and suppressed anxiety at the forthcoming meeting. It may not go well for him. He cruised through the familiar suburb and parked, knocking on the door of a house he swore he'd never return to. The paint peeled beneath the rusty knocker and wet rot ate the bottom of the doorframe. Nothing like he remembered.

Surprise and dismay flashed across the face of the slender girl who opened the door, her short blonde hair tousled and dark shadows beneath her eyes. She gaped in shock, but her greeting sounded harsh. "What do you want?"

Bodie put his hands behind his back to hide the trembling of his fingers. "I'm in town for a few days. I didn't want to pass through without saying hi."

Her face curled into a sneer. "It's never bothered you before."

"Amy. I need to talk to you."

"Well, I don't want to talk to you!" She pushed the door against him and Bodie reached out a hand to stop it closing.

"Please, Amy. It's important."

"It's always important to you, Beauden. Nobody else's problems are though."

"That's not true." He stepped across the threshold and she put her palms against his chest in protest.

"I'm a charge sergeant," she said, her voice wavering. "I can drop you right where you stand."

"But you won't." Bodie took her chin in his fingers. He closed the door with his heel and pulled her in towards him with strength and purpose. One arm wrapped around her back and the other cradled her head, stroking the soft blonde curls and listening as she steadied her breathing. Bodie felt an old ache leave him as they stood there for the longest time, neither wanting to break the spell.

Bodie relaxed his hold and felt for her left hand, untangling it from the back of his shirt. Bringing it closer, he examined the space on the third finger of her left hand, where the wedding ring once chided him. "Sorry," he whispered, wiping away the tear which dripped from her chin. "I didn't know. I would've come back for you."

Her eyes filled, turning her blue irises into a lake. Bodie studied the familiar freckles and the lips that fascinated him once. Her lips never belonged to him, but to someone else.

"Mummy?" The little voice sounded half whisper, half sob and echoed in the cold hallway. Amy inhaled and whipped around, wiping her sleeve across her wet face.

"Yeah baby. I'm coming."

"It's hurting."

"I know. Come and get medicine." Amy held out her hand and Bodie watched as the child pushed his fingers into her palm, staring at the stranger over his bare shoulder. Wavy, jet black hair framed his olive face in stark contrast to his mother's blondeness and his eyes were darkest brown and almond shaped. His lips pursed in suspicion.

"Who's that man?"

"Nobody. Don't worry." Bodie's chest clenched and he set his jaw, standing by the front door like a piece of unwanted furniture. "Hop up." Amy held out her arms and lifted the child onto the draining board, steadying him with one hand while she reached for a bottle of pink liquid. Sleep tousled, his little body wore a pair of blue underpants. Chickenpox sores marred his delicate frame.

Amy's attention switched to the child and she concentrated on his needs, kissing his nose and muttering endearments. Keeping his thumb in his mouth, the child stared through the open door at Bodie, breaking the connection only for a second while a white medicine spoon replaced his thumb. Swallowing caused the child to wince, but he let Amy scoop him onto her hip and carry him away afterwards.

Bodie heard her speaking to him and the boy complaining in reply. He remained sentry-like by the front door, not knowing whether to leave or stay and say his rehearsed words. His nerve deserted him, trickling away minute by minute. Then he heard it. Just a word, a name, but he heard it and woke up from his stupor.

"Jas, lie down," came Amy's soft voice again. "Go back to sleep so the spots leave and you can get better."

As a white woman married to an Indian, Hana fought many battles and lost. Bodie's surname of Singh represented one of them. Deepak's chosen Sikh name for his first born grandson was another, his middle name the cause of a family rift. Beauden Jaspal Singh Johal. Hana consigned his heritage to the middle of his self, safely hidden apart from moments when officialdom exposed it.

"Jas, lie down," Amy pleaded. "I need to get rid of the man."

Like a wave crashing over him, Bodie felt her rejection. The child shared Izzie's unruly locks and Vik's eyes. The tiny face resembled a miniature version of the one which stared back at Bodie from the mirror as he shaved and readied himself for his empty, work driven life.

In that split second he knew he'd stay, trapped in position to the left of the front door, the streak from Amy's tears drying on his shirt. Stay, say his piece and see what happened.

Chapter 45

Hana set off for Achilles Rise after Bodie left for Northland. She took the cat cage and vacuum cleaner, planning to have a couple of hours of serious cleaning before the letting agent arrived to take an inventory. Any damage after Saturday would be the responsibility of the tenant.

It seemed familiar pulling into the driveway, a comforting reflex action. Safety enveloped her as she raised the garage door with the remote and Hana decided she should use the garage more at her new property.

A mixture of nostalgia and fear overcame her as she walked through the empty house, her happy memories tainted by the recent attack. The sun shone and the house looked bright and cheerful. Hana cleaned, wearing her yellow rubber gloves and pushed the vacuum around afterwards. With no furniture in the property, it took little time and she surveyed the mountain range through the front windows. "I never thought I'd leave," she sighed, pinpointing Culver's Cottage in the far distance through the geography of the landscape. "I suppose it's time for a change."

Hana dreaded the final walk through. She moved around the property remembering another time when it lay empty, awaiting furniture and occupants. In her mind, she saw Izzie and Bodie choosing bedrooms and laughing as they explored the garden. Vik planned where to hang the tumble dryer in the laundry and grabbed her around the waist for a celebratory kiss. His death pulled at her heartstrings, as though afraid he'd be forgotten in the excitement of her life changes. Hana stroked the kitchen bench top, her memories sharp. "We went through a lifetime of hurt, change and love together," she said to the empty house. "I don't know if I have the energy to do it all again. How do you justify your stretch marks to someone who wasn't there when they became part of your body?" She thought of exposing herself to Logan and cringed. Caroline's face misted into view, perfect, unlined and untainted by the rigors of motherhood.

Hana found walking around the empty Achilles Rise house depressing. Any expected psychological benefits failed to kick in. The blond man's attack marred her memories of laughter and happiness, bringing the aftermath of Vik's death to the fore. "No!" she pleaded with herself. "This is a happy house. Stop letting him spoil it!"

She admitted defeat whilst wiping the last of the kitchen counter tops. Her fingers shook as she dialled the agent's number. "Hi, it's Hana Johal." She breathed in through her nose but the air didn't help her nerves. "Something's come up," she lied. "I can't wait here for our walk through. Yes, I'm happy to sign off if you want to post the contract to my new address. I've cleaned. Yes. Thanks."

Longing for the isolation of Culver's Cottage and the promised gates due to shore up her security, Hana let go of her former home's hold on her emotions. The sound of the cat-flap made her jump and she let out a scream. A huffy Tiger stalked into the family room, his wide eyes searching for danger. He peered around Hana, looking for the thing which made her cry out. Hana hunkered down and called him, but he demonstrated his irritation by skirting the room and sticking close to the walls. "Come on boy," Hana pleaded. "I know you don't like change and there's been heaps lately. But we're going to our new home. You'll love it. No dogs, no neighbours, just abundant mice to catch whenever you like."

Tiger approached with reluctance, listening to the soothing tone of her voice. He softened, whipping her with his tail as he circled and wound his body around her legs. Hana reached for her handbag and produced his favourite treats, letting him eat far too many before picking him up. "Come on old man," she cooed. "Time to leave." She cradled his furry body into her chest, feeling him stiffen and start to wriggle. She moved towards the cat cage, open and ready on the carpet. Sensing her purpose, Tiger employed the claws on all four feet, but Hana held on for dear life. "You're coming home with me, so get over it!" she hissed, wrestling with his wriggling, dangerous form. She won the battle and squeezed the reluctant Tiger into a cage he hated with a passion. The twelve-year-old male sat on a sheaf of newspaper in the bottom of the cage, glowering at Hana through the bars. "Sorry, old man," Hana sighed. "Believe it or not, this is for your own good! Those children would be far too athletic for you." She examined the scratches up her arms and winced. "Like I didn't have enough damage to my hands," she complained.

Hana bumped the vacuum cleaner down the stairs one-handed, not wanting to stress her wrist further. Her heart felt torn. With two ruined hands, she cradled the cat cage and carried it to the garage, Tiger's claws swiping at her chest through the bars. "Goodbye," she said, her voice wobbling as she pressed the remote and watched the garage door close behind her. It felt like scant consolation that she still owned the property.

Pulling up to the intersection, Hana felt numbness invade her body. She rested her forearms on the steering wheel and closed her eyes at a loud mewl from the cat cage next to her. The cat turned around and around in distress and Hana wiped her eyes and steeled herself for the drive home.

Her face looked blotchy and red-rimmed eyes peered back at her from the rear view mirror. She sighed at herself as a car drew up behind her and she pressed the gas pedal to move up to the junction. A gasp caught in her throat at the sight of the olive face staring through the windscreen behind her. "Oh no, oh no. Not again!" Hana turned her whole body to look, the colour draining from her cheeks at the victorious expression on her attackers' faces. The blond man in the passenger seat waved and Hana watched his door swing open.

She fumbled for the central locking, shooting the switch with shaking fingers. Tiger chose that moment to yowl an objection at his prisoner status. Already signalling left towards River Road and home, Hana made a split decision and turned right instead. Panic made her pull out without looking. "Sorry, sorry!" she wailed as she narrowly missed a collision with a car moving along Discovery Drive. She flew down the road, driving far too fast. Every junction and roundabout presented her with decisions she couldn't think through in time. Resolution Drive loomed to her right, the speed of the highway inviting her to put her foot down. Glancing in her mirror, Hana saw the black BMW only two cars behind. When the other vehicles between them indicated left and peeled off, Hana knew the quicker road would allow them to speed up. The driver put his foot down, moving swifter than she dared travel in the built up residential area. Making another split decision, Hana went straight on at the roundabout and flew into the small estate along Farringdon Avenue, twisting and turning in the maze of streets. She drove too fast for the road conditions and prayed for the intervention of a police officer, the only thing which could put an end to the chase.

Hana turned so many times she almost lost her bearings, almost but not quite. Other cars pulled out behind and around her as rush hour traffic increased, separating her from her pursuers for moments at a time. She rounded another corner and didn't see the BMW in her rear view mirror, but sensed it still pursued her. The Honda nipped through the turns at Hana's bidding, following a route familiar to her, but a rabbit warren to anyone else. She spotted her salvation, a brick bungalow at the end of a cul-de-sac. The garage door rose to admit the owner's small Nissan Micra, which she eased into place between a tumble dryer and single chest freezer.

The empty space beside it waited for her husband's station wagon, but he wasn't due home for another hour.

Hana sped onto the drive, braking at the last possible moment as she shot into the vacant space in the double garage. Ramming on the foot brake, she killed the engine. The Honda lurched as she spun from the driver's seat, rolling forward until the bumper touched the wall. Tiger's frantic yowling communicated his angst as the homeowner screamed and Hana slammed her hand over the door release button. The roller door crunched and creaked closed, shutting out the daylight and the black BMW, which cruised around the roundabout in the distance.

"Hana?" The woman from her church recognised her and Hana groaned and bent double. The Honda clicked as the engine cooled, its nose resting against the wall. Hana vomited on Cilla's garage floor.

Cilla phoned the police while Hana cleaned herself up in the bathroom. Her knees wobbled like jelly and her clean-up operation halted at the continual need to retch over the toilet. The sobs caught in her throat as she sat on the pedestal mat, her back against the side of the bath.

"Hana." Cilla knocked on the door. "The police are on their way." She tried the door handle and stepped inside. "You poor girl. Why are those men chasing you?"

Hana's answer sounded like the paranoid ramblings of a lunatic and she silenced herself, hearing her words flow in a chaotic mess. "Please can you shut the curtains?" she begged, refusing to leave the bathroom until Cilla complied.

"I've done it." The white haired woman returned looking frightened and Hana rubbed her eyes with sore fingers. Cilla noticed the stitches in her palm and the wrist bandage. "Hana, you're scaring me. Did they do that?"

Hana nodded. "Yes. Please can you make sure you closed the blinds in the garage? I don't want them looking through windows and seeing my car. They'll find me!" She panicked. "You can't let them find me. Please don't let them find me."

Cilla disappeared and returned with news of Tiger. "Should I let him out, dear? He's howling."

"No." Hana shook her head and wiped her nose on her sleeve. "I won't catch him again." She pulled her phone from her jeans pocket, wincing at the pain in her wrist. "I'll ring Bo."

Bodie groaned in frustration. "I'll talk to someone at the station, Mum," he promised. "I just reached Whangarei. I'm so sorry, I can't come back again. Not yet. I only just got home. I'll make some calls, we'll get this sorted."

"You're late. Did something happen on your way home?" She reverted to type, the concerned mother overriding fearful victim.

"I'm fine. I stopped off for coffee," Bodie replied, relaying a partial truth. He gritted his teeth, running through a list of people he could send in his stead. Only one fitted the criteria she needed and the realisation stuck in his craw. "I'll send someone," he said, his voice wooden.

"Okay." Hana rang off and sank her head onto her knees. Cilla shuffled her feet in discomfort.

"What do you want me to do?" she asked. "Bill's gonna open the garage when he gets home. I hope he doesn't ding your car. What shall I do to stop him?"

Hana swallowed. "I'm so sorry. I didn't know what else to do."

She visited Tiger and he hissed and spat from his cage, baring his teeth in anger. "He's a ferocious little thing, isn't he?" Cilla commented, stepping back as the black and white demon launched himself at the cage bars.

Hana wiped her eyes on her sleeve. "He hates the cage. I can't let him out though, not while he's this upset. He'll run away."

They formulated a plan and Cilla wheeled a wheelbarrow in front of the garage door, to stop her tired husband opening it and driving straight in. Hana hid around the corner of the house, checking the road as Cilla treated the episode like a detective novel. "Bill's on autopilot after a long shift," she called. "Oh, I should shut up. The neighbours will think I'm talking to myself." Her face coloured at the sight of the long, sleek vehicle pulling onto the drive. "Someone's here!" she hissed, sending Hana fleeing back to the safety of the bathroom.

"It's the cops." Cilla knocked on the locked door. "And another man." She stepped back at the sound of running water and shrugged at the handsome male at her shoulder.

Logan knocked. "Hana, open the door," he insisted.

She dried her face on her shirt, mascara streaking her cheeks and making her reluctant to dirty Cilla's neat towel. She sniffed and cursed as the water aggravated her stitches. "I'm fine," she lied. "Bodie shouldn't have called you." She leaned her bum against the sink, making no move towards giving him entry.

The lock resounded with a click and Logan stepped through the door, dipping his head to clear the frame above. Hana gaped in surprise at the ease with which he invaded. His arms felt safe and Hana closed her eyes against the wave of relief which shook her body. "You shouldn't be here," she whispered and he stroked her hair.

"I'm exactly where I should be," he replied. "Come and talk to the cops."

"Did they hide their car?" Hana demanded, pulling back and staring up into his face. "What about your truck?"

Logan rubbed her shoulders in a calming, rhythmic motion. "My bike's hidden down the side of the house and the cops came in an unmarked vehicle." His crows' feet showed at the corners of his eyes as he winced. "They look like teenagers though."

"No!" Hana wailed. "They won't believe me. They'll think I imagined it."

"I believe you." Logan pressed her cheek into his chest. "Bodie believes you." He smoothed his thumb beneath her eye and wiped the dark mascara on his jeans. "Come and speak to them. Let's get this over with."

Hana ran through her story while the cops made notes. "A BMW followed me out of Achilles Rise and chased me here."

"So what?" the younger of the two replied. "How can you be sure they followed you and weren't driving in the same direction?"

Hana heard Logan give an exaggerated sigh. "I saw the driver's face," she implored. "It's the same man who dinged the back of my car and broke into my home. The passenger did this." She lifted both hands to show the wrist bandage and stitches. "You're supposed to have caught them by now."

Both cops looked sceptical but heard her out, scribbling in their pocketbooks as she explained the reason for her sudden, uninvited entrance into poor Cilla's garage. "They'll kill me next time," she asserted, her eyes widening in fear.

Logan reached for her shaking right hand, stroking the inside of her wrist to avoid the stitches. She clung to the lifeline he offered as the cops gave platitudes and promises of increased vigilance.

After the cops left, Logan excused himself. "I need to call Bodie back," he said, releasing Hana's hand. "I promised." He walked outside into the darkening garden, accepting the coffee Cilla pushed into his hand. Bodie answered the call straight away. "They don't believe her, mate. They think she imagined it. They've logged it, but aren't taking her seriously. You need to go back to that detective, the one who visited the house after the attack. Odering." He said the name through gritted teeth.

"Okay. I'll do it now." Bodie gritted his teeth, sounding livid. He outranked both of the detectives who sat in Cilla's lounge for an hour, drinking her coffee and dispelling Hana's fears with empty clichés. "Put me onto Aunty Cilla," he demanded. "She knows me. I'll ask her to swap cars with Mum for the weekend until we can sort something else out."

"This has gone on for too long," Logan said, lowering his voice as Hana wandered into the garden and heaved in gulps of night air. "I think someone's using her as bait."

Bodie denied the claim with an immediacy that only heightened Logan's suspicions. Cilla agreed to the swap as Bill arrived home and assured them they wouldn't need the tiny car until Monday. Logan loaded Hana's possessions into the Micra and put the spitting cat on the back seat next to the vacuum. Tiger spat at him and took a swipe at his fingers through the bars. "Don't start, buster," Logan threatened from between gritted teeth. He pulled his hand back in time. "You've no idea what problems cutting me will cause."

Hana handed the Honda keys over to her friend with great reluctance and followed Logan to the Gordonton house. He rode his bike ahead of her at a steady pace.

Logan locked his bike in the garage, picked up some clothes and drove Hana home to Culver's Cottage. He struggled with the driver's seat, his legs so long he had to push the seat right back. "The truck's not a good idea," he said. "If they've watched you, they'll know the registration number. I don't want them to follow you to Culver's Cottage otherwise it's game over." He pulled a black baseball cap down over his face and Hana covered her distinctive red hair with a hooded fleece Cilla lent her. Darkness shrouded her house and Logan made her lock herself in the car. "Stay here," he insisted. "I'll check the property. Any trouble, just dial the cops and drive." He waited until she'd clambered across into the driver's seat.

His knock on the window made her start and her wide, green eyes glinted in the moonlight. She unlocked the door and Logan squatted down next to her. "It looks undisturbed," he said, his lips curving upwards into a smile. "Let's get you inside."

"I wish the gates were already installed." Hana rubbed her hand over her eyes, frustrated when she caught the stitches in her palm for the millionth time. "Ow-er!" she complained, flashing her beautiful redheaded temper.

Logan pursed his lips in response. "You're gorgeous when you're mad," he said, his admiration lightening the mood.

Hana raised an eyebrow. "You wouldn't say that if you had to live with me," she said, her sentence tailing off as awkwardness overcame her.

"Would too." Logan pulled her from the car and kissed the top of her head. "You're gorgeous. Mad or not mad. I like both."

"Idiot!" Hana slapped his chest and then swore, stamping her foot as the stitches smarted. "Take them out!" She waved her hand in his face. "Please, take them out for me."

"No." Logan caught her by the wrist and turned her hand over. He pulled her into the house so he could look under the hall light. "Not tonight."

"But they hurt and itch." Hana tried to drag her hand back and he raised an eyebrow and looked closer.

"Did you already have a go at these?" The suspicion in his tone made her blush.

"No."

"Liar!" Logan smirked. "What did you use? Garden shears."

"Kitchen scissors." Hana pouted. "I felt desperate."

Logan shook his head. "Tomorrow. I'll look at them tomorrow but I want decent scissors, wahine."

Tiger yowled from the car and Hana steeled herself to brave his fury. Logan used the handle to carry the cage in and Hana opened the grate. The angry cat sprang through the gap in a single fluid leap. He shot her a filthy look and ran towards the back of the house, his fur standing on end in warning. Hana found him sitting in the middle of her bed with a cross look on his face, conflict licking his paws until they were soaked and shiny. She put down bowls of kibbles and water and set out the litter tray near the front door. "I should keep him indoors for a while," she said to Logan as he watched her activity. "What if he tries to find his way back to Hamilton?"

"No idea, sorry," Logan replied, nosing around in the fridge. The door sounded its warning beep when he kept it open too long. "Sorry." Logan appeared with a packet of chocolate biscuits. "I guess this is dinner." He pushed the fridge door closed with his heel, leaning across to fill the kettle.

Hana rested her spine against the pantry door, looking around the newly painted kitchen. "What a bloody mess," she sighed, her eyes blank as she contemplated her tumultuous life.

"I thought it looked ok," Logan replied, looking in surprise at the clean walls and shiny floor.

"My life!" Hana exploded. "My stupid, messy life!"

Logan set the kettle to boil, wiped his hands on his trousers and walked across to Hana, wrapping his arms around her. She felt rigid, unyielding and shock iced her bones. "You're freezing," he breathed into her neck, rubbing her arms to warm her. "I'll make a hot drink and you need to eat something. Fancy a biscuit?"

Hana shook her head. "I can't. There's a hard lump in my chest that won't go away."

"It's okay." He rocked her with a gentle motion and she closed her eyes and enjoyed the comfort and security his arms offered. When he broke the contact, Hana felt the lack of it.

Logan made her a hot tea, dunking the tea bag into the mug and adding milk before it stewed. Hana winced, but kept her British criticism of his tea making skills to herself. "How about a hot bath?" he offered, putting the mug down in front of her. "It might help."

Hana shrugged. "I can't think straight."

He disappeared into the bathroom and Hana picked at a blob of paint on the table. She heard the sound of running water and the pipes set up their awful screechy song. "You stupid, stupid woman!" she berated herself, squeezing her fists into her eyes. "Why did you wish for excitement and love? You know it all comes at a cost!"

After ten minutes, Logan reappeared with her dressing gown and a clean towel. "Come on, a nice bath will help you relax. I'll open a bottle of wine and bring you some." He jerked his head towards the table. "You didn't touch your tea."

Hana allowed herself a smile as she saw the candles around the side of the old bath. A soft light flickered in the room, changing the atmosphere and obscuring the peeled wallpaper and stains on the ceiling. Foam covered the surface of the water and the floral scent calmed her. She dipped her hand in the bubbles and sniffed them. Orchid and lily went up her nose and she coughed. Logan cleared his throat. "I'll bring you wine and then leave you to enjoy it," he said, turning away.

Hana spoke to his retreating back. "I'm sick of feeling like this. When will it end? When they kill me?"

Logan chewed on his bottom lip, his fingers holding the door handle. "I don't know, Hana. Do you want me to help?"

"How?" Her eyes widened.

Logan licked his lips and took a step forward. "I know people." A dark shadow crossed his face. "They can help but it's best I don't involve you."

Hana's eyes narrowed to slits. "Illegal people?" Her question sent darts of pain into Logan's heart and his nod looked slowed down in time.

"Yeah. People who operate outside the law. But if you want it sorted that's how."

She thought for a moment, frightened by how tempting his offer seemed. She inhaled. "Could people die?"

He looked at the floor and then back at her face. His nonchalant shrug seemed forced. "It's not our problem, Hana."

She sighed. "But it is, Logan. Who are these people? Hitmen?" She laughed and he smiled.

"No. Just business men who know things."

Hana worried at her bottom lip. "Should I be scared of you?"

"No." He snorted. "No, I promise." He smiled and Hana's fears evaporated like the bubbles on her hand. "I just know people who know people who know people." He stepped into her personal space and his hands held her waist in a gentle caress. "It doesn't matter, Hana. We'll let the cops sort it out."

"Okay." She cocked her head and stared into his mesmerising eyes. "You're not what you seem, are you, Logan Du Rose?" Bodie's words came back as a warning and Hana pushed them away, no longer heeding the advice of others who weren't there in the dark, lonely hours of the night. She ran her hands up Logan's strong forearms and ignored the jab from her stitches. "I rather like your air of mystery." Her lips quirked upwards in amusement and Logan stirred beneath her hands.

"Twenty-six years," he whispered, lowering his head to kiss her neck. "That's how long I've wanted to be this close to you." His lips against her flesh sent tingles down Hana's spine and she exhaled a ragged breath. He kissed her jaw, cheek and then coasted his lips across hers. "I love you, Hana McIntyre," he said, his voice hoarse.

"How can you love me?" she asked. "You don't know me."

"Yeah, I do." Logan's eyes crinkled at the edges. "You're everything I dreamed you would be."

Hana shook her head, the attraction between them hiking. "Twelve weeks you've known me. It's not much to base a relationship on."

"It's more than enough," Logan breathed into her ear. "Let me show you how much you can trust me."

Hana let the idea sink into her brain. He offered more than companionship. Adoration laced every sentence he uttered to her and loneliness drove her into his arms.

"There are things you don't know," she whispered, lifting her hand to stroke his rough cheek. "I don't know if I can tell you."

"I. Don't. Care." He sounded certain and Hana inhaled, desperate to trust him.

"How do you know that? You don't know what it is."

Logan's lips increased their pressure, driving her negative words away. Hana put her palms against his chest. "You're not listening to me, are you?"

"Nope." His lips quirked upwards and she laughed. "I've done nothing to betray you, Hana. And I won't. I promise." He bent his head and kissed her face before moving to the soft, sensitive skin of her neck. A series of hypnotic prickles tingled through her nerve endings and she felt her stomach go into free fall.

Logan Du Rose offered a yawning chasm of temptation. She'd been there before and it didn't end well. Logan felt the glimmer of hesitation morph into fear and stopped himself exerting his selfish impulses. To his own surprise, he heard himself utter two words he promised he'd never speak again. "Marry me."

Chapter 46

Hana's face registered first shock, then surprise followed by realisation. "I've got stretch marks," she said and then clapped her hand over her mouth in horror. "Forget I said that." Her cheeks blushed to the roots of her hair.

Logan threw his head back and laughed. Hana stared up at him, cocking her head to one side like a little bird, studying more than the external features but the very heartbeat of him. The idea settled on her like a comfortable mantle, ridiculous but right. Her hand strayed to his cheek and she felt the stubble pushing through his skin. Staring deep into his captivating grey eyes, Hana ran her finger down the familiar scar under his eye, feeling him tremble at her touch. "Hana I don't care," he whispered. "I've wanted you since the first day I met you. I'm in it for the long haul, babe. So, marry me."

Hana sighed. Unwrapping Logan Du Rose was like peeling an onion layer by layer, with the chance of tears the further in she got. There seemed too much to resolve, so many conversations which threatened to upend their fragile equilibrium. "I don't know what to say." Hana smiled and Logan's brow knitted.

"Then say nothing." He licked his lips and then dropped to one knee in front of her. "Apart from yes."

Hana laughed, the sound hollow. "I'm scared," she whispered and his hands on her hips invoked safety. She picked her words with care. "I want to," she admitted. "But it sounds ridiculous and my kids will have a fit."

Logan stayed on one knee, his attention fixed on her. "Then don't tell them," he said, his tone serious. "Do it on your terms."

Hana bit her lower lip, the thought taking shape. "I couldn't." Her brow knitted, but she didn't mean it. "Could I?"

Logan exhaled in a rush, his grey eyes glittering up at her. "What do you want? Nobody else, just you. And Hana, my leg's going dead."

"Sorry, sorry." She took a step back, causing Logan to grab hold of her sweatshirt. She put her hands over her face. "What about Caroline?"

Logan sighed and looked at the floor. "You let me get down on the floor and then ask me that?" Sadness flickered in his eyes. "She doesn't feature. Hana, I'm getting older by the second. Yes or no?"

"This is ridiculous." Hana ran her fingers over his, experiencing an electrical tingle. "But I want to."

A slow smile spread across Logan's lips and he hauled himself to a standing position. "Really?"

"Don't make me doubt!" Hana slapped his chest and he caught her fingers and kissed them. "Just make it happen, Du Rose," she said. "Before I change my mind."

Logan swallowed. "It's as good as done." He ran a nervous hand through his dark hair, leaving it spiked at the front. "Wow. Just wow." He pulled Hana into his body, aligning her against him for the first time of many.

When he stepped back and looked at her, it was as though he asked again with his soul. A fragile, silken thread of connection strengthened and reinforced and something old, ethereal and outside their understanding became as solid as an iron bar. Hana's voice wavered. "You wouldn't let me say no anyway, would you?"

Logan's gaze softened. "I've loved you since I was fourteen, Hana," he whispered. "It can't be a surprise that I don't want to spend another moment of my life away from you. I searched for you, Hana. I scoured London in case you were there. I want to spend my life with you. I always did."

Hana nodded and Logan's eyes widened at the same time as his brow knitted in confusion. "Do you think you can love me?" He bit his lip.

"Yes, I do," Hana replied. To her surprise, she felt no instant sense of misgiving or the usual second-guessing of her own split decisions. Any notion of hasty backtracking seemed absent. She just felt peace and relief at the prospect of not managing on her own. Someone loved her and she hugged the knowledge to herself, waiting for the warmth to sink in. The newness of it made her want to tuck it into her chest and hide it from the world, unwilling to let its habitual cynicism destroy a beautiful thing.

"Your bath's getting cold." Logan released her with reluctance and showed great self-control leaving the room so she could undress. His body zinged with unfathomable electricity as though the fulfilment of a lifetime goal left him lost and without direction. He busied himself in the kitchen, boiling a kettle he wouldn't use and making a ham sandwich he couldn't eat. The shadow of Caroline Marsh sank to the depths of a lonely history, but his subconscious recognised the latent threat.

Hana emerged from the bathroom refreshed and less daunted, clothed in pyjamas covered with monkeys. Comfortable and warm, they reminded her of Izzie and offered safety against her precarious life. They covered her in more than fleecy fabric and ferocious looking mammals.

Hana sat at the kitchen table and studied Logan. His fingers shook as he continued with a stack of marking he'd shoved into his overnight bag. He glanced up at her, his eyes filled with fear and worry. His tight smile communicated his angst before a blank expression shut Hana out. They sat in silence as Logan scribbled away on the exercise books. He changed ticks to crosses and back again before giving up and closing the ink blotted pages with a snap.

"Do you regret asking?" Hana said, her voice wooden. "You're scaring me."

Logan exhaled and sat back in his chair, running a hand across his face. "I don't regret it." He looked up and forced a smile onto his lips. "I love stretch marks."

Hana gasped and widened her eyes, not understanding his humour. Her washed hair lay in shining, red tresses, tumbling over her shoulders like a curtain. Logan reached across the table for her hand. "I'm kidding, Hana. I joke when I'm nervous."

"So you don't like them?" Hana chewed her lower lip, vulnerability in the set of her shoulders.

Logan sighed and pushed his chair back, patting his thighs. "Come here. I need to hold you."

Hana stood, padding around the table, intrigued by his use of the word need, instead of want. She stopped in front of him. "I do have stretch marks," she repeated. Her eyes bored into his soul.

"I told you I don't care and I don't. I'm not that shallow." Logan pulled her into his lap and wrapped his arms around her. He pressed his face into her damp hair and sighed. "I'm no oil painting when I get my kit off."

Relationships in later life carried so much baggage and Hana felt the presence of it in the room, pressuring them to fail, to give up. "This might be too hard," she whispered into his shoulder and he pulled her closer.

"You're my soul mate, Hana." He fumbled the words and rested his chin against her neck. "I've known that forever. I won't give you up without a fight. If your acceptance is a knee-jerk reaction, then so be it. I'm taking it."

Hana snuffled into his shirt. "It kinda was."

"Too late. It's a done deal."

"It doesn't mean I don't want to." Hana kissed the underside of Logan's jaw. "I actually do. Hana Du Rose has a ring to it."

Logan's inhale sounded painful and Hana felt him swallow. "But?"

She shifted on his knee and winced. "I want to ask some questions but I need the truth."

"Okay." Logan leaned back in the chair, his arms around her waist but his emotions disconnected. "Ask away."

Hana thought for a moment and licked her lips. "Okay, why do you want to marry me?"

"Wow." Logan's eyes shuttered. "That's easy. I already told you the answer to that. I love you and always have. It makes perfect sense to me."

Hana watched Logan's face with intensity, her expression unreadable. She swallowed. "You were honest about that, even if your mother forced the moment. If all this happened without Caroline's arrival, I wouldn't feel so uneasy."

"Yeah. Caroline." Logan's fingers fluttered against her waist. "Somehow she always makes it about her."

"So what's the solution?" Hana's expression held doubt. "I can't compete with someone like her. She's gorgeous, confident and knows what she wants. I'm the complete opposite."

Logan's arms snaked around her waist and he gripped her harder. "I didn't marry Caroline, Hana." He gritted his teeth. "I'm not interested in revisiting that episode in my life or aligning myself with someone like her. It's you I want. I need you to trust me."

Hana ran her fingers over his hands, feeling the knotty knuckles relax a fraction. Grazes still marred his left hand, still fresh. "When do you imagine us getting married?" Images of Bodie's expression of betrayal and Izzie's disappointment consumed her inner vision.

Logan's face creased in concentration. "Soon." He looked up at her, his grey eyes shrouded beneath long dark lashes. "I want you to know I'm sincere. Invite whoever you like but I want to do this as soon as possible."

Hana nodded. Her jaw worked beneath her delicate skin. "My kids will have a fit. I can't face telling them beforehand." She winced. "I know you don't want to talk about Caroline, but I need to. She thinks she has a claim on you. She's made it clear I'm not a worthy opponent. I can't marry you and then watch my life crumble because your ex wins you back."

Logan shook his head from side to side, the motion slow and filled with exhaustion. "Won't happen, Hana. I promise you that much. Any claim she feels is in her head and I told her that when she turned up." He let go of her waist and rubbed his eyes. "I don't know why I allowed her back into my life. I couldn't find you and something broke inside me. Settling for second best seemed a fair choice." He snorted. "Then she left me standing at the altar like a fool."

His eyes misted as memories filled his head. They played a challenge game as children, his brothers and cousins. They got together in the den they made against the explicit order of their respective parents. It always led to trouble. The older kids took the power of the spinning bottle much too seriously and Logan as the youngest, always ended up with a hideous forfeit. It was as though they detested him, masking it in play but exorcising their hatred in subtle ways. He failed every challenge his cousins set, just as they intended. He closed his eyes against a particular memory buried deep within his subconscious. The momentary exhilaration reminded him how he outwitted the old bull who roamed the upper reaches of the mountain. Caroline's blue hair ribbon fluttered in his fingers and he limped from his hasty dive across the wire fence. His male cousins eyed each other with disappointment. "Should've died," Kane Du Rose muttered. He elbowed Logan's older brother. "You said it would work, Barry. The meamea should be dead."

Caroline's pale features flashed into his vision and he licked his lips at the memory. "Punish him then," she said, her smile victorious. "Stab him with this."

Logan backed away at the sight of the rusty machete she pulled from behind her back. In real time, he put a shaking hand to his right side and shivered. "She's nothing to me," he spat, his tone ugly. "She conned me one time too many."

"You say that, but I saw you both," Hana contested. "She won't give up." She felt the other woman's hold on him like tendrils clawing at his flesh. "I won't be second best again, Logan." She hardened her tone. "I saw you leave in Pete's car together. She put her hands all over you. I saw the text you sent her. I need to know if you slept with her that night or since. Be honest or we have no future."

Logan took a shuddering breath and leaned back in his chair. Hatred washed over him like nausea. "No, I didn't sleep with her and I won't. She and I are done." He cocked his head and studied Hana's face. "Tell me about this text. I never texted her."

Hana raised an index finger. "I want to know about that night first. You owe me that. I felt a fool, waving to you in the car park and watching you drive away with her. I thought we'd started something special and it cut me to the core."

Logan nodded, tiredness in his eyes. "It's as I told you before. I stormed off and she followed me to the car. What you missed was the heated conversation we'd had five minutes before and Angus telling me to take it outside. I didn't want another scene, so I took her somewhere neutral." Logan ran his fingers through his hair, making it stick up at the front. Hana saw a slight tremor in his hands as they rested as fists on the table. "We went to an English pub nearby and she talked about the wedding and my parents. She apologised, said I should take her back and then tried to kiss me. I pushed her away." Logan ran the back of his hand across his lips and Hana's brows narrowed, recognising her own action after the blond man's lips touched hers. She saw revulsion in Logan's eyes and rested her palms on his shoulders. He sighed. "I dumped cash on the table for a taxi and walked away."

"Just like that?" Hana's eyes narrowed in suspicion. "You left her there?"

Logan nodded and wrinkled his nose. "You think it was mean?"

Hana shook her head and shrugged. "I don't know. Probably safer. I don't think she can take no for an answer."

"She can't." Logan's sigh sounded ragged, as though pulled from his chest by a fishhook and line. He pushed his fingers around Hana's waist and buried them beneath her pyjama shirt. She flinched at his direct contact with her skin, a flush beginning on her chest and creeping up to her neck.

"What will you do?" Hana asked. "About Caroline."

"Nothing." Logan's jaw drew a hard line beneath his cheek. His eyes softened. "I'll marry you like I always wanted. She did me a massive favour leaving me at the altar. I can't imagine finding you and being attached to someone else."

Logan's fingers fluttered against Hana's hips. "I thought you'd got someone else." Guilt infused his expression and mingled with pain. "I didn't know you'd seen Caroline get in the car. But I knew she'd said or done something because of how you behaved towards me afterwards."

"Sorry." Hana lifted the fingers of her right hand and stroked Logan's cheek. "I felt humiliated."

Logan nodded. "I drove up here on the bike needing to speak to you." He licked his lips and spots of colour appeared on his cheekbones. "This will make you laugh." He cleared his throat. "I saw you and Bodie in the upstairs window and thought you'd found another guy."

Hana's eyes widened. "What? No!"

"I only saw silhouettes." Logan closed his eyes and laid his head back against the chair. "I felt an idiot."

Hana's laugh embarrassed him and he pursed his lips. "Yeah, yeah. Have your fun." His eyelashes fluttered and his lips quirked upwards. "I drove around for a while and found a lake just outside Huntly. I sat up there and met this cool guy who knew you."

"What's his name?" Hana cocked her head with curiosity. "And why would he be at the lake in the dark?"

Logan shifted his bum on the chair, unseating Hana so she pitched into his chest. Logan capitalised on the happy accident and tucked her head beneath his chin. "Youth group," he said with a contented sigh. His fingers traced a soporific pattern on her back. "His name's Allen and we got talking. The kids ran around the lake with torches and we chatted. He said his youth leaders could manage without him."

"I know Allen. He pastors my church. Why did you start talking?" Hana asked. "I can't see you gravitating to a group of boisterous kids."

Logan shrugged and Hana's head bounced on his chest at the movement. "He admired my bike." He kissed the side of her face. "It's a great bike."

"I didn't know." Hana yawned.

"It's an awesome bike!" Logan sounded offended and Hana corrected his wrong assumption.

"I meant that I didn't know Allen liked bikes."

"Oh. Well, he does." Logan sighed against the back of her head. "I gave him a ride to the church and went back to his place. We shared a few drinks and Pete fetched me."

"You got drunk with my pastor!" Hana sat up, her movement jerky. "I bet his wife wasn't thrilled."

"Not much." Logan wrinkled his nose. "I don't get drunk but we made enough of a dent in the whiskey to put me over the limit."

"What did he say about me?" Hana kissed his cheek and ran her lips along his jaw to his ear lobe.

"Nothing incriminating." Logan groaned and released a sigh. His legs shook beneath her. "He likes you. Says you're a sweet woman and the car I described sounded like the one he sold your son."

"Ah. So you didn't suffer for days thinking I got myself another toy boy," Hana whispered. "Unlike me, who believed you picked Caroline."

"I would never pick her over you." Logan met her lips with a kiss and his fingers on the back of Hana's neck pulled her closer. "I love you," he breathed. "Why don't you believe me?"

She shrugged and put distance between them. A few centimetres felt endless and the light flickered in Logan's eyes. "I don't deserve it." She sounded so sure, the belief pulled from somewhere deep in her soul. Logan opened his mouth to contest the claim but Hana redirected the conversation away from her. "I'm sorry Caroline hurt you, Logan."

He nodded. "Yeah. I think she knew I saw her as Plan B. It's an awful way to treat someone."

"So why is she trying so hard to get you back?" Hana asked. "She looks confident."

Logan rubbed his eyes with the back of his hand. "It's about my name. She wants to be a Du Rose."

"Na!" Hana dismissed the notion with a wave of her hand. "That's daft."

"Maybe. But she still conned my father into believing I left her with wedding debts. He sold a massive tract of my land to pay for it."

"The land by your uncle's place?" Hana narrowed her eyes and stared at Logan. "That's why you got upset on the way back from our trek?" Logan nodded and Hana sighed. "And Alfred sold it to pay Caroline?"

Logan shook his head. "Not quite. Hana I want you to understand that I asked her to marry me out of desperation. I never pretended I loved her and don't think she ever intended to walk down the aisle with me. She needed to take away my mana in front of the whānau. What I don't understand is why."

"Revenge?" Hana asked and Logan shook his head.

"For what? She always knew the score."

"Promise me you're not a cheat?" Hana stared hard at Logan, watching him and praying for discernment.

"Babe, that's the easiest promise I'll ever make," he said, his body language broken and defeated.

Hana stroked his face and kissed his forehead. "Caroline didn't take your mana," she whispered. "If Angus Blair can respect you like he does, then you still have it. As for your family, they didn't seem real bothered about your wedding. They only care about you. If I promise not to jilt you or cause you to lose your land, can we please not mention Caroline Marsh ever again?"

Logan sighed with relief and nodded against her arm. He put his fingers under Hana's chin to meet her gaze. "I'm not going anywhere, Hana. I love you and this is all I ever wanted. Without you, I'm nothing." His long lashes brushed against his cheeks and Hana felt her heart give a victorious leap. It defeated her head and silenced all the murmurings why a quickie marriage seemed a terrible idea. She leaned down and kissed Logan's sensuous lips, hurling herself into the unknown and hoping she didn't regret it.

Logan held her for a long time, cradling her head against his collarbone. When her breathing changed, he nudged her awake. "Hana?" His voice sounded soft. "When you cried on the tube train in your yellow dress, I wanted to take you away and make you feel better." He looked up into her sleep filled eyes. "I never expected you would make me feel better first."

Hana smiled and kissed him. "I remember your eyes," she whispered, their lips touching. "Grey and fathomless." Her thumb stroked the scar above his cheekbone and saw relief cross his face. "I blocked out much of that unhappy period in my life." Her brow creased and Logan reached up and smoothed away the lines.

"It's okay," he replied. "This is our time. Let's leave the past where it is."

"Deal," Hana agreed. "But that includes the text I thought you sent Caroline. Can we leave that there too?"

"But I didn't send it. What did it say?"

Hana winced. "I read it on her phone and deleted it. I'm not proud of myself."

Logan chewed his bottom lip and grinned. "So, now you're admitting you aren't perfect?" Hana nodded and he laughed. "Thank goodness for that," he said.

They parted for the night in the cold hallway, embracing with an air of nervous excitement. "Night, Loge," Hana said, yawning. Logan smiled and released her slender body.

"Night, babe."

Hana pushed the bedroom door closed against him and he stared at the rimu knots, his mind elsewhere. He told Hana the absolute truth about his drink with Caroline, but withheld one vital piece of information. "Stay out of my life!" he'd hissed at the blond woman, hurling forty dollars cash onto the table for her taxi fare as though paying a prostitute. Turning away to shove his wallet into his pocket, he heard her raise her voice enough to draw attention from the other patrons.

"It's not over!" she shouted. "This will never be over for you. There are things you don't know Logan." When he ignored her and kept walking, she raised her voice louder. "I'll tell her!" she threatened. Logan heard her chair scrape across the floor. "She won't want you when she knows the truth!"

Logan had slammed the outer door of the pub behind him and hoped the thick cloud of doom she conjured up didn't follow him out. But it did, almost wrecking everything.

Hana woke with a groan to another windy day punctuated by torrential rain. She met Logan in the kitchen and scarfed toast straight from the toaster. "Hello fiancé." He kissed her sleep-softened cheek and Hana cringed with embarrassment. "That's not fair! You've already showered and smell so good." She put a hand in front of her mouth. "Don't kiss me until I've cleaned my teeth."

Logan laughed and buried his face in her neck. "Idiot," he breathed, enjoying the scent of her hair. "I'm taking you ring shopping today."

"Really?" Hana glanced down at her bare finger and frowned. "We don't have to."

"Yeah, we do." Logan arched his back and watched the change in her expression. "Unless you changed your mind in the night."

Hana shook her head and the small smile that creased her face looked coy. "No, I haven't."

"I checked the website for the registry office." Logan's eyes narrowed, watching Hana for any adverse reaction.

She smiled. "My father used to call it the Registrar of Hatches, Matches and Dispatches." She giggled, the first time she'd mentioned Robert McIntyre with any happy connotation.

Logan snuffed out a laugh. "I used your computer; I hope that's okay. I printed off a Notice of Intended Marriage and I need your help to fill it in.

"Oh." Hana's eager smile disappeared. "Do you need Vik's death certificate?"

"Nope." Logan reached for her and wrapped her in a strong embrace, smirking at the monkeys on her shirt. "Just the date."

"I can tell you that," Hana breathed, the number engraved on her psyche.

"The office is open from nine until four, Monday to Friday," Logan said. "So we either need to find a celebrant or take time off work." His shoulders hunched in disappointment.

"What did you do before?" Hana asked, looking up at him.

Logan closed his eyes. "It doesn't matter. She did it all and had months to plan it. I want to marry you this week."

Hana stroked his bicep and looked up in sympathy. "We'll work it out, Logan. Don't worry."

He smiled down at her. "Also, one of us needs to go into the office three days before the ceremony to sign a statutory declaration and show birth certificates and the other documents they want."

"It sounds complicated, doesn't it?" Hana's sigh emptied her lungs of air.

"No, I'll deal with it on Monday. Give me your documents and I'll take them to the office." Logan gritted his jaw in determination. "Shall I just grab the next available date or ring you first? And what about family and guests?"

Hana's eyes widened in fear. "They'll try to talk me out of it. Would it be terrible to just ask forgiveness instead of permission?" She wrinkled her nose and Logan snorted.

"Geez, woman! You keep surprising me. Is that what you want?"

Hana nodded, convincing herself with every bounce of her head. "Yeah. I do. I don't know how I'll tell them afterwards but I'll find a way." She chewed at her thumbnail and worry knitted her brow.

Logan smoothed the lines from her forehead and smiled. "I'll help you," he promised, still waiting for her to back out and devastate him.

"I'm not changing my mind." Hana kissed him. "You're stuck with me."

Logan inhaled and grinned, his perfect white teeth grazing his lower lip. "I'll believe that when I've put the ring on your finger and kissed the bride. Maybe not even then."

Hana's eyes communicated the gravity of her promise. "I'm not Caroline, Logan. I won't back out."

When the rain eased, Logan insisted they walk up the mountain to the boundary of Hana's property. She grumbled up the hill, slipping and sliding behind him. "Why are we here? I thought you wanted to go shopping."

"I do." Logan turned and offered his hand, biceps flexing as he took Hana's weight. "But it's pointless going out for the day and leaving the house vulnerable. And I don't want to leave you alone at the house and walk up here either."

They found a place to climb over the fence into the thick bush but stuck close to the fence line. Logan examined the ridge above with keen, bushman's eyes. "The Te Araroa walking track is up there," he said, pointing. "But the bush looks impenetrable above the property. Anyone coming this way will need hiking boots and a darn good compass. The supplejack alone will slow them down." His brow knitted. "Besides, who'd approach from this direction? You'd see them from the house."

"Not if I'm not here." Hana slipped sideways and used her grip on Logan's jacket to right herself. She stamped her foot with impatience. "Please can we go back? It's starting to rain." She held her palms out to catch the smattering of drops and unbalanced herself.

"Okay, okay," Logan replied, grinning at her discomfort. "But I promised your son I'd check it out. Let me just ring him."

"Don't mention the-you-know-what," she warned. "I'm amazed he called you last night. You're the last person he'd want to involve."

"Yep." Logan winked at her and Hana clung to his arm as they descended the steep slope. She listened to Logan giving one-word answers to Bodie. She kept silent, concentrating on her footing. They skirted the fence line with care but a branch of the subtle bush lawyer seized Hana's sleeve and tore at it, snagging her hand and wrist as she struggled to free herself. "Steady, steady," Logan soothed, holding her fingers and extracting her from the plant's nasty grasp. "You can't do it that way, you have to relax and tear it off bit by bit."

As he freed Hana, another branch leaned in for the kill, drooping under the rainwater and digging its thorns into the back of his hand. Logan hissed in pain and rolled his eyes.

"Nice place you've got!" he complained later, as he ran the cuts under hot water to remove any dirt. "Even the wildlife sticks up for you. You should be fine out here."

Hana smiled to herself. "We," she replied.

"Pardon?" Logan patted his hands with a tissue and turned to face her, leaning backwards against the counter to hide the relentless blood soaking into the soft cloth. "What do you mean?"

"Nothing," she answered, smirking as she chewed over her thoughts. "You said I would be fine out here. But you'll be here too."

"True." Logan kissed her and excused himself to deal with the familiar throbbing headache and unforgiving cuts.

Hana touched up gaps in the paint as she waited for Logan. He emerged in the kitchen half an hour later, looking tired. Sticking plasters littered the back of his hand, blood showing through the fabric. "When are we going out?" Hana asked, washing her brush in the sink.

"Now, if you want," he said. He looked at his watch and whistled. "Wow. Where's the day gone?"

Hana glared at her hand and produced the kitchen scissors. She held them out to Logan. "You promised. They're itching and I want them out. I made a mess trying to do it with my left hand."

"I noticed." He groaned and turned her hand over, inspecting the wound. "Fine," he grumbled. "But I want different scissors."

Hana fetched tiny manicure scissors and closed her eyes as Logan wielded them with difficulty. "My fingers don't fit in the stupid holes," he muttered, slipping the sharp edge between the first stitch and her palm. Hana jumped at the sound of the snip and the dark stitch hung loose. Logan cut all seven and stood back as Hana cringed. "You need to pull the bits out," he said, nudging her shoulder. "Then wipe the wound with an antiseptic cloth. How's your wrist?"

"Okay," Hana lied, using it despite the pain. "It's a sprain."

"Hmmmn." Logan raised his eyebrow like he didn't believe her. "Keep that strap on it," he advised.

Hana cleaned up and readied herself to go out. Reaching the front door, she held back and panicked. "What if the men are searching for me?" Her eyes widened and she dug her heels into the floorboards. "There might be more of them looking everywhere."

Logan shook his head. "They think you moved to the Farringdon area," he said. "Why would they look up here?"

"The house sale documents," Hana replied. "They can see them online."

"Na. It's not that easy. They'd need to get a licenced real estate agent to search for them and who would do that? Monday will be a problem because they know you work at the school. They'll be watching the entrances and exits."

Hana sighed and her heart rate spiked. "We can go out another day," she said, swallowing gulps of air.

"Come on." Logan took her arm and led her through the front door. "We'll drive to Sylvia Park in Auckland, we're using Cilla's car and I'll block the driveway."

"How?" Hana wrung her hands and stared at him. "What with?"

"Don't worry." He kissed her and tapped her on the bottom. "Get in the car while I set the burglar alarm."

Logan pulled fallen tree branches across the driveway half way up. Hana watched his considerable strength, neck and arm muscles bulging as he pulled the punga across the road. He eased a white handkerchief from the pocket of his leather jacket and wiped his fingers, staring around him. When he got back into the car, he gave Hana a confident smile. "It looks solid, but it's not. I didn't mess around too much with it or it'll fall apart."

Hana nodded. "Thank you. I can't wait for the gates to arrive."

Logan reached out for her hand and held it, smoothing her cold fingers with his. He made the hour's drive to Auckland driving one-handed for most of the way. They scored a good parking space and Hana relaxed enough to hold his hand around the vast shopping mall. She browsed the various shops, buying small decorations for the house and derailing Logan's plans. "Enough," he told her, pushing her towards a jewellery shop they'd passed twice. "I'm buying you an engagement ring."

Hana stopped and spun away from him, her face ashen. Logan's lips parted in dismay. She put her hands behind her back and a standoff ensued. "I don't want an engagement ring, Logan."

"Oh, Hana." He covered his eyes with one hand and she gasped in horror.

"No! Logan, listen. I will marry you, but an engagement ring is a terrible idea. I can't wear it before the ceremony because everyone will see it. So let's just get wedding rings. Yeah?" She pushed her face under his arm and exposed his frightened expression. "Don't be silly. I want you to be my husband still."

"I wanted you to have a ring." He sounded sulky and disappointed and Hana wrapped her arms around his waist.

"But you understand why it won't work?" she asked and he nodded.

"Yeah. But you could wear it in the evenings," he argued and Hana shook her head.

"Nothing about what we're doing is traditional," she said. "I just want a plain wedding band, please. I'll be satisfied with that."

Logan kissed her forehead and compared her to the money grabbing Caroline. She'd kept all the wedding paraphernalia and engineered his loss of the land in addition. They stood in the centre of the mall, people filing past them on every side. Logan buried Hana's face in his chest, their heartbeats aligning despite the busy foot traffic around them. "I love you so much," he whispered, kissing her lips and closing his eyes against the fear of losing her before he reached the finish post. "You keep surprising me."

Hana stood on tiptoes and kissed the underside of his rough chin. "Yeah, well I'm the lucky one," she said with a smile. "So let's go buy some wedding rings." She clasped his hand and led him towards the glittering jewellery shop.

The window display sparkled beneath the strip lights. Necklaces and earrings glinted from every angle. "These cost a fortune!" Hana complained, gravitating to the cheaper displays. "Can't we try somewhere else?"

"No!" Logan looked hurt. "I'm giving you a decent ring. I told you I'll feel more secure once I put the ring on your finger and kiss the bride." His eyes twinkled and he leaned down and kissed her cheek. "But I want the ring to last for the next fifty years, so it needs to be decent."

"Okay." Hana nudged his arm. "But I'll pay half." Logan gaped in surprise and watched her push her face towards the glass. She pointed at a pair of bands near the bottom edge. "Those are nice. I can afford that." She stood on tiptoes and overbalanced, nutting the window hard with her forehead. An alarm sounded all around them. Hana clutched her forehead and Logan watched a security guard waddle towards them.

He threw his head back and laughed, the motion rocking his body. "Geez, Hana!" he snorted. "Way to go, babe."

The security guard arrived at the same time as the manager of the jewellery shop. They found Logan laughing and Hana rubbing her forehead. Logan held his hands up, palms facing outwards. "Stand down," he said to the guard. "My fiancé just banged her head on the window."

"You think I'm a robber?" Hana's jaw dropped and she looked appalled. "That's terrible!"

"We want to buy wedding rings," Logan reassured them as an audience gathered. "We're not vandals. Well, I can't speak for my fiancé, but I'm not."

"Would you like an ice pack for your head?" the manager offered. "It's looking painful."

Hana gulped and rubbed the red mark on her forehead. "No thanks," she grumbled, glaring at Logan. He wrapped his arm around her shoulder and ignored the dig in the ribs she administered. The security guard bumbled away, puffing from the excitement.

"Come inside," the manager said, crooking a long finger towards Hana. "How can I help you?"

Hana glanced down at her ring finger, flexing her painful wrist and ruing the spiteful cut from the spiky plant across the space where her wedding band should go. She sighed, sensing disaster looming.

"We want wedding rings," Logan said. "And don't have time for them to be sized."

"Ah." The jeweller smiled, a haze of romance in her eyes. "When's the big day?"

Hana swallowed and looked up at Logan. "It's a secret," he said, winking at the woman. Hana's jaw dropped at the way the jeweller's eyelashes fluttered under his grey gaze and the speed with which she bent to the task of finding something suitable.

She produced a simple arrangement of twenty-two carat gold bands with a herringbone pattern etched into the surface. Hana closed her fingers into a fist. "They cost an absolute fortune, Logan! Can't we find something cheaper?" she hissed. "I think my first wedding ring came out of a cracker!"

"Nope, we're doing it properly," Logan whispered back. He smiled at the jeweller and nudged Hana's arm. "Try yours on, darling."

"I don't know what size I am," Hana said, keeping her hand out of range.

"This size." The jeweller held out her palm and balanced the ring in the centre like an oyster displaying its best pearl yet. "I can tell by looking. I've done this job for years."

Hana sighed and placed her hand flat on the glass cabinet, embarrassed about her chipped nail polish and the myriad cuts littering the back of her hand. The jeweller pushed the ring over her knuckle and sat it in place. "Beautiful," she said, standing back to look. "It suits your fine bone structure."

Hana lifted her finger and stared at the wedding band, realising how much she'd missed the many symbols of love and union. Logan smiled down at her. "Do you like it?" he asked.

The jeweller glanced at Hana and then busied herself finding a matching one for Logan. She gave them breathing space. "I love it," Hana whispered. "But I can't afford even a quarter of it." Her face crumpled in disappointment.

"It's fine," Logan whispered back. "It's my gift to you, Hana. Will you let me do this?"

"I don't know." Her breath caught in her chest and Logan slipped his arm around her shoulders as though afraid she might bolt. Hana eased the ring over her knuckle and her bare finger mocked her.

Logan didn't let go, allowing the jeweller to slip his ring into place. She sat it on his left ring finger and he stared down at it. "Pity I've so many scars," he mused, folding down the bent middle finger. He glanced sideways at Hana, watching as she laid her ring on the velvet cushion. His eyes flicked up to the jeweller. "We'll take them," he said, his voice decisive.

The woman broke into a wide smile. "Good choice, sir." Fancying her chances, she pointed at Hana's empty finger. "It's usual for the lady to have an engagement ring as well." She motioned towards a tray of diamond-encrusted gold.

Hana appealed to Logan with her eyes. "Please let's not. We discussed this."

The woman raised a hand in a reassuring motion. "It's okay. Eternity rings are popular as a sign of enduring love. The husband gives one at the first wedding anniversary or birth of the eldest child."

Hana gasped with embarrassment at the mention of babies and colour rushed to the roots of her hair. The idea of bedroom antics overheated her and she backed away from the counter. Logan's restraining arm around her shoulders prevented escape.

"Okay," he conceded. "I'll buy my wife an eternity ring on our first anniversary." He winked at Hana and she tightened, imagining how she might feel after a whole year. Her face clouded at the thought he might already be sick of her.

"What's up?" Logan asked her outside, observing Hana's dark expression. She turned to him, leaning closer to whisper.

"We never talked about children. I think I'm too old. Oh, Logan! What are we doing? Obviously you want a family."

"Hana, stop!" Logan wrapped his arms around her, alarmed by the helplessness in her eyes. They caused a traffic jam in the middle of the busy mall. "A year ago I'd have killed to be standing here holding you. Having a family isn't on my radar. I honestly don't care. How can I make you understand being with you is all I ever wanted? Trust me; I'm grateful for what I have right here."

Hana sighed with relief and then ruined the moment. She winced and Logan looked concerned, a questioning in his eyes. She gulped. "I've these really ugly lines on my stomach from having Bo and Izzie so close together. They're sort of here." Hana touched her stomach down near her hip and her eyes misted with tears.

Logan appeared serious, his brow creased in concentration. "That could be a real deal breaker. I wish you'd said something before I bought the bloody rings!" He placed his hands in the small of Hana's back and pulled her hips into his body, his face softening with lust and expectation. "Maybe I should have a look when we get back to your place. In case I'm not sure."

Hana's jaw dropped and her eyes narrowed. "You git!" She smirked despite herself and Logan laughed. "I believed you!"

Choosing items for a secret wedding and life afterwards felt exciting but tinged with a sense of guilt. It crept up on Hana as she looked at the things she didn't need. She stroked a packet of wedding invitations in a stationery store and wondered what her children might say. Logan cleared his throat behind her. "Having regrets?" he asked, his voice soft. "We can wait and do it the other way."

Hana shook her head. "Bodie won't understand. He's already formed an opinion of you and time won't help that. I'm worrying about Izzie." Hana sighed and then dismissed that thought. "No, she's gorgeous. She'll love you." Pulling her favourite handkerchief from her pocket, she worried at it in her fingers, twisting the navy kiwi birds into a knot. Logan winced at the action and took it from her, tucking it back into her pocket.

"What do you want to do?" he asked.

"Maybe one day when I'm safe from those men, could we have a party and get our marriage blessed?" Hana asked, her eyes wide and searching.

"Yeah, course we can." Logan buried his face in her hair. "For sure."

He led her to a coffee shop and bought drinks. He fiddled with a sugar sachet while they waited. "There are so many gaps in my knowledge of you," he confessed. "What was your first wedding like?"

Hana sighed. "Not ideal. They hid my baby bump beneath a sari so nobody would know, but they did, anyway. A guru performed a Sikh ceremony and the next day, a registrar repeated it for the legalities. Deepak dropped us at the London registry office and my belly looked huge under the borrowed sari. He went to park the car and by the time he got back, it was over." She removed the sachet from Logan's fingers. "What about you?"

"Me? Geez." Logan started in surprise. "I did the dream white wedding with no bride. I guess between us, we've good reason to avoid traditional. People will understand and real friends will accept it."

Hana nodded and the worry left her eyes. "You're right."

They wandered together without urgency, laughing at similar things and enjoying each other's company. Logan seemed more settled with the rings inside his leather jacket pocket, tucked behind the zipper. "Now you can't get out of it." He smiled in triumph and Hana resisted the urge to joke that she could. But he read her mind anyway and knitted his brow. "Please don't freak me out?" he begged her and Hana kissed him, mischief playing in her green eyes.

They wandered into a furniture shop around three o'clock. A Beatles song piped into the store and Hana smiled. Logan nudged her. "What's funny?"

"Nothing." She shook her head, her eyes sad. "My mother's name was Judith. My dad got to their wedding late because he queued for the single at the record shop."

"That's cute." Logan squeezed her hand.

"My mother couldn't hear." Hana swallowed and chewed her lower lip. "I think the diagnosis is profound deafness. But she always loved the cover."

"Like Jack?" Logan asked and Hana nodded.

"Yeah, like Jack."

Logan let go of Hana's hand to examine a side table and she wandered away. She stroked the legs of a renovated bureau and wondered about giving her furniture at home a facelift.

"Hey, Hana," Logan called, beckoning her over. "What do you think to this? It's magnificent, aye?"

"Wow." Hana admired the French style four-poster bed. Painted in muted cream, it was overlaid with gold dust rubbed into the folds and outer edges like a highlight. A pale green voile covered two sides as curtains, the other two pulled back to display the bed.

"It comes with mattress and bedding," Logan said, prodding at the lace quilt cover with tiny green embroidered flowers. "The bedside tables are part of the deal. Do you like it?"

Hana started. "Do you have money to burn or something? I'm not marrying a spendthrift!"

Logan laughed at her reaction. "Come on," he urged. "Let's try it out."

"My bed's fine," Hana argued. "You'll like it."

Logan shook his head. "I'm not making love to my wife in another man's bed, thanks."

Hana swallowed and chewed her bottom lip. "I'm sorry. I never thought about it."

Like naughty children, they removed their shoes and clambered onto the bed. The shop assistant glided over, ready with her don't-sit-on-the-displays speech ready.

"I want this bed," Logan declared. "We're buying it."

Another customer intercepted the shop assistant and she pouted in annoyance. "I'll be there in a sec," she announced. "I need to get this old couple off the display bed."

Hana lay on her back and peered up at the wooden canopy overhead. "Oh, look," she said, prodding Logan's arm. "There are lights like stars overhead."

"I love it," he confirmed, closing his eyes. "I want it."

"I wonder how the lights are powered," Hana said. "There must be a cable here somewhere." She leaned over the side of the bed and tracked a cable along the back of the headboard. "It must plug in," she called over her shoulder. "I can't remember where the power points are in the master bedroom. Can you?" She leaned further over, listening to Logan asking the shop assistant questions. "It's quite long," she shouted. "It should reach."

She glanced backwards as Logan lay on his side. She took in his strong physique and rugged facial scar, noticing the assistant's avid interest in him. A fit of jealousy narrowed Hana's eyes and Logan watched as his future wife lost her balance and disappeared with a squeak and a bump between the bed and the side cupboard.

Hana lay on her face, trapped between the furniture. "Why?" she wailed inside her head. Buried beneath the pillows and heavy matching bolster which followed her down, Hana wished for a hole in the ground to swallow her up. Mustering what dignity she still possessed, she waved the extended cord in her right hand and announced, "Just as I thought, it will reach our sockets!"

Logan smirked at Hana's attempt at a dignified recovery and his memory of her bottom disappearing over the side. His grin said it all. Hana tried not to feel offended as she raised herself up, replaced the pillows and bolster and patted them into place with one eye on the lecherous shop assistant. "Nice ass, babe," Logan said and winked. "We'll take it," he announced. "I'll come and pay."

Smitten by his charm, the assistant clicked off on her high heels to fill in the paperwork. Logan left Hana to finish straightening the bed, giving her another smirk and adding to her pain by blowing her a kiss. "I'll take the ass too," he whispered.

"Woman, you're a disgrace!" Hana admonished herself, using a nearby mirror to sort herself out and primp her straightened hair back into a semblance of normality. By the time she approached the counter, Logan leaned against it filling in the paperwork for delivery. "Oh," Hana said in mock surprise. "You can do joined-up-handwriting."

Logan ignored her snide comment. "It's the last one in the north island. We can have it this week." Happiness showed in his face as he produced a credit card.

Hana choked at the bill and fought to claw back her pride, until the assistant commented through gritted teeth, "You might as well have that one, seeing as you've already had so much fun in it!"

Logan snorted, halting his retort at the sight of Hana's raised eyebrows. He signed the paperwork and paid for the bed, following his fiancé out into the mall. "You are such a flirt!" Hana complained.

Surprise flooded Logan's face. "No, I'm not!" he replied.

"Yes, you are!" Hana shoved him into a rack of women's undies hanging on display outside an underwear store. A polka dot lacy bra strap caught round a button on his leather jacket and he dragged the rack behind him. The security guard reappeared, determination on his face and Logan licked his lips and tried to extricate himself.

Hana abandoned him, enjoying her revenge by walking away laughing.

Chapter 47

"I've had a fantastic day." Hana smiled, leaning back in the passenger seat with a contented expression on her face. "I can't wait to wear the ring." Logan wrinkled his nose and gave Hana a cute smile, basking in a moment that still didn't feel real. "Everyone will think we're crazy," she sighed. "You do know that?"

"Yep." Logan reached for her hand. "But I don't care. Do you trust me?" He cast her a sideways look as he changed lanes. "You believe I'm not messing around with my ex and that I'm in this for real?"

"Yeah, I believe you." Hana peered through of the side window. "But you were right when you said it suited me to believe the worst. I focussed on my own fear of humiliation instead of letting you explain." She glanced across at him. "There are things you don't know about me."

Logan knitted his brow and looked worried, contentment sliding from his face. "We agreed it didn't matter," he said, an edge to his voice. "We'll learn things about each other as we go. I have a past too, Hana. I don't think writing you a list would be helpful."

Hana ran a slender hand over his thigh. "I believe you and you make me happy. I don't want to worry about anything else, not today, anyway." She watched the darkened countryside zip by, sure her rash behaviour would come back to bite her, especially when forced to admit what she'd done. A rebellious voice in her head told her not to listen to their criticism. They didn't live alone with memories and boredom for company. They couldn't know the poor companion loneliness made.

Hana watched Logan as he drove. He concentrated, switching lanes and manoeuvring Cilla's tiny car homeward. On impulse, she reached out and put her hand on his thigh again, trying not to distract him.

Logan took his eyes off the road and glanced across at Hana, a worried expression replacing the look of concentration. She swallowed and sat up straight. "I love you," she said and watched as happiness spread across his face like a breaking dawn. "I feel so grateful that another person wants my love as much as you do. But I don't deserve it."

Logan placed his left hand over hers and squeezed it. "I don't just want your love, Hana; I need it. I've always needed it." He sighed. "I'm afraid."

"Why?" Hana stroked his fingers.

"I feel vulnerable," he admitted, checking the mirrors and changing lanes again. "I should be happy but I'm peering over my shoulder for the next disaster. We need to be left alone to settle together but I suspect it won't happen."

Hana swallowed. "Let's get married as soon as possible and deal with the rest one day at a time."

"Deal." Logan smiled at her. "That sounds like a plan."

Using the back roads via Huntly, he drove over the Tainui Bridge, becoming watchful again as reality snaked back into their lives. That night they cuddled up on the sofa and watched a Saturday night movie on the fuzzy television. The picture seemed at its best with Logan holding the portable aerial, but his arm ached. "I can't do this," he grumbled, switching arms.

"Spoil sport," Hana replied. "I enjoyed looking at you with your arms in the air. You're quite tank for an English teacher."

"Yeah, well my workouts don't involve holding aerials!" Logan snorted and dropped it, diving on Hana and tickling her until she almost barfed. They tumbled onto the floor and Hana groaned as his rough chin grazed her neck.

"Stop," she whispered. "You need to make an honest woman of me first."

Logan snuffled in her hair. "That's asking the impossible," he joked. "Define honest woman."

"Haha," Hana retorted. "You're just bored because the TV reception is terrible."

Logan flopped onto his back. "I'm insulted!" He sniffed. "I don't need entertaining. I'm not a child."

"There's no decent receiver at the property and I'm worried about the safety of anything fixed to the roof in the high winds," Hana mused. "Do you watch TV much? Is it weird that I don't know how you spend your time?"

"No, Hana." Logan ran his hands down her side and flexed his fingers over her hip. "It's not weird and I don't watch much TV. We didn't have one growing up."

"I can get it fixed if you want. I might afford Sky once the rent comes in from the Achilles Rise house."

"Na, I'm good. There are heaps of other things we can do to fill the time." Logan smirked and Hana felt a steady flush creep up from her chest, staining her cheeks and making her feel self-conscious. Logan nibbled the sensitive skin on her neck. Hana shivered and he stopped, his eyes sultry with a hint of amusement. His lips felt soft and warm on her skin, but she froze at a sudden miserable flashback of the look on Vik's face when she told him she was pregnant. She pushed herself upright.

"We should've talked about babies," she said, running a hand through her hair. "It never occurred to me."

Logan rolled onto his back and pulled her on top of him. "I told you it doesn't matter," he whispered.

Hana rested her cheek on his chest and relaxed. "The thought of having a baby at my age is ridiculous," she said with a sigh. "I don't think it's possible." Logan traced circles on her spine with his fingers and she lifted her chin to look at his face. "About sleeping together," she began, her voice tremulous.

Logan placed his index finger over her lips. "I get it, Hana. You don't have to explain. I want this to be right as much as you do. It's fine," he soothed. "I'll wait for you. It's okay."

Neither of them saw the end of the film. The fire roared in the fireplace giving off a soporific heat and they dozed off before ten, Hana laid sideways across Logan's body with her head on his stomach.

A metallic banging woke them, causing Hana to let out a cry as Logan leapt up with a start. "Sorry, babe," he said, reaching back to stroke her temple. Hana picked herself off the floor and Logan held her hand. "Someone's outside," he hissed. "I need to check it out."

Bleary with sleep and shaking with adrenaline, Hana nodded. Her green eyes glowed like lamps in the semi darkness. Logan turned away from her and Hana caught his wrist, feeling the familiar ache shoot up her arm. "Logan," she hissed, her voice urgent. "Stay inside. I'll call the cops."

His sarcastic sneer surprised her. "Hana, by the time they drag their asses up here, these guys will be in the house or gone." His jaw tightened and the look of determination in his face frightened her. "I'll take care of it. It might be a possum." He slid his wrist from her grasp and gave her shoulder a squeeze. "I won't be long."

By the time Hana reached the front door, she saw Logan already outside on the veranda and running down the stairs. A long, black object hung from his left hand. Hana's heart pounded, the reverberation thudding in her throat. She pulled on the door handle and it stayed closed, the catch on the Yale lock holding it fast. Her shoulders slumped at the realisation Logan locked her in. She respected his wishes and instead of opening it and following, tracked him around the property by running from room to room and staring through windows. She lost him through the gloom behind the garage, her nose pressed against the glass door onto the roof garden.

The click of the front door made her cry out and press herself against the wall. Her hands wrung in front of her, sending pain into her shoulder and testing the fragile scar tissue over the knife wound. Hana held her breath and listened.

"Hana?" Logan's voice wrested a groan of relief from her chest and she squeaked out a reply.

"I'm here."

His long legged stride pounded down the short hallway from the lobby to the garage stairs and he stopped at the whiteness of her complexion and the terror in her eyes. He grabbed her roughly and held her tight. She shook and freezing air rolled off his clothing. Hana pointed at his feet. "You went outside in your socks." Her words sounded breathy.

Logan nodded against her temple. "Yeah, they're soaked. I didn't have time to grab shoes."

"Take them off." Hana let go of his waist so he could bend to strip the saturated material from his feet and she felt him shivering as she supported his arm. "Leave them at the top of the stairs," she said, her voice shaking. "I'll wash them tomorrow."

"Thanks." He trembled in his bare feet and shirtsleeves. "It's freezing out there. Must be below zero."

"Who made the noise?"

Logan rolled his eyes. "A possum in the bins. Little buggers. They'll have a go at anything."

Hana released an exhale. "Maybe I didn't put the lid on properly." She swallowed. "I guess there are lots of them up in the bush."

Logan nodded. "Yeah. Like at home. Dad runs possum shoots to control them. It's up to the Department of Conservation here." Water glistened on his clothing and Hana patted him with her palms.

"You should get your wet things off," she said, peering into his face. "Then come and sit by the fire." She sighed, the peace of twenty minutes ago broken so abruptly it left her drained. A possum in the rubbish was nothing, but the possibilities for the couple's shattered nerves seemed endless.

Logan opted for a hot shower and Hana busied herself making a pot of tea in the brightly lit kitchen. He emerged in a tee shirt and shorts and drank coffee despite the lateness of the hour. "I can't live like this anymore," Hana said, her voice cracking with stress.

Logan sighed. "But you don't want me to help."

Hana put her mug on the table and examined the colourful red strawberries, deep in thought. "What kind of help is it, exactly?" She looked up and studied his face, seeing the strange light activate in his eyes.

"I told you, it's best you don't know."

Hana swallowed. "Sometimes I wonder if I know you at all, Logan. It scares me."

He exhaled through his nose. "It should make you feel safe," he replied. "But I'll be who you need me to be for as long as it takes."

"What does that mean?" Hana's senses went on red alert. "Aren't you an exceptional English teacher with a background in accounting? Who else are you?"

"Nobody else." Logan tipped the rest of his coffee down the sink and swilled it away with water. He pulled the dishwasher open and thought better of it. "Can I replace this old machine when I move in?" he asked, sniffing the elderly interior. "It stinks."

Hana nodded. "Okay. But you didn't answer my question."

"Yeah, I did. I am who you say I am." Logan squatted by her side. "But I'm tired and so are you. I just got engaged to the woman of my dreams and don't intend to fight with her at this time of night."

"You think I want a fight?" Hana's brow knitted and Logan gave a slow blink as though gathering his patience.

"No, Hana. But this won't end in a sensible conversation while we're both tired and rattled." He reached up and kissed her forehead. "I'm going to bed. Tomorrow we'll make a plan for getting to work on Monday. Not only do we have two guys to avoid, it's not a good idea to rock up to school together with that natty clause in your contract. Dobbs and Watson are like romance terminators at the moment."

Hana accepted his kiss and watched him walk from the room. His muscular olive legs taunted her with what she wasn't yet entitled to; sight of the rest of his gorgeous body. She leaned her face on her forearms fighting the sting of dissatisfaction and woke in the same position in the early hours. Her stumble to bed caused a flash of mischief at the sight of Logan's closed bedroom door and she forced herself into her own room and face planted on the empty double bed, still fully clothed.

Hana woke late the next morning, her phone buzzing in her pocket. She groaned and rolled over, hauling it free and noticing the flashing low battery light. "Hi." Her voice sounded sleepy.

"Is it possible to get my car back?" Cilla sounded piqued and Hana glanced at her watch.

She gasped at the time. "I've missed church," she said with a sigh. "Sorry. We had a disturbance last night and I went to bed late." Hana stifled a yawn. "I'm so sorry. I'll organise something with Logan and get back to you." The sound of coffee cups clinking in the background gave Hana an uncomfortable guilt sensation through her spine. She'd missed church and coffee duty afterwards.

"Are the police any nearer to catching those men?" Cilla asked, lowering her voice. "We kept your car hidden all weekend and used Bill's ute."

"I haven't heard from the cops," Hana admitted. "And the disturbance turned out to be a possum in the bins. Logan checked it out, but we thought the worst."

"Logan lives with you?" Cilla's tone oozed judgement and Hana blanched.

"No. But at the moment, he's the only protection I have." Hana's reply sounded snippy and she rang off after promising to swap cars back. She flopped back on the bed and put her hands over her eyes.

"Hey." Hana didn't hear Logan's soft knock on the door and started as he spoke to her. She sighed and rolled onto her stomach.

"I didn't wake up in time to go to church and Cilla wanted her car back." The bedding muffled her sentence. Logan shrugged and sat next to her. Already showered and dressed, he smelled of aftershave and shampoo. "I said we'd organise something." He ran his hands over Hana's spine.

"Did you say you'd take it back today?"

"No." Hana sounded sulky. "But I should be there, anyway." She pushed herself into a sitting position and then flopped forward onto Logan's stomach. "They've always been kind to me. Maybe we should just do a proper wedding later." She felt Logan's stomach tense beneath her cheek. "They're good people. I've always been able to count on them. Even when the lawyers froze our accounts after Vik's death, they brought food and lent me money."

"That's nice." Logan's reply sounded lame, even to himself. "Was that Allen?"

Hana shook her head. "No. He came a few years ago. The previous pastor was a good friend of Vik's." She sat up, her brow creased. "What will we do about getting to work? And how do I take Cilla's car back to her? Returning to the same location is dumb." Hana got into her stride. "How many more cars can I borrow?" she complained. "Will I have to disguise myself forever until they get bored and go away?"

"No, babe," he reassured. "We'll get it sorted out somehow." He ran a gentle hand around her neck and pulled her back onto his stomach. "Just trust me," he said.

Logan nipped out on an errand and Hana pottered around, tidying and cleaning up. Unlike his mistress, Tiger seemed calm and settled, laying in spots of sunlight and moving onto the next one as they winked out. "You look happy, old man." Hana stroked his head and he yawned. "Don't know why you made all that fuss about coming here."

Putting away a screw she found loose on the floor, Hana opened the drawer in the hall table. Her fingers clasped the long, black object she saw in Logan's hand the night before. The heavy, six-cell Maglite looked brand new and her wrist protested at lifting it. She remembered Bodie's words after police training college as he explained how a pop on the head with a Maglite could be classed as accidental, whereas drawing his baton engendered a heap of paperwork. Hana closed the drawer on the shiny object, both afraid and emboldened by Logan's serious desire to protect her.

Logan arrived home, two plastic wheelie bins sticking out of Cilla's tiny car. The trunk lid wobbled as the car reached the end of the driveway.

"I went to your favourite shop," Logan said. "The shop owner says hi."

Hana ran her fingers over the green plastic. "How will this help? Do they fall over more quietly?"

Logan rolled his eyes at her. "No, you egg! We'll keep the rubbish in the garage inside these and just put the bags out on bin day. We'll drive them down to the road as usual."

"What will you do with the metal ones?" Hana asked.

"I'm gonna drill holes in one of them and make it into an incinerator." Logan looked pleased with himself. "There's a sign on the Waipa Bridge. Open fires aren't permitted within one kilometre of the bush so we can burn in this."

"Cool." Hana found his enthusiasm infectious, following him as he walked to the passenger seat. "I filled up the car and gave it a clean out too. But I also got something else from the shop." From the front passenger seat, Logan produced a long, wide plastic bag, containing rolls of paper. "Close your eyes," he said, "no peeking!"

He placed one of the rolls into Hana's open palms, watching as she opened her eyes. "I'm scared you won't like it now," he said, chewing his lower lip. Tiny cream flowers swirled around a pretty green background, the same colour as the voile on the new four-poster bed. Punctuated now and then by a small pink rose, the effect seemed stylish and calming.

Hana beamed. "Wow. I love it. Where did you find it?"

"That shop you love so much." Reaching into the car again, Logan produced two five-litre cans of cream paint which picked out the tone of the flowers. He studied Hana's face for a reaction and sighed with relief when he saw she approved.

"It's amazing." Hana's face held pure delight. "I couldn't trust Vik to choose colours," she gushed. The look on Logan's face wiped the smile from hers. "Sorry." She pursed her lips and stared at the ground. "I shouldn't compare you. You're nothing like each other."

Logan's jaw worked against his cheek. "It's fine, Hana. I'm more worried that you'll think I'm taking liberties. You own the house, not me."

Hana's eyes widened. "Does that bother you?"

"No." Logan stroked her cheek. "Not at all. But I don't want to overstep the mark."

"You won't." Hana's eyelashes fluttered. "Won't it be yours when we're married, anyway?"

Logan's laugh disturbed the birds in the bare kowhai trees. "No, Hana, it won't. I'll never lay claim to anything of yours. That's between you and your kids."

"But won't we share?" she asked, suspicion growing in her eyes. "Isn't that part of marriage?"

"Maybe." He caught her around the waist, his grip firm. "You can have access to everything of mine, wahine. But I won't come between your children and their legacy." He turned her body and pointed her at the porch. "Grab the wallpaper. I thought decorating might distract us from our return to work and reality tomorrow."

Taking an opposite wall each, they painted Hana's bedroom using the pads left over from the kitchen. They raced each other, competing to finish and chatting as they covered the hundred-year-old walls. Hana lifted her pad and contemplated the wall behind the headboard. "This is the worst," she said. "I couldn't get rid of all the dents."

"Do the feature wall there," Logan suggested, brushing cream paint around the glass panes in the wooden doors to the balcony.

Hana screwed up her face. "It seems such a waste to hide gorgeous wallpaper behind the four-poster bed. Why don't we do the opposite wall too, providing there's enough?"

Logan nodded and went back to his painting. "I bought five rolls. With the tiny print pattern, the shop owner figured it shouldn't use up too much paper in the matching process. And look, if we run out, I'll go back and get more."

"Yeah." Hana looked from one end of the room to the other. "I like that idea. How are you at wallpapering?"

Logan shrugged. "Dunno. Never done any."

They stopped for lunch while the paint dried on the walls and skirting board. Later while Logan gave them a second coat, Hana painted the architrave and skirting board around the walls she wanted to paper. She stopped as the natural light disappeared and the overhead bulb created confusing shadows against the painted surfaces. "I'm so tired." She yawned and face planted into her pillows. "Can we stop now?"

"What about the ceiling?" Logan looked up at the fresh plaster in two corners and Hana groaned.

"I can't face it," she grumbled.

Logan pressed on until after eleven o'clock that night, giving the ceiling a coat of paint with the pad. He struggled to paint around the sleeping Hana. Twice he moved the bed and she didn't stir. Washing out the brushes and pads in the kitchen sink, he ate toast and jam and took a phone call from his father. Logan closed the kitchen door and kept his voice low as he gave instructions on a hotel matter. He returned to the master bedroom and finding Hana still asleep, covered her with a blanket and turned out the lights. He left the bedroom door open to allow the paint fumes to disperse and cracked the security latch on the high window in the kitchen. The through draught chilled the house but expelled the fumes.

Pete rang him late, whining about working with Caroline. "I'm sick of her," he griped. "She's real mean. Do something."

"She's the least of my problems, bro'! And she's not my responsibility. See Angus if you can't cope."

"Can't cope? Who can cope with her? She keeps asking after you and wants to know where Hana's gone. On Friday she said Hana's gone off sick with stress because she knows she's gonna lose to her. She wants you back mate. I don't see her leaving without you."

Logan sighed. "She'll have to, Pete. Even the sight of her makes my head ache."

"Yeah. After what she did, I'm surprised she's got the guts to walk back into your life. Geez, she humiliated you."

"Thanks, Pete." Logan gritted his teeth. "In case I forgot how embarrassing it was." He lay back against his pillow and rolled his eyes. "I need to go. Hana's asleep."

"What? In the bed with you?" Pete sounded aghast. "I'll just tell Caroline that. She'll get the message."

Logan sighed. "No, Pete. Hana's in her room and I'm in the guest room. And don't give Caroline more ammunition against Hana. The trustees will fire her."

Pete tutted. "Roddy from history quit on Friday. He's dated Claire from the art department for years. He said she didn't want to get married after her messy divorce and they agreed at the start they wouldn't. They bought a house together last year. Watson went after Claire over it and Roddy said one of them needed to leave and he can get work elsewhere."

"Geez," Logan sighed. "That sucks."

"That's not all." Pete made a squelching noise and Logan winced, not dwelling on the possible reasons for the sound. "They're still going after her because she's living in sin with him. It's a bad example to the boys."

"More reason not to tell anyone I'm here with Hana."

"Yeah, too right." Pete sneezed. "When are you coming home? This place got dusty real fast."

"Clean it, lazy git!" Logan exclaimed and then lowered his voice. "I need to go. I'm tired."

"Okay." Pete paused. "You're good on legal stuff. Can the trustees do this to staff?"

"Yep." Logan sounded certain. "It's in their contract and it's a private school. Someone could take it through the courts but who's gonna do that?"

"You." Pete whooped like a child. "You're our champion."

"Whatever!" Logan scoffed. "My contract's only for a year and you know that. Fight your own battles."

"Hana doesn't know that, does she?"

Logan sat up in bed. "I hope you're not threatening me, mate. Because you know how that will go for you."

"No, no." Pete backtracked, forcing a lightness into his tone. "How is Hana?"

Logan ran his hand over his face. "Jumpy. Real jumpy. She'll be fine. We'll get it sorted."

"You gonna break someone's legs, brother?" Pete let rip with a wicked raucous laugh and Logan winced.

"If you breathe a word to anyone, I'll break your legs. You know I'm not joking, man!" He heard Pete gulp and suspected he inspected the odd kink in his left shin, the result of a fight they had in fifth form. Logan peered down at the bent bone in the middle finger of his left hand. Pete started it and he finished it. It seemed ironic the fight was over Hana, or the unnamed girl on the train.

"You still haven't forgiven me for that yet, have you?" Pete griped.

"You haven't apologised!" Logan's voice betrayed tiredness and irritation.

"Fine, I'm sorry," Pete conceded with obvious reluctance. "I know she's real now. But obviously I didn't know then. It sounded so far-fetched, you saying you'd seen this girl on a London train and she was your soul mate."

"You done?" Logan's temper flared at the memory of old hurts and he wanted the conversation over.

"How will you get to work undetected?"

"Not sure yet."

"And what about Watson and Dobbs? If you keep arriving at work together, they'll come after you. The trustees will fire your ass."

"You think I don't know that? Stop winding me up!" Logan hissed.

"Will you talk to Caroline then? Tell her to stop picking on me."

"No. I'm not going near her. I promised Hana. I don't break my promises."

"Yeah, bro', I know. I know." Pete's voice softened and Logan terminated the call. Marriage would legitimise their relationship in the eyes of the board members, but the problem of the two men stalking Hana remained. Logan reached for his phone and then lay it down again. She said no and he wished to respect her desires, however hard it might be.

Caroline's continued presence unleashed a whole other set of issues and he didn't know where to start with those. Logan turned over in the single bed with a dreadful sickness sitting in his stomach. Sleep felt a long way off.

Chapter 48

Logan dragged himself from the single bed before six o'clock on Monday morning, showered and dressed for work. Sleep proved fruitful and a plan dropped into his brain in the early moments between slumber and waking.

The light from the landing disturbed Hana, burning through the open door and reflecting off the new paintwork. She grunted as Tiger's claws kneaded her stomach, trying to make her stay still so he could keep her as a pillow.

Turning on the bedside lamp, Hana saw yesterday's clothes twisted around her body. Shrouded in a blanket she smelled the receding odour of paint, overlaid by the scent of toast. Brushing her hair back from her face, she stumbled out of bed and padded to the kitchen. The thought of the day ahead daunted her.

"Hey, gorgeous." Logan smelled of toothpaste as he kissed her and plonked a cup of tea on the table. "Sit down and I'll make your breakfast."

Hana sighed. She required time to wake up in the mornings and Monday's were no exception. "Okay, so you're not a morning person then." Logan dismissed Hana's dirty look with a smirk and pushed the drink towards her.

"Thanks," she grunted. "I need a shower, two cups of tea and the clock hands to move past seven." She yawned and watched Logan move around the kitchen. "You on the other hand, look like someone who rises with the sun. I don't think I like you."

A cold shower woke her properly as the hot water dried up without explanation. She screamed and shot from the bathroom in her towel.

"Sorry," Logan called up the stairs. "I put the washing machine on. I didn't think about diverting the hot water."

Hana squeaked in reply and slammed the bedroom door. Half an hour later she emerged, feeling more human. She discovered Logan in the kitchen, washing up at the sink. "Sorry for being grumpy." Hana wrapped her arms around him from behind, enjoying the solidity of his muscles and the sense of companionship.

"I'll get used to it," he said, drying his hands and turning. He stroked the side of her face and pulled her long red tresses from the collar of her cardigan, smoothing them down her back. His kiss made Hana's stomach feel like she rode a swing, a sensation of painful ecstasy. Logan's shirt hung outside his trousers and Hana slid her hands underneath, caressing his tanned skin. She felt him exhale and explored further, touching the hard muscle either side of his spine. Logan paused in his kiss and nipped her bottom lip with his teeth, his excitement growing.

"Let's stay home," she whispered, her voice hushed and soft. "Don't you want to?" She stroked her fingers around his ribs, feeling him still as her cool palm encountered a ridge of skin. Raised and rugged, it tracked up the right side of his body from hip to armpit and the way he held his breath communicated his fear to Hana. Logan froze, waiting for her reaction and Hana worked hard not to give him one. "Did someone hurt you?" she whispered and he nodded, a slight, almost imperceptible action. "Then I'm sorry," she said.

Hana kept her hand over the scar and restarted the kiss, eager to go back to where they were. She realised she didn't care what damage he hid beneath his shirt and communicated her acceptance with her body. Logan pushed her hair up from the back of her neck, tracing his fingers upwards through it. It felt good. Hana looked up at him and repeated her request, "Stay home with me."

Logan pulled away and she felt his soft breath on her cheek. His grey eyes revealed how the battle within him matched her own. "We could," he breathed. "But it's not what you wanted. I've waited twenty-six years for this; a couple more days is nothing." He kissed her. "Besides, I want us to have our own bed."

"True." Emotions coursed through Hana's chest. A tiny spark of rejection activated a Jezebel spirit which demanded she make him do her bidding, but she mentally rebuked it. "You're right," she sighed. She didn't want to begin her new marriage the same way as the old one. A memory flashed into her mind and took her breath away with its unexpectedness. Inevitable pain surfaced and Hana pressed her face into Logan's chest. Someone else stood before her with a confession of requited love and imploded Hana's world in a sentence.

"What's the matter?" Logan's voice forced her from her memories. "Did I offend you?"

Hana shook her head. "No. Not at all. Everything you said is right. I can't wait to be your wife."

Logan rubbed his hand up and down Hana's back. It consoled and comforted her, settling the quavering sensations in her gut and giving her hope. "I love you." He kissed the top of her head and enfolded her, stroking her hair and providing the barrier against a fear inside Hana's soul that he didn't even know existed.

Logan drove to Cilla's in the early morning execution of his plan. "It's full of petrol," he said, handing her the keys. "Thanks so much for your understanding."

Cilla fluttered her eyelashes at the handsome male and accepted the keys. "So, I'm taking Hana to Alder Dale?" she said, double-checking. Logan nodded and retrieved his bike helmet from the back seat, giving Hana a smile as he walked around to the side of Cilla's house.

"Good morning, Hana," Cilla said, climbing into the driving seat. "You look a little better than you did the other night." She cranked on the seat handle and closed the gap between her stomach and the steering wheel. "Anything from the cops?"

"No." Hana sighed and her mouth turned downwards. "I'm sorry I involved you in this."

Cilla shook her head and started the engine, backing the tiny car off the drive and into the street. Hana watched as Logan wheeled his motorbike onto the driveway. She craned her neck around to watch him ride behind them for the three kilometres to Alder Dale Residential Village, where they turned onto the small driveway of one of the units there. Hana knew Cilla wanted to ask questions about Logan and evaded her enquiries with marginal success. "Logan's a colleague," she said. "He got dragged into this mess and has helped me heaps."

Cilla pursed her lips. "It seems like more than a work relationship, love," she replied. "I hope you know what you're doing. We loved Vik so much. His death took something from all of us."

Hana's jaw dropped and she inhaled to force down her temper. "Are you saying I shouldn't meet anyone else or try to start again?" she asked, her tone tight and wooden.

Cilla shrugged. "I don't know, Hana. When you've had the perfect man, it's hard not to end up disappointed with anyone else. We might all struggle to accept someone new."

"Thanks for your help, Cilla," Hana said, jumping from the car. "Logan filled your car to the top. I'll see you around." She closed the door behind her and stood on the driveway, shaking from head to toe.

"Hana, dear, what a performance." Angus greeted her with a kiss on the cheek and mistook her anger for distress. He jabbed his remote at the car behind him. "Hop in, dearest," he said, turning to wave to Cilla as she backed off his driveway.

Hana shot a glance loaded with panic at Logan as he cruised to a stop on the small street. He pushed his visor up and raised his eyebrows. Angus shooed Hana into his car and gave her no opportunity to vent her bile about Cilla's comment. She slumped into the passenger seat of his sporty black Audi with its tinted windows and travelled to work incognito in the principal's mid-life-crisis car.

Pete eyed Hana with curiosity as she slammed into the office, observing her as though she was a specimen. "Don't stare at me like that," Hana snapped, shoving her handbag into the bottom drawer of her desk. "All this trouble is making me depressed. Car switcheroos are ridiculous."

"I'll tell Logan." Pete blew at the key ring in his hand, a tube of superglue lying on its side and leaking onto his desk.

"Don't you dare! I'm grateful for his help. It took a lot of work to coordinate an operation like this morning's."

"Yeah." Pete turned to her with the key ring gripped between finger and thumb. An Audi emblem peeked out from beneath his fat finger, the old Toyota one lying broken on his desk. "That's what he does best. Nobody messes with him when he rounds up the boys." Pete licked his lips. "Hana. Were you in bed with Logan when I called him last night?"

"What do you mean round up the boys?" Hana demanded. "And my relationship with Logan is nobody else's business! I'm tired of people thinking they have a right to comment. They don't!"

Pete spun back to engross himself in his activity and gave Hana the silent treatment. Irritated, she stomped off to the staffroom, calling over her shoulder, "I hope it sticks to your fingers!" Pete stuck his tongue out at Hana's retreating back and then got the scissors out of his desk as her wish came true.

The groundsman barrelled into their office before interval, his face puce with anger. The door opened so hard, it hit the cupboard behind. Her nerves shot, Hana screamed and tried to run away, tripping over the wheels of Pete's chair as he whirled around in surprise. She smashed into the open drawer of the tall filing cabinet and jarred her painful wrist, bursting into tears of pain and terror. The sleeve of her cardigan caught on a file and pinned her in place like a fish on a line.

"What the hell's happening?" Sheila's blonde ponytail swung behind her as she emerged from her office and went to Hana's defence. "Larry Collins, get out of here!" she demanded.

"No!" the groundsman shouted, the wobbly flesh beneath his chin swaying with the lurching of his body. "Where's her car? Why's the principal parked in her space?"

"How does she know?" Sheila yelled, disconnecting the yarn from Hana's sleeve and releasing her. "Someone nicked her car, you stupid man. Bugger off and annoy someone else."

"Oh." Larry Collins peered sideways so he could see around Sheila. "Ask her if she came on a motorbike this morning."

"No, I won't!" Sheila bit back. "Don't be so bloody ridiculous, man!"

Pete snorted and flapped his keyring in the air. "You don't wanna mess with the owner of that bike," he muttered.

"Whose is it?" Larry's voice rose in temper. "I'll clamp the bloody thing. Our principal shouldn't have to park with the other nobodies!" He waved a beefy hand towards Hana. "Nobodies like her!"

"Get out!" Sheila moved towards him at speed and Hana put a hand out to steady herself. Her sleeve reattached itself to the filing cabinet again and she groaned in misery.

Larry Collins exited the room backwards, alarmed by the darkness in Sheila's eyes. "You're all weird," he hissed, menace in his voice. "I'll clamp that bloody bike right now."

"Oh, Hana." Sheila wrapped her arms around Hana and stroked her back. "Angus said you'd been sick. Ignore Larry. He's a stupid little man."

"He is!" Pete exclaimed. "Especially if he thinks he's clamping Logan's bike."

Hana wailed in misery. "He only tried to help me!" She looked up in time to see Pete's fingers flashing across the keypad of his phone.

"It's okay," he announced. "He moved it. He went into town in his free period."

"What's going on?" Sheila demanded.

Hana turned away, remembering Logan's promise to visit the registry office. Her cheeks flushed and she hid a smile behind her hands. Sheila disconnected her from the file and stamped into her office, slamming the door behind her. "Thanks Pete," Hana said, grateful more for Logan's whereabouts than Pete's intervention.

Logan appeared in the office before lunch, having made an interesting discovery at staff briefing which aided his cause. "Hey, Hana," he said, resting his bum on the corner of her desk.

"Hey." Hana's eyes held expectation and excitement but Pete's presence made discussion impossible.

"Did you know the school's closed on Friday?" Logan asked her, his lips rising in a smile.

Hana shook her head and knitted her brow. "No. Why?"

"Oh! It's awesome," Pete raved. "I love the V8 races. The cars race around town for three days starting on the Friday. The main race is always on Sunday. The white lines are on Mill Street already. I'm going down later with my ride to do some racing. I do it every year. You should come, Logan."

Logan laughed. "Er, no thanks," he replied. "You rev that heap of crap and it'll drop its bumper on the track."

"Yeah but school's closed. If you don't wanna come revving with me, you could come to the Friday heats. You might as well. The sports department always get drunk in the beer tent. Best day of the year; better than Christmas."

"Whatever." Logan peered at Pete's hand. "Why is your finger stuck to your thumb?"

Pete stared down at his hand and jabbed his thumb at Hana. "She cursed me," he said. "But Larry Collins yelled at her so karma got her back."

Logan's brow furrowed and he jerked his head towards Pete. "Wash your hand."

Pete shrugged. "Na, thanks. I'm picking it off."

Logan spun around and lifted his friend by the collar. "I said go and wash your hand." He pushed Pete towards the office door and spat him into the common room. "And take a decent while." He slammed the door in Pete's face.

"You got the registry office?" Hana asked, her eyes shining with excitement. She pushed her hands around Logan's waist and rested her cheek on his chest. "And we're getting married on Friday?"

"Yep." He swung her around and slid her down his body. "Sure are, Ms McIntyre." He kissed her, laughing when she wiped her lipstick from his lips with her thumb.

"Thank goodness something's gone right," she sighed.

"Why's Larry yelling at you?" Logan's brow narrowed.

Hana's eyes widened. "It doesn't matter now. But he burst in here and terrified me. My fear reaction is way over the top nowadays. I went loco."

"That's understandable." Logan's lips felt good over hers and Hana sighed with satisfaction. "On Friday at ten o'clock, you'll be Mrs Du Rose." His eyes crinkled at the edges and he bit his lip. "I can't wait," he whispered in her ear.

The sound of a drawer closing made Hana jump and she shot a look at Sheila's office door. They stilled and listened as Sheila slammed her fingers into her keyboard with aggression. "I wish I knew what was up with her,"

Hana whispered. "She's being really odd." Hana turned back to Logan, her face dropping at the unease in his eyes. "What's the matter?"

"Nothing." The wary look left his face. "Nothing at all."

Hana touched his fingers, winding hers through them and feeling his rough skin against her softer pads. His eyes returned to their silvery tone and he smiled and kissed the back of her hand. "See ya later." He winked before leaving the room and Hana sighed with satisfaction. Her stomach did flips at the thought of marriage to him, able to undress him at will and inspect the quality gift beneath the expensive wrapping.

Logan stuck his head through the door after lunch, on his way back to class. He found Hana alone and bailed her up against the filing cabinet, kissing her out of view of the windows. "So, you haven't changed your mind then." He smirked as she slipped her hand underneath his jacket.

"No." She tried to sound huffy but his kisses on her neck made her fail.

"I'll stay at the Gordonton house for the rest of the week." Logan snuffed into her hair and Hana stalled, her body rigid.

"No, you can't!" she exclaimed. "Please don't leave me there by myself?" She hated the pleading tone in her voice.

"The gates go in today," Logan replied, misunderstanding her fear for irritation. "Angus and I moved your car from Cilla's garage earlier and hid it in his. Each morning, you can drive to Alder Dale and get a lift into work with Angus. Your car will sit in his garage all day." He ran a hand through his dark hair, leaving his fringe flicked back from his forehead. "It will make you harder to trace. They won't find you."

"But I'm scared," Hana argued.

"I know you are." Logan switched to talking about work matters and stepped back as staff and boys wandered past the office door on route to their next class. He continued once they disappeared. "The gate will protect you at home, so the most risk is when you're travelling. Your son came up with no ideas and his colleagues don't seem interested, so I'll take care of you myself."

Hana nodded in response, but grave misgiving filled her heart. Her afternoon plunged from ecstatic to miserable. Caroline Marsh returned and sent Pete running for cover. With Hana at her mercy, she barked orders and gave her stares of unveiled malice. The head of geography visited with concerns about a student and Caroline engaged him on the topic of honeymoon destinations. "Logan and I fancied Bali," she said, every word cutting into Hana's psyche. "But then we decided on Fiji. He's not the beach sort. He likes to be busy, so we thought we'd scuba dive and hire scooters."

"Logan Du Rose?" Clay O'Sullivan knitted his brow in confusion. "Are you and he together?"

"Engaged." Caroline twinkled her fingers in his face, displaying a huge diamond on her ring finger.

"Oh, congratulations." He bent and kissed her cheek, shrouded in awkwardness. "When's the happy day?"

"We should've married in January," Caroline said. "But we postponed due to a family crisis." She fluttered her eyelashes. "It'll be soon though. I'll be sure to send you an invitation."

Hana breathed through pursed lips, her redheaded temper soaring and driving her blood pressure skywards. She shoved the buds for her dictaphone so hard into her ears it hurt, drowning out Caroline's lies as Evie's gentle voice dictated case notes. Hana spewed the words onto her screen like an automaton, her fingers flying over the keyboard. Caroline's tap on her shoulder made her jump.

"I hope you heard all that." The blonde woman's blue eyes sparkled. "You don't stand a chance against me. Logan can't get enough of what I have to offer." She oozed confidence and Hana felt depleted in her presence. Caroline's touch caused physical pain and Hana jerked backwards.

"Don't touch me!" she snapped. "And don't speak to me. I don't work for you."

Caroline laughed, the sound polluting the atmosphere with its bile. She jabbed her finger at the half cup of cold tea on Hana's desk, jumping back in fake horror as the liquid soiled the papers everywhere it touched. "Damn," she said, laughter in her voice. "I'd help you clear up, but I'm teaching next door to Logan now. I know how much he looks forward to seeing me. It's impossible to find time together in this place." She spun away and left Hana mopping up the mess, fighting the increasing sense of doom.

Hana binned her day's work and started again, tears pricking at her eyes. Her confidence plummeted into her shoes and Caroline's words ate at her trust in Logan. Sheila rang to demand the reports she gave Hana to type and she admitted they'd been ruined. "I'm printing them again now," she said, wincing as the copier ate the top copy of each.

Caroline returned, tossing her head and throwing her folder onto her desk. She winked at Hana and licked her lips, the inference clear. "You should wake up and crawl back into your granny car," she spat. "Logan always comes back to me. I don't want to see you hurt, but I've been here before." The smile faded from her face as Chris Carter stuck his head through the door.

"How can I help you?" Hana fixed a polite smile on her face and stood, stepping towards the sports teacher. "Sheila isn't back yet." She pushed her shaking hands behind her back and faked confidence.

"Oh." Carter's gaze slid towards Caroline. "I wanted to see Caro."

Hana backed away, edging to her chair by degrees. "That's fine," she said, her eyes sliding to Caroline's face. Anger lit a fire in the other woman's cheeks, producing high spots of colour.

"Not here!" she snapped. She shot a spiteful glance at Hana and left the room, Chris Carter trailing her like an obedient puppy.

The tension left with them. Hana pressed her forehead to her desk and looked up when her computer squeaked in protest. A line of unintelligible typing punctuated her letter to a university and she rubbed the outline of the keyboard from her forehead and deleted the nonsensical sentence. "What are you up to, Ms Marsh?" she commented out loud. "Because that guy's the school Lothario."

When Caroline returned, she remained quiet, leaving Hana alone to catch up on the work she ruined. Hana's fingers flew over the keyboard as she liaised with social services for one of the guidance counsellors. A livid stench seeped through the closed office door from the common room, making Hana feel sick. It smelled like a mixture of diarrhoea and drains. Caroline covered her mouth with her hand and exited through the door to the lobby.

Hana sighed and poked her head into the common room. Boys hung out of the large windows gagging, pinching their noses and covering their mouths. The Year 12 dean turned towards Hana. "What's that smell?" she asked.

"What smell?" He blew his red nose into a tissue. "I've a stinking cold. I can't smell anything."

Hana covered her nose with her hand. "The boys are dying." She looked around the room at the students gasping for air. "How could you not notice?"

"Don't look at me! I didn't make the smell." He acted affronted and looked around him, noticing the expiring students. "Oh. Is it that bad?"

"Okay, who dropped the stink bomb?" Hana demanded. Instead of schoolboy laughter, blank stares met her, accompanied by the occasional retch. Hana and the dean trawled around the room looking for evidence of a stink bomb or a dead body. Nothing. Hana sniffed her way around and the dean tried to help, but spent more time blowing his nose.

A clap of thunder silenced the room and Hana jumped and grabbed her colleague's arm. "What was that?" she demanded.

A large boy from the back row stood, raising his hand in the air. "Please sir, can I go to the bathroom?"

The dean nodded and they watched as the boy grabbed the back of his shorts with both hands. He set off at a fair speed for such a large chap. As he barged through the double doors and hit the staircase sprinting, he wailed, "Oh no, not again!"

Hana pointed towards his retreating back. "Can someone check on him, please?" Usually so eager to get out of the study class on a pretext, none of the boys volunteered.

"I'll go," the dean said with a sigh, grabbing a stack of tissues. When he didn't return, Hana collected his belongings and put them on the table in the student centre.

Caroline Marsh ventured back into the office before home time, holding her hand across her mouth. The stink remained but Hana got used to it after the first hour. Caroline wrinkled her nose in disgust. Peter North appeared at a run and fumbled around in the crap on his desk. He snatched up his Rubik's Cube and turned to leave. The smell hit him like a slap around the face and he spoke to Caroline. "You should see a doctor for that! You're starting to stink on the outside like you do on the inside," he snapped. "Oh." He pressed an index finger into her face. "Logan loves Hana, so get over it." He winked at Hana and spun the lines on his cube. She'd never felt so grateful to the funny little man.

Hana sat in her office after everyone left and waited for Angus. She heaved a sigh of relief at the sight of him in the doorway just after three thirty. "You're leaving early because of me, aren't you?" she said, guilt in her voice.

Angus raised an eyebrow. "Does it matter, Hana?"

She shrugged and picked up her handbag, locking the office door behind her.

"What's that smell?" Angus asked in the common room, puckering up his Scots nose in disgust.

"A bad biryani apparently," she replied.

Angus drove her to his apartment and opened his garage, handing her the keys to her car. "We moved it earlier today," he said, watching her with interest. "Your friend Cilla had quite a lot to say on the subject of our Mr Du Rose. If you're having a relationship with him, Hana, there's only so much I can do to protect you."

Hana nodded. "Don't worry about it, Angus. It'll all be over soon."

She drove through Ngaruawahia and turned right onto Hakarimata Road, feeling the tension melt away with her proximity to the bush. High on the mountain ahead of her stood a wooden cross, painted white and lit up as evening approached. The Christian youth camp nearby owned and maintained it and the glow reflected off the surrounding bush like a beacon. It called Hana home. No other vehicles showed in her rear view mirror and she turned into her driveway feeling relieved at her paranoia.

She forgot about the new gates until she almost ran over the electrician. Hana screeched to a halt and jumped out, leaving the engine running. "I'm so sorry," she gushed as the man brushed dirt from his trousers. "I forgot you'd be here."

"That's okay," the man grunted, waving across the gate installer. "I ran the cable down the side of the road, but I'll need access to the house." Hana nodded and peered into the gloom, seeing many faces turned towards her.

"How many people worked here today?" she asked, watching a man with a shovel fill in a deep trench alongside the driveway.

"The boss put everyone on this job," the installer said, waving an arm at his crew. "Mr Johal explained you needed it fast. An install like this usually takes two guys three days. So he sent seven of us." The man smiled, his face and hands dirty from digging. "And he charged extra."

"Just inside the house to do now," another man said, sidling up in a cowboy hat and overalls. "We need to run the cable through the roof space and install your intercom." He slapped the electrician on the back. "Josh wired the power into the same source as your water pump."

"Water pump?" Hana's brow knitted. "I have a water pump?"

The electrician smiled and turned away while the gate installer tried to explain. "Yeah, miss. It's the pump which sends the water from your rainwater tank to the house."

Hana nodded and colour rushed to her cheeks. "That water pump," she said, embarrassment making her throat tight. "I know what you mean. It's amazing. You've done a fantastic job." She stepped sideways and focussed on the gate being slotted into its runner.

"Glad you like it." The other men went back to their tasks and the installer stood next to her. "See how the driveway is cut into the rock here?" He pointed to the steep sides of her driveway. The first part of the slope looked like a tunnel, passing through a high-sided mountain populated by dense bush. "This protects you from anyone bypassing the gate." His finger indicated the runner as two men heaved the gate into place. "The road workers blasted the front into a sheer side years ago when they created the main road, so it's ideal for running the gate across it. The only time you'll have a problem is if there's a landslide. Your gate won't be able to open across it then." He grinned at her. "You'll have a great excuse not to go to work."

Hana nodded and watched the heavy metal gate slide left across the front of the orange rock face and then back to cover the aperture. Four men on the driveway tipped soil back into the trench. "How far down did you dig the cable?" she asked. "In case I need to dig there."

The man snorted. "A metre away from the edge of the drive and another metre down," he said. "You won't hit that by accident."

"Okay." Hana inhaled and felt her sense of safety return. "I love the navy blue," she said, peering into the gloom. "What do you need from me?" She pointed to the runner. "Is that okay to drive over?"

"Yep, for sure." The installer called to the electrician and waved him across. "Let's get the wiring finished and then we can tidy up tomorrow."

Hana gave them a ride up the long hill and brewed tea and coffee for them. The electrician disappeared into the roof through a hatch above the garage stairs and they heard him crashing around on the joists. "Did my lad walk up yet?" he shouted, his voice muffled.

The installer walked beneath the hatch and called up to him. "He's on his way. Want me to spot for you?"

"Yeah?" Hana heard him cough on her abundance of fibreglass insulation and winced. "Ask the lady where she wants the control panel and I'll drop the cable down that wall.

Hana chose a location next to the front door, adjacent to the burglar alarm panel. "It will look like mission control," she joked, but nobody laughed.

"That was easy," the electrician said later, dusting pink fibres from his clothing onto the porch. "I followed the cables from the security alarm. Job done. And thanks for the bacon butties, miss. We don't usually get those."

The other men mumbled over their sandwiches and waved crusts of bread in appreciation. They huddled on the porch as a group and drank tea as night descended.

"So, I can use it already?" Hana asked and the head installer nodded.

"Yup. Ready to go. I'll pop back in a week's time to check it over and make sure it's still sitting straight. They sometimes need adjusting in the first few days." He opened a box and pulled out two remote controls, covered in plastic wrapping. He handed one to Hana. "This remote will open, shut, half open and lock open. You'll get used to the functions and I'll leave a manual. There will also be a number programmed into the keypad and if you write it down for me, I'll get Wally to walk and put that in. If someone opens the gate from outside and drives through, the keypad up here will sound a single beep as it opens. They need either a remote, or the keypad number to get in. Otherwise, they press the button on the intercom and an alarm sounds in the house. They don't know it's a camera and will take a photo of them, so if they're up to no good, you've got their picture."

Hana scribbled a four-digit code on a scrap of paper and gave it to him. It changed hands twice before finding the right person to carry out the task. A slender man with curly red hair set off down to the road. Ten minutes later, Hana jumped as the intercom buzzed in the hall. "Action stations, Phil," one of the younger men said to the installer.

He bounced into the house, wiping his feet on the doormat and pressed a button. Hana's jaw dropped at the sight of Wally peering into the screen, his red hair back lit by passing cars. "Right, miss. This is what you do," Phil said, tugging on Hana's arm in his excitement. He pressed an icon with a face on it. "Ask who they are and what do they want?"

Hana leaned forward until her lips almost touched the speaker indents. Wally's face pixelated in front of her eyes. "Er, who are you?" she stuttered, feeling a fool. "And what do you want?"

"It's me, Wally," the man replied, looking hurt. "I'm with the guys who installed your gate."

A peal of raucous laughter issued from the porch. Phil stared at Hana in disbelief. "I didn't mean him," he said, smirking. "You ask other people that. We know that's Wally, don't we?"

"Yes." Hana nodded and bit the inside of her mouth. Phil pointed to an icon of a key.

"Press that and Wally can come back in." Hana pressed the button and stifled a giggle. Phil's phone rang and he turned away to answer it. "Okay, Wally. Wait until it closes and then test the new code on the keypad." Hana watched as the two men enjoyed a phone conversation made up entirely of half words and grunts. Thirty seconds later, the keypad buzzed again. Like a game show contestant, Hana slammed her index finger over the face icon and Phil stared at her again.

"But Wally can let himself in," he said, looking perplexed. "He's got the code remember?"

Hana nodded like a naughty schoolgirl and swallowed the rising fit of giggles. The camera showed her empty driveway and the sound of Wally puffing up the hill. "How long does the gate remain open?" she asked, thinking of someone attempting to follow her through.

"I've set it to thirty seconds," Phil said. "But you can park on either side and close it using the remote once you're through." He smiled. "It's a great system. You'll love it."

The men left after dark and Hana watched them exit through the camera, pressing the unlock button and seeing their utes pull onto the main road one by one. She heard the click as the gate closed and the camera shuddered. Phil's parting instruction resounded in her brain. "Don't panic if it's flaky in an electrical storm. Some of them can be quite magnetic and they frig a lot of stuff up. But the gate won't open by itself, okay? Call us if you have any problems."

"Magnetic." Hana murmured the word to herself as she watched the darkening bush through the kitchen window. "Why does that remind me of something?" The memory evaded her, hammering a warning but not revealing the source. She realised she knew something crucial, but couldn't dislodge the piece which made it so.

Hana heated soup she found in the pantry but wasted it, realising too late she wasn't hungry. She felt tired and as the house settled around her, loneliness chewed at her bones. She watched Tiger as he poked around in his water bowl, trying to retrieve a feather that found its way there. Bored, she wandered into her bedroom. Stepping through the doorway, the difference in the room struck Hana. She clapped her hands at the sight of the crisp paintwork. Dressing in the early morning darkness, she failed to appreciate the prettiness of the cream walls and the cleanliness of the freshly painted ceiling. The roughness of the grey plaster walls either end of the bed offered a stark contrast. Hana sighed with contentment as she sat on the bed to remove her tights and blouse. A sense of transformation in her house and life vied with the loneliness. In comfortable clothes with thick woolly socks on her feet, she peeked into the bag of wallpaper and removed a roll. "This will look amazing," she mused to herself, holding it up against the cream paint. "You've got similar taste to me, Du Rose."

Hana found the wallpapering equipment Logan left in the garage next to the new wheelie bins. She carried it upstairs and laid it out on the floorboards of her bedroom. Then she sat down cross-legged in front of it. Her last wallpapering attempt didn't go so well and she stroked the silken pages with anxious fingers.

Hana remembered using their pine dining table in England to paste the back of the paper, starting full of enthusiasm. She'd balanced on the table fixing soggy paper to the walls and taught three-year-old Izzie to read and write at the same time. But Vik's criticism stung later, as his brown finger pressed on a particularly bad crease. "This looks ridiculous!" he spat, tiredness and travel making him cruel. Hana remembered her tears and the resentment she felt at his continual, neglectful absence.

She sighed. "Logan isn't like Vik," she said aloud. "And anyway, this is my house."

Grabbing a tarpaulin from the garage, Hana laid it as flat as she could over the kitchen table and went back for the ladders. No small Izzie stuck wonky alphabet letters onto the tarp, but Hana measured, cut, pasted and stuck the first sheets of wallpaper in her new home. She surprised herself with how much she enjoyed it, working her way across the easiest wall first. "Paper towards the window," she whispered, focussing on Vik's other criticism. "Then the joins don't cause shadows." Hana sighed and stood back to admire her work, wondering why her late husband's cruellest words still lingered in her heart, burying the kind moments under resentment and sadness.

She used up three of the five rolls and made it half way across the second wall when her ringing phone made her jump. Hana looked at the screen, seeing Logan's name flashing. "Hi." Her voice sounded breathless.

"Your gate looks great," he said, the sound of his motorbike rumbling in the background. "Please can you let me in?"

She walked to the hall and pressed the remote on the wall, watching through the road-facing camera to make sure nobody followed him up. The view wobbled as the gate clattered closed against its metal fixings. By the time Logan's headlight bounced up the incline, Hana had washed her hands and waited for him. The bike's engine strained up the hill as he kept it in low gear. Hana waved from the porch and Logan pulled off his helmet and waved back. He seemed intimidating in his bike gear and his movements looked slow and careful as he put the heavy machine on its stand. His body language oozed tiredness. Logan unzipped his jacket and stuffed his gloves into the pannier. He squeezed the bike keys into his tight jeans pocket and picked up the helmet, taking the porch steps two at a time.

"Hey," he said, breathing in her scent at the top of the stairs. "I missed you." He sighed and held onto her.

"I've done something," Hana whispered. Her smile faded. "But you might think it's crap."

Logan squeezed her shoulder. "Why would I think that?" He kissed her temple. "Show me." He held her hand all the way to the bedroom where he stared around without a single word of criticism. "What an amazing job," he said. "You're a woman of many talents."

"Thank goodness!" Hana gushed. "I thought you'd find all the bits I did wrong."

"Na." Logan shook his head. "I'm a perfectionist, but only over the things I do myself." He looked around and sighed. "I'm told I'm a real pain to live with."

"Who by?" Hana needed to ask but dreaded the answer.

Logan's eyes crinkled at the corners. "My mother. She hates it."

Hana licked her lips. "Want me to make you some food?" She ran her thumb over the back of his hand, hearing his leather jacket crinkle as she moved the sleeve.

"No, thanks. I can stay and help for a while if you want."

"I'd love it." Hana reached up and kissed him, gratified when he caught the back of her head and pressed her closer. His lips felt cold against hers.

Logan removed his jacket and helped with the last few sheets. "Are you okay about Friday?" he asked, handing her the brush to push out the air bubbles.

"Yeah." Hana stared down from her position on the ladder. "Are you?"

"Course." His brow narrowed. "I'm making sure you'll turn up."

Hana laughed. "Trust me," she said, winking and copying his catch phrase. He made her squeak, brushing a sticky strand of hair away from her face and then lifting her into his arms. He lowered her to the ground but kept hold of her, looking into her eyes with such seriousness she felt her heart give a skip of fear.

"Can you put Tiger into the cattery for a couple of nights after the wedding?" he asked.

Hana looked at the old cat. He perched in the centre of her bed with all four paws beneath him. He watched their decorating activities through slitted eyes. She pulled a face. "Only if you put him in the-you-know-what."

Displaying his sixth sense for trouble, Tiger thudded onto the wooden floor and left the room. Logan's shoulders slumped. "Yeah, maybe not."

"Why?"

"Just a thought." He kissed Hana's nose and refused to discuss it. "No, don't ask questions." He grunted as she tickled his ribs and ran away from her. Hana followed him to the garage and pestered him as he collected the paint for the ceiling. He raised the brush in her face. "Askers don't get," he warned her, laughter in his eyes.

The bedroom looked stunning when at ten o'clock, Logan finished putting the last coat of paint on the ceiling. The room glowed with the exquisite colours and the house felt alive. Hana got excited about the four-poster bed with its voile swags and side tables. "What time's it coming?" she asked for the third time and Logan smiled.

"Four o'clock on Thursday, same as last time you asked."

"Oh. Sorry." Hana screwed her face up and looked apologetic. "Will we have time to put it all together? It might take hours. My old bed can go into the double spare room."

"Good idea," Logan said, his back to her as he cleaned excess paint off his brush. He forced himself to shake off the image of the dark-skinned man on the tube train. His jaw worked as he gritted his teeth, remembering how Hana reached for the long, brown fingers in her distress and Vik ignored her. He'd stared through the train window, dabbing his bleeding lip with a tissue and leaving Hana's needs untended. Logan balled his fists and fought the urge to smash the double bed into pieces with his bare hands and use it for firewood. Hana's sigh startled him from his morbid thoughts. "What's wrong?" he asked.

She shook her head. "You didn't answer my question, but it doesn't matter. When you look distracted like that, I panic inside. I imagine you've changed your mind."

"Not gonna happen." Logan hauled her sideways and crushed her into his ribs. "You over think everything, Hana. It's part of learning to trust someone."

"I know." Hana rested her chin against his chest. "It's difficult. I've been alone for a long time and my only forays into relationships didn't go well."

Logan pushed her back by her upper arms and stared at her, his grey eyes hard. "Why am I only hearing about other guys now?"

Hana snorted. "No other significant guys. Don't go macho on me." She rolled her eyes. "No ex fiancés anyhow."

Logan hissed in an exaggerated breath and feigned shock. "That's harsh, wahine. Below the belt. I need to sort you out." He dragged her closer and jabbed his fingers into her ribs, tickling until she squealed. The play fight turned into something steamy, sparked by a stray kiss. "You need to stop teasing me," Logan grumbled, looking uncomfortable. Hana taunted him with a seductive nip on his bottom lip. He groaned. "You're gonna be in such trouble on Friday night."

Hana pursed her lips. "I can't remember what to do," she confessed. "I might need a diagram."

"Shut up and get the dirty brushes together," Logan ordered, wincing against the strain of keeping his promise. "Stop talking about you-know-what."

Hana followed him to the kitchen, waiting until he immersed his hands in the sticky water. She grabbed the hem of his tee shirt and raised it, biting the skin above his waist. The awful scar met her, filling her vision with a wound which must have half killed him once. Hana paused and resumed her teasing, dragging her lips over his ribs. Logan moaned and diffused his frustration by rubbing sticky fingers through Hana's hair. She shrieked in dismay. "That's mean," she cried, pouting and feeling her wet curls. The sight of the desperation in his eyes made her sorry.

"Stop taunting me," Logan threatened, his eyes closed. "You're making it worse." He peeked from beneath his lashes and caught her easy smirk. "You're doing it on purpose!" he said, shock in his voice. He reached for the zipper of his jeans. "Wanna see what you did?"

"No!" Hana screeched and fled from the room. She locked herself in the bathroom.

"That won't help you," he jibed from the hallway. "There aren't many locks I can't pick, especially stupid ones like this."

"Whatever!" Hana giggled from her seat on the side of the bath.

She emerged to say goodbye to Logan, their kiss charged with desire and longing as he straddled his bike. "Not much longer now," he soothed, seeing fear settle in her eyes.

"I've heard it's like riding a bike," she replied, running a finger over the handlebars.

Logan snorted. "Sex again, Ms McIntyre? I meant until I'm here looking after you every night."

"Oh." Embarrassment flickered across Hana's face and she giggled. "Why can't you stay? Nobody will know."

Logan shook his head. "Can't babe, sorry. Things to do, people to see." He winked at her and pulled his helmet over his head. Hana stepped back as the bike surged and watched him control the powerful machine. He waved at the first bend and Hana sighed, wrapping her arms around herself in the eerie darkness. She heard the revs change as he hit the steep downhill and climbed the porch to press the gate release. Red tail-lights filled the camera aperture as Logan cleared the gate and Hana watched as he turned left instead of right.

"Funny," she said aloud, wondering why he'd drive to Huntly first. Figuring he'd take the minor arterial road east, she locked the front door and thought no more of it.

The week crawled by for Hana in a haze of disgustingly early mornings. She arrived at Angus' unit before seven and listened to the international cricket scores on his car radio, neither awake nor interested. Some nights she worked in the office until he left at six o'clock, trying to remain grateful for the lengths he went to in taking responsibility for her transport arrangements. Logan spent the evenings with her, leaving the lounge often to take hushed phone calls which he told her not to worry about.

Wednesday's highlight proved to be Peter North, who caused an unintentional stir. Sconned by a cricket ball to the face, he lost consciousness and threw up in front of a Year 9 class. He woke to the sound of an ambulance and blood streaming into his eyes. Dobbs fetched him from the hospital and dumped him in the student centre. "The moral of the story is this," he shouted, not caring when Pete shoved his fingers into his hairy ear holes. "Don't listen to your iPod whilst standing in the cricket nets, especially whilst supervising Year 9s!"

Dobbs left and Pete sank his head onto his forearms, remembering his wound at the last minute. "The ball didn't give me a headache," he grumbled, his bottom lip drooping. "He did. For two bloody hours he's said the same thing over and over again." He sighed. "Never let him take you to the emergency room. It's not worth it."

Hana made sympathetic noises and turned to answer the ringing phone. "Oh, hello Henrietta," she said. Pete snatched the handset from her before she could say anything else.

"I'm hurt!" he wailed. "It's terrible. Oh, you heard? You are? That's wonderful." His expression perked up and he blew a soggy kiss onto Hana's phone before handing it back.

"Gee, thanks." She reached into her drawer for a wet-wipe.

A knock on the door heralded a small boy with a guilty look on his face. His bottom lip wobbled and he pointed to Pete. "Mr Dobbs said you'd punish me," he muttered and heaved in a breath. "I batted the ball which hit you in the face."

"Oh, that." Pete swung on his chair and waved his arm in dismissal. "It's nothing." The bandage across his forehead slid down over his eyes and he pushed it back up with a dirty finger.

The child edged closer. "Mr Dobbs said to expect a very long detention." His fingers twisted in front of his striped blazer and Hana cocked her head in sympathy.

"The sort you might need to invite your wife and children to?" she asked and the child nodded.

"About that long, yeah."

Hana looked at Pete, astonished by his good humour. She watched as he dragged a chocolate bar from his top drawer and examined it. Fluff covered the wrapper and aged the label stuck to it with tape. Hana read the words upside down and glared at him. Pete dangled the bar in his fingers, testing its floppiness. "I was saving this," he said with reluctance. "But you can have it." He turned and waved it at the boy who took a step backwards. "Have it," Pete said. "To show there's no hard feelings."

The child took the chocolate bar and read the label. "But it says, 'Happy birthday Hana,'" he whimpered.

"So it does," Hana commented through gritted teeth. "But is it happy birthday last year or the year before?" Her voice sounded acerbic and the child held out the bar.

"Take it and run," Hana suggested, glaring at Pete.

The boy fled and before she could berate Peter North, he turned to her with excitement in his eyes. "Henri's coming home to look after me," he said, standing and jumping on the spot. His bandage cascaded into his eyes and he walked into his swivelling chair like a blind man. He pushed the swathes of cloth from his milky eyelashes and grinned at Hana. "Do you think this is bad enough for sex?" he demanded, jabbing a spindly finger at his forehead.

Hana ignored him, her green eyes flashing. "How many, Pete?" she demanded. "How many years?"

He shrugged and refused to look her in the eyes. "A few," he said, sounding sulky.

"Sheila's too? And Rory's?"

He winced and stared at the ceiling, chewing on his bottom lip. "I can't remember," he said, flaring his nostrils.

Hana snorted with disdain. "You're disgusting, Peter North! All these years we thought nobody gave a stuff about the student centre staff. Oh, my goodness!" she exploded. "You ate the guidance counsellors' chocolate too, didn't you?"

"I don't feel well," Pete complained, a globule of blood dangling from the end of his nose. His bloodshot eyes blackened underneath as Hana watched.

"I've no sympathy for you," she snapped. She pointed to the box of tissues on his desk. "Use one of those."

Caroline's dramatic entrance saved him from further admonishment, flouncing into the room like a leggy princess. A Year 13 boy followed her, tears in his eyes and an illegal ponytail in his hand. A bobby pin stuck to the end and revealed his attempts to keep it hidden before somebody snipped it off. Pete ignored them both and attempted to patch up his rocky relationship with Hana using small talk, whispering so Caroline couldn't hear. "Hana, Hana, I want to tell you something funny." He leaned closer and Hana stiffened. "Henrietta washed one of her dresses with our stuff and when she hung it on the line to dry, she discovered four of Boris's odd socks and a tee-shirt of Logan's sticking out of the sleeves." He rubbed his eye and winced. "Oh, and a pair of my undies."

Hana made gagging noises in her throat and Pete leaned closer. "Hana, Hana, I'm bleeding."

She gasped as blood poured from Pete's nose. "Don't panic," she told him. "Lean forward over your dustbin and I'll call the nurse." Hana grappled for the phone but changed direction to stuff a whole box of tissues under his nose.

Caroline stopped speaking and leaned sideways to watch. The Year 13 stood up in horror and then sat down again, his skinny rat's tail wiggling in his fingers. "Do something!" Hana barked at Caroline and the blonde woman shrugged.

"Like what?"

"Like call the nurse!" Hana spat.

Something in Caroline's eyes made her afraid. "I thought you'd be used to that by now." Her smirk made Hana's stomach churn and she mistook it as a reference to Vik's death. She opened her mouth with a retort but Pete's dead faint onto the carpet took her by surprise and knocked her flying. The Year 13 ran for help, still clutching his ponytail and Caroline turned back to her desk.

Pete woke up and stopped Hana dialling another ambulance. "It's doppin' dow," he muttered through a swathe of tissues.

"Pardon?" Hana squeaked.

Pete pulled the tissue box away to show the blood reduced to a trickle. "I ded it doppin' dow."

Hana rubbed his back. "It looks like it's stopping now," she said. The Year 13 reappeared looking green and ill.

"Nobody's on reception and I can't find the nurse," he announced.

"I dink I deed dodo dome," Pete said and smiled up at Hana. Blood speckled his teeth. "Dendietta's dumin dome. An de dess das dink. It dooked dike a derson."

"Pardon?"

"Oh, for goodness' sake!" Caroline slapped the desk with her open hand and the student fled into the common room. "You really are a stupid bimbo, aren't you? Logan won't stay with someone like you, not in a million years and if you can't stand the sight of blood, you won't survive long around the Du Rose boys." She gathered up her files and paper, pulling her skirt into place with a sexy wiggle. "And what the dumbass is saying is, 'the dress was pink! And it looked like a person.' Although who loses that much blood and still wants to talk about his fat girlfriend's tent dresses? Losers, the lot of you." Caroline left the room in a huff of perfume and temper.

Hana bit her lip and looked down at Pete. His face turned up towards hers like a broken puppy caught crapping on the carpet. "It's okay," Hana patted him on his wispy hair. "You're not a dumbass or a loser."

"Do ar."

"Hey?"

"I du dunass an du de dooser."

Hana peered at Pete as his meaning sank in. Her lips parted with indignation. "Charming! I am not a loser. Sort yourself out now!" Hana pushed his face into another box of tissues and he stepped across the room like an automaton. "Find the nurse!" Hana shouted as he walked into the doorframe. "And mind that."

Hana slumped into her chair and put her face in her hands. An image of Henrietta's dress fluttering in the breeze occupied her inner vision and she tried to see the funny side. Then she sat up straight, her hand over her mouth. "Oh, no!" she gasped. "What should I wear on Friday?" She ran through a list of possibilities, dismissing them all as too old, too prim, not wedding enough or just not gonna happen.

Hana panicked. She looked at her watch and then remembered her car sitting in Angus' garage. By the time she got to it, the shops would have shut. "I can't wear jeans to my own wedding," she groaned, laying her head on her forearms. The idea came and went numerous times before Hana acted. In her defence, she felt she had no choice.

'HELP ME,' said her text to Anka's number. No reply came and Hana let relief and sadness flood her emotions as a dirty, confusing mix. Anka had ignored all previous messages and Hana stuffed her phone into her desk and continued with her work.

"Wots wrong?" Hana's hands shook as she read the reply twenty minutes later.

Typing and then deleting the answer over and over, Hana realised the terrible error in her haste. If Anka told Tama about the wedding, he'd enjoy leaking it to Logan's parents. "Don't answer," Hana told herself, twirling her phone on the desk. It spun in a circle and vibrated again. 'Hana? Are you okay?'

Hana swallowed, knowing in her heart Anka still cared for her. They'd been friends for years, sisters in the church, confidants in times of hardship. Hana ached for that genuine female closeness they'd shared. Against her better judgment, she picked up the phone. 'Going to a wedding. I'm desperate for your help.'

Anka would ignore her. It wasn't an emergency and not serious enough to patch up their friendship over. Hana shoved her phone in the drawer, not expecting a reply. She'd wear an old dress. Logan wouldn't mind.

The message came before the final bell. '12 Brook Street,' it said. 'It's not far. I'll be home by the time you get there.'

Hana savoured a response she hadn't expected. She got directions from the internet, realising Anka didn't know she'd need to walk. It looked a few kilometres away. Her heart skipped in her chest with excitement and she reached for the phone, dialling Angus' assistant. "Hi," she said. "Please can you tell Angus I'm nipping out of school, but I'll be back before he leaves at six?"

"He's in a meeting!" the woman snapped. The line went dead.

Hana exhaled in exasperation. "Horrid woman!" she grumbled. She texted Logan to tell him she needed to grab a dress for Friday, but she'd go home with Angus as usual. She caught sight of Anka's message as she closed her phone. Her heart quickened and excitement bubbled in her chest. The slam of the office door at the same time as the final bell, made her jump and the phone skittered across the carpet.

Caroline smirked and pushed her perfect bum into her chair. The sideways glance she sent in Hana's direction made her flesh creep. Caroline pulled a lipstick and small mirror from her handbag and leaned back. "Logan's such a great kisser," she said, her tone sultry. She ran the lipstick over her lips, the inference clear.

Hana turned away, refusing to doubt Logan because of a tissue of lies. Her shoulders straightened. "Ah well," she replied, barb in her voice. "Pity you wasted your opportunity." She snatched her phone from the carpet, ignoring the rattling sound it made. She shoved it in her bag and pulled her coat over her arm. "Waking up next to Logan Du Rose is dynamite."

Hana slammed the door behind her and steadied her nerves before descending the thin staircase to ground level. Boys flanked her on every side and her battered phone gave up its sim card, depositing it quietly in the bottom of her handbag. Logan's multiple frantic calls went into the ether.

Chapter 49

Hana clumped over the soft soil of the playing fields, her boot heels sticking in the mud. Boys milled around and she listened to their entertaining conversations. Their height and bulk sheltered her, offering a false sense of safety and Hana forgot everything apart from the excitement of seeing Anka. Some boys walked alone, heads down as they ran through their own thoughts in glorious oblivion. Others jostled and chatted in tight, insular groups. At the end of the field, Hana hesitated, following the flood of boys into a narrow lane. It terminated on a wide street and they turned left and right, dispersing to nearby streets with cheerful waves and cocky retorts to each other. Unsure, Hana halted and the throng carried her forwards, trapping her amidst a group which turned right.

"Excuse me." Hana tapped the arm of a boy she recognised and he stopped in front of her, his friends hovering nearby. "I wanted Brook Road." She frowned and reached for her handbag zip. "Maybe it's Brook Street."

"Ah yeah." The boy nodded. He waved his arm in an obtuse arc. "You follow that road to the end and then turn left." He looked down at her shoes. "It's quite far, miss. You gonna be okay?"

"Yes, thank you." Hana gave him a wobbly smile and followed the direction of his wave, pulling her long coat tighter against the stiff wind.

She set off walking and kept going, recognising road names from her internet search. An older part of town she didn't know passed by, daylight abandoning her to the fate of intermittent streetlamps. With darkness came an increasing sense of unease and Hana clattered along, her heels clicking against the pavement. The sign for Brook Street loomed in the distance and Hana picked up her pace, trying not to slip on the wet ground as she broke into a run. "Stop, stop," she urged herself, seeing a driver slow down to stare at her. "Don't draw attention to yourself." All sense of bravado abandoned her as she thought of the men hunting her and realised how stupid she'd been.

The entrance to Brook Street couldn't come soon enough. Hana made the turn and left the main road behind, the dark street eerie with its flickering lamps and shadowy lawns. Number twelve identified itself as a rental property, the weed patch in the front garden long and unkempt. The door longed for treatment, the paint peeling away from the edges. Hana pressed the doorbell with a shaking finger and heard nothing.

She gave up and clattered down the path towards the road, feeling foolish. The lights of a car blinded her and Hana jumped back as the vehicle spun onto the cracked driveway. The engine died with an unhealthy splutter and Anka slipped from the vehicle. She gave Hana a quick glance and waved her hand at the car. "Ivan kept the Beema," she spat.

Hana stared at the old Toyota and gave an ineffectual nod. Her eyes roved over Anka's body, noticing the considerable weight loss covered by the slick skirt and jacket. She glided up the front steps as though the rickety boards didn't need attention, her high heels digging into the rotten wood. Anka offered no other greeting, shoving her key into the lock and pushing the door open with a great creak. Hana watched from the driveway as Anka flicked a switch, flooding the tatty interior with light. She stuck her head outside and jerked it in Hana's direction. "Are you coming in, or what?"

Hana took a deep breath and followed, avoiding the gaping hole in the porch steps. Once inside she bent to undo the zip on her boots. Anka stopped her with a hand on her sleeve. "Leave them on or you'll freeze." Hana stood and followed her down a long hallway, finding herself in a small kitchen. Anka rested her bum against a cupboard. "Would you like a drink?"

Hana's fraught nerves flooded with relief. She nodded. "Do you have tea?"

An hour later, they sat at the dining table in some semblance of friendship. Hana explained everything about her recent excitement in a spirit of honesty and Anka listened. "I don't know what the men want," Hana concluded. She turned her palm over and showed her the healing wound. "Seven stitches says it's something major."

Anka sighed with tiredness, rubbing her eyes with her hand and smudging her makeup. "I'm sorry I abandoned you." She lowered her gaze to the untouched biscuits on the plate between them and tears made her eyes sparkle.

"How are you managing?" Hana asked, reaching for her hand. "I can get some money together if you need it. You know I don't mind."

"I know." Anka squeezed her fingers. "It's not the money. I got work at an osteopath's office." She sniffed and worked hard to change the subject. "I'm enjoying the job. It's less stressful than school. So, whose wedding are you going to?"

Hana looked at the men's socks hanging on the airer by the back door and faltered. "You live with Tama?" she asked and Anka's eyes hardened.

"Does it matter?"

"It might." Hana swallowed. "If I'm marrying Logan."

Anka leaned forward, her eyes wide with amazement. "What? Why?"

Despite herself, Hana laughed. "Because I love him," she spluttered. "Why else?" Worry shrouded her happiness. "But please don't give the game away. You'll hurt me more than you can imagine."

Anka nodded, the motion slow and deliberate. "Okay, Hana. I'll say nothing." Her smile looked strained and forced, but Hana had come too far not to believe her. "Let's find you a dress."

Hana spent the next hour in her bra and knickers, trying outfits one after the other. She became desperate, believing she might end up getting married to a hunk like Logan in her jeans and paint stained tee shirt. "He'll think I didn't bother!" she wailed, pulling off the last dress in response to a shake of Anka's head.

From the back of the wardrobe, Anka dug out a bottle green dress and held it up in front of her. "I never wore this," she confessed. "Something in the earthiness of the green against my skin made me look dirty, but with your striking auburn hair, I think this could be it." Anka held it out and Hana hesitated. "This is it, Hana. It's the only thing you haven't tried. I own nothing else."

Fitted and dainty, the dress comprised a swishy fabric which swayed when Hana moved. The layered material cast shadows of darker and lighter tones. Nipped in at the waist, it showed a lot of leg, but the long sleeves would keep out the autumnal chills outside the registry office. Anka broke open a new packet of sheer tights which offered a suntanned look and handed Hana two of the three pairs. Hana tried to hand one back, but Anka waved it away. "Take both in case of last minute ladders."

Around five o'clock, Anka's mood changed and she became increasingly distracted. Hana sensed the intimacy between them draw to a close. She collected the dress into a carrier bag and readied herself for leaving. "Is everything okay?" she asked Anka as her friend shoved her towards the front door.

"Fine," Anka snapped. "You should go now." She pushed Hana onto the front steps and something in her eyes made Hana alarmed.

"What's wrong?" she demanded and Anka shook her head.

"All the best for Friday," she said, her voice sounding strained. Hana hugged her, feeling bones beneath her embrace.

"If you need me, text," she called as Anka closed the door in her face.

Once in the street, the darkness shrouded Hana like a thick cloak. She didn't know this part of town and panicked. Guessing she shouldn't use the narrow lane and playing fields back to school, she readied herself for a long walk. Defeated, she set off towards the lights of the main road. An old scooter zipped past her and slowed. Hana stopped and watched it bounce over the curb and into Anka's driveway. Through the branches of a bare tree, Hana saw a side view of Tama as he hopped from the scooter and skipped up the porch steps. Despite the muscles and bravado, he looked like a child. A foolish, love-struck child. Hana felt sadness descend on her shoulders, a weight of responsibility for Tama, Anka and the snare they created for themselves. "Trapped," Hana whispered, holding her cold hands up to her mouth. The word clarified itself in condensation against the biting air. Anka had wandered into the oldest trap in the devil's book.

Hana caught a bus travelling anticlockwise on the Orbiter route and got off at the last stop she could. She walked for ten minutes before getting anywhere near the school. She looked at her watch and saw the time move past six o'clock, panicking that Angus might have left without her. Hana paused under a streetlight and poked around in her handbag, searching for her phone. She pulled it out with a sigh of relief and pressed the button to activate the screen. It lit up, but the functions refused to respond. "What do you mean, no service?" Hana groaned. "How can there be no service?" She looked around her for answers, finding nothing.

Deciding not to panic as an act of will, Hana kept walking along the rural road, focussing on the bright lights in the distance. They shone out onto Maui Street like a haze, highlighting the blackness enclosing the rest of the town. Traffic increased and she felt heartened to see vehicles buzzing in and out of the gates like bees returning to the hive. Her foolish expedition coincided with a community education night and Hana felt her mood of doom lift. The carrier bag containing the dress bounced against her coat and she convinced herself Angus would still be there.

Hana saw his empty parking slot from the gate and the heady sense of foreboding returned. She checked her own in case he'd parked there instead, but a car she didn't recognise occupied it. He didn't wait for her. Hana stopped on the pavement and watched the vehicles pass, knowing she used all her cash on the bus ride. She didn't have enough for a trip to Alder Dale. "Think, think!" she hissed, looking for a solution. Her fingers pushed into her handbag and closed around her office keys. Hana turned and walked towards the main building in the distance, stopping to allow traffic to pass before crossing the lane.

She became aware of the car before she saw it, evil hanging over it like a fog. It slid around the corner away from her, travelling with exaggerated slowness. The brake lights flicked on and off as the driver paused to watch people. Hana's breath stuttered into her lungs in panicked gasps and she misread the edge of the curb, almost falling under the wheels of another vehicle. "Sorry, sorry!" She waved her hand in apology and stepped back. The BMW slid around the turning circle and she saw the oriental features of the driver lit up in the reflected glow of oncoming headlights. Hana's fingers fumbled the wide hood of her coat up and over her head, masking her distinctive red hair. She forced herself to stare at the ground as the car passed by.

It drove past so slowly she held her breath, hearing her heart beat out a warning tattoo. At any moment, she expected the blond man to appear and drag her into the car. Hana squeezed her eyes shut against the memory of his flick knife, knowing he might just slit her throat instead. Distracted by a toddler wriggling from its mother's grasp and running into his path, the driver slammed on the brakes. Hana gasped, feeling relief flood through her as the woman hefted her child out of harm's way. "You must never do that!" the woman screeched, hysteria in her voice. Hana turned away from the spectacle and crossed the road behind the BMW, her legs feeling as though they belonged to someone else. The lights from the main building encouraged her on and she muffled the sound of her moans of fear with a firm hand over her mouth.

"Not far now," she promised herself, focussing on the front doors. "Just a little further." Fear blinded her, allowing her only one point of reference in her vision and Hana concentrated on putting one foot in front of the other and keeping the door handles in view. "Almost there," she whispered to herself.

Hana didn't dare look back. She kept walking against the flow as everyone else headed to classrooms on the periphery of the site. To help her stay calm, she recalled the list of various adult courses on offer and tried to pick her favourite, unable to choose between Italian for beginners and Chinese cooking. Everything in her wanted to run, but she stopped herself, knowing it would draw unwanted attention.

Hana fell against the front doors, finding as she grappled with the handles they wouldn't open. Her breath came in gasps as her panic ran out of control. She wrenched at the rigid door handle without success, knowing she didn't have a front door key. The firm grip on her right arm sent her into orbit. "No!" she cried.

Hana lashed out, startling Pete and catching him in the eye with her hand. He swore and opened his mouth to complain, halting as he saw distress reflected in her face. "What's wrong, Hana?" he asked, rubbing his eye and righting his wonky head bandage.

She couldn't speak. Her chest tightened and she hyperventilated on the steps. Pete glanced behind him and then back at Hana. "Stop, Hana. People are staring. They'll think I'm kidnapping you."

As she stumbled sideways, he grabbed her arm. "Come round here," he hissed, looking over her shoulder. "Do you want me to get Logan?"

The plastic bag containing the dress banged against Hana's leg and a sob escaped the boundary of her palm as it pressed against her mouth. "No," she gasped. "He'll hate me."

Pete guided Hana to a side entrance, shoving her up the steps and unlocking the door. Lit up like a Christmas tree, the corridor inside made her panic further, convinced the men would continue their search on foot. She ducked down beneath the level of the windows and Pete's eyes widened as he understood her anxiety. "They're here?" he demanded. "Those dudes are here?"

Hana nodded and squatted against the wall, hugging her makeshift wedding dress to her chest. The coat hood hid her face but the wracking sobs couldn't be mistaken for anything but misery and terror. Pete locked the outer door behind them and cast around for an escape.

"In here!" He used his master key on a single door between two classrooms and shoved his way into the room. Hana crawled across the floor, dragging her bags behind her. "They're out there," she cried, her sounds like those of a wounded animal. "They're here for me!"

Pete dragged her inside and closed the door. He activated his mobile phone as a torch and put his finger over his lips. "The light bulb hasn't worked for ages in here," he whispered. The pathetic light lit up his face from below like a ghoul and Hana focussed on something else to prevent her releasing the scream building in her throat. Gym equipment lined the walls and a basketball hung from a discarded soccer net. Hana pressed the plastic bag against her eyes and wished herself somewhere else. Another country. Another life.

Pete waited until the sounds of foot traffic and laughing voices outside died down. Then he made a phone call.

Angus refused to send Logan and arrived on his own, unlocking the cupboard and collecting a rumpled Hana from the floor. "Logan's at my place," he whispered in Hana's ear. "You're safe now."

"Oh." Pete looked disappointed. "I wanted Logan to see me do something good for Hana," he said, his lips turning downwards. "Where is he?"

Angus rolled his eyes. "Do you think Logan arriving like the cavalry would be the best idea, Pete? You don't suspect that might draw more attention to Hana's presence?"

Pete shrugged. "Maybe. But he's missed me being a hero now." He shoved his hands in his pockets and sloped into the corridor.

"No, he hasn't." Angus patted his shoulder and locked the cupboard behind them. "He knows how amazing you are and he's very grateful."

"Is he?" Pete grinned and touched the bandage on his head. "Will he let me take Henri out in his Triumph?"

Angus winced. "Perhaps not that grateful," he muttered under his breath. He flapped his hand at Pete. "Why are you still at school?"

Pete bounced on the balls of his feet. "Boris took my car home because the doctor said I can't drive. Henri's cancelled her flight to the south island. She's picking me up in a while. I think I might get lucky tonight."

"Och, how delightful," Angus replied, looking like he'd sucked a lemon. He led Hana towards the outer door. He leaned into her ear. "I wonder if the doctor's seen his driving, because he's right. He can't drive."

Hana swallowed, unable to summon up even a nod of agreement. Angus tried to take the bag from her hand and she yanked it away. "No!" she hissed, her tone threatening. "It's all about this, can't you see that?"

"About the bag?" Angus' eyes widened and he teased it from Hana's hand, peering inside even though she kept a tight hold of it. "The men want this green dress?" He raised a ginger eyebrow and Hana groaned in frustration. "Okay, let's get you home," he conceded, his eyes rounding with kindness. "Everything will be fine there."

Pete and Angus smuggled Hana out the side entrance. They scurried past lighted classrooms filled with adults learning skills they missed at school and paid hard currency for later. It seemed ironic. "I hid my car by the boarding house," Angus puffed as Pete acted as lookout. "The back gate is locked so nobody parks there." He deactivated his central locking and left Pete to put Hana in the car, bewildered when she catapulted in headfirst from Pete's hefty shove and almost landed in his lap. "Thanks, Mr North," he called, taking off so fast the passenger door closed itself.

The back gate rolled open as Angus' distinguished car reached it and he floored the gas, breaking the sound barrier on minor arterial roads. Hana closed her eyes against the sensation of sickness and Angus grinned like a moron all the way up the expressway. "I've wanted to do that for the last year," he said with a chuckle. "It's one thing to know what one can do and quite another to prove it."

Logan paced up and down outside Angus' tiny unit, wearing a rut in the front lawn. His face looked livid, his grey eyes wild and flashing. He thanked Angus with forced civility but bundled Hana into the Honda without speaking to her. She moved beyond her wild panic to a state of childlike anxiety. She sniffed into the hanky with kiwis round the fringe and clutched her wedding dress in a death grip. Her wrist ached and her palm felt sore, compounding her misery. She'd been stupid and Logan would dump her and call off the wedding.

He drove, slipping into Rototuna and north to Ngaruawahia via Horsham Downs and Lake Road. Hana pressed her face into the handkerchief and tried not to make audible crying sounds, noticing he picked up River Road much later than usual.

Logan clicked the remote as they pulled onto the driveway and the gate slid open with ease. Hana glanced at the post box but thought better of it as the car jumped up the gravel. Logan didn't wait for the delay, but pressed the remote again and the gate closed behind them. Once at the house, he locked Hana in the car and checked every room of the old villa.

Hana used the interlude to wipe the tears from her face and bravely await her spectacular dumping. Logan's anger preceded him like a swarm of bees as he ran down the steps towards the car. He offered her his hand and leaned in to pick up her bags. Locking the car behind him, he followed her up the steps into the house and closed the door with his foot. Hana heard the lock click shut.

Her boots looked filthy and caked with loose mud, the pointed toes scuffed and stained. A giggle burst from Hana's lips as hysteria bubbled near the surface. She clapped her hand over her mouth, wincing as the plastic bag hit her in the chin. "You're stuck here," she said, feeling a laugh work its way up her throat. "Will you dump me and walk home?" She snorted, the sound incongruous in the tension. "Sorry, sorry." She squeezed the bridge of her nose between finger and thumb and concentrated on the pain of the pinch to refocus her.

"You think this is funny?" Logan's jaw worked, creating lines in his cheek. Hana couldn't look at him. She noticed a hole in his sock, his big toe peeking through. Something about the sight caused her to reach breaking point and laughter burst from her lips.

It sounded hysterical even to her own ears, wrought from her body as though by an unseen hand which pulled it out on the end of a magician's thread. Logan's eyes flashed and he stomped to the kitchen where Hana heard him switch on the kettle to boil. Her laughter subsided, leaving behind an extreme emptiness and a wretched misery which turned to tears and dismay. Still clutching the bag, Hana slipped off her boots and kicked them aside. She padded to the bedroom and closed the door.

She exchanged her work clothes for the tatty monkey pyjamas, admiring the pretty wallpaper as she climbed into bed. The green dress spewed from the plastic bag, casting itself in green waves over the sheets. Hana snuggled into the safety of her bed and blocked out the world, letting the day's events run before her inner vision. "Everything's a big mess," she whispered.

Logan knocked on the door and Hana heard the clink of crockery. She didn't answer and he entered, anyway. "I brought you toast," he said, laying a plate on the bedside table. "I think I made your tea how you like it."

Hana smelled the toast and kept her eyes closed, feeling the mattress sag as Logan sat next to her. He said nothing else and Hana tensed. "If you want to dump me, just do it," she said, punctuating the sentence with a disgusting sniff.

"Oh, Hana!" Logan bent almost double, one hand resting on his thigh while the other covered his eyes. He looked tired and spent and Hana experienced a flash of guilt. She sat up and reached for him, her fingers fluttering over his biceps. "I'm sorry, I'm sorry, I'm sorry." The tears flowed and she didn't brush them away. "I realised I didn't have a dress for Friday. Riding with Angus every day meant no car and not enough time to buy one. My phone died and then Anka went weird. It took ages to get back to school and the men were already there, looking for me. I'm so sorry."

Logan sighed and wrapped his arms around her, pulling her close to his chest. "All this over a bloody dress?" he asked, disbelief in his tone. "That's crazy, Hana."

"No, it's important!" She sniffed again and he reached into his pocket for a handkerchief. "I can't turn up in jeans. You'll think I don't care." She wiped her eyes with the back of her hand and Logan shook his head, leaning forward to dab with the hanky.

"Keep still," he told her, his voice tender and his touch gentle. "Hana, I don't care if you turn up naked," he said, his grey eyes stormy.

"Yeah, you would!" Hana swallowed and he placed his index finger over her lips.

"I know, I know. Stretch marks." He cocked his head on one side. "You must learn to talk to me," he said, his tone soothing. "We're a team. I can't believe you sacrificed your security to borrow a dress. Angus said you met Anka."

Hana nodded. "She's living with Tama in a scruffy rental in the south of the city. It took ages to walk there and she threw me out before he arrived home." Hana reached for her tea. "She looked scared. You don't think he hits her, do you?"

Logan closed his eyes and shook his head. "No, babe. It's not his style." He climbed onto the bed and lay next to her. Hana put her tea back on the cabinet and laid her head on his chest. Logan sighed. "Why did you think I'd dump you?"

She shrugged. "I messed up and you gave me the silent treatment. It felt like a logical conclusion."

Logan's head scuffed the pillow. "That's ridiculous. Don't say it again. You scared me and I didn't know how to explain how it made me feel. Where I'm from, we never speak about our emotions."

"I'm sorry," Hana whispered and he turned to face her. His palm against her cheek felt warm and safe. Logan climbed beneath the bed sheets, keeping his clothes on. He held Hana in her monkey pyjamas, his kisses urgent and desperate. When he rolled on top of her, Hana almost came apart at the seams. His insistent fingers pushed beneath her pyjama top and strayed where they hadn't before. His tongue felt warm and sweet in her mouth and Hana gave in to the moment. Her heart slid into her stomach, causing a roller coaster ride of sensations. Her mind-voice screamed warnings and threats to her lust addled brain. Logan's work calloused fingers felt rough against the soft skin of Hana's hip as he slid them inside the waistband of her pyjamas and smoothed the skin over the jutting bone.

Her father's face swam before her, sneering and angry. "Slut!" he hissed. "You're no daughter of mine! How could you?"

Hana gasped as though drowning and fought for air. Logan's expert ministrations stopped and he rolled off and gathered her into his arms. "Sorry, sorry," he breathed into her hair. He kissed her face and forehead, pressing soft lips to her skin and holding her, determined not to let her go.

"It's not your fault." Her voice cracked and she sobbed, a litany of compounded agony pouring from her soul.

Hana awoke early the next morning, unused to the sensation of someone else in her bed. She heard Logan's steady breaths and felt the downward pull in the mattress where he lay next to her. She reached out and met the scratchiness of his jeans with her questing hand. As she climbed from the bed, his fingers released a handful of her pyjama shirt.

Hana turned on the kitchen light and made a pot of tea. The toaster sat on the counter so she stuffed a few slices of bread into it and fetched herself a plate. Tiger prowled around and she gave him tinned meat and biscuits. "You should go out soon," she told him, stroking his soft head with her fingers and allowing his fur to sooth her. "There's lots to explore but you mustn't go near the main road."

Logan walked into the room, looking dreadful. A coating of dark stubble shadowed his face and his hair stuck up at jaunty angles. Dark circles hollowed his eyes. "Far out!" He sank into a dining chair, the effort turning his complexion grey.

"What's wrong?" Hana asked and he ground his jaw and shrugged.

"Just don't feel great," he said, not getting eye contact with her.

Hana collected the toast and put it on a plate for him, but he buttered it and then only picked. Hana faltered, remembering the electricity of the night before and her awful rejection of him. "I'd understand," she began. "If you want to call the wedding off, I wouldn't blame you." She gulped, twirling a spoon in her fingers and dreading his answer.

Logan looked at her with his piercing grey eyes, accusation in the set of his jaw and his voice a low growl. "How could you even suggest that? The way I feel about last night has nothing to do with marrying you. It's keeping you safe I struggle with. You're impulsive, behave rashly and exhibit a bizarre death wish." He put his head in his hands and sighed with exhaustion.

"Anka lent me a beautiful dress." Hana sat next to him, aware he tensed when she mentioned Anka's name. She put her hand on his forearm. "I'm sorry. I told her about the attacks but she's focused on her own problems at the moment."

Logan made a sound a bit like a scoff, but offered no comment. Hana tried harder, afraid he might still call it all off. "Does it matter if you see the dress before the wedding? It's in the carrier bag on the bed." She stood and backed away from him, frightened by the dark look in his eyes.

Logan leapt to his feet, dragging Hana towards him. His grip around her torso made her breathing haphazard. "You need to let me sort these guys out," he whispered into her hair. "I can't watch you struggle. I've only ever had myself to worry about before now. I don't know how to do relationships."

Hana breathed in the masculine scent and fading aftershave. Love burgeoned in her heart like a delicate flower. "The cops will take care of it," she replied, her tone determined. "I'll ring Bodie today and tell him what happened."

"This is crazy." Logan scratched his head.

"I liked sleeping with you," Hana whispered, her tone teasing. She kissed him on the underside of his stubbled chin. Logan relaxed his grip, his smile tight. He reached into his jeans pocket for his cell phone.

"Yeah, we almost didn't just sleep either. Hope your son's an early riser!" He raised his eyebrows and dialled Bodie's number.

Bodie sounded angry, his tone acerbic. "Are you freaking kidding me? My mother went missing and you didn't call us?"

Logan snorted. "Yeah, because the cops are so interested in her problems. They've got her in witness protection with a bodyguard and everything!" He walked into the hall on the pretext of moving his boots to continue the call without Hana hearing.

"I'll get a shower," he told Hana later, shoving the phone back into his jeans. "It might make me feel better."

Hana nodded and got ready for work. "I'll continue the charade with Angus for now and take each day as it comes. But I promise to behave," she called through the bathroom door. Logan didn't reply.

He emerged looking sick and complaining of a splitting headache. He leaned against Hana's bedroom wall with a sorry look on his face. "I don't think I can face a day of noisy classes followed by the ultimate in boredom, a faculty meeting," he grumbled. "I'll drop you at Angus' place and go home for some medication."

"What medication?" Hana stopped with her lipstick in her hand. "I've got painkillers here. They're in the plastic box in the pantry. Want me to find you some?"

"It's okay." Logan wrinkled his nose. "I've got other stuff at home."

Hana's brow knitted. "I didn't know you took medication. What's it for?"

"It's nothing!" Logan's patience sounded frayed and he ground his teeth. "Just let me do what I need to do."

Hana swallowed and finished applying her makeup. She felt chastised and the familiar sensation irritated her. "Sorry for caring," she bit.

Logan sighed and left the room and Hana heard him putting his jacket on in the hall.

He drove her to Angus' place and apologised for his absence. Angus took one look at him and agreed. "Get yourself to the doctor's, man," he said, studying him with practiced eyes. The familiar signs were there. He patted Logan's arm and unlocked the car for Hana, ushering her into the passenger seat without giving her time to argue.

"Thanks," Logan said, jerking his head towards the car. "For everything."

Angus nodded and leaned closer to him. "I'm hearing great reports of you as a teacher and I appreciate the way you conduct yourself. Parents of private schools like to attend parents' evenings to ensure the investment in their child is proving worthwhile." He patted Logan's arm. "But it's noticeable how popular you are. A record number of busy mothers turned out to support their boys at the last one." Angus chuckled. "Any reason to get them in is a good reason, even if it's to lech at my head of faculty."

Logan sighed. "Great. So you're pimping me out?"

Angus grinned. "Why not, Du Rose? If you've got it, flaunt it."

"No thanks." Logan winced. "Not my style. And don't be a sexist old man."

Angus roared with laughter. "Don't let anyone else hear you speak to me like that." He slapped Logan on the shoulder. "Get some rest," he said. "You look like crap."

"Gee, thanks." Logan smiled at Hana and narrowed his eyes at Angus. "Take better care of Hana today, please. You need to keep tabs on her."

He stood back and watched them leave, Hana's anxious face pale and looking straight ahead. Logan drove to the Gordonton house across country, passing flat calm lakes and turning back on himself. He cringed at the memory of Angus' face expression at the sight of him in the previous day's clothes and pushed the thought away. It wouldn't matter after Friday.

The house felt empty and Logan let himself in using his key. Signs of a Henrietta-style feast littered the kitchen. Investigating the common areas for stray belongings, Logan knew he'd find none. Too compulsive to leave his stuff lying around, he went to his bedroom at the far end of the house. He took his medication and crashed on the bed without waking for a full two hours.

Chapter 50

Logan's possessions took up little room in the Honda and he stood back and quantified his thirty-nine years of life. Always on the move. Always tearing up barely formed roots in the name of progress. Logan sighed and closed the lid on evidence of his failure to settle.

Thoughts of Caroline invaded his brain, her lithe body wrapped around him and her sweet promises of fealty numbing his tired bones. "No," Logan sighed as he screwed up the note he tried to write for his flatmates. "You're full of lies, Caroline. You'll never change." He remembered the flush of his first time with her as his memory of the redheaded girl on the train dulled to a hazy, adolescent image. He didn't know then she'd rolled in the hay with the farm boys and some closer to home. She seemed different when he returned from England, his search for Hana suspended by failure. Softer, warmer, more open to settling.

Logan snorted and shook his head. "Idiot!" He exhaled the word, wishing to undo the wasted years he wouldn't get back. "Too old to father children with Hana now." The thought cut him and a shake of his head dispersed the self-pity. "You can't have everything," he whispered. "You got what you wanted most."

His grandmother's oft repeated prophecy dug into his core until it pained him and he winced against denying her what she'd desired from him. "I can't start a new legacy without children, kuia," he said, his tone sad. "You got it wrong." Tama's image filtered into his mind and he spat in the gravel next to the Honda. "No," he said aloud to the elderly villa. "He's done it this time."

Logan unlocked the storage shed next to the house and inspected his bike for damage. Boris rode it over from Angus' house the night before and a thick crust of mud betrayed the fun he'd had. Logan shook his head and covered it with a tarpaulin. His truck sat behind it and the Triumph further back in a rear corner. He looked up at the sound of mice in the roof and pulled a cover over the old vehicle. The wind from the open doorway caused it to waft up and he cast around for something to secure it. An abandoned hunk of wood fit his need and he wedged it between the front seat and steering wheel to stop the cover flapping.

Logan left the villa with his heart thudding in his chest. He'd arrived after the aborted wedding in a state of confusion and left only a little better off. He found Hana but with her came a whole raft of problems, ones which perplexed and confounded him, dragging him back into a world he resisted with a frayed act of will. Logan Du Rose gained his soulmate and stood to lose everything else. Trying many times for honesty and transparency with her always ended in defeat. Either he didn't want to say it or she didn't want to hear.

He watched the house recede in the rear view mirror and gave a heavy sigh. "This could be one amazing opportunity or a damn big mistake," he said to his reflection. A smile spread across his lips. "Who cares? I'm happy for the first time in my life." With that certainty he turned left, joining the back roads to Culver's Cottage.

Just before the intersection with River Road, Logan's phone chirped in his pocket. He fished it out and put it to his ear. Bodie's voice made him start and he almost dropped it in guilt. "You driving?" Bodie demanded, hearing the car noises.

Logan jammed the phone into the dashboard cradle and pressed the button to put it on loudspeaker. "Nope," he answered, glad the policeman didn't witness his driving offence. "Speakerphone, go on."

Hana's son had some issues to discuss with the man he hardly knew, including an insightful snippet of information he gleaned from an old Hamilton contact. "They're still looking for the man you both identified. He's a nasty piece of work. The new detective at Hamilton City wants him real bad. The word is he's tracked him here from further north."

Logan nodded and wrinkled his nose. "Yeah, I know Detective Sergeant Odering."

"How?" Bodie's question sounded rude and Logan smirked.

"Really? You're telling me you haven't already checked my record and found nothing?" Logan hissed through his teeth. "Damn, that's right; you need grounds for searching personal details because of the Privacy Act. Bummer. Who'd you get to do it for you?"

"I wouldn't waste my time," Bodie snapped and Logan heard the irritation in his voice.

"I would if Hana was my mother," Logan said, pressing the younger man's buttons and enjoying himself. "But there's no need. I'll tell you whatever you want to know. I remember Odering from high school. He's a year older than me and had a body odour problem. Probably still does if you get close enough. What else do you want to know?" Logan gritted his teeth and struggled to control his temper, reminding himself that Bodie's reticence deserved respect, not ridicule.

"Nothing," Bodie conceded, but Logan knew it wasn't finished. "Let me tell you about the guy who attacked Mum."

The list seemed endless. Every offence involved actual bodily harm, the common denominator being the flick knife Hana identified. "My mate in communications says he's skilled with it." Bodie's sigh held defeat. "You probably saved her life, which is the only reason I'll give you this one pass."

Logan grunted in acceptance but gave a two-fingered salute to the phone as he managed the bends on River Road. "Whatever, kid," he murmured.

Bodie continued relaying information, his tone impassive. "He usually damages other guys. There's no record of him attacking a woman, so this is different. The file on him points to minor stuff but Odering told his crew that this is big. He's after something lucrative, but clever. A woman already died and I'm sure I searched for her body in the Waikato River a few months ago. Odering's convinced Hana's problems are tied up in this. These two guys are looking for something which went missing and when they find it, they'll hand it off to someone else waiting in the shadows. The payout sounds big if you believe the rumours. The local cops think Mum knows what the object is."

"But she doesn't." Logan thought of Hana's confusion, her denial convincing and her frustration genuine.

"I know."

Logan picked his words with care as he travelled past Turangawaewae Marae. He nodded his head with respect at the stronghold of the Māori king and the flag flying over his house. "Could this be something your father left behind?" he asked, keeping his tone light.

A stony silence met his question. When Bodie answered, his voice sounded clipped. "He left many things behind, including a devastated family. But nothing illegal."

Logan exhaled and stemmed his rising irritation. His conscience pricked at the memory of his secret wedding to this man's mother and he relented. The already strained relationship would become openly hostile after Bodie realised he'd been tricked. "Sorry," he conceded, his tone grudging. "Bad enough to lose your father without some jerk suggesting he left a legacy of trouble behind. Forget it." The phone bounced in its cradle as the Honda bumped over the railway tracks on the road to Waingaro. "I'm out of ideas. I don't know how to solve this."

"Don't bother," Bodie replied. "Just keep my mother safe and don't let her know this is bigger than she realises. The criminals aren't the only ones watching her, but don't tell her that."

Logan raised his eyebrows and peered in the mirror, checking the road behind. Nothing. He suspected Bodie of trying to scare him.

"This new detective Odering came from Auckland," Bodie said, lowing his voice. Logan guessed he had company nearby. "He's real quiet and buttoned up. Plain clothes. The bosses gave him an office downstairs on his own instead of with the other detectives. Every call relating to Mum's case goes straight to him as of last week. I saw him before I left, but he pretended he didn't need to hear anything I wanted to say."

"Maybe he didn't," Logan suggested. Another thought rose from his gut. "You think he's using your mother as bait?"

"Yeah," Bodie replied and Logan's heart grew icy cold in his chest.

"Geez." Logan rubbed a hand over his face, his headache dulling to a steady thump. He sighed. "I don't know what to think right now. Can you still do that thing I asked?"

He waited for Bodie's reply. "Yeah, I'm fine. It's no big deal."

"Thanks." Relief flooded Logan's tired brain but the ice in his heart remained solid. Culver's Cottage appeared in the distance, the front bay window winking in the watery sunshine. Logan rounded the bend and it disappeared from view. As he reached out to disconnect the call, he heard Bodie say, "Keep her safe, Du Rose. Or I'll make you sorry."

"Yeah, whatever," he said, pressing the red button and cutting Bodie off. He checked the road behind and turned without indicating. Nothing followed. The gate slid open and Logan revved the Honda up the incline, pausing to watch the gap close behind him.

Negotiating the final tight turn through the bush, Logan jumped as his phone rang again. He reached the house and peered at the digital display. The unknown number taunted him and he snatched the phone from its cradle. "What?"

"Hi, we've got a bed for you," the voice said, sounding tired and cranky.

"That's not until this afternoon," Logan replied, running a hand through his hair. He groaned as he remembered the reason why he meant to visit the night before. Hana's wooden bed still occupied the space where he intended his marital bed to supersede it.

"Do ya want it or not?" the driver snapped. "I can take it back to Auckland. It doesn't bother me."

Logan sighed. "When do you arrive?" he asked, his tone sullen.

A rustling of paper filled the airways and then the driver spoke. "Under an hour," he said and disconnected before Logan could complain.

Thirty minutes later, Logan sat on Hana's bedroom floor nursing a nasty cut on his index finger. Blood pooled in the wound and dripped onto the tissue he held against it. "Just what I needed," he sighed. His hasty dismantling of Hana's old bed had disaster written all over it. He'd wanted her to empty her bedside tables the night before and help him shift the old bed into the next room. But her terrifying experience resulted in them both sleeping in a bed he resented and doing nothing to ease his transition into her home and life.

Stripping the sheets off and dragging the mattress next door proved the easiest part. Unbolting the heavy wooden frame needed two people. The spanner slipped as Logan worked in haste and he slashed his hand on a sliver of wood poking out from beneath the footboard. He dismissed Vik's jealous stab at him from the grave as superstition.

Logan stood and dragged the individual pieces next door, shoving the single bed aside. He changed the blood soaked plaster twice before conceding he needed his nasal spray. The black and white cat hopped onto the sink and sniffed at his blood and Logan pulled his hand away. "I hope you can keep a secret," he said, watching the amber eyes give a slow blink. He jumped as the intercom heralded the delivery driver. Logan looked at his watch and swore.

The new bed looked nothing like it did in the shop and Logan's romantic dream-bubble burst with a devastating pop. "How do I know it's all here?" he demanded as two men dumped the pieces in the hallway and bedroom.

"Cause I say it is," the delivery driver snapped and Logan raised his eyebrows, welcoming the challenge.

"You know what?" Logan took a step forward. "I'd like you to inventory every single piece while I watch."

The driver's face dropped and his temper wilted. "Dude, it's all here. I promise." Frustration leaked into his tone and Logan took another step forward. In a fluid movement, he hid the bloodied finger behind his back.

"We're meeting chicks," his companion said, his lips turning downwards. "Hot ones. Please, man. Let us go or we won't make it back to Auckland."

Logan heaved out a sigh. "It's all here?"

Both men nodded their heads like maniacs. "For sure," the younger one promised.

Logan looked at the acne on his chin and the dusting of hair he coveted over his top lip. They were just kids. "Fine," he said, watching their eyes light up. "But you carry every single piece into the bedroom and don't damage the wallpaper."

"Choice!" the older one exclaimed, his blond hair flopping into his eyes. "Thanks mate!"

Logan narrowed his eyes. "I'm not your mate. The name's Du Rose and don't forget it. Because if I find even one screw missing, I'll make a new one out of your face."

"Du Rose?" The older man faltered. He glanced at his companion and nodded. "Okay."

Logan leaned against the wall as the men carried the various parts of the bed into Hana's room. His imposing presence unnerved them and they banged the canopy against the doorframe in their hurry. "Careful," he said, his tone flat.

"Sorry, bro'," the driver said, his eyes flicking over the determination in Logan's steel grey irises. They finished and presented the delivery slip to Logan for signing, blanching as he scribbled his name and added the word, 'unexamined' to the end.

"Ah, no!" The younger man's shoulders slumped. "Youse can't say that. We're supposed to build it for you. They'll know we didn't."

The driver glared at him and Logan's eyes flashed. "And I know you didn't. Get out."

"Can't you change that bit on the end?" the other man begged, flapping the paper at him.

Logan flexed his jaw and lifted his right hand up to his own face, balling the fingers into a fist. He studied the various cuts, scenting the men's nervousness like an animal. The driver backed down first. "Let's go." He tugged his companion's sleeve. "I just remembered why I know his name." He lowered his voice and pushed the other man onto the porch. "His whānau will eat youse for breakfast."

Logan heaved a tired sigh as the lorry fired up and headed down the hill. He waited by the intercom and buzzed them through the gate at the bottom. "Geez," he groaned, pressing his fingers into the bridge of his nose. A smirk turned his lips up at their reaction to his name. They couldn't know it, but his pretence carried it off and his confidence sealed the deal.

Logan spent the rest of the day reassembling the guest room before turning his attention to the master bedroom. By the time Hana texted asking for a ride home from Alder Dale, the four-poster bed stood as the centrepiece of her sanctuary. Logan stuffed the duvet into the new covers, hung the voile, replaced the electric blanket on the mattress and plugged in the spotlights. He unpacked his clothes and placed them in one of the new bedside tables, hanging anything of importance inside the freestanding wardrobe. Her scent hit him each time he opened the door, rustling past her dresses to hang his shirts. He leaned his forehead against the wood and savoured the moment, solidifying his sense of gratitude.

After putting the finishing touches to the guest room, Logan hurried to Flagstaff to fetch Hana. He swung through the security gates and careened along the narrow lane between properties. Making up for the fright he gave an elderly woman pushing a walking frame, he smiled and waved. Responding to the only human contact she'd had all day, the woman waved back instead of utilising the rude hand signal her great-grandson taught her at the weekend. She regained her balance and tottered home, forgetting why she began the laborious journey to the shopping centre at the top of the hill. The mirror in her kitchen revealed the scarf and hairnet adorning her head and her shoulders slumped as she groaned. "Oh, darn!" she exclaimed. "Hairdressing appointment." Sighing she turned to begin the walk again, like a snail replaced at the bottom of a wall.

Hana sat in Angus' lounge with a glass of wine in her hand and Logan gave her a gorgeous smile. "Hey," he said as Angus let him in. It cost him not to stride across and kiss Hana's soft lips. "Sorry I'm late. I finished some stuff up at the house."

"That's okay." Hana stood. She lifted her glass and drained the last of the merlot. "Thanks Angus. It's kind of you to go to this much trouble."

"It's no problem," Angus replied, squeezing Hana's arm. He took the glass from her hand and put it on the kitchen counter. "Isn't it your birthday soon?"

Hana's face clouded. "Yes."

Angus looked nervous and bit his lower lip. "Sorry. It's tactless to ask a lady how old she is."

"It's not that." Hana pouted. "I thought nobody knew, but then I discovered Pete eats the chocolate bars we get. I've seen other people receiving them and assumed nobody cared about the student centre. I guess you just proved me wrong."

"Oh yes." Angus swallowed with discomfort, wanting the conversation over. He didn't get eye contact with Logan, but felt the bad vibes reaching across the room for him. "I'll arrange for you to have the bumps on Monday."

Hana laughed. "It's not this weekend," she said. "But it's soon."

Logan hurried her from the house and stuffed her into the Honda. In his haste, he set off before she fastened her seatbelt. "Steady!" Hana squeaked, sliding around on the leather seat.

"Sorry." Logan ran a hand through his hair and settled his nerves, winning the internal battle with considerable effort. He slowed the vehicle and waved to the little old lady who seemed no further up the road than when he saw her before.

Hana glanced up. "Oh, do you know her?"

"No." Logan shook his head.

Hana swivelled round in her seat, watching as the woman battled with her walking frame. "Do you think she's okay?" Logan slowed as they passed, seeing the woman wobble against her frame as she held on with one hand and lifted the other. She jabbed a finger at Logan and then raised her middle finger in an obscene gesture.

"Oh, my!" Hana exclaimed. "How rude!" She averted her eyes and faced the windscreen, shock turning her lips into a straight line.

Logan laughed and the surrounding tension dispersed. He kept his left hand on his thigh, hiding the bloodied plaster from Hana's sight. She frowned at him. "It's not funny. I wonder if Angus knows he lives in a den of iniquity."

Logan snorted and turned onto River Road, taking Hana away from Hamilton. And away from danger. He took extra care observing the other vehicles on the road, noticing nothing odd.

At Culver's Cottage, Hana loved the bed. "Oh my goodness!" she exclaimed. "It matches the wallpaper. And I can't believe you sorted out the spare room as well. You didn't need to worry. I'm not expecting visitors."

She sighed with happiness and wrapped her arms around Logan's waist. "Thank you so much. I wasn't looking forward to spending the night sorting it out." She caught sight of the plaster on his finger and snatched his hand towards her. "What did you do?"

Logan pulled it away. "I snagged it on a piece of wood sticking out from under your old bed." He put it behind his back. "It's nothing. Don't worry."

Hana opened her mouth to object, sensing he didn't want mothering. She killed the sympathy on her lips and suggested dinner instead. "Pumpkin soup?" she offered. "I know there's a tin at the back of the cupboard."

"Yeah." Logan slipped his arm around her shoulders. "I'll get some bread from the freezer downstairs."

Afterwards, Hana moved her clothing from the old bedside drawers. They smelled of soap and washing powder and she placed her underwear in the woody scented cabinet. Logan laid on the bed and watched her move around the room, his grey-eyed gaze following her. "Gosh, look at the crap in here," she said in surprise. She chewed her lip.

"What?" Logan turned on his side and faced Hana as she tipped the drawer on the bed next to him.

"I got rid of Vik's underwear but over time I filled his drawer with rubbish." Her fingers scrabbled through the odds and ends. "Batteries, torch, lavender bags." She smiled. "I made these with Izzie for an enterprise project at school. Her group won." Hana turned the bag over in her palm and lifted it up to her nose. "It still smells." A tattered driving licence drew her attention and she picked it up in gentle fingers. "Oh. It's Vik's." She turned it over and the handsome man with the dark skin stared from the photograph in her hand.

"Didn't you get rid of all that when you moved?" Logan asked, tracing a daisy on the bed cover.

Hana shrugged. "Bodie loaded the drawers without emptying them. He thought it might be quicker."

Logan swung his legs over the side of the bed and stood without speaking. His brow furrowed and he left the room. Hana watched him walk away, confusion shrouding her face. She upended the drawer into a black dustbin bag and scooped the rest of the items from the bed after it. The driving licence went into her back pocket.

Logan built up the lounge fire ready to light. He stood in a half glow, back lit by the bare hallway bulb. Hana watched him from the doorway, her heart fluttering in her breast. "We'll be married tomorrow," she said, her voice soft. He nodded. She ventured further into the lounge and rested her palm against his arm. "What did I do wrong?"

"Nothing." His eyes flashed and then he repeated it, desperate to convince himself. "Nothing, honestly Hana. I want to marry you."

"You don't sound sure anymore." Fear paled Hana's complexion further and the hand against Logan's arm shook.

"I'm sure." Logan pulled her into his side and kissed her temple. "I need to get used to you talking about your husband." He breathed into her hair and Hana froze.

"I didn't think. I'm sorry." She pursed her lips. "Do you think we can do this?"

"Yup." Logan forced himself into a better humour. "He's part of your life but I didn't realise his stuff was still around. I need to learn to cope with it."

Hana nodded against his chest and sighed. "I'll try to make it easier for you," she said. "I'll adjust."

"Me too," Logan whispered. He pressed his lips against hers and closed his eyes, leaning into the kiss. His arms felt strong around her waist.

Hana broke away to catch her breath. "Last night apart," she murmured into his shirt. "I'll fight you for the new bed?"

She heard the smile in his words. "Na, you take it. It's my gift to you, anyway."

Hana allowed herself to feel lucky as she kissed with Logan in front of the wide bay window, the lights of Ngaruawahia reflecting off the river. She paddled the risky waters of life, no longer drifting along it like flotsam. She admitted to herself how good it felt.

Chapter 51

Logan's face paled as the Sikh guru bound the cloth around his hands, tying his strong olive fingers to Hana's tiny ones. He tied it too tight and the blood thudded in Hana's fingernails. The man opened his mouth to speak and through the haze of red and gold, Hana heard her father's voice. "You're a disgrace to my good name, a disappointment. You're no daughter of mine." It echoed down the years, still inducing the same clenching of heart and spirit. Then Logan's face morphed into Vik's and Hana choked, knowing she needed to scramble free before they sucked her back in.

Hana sat up, sweat beading on her brow and her hands clammy. The dream reminded her of her former hopelessness, saddening her at the trampling of better memories. Vik made her happy. Eventually. She forced herself to remember the good times, Bodie's first smile, Izzie's first tooth, the journey to New Zealand. She smiled at the vision of their little family experiencing Russell; glad to be on the white sandy beach next to a flat green ocean.

Hana lay back against her pillows and thought of Logan. "Nothing like Vik," she whispered. He offered protection and made her feel safe. When he touched her, the electricity seared her soul. An earth scientist and engineer, Vik represented solid husband material, clever, articulate and a great provider. His sense of realism vied with Hana's fanciful, creative side and he viewed her impulsiveness as a challenge to his authority. Logan allied with her artistic nature, but promised to ground her when she dived off into stupidity. Hana shook her head, knowing her new marriage couldn't work as long as she compared her new husband to her dead one.

"That's the trouble," Father Sinbad told her over the phone the day before. "You lost your partner before either of you were ready. Everything Vik was became immortalised in a sheen of perfection. He never had time to dull or grow old in front of you. Age and life did nothin' to him. He remains as youthful and vibrant as the day you last saw him, despite the heavy tread of time on the stairs of life and the expansion of flesh and receding of hair in yer own world."

Sinbad's wisdom rang true. "Apart from the receding hair," Hana said, snuggling down in the big bed. "Thank goodness I don't have that." The duvet inner felt different and she patted it, sensing it wasn't her own. Burrowing into the covers, she found the label and gasped. Brand new and expensive, it weighed her down beneath it. Hana remembered the look on Logan's face as Vik's driving licence landed on the new cover, her old life soiling his attempts to help her begin again. Guilt prickled at the nape of her neck and she climbed from the bed and pulled her jeans off the back of the chair. The plastic driving licence felt hard in her hand. Vik's thirty-seven-year-old face stared up at her and Hana chewed her lip. "Sorry, Vik," she whispered. "But it's time to let you go." She winced. "It's what you wanted after all."

The plastic hit the side of the bathroom bin and made a dull thud as it settled. Hana cleaned her teeth and stared at herself in the mirror. She felt as though she'd crested a mountain after a long, arduous journey to the summit. Descending presented another raft of problems. Did she run down, accepting the scrapes and falls on the way, or opt for the safe path? Hana sighed, not knowing the answer.

"Hey, how did you sleep?" Logan tapped on the bathroom door and Hana dried her lips and turned towards his voice.

"It's not locked," she called. Logan pushed his face around the door and she smiled at him. "I've worked out there's not much point."

Logan grinned and stepped over the threshold. A white tee shirt covered his upper body and tight shorts encased his gorgeous bum. Dark hair dusted his long legs, defining the muscle in his calves and thighs. Hana folded her arms and leaned against the sink. "Good morning," she said.

"You didn't answer my question." Logan edged nearer and placed his fingers either side of her waist. He bent his knees so he could look into her eyes. "How was the bed?"

"Big," Hana replied, tilting her face upwards. "And lonely."

Logan's lips quirked upwards. "No regrets?" he asked, his tone tender. "If you like sleeping alone, now's the time to say something."

Hana bit her bottom lip. "I don't want to sleep alone," she replied, her eyes narrowing behind fluttering lashes. "I want company every night. Think you can manage that?"

Logan's nostrils flared as he inhaled and swallowed. "Every night?" he said, lowering his voice. "You sure about that?"

Hana's eyes twinkled and she nodded. "Very sure." His fingers strayed along her sides and clasped behind her back, pulling her body close to his. Hana's arms slid up and stroked the sides of his neck. His body felt hard and strong against hers and desire shot through her stomach. She stood on tiptoes to kiss him and Logan lifted her, clasping his hands under her thighs.

"I can't wait," he whispered between kisses. "You're beautiful and I love you."

"You promised you'd say that every day." Hana kissed his neck and rested her cheek against his shoulder. He felt solid and safe beneath her and she pushed her fingers into the soft curls at the back of his head.

"And I have." His biceps bulged against her ribs. Hana sat up and parted her lips with a ready contradiction. Logan silenced her with a kiss, keeping his lips against hers as he spoke. "Apart from the nine days, twelve hours, fifteen minutes and thirty four seconds when you wouldn't speak to me."

Hana wrinkled her nose. "Fair enough. But did you think it?"

"Course I thought it," he scoffed, nuzzling her neck. "You just wouldn't let me say it."

"You need to put me down so I can get ready." Hana wiggled her legs and Logan groaned.

"Don't do that," he begged, his eyes narrowing. "What will you wear?"

"Clothes, silly." Hana slid down his body and watched the discomfort on his face. "The dress I almost died fetching from Anka."

"Yeah, don't say her name." Logan closed his eyes and gritted his teeth. "Anytime there's big trouble in my life, there she is like a bloody bad omen."

"She didn't use to be." Hana looked down at her pyjamas and spied a streak of blood. She tracked it back to Logan's finger. "You're bleeding again. Want me to find a clean plaster?"

"Na, I've got some." He pulled the fabric from his finger and squeezed the two edges of the cut together. Blood pooled in the slit. "I'll sort it out. You get ready."

"I need the shower." Hana flounced from the bathroom, wiggling her hips and looking over her shoulder.

"Yeah, I need a cold one now," Logan complained. She laughed and disappeared into the bedroom and he lifted the lid of the dustbin to flick the bloodied plaster in. Vikram Singh Johal's face stared up at him and he inhaled, before dropping the plaster over the image and replacing the lid. "You never deserved her asshole," he said.

"You're ready too early, idiot!" Hana groaned to herself an hour later. She put the finishing touches to her makeup and fought the good fight with her hair, pulling it into a loose bun and teasing tendrils down the side of her face. A matching green clip fell out when she upended the bag, tumbling onto the dress. "Oh, Anka," Hana breathed, recognising a trace of her old friend's former kindness. She slipped it into her hair, a delicate flower made from fragile cloth petals the same colour as the dress. It looked striking in Hana's dark auburn tresses. A momentary fight with a stray and unexpected grey hair left Hana feeling annoyed and then she took a deep breath, readying herself to pull the dress on over her underwear. The task proved much harder than it did with Anka helping. The dress seemed tighter and less co-operative. "Oh, why me?" she hissed.

Her head wedged in the bodice and her arms stuck out of the sleeves. She pushed and shoved but the further in she went, the more restricted her movement became. After a few moments of undignified wriggling, Hana felt claustrophobia take hold and a rising panic built. The more she panicked, the hotter she felt and the more stuck she became. "Oh, help!" she wailed. "This wasn't meant to happen!"

A knock on the door made her whip around, unable to see which direction to face. Her pale winter body and belly-hugging black knickers poked from the bottom of the dress. "Hello?" she called, sweat trickling down her spine.

"Are you okay?" Logan asked. "I'm ready early."

"I'm fine," Hana lied. She swallowed and backed in the assumed direction of the bed, bumping into one of the posts and tripping sideways. "Oof!" she cried as she slid to the floor, creating a dull thud as her backside hit the rug.

Before she summoned another more coherent sentence, Logan opened the door and Hana heard his long strides across the room. "No!" she wailed. "This is embarrassing. You can't see me like this."

"I can't see you at all." Logan's voice sounded normal and without humour.

Hana felt his hand grab her wrist and yelped. "Ouch."

"That still hurts?" Logan switched to her other arm and hauled her upright. "You need to get it checked."

"It's much better." Hana stood with her arms in the air and her head buried in the green dress. Her knickers and legs stuck out the bottom. "I'm stuck," she announced, as though Logan might not have noticed.

"And bloody gorgeous." Logan paused and ran a finger down Hana's thigh. She squeaked and lashed out, missing and pitching backwards. He caught her and gave a dirty laugh.

"If you're a gentleman, you'll say nothing right now," Hana grumbled, feeling hopelessly compromised between the dress and the man. "I'm so embarrassed," she gasped.

"Hold still." Logan peered around the side of the dress and found the zipper which Hana missed. He eased it down and released her from the fabric death grip. She felt the tension go and opened her eyes.

Logan pulled at the hem of the dress, straightening it over her hips with concentration in his face. Slow and sensuous, the action felt obscene. He tugged the zipper up so the dress fit snugly, hugging Hana's slender figure. His fingers brushed her waist and Hana held her breath. When his eyes met hers, she fancied she saw right into his soul. Tension hung in the air between them and Logan's lips twitched. He bowed his head to kiss her and then halted himself. "What's wrong?" Hana whispered, fearful as he pulled away.

Logan swallowed and brushed his own lips with his hand. "I don't wanna smudge your lipstick," he said, his pupils huge against his grey irises. "You look beautiful."

Hana sighed and patted her mussed hair. "I did. Now I'll have to do it again."

"Leave it long." Logan moved closer and fondled an escaped red curl. "I love it best this way." He left the room, striding through the door and closing it behind him. Hana felt the electricity buzz through her and found it hard to focus on her appearance.

"Start again," she told herself, steadying her nerves. She restyled her tumbled hair, straightening it again and coiling the ends. She left it long in deference to Logan's request, pulling strands from the side and affixing the clip to the back of her head. With her first application of lipstick and foundation on the dress lining, she reapplied it and stroked the tights into place. Pushing her toes into high heels completed Hana's wedding attire. She smiled at her reflection. "This is it. Too late to change your mind now."

Hana's mind cast back to her first wedding day, a Sikh ceremony followed by a trip to the registry office for the legalities. She remembered the sense of numbness; her only comfort the kicks in her belly from her unborn son. She'd known Logan a matter of months yet still understood him better than Vikram Singh Johal on the day he made her his wife. The early days with Bodie hid beneath a dark emotional cloud.

He conveniently appeared during a mid-course break. Hana breast-fed whilst reading Keats and Wordsworth and Vik changed nappies amidst papers covered in biological formulas and ecological reports. Bodie chucked up on English essays and science ones without prejudice and the newlyweds struggled on, regardless. Hana asked Vik during a depressed moment, "Would you have married me if I didn't get pregnant?"

He refused to answer the question and it crushed her spirit. Hana subdued herself and tried to be a good wife, sensing he'd sacrificed his own choices for the sake of decency. This time needed to be different.

Hana found Logan sitting at the table nursing a cup of coffee. He peered into it as though it possessed hidden depths, his long legs stretching out beneath the table. His white shirt pressed against his muscles and his trademark tight trousers accentuated every curve. Gold cufflinks sealed the cuffs of his shirt like a tiny, glittering detail.

Hana's heart skipped with excitement, blotting out the nervousness. She squeezed herself onto his knee in the small space between his body and the edge of the table. Her head on his shoulder felt right and Logan's hands either side of her waist made her sigh with relief. "You look stunning," he said. He reached for her right hand and examined the healed cut, bringing it to his lips to kiss.

Hana sat up and studied his face, looking for doubt or fear in his grey eyes. Instead, she found hope and contentment. "You look quite hot yourself," she said with a smile. His fringe flopped into his eyes and Hana pushed it back with careful fingers, letting them stroke the scar above his cheekbone. "Are we doing this or what? I'm keen to get to the next bit." She ran her index finger across his lips and felt his light exhale against her skin.

Chapter 52

Logan took a circuitous route to the registry office and Hana felt his gaze on her as she fidgeted in the passenger seat. Desperation and anticipation vied in her mind. "There's nowhere to park," Logan announced as he circled the court building for the third time. "I'll drive to the multi-storey and we'll walk."

Hana paled. "But what if those men see us?" Her green eyes widened in fear.

"Then I'll give them a slap they won't forget," Logan growled. "But I'm still marrying you."

The sound of the V8 engines raced around the streets, the vibrations shaking the pavement. Hamilton heaved with visitors and Logan dodged families and petrol-heads as he led Hana towards the office. Her heels clicked a staccato beat against the pavement, his stride too long for her to match. She tugged on his arm and halted, pitching forward as he missed the distress cue. "What's wrong?" His head whipped around and his chest muscles tensed.

"Too fast," Hana gasped. "I can't run in these."

"Sorry." Logan returned for her and gathered her elbow under his palm, offering a slower pace and more support. People parted and stared at their strange attire, dressed for a posh dinner on a Friday morning. Logan ignored their interest but Hana found it harder.

The wide colonial steps curved upwards in Hana's vision and she puffed towards them, ready to tackle the final hurdle. Logan halted with such suddenness; she spun around and crashed into his chest. "What?" Panic flashed across her face.

"Wait here," he commanded. He dropped her hand and called over his shoulder, "I'll be back I promise." Leaping down the steps, he disappeared around the corner into Hood Street. Dread and terror rose into Hana's throat like acid. She looked at her borrowed dress and her fluttering fingers sought a coil of red hair as a reflex.

"He wouldn't," she hissed. "He wouldn't leave me here." She blew through pursed lips, tasting the expensive lipstick she seldom used. Her heart pitched into free-fall and nausea made her want to sit on the steps and await the ridicule of the town. Her car and house keys nestled in Logan's pocket. She couldn't escape without money and keys.

Hana became acutely aware of cars moving along the road and people hurrying past. Some glanced at her as she stood paralysed on the steps, stunningly overdressed for humiliation. Panic blurred her vision and she fought for focus, settling on a lone figure across the street who mirrored her own stillness. Anka.

Hana's eyes filled with tears. She raised her hand to wave and changed it to a frantic beckoning motion. Her heart lifted and desperation flooded through her. Anka would know what to do. But Anka shook her head. She pressed her lips to her palm and blew a kiss to Hana, sending it across the distance with a tinge of sadness and regret. Hana saw the glistening of tears on her cheek and panicked, negotiating the steps in her heels with difficulty. "Don't go!" she shouted, her voice carried upwards on the breeze and flung away without effect. "Anka!" The name sounded strangled on her lips and Hana glanced at her growing and curious audience.

"Hana?" Logan's eyes stared up at her, his brow creased with concern. He followed Hana's gaze and let out a sigh, seeing nothing. "You ready?" he asked, his tone flat and his expression showing he expected trouble. An elderly man stood behind Logan, one arm reaching up to clasp his shoulder. An old woman behind them carried a cup and saucer bearing the logo of a local cafe.

Hana nodded and stared at the newcomers. "Yes."

Logan edged closer and the man followed, shuffling forwards in line. "Were you leaving?" he whispered.

"No, no. I promise I wasn't." Hana heaved a sigh. "I thought you left me here and maybe it was a cruel joke."

Logan cocked his head. "Really, Hana? Are you kidding me? I just forgot the bloody witnesses!" He jerked his head towards the old people at his heel. "This is Bill and Esme Wilson. They said they'd do it."

"Love to, but can we be quick? Our bus leaves soon and my coffee is going cold." Esme grinned at Hana and her false teeth ground between her lips.

"Yep, let's do this," Logan said, relief colouring his olive cheeks. He held onto Bill as they began the arduous journey up the endless stairs to the courthouse and Hana clutched Esme's arm.

The ceremony happened at speed. It left Hana with a headache. The legal marriage of Logan Henri Jackson Du Rose and Hana Elizabeth Johal took only moments, punctuated at intervals by the antics of their witnesses.

"I thought we'd been kidnapped," Bill said, his voice echoing in the open space. "Did you, woman? He just grabbed us, didn't he?"

"Shush, Bill," Esme retorted, sending a plume of spit caused by her ill-fitting teeth. "They're getting married. They just met."

"Oh. Nice. Is there food?" Bill shared a phlegmy cough and Esme banged him on the back like Hana's mother once pounded the hall rug over the washing line.

"Oh, I dropped my cup," Esme announced as her crockery clattered against the tiled floor. "It's a little chip. They won't notice." She retrieved it with difficulty from beneath Bill's chair.

The registrar eyed Logan's nervous smirk and raised an eyebrow. "Your witnesses must be of sound mind," he stated, halting the proceedings.

Logan swallowed and glanced at Esme's rounded bottom exiting the row of seats backwards. "They're fine," he said through gritted teeth. "Can we keep going, please?"

"I've got another wedding in ten minutes," the man replied, narrowing his eyes behind his glasses. "Let's press on. Rings?"

Logan slipped Hana's ring onto her finger but his proved harder. He winced as she shoved it over his knuckle, getting it stuck midway. Hana grunted as she tried twisting it. "Should've got one with a screw thread," she muttered and Logan snorted, the sound loud and jarring in the silent room.

Another chesty cough from Bill, accompanied by an unmistakable fart from Esme made Hana's eyes water. She fought to hold in her rising giggles and missed everything else the registrar said. She jumped as Logan leaned in to kiss her and almost hit him in the face. "Esme sounds like a whoopee cushion," she sniggered against his lips.

"Young man, we've missed our bus," Esme informed Logan as he guided her to sign the legal document.

"I'll take you home," he promised. Hana raised her eyebrows.

"Unless they're on a day trip from Auckland," she muttered.

Logan snorted and helped Bill into a seat in front of the document. The registrar looked at his watch and tapped his foot. "What do you think, Esme?" Bill demanded, holding the fountain pen in his hand. "Shall I say we had a nice time? The room's a bit shit. We asked for a sea view."

Hana gasped and shot a look at the registrar. To her relief he concentrated on another party hovering around the door. She leaned close to Bill's ear. "Just sign your name," she hissed. "In your best handwriting."

"Right," he grunted and poured over the document like a child doing its first attempt at joined up writing. He looked pleased with the finished product and blew at the ink.

The registrar checked the old folks' identification again and raised an eyebrow as Bill attempted to raise himself from the chair. "Lovely service, vicar," the old man commented as Hana hauled him upright and almost pitched over backwards under his weight.

"Mr and Mrs Wilson!" The shocked shriek made them all start as a middle-aged woman pushed past the eager audience at the door and ran towards them. "We almost called the police," she panted, shoving past the registrar and giving Logan a filthy look. "The bus is about to leave! What are you doing?"

"Having fun," Bill remarked and whacked the woman on the shin with his stick as she lurched for Esme's arm. "Bugger off."

"I'll formalise the document on Monday and post out your marriage certificate," the registrar said, pointing towards the door.

"Thanks." Logan swallowed and looked at the elderly couple as they resisted the woman's attempts to corral them. "We should leave," he said in his best schoolteacher's voice.

Bill, Esme and their escort left the room, the action made more difficult by the new wedding party that wouldn't let them through. A bride in a Pavlova dress clung to the arm of a skinny man in top hat and tails. The registrar followed close on their heels and announced to the new group, "Right, we're ready now." The resulting surge acted like a plughole, threatening to suck Hana and Logan back in. Hana arrived panting on the front steps and Logan's shirt tails hung out of his trousers.

Hana snorted. "Did someone grope you?"

He rolled his eyes and checked his pockets. "Wallet is still here, so probably."

Hana turned and cast around. "What happened to the old people?"

"I think they got swept back in." He bit his lip to hide the bubbling laugh in his chest. "Sorry. What a disaster."

"No, I loved it." Hana's eyes shone and she rested her palms against his chest. "I think the witnesses might've been senile though."

Logan winced. "They seemed keen when I asked them. But thinking about it, the group looked large and I'm willing to concede I might've gate crashed a residential home outing."

Hana snorted and Logan wrapped his arms around her waist. "Maybe it's a good omen," he sighed. "Laughter from the start." He kissed her forehead and she sighed with relief.

"I hope so," she replied.

Retrieving the Honda from the multi-storey, Logan drove north and stopped outside a mock English pub called The Dog and Duck. Once he put on the handbrake and turned off the engine, he leaned his head back against the seat. His hand reached across for Hana's and she curled her fingers around it. "Hungry?" he asked. He jerked his head towards the pub. "I thought you might fancy an English breakfast."

She smiled. "You're funny. I don't care where we go as long as I get to keep this feeling of happiness."

Logan leaned across the handbrake and took Hana in his arms. He examined the ring on her left hand and kissed it. "I said when I saw the ring on your finger and got to kiss my bride, I'd feel better." His soft lips covered hers.

"Do you?" she asked, her expression pensive.

Logan nodded, the action slow. "Yeah." His fingers dug into the back of her hair and he rested his forehead against hers.

"We can go straight home if you like." Her eyelashes fluttered, tempting him to forget everything and Logan bit his lower lip.

"Let's eat first," he said with a smile. "I'll need my strength."

Their bizarre wedding breakfast comprised fish and chips in a basket. They ate, dressed to the nines amongst a clientele of men with beer bellies and a gaggle of school mums. Logan smiled and took Hana's hand in both of his, admiring her matching wedding band. "How does it feel to be Mrs Du Rose?"

Hana's eyes sparkled. "I'm not quite yet," she whispered with mischief. "But you've eaten like a horse so why don't we go home and seal the deal?"

"You sure?" His kiss captured the last of her lipstick.

"It's a little late if I'm not." Hana's confidence faltered and Logan wrinkled his nose and squeezed her hand.

"Stop thinking about the stretch marks," he whispered.

Hana gaped in surprise and then forced her face into a blank slate. The nerves came and went and the consummation of their marriage hung before her like a dark cloud. Anticipation and terror vied for prominence.

Logan paid and they left, Hana's heels clicking against the gravel car park. When he didn't turn off over the Waipa Bridge, Hana panicked. "Logan, where are we going?"

"I'm taking you away for the night," he replied, keeping his eyes on the road.

Hana fidgeted in her seat. "But what about Tiger? I don't have a change of clothes!"

Logan ignored her protests. "Trust me," he demanded, knowing it wouldn't be the first time in their marriage he'd ask her to do that. He sighed. "I want you to myself, Hana, at least for one night."

After half an hour, they pulled off the main state highway and passed Rangiriri Pa. The bush rose up to meet them on either side and Logan took the narrow roads with confidence and familiarity. "Where are we going?" Hana asked, her fingers writhing in her lap. Logan rested his hand over them and stopped their movement, raising an eyebrow and shaking his head.

"Wait and see," he said. "Somewhere peaceful."

The Rangiriri Hotel and Golf Club sign made Hana gulp in fear as Logan turned down the long driveway. Cherry blossom trees waved either side and he swung into a parking space next to Mercedes Benz and Audi convertibles. Hana swallowed. "Logan, this is way too posh for me." She looked at Anka's loaned dress and felt her nerve fail.

"Don't talk crazy, wahine," he said, hunkering down next to her side of the car. Gravel shifted under his cowboy boots and a stiff breeze attacked his hair.

"But it must've cost a fortune," Hana hissed, watching as men in shorts pushed golf trolleys past the car. "I can't play golf."

Logan snorted. "You don't have to. I'm friends with the owner and rented a suite. Come on." He leaned across to unfasten her seatbelt and smirked as she fought him.

Hana stood at the plush bar and let Logan order her a merlot. He clinked her glass with his whiskey on the rocks. "Happy wedding day, Mrs Du Rose," he said with a grin. "Do you want to eat in the restaurant or see the room?"

Hana's gaze darted around, clutching the stem of her glass so tightly, Logan removed it from her hand lest she snap it in two. He smiled. "Room it is then." His smile faltered as Hana gave him a look of pure terror.

The ride upstairs in the lift seemed endless and Hana counted the squares in the carpet detail. Logan carried their drinks and chewed his bottom lip. He used a key card to access the room at the end of a long corridor and Hana gasped at the opulence in front of her. "Wow!" she exclaimed. "How do you know the owner?"

"I grew up with him," he said, nudging her forward. "They don't have a honeymoon suite but this is as executive as it gets. Do you like it?"

Hana exhaled and stroked the side of the large spa bath. The bed looked big enough to sleep twelve. "You have rich friends," she said and Logan wiped the look of guilt from his face in an instant. He told her the truth but played it down to avoid revealing all his secrets in one drop.

"I earned a good income in London." He put the drinks on the bedside table and loosened his top button. "When I came back, my friend approached me for an investment so he could take over his father's golf club. I gave him financial advice and helped him set up the hotel. We have a different clientele, so he refers conference stuff to our hotel in the mountains and our guests get discount on a day pass to play golf."

"How far is your hotel from here?" Hana asked, watching through the floor to ceiling window as two old men teed off towards the ninth green. One leaned on his trolley until the very last minute before launching his ball onto the fairway. He looked too shaky to swing the club but his aim went true.

"Just over half an hour." Logan kicked off his cowboy boots and lay back on the bed, his left hand picking at the thumbnail of his right. "Hana." His voice wavered as an uncharacteristic nervousness consumed him. "We don't have to do anything. It's not compulsory."

Hana turned from the window with a giant exhale. "It kinda is." Her gaze settled on an overnight bag next to an ornate oak wardrobe. "Is that our stuff?"

"Yeah." Logan sat up using his stomach muscles and ran a shaking hand through his hair.

Hana gasped. "You poked through my knicker drawer?"

Logan snorted. "I did. You keep some crap in there. Till receipts, soap, nail polish. I struggled to find any undies."

Hana stared at the ceiling and blushed pink to the roots of her hair. "I can't believe you did that. What about my makeup bag? I bet it's still at home, isn't it? I'll wake up tomorrow morning so pale you'll think I'm dead.

Logan jerked his head towards the bag. "It's all in there, Hana. I told you to trust me."

Hana cocked her head. "You say that a lot. It makes me worry more."

Logan wrinkled his nose and pressed the heels of his hands into his eyes. "Do you want to go to the restaurant for food?"

"No." Hana caught sight of the fear and apprehension in his face and pitied him. She walked towards him, placing her feet like a dancer and causing her dress to shimmy around her thighs. Logan swallowed as she got closer and opened his mouth to speak. "Say nothing," she whispered. "Just love me." She attacked the stiff buttons with trembling fingers and straddled his thighs. As each gap widened in his shirt, she leaned forward and kissed the dusky, olive skin it revealed. Logan's legs shook beneath her and she sensed twenty-six years of hope and failure weighing him down. When she trespassed into unknown territory, exploring further than propriety ever allowed before, she felt him give in and let arousal master fear.

He flipped her onto her back while his shirt gaped open, revealing a muscular chest with a dusting of dark hair across his pectorals. Freeing himself from the clinging white material, he cast it on the floor without care. Hana gazed into eyes the colour of grit, attraction making Logan's pupils flare against his irises. "I love you, Hana Du Rose," he whispered, pulling down the zipper on the side of her dress.

Hana's brazenness astounded her. Logan's adoration gave her confidence and she felt beautiful in his arms. She hardly recognised the teasing, sensual personality who took over her body. Most of all, she had fun.

They emerged from the bedroom hours later, catching the end of dinner service and eating as though starved. In the space of a day, their relationship grew and Hana's toes massaged Logan's shin beneath the table.

The next morning, after a breakfast delivered by room service, they lay entwined in the massive bed and Hana faced the prospect of returning home. A cloud of danger hung over Hamilton and dulled the shine of her illicit weekend. She rested her head on her husband's downy chest while his fingers traced the outline of her shoulder. "I don't want to go home," she whispered and snuggled closer.

"I know." Logan sighed and chewed the inside of his cheek, stopping himself before he drew blood. "I don't wanna either."

"What about the cat though?" Hana half sat up, the white sheets slithering down her body and revealing part of a breast. "He's cooped up in the house. He'll get up to mischief."

"No, he won't. Trust me, I've sorted it," Logan reassured her, distracting her again with his kisses. His eyes danced and sparkled as he caught up on twenty-six wasted years and worked hard to learn every single freckle and beauty spot on his new wife's body.

"You do say 'trust me' a lot," Hana commented as she lay beneath him, a carpet of auburn hair covering the pillow. "Should I be worried?"

"Definitely." Logan pulled her close. Hana traced a vein along his large bicep and followed it with a kiss.

"Sounds dangerous," she whispered, her eyes teasing. Logan laughed and pressed his lips to hers. He rolled, so she lay on top of him and wrapped his fingers in her beautiful hair.

Getting dressed proved difficult. Every item Hana donned, Logan worked hard to remove. "Wear the green dress and do your hair the same as yesterday," he encouraged, kissing a spot on her neck which he discovered he liked.

"I've got my jeans on twice so far!" Hana complained. "That poor dress won't cope with your savagery. I can't spend another day clacking around in those shoes." Hana giggled as Logan's strong arms caged her from behind. She jerked her head towards the green dress lying on the carpet. "Look, it's creased."

"There's no savagery!" Logan sounded hurt. "I'm making sure you know you're married. Do you feel like Mrs Du Rose yet?"

"If not being able to walk is part of the criteria, then yes." Hana turned to him, naked but for the dress dangling from her fingers. "Why can't I wear my jeans?"

"Please?" Logan kissed her neck again and Hana shivered. "I'm taking you somewhere special this evening and you'll want to look good."

Hana's eyes dulled. "Don't I look good in jeans?"

Logan raised an eyebrow in reprimand. "You know you do, Hana. Just wear the dress, wahine." He showered and dressed in the shirt and slacks, adding a suit jacket and tie to the ensemble. Hana went along with it and they ate at the golf club restaurant, standing out against the seasoned golfers in their chequered leggings and Fair Isle pullovers.

Logan carried the bag to the car mid-afternoon and took Hana for a walk around the grounds. Native gardens screened them from the wind and they meandered through the plantings following a winding gravel path. "It's a shame you sold Vik's old golf clubs. You could have used them here. Pete let slip you have an impressive handicap."

Logan glanced away and pursed his lips. "Pete's got a big mouth," he said, his answer biting.

Hana sat on a bench and watched his face, increased intimacy making him easier to read. "You didn't sell them, did you?" she asked. He licked his lips and looked away. "They're still in the garage at the Gordonton house, aren't they?"

Logan shrugged. "Might be."

"Oh, Logan." Hana shook her head. "Why?"

He sighed. "I wanted to help you. I paid what I thought they were worth. Do you want them back?"

"No." Her own certainty surprised her. "And I'm sorry for mentioning my dead husband on our honeymoon."

Logan sat next to her and kissed her temple. "We've both had a previous life, Hana. It's bound to invade sometimes." He winked at her. "Don't do it again."

"Deal." She squeezed his hand with gratitude.

At six o'clock, after a sumptuous afternoon tea, Hana climbed into the Honda and prepared to go wherever Logan took her. She realised that trusting him got easier the more she did it. Her acquiescence dispersed like a popped bubble as she recognised a landmark and sat up straight. A fearful knot grew in her chest, making breathing difficult and she squirmed in the passenger seat. "Logan," she said, her voice shaky. "Logan, I don't want to do this."

As they pulled onto the bumpy track, sickness added itself to the mix, curdling the beautiful afternoon tea with its sweet, triangular sandwiches. The wide sandstone house rolled into view and Hana's chin trembled. "This isn't fair!" Her voice sounded strangled. "Please, Logan, not yet."

"Don't be daft," he soothed, riling her further with the empty platitude.

"I'll get out!" she said, grabbing hold of the door handle as they rounded a dangerous bend.

Logan leaned across and rested his hand over Hana's trembling fingers, not letting go as she writhed against it. "That would be dumb," he said, his voice level.

Hana twisted the new wedding ring round and round her finger and thought of ways to escape. "I won't get out," she snapped, all trace of the confident, sensual temptress gone. "We said we wouldn't do this. They'll hate me."

"No, they won't." Too soon the Honda swung around the driveway and pulled up in front of the staircase. The front doors of the hotel stood open and moths fluttered around the exterior lamps. The car park looked jammed and the building carried an air of buzzing anticipation.

"Don't make me do this," Hana begged as Logan got out of the car. He opened her door and leaned a forearm against the sill above her head. "We've had an amazing few days. I don't want an angry exchange with your parents to ruin it."

Logan snorted. "I'm not sixteen, Hana," he said with a laugh. "I can marry whoever I like. And right now that's you Mrs Du Rose." He stroked her cheek and pointed at the stilettos in the foot well. "Get your shoes on, babe."

Hana stalled, taking ages to get the shoes on and Logan sighed. "You can't run in them, Hana, so stop contemplating it."

Hana's lips dropped open in surprise. "I wasn't!" she lied. He laughed and raised an eyebrow in denial.

Leading his bride up the steps, Logan felt her pulling against him. He stopped and turned to face her, alarmed to see the glazed look in her eyes. "I can't do it," she gasped, clutching her chest. "I can't do it again."

"Hey." Logan stepped down to her level and wrapped his arms around her, feeling her tremble beneath his hands. "I get it, Hana," he breathed, his tone calming. "I didn't but I do now." He lifted her chin with his index finger. "But you're not eighteen and about to face the wrath of angry family members. Nobody hates you and nobody will. You're beautiful and amazing and I'm proud to call you my wife."

Hana bent double as a sob caught in her throat. Terror got the better of her and the Indian women in her mind pointed and whispered at her large, shameful belly. Logan pushed his fingers into her hair and dragged her closer. "Come back to me, wahine. Let go of the past," he whispered. "You belong to me and I love you."

His scent comforted her and the softness of his shirt soothed her cheek. Hana struggled to ground herself in the promise of his love. Fear made her bone-tired with its muted whisperings and she sighed in defeat. "I'm scared," she stammered and Logan stroked her hair, trying hard to avoid the complicated flower thing trapped at the back.

"I know," he whispered. "But this way is best." His soothing voice stilled Hana's panic, but he gasped as he stroked her cheek and felt the wetness of her tears. "Geez, Hana," he groaned. "I'm sorry. I should've warned you." He grappled in his pocket and produced the ever-present handkerchief. Hana dabbed at her eyes with shaking fingers. "You amaze me," he said with a sigh. "You care about how other people feel and it's what makes you so special. It's also what makes you vulnerable." He held her, rubbing her back and letting her calm down enough to listen to him. "It's just a party Hana. Everyone came to celebrate your birthday early. I thought if we got them here, we could tell them all in one hit. Nobody hates you, Hana. I did this to stop them feeling hurt and because I knew it bothered you. Please, give me a chance?"

Hana paled. "So, it's more than just your parents?"

After a few seconds of hesitation, Logan moved onto the next step and held out his hand, "Please? Come."

Hana swallowed and dabbed her eyes again. "Do I look like I've been crying?"

Logan sighed at the sound of the inevitable question tender women always asked. Their eyes might resemble oranges, red and puffy, but the dutiful male must deny it. "No, you look fine," he replied.

Logan exuded mana and authority as he led his new wife up the steps of his family home and into the stunning lobby. He was the chief, the rangatira returning home with his long-awaited bride. Nobody would challenge him again and as he threw his shoulders back and raised his head, he felt the assurance of his ancestors.

Unaware of what she'd stepped into, Hana's heels clattered across the floor towards the double doors of the ballroom. Logan pushed them open one-handed and Hana took a huge breath inward, gulping for air as though the next breath might be her last.

Dearest Reader,

I'll give you just a second to take a deep breath. But only a second.

Hana's wearing the ring but did she really get the guy?

You thought you'd met the Du Roses, but the fun's about to start. Logan's family is not what you think. These guys put the capital 'T' in Trouble.

Are you ready?

Hana might have got away from the blond man but he's not done with her yet.

This saga is laid out before you like a tray of fine wine and expensive chocolate.Dip in. Be decadent. You deserve it and it's all yours.

Hana's already made a life changing error of judgement and Logan?

Logan's about to get really hurt.

You can purchase the next in the series;

HANA DU ROSE

from my website,

ktbowes.com

Other books by this author:

The Hana Du Rose Mysteries:

Logan Du Rose

About Hana

Hana Du Rose

Du Rose Legacy

The New Du Rose Matriarch

One Heartbeat

The Du Rose Prophecy

Du Rose Sons

Du Rose Family Ties

Du Rose Vendetta

Phoenix Du Rose

****

The Calculated Risk Series:

The Actuary

The Actuary's Wife

The Actuary in Trouble

The Heart of The Actuary

****

Troubled series for teens:

Free from the Tracks

Sophia's Dilemma

A Trail of Lies

Gone Phishing

****

New Zealand Soccer Referee series:

All Saints

****

Escaping the Back Country NZ series:

Pirongia's Secret

Deleilah

****

A Keeper's War Fantasy Trilogy:

Perpetual Winter

The Bee Queen

Hive

****

UK based mystery/romances:

Artifact

Demons on Her Shoulder

****

The Curly Fan Club

Dead Straight

Bad Hair Day

Side Parting

Take a look at all K T Bowes' novels at ktbowes.com

About the Author

K T Bowes has worked in education for more than a decade, both in New Zealand and the United Kingdom and has written since she could first hold a pencil. She is married with four beautiful children who are all now making their own way in the world.

She lives very close to Hana's house in the Hakarimata Ranges and based Culver's Cottage on a real house which sadly burned down after she started writing the series. The people are made up, but the towns and locations are real. If you ever visit, be sure to check them out.

From the Author

I hope that you enjoyed About Hana as much as I enjoyed writing it. I would be grateful if you would take the time to leave a review at your usual retailer. My work is ranked on reviews and your comments will allow me to reach a wider audience.

It doesn't have to be an essay - I will be grateful for a few words.

Check in and say hello to me in any of the locations below. Maybe suggest I get back to writing and stop watching cat videos.

FACEBOOK
https://www.facebook.com/NZauthorKTBowes/
TWITTER
https://twitter.com/ktboweswrites
INSTAGRAM
https://www.instagram.com/k_t_bowes
PINTEREST
https://www.pinterest.nz/hanadurose/
LINKEDIN
https://www.linkedin.com/in/ktbowes/

Thank you.

www.ingramcontent.com/pod-product-compliance
Lightning Source LLC
LaVergne TN
LVHW040746250326
834688LV00034B/483